ACTIVE MEASURES

PART ONE

Published by H-Hour Productions, LLC. Printed by CreateSpace.
www.mattfulton.net

Library of Congress Control Number: 2016910093

ISBN-13: 978-0-977169-1-7
eISBN: 978-0-9977169-0-0

To Liam —

Active Measures
Part I

a Novel

by Matt Fulton

1-29-18

The mind is its own place, and in itself
Can make a heaven of hell, a hell of heaven.

—John Milton, *Paradise Lost*

PROLOGUE

THE RUSTING FENCES and chipped white guard towers seemed out of place against the calm and picturesque villages of Germany's Rhine Valley. Cinder block barracks and concertina wire still sat as tourist attractions, but the maze of tank ditches and patchwork of minefields had long been removed. From their perch atop a four-hundred-meter hill above the Fulda Gap, American forces positioned here would have had a direct line of sight into the *Deutsche Demokratishe Republik* and the Soviet 8th Guards Army garrisoned immediately within. Since the late 1940s, American and Russian soldiers flooding the hills eyed each other through barricades of steel and dirt, anticipating a conflict that never came. A border crossing anywhere else acted simply as a filter on an artificial line drawn along a map. However, this was more—it was a demarcation between two worlds: democracy and communism. This was Observation Post Alpha, and if war ever came between East and West, this latticework of fences and checkpoints would have been ground zero in a fight that would reshape the world.

In a Top Secret report entitled OPLAN 4102, US European Command scripted in precise detail how American forces would react hour-by-hour to a Soviet attack on the inner German border. West Germany would essentially morph into a massive military encampment as the US Air Force would ferry reinforcements, ready them for attack and place them under NATO's command hierarchy. The plan described the movements of every individual combat unit in the rugged, rural terrain, creating an in-depth defense plan that even provided for nuclear and chemical release procedures. The region was one of two likely routes for a Soviet tank offensive, the second being the North German Plain near Hamburg, which declared itself an open city that would not stage any resistance to Russian forces. A third, less likely route existed through the Danube River valley in Austria. The geography of these lowlands was more favorable to a Soviet armored column than the alternate route to the north, which was likewise suited to a mechanized infantry assault. Allied and US emphasis on the Fulda Gap was not without reason.

History always relied on this corridor that cut directly through Germany's core and provided a gateway to Western Europe. In October of 1813, Napoleon Bonaparte—limping away from a disastrous defeat at the hands of both the tsar and Mother Nature—sought to wrestle back control of Germany. His two-hundred-thousand-man *Grand Armée*—merely a shadow of its former glory—met the formidable Sixth Coalition at Leipzig in what became the largest military confrontation before World War I. Over the next three days, the allied Russian, Swedish and German forces nearly surrounded Napoleon and fought to a clear, decisive victory that ended the French Empire's ambitions in Prussia. Napoleon's army made a narrow retreat toward Paris through the Fulda Gap and the coalition gave pursuit. A year after, Napoleon was captured and sent into exile on the island of Elba. Two centuries later, the Warsaw Pact had a similar strategy to that of the Sixth Coalition, and the Pentagon had forty years to decide on a response.

Defense of the Fulda Gap had been the primary responsibility of the American V Corps, which in the 1980s consisted of the 3rd Armored Division, the 8th Infantry Division, and the 11th Armored Calvary Regiment, which guarded the inner German border since 1972. Prior to that point, the border was the responsibility of the UK's 3rd Constabulary Regiment and 1st Constabulary Brigade. The mission of these heavily mechanized reconnaissance units, equipped with Bradley Fighting Vehicles and M60-series main battle tanks was two-fold: In peacetime, their role was to keep watch over the border for signs of Red Army movement that would signal an imminent attack. At war, the regiment had the responsibility to hold back a Soviet onslaught until the 3rd Armored and 8th ID—the V Corps' backup—could mobilize and deploy. The armored cavalry would then act as a screening force, maintaining continuous visual contact with the Warsaw Pact's forces, reporting on their movements and orders of battle.

Opposing American units on the opposite end of OP Alpha was the Soviet 8th Guards Army, reinforced by four armored divisions including the 1st Mechanized Infantry Division of the 1st Guards Tank Army, which four decades earlier had fought back Hitler's armies at Stalingrad and gave pursuit all the way to Berlin. The 8th Guards had a well-deserved reputation for driving holes through Europe and in the 1980s was equipped with three motor rifle divisions and an armored tank division, plus support elements to ensure the future would not set a new precedent.

The residents of this quiet valley knew it was a dangerous place to live and if the order to invade ever came from the Kremlin, it was common knowledge that the Soviets would have trampled through the NATO units protecting them. Flanked by the Hohe Rhön and Knüllgebirge mountains, the Russians could move massive quantities of men of weaponry through the plains, affectively cutting West Germany in two and storming a path to the French border. The communists would hardly have stopped there; not only would the Soviets have reached the epicenter of American military power in Germany, including Ramstein Air Base and a host of barracks and munitions depots, but the Red Army would also be within striking distance of Frankfurt, West Germany's main banking center and a key financial hub for the whole of Europe. Compounded with the loss of Hamburg, NATO would stand to forfeit Germany's industrial heartland and the Rhine. The Americans would then be forced to fall back into Belgium and France and go on the defensive. NATO would lose the initiative and the armies of World Socialism might soon see the Atlantic, or at the very least, redraw the map in a way that favored Moscow.

While history and geography were both on their side, the Soviets knew that crushing the Americans and their allies was easier planned than accomplished. In order to further ensure the success of conventional forces in Germany and the rest of Europe, the Soviets enacted a bold plan that would target key facilities and personalities in the opening stage of World War III. This involved coordinated acts of sabotage, subversion and assassination. Power stations, airfields, ports, bridges and the central nodes of C3I—command, control, communications and intelligence—were canvassed by Russian special operations forces during the Cold War and prepped for elimination when the order finally came down from Moscow. However, this strategy was not exclusive to Europe alone. Russian military intelligence also penetrated deep into the United States where prepositioned arms sat in wait for use by bands of deep cover saboteurs. These weapons would be used for similar purposes as in Europe and were intentionally placed near the location of American leaders in the event of war. The tactic was designed to decapitate the United States and NATO, leading to confusion and disorganization on which the sprawling armored divisions stationed in the Fulda Gap and the rest of the Warsaw Pact would capitalize.

The GRU—the Main Intelligence Directorate of the Soviet General Staff—took the lead in this operation. Relatively unknown to all but a few intelligence circles in the West, this agency's power rivaled that of the KGB. To keep the Red Army in check and block any attempts at a *coup d'état,* the Politburo heavyweights always kept a watchful eye on their officers. They entrusted this task to the Second Chief Directorate of the KGB, which held the portfolio for counterintelligence and internal political control. Agents were placed in military units to watch everything and report on even the slightest hint of mutiny on the part of Soviet officers. However, the GRU sat outside this tight network of surveillance and was fully autonomous of their rivals on Dzerzhinsky Square. They kept their own watch on Soviet elites, managed a web of spy satellites and SIGINT stations around the world, and commanded a force of at least twenty-five thousand Spetsnaz commandos. These special operations units functioned much in the same way as the British Special Air Service or the American Delta Force. At the beginning of a war against NATO, Spetsnaz units imbedded in Western Europe would have activated these weapons caches, moved them to their targets and detonated them, crippling American forces.

In the 1990s, a number of former Soviet intelligence officials from both the KGB and the GRU came forward and revealed that high explosives and small arms were not the only things secreted away behind enemy lines. The defectors revealed the existence of small, man-portable nuclear weapons with yields of one to ten kilotons that could be detonated with only thirty minutes of preparation. "Suitcase nukes," as they became popularly known, would have been the Soviet trump card in any Cold War conflict. Their explosive power was not nearly enough to obliterate a large metropolitan area like Paris or Brussels, but the devices packed enough punch that they would cause considerable devastation. GRU Spetsnaz operators placed the weapons near key ports and depots in Central Europe and command bunkers in the United Kingdom and France. Minutes after the order was given, NATO's hierarchy would lay in a smoldering ruin and vast swaths of the North German Plain and the Rhine Valley would be showered in radioactive fallout. Moscow's strategy would ensure that if communism could not have exclusive dominion over Europe, neither would any power. In World War II, the Soviets fought for years to seize valuable ground and cement their hold on the eastern half of the continent. For the next global confrontation, the Kremlin's top thinkers sought to advance at a brisker pace.

And it is here that the story has its proper beginning.

In November of 1989, the Berlin Wall fell, not by exploding artillery shells or the overpressure of a thermonuclear warhead, but by the might of individual East Germans striving for the same rights and freedoms enjoyed by their families in the West. Over several whirlwind months, tens of thousands of East Germans poured down through the splintering Warsaw Pact to rejoin their relatives and reap the benefits of a free market society in the Federal German Republic. This created an unstoppable chain of events. The Iron Curtain—miles of razor wire and machine gun turrets constructed to keep the oppressed in rather than American GIs out—was now a redundant relic of a bygone occupation. There was neither a need nor a way to fight it anymore. The Soviet Bloc was coming down and it was only a matter of when rather than if. Cries for reunification came swiftly and soon Berliners stood atop the wall that had kept them apart for generations. The communist dream of a single Germany was realized, but not in the way its followers anticipated.

With the triumph of democracy in Europe, the Soviet Union now struggled to maintain its fragile empire of client states and withdrew its forces from the continent to maintain order at home. This new reality fell hard on many in the military and intelligence circles who recently witnessed defeat in Afghanistan at the hands of zealots dwelling in caves and now came to see their own domain, the Warsaw Pact, crumble before them. Yet few in the West understood the paranoia of Soviet intelligence officers, the lengths to which they went to further the Marxist cause, and their utter obsession over a showdown with the United States. To the GRU, still strong despite the gutting of the KGB and the dissolution of Soviet forces in Germany, a third world war was still, eventually, inevitable.

These officers had the means to ensure that when that unavoidable confrontation erupted, Russia would keep the upper hand. Since the 1950s, protocol dictated that no single military branch or intelligence service held complete control over the Soviet Union's vast nuclear arsenal. During the Cold War, this was accomplished in the field by the Red Army's possession of mobile ICBM launchers and the KGB's control of individual nuclear warheads. Yet the GRU's small, man-portable atomic weapons had no such system of joint-ownership and the highly classified nature of their production, storage and deployment kept them free from oversight of arms reduction treaties. It was simply as if these weapons never existed, and it made them the perfect tool for an illegal operation outside of the Kremlin's oversight.

On February 25th, 1990—when most Soviet units were pulling back from the inner German border—a small Spetsnaz unit deployed under the cover of a raging blizzard into the dense overgrowth of Baden-Württemberg's Black Forest with a mission to conceal what would be the GRU's insurance policy. The forest's location, a few kilometers from the French armored brigades poised on the opposite bank of the Rhine, or several hours' drive on the A5 autobahn to the American military communities in Stuttgart and Heidelberg, provided a wealth of attack options should the GRU's prophecy come to pass.

A small holiday cottage, one of dozens peppered among the snow-laden fir trees, was covertly purchased through the GRU residency at the Soviet embassy in East Berlin. The Spetsnaz operators arrived as the storm spun into its full fury. They posted sentries around the cottage, covered the windows with sheets of ply, and descended to the basement. A section of the brick wall was chiseled away and they excavated a cavity in the foundation just large enough to fit a watertight container approximately the size of a steamer trunk. Attached to the trunk by a set of wires was an antenna similar to the kind used by submarines to receive transmissions under the Arctic ice shelf, and a battery pack that maintained the integrity of the trunk's plutonium-239 core and neutron generator. The one-kiloton RA-115 Atomic Demolition Munition was designed by its Soviet engineers to be neglected, and with a dry, temperate climate it could linger for years without mainte-nance. The Spetsnaz operators laid new bricks in the wall, entombing the trunk inside, and cleared away any trace of their passing.

And the bomb would sit for a quarter century while life above eased on, unsuspecting and ignorant of what slept just out of sight, ready and waiting.

CHAPTER 1

THERE IS GREAT power in letting go.

But no one had taught him that. No one had plunged down their hands to dig up the shards and piece him back together. No one had ever tried.

Not yet.

Jack Galloway weighed his surroundings with a wary intent: a few muted women, their bodies engulfed by the deep, black, obscuring fabric of a *chador;* the cliques of men, young, old and plenty lost somewhere in the gap between; and their voices—the usual voices, the normative patterns—at times exuberant toward the cricket match on the television suspended from the far wall, at times silenced by an assuaging drag on a water pipe, at times hushed in acquiescence of the CCTV camera suspended to the other; at no time content. Their faces were unfamiliar to him yet their patterns, their movements, their fleeting glances, their questioning eyes were not—all caught by his own, all measured, processed and stored lest his eyes ever fall upon them again. Then he would know. Then he would vanish. Familiar faces in unfamiliar places were deadly in the denied corners of the world.

Jack took his cuff and wiped down a ceramic cup. He hadn't seen his potential minder since he ducked into the café, although that was likely by design. In Moscow it was called "dolphin surveillance"—now you see me, now you don't. The KGB would tail the subject with a sloppy team, making the surveillance obvious and then promptly pull the team off, replacing them with a much more skilled unit, of which the subject wouldn't be granted the slightest hint. It was meant to deceive the subject into a false sense of security—the illusion of reality: an unreality—like the shadows dancing over the cave wall before the captivated prisoners, chained and ignorant of the raging fire at their backs. All mere projections; charades; lies in the dark.

Jack left the café, averting his face from the CCTV camera—the security services had unfettered access to the hard drives—and returned to the street under a gentle fall of rain.

It was just as his father had shown him in the front room of their embassy housing in Hampstead. His father would extend his arm and on cue, four coins would drop from his sleeve onto the table. He would count them and smile, "Are you with me?"

Jack continued down the street toward Tajrish Square, the hub of the affluent neighborhoods of northern Tehran. The streetlamps lit the way before him, and behind him. His minders hadn't made themselves known, if they were even there. He hailed a passing cab. It pulled to the curb, splashing through the runoff that had gathered into shallow lakes of light. He directed the cab three blocks south, then promptly ordered it to stop, hopped out and doubled back five blocks north where he arrived at Ammar Street, a quiet, leafy residential lane flanked by distinguished walled homes. Here even the most capable surveillance unit would be pressed to find cover. Jack wasn't keen to make it easy for his shadows. He kept on down the street.

His father would place the coins in a line on his right palm and count out each one, again, deliberately. Then, he folded his fingers on both hands, the right one touching the edge of the coins. He smiled again. "Are you with me?" Jack would nod. His father sharply flipped his hands, the backs turned to the ceiling. He smiled, turned over his right hand and opened it. Three coins. He turned over his left hand. One coin. "Did you see it jump?"

On the opposite side of the street, Jack saw a white, stone villa surrounded by a high wall and a manicured garden. The lights inside were doused and the curtains drawn—save for one. Suspended in a window on the upper floor was the soft orange flicker of a candle. Jack took note and walked on. He would wait for contact. That candle in the window was all he could concretely know, the only static light in a field of shifting shadows, flickers, projections and charades—lies in the dark; a solemn sign his father had shown him twenty-five years before.

That candle had been snuffed out. But no one had ever taught Jack why. Not yet.

CHAPTER 2

5:45 ALWAYS CAME too early. A swift smack of his hand silenced the monotone chirping echoing through the bedroom. He double-checked the time
and eyed the green-tinted darkness around him through two weary slits;
Mary, his wife, still slept soundly beside him. With a subtle hint of jealousy,
Ryan Frecman rose and went about his routine. Later, after knotting a crisp
blue tie and throwing a suit jacket over his shoulders, he returned to his
wife and leaned over the bedspread to plant a kiss on her forehead. Mary
rewarded him with a loving groan and rolled back into the tangle of sheets.

Freeman descended the staircase and met his security detail in the kitch-
en. His personal space had shrunk in the past month. Upon being confirmed by the Senate as director of the Central Intelligence Agency
(D/CIA), a section of the basement in his three-bedroom home on Highland Drive in Silver Spring had been walled-off to create a security command post and classified document vault. It was now half-past six and
Freeman trailed two of the agents into the world of manicured lawns and
joggers that was suburban Maryland. The sky was pink and the air was
characteristically still for a bitterly cold winter morning. It was the first of
February.

An armored Chevy Tahoe idled in his driveway with pulsating red and
blue LED lights behind the windshield. An identical chase car sat alongside
the curb. Freeman climbed into the rear right seat and welcomed the heated
cabin. His work day had actually begun at ten o'clock the previous evening
when a printer in the basement command post automatically started, as it
did every night, and spat out a draft of the president's morning intelligence
briefing. The President's Daily Brief (PDB) was the most important document the intelligence community produced and was referred to by many as
simply "the book." Essentially, it was a classified version of any major
newspaper with the key exception that its stories were on topics most re-

porters would sacrifice their first-born child to break. Freeman would review the draft for an hour each night. On occasion he would call the PDB night editor and give his opinion on the content and provide direction on which pieces may require more, or less, explanation.

But while official Washington slept CIA's overseas operations were in full swing, and that meant with each sunrise a mountain of cable traffic crowded offices from Fort Meade to Fairfax, all of which had to be sifted, analyzed and prioritized for the policy makers. Freeman was an expert in determining that priority, but to aid him, a sizable anthology of state secrets in three-ring binders and fat manila folders sat at his side. He began cutting through the pile by reaching for a stack of reports his staff had plucked from the Operations Center's overnight influx of secrets. The reports, fronted by laminated bright-red Top Secret cover sheets, addressed a large swath of issues that the various directorates, desks, stations and centers at his command deemed worthy of his attention that morning. In a matter of minutes he had poured over the pages and filled the margins with cursive shorthand that only his secretary was able to decipher into legible English. Next came something always guaranteed to sour Freeman's mood: a collection of clippings from *The New York Times, The Washington Post* and a changing variety of foreign newspapers—the daily leaks, as he called them. Thirty years of experience in the US Intelligence community had taught him that staying abreast of the media was just as much if not more crucial than the intelligence. What was reported in the morning broadcast usually fueled policy makers' agenda and it was consistently the first item they wanted to discuss.

Finally, the D/CIA turned his attention to a leather portfolio containing a collection of one- or two-page articles printed on heavy paper. Freeman walked through the finalized PDB, reading each article in detail, making notes on what to consider, as well as what last minute advice should be phoned in to the briefing team under the aegis of the director of national intelligence that would join the president in the Oval Office promptly at nine that morning. His eyes fell upon an article with intelligence contributed by a targeting officer out of Station Beirut entitled, *"Hezbollah Scours Source of Lost IRGC Aid Funds."* The report concerned information gleaned from a Lebanese source identified by the "crypt" or code name AM/TOPSAIL. TOPSAIL claimed that Sheikh Wissam Hamawi, Hezbollah's secretary-general, was leading an internal investigation aimed at finding two million dollars in missing aid money that had been funneled to the group through private charities controlled by the Iranian Revolutionary Guard Corps, known as the IRGC or the Pasdaran. Slapped on the first page of the article was a yellow Post-it note with "Call me!" scribbled over it. Freeman recognized the handwriting and immediately reached for the encrypted BlackBerry in his jacket pocket. It clicked twice and rang on the seventh floor of

Langley's Old Headquarters Building.

"Morning, boss," answered Grace Shaw, a legendary field officer, and CIA's deputy director for operations (DDO).

"Why are you in so early?"

"Pipes in the condo upstairs froze. Had a quick panic attack until I realized I'm lucky if I sleep there two nights a week anyway. You see my note?"

"Yeah, what gives?"

"Let me tell you what I know and you can be the judge."

"Okay…"

"The Tel Aviv COS got a request overnight from Jerusalem—from Avi Arad's security advisor, not Mossad—to be read-in on *all* TOPSAIL intake as it concerns a source of funding to Hezbollah from the Rev Guards."

"What?"

"Yeah, right on Ilan Halevi's letterhead—clear as day—my eyes, trained. Who do you suppose talked?"

"Tanner."

"Wouldn't be the first time." Shaw referred to Dr. Eli Tanner, the president's national security advisor. Tanner was most recently the president of the Council on Foreign Relations—a lifelong academic who had never set foot in the field and didn't grasp the concept that loose lips do, in fact, sink ships. He was a personal friend of Prime Minister Arad and it wasn't the first time that their relationship had irked Freeman. However, as Tanner's office sat mere steps from the president of the United States, he remained untouchable.

"What do they want?" Shaw sensed the annoyance in her boss's voice.

"A trade."

"Tell Halevi to go fuck himself."

"Really?"

"No. Just tell him no."

"Damn, I got excited there. But just between you and me and anybody who'll listen, Tanner needs to shut his mouth or one day he'll let something slip that'll get somebody killed."

"Roger that."

"Your schedule says you're coming straight in, is that still true?"

"Yep."

"Okay," Shaw shifted in her chair, "because I just heard from Ops at NRO and they say the weather should be good when they pass Haj Ali Gholi. They'll get maybe a twenty-minute window for VTC. You've been wanting to see it live?"

"I do. See you soon."

"Bye, boss."

The encrypted line went dead just as the Tahoes reached the Beltway and crossed an icy Potomac River.

• • •

Ouzai was one of the poorest sections of Beirut's desolate southern suburbs. For displaced Shia from the south and Palestinian refugees, too impoverished to take up residence in their own scattered camps, the grimy warren of cinder block houses and illegally built apartment buildings was often the only escape from an Israeli prison. Many of the structures in that chaotic, destitute slum were built close enough together that residents could reach out and touch hands. Electrical wires ran exposed along crumbling walls and stairwells. Burning garbage and the thick, oily smoke it produced would choke the cool breeze flowing off the Mediterranean as middle-aged men and women faded away from diseases the developed world had long since forgotten. Power failures and short circuits were a common occurrence. Those better off could purchase generators and place them on their balconies; when the power was cut, it was a contest to get one's voice heard over the whine of diesel engines. And in the hot summer of 1982, a young Shiite boy called it home.

Barely over the age of twenty, he was still a child—razor-thin with eyes the color of jade. The boy had, to this point, led a simple existence helping his father push a small vegetable cart through the dusty paths and squalor of the city's southern suburbs. He was known in the neighborhood for his sense of humor—frequently cracking jokes at family weddings—and for his pious adherence to Islam. A distant cousin was a prominent scholar of Twelver Shiism, had studied in the Iranian seminaries of Qom and even wrote books that could be found in some Muslim enclaves of Europe. The boy admired his cousin yet knew a similar path was impossible for him. But his mind was sharp and on a scholarship he enrolled in the American University of Beirut to study engineering, only to drop out after a single year. As a Shia, a job in Saudi Arabia or anywhere in the Gulf was incredibly unlikely and that was where all the work could be found. For a young man in his situation, he picked up the only tool he could wield: a Kalashnikov rifle.

His name was Ibrahim al-Din and it would soon become synonymous with the spate of bombings, hijackings and kidnappings that would scourge Lebanon and its foreign occupiers for the next thirty years. Al-Din and his friends rested in the glow of the Mediterranean sun with their legs pulled up beneath them, contemplating their bleak futures. In that single-story house next to the Airport Road there was no running water or electricity—the Israeli Air Force ensured as much when they began their siege of Beirut. A few short miles to the north, a string of luxury flats along the sea were being pounded by relentless artillery fire and the rumble of cannons was clearly audible over his family's struggling generator. War was a fact of life for these young men and they accepted it and the death it brought like many accepted a rainy day. Al-Din knew in his heart that the end was near, that it was simply a matter of time before the PLO—then the vanguard of the

Islamic resistance—would capitulate its Lebanese base and flee. The Arabs had consistently failed to protect their own people and once more humiliation and defeat would be their fate. It was a precedent for which the eager young man grew tired.

All three spent their teenage years fighting in the Lebanese civil war on the side of Fatah as snipers targeting Christian neighborhoods in the cratered wasteland of East Beirut. The combat that was native to these men crafted them into masters of urban warfare. Al-Din, especially, was a prodigy in the art of death and there was not a weapon he couldn't unjam, nor an AK-47 he couldn't fieldstrip blindfolded; he could crimp a blasting cap with the skill of a demolitions expert and put a rocket-propelled grenade on target at over a hundred meters. By the time he was sixteen he had organized a hundred men into a student brigade for Force 17, the personal bodyguard service of Yasser Arafat, who spoke openly of al-Din's skill and intelligence. Now, as the Israelis inched closer to Verdun Street, where the PLO was headquartered, it was obvious to al-Din, and the others that their former commander had failed. It was time to fly a new flag.

Al-Din, the two others in the room, and countless more spread throughout Lebanon and the Arab world were exiles in their own homeland. Ouzai's position on the northwest perimeter of Beirut International Airport served as a constant reminder of how they had been subjugated by forces outside their borders. Day and night, jets full of rich Lebanese flew in from New York, Paris, Rome and London. Chauffeured Mercedes and hand-built Bentleys would queue in front of the terminal and ferry the decadent back to their mansions in the Baabda hills above the city. Their heavy bags of Swiss chocolate, French cognac and Italian couture kept a reality present to the angry men that, in Lebanon, the Lebanese were second-class citizens.

The Ottomans, the French and now the Israelis with their American protectors, were their occupiers. The sound of commercial airliners was replaced with screeching F-16s manufactured in the United States, and the airport was closed—now a pockmarked sheet of asphalt—but nothing would change once the Israelis completed their mission.

However the young men had a different plan and they were determined to change Lebanon for good.

Yet they were not naïve and knew they could not take back Lebanon or Palestine from its occupiers alone. The Palestinian elite failed them just as much, if not more, than their rich Arab brethren in the Gulf. The Saudi royal family and the Emiratis only gave their oil-soaked cash to the Palestinian cause out of guilt. Twice, the massed armies of the Arab world had stood up together to run the Zionists back into the Mediterranean and twice they had failed. But Al-Din was aware of a new movement stirring on the eastern shores of the Persian Gulf led by a charismatic ayatollah named

Ruhollah Khomeini. Three years earlier Ayatollah Khomeini led a revolution—a Shiite revolution—that overthrew the shah and expelled Western influences from Iran. The ayatollah was now promising to do the same across the Middle East and eventually the whole world. The "Imam," as he was affectionately known within his new Islamic Republic, succeeded where countless revolutionaries before had failed.

The boy stood and wished his family and friends farewell, but he would return. With a small amount of money he saved from helping his father, he took a shared taxi east to Baalbek in Lebanon's lawless Beqaa Valley. A man al-Din knew as Sheikh Mostafa agreed to meet with him there, out of reach of the Israeli Air Force and Mossad's hit squads. Together, they would plot the future of the Lebanese people. Al-Din knew little of this Sheikh Mostafa other than that he was an ethnic Arab, a Shiite like himself, and an officer in Ayatollah Khomeini's new Revolutionary Guard Corps, a separate military force committed to preserving and expanding the wave of fundamentalist Islam that washed over Iran. Al-Din went to see if the Iranians were serious about conquering the Jews and forcing out the French and American soldiers that would soon arrive in Lebanon. Al-Din wanted to know if the sheikh and the ayatollah behind him would flinch at the sight of blood.

He sat across from Sheikh Mostafa and listened intently without blinking an eye. That was a distinguishing feature of Ibrahim al-Din—his eyes would gaze on unnervingly and pass through a person without reverence for the soul within. It was a stare that proclaimed he would murder you as easily as he would shake your hand. The future that Sheikh Mostafa presented was clear: a war with Israel, a war with the United States, a war with the West and any other enemy of Shia Islam. That part of the plan was not particularly important to al-Din. He was a believer and a follower of God, but he was not tutored in Islam like his cousin, nor did he necessarily fall down at Ayatollah Khomeini's new interpretation. Al-Din saw the Shia faith as a means of recruitment and as a way to market a wholly political struggle to a people wholly uneducated in politics. The fact that he would carry the banner of Shiite revolution to the shores of the Levant was a contractual obligation to which he did not object. Iran's goal in Lebanon was clear and all that was needed were martyrs to turn it into a reality. The sheikh asked if al-Din and his followers were ready, but he already knew the answer.

From that summer day in 1982, Ibrahim al-Din became a captain and a founder in what would become the most effective guerrilla army in the world: Hezbollah—the "Party of God." The thin, honey-eyed man returned to Beirut with his instructions. He would only recruit relatives and trusted fighters from Fatah. With Iran as a rear base, this war would be fought entirely from Lebanon. The IRGC would provide the weapons and funding, but there would be no payroll and transactions would be handled only in cash. Al-Din was never to contact the sheikh electronically and a trusted courier would relay their messages. All of his activities, his movements and the names of his fighters would be kept under the utmost secrecy; only Sheikh Mostafa and a handful of officers in Tehran would know that al-Din even answered to the Iranians.

His ascendance to the world stage as a master terrorist was swift and brutal. At 1:03 in the afternoon on April 18, 1983, a delivery truck laden with two thousand pounds of plastic explosives rammed through an outlying guard post and lodged itself in the lobby of the US embassy in Beirut. Before anyone could respond, its cargo detonated, taking the lives of sixty-three people, including most of CIA's top echelon in the Middle East. The force of the expertly crafted bomb collapsed the central façade of the chancery building and shattered windows as far as a mile away. In October of that same year, another bombing ordered by al-Din ripped through a barracks housing American marines at Beirut airport. Two minutes later, another blast struck a company of French paratroopers. In the costliest day for the US Marine Corps since Iwo Jima, 241 American servicemen perished.

After the attack, the United States withdrew its force from Lebanon and, for the first time in history, Ibrahim al-Din—and by proxy, Iran—had accomplished what every other Arab state had failed to do: they prevailed against the technological and conventional might of a Western military power. His campaign to cleanse Lebanon continued through the decade with a rash of kidnappings that targeted journalists, members of the clergy and even CIA's Beirut Station chief. A wave of commercial airline hijackings in the eastern Mediterranean that al-Din also masterminded, and even participated in, expanded the fight. However, in the skies between Cyprus and Lebanon, al-Din was about to witness a philosophical shift in the strategy of his Iranian backers and it would signal a greater shift in the value of the trade he perfected.

On April 5, 1988, eight hijackers stormed the cockpit of Kuwait Airways Flight 422 under orders from al-Din. Armed with grenades, three of the terrorists informed the captain that they were now in control. The hijacking was an effort to free members of the savage Dawa 17 organization who awaited execution in a Kuwaiti prison cell for their efforts to attack the American and French embassies in the country. Al-Din's cousin was among them.

His men aboard the plane were professionals, and they kept their hostages under complete control—quiet, submissive and terrified. To hide their Lebanese accents, they only spoke classical Arabic, swapped clothes and wore masks so their captives could not tell them apart. They kept the window shades drawn to degrade the hostages' sense of time, and they turned the lights and air conditioning on and off to maximize discomfort. They prowled the aisles like vultures, shouting and picking out individuals to shine lights in their eyes, making them believe they were seconds from execution.

From his base in Ouzai, al-Din ordered the plane down at Mashad in eastern Iran where it sat beside the runway for several days. In past operations, the IRGC would allow the hijackers off the plane to refresh in shifts, but this time they did not. The peculiar change in protocol was the first sign to al-Din that something was different. After an inordinate amount of time, the airliner took off again, this time bound for Beirut and the airport that Hezbollah now controlled. Once in Lebanese airspace, the political bosses of Hezbollah and al-Din's handlers in Tehran made it clear that they wanted nothing to do with the hijacking. The plane circled for hours until al-Din realized that his masters would not let the plane land. Frustrated, he directed the hijackers to Larnaca, Cyprus.

The Cypriots did not have a particularly well-equipped hostage rescue team and the small airport there had good fields of view from all directions around the runway. It was a prudent tactical move that would keep the hijackers in control. Al-Din also had a competent surveillance team at his disposal in Cyprus that would alert him of any troop movements toward the airport. On the fifth day of the ordeal, the Kuwaitis still refused to negotiate. In anger, al-Din radioed his men aboard the plane and ordered them to execute two of the hostages. They did so in earnest, but it had no effect. The Kuwaitis were not intimidated and the Iranians refused to associate themselves with al-Din. The plane's next stop was Algeria, where after PLO negotiations, the hijackers were granted safe passage back to Lebanon in exchange for abandoning the airliner. For the first time, an operation al-Din meticulously planned and executed had failed to achieve its purpose, but why?

Central to Iran's developing goal of regional hegemony in the Middle East was a desire to transform itself from a terrorist state to a conventional military power. One could not accomplish such a thing by executing airline passengers. Iran's interest was now rooted in air and naval tactics, armor and advanced weaponry, and the political posture to be noticed. For Iran to be taken serious it had to act serious, and that was not done by basing its policy in the Arab world on a terrorist, noble as his cause may have been. With his specialty service no longer required by his employers, al-Din's role, too, shifted from hijacker and kidnapper to liaison, military commander and strategist.

He was given the chance to spill Israeli blood numerous times throughout the nineties as the Israel Defense Force (IDF) continued its costly occupation of Lebanon's southern Shiite heartland. Hezbollah militants would continuously ambush Israeli patrols or bombard a fortified outpost with anti-tank missiles and swarming raids. In the summer of 2006, it was al-Din who made the Zionists' advance to the Litani River a tactical hell. Still, his

, overseeing the transfer of Iranian
The rest of Hezbollah's commanding seen as the modern reincarna-
re concerned with conquering the

the kill and capture lists of every
nterpol red notice hung over his
l beyond the safe harbor of Hez-
survive, he vanished back into the
emerged. In time—and with new,
—the memory of his many ene-
eories in circulation on what be-
the Germans held to a flimsy ru-
ars ago under an assumed name
sh quickly became too obsessed
ong as al-Din kept off the radar,
led by Mossad's merciless and
ewer than four times to assassi-
ut as with any ghost, finding it

fell on Lebanon, Ibrahim al-
to finishing his mission, and so long as there was
an Israeli state, his was a struggle without end. He would never lose sight of
the vision he set out to realize over thirty years earlier. But he needed the
means, he needed inspiration, he needed an opportunity—and in due time
he would get them all.

CHAPTER 3

FREEMAN WAS ALREADY in his office and on his third cup of coffee, the second since arriving at Langley. The morning sun cast a bright, natural light into the room, which held a remarkable view over the Potomac Valley and Northern Virginia. A ridge carrying the George Washington Memorial Parkway blocked a direct view of the river, but through the empty branches he could scarcely make out the rocky shores of Maryland. In almost an hour, he made his way through the call sheet on his desk that required his immediate attention and was close to appeasing everyone in the second list of people from the agency and around the Intelligence community that needed "just a minute" of his time. Freeman's secretary had made close to three or four rounds of changes to his schedule. He had no particular sense that any of these alterations were being made, nor did he much fuss over them; Freeman just went where he was told and made frequent consultations to his daybook, a masterful collection of research papers, background sketches and biographies that his staff prepped each day.

He just ended a conversation with the director of the National Security Agency and looked down to his mug, noticing it was almost time for a refill, when his phone rang for seemingly the twentieth time that morning.

"Yeah?"

"Satellite's coming up," Grace Shaw reported from her office down the hall.

"Get everybody in the conference room."

"Already waiting for you."

The D/CIA smiled. His suite of offices occupied the entire southeast corner of the Old Headquarters Building's seventh floor, where all of the agency's top executives were based. With the daybook tucked under his arm, he walked out into the private hallway that connected his office to his conference room.

Grace Shaw met him outside with Peter Stavros, chief of the Iran Operations Division (C/IOD), known internally as Persia House. "Again, these are live and we're not entirely sure what we're going to see," Stavros cautioned, "but once we have it, we'll get the proper analysis."

"I hope they're smiling." Freeman turned into the room.

Freeman took his seat at the head of the conference table and looked forward to a set of twin LCD monitors with various readouts that meant something to someone with a greater technical understanding then he. Shaw and Stavros took the seats closest to him as a group of division chiefs and senior analysts lined the table. Next to the monitors, a technician from the National Reconnaissance Office (NRO) prepared the live video feed.

"We got lucky on this pass, sir—near-perfect viewing conditions, given the location. Ground temperature is about eighty-three and humidity isn't much higher," the technician, an Air Force captain, informed. "The bird was repositioned specifically for this and at about 0845—that's 1615 local—it'll sit five degrees from being directly overhead. Shadows will be at a good angle, too."

"This was so much harder in the eighties," Shaw added.

The technician lifted a phone and relayed orders to the pilot in his "cyber cockpit" at the National Reconnaissance Operations Center, twenty-five miles away in Chantilly. At once, the monitor sprang to life with a streaming video feed directly from NRO's Aerospace Data Facility-East, the primary downlink station for the eastern seaboard at Fort Belvoir. It displayed a clear, crisp image of the Islamic Republic of Iran from one hundred and two miles above the surface of the Earth.

"There's Tehran…and its smog," Freeman observed, looking intently at the view from one of the KH-13 reconnaissance satellite's eleven wide-angle lenses. This was #63B, to be precise. The white peaks of the Alborz Mountains came next as the satellite orbited overhead at twenty-six thousand miles per hour. In several seconds, the picture on the ground morphed into an empty beige wasteland as the satellite moved east over the Dasht-e Kavir desert at the center of the Iranian plateau. The view on the screen slowed over an expansive, hazy white smear called the Haj Ali Gholi dry lake. Finally, the image shifted one last time and settled on a group of dusty mountains at the southern edge of the lakebed. A high-resolution camera took over and peered into a narrow valley locked between two high mountain ranges, miles from any from any semblance of civilization.

The senior intelligence analyst from the Iran Branch of the Underground Facility Analysis Center (UFAC)—the Defense Intelligence Agency's clearinghouse for information and analysis on hard and deeply buried targets worldwide—rose from the conference table and stood next to the monitors. "Director Freeman, I must preface this briefing by saying that the analysis to follow includes our preliminary findings, rather than a definitive judgment of the site. As you are aware, NGA noticed the new construction only seventy-two hours ago and, to be perfectly frank, that's the only reason we are aware of its existence." The analyst took a sip of water before referring to his handwritten notes.

"First, allow me to provide some background as to the setting of what we're seeing here. To quickly clarify a question we faced earlier, we can now say with certainty that the site is not visible from any publicly accessible land. Directly to the north of the valley is Haj Ali Gholi, an expanse of salt flats, which remains dry year-round. Tehran is a hundred and eighty miles to the west and the nearest town is Damghan—population, fifty-seven thousand—about forty miles north. The climate is almost rainless and extremely arid, with temperatures ranging from a hundred and twenty degrees in the summer to seventy degrees in January. Humidity is generally always high, which has provided poor viewing conditions over the last few days. As for nearby military installations, the Iranian Space Agency's launch site at Simorgh is sixty miles to the southwest and we're aware that the IRGC Aerospace Force operates a missile test facility of some size fifteen miles northwest of that. It's our determination right now that neither is in any way connected to the site.

"Allow me to direct your attention to the foot of the mountain range at the western edge of the valley where we've seen the highest level of activity." The analyst switched on a laser pointer and circled a tunnel entrance sunk into the mountainside. "As for 'Monet,' the northern-most of the two portals, we've noticed slightly more activity overnight in the form of vehicle traffic on the access road leading into the mountain. This leads us to believe that Monet is complete and fully operational—"

"Any idea how long?" a CIA imagery expert interrupted.

"Not yet, but we're checking older imagery to try and get an answer. As you can see," the analyst continued to the rest of the group, "the tunnel entrance is clearly fabricated with poured concrete and reinforced with steel rebar. There is a guard post constructed *here* and you can see a paved road, branching off from the main access road that leads into the mountain. And as I said, we can now confirm vehicle traffic into Monet in the evening hours, only."

"Excuse me, could you focus on that guard post?" asked Stavros.

"Certainly." The technician picked up the phone again and passed the orders to the pilot. The picture quickly changed as the camera zoomed in, demonstrating just what NRO's new bird was capable of. A pair of stationary dots became the discernible picture of two bearded men standing together at Monet's entrance with Heckler & Koch G3A6 assault rifles slung over their shoulders, completely ignorant of their spectators over six thousand miles away.

"The ground security force, which we estimate to be battalion-sized," the analyst informed, "wears desert camouflage fatigues with H-and-K G3 assault rifles, which is the standard-issue weapon of the Revolutionary Guards, but we cannot use that as an indicator of the site's operator. We haven't seen any signs of unit insignias on the uniforms. If we could pan back out, I'd like to add that Monet has been a complete enigma to us. We still haven't a clue of its purpose, nor have we been able to judge its internal layout and until we do that, any final analysis will be incomplete." The analyst turned to the NRO technician and asked, "Can we move the image to Picasso?"

The view through the satellite's camera quickly shifted a kilometer south, following the main access road on the valley floor.

"Jesus, would you look at that," Shaw marveled at the screen before her.

The KH-13's lens refocused over a second tunnel entrance blasted into the mountainside. Sitting directly adjacent were two large teardrop shaped mounds of excavated earth, or spoil. "Since discovery, we've viewed sustained activity at Picasso," said the analyst. "The spoil piles—*here* and *here*— grow daily and from what we can tell, they contain approximately a thousand cubic meters of crushed rock in total, covering some five hundred square meters. Based on that information, we estimate that construction began sometime between October and December of last year."

"And still only at night?" asked Stavros.

"Yes, sir. As is true with the entire site, it seems to hibernate during the day, with the majority of activity taking place overnight, including all of the construction at Picasso. I'd guess this to be nothing more than a countermeasure, and not due to any operational knowledge of the constellation's orbital path." The analyst referred to regularity with which a KH-13 satellite passed overhead. "Any pieces of construction equipment not in use are stored under this camouflage netting here during the day, and the heavier pieces are moved inside the tunnel. And, as you can see now, there's a rail line for mining carts, which leads from the pile and into the tunnel portal. Strikingly absent from the site is any amount of concrete, steel rebar, or the equipment to put it in place. The Iranians seem solely focused, for the time being, with digging, and haven't made any attempt to harden the portal beyond the natural rock. This suggests to us that Picasso is more temporary in its construction than Monet. Given that the spoil piles grow daily, we can judge that construction of Picasso is still well underway. If the tunnel is dug straight into the mountain from its portal, it's on an axis to meet Monet with a difference of maybe twenty degrees. This could mean that Picasso is an expansion of its sister facility, but that can't be confirmed right now."

At the opposite end of the conference table, Freeman sat patiently without saying a word. The analysis was desperately frustrating. He felt as if he were being led by the hand through a labyrinth, coming upon an unmarked door only to see after it was opened that another endless passage awaited him, lined at either side with more anonymous doorways. There were no answers at the end of these questions, only more uncertainties, more deception and more time wasted. "So is this a third enrichment hall I'm seeing?" the D/CIA spoke for the first time. "Is this Iran betraying our agreement?"

"Unlikely, Director Freeman. The nature of the construction wouldn't suggest it. A fuel enrichment plant requires a massive amount of floor space to accommodate thousands of gas centrifuges spinning in tandem. The Natanz facility has two halls, each with about twenty-five thousand square meters of space. Fordow has around five thousand. To create such a huge space, you'd have to dig down, clear out that wide area, build a containment facility, and then cover it back over. I'll pull up a rendering." The analyst brought on the second screen a 3D computer model of the valley floor showing the steep rise of the mountain with an animated graphic denoting the portals for both Monet and Picasso. "The elevation of the mountain is fifteen-hundred meters above sea level," the analyst read from his notes. "That would cover these sites under more than six hundred feet of solid rock. The topography we're dealing with here doesn't support that sort of construction. It'd be much too labor intensive."

Freeman harshly rubbed the bridge of his nose, a nervous tic he had since childhood. "Okay, it's probably not an enrichment hall. So what else would you build in the middle of nowhere? A bomb?" Every head around the table turned to face him. He suddenly wished he could take the word back the second it spilled from his mouth.

"Ryan." Shaw laughed, "let's not get away from ourselves."

"Maybe," the analyst responded as the temperature in the room seemed to skyrocket. He, too, immediately felt the gravity of what he had said. "Of course, that's, not really, likely. Nor is it my place to suggest such a thing, sir," he walked back his words.

"But it is. And it's my job to decide whether or not I believe you. What does your experience say?"

"Well, with the exception that there aren't any outbuildings, the site is eerily similar to preparations at Punggye-ri before the North Koreans tested their first device. And the geography is similar to the Ras Koh hills, where Pakistan conducted a few tests in '98. The overburden of the rock would allow detonation of a yield of twenty to forty kilotons. That's the maximum detonation size that the mountain could support without venting."

"Sir!" Stavros insisted.

"I want to hear what he has to say," Freeman cut him off. He looked to Shaw and made eye contact with her. It was obvious to him what thoughts were running through her head, but they couldn't be spoken in the room.

"But the division chief is right," the analyst agreed. "It's far too early to make that sort of call. *If* it's a test site of any sort—*if*—these spoil piles will start to disappear and that will give ample warning that a shot is imminent.

They'll take the spoil and fill the tunnel back up. And none of this accounts for Monet, none of it."

"We'd get the seismic readings and air samples in real-time anyway," an agency expert down the table dismissed.

"It's not that simple," the analyst countered. "The area sits on the convergence of the Arabian and Eurasian plates, and the Astaneh and Shahrud fault systems pass each other not forty miles north of the lakebed. A test here could be passed off to a seismic monitor as a geological anomaly. It would be very high burden of proof at the United Nations."

"Air sampling?" asked another agency expert.

"That desert is volcanic in origin. The underlying bedrock and soil are mostly full of basalt—relatively high background-radiation count. Any emissions the test would give off—save for a large vent of radioactive dust—would get lost in nature. Radionuclide stations wouldn't notice a thing."

Freeman saw that Shaw had her head in her hands. "But as long as that spoil pile grows, we have time…if it is what you're saying it is."

"Director Freeman, it is not the judgment of my colleagues and I that what we're seeing is in any way related to a nuclear weapon, much less an imminent test. You asked me what my intuition tells me and I am simply giving you relevant facts."

"You are, and you've done a superb job in doing so."

"Thank you, sir."

"Okay," Freeman sighed, "let's send this out to ODNI, DTRA, STRATCOM J2, NCPC, ASD(NCB), NSA, NGA, Los Alamos and AF-TAC, immediately. This is TS/SCI—if you don't need to know, you don't. I want us back here in forty-eight hours." The meeting adjourned hastily and in less than a minute, Freeman had whisked his brain trust down the short corridor to his office.

"But, and I say this again, if the ayatollah gave the order to restart, we would know. This isn't up for debate, Grace," Stavros argued a few tense moments later, sitting on the arm of Freeman's sofa.

"The man could drop dead of another stroke any second, Peter, and CITADEL is still human no matter how special he is," Shaw shot back.

"No, Pete is right," Freeman drifted back from the windows. "Khansari hasn't made a single decision on his own in months. We would know if they restarted the nuclear program. That's why CITADEL is there." He rubbed the bridge of his nose again. "Grace, we aren't gonna figure this out with a satellite. Pete, any alternatives?"

Stavros shook his head. "I have a couple NOCs traveling in and out, but they can't get close. Jack's the only one inside. I can have him ask."

"Grace?"

Shaw bit her lip. "If you boys think it's worth the risk, then I agree."

"Okay," Freeman nodded. "And let's rope in the distribution list; it's too big as it is. Leave it at WINPAC, CP, you guys, *very* few at ODNI. NE doesn't need to know yet. I'm not reading about this in the *Post.*"

"Got it, sir," Stavros confirmed.

"Good."

"Right," Shaw agreed. "Pete, let's send word to Tehran and see what we can shake loose." They both went to leave Freeman's office when Shaw stopped at the door and turned her head. "Ryan, once this is out we can't get it back."

"I know."

A quick glance at his passport by a wary police officer would have shown the name of a Swiss national, Simon Marleau, born 25 February 1985. A closer inspection of the pages to follow by a vigilant immigration official would have revealed numerous foreign visas, all of which would have appeared authentic, detailing a pattern of travel from his home in Tehran to Zurich, Brussels, Paris, Istanbul or Dubai, and would have spanned the four years since its date of issue. Upon further questioning, "Simon" would have gladly offered up minute details in German, French, Arabic, Persian or English of his childhood in Emmen, a working-class suburb of Lucerne, or his time abroad studying economics at Georgetown University in Washington, DC. He could have also spoke at great length of his employment as a contracted account manager in the Tehran representative office of the Arab Banking Corporation. A run on the cheque cards at his disposal would have also shown a lengthy credit history to match. And each time the questions were posed, even under a polygraph test, Simon would have recounted these stories with the exact same attention to detail. But, as is with all works of fiction, they were lies, expertly crafted by the wizards of Langley for the non-official cover (NOC) operative whose job it was to guard the most valuable asset the Central Intelligence Agency had known since the Cold War.

But his cover hardly concerned him at the moment. A clear glaze of cold sweat formed across Jack Galloway's brow and the quickening thud of his heart ensured that it would stay there for the immediate future. Using every muscle in his legs, he hastened the pace of his jog and rounded another bend on the dirt path as a healthy sense of paranoia kept an attentive pair of eyes over his shoulder. The path was one of a handful Jack would use to maneuver through the park and it was especially useful for spotting a tail. At this level of the mountain, the path's switchbacks became sharp enough that any surveillance team attempting to maintain continuous visual contact with him would be hard-pressed to remain hidden. Jack planned it that way. He had been jogging aimlessly through one of Tehran's affluent residential neighborhoods at street level for over an hour, only deciding to enter the park and ascend the mountain when he was convinced he hadn't seen anyone twice. If he had spotted so much as a suspicious glance from a passerby, he would simply finish his run and return home to wait patiently for the next opportunity. It was an exhausting routine, but Jack welcomed it. It was what kept him alive.

After clearing another tight bend, Jack turned his head and saw only nature at his back. Nothing. He was "black"—free of surveillance.

He took a second to catch his breath and take in the view before him. Jamshidieh Park sat on the lower slopes of the Alborz Mountains, which formed Tehran's northern-most extremity. The entire Iranian capital, home to over eight million, spread out before him in a seemingly endless field of concrete residential blocks and snaking highways, all cloaked in drifting clouds of orange smog.

Panting and wiping the sweat from his forehead, Jack bent down and slid off the heel of his right tennis shoe, revealing a small, hidden cavity. He eased two fingers inside the confined space and removed a folded piece of paper wrapped in tin foil. A few steps off the path, Jack found a rock the size of his fist, smooth and much darker than the ones surrounding it. He pushed the rock aside and brushed clear an inch of dirt, unearthing a black, metal surface twice the size of a quarter with a string attached. Jack pulled on the string and eased out a waterproof, eight-inch spike. He unscrewed the threaded cap from the top of the spike and opened a hollow space that was large enough to hold a few film canisters, a thumb drive, or a small message. Jack placed the folded paper inside and buried the spike before replacing the rock exactly as he found it.

Without a swarm of Iranian counterintelligence officers behind him, Jack succeeded in servicing his dead-drop one more time. He stood and stretched his legs before returning to the path. In an hour, a cut-out—an anonymous Iranian Jack regularly paid to pass messages to his asset—would drift by the same rock and retrieve the spike's contents. And before dawn the next morning, an underpaid worker of the Tehran Sanitation Department—whose meager salary Jack also supplemented—would take a piece of chalk and mark a lamppost on Ammar Street opposite a comfortable, walled villa owned by the state. And to the dozens who would drift past that morning, the chalk mark would be meaningless—save for one.

Andrei Ilyich Minin rose from the warmth of a Mercedes-Benz S600 into a frigid gust of eddying snowflakes that bit his round boyish cheeks and tore at his neat sandy hair. He buttoned his overcoat and looked east to a taxiing AirBaltic 737. The winter sun clung shyly to the horizon, swathed in smog and clouds, its weary glare broken by the tailfins of business jets. Minin counted nearly two-dozen pristine Gulfstreams, Bombardiers and Dassaults on the apron at Vnukovo-3, sitting with only inches to spare between their wingtips. That morning an international power menagerie had descended upon Moscow like seals on a rock for the annual meeting of the Valdai Discussion Club. Over the coming week, an assortment of oligarchs, journalists, diplomats, academics and various intellectual hangers-on would gather under the theme, "The World Order: New Rules or a Game without Rules?" After five years of civil war in Syria ripped the old notion of order to shreds, the meeting's roundtables and plenary sessions were geared to find an answer to that perplexing question.

For the keynote that evening, President Mikhail Borisovich Karetnikov was due to deliver a landmark address that would dramatically reassert the Russian Federation's role on the world stage. It was being hinted by the Kremlin that the speech would launch a rhetorical assault on the upheaval of the past nine months with a soaring indictment of Turkey's invasion of Syria that hastened the collapse of the regime and ended the war. Rumors also abounded that Karetnikov would denounce President Andrew Paulson—by name—and condemn the current unipolar world order of the United States that consistently bred such catastrophes in the Middle East. The consequences of this "Karetnikov Doctrine"—as the press deemed it—were up for speculation, but if whispers in the Arctic wind were to be believed, a much darker future lurked on the horizon.

As Minin watched the 737 hurl itself down the runway, his eyes caught a silver Opel Antara parked beneath a fluttering windsock. The SUV's windows were tinted and its license plate was stamped with the prefix code of the Kremlin's Special Purpose Garage. *They weren't even trying to hide,* he thought. Sitting inside were officers of the *Federalnaya Sluzhba Okhrany*—the Federal Protective Service, or FSO—armed with high-powered binoculars and parabolic microphones. Minin immediately knew their target, and who sent them.

Looming over the other planes on the tarmac, like a whale in a school of goldfish, was an Airbus ACJ330. Its fuselage stretched sixty-nine meters from nose to empennage and was painted pearl white with a tapering black band running along the windows. Mounted discreetly on the tail cone and tucked behind the Rolls-Royce engines under the wings were tiny infrared panels meant to stave off heat-seeking missiles. Airstairs were pressed to the cabin door and a bulky man in a wool coat stood guard at the bottom step. Minin made a wary glance at the Opel, and began walking to the plane.

He approached the guard—likely a former operator of the British Special Air Service, as Minin understood most were—and offered his name. After he was wanded with a magnetometer, the guard muttered something in his lapel and nodded for Minin to climbs the stairs.

A young stewardess appeared in the cabin door, dressed impeccably in heels and a tan form-fitting skirt despite the cold. "Welcome aboard, Mr.

Minin," she greeted him in English with a slight French accent. "May I take your coat?"

"Thank you," he replied, pulling his arms from the sleeves.

"His Lordship will be with you presently. Please make yourself comfortable in the lounge just down the corridor," she said with an effortless smile. "May I bring you a beverage while you wait?"

Minin thought for a moment. "Espresso would be wonderful."

"Of course, sir," she held her smile. "My name is Nicolette. Please don't hesitate to ask me or my staff if you require *anything*. It's our pleasure to serve."

"Thank you."

The corridor ran a few steps aft and opened on the lounge, spanning the width of the cabin. The aircraft's interior was designed by the London firm Candy & Candy and was appointed with silk-and-wool carpeting, hand-stitched leather seating and lacquer tables and consoles in understated, earthy tones.

Minin chose a sofa along the starboard fuselage. Bloomberg played on a television recessed in the bulkhead. Amid the scrolling stock ticker and graphs overlaid on the screen, the anchors squawked about the two breaking stories that teased markets from New York to Hong Kong into a frenzy.

At four o'clock that morning, Oleg Dubik—CEO of Gazprom, the world's largest natural gas producer—emerged from a conference room at the Mandarin Oriental hotel in Shanghai and announced that he and his counterpart with the China National Petroleum Corporation (CNPC) had reached an agreement after months of negotiations. Their joint memorandum, which was being parsed by the Bloomberg anchors, revealed a thirty-year deal, worth four hundred billion dollars, that would ship thirty-eight billion cubic meters of Russian natural gas to China annually. A network of pipelines dubbed the "East-Route" would connect the Kovyktin and Chayandin gas fields in eastern Siberia to the metropolitan sprawl surrounding Beijing and the Yangtze River delta. Once constructed and operating at full capacity, the deal would provide one-fifth of China's yearly consumption of natural gas.

Another stewardess entered the lounge and laid a silver tray on the table. She set his espresso cup and saucer with a bowl of sugar cubes in front of him. Across the table, she placed a bottle of Fernet-Branca and a crystal stemmed cordial glass, smiled, and excused herself.

Barely was the ink dry on the memorandum in Shanghai when, at midnight in Moscow, a press release was quietly issued from the Kremlin. The one-page statement sat unnoticed in newsrooms overnight until, with dawn, it exploded.

"I've had hemorrhoids more pleasant, my dear!"

Minin's head spun.

Two gray and white Italian Greyhounds—Artemis and Eos—pranced into the lounge and happily came for Minin with their wet noses. He knew they were gifts to their master from the grand duke of Luxembourg, and twins of the same litter.

Lord Roman Leonidovich Ivanov trailed in a moment later. He was a tall, sharp man of eighty-six with the booming voice of an auctioneer, the confident poise of a Shakespearean actor and the suffocating presence of a master politician. A wavy silver mane covered the sides of his head; wrinkles ran across his forehead like rivulets and connected his wide nose with the corners of his mouth; and pale, fleshy circles ringed his eyes where tanning goggles frequently rested.

"Down, girls," he spat at the dogs while knotting the sash of a bespoke silk kimono around his waist. "Go!" He pointed his bony index finger and whistled and the dogs scampered out of sight. Next his finger turned on Minin.

"I'll ask you straight, boy!" Ivanov's voice swelled through the cabin. "Did you play me for a bloody fool?"

"I—I didn't do anything."

"You're damn right you didn't!"

The second breaking story that morning was an unceremonious announcement that the Kremlin was withdrawing support for South Stream, a pipeline designed to transport Russian gas under the Black Sea to Bulgaria where it would have run in two branches: one south across Greece and under the Adriatic to Italy, and one north across Serbia and Hungary to Austria. The project had been in development for much of the last decade. Customers were arranged in Europe, permits were approved with the transit countries and some sections, such as in Bulgaria, were already under construction. One press release in the middle of the night ended all of that; the consortium could keep building, but the pipes would stay dry.

Ivanov sat across the table from Minin and unscrewed the bottle of Fernet-Branca. "Who knew about this?"

Minin shook his head. "It came from Volodnin's office."

Ivanov scoffed. He poured the bitter into the cordial glass and threw it back in a single gulp.

"If anyone else knew in advance, they kept it from me."

Valery Volodnin was head of the Presidential Administration, Karetnikov's chief of staff and closest confidant. He was also the first deputy prime minister and chairman of both Gazprom and Rosneft, the state oil monopoly. Volodnin had served with the KGB and was suspected to be the leader of the *siloviki,* a faction of former Soviet intelligence officers that now held a number of key positions in Moscow. He was a ruthless manager, enforcer and protector of Karetnikov. It was whispered that when an outspoken journalist or politician ran afoul of the president for the last time, it was Volodnin who personally saw that they troubled his boss no more. Minin was his deputy.

"I was in the air not twenty minutes," Ivanov's eyes tightened. "From that shithole in Ashgabat. The phone rings. I expected great things. But it's my general counsel. Guess how he found out."

Minin didn't answer.

"The fucking BBC!"

Minin blinked and tried to look away.

"I have had an understanding with Gazprom for ten years," Ivanov smoldered. "I fought your battles with Brussels, I assured friends of mine that opening their wallets to Karetnikov was wise, I got those imbeciles in Sofia elected," his tongue hung on the word. "Now I'm cheated out of fifty billion...and I want someone's head, *Andruishka.*"

Ivanov was long called "the Oracle of St James's" for the neighborhood of London where Bridgewater House, his head office, fronted Green Park. His investment firm, the Ivanov Group, amassed a trove of nearly seven trillion dollars in assets under management—and a personal net worth of a hundred and twenty billion, making him easily the wealthiest man on Earth. Over a career spanning sixty years, Ivanov became widely seen as one of, if not the most, influential financial voices alive, on par with or even surpassing some central bank governors, finance ministers and heads of state. He held shares in the world's largest banks, energy companies and shipping lines. One such investment was a fifty-fifty stake held with Gazprom in South Stream AG, a joint venture registered in Zug, Switzerland to design, finance and construct the pipeline. For Karetnikov, it was a tool of geopolitical might to keep Europe addicted to Russian gas and further cement Moscow's influence in the former Soviet satellite states as part of a larger ploy to weaken European unity. For Ivanov, the pipeline was simply good business. And so for years Ivanov toiled behind the scenes to court potential investors and allay concerns, providing a friendly face where his Russian partners could not. While he and Karetnikov personally detested each other, Ivanov always understood that the West wanted Russia alongside it vastly more than it wanted to resist it. Since the end of the Cold War, he endeavored to make that a reality, with great headway, until Mikhail Karetnikov evoked the worst vestiges of his country's past.

It began two years earlier when Karetnikov seized the Crimean peninsula from Ukraine in broad daylight and dared the West to make him pay. As sanctions were levied against Karetnikov's associates, the European Commission passed regulation after regulation to prevent South Stream from being built and leaned on the Bulgarian government, where the pipeline would come ashore, to end their involvement. Gazprom executives and Kremlin emissaries began clandestine pilgrimages to Bojan Siderov, the prime minister of Bulgaria, and showered the country with politically strategic investments. Ivanov warily helped the GRU, Russian military intelligence, funnel millions to Ataka, a far-right party opposed to European integration and the exploration of Bulgarian shale gas. After parliamentary elections, Ataka gained enough seats to bolster Siderov's coalition and pass a bill clearing the way for the pipeline. Everything was in order, and even as of that morning, pipe-laying ships were at work in the Black Sea.

"I can't give you an answer," Minin sighed.

"What do I say to Eni and OMV?" Ivanov leaned in. "What do I say to the crews in Burgas?" He shrugged. "'Mikhail's mistress bit down a little too hard last night and, shame, it's worth fuck-all now?'"

Minin looked down at his toes.

"I helped that bastard when no one else would."

During the last week of negotiations in Shanghai, the Chinese delegation suddenly informed Gazprom that in any arrangement they would only agree to pay half of the going European market rate for Russia's gas. To strengthen their position they revealed that a consortium of Central Asian energy monopolies, led by President Dhzuma Ovezov of Turkmenistan, was offering the same rate. The Chinese demanded that Gazprom match the offer or talks would end. Through Karetnikov's furious outbursts when the news reached the Kremlin, Minin quickly thought to make a call.

One of the Ivanov Group's most important holdings was a sixty-percent stake in Vidar, a Geneva-based global commodities trading firm co-run by managing-directors Torbjön Thåström and Arseni Sokoloff, another former Soviet intelligence officer and occasional judo sparring partner with Karetnikov. Vidar held tender contracts with Rosneft, Gazpromneft and Surgutneftgaz and traded a vast swathe of Russian seaborne crude on the open market. At Minin's request, Ivanov flew immediately to Turkmenistan and spent several days holed up in the garish Oguzkhan Palace in Ashgabat, sweet-talking the notoriously corrupt Ovezov. He countered the Chinese with a proposal that Vidar would purchase the lot of Central Asia's gas exports at the standing market rate for the next thirty years, and promised that he would personally secure a grant from his friends at the Asian Development Bank to help construct a new power plant on the Caspian Sea. To seal the deal, Ivanov brought twenty suitcases bursting with British pounds sterling for whatever use Ovezov saw fit. With that, Ovezov was hooked.

"Do you know what kind of delusional nonsense that crater-faced cretin goes around spouting? He thinks we're mates now," said Ivanov. "He wants to come up to Scotland for a stalking trip at Glengorm."

Minin pointed to the television with his chin. "They're talking about him."

Ivanov craned his neck.

The anchors cut to footage filmed three days earlier. One clip panned over the charred husk of the baroque Château Bartholoni. Another featured a row of police cars and fire engines, and emergency lights pulsing in the dead of night as lips of flame crept above treetops in the distance. The last showed the tranquil surface of Lake Geneva, shimmering red and orange like a sheet of molten copper.

"That's done now," Ivanov dismissed.

"I heard there was smoke in his lungs." Minin looked at the TV. "He was still alive."

Ivanov pursed his lips. "I want to read something to you, *Andruishka*. Don't move." The Oracle of St James's floated down the corridor.

Arseni Sokoloff was outraged to hear of the scheming in Ashgabat; Vidar was nominally under his control, a firm that Sokoloff alone had built into a behemoth of the global energy markets that enticed Ivanov's investments. He refused to tether Vidar to Dhzuma Ovezov's incompetence for the next thirty years. Yet without him, Gazprom's hope for a lucrative contract with the Chinese would implode. Sokoloff had to be removed from the equation. Minin quietly reached out to Colonel-General Vyasheslav Trubnikov, director-general of the GRU, and asked for his assistance. In turn, Trubnikov contacted a man whom he only ever referred to as, "the American."

Ivanov returned with a small leather-bound book bearing the title, *Michael Robartes and the Dancer* by the poet William Butler Yeats. He flipped to a yellowed, dog-eared page and mouthed, "The Second Coming," then read aloud:

Turning and turning in the widening gyre
The falcon cannot hear the falconer;
Things fall apart; the centre cannot hold;
Mere anarchy is loosed upon the world,
The blood-dimmed tide is loosed, and everywhere
The ceremony of innocence is drowned;
The best lack all conviction, while the worst
Are full of passionate intensity.

Surely some revelation is at hand;
Surely the Second Coming is at hand.
The Second Coming! Hardly are those words out
When a vast image out of Spiritus Mundi
Troubles my sight: somewhere in sands of the desert
A shape with lion body and the head of a man,
A gaze blank and pitiless as the sun,
Is moving its slow thighs, while all about it
Reel shadows of the indignant desert birds.
The darkness drops again; but now I know

That twenty centuries of stony sleep
Were vexed to nightmare by a rocking cradle,
And what rough beast, its hour come round at last,
Slouches towards Bethlehem to be born?

Ivanov's cold indifference was unshakable. He snapped the book shut. "Do you want to spend the rest of your life in that man's shadow? Or would you like to cast a pall of you own?"

"Where you're asking to go—I can't follow."

"You're not innocent anymore," Ivanov said.

"No." Minin shook his head. "No."

"Could Trubnikov's man?"

Minin stared at the TV. "He's done that much."

"Andruishka, we've talked about this for years."

"It's not right."

"Go see him. See for yourself."

"He was still alive…"

"He's not now."

Minin's eyes welled for a moment.

"Andruishka?"

"Fine," he breathed. "I will."

CHAPTER 4

THERE IS AN old Russian saying: *"Tyajela ti shapka manomakha,"* which translates as, "The crown of the tsar is very heavy." For Mikhail Karetnikov, his was becoming too heavy to bear.

The president was a creature of habit. He woke precisely at eleven in the morning and began his day with a modest meal of fresh-blended carrot juice, cottage cheese and an omelet of quails' eggs gifted from the farmlands of Patriarch Pimen II, primate of the Russian Orthodox Church. He had no taste for tea, coffee or alcohol and the intoxicating effects they sowed on the mind. After breakfast, he made time for swimming. In the dead of winter he preferred for the water to be heated to a near-scalding temperature. He donned goggles and threw himself into a vigorous front crawl up and down the length of the indoor pool, relaxing his muscular frame, which after sixty-three years—to his displeasure—began to ache with hints of mortality. The few journalists allowed behind the veil to write profiles on him had speculated with fawning romanticism that it was in those moments of solitude, when all was true and laid bare, that the pivotal decisions of his reign were made—fateful decisions of life and death that reverberated from Kaliningrad to Vladivostok, sent tremors through the capitals of Europe, and lapped at the western shore of the Atlantic.

By then the first bevy of aides and ministers were summoned, but he made no effort to hasten his rituals; they idled in nearby waiting rooms, often for hours, without a syllable of protest. He loathed the concrete beehive of Moscow: its gridlock and pollution, its human stains. He elected to avoid the city whenever possible and forced his subjects to come to him. As Louis XIV relocated the royal court from Paris to Versailles, he chose Novo-Ogaryovo, nestled in the forests twenty-six kilometers west of the Kremlin, as his official residence. The sprawling country estate was centered on a mustard-colored neoclassical villa built in the late 1950s as a *gosdacha* for Soviet elites and featured several guest cottages, a greenhouse and a gymnasium, horse stables and a chapel, a barracks for the contingent of FSO guards and two helipads. In recent years he only emerged from behind the compound's six-meter walls when the pedantic pace of protocol warranted. Otherwise, that snowy sweep of white birch and pine trees was the only sliver of his kingdom to meet his steely eyes.

He bathed and dressed in his own time as well. His showers were frigid and bracing. His wardrobe was curated almost exclusively with suits of dour cloth cut and sewn by master tailors flown in from shops on Savile Row, often on recommendation from the oligarchs who came to pay him fealty. On occasion he deigned to inject a touch of color at the neck with a rich, woven-silk tie in a classical shade such as Bordeaux. Unlike the flowing velvet robes of the tsars before him, his uniform did not need to elicit strength; his words and his deeds accomplished that alone.

He began working shortly past noon. His office at Novo-Ogaryovo was spare and impersonal with cream paneling and a heavy wooden desk. A bank of clunky, fixed-line Soviet telephones connected him to secretaries in the anteroom outside. There were no computers. As a boy he struggled to comprehend words written on pages, and although he trained that childhood weakness away, the glowing intangibility of electronic screens still irritated him. First he read the popular tabloids *Komsomolskaya Pravda* and *Moskovksy Komsomlets,* understanding that their consumption by millions of ordinary Russians was often a reflection of the national mood, followed by the more prestigious broadsheets *Kommersant* and *Vedomosti* with their lightly censored commentary and analysis of economic and political issues. Then his attention turned to four leather portfolios, each containing a report prepared by his legion of spies and enforcers. The first report from the *Federalnaya Sluzhba Bezopasnosti*—the Federal Security Service, or FSB—concerned domestic threats, such as the latest on counterterrorism operations in the Caucasus. The next was from the FSO and contained recent information on opposition figures that displeased him. Another from the GRU outlined the directorate's support to separatist militias in the eastern Donbass region of Ukraine. Finally, a report from the *Sluzhba Vneshney Razvedki*—the Foreign Intelligence Service, or SVR—kept him abreast of phone conversations placed from the hotels of the Ukrainian and American diplomats currently meeting in Berlin with his foreign minister, Uri Popoff.

There were no daily staff meetings. By then any matters that were left unresolved from the previous night were already settled in his mind, and those initial hours were spent echoing his edicts across the organs of government. He saw little purpose in consulting others. Time had left him weary of dissenting views and suspicious of those harboring them. In fact, he considered it a sign of poor resolve when he heard how his counterparts endlessly entertained the opinions of lesser men. The Russian people placed their faith in his judgment alone. Only he was entrusted to lead them. To share that responsibility would be an abdication of the moral contract empowering him to rule. To commit such a crime would be to associate with the worst criminals of Russian history, a treasonous lot who surrendered their authority and allowed it to be hijacked by hysterics and madmen.

That was the burden he shouldered, the weight of Mikhail Karetnikov's crown. If he set it aside, even for a moment, the gates of his country would swing open to a familiar foreign horde that would pillage and subjugate until Russia was, again, unrecognizable.

For sixteen years his was a lonely crusade; a battle fought from gilded hall to gilded hall, a monotonous string of meaningless receptions, ceremonial pageantry and tedious formality. Through it, he moved with a swaggering stride and gleamed as if made of bronze. Silence encircled him. Men flinched at his sight. Faces turned solemn and eyes sank to the floor. Friendship was not a luxury he afforded himself. After thirty years of marriage he divorced his wife, Lyudmila, when her anxiety attacks became too grating on his patience and sent her to a dacha in the Ural Mountains. Men visited shortly after she arrived and threatened to come again if she ever spoke to the press. His two daughters were state secrets and lived quiet lives in the Netherlands. Clear of his gaze, his ministers and aides would gather in Moscow's *nouveau riche* restaurants and nightclubs. His courtiers thought highly of themselves if they learned to mimic his mannerisms, to inform their own inflections by the cadence of his voice. They would laugh and prattle deep into the night, eating and drinking until pains shot up their sides and their faces became a flushed field of ruptured capillaries.

All the while, Karetnikov held the gates.

He was at his desk when Andrei Minin entered.

The young man made the customary intimation of submission when entering Karetnikov's sacred presence and subconsciously dipped his head.

"Good morning, Andrei Ilyich."

"Good after— Good morning, Mr. President."

Karetnikov didn't look at Minin. His eyes were on the paper before him, making final alterations to the speech he would deliver that evening to the Valdai Discussion Club at the Moscow Expocentre. "What did Roman Leonidovich have to say?"

"He's angry—"

"I can't hear you." Karetnikov looked up.

It was an awkward arrangement, standing there on an open tract of the parquet floor while Karetnikov hovered behind his desk; seated, but looming nonetheless. Minin stepped a bit closer. "Roman Leonidovich is upset that we abruptly ended our involvement in South Stream."

"It wasn't abrupt. I decided months ago."

"He feels personally betrayed after lending his support in Gazprom's deal with the Chinese."

Karetnikov lost interest. He looked back at his speech. "He served his purpose and was compensated accordingly."

"With respect, sir," Minin's voice wavered, "he does not see it that way."

"How will he survive?" Karetnikov said with a sardonic roll of his eyes.

Minin exhaled. "Sir, what should I tell him?"

"I don't care. With Arseni gone, I see no reason to continue any relationship with Roman Leonidovich. I've already instructed Gazprom and Rosneft to find another firm when their contracts with Vidar expire. We're moving on."

Minin clenched his left hand into a fist. "Mr. President—"

"That's all."

Minin dipped his head again. "Thank you, sir." He let himself out and stopped in the corridor. Minin did as Ivanov asked. He finally saw it for himself, and it made his stomach turn. Although it didn't much matter anymore, a small piece of him felt anguish—a resigned sorrow that it had come to this.

The armor-plated Peugeot 508 sedan arrived promptly on call in front of Beit Rahbari, the leader's household in central Tehran. Saeed Mofidi, senior advisor to the supreme leader, sank onto the backseat and welcomed an earlier end to yet another day. His Excellency, Supreme Leader Ayatollah Ali Mostafa Khansari, had found himself in a haze since mid-morning— largely incoherent in his speech and frequently forgetful of where he was: symptoms of dementia that slowly reft a path of ruin through his brain. The ayatollah had good days and bad, but this, Mofidi knew, was one of the worst in weeks and particularly difficult for him to watch. Khansari's only engagement that evening—dinner with a group of Islamic jurists from Qom—was hastily canceled. The reason given was, as usual, canned, vague and deceptive. But Mofidi knew the truth and he would record it all, just as he had always done.

"*Asr be kheyr, Baradar* Saeed!" his driver, Babak, a young sergeant in the Revolutionary Guards greeted the old general.

"And a good evening to you, *baradar.* What's the time?"

"Half-past six," Babak checked his watch.

"That's right. Let us take time to praise God and all His blessings."

"As you wish." Babak eased the car around the circular driveway and through the front gates where a pair of soldiers from the IRGC's Ansar-ol-Mahdi Force, the unit charged with protecting top regime figures, saluted sharply. The Peugeot turned onto Pasteur Street and quickly cleared a series of barriers and checkpoints.

Rush hour was the same in nearly every major city around the world, but in Tehran an abundance of aging, poorly built vehicles and a dismal public transportation system made the twice-daily migration a special kind of hell. The traffic problems were compounded by the city's geography. Surrounded on all sides by tall mountain ranges, Tehran did not have much free-flowing air, which shrouded the busy streets in a cloud of exhaust and other noxious fumes. Mofidi looked out his window and noticed that tonight the roads had reverted back to their typical gridlock. For the three days prior, schools, most businesses and some government offices were closed, all in a futile attempt to clear up the dense blanket of smog that lingered over the capital. Many vehicles in Iran were fed a domestically produced blend of gasoline that did not meet the refining standards of the cargoes imported from abroad. Instead, the domestic gasoline contained high levels of aromatics and burned with concentrations of floating particles. When mixed with the city's abnormally high levels of nitrous oxide and ozone, the smog led to a variety of health problems from headaches and dizziness to more serious cardiac and respiratory ailments. Tehran's mayor and the health ministry had taken steps to combat the problem, but they were hardly drops in the ocean. Spontaneous three-day public holidays did nothing but bring an estimated three hundred million dollar hit to the economy and strict traffic controls—alternating days between even and odd license plate numbers—did little against the three-and-a-half million cars and buses on city roadways. As usual, the mullahs and assorted hardliners railed that it was all America's doing. Mofidi mused quietly to himself considering that. Iran's failure to expand its handful of refineries had forced it to become a major importer of foreign gasoline. The thought was maddening: an OPEC member, one of the largest producers of oil and natural gas on the planet was *importing* gasoline to run its economy. On top of that, the holder of the world's second-largest natural gas reserves, behind only Russia, was already a net importer of gas. Large sections of these imports were needed for injection into the country's fading oilfields. Yet from the madness, Mofidi was beginning to see a ray of light after decades of misery.

Three years earlier a sweeping majority elected a moderate cleric from Isfahan, Hojjatoleslam Behrouz Rostani, as president of the Islamic Republic. Rostani's election came as an utter shock to hardliners in the seminaries and the Revolutionary Guards. He campaigned on a populist message of improving the lives of ordinary Iranians, reaching out to their traditional geopolitical rivals in the United States and across the Persian Gulf. He promised to alleviate the Western sanctions that had decimated the Iranian economy. Armed with that mandate, Rostani presented a new face to the world, offering reconciliation and declaring an end to the craven rhetoric of his predecessors. First on the agenda was to finally settle the issue that drove a wedge between his country and the modern world: Iran's nuclear weapons program. A backchannel was established with Washington through the sultan of Oman, which resulted in months of fierce negotiations in Lucerne and Geneva and Vienna, until—almost a year ago—Rostani's foreign minister, Javad Zanjani, reached an accord with his American and European partners called "the Joint Comprehensive Plan of Action," or simply, the JCPOA.

Provisions in the agreement were overseen by the International Atomic Energy Agency, the IAEA, and gradually came into effect over the past twelve months. Iran's stockpile of low-enriched uranium—which was concentrated under twenty percent of uranium-235, and useful only in commercial light-water reactors—was reduced from ten thousand kilograms to less than three hundred, and would be maintained at that level for fifteen years, while two-thirds of its centrifuge holdings would be placed in storage. The enrichment facilities at Fordow and Natanz and the Arak heavy-water reactor were all converted to research and scientific purposes. The goal of these key provisions was to lengthen Iran's "breakout time"—the time necessary to produce enough fissile material for a single nuclear weapon—from two to three months to a year. In exchange, as the IAEA confirmed Iran's compliance, the United States and the European Union would drawback their sanctions.

Mofidi could already see the consequences of that Western chokehold being lifted. New delegations seemed to land at Tehran's Imam Khomeini International Airport one after another. Just last week, a group of executives from Siemens and BASF arrived with the president of the German Chambers of Commerce and Industry. Before that, the French automobile manufacturer, Groupe PSA, inquired about licensing arrangements. The major Iranian banks Mehr, Ansar and Saderat were reconnected to the SWIFT transaction network. Total and Royal Dutch Shell proposed investments in the country's oil and gas industries. And for it, President Rostani's approval ratings had skyrocketed. Through the smog, Mofidi saw a tinge of hope on the streets, an infectious air of good fortune. But it was not destined to last.

Some were determined to scuttle it all. Major General Qasem Shateri, commander of the IRGC's Quds Force, launched into fiery tirades whenever the agreement came up in Supreme National Security Council meetings. He even once openly accused Rostani of being a seditious Israeli agent. As if to pour salt in his wounds, Rostani pressed his luck with the Americans further. After the JCPOA was ratified, he dispatched Zanjani back to the negotiating table to ruminate with the Americans on the issues of human rights, ballistic missile technology and Iran's support for groups like Hezbollah and Hamas that still divided them. Headway was being made until, almost out of thin air, news reached their hotel in Lucerne that Turkish tanks had rolled over the Syrian border and the rebels were staging an uprising in Damascus. The Iranian delegation left and never returned. The

JCPOA was honored and enacted by both sides, but as Mofidi knew the zealots always wished, Iran was once more at an impasse with the United States.

Babak had skillfully maneuvered the Peugeot north along Vali Asr Avenue through the dense flow of traffic to the corner of Sadabad Street off Tajrish Square, only a few blocks from Mofidi's home. He pulled alongside the curb in front of Masjid Giahi, a local Shia mosque. This was routine for Mofidi on days when time permitted. He hopped out of the car and walked through the front doors. Babak stayed with the Peugeot, admiring the piety of the general—unaware that an act of treason was underway.

In the expansive entry hall, Mofidi stopped, hung his suit jacket on a hook, removed the pair of black loafers from his feet, and placed them on a shelf with the shoes belonging to those already in the prayer room. A quick look at his wristwatch before that too was put away told him it was nearly seven o'clock. *Right on time.* Clean and ready to stand before Allah after washing his feet, face and arms, he stepped into the hall to join a group of Muslims already in prayer before the *qiblah* wall, which faced southwest toward Mecca. As he stood up straight, his hands at his side to begin his prayer, a wave of peace came over him.

Outside, a middle-aged Tehrani named Akbar entered the mosque a few minutes behind Mofidi and went through the motions to cleanse himself. Akbar operated a stall not far from the mosque, selling snacks and newspapers to passersby. The extra envelope of cash he received each week to cooperate and remain silent helped him feed four hungry young mouths at home. He was a religious man, but tame in his political sensibilities, and he welcomed the opportunity to undermine the mullahs who strangled his country. The way Akbar saw it—he was the patriot. He too removed a pair of black loafers and placed them on the shelf directly to the left of Mofidi's. To any onlooker, the shoes were identical.

Several minutes later, Mofidi's failing knees began to ache and he concluded his discussion with the Almighty. He finished his recitations and gave a glance over his shoulder to acknowledge the angels that followed mankind, recording their deeds—good and bad. He saw Akbar at the end of the row and guilt quickly overcame the peace. *This, Saeed, is the* right *path,* a voice told him. In conclusion of the prayer, he cupped his hands at his chest and wiped his face with his palms. While no one noticed, Saeed Mofidi was wiping tears from his eyes. He stood and left the prayer room, making sure to avoid any eye contact with Akbar just a few feet away. He donned his jacket in the entry hall and led his hands to the loafers on the left. Without a hint of emotion on his face, he put the shoes on his feet and exited the mosque to the waiting Peugeot. It was an exchange that even the most skilled counterintelligence officer would fail to notice.

"Take me home," he ordered Babak.

Mofidi's home, a white, stone villa surrounded by a high wall on Ammar Street, was a short drive from the mosque, and they arrived through the gates in minutes. The tree-lined residential street was eerily calm. "Do you have a family, *baradar?*" Mofidi hesitated as he opened the car door.

"Yes, my wife bore us a baby girl earlier this year and by the grace of God she is the most beautiful thing I have ever seen! *Inshallah,* we will be blessed with more."

"I envy you." Mofidi disappeared inside the darkened villa without another word. Alone again, he fixed a small helping of *gheyme polo,* rice with yellow split peas and meat. It was shortly after eight in the evening and he passed the next few hours reading the state news reports. He had to wait until midnight.

The clear moonlight over the Kuwaiti desert was a sharp contrast from the cloud of noxious fumes that lingered over the Iranian capital. At Camp Arifjan, among a beige grid of prefabricated concrete buildings, warehouses and Quonset huts, an array of antennas reached high into the starry night sky. Near the camp's perimeter fence, guarded by a detachment of Triple Canopy security contractors, was a modular trailer adjacent to a five hundred-kilowatt shortwave radio transmitter. The Central Intelligence Agency knew the trailer by the code name, "LONGHORN."

A steady stream of coffee kept the sole technician on duty awake. She checked a bank of digital clocks mounted over her workstation, saw that it was nearly midnight in Tehran, and prepared the latest CITADEL message for transmission. Whoever this asset was, what he did and the meaning of the message she was about to send, she did not know. However, the resources and secrecy that Langley brought to bear in support of this single mission was unlike anything she had ever seen.

Mofidi was ready at the small desk in his bedroom on the top floor of his home ten minutes before midnight. The curtains were drawn and every light in the villa was doused except for a dim lamp in front of him. At his fingertips was a pad of graph paper, a pencil and a Sangean model ATS-505 shortwave radio. He had retrieved the right loafer from the pair he swapped with Akbar at Masjid Giahi and removed the heel to access the cavity inside. The paper wrapped in tinfoil, which just over twenty-four hours ago was concealed inside a dead-drop spike in Jamshidieh Park, now sat in his hands. The courier had again delivered it without error. He unwrapped the tinfoil and laid the paper on his desk. In outward appearance, it was just a small sheet of random digits written into fifty-six groups of five, but to anyone with knowledge of cryptography, it was a one-time pad, the only method of encryption mathematically impossible to crack. Its security came from its key—a set of numbers that were truly random—and the strict rule that it could only be used once with the sole copies of the key being held by sender and recipient.

Mofidi checked the time again—thirty seconds to midnight. He directed his shortwave radio through a sea of static until he reached the frequency at 9.359 kHz and adjusted his headphones. Initially there was just more indiscernible white noise, but suddenly—out of the ether—came his signal.

Beep. Beep. Beep.

Mofidi readied his pencil to the graph paper and waited. The three successive tones told him the transmission was about to begin. Soon after, a disembodied female voice took its place.

"Five-one-niner. Five-one-niner. Five-one-niner."

The voice spoke Mofidi's radio call sign—519—and continued again a second later.

"Three-six-five-five-seven. Three-six-five-five-seven." The transmission repeated each group of numbers twice for clarity. *"Six-zero-niner-one-seven. Six-zero-niner-one-seven. Two-niner-zero-one-two. Two-niner-zero-one-two. Two-niner-three-zero-five. Two-niner-three-zero-five. Two-niner-three-zero-five. Two-niner-three-zero-five."*

The broadcast continued, reciting all fifty-six groups. Once more, the voice vanished into a sea of white noise. Mofidi wrote each number down onto his graph paper and now had before him a block of seemingly meaningless numbers.

```
36557   60917   29012   29305   21905   77664   29387   47216
06327   38003   54920   63833   79320   00023   18741   92764
12998   42609   22351   96820   37727   57230   19952   79779
27125   33774   99618   58312   25301   53815   07840   62056
78122   94325   40681   84078   04838   39965   04751   11285
74404   31189   35078   44121   29594   30445   02885   14965
81639   06472   42375   34374   11249   23946   16318   88246
84418
```

His attention now turned to the one-time pad's key, which had another set of numbers equal in length. Mofidi lined up the two sets beginning with the second group in the broadcast; the first was the original grouping from the key in front of him and meant only to indicate that he was using the correct one-time pad for that particular transmission. He started with the first group—60917—and added it, using non-carrying arithmetic, to its corresponding group in the one-time pad so that it equated to a third set of numbers—95121. This set was the message's plaintext and indicated each letter's numerical value in the English alphabet. Mofidi repeated this process methodically, through each group, with every digit, until the message revealed itself. It was a message to him…

HAVE OBSERVED UNIDENTIFIED FACILITY UNDER MOUNTAIN
NEAR HAJ ALI GHOLI DRY LAKE, SEMNAN PROVINCE. REQUEST
INFORMATION ON PURPOSE, NATURE OF FACILITY. BE SAFE —
JACK.

Mofidi sat back in his chair and contemplated the message from his American handler. *An underground facility at Haj Ali Gholi? A wasteland? That doesn't exist.* He—CITADEL—Omid, the pseudonym Mofidi used to sign all his letters to CIA and the Persian word for "hope"—was in the best possible position to discover what was happening at this facility the Americans were so excited over, if it even existed. The supreme leader's health was ailing, a fact known by few outside his inner circle. Both unwilling and unable to work hands-on with many matters of state, Ayatollah Khansari left most issues up to a small group of trusted advisers, one of them being Saeed Mofidi. In fact, he had come to rely on the retired general as a personal emissary to all branches of the armed forces. The question that dominated his mind was why he was not aware of a secret underground facility far-off in an unforgiving terrain. He took the deciphered message and the one-time pad to his kitchen sink and turned on the faucet. The pages dissolved instantly in the water, forever destroying any trace of the broadcast.

It was raining. It always was in his nightmares.

Mofidi was soaked to the bone and his soul cried out for answers. Raindrops gathered on his eyelashes. He looked up to the towering red brick edifice before him. It was the main wall of Evin Prison, and while the design was unremarkable, it had only one purpose: to strike fear into the heart of anyone who looked upon it. It was August of 1999 and a month earlier the regime's security forces had quelled a student uprising at Tehran University. Mofidi's son was studying law there and in the midst of the chaos plain-clothed men with beards and clubs, the dreaded Basij, charged into his dormitory, dragging him and Zahra, his young fiancé, away. Mofidi would never forget the phone call he received informing him that they were being held at Evin for conspiring against the Islamic Revolution. His legs went weak, his head faint, and his stomach sick when he heard the news. Evin Prison was where the shah and now the ayatollah's security services held its political prisoners. Unspeakable acts were being committed against his only son and the woman he loved. He had to free them from that hell.

A mob had formed outside the prison when he arrived, all demanding to see their loved ones. Men chanted and shouted and women wailed in agony, slapping their faces and beating their chests. Mofidi was one of the lucky ones and had managed to obtain clearance from his division commander to visit his son. The throngs outside did not have that luxury. As he approached the tall iron gates, a guard on the wall above fired off a burst from a PKM machine gun up into the air. The crowd slipped into chaos with people screaming and running for cover. Mofidi dropped down closer to the gates and covered his head. When the shooting stopped he went inside and into a small front office to secure his visitation pass. The guard checked his papers against a list of appointments for that day, nodded, and led him to the prosecution wing. Once there, a prison guard escorted him to a ward on the far side of the prison.

Mofidi had to fight with every fiber of his being to maintain just the will to stand. His mind raced with every horrific kind of thought. *Will they release him? Was he tortured? Was there a mistake? ...Was he guilty?* Once inside the main hallway, lined with cells, the smell of body odor and raw sewage overtook him. Distant cries for redemption and mercy cut through the odor, making it all the more unbearable for him. *My son is here!* he cried to himself. A row of blindfolded prisoners paraded past him. His heart raced. The guard told him to wait there while he arranged the visit with his son. He felt dizzy as the shrieks and smells swirled around him.

Minutes later, Mofidi saw a trio of guards, wielding AK-47s, escort a group of barefoot, young—some teenage—girls down the hall. They looked broken, as only a caged animal could appear. Some had tears streaming down their faces and others were caked in dried blood. The shock immediately hit him—one of the girls was Zahra. He pointed to her, pleading with the guard. *"Baradar!* That girl is my son's fiancé. She is innocent!"

The guard rested his hand on the shoulder of Mofidi's uniform and whispered in his ear, "I am sorry, but the execution order has already been given. Nothing can be done."

Mofidi wanted to rush out and grab her—take her away from that hell on earth, but his legs wouldn't allow him to move, not allow him to save her from those monsters. Her face was gaunt and expressionless. She walked past Mofidi with a hollow fear in her eyes. A minute later, gunshots echoed through the hall and a rush of birds in a nearby courtyard flapped their wings off to the heavens. Just as the guns went silent, the call for prayer boomed over the loudspeakers.

"Allahu akbar! Allahu akbar! Allahu akbar!" the prison guards cried.

Mofidi said a silent prayer to himself. He was led off to a cell and instructed to wait. He still felt dizzy and could not even begin to comprehend what he had just witnessed. His son's fiancé was dead. Would he tell him? How could he tell him? After what seemed like an eternity, the cell door opened and the guard led his son into the room.

Mofidi had never seen anything so horrific in his life.

His son walked to his father, hunched over, dragging his left foot, which was broken at the ankle. His body was rail-thin and his clothes hung loosely to his frame. His son was only twenty-three but there were streaks of white in his hair that had not been there before. One eyelid was closed and a stream of dried blood trailed down from the socket. Cigarette burns covered his body.

With what strength that remained, Mofidi reached out to grab his boy.

The guard lifted his arm to block the embrace. "You must not touch the prisoner!"

Mofidi glared at him with pure sorrow and desperation in his eyes. The guard dropped his arm. Mofidi caught his son and they both collapsed to the floor.

"Omid, it's me, it's your father. I'm here now. Do you hear me? It's me. It's me and I'm going to take care of you."

Omid spoke in a pained whisper. "They said we were conspiring with the People's Mujahedeen but none of it is true. Papa, please get Zahra out of here." His voice broke. "I cannot bear to see them torture her. I don't care what they do to me but by Allah's love, I can't see it anymore." Tears filled his eyes. "I don't know how human beings are capable of such things. Papa, they raped her. They took her and they raped her in front of me. They made me watch." Omid gathered his gaze deep into his father's eyes. "I told lies, Papa. Zahra is pregnant. She cannot stay here. I'm so sorry."

Mofidi sobbed. He tried to open his mouth and form words, but all that came was a high-pitched crack. What was there to say? Mofidi wiped his nose. His forehead met his son's. "Omid *jon,* I love you so, so much! You are my whole world. I promise I'll do everything I can to get you and Zahra out. You need to stay strong. Promise me. I love you, my dear boy!" He held his son close until the guard spoke up again.

"You must leave."

Mofidi helped his son to his feet. The guard took Omid and led him down the hallway. Mofidi was escorted back to the gates and left into the rain, and the mob of hopeless souls.

As Mofidi was an IRGC officer, he was not treated like the other families and sent a bill for the bullet that took his son's life later that evening. A part of Mofidi died in that prison, but another was born. He could no longer stand by and provide lip service to a madman and his regime. Mofidi resolved then that he would make them suffer, that he would show the world their evil—even if it cost him his life—if only to see his boy again.

CHAPTER 5

SECRETARY OF STATE Angela Weisel's Cadillac limousine pulled to the awning above the ground floor entrance of the West Wing. It had been a long night. Her Air Force C-32 departed Berlin's Tegel Airport at eleven the previous evening and flew eight hours over the Atlantic, landing at Joint Base Andrews shortly after one in the morning. She left her home in Kalorama Heights a few hours later, briefly checked in with her staff at the Harry Truman Building in Foggy Bottom, and then rushed to the White House. After six years of shuttling around the world as the face of American diplomacy, the notion of a full night's sleep was an alien concept.

Stepping through the foyer, a young officer of the Secret Service Uniformed Division greeted her as a regular and typed her name into the visitor log. After checking her coat she turned left and ascended the stairs to the first floor, then made a second left, breezing down the hall and into the office of Dr. Eli Tanner's secretary.

The president's national security advisor had been chained to his desk since five, mostly with his eyes fixed on a pair of computer screens that connected him to the massive government machinery under his supervision. He heard a knock on the doorframe.

"Morning, Eli."

"Hi, Angela," Tanner sighed as he tapped out the closing words of an email.

"Is he ready?"

He glanced at the schedule. "Yeah, he was having breakfast with Frick and Frack. Let's head over." The national security advisor gathered his copy of the day's PDB and a few additional folders. "How was Berlin?" Tanner asked as he exited into the hall with Weisel.

"Poured the whole damn time. How's everything here?"

"Nobody gives a shit about us anymore. I think half the press corps jumped ship to follow Brandon around on a bus."

"You know, I've been meaning to ask you," she said. "But how's Ryan making out?"

"Freeman?"

"Yeah."

Tanner arched his eyebrows. "Seems fine. Sheridan's happy with the pick. He's a career employee and his troops respect him. But he's only a got a year until Brandon, or God knows whoever else, boots him to the curb. As far as I'm concerned, if he keeps Langley off CNN, he'll have done his job."

The national security advisor's office, located on the northwest corner of the West Wing, was farthest from the Oval Office. Weisel and Tanner made their way through the surprisingly narrow halls, past the office of the vice president, who was off barnstorming through New Hampshire, followed by the office of the chief of staff, who was already with his boss. After a left turn, they continued on past the office of the two senior advisors on the right and the workplaces of the deputy chiefs of staff on the left. Most West Wing offices were more like closets, but their prestige came from sitting literally twenty-five feet from the nerve center of American government. The door leading to the Roosevelt Room was on their left and the communications team was sequestered inside, crafting a messaging strategy for a new initiative recently announced in the State of the Union. Tanner then led her right, into the anteroom where cabinet members often queued up like jets over an airport.

"Good morning. Let me check and see where he is." The president's personal secretary rose from her desk and looked through the peephole in the curved door leading to the Oval Office. "They're just finishing up."

"Thanks, Carol," Tanner replied.

A minute later the curved door opened and President Andrew Paulson appeared in the gap, shaking the hands of Hugh Lewis and Gerald Whent, the speaker of the House and the Senate majority leader. After exchanging pleasantries with Tanner and Weisel, they both started back to the Capitol.

"You two ready?" the president asked once they left.

"Absolutely." Weisel was first through the door.

"Ange, that was great work in Berlin," Paulson said as he shook her hand. "Let your team know I appreciate it."

"Thank you, Andrew."

"Have a seat. Help yourself to coffee."

Larry Dawson, the president's chief of staff, a Pittsburgh native and the heir to a steel fortune—who had earned further millions in numerous business ventures of his own—was already seated on one of two beige sofas in the room. A ray of sunlight broke the scattering clouds over the National Mall and shone through three thick polycarbonate-coated windows behind the *Resolute* desk, glinting gently off the gold-and-white-striped wallpaper.

Paulson recently turned the corner into the final year of his presidency. His approval rating consistently hovered around fifty percent, which was sufficiently high enough that his vice president, Brandon Jacobs, saw fit to tether his name to Paulson's record and launch his own campaign for the White House. Jacobs had just won the Iowa Caucus and now swept into New Hampshire with the wind at his back, rapidly clearing a path to his party's nomination. With his potential successor dominating the airwaves, Paulson turned his attention to the bittersweet task of solidifying his mark on the country and glossing over his legacy's scars before less-forgiving historians had their chance.

The president took his usual perch in a caramel leather high-back chair in front of the fireplace. "Well, guys, how are we doing?"

Paulson consistently used that question to open every meeting with his national security advisor since they first entered the Oval Office together on the day of his inauguration. Its cheery delivery masked an intensely serious meaning at its core: What have you done in the last twenty-four hours to keep our enemies at bay?

"Mr. President, before we get started, I'd like to bring you up to speed on a conversation I had earlier with Admiral Wade," said Tanner.

"Shoot."

Tanner reached into a red folder and retrieved a glossy photograph of a portly Arab man in his late-fifties wearing a dark suit, and mostly bald with a thick black mustache that showed obvious signs of dyeing. He handed the photograph to Paulson, who examined it closely.

"Sir, this is the last known depiction of Major General Ali Mamlouk, taken at a Baath Party conference about a month before he disappeared. CIA thinks the Iranians arrested him. You may recall this man was part of Jadid's inner circle and the last commander of the Syrian National Security Bureau. He's been indicted on forty-six counts of crimes against humanity. We believe, as does The Hague, that he relayed the orders authorizing the use of sarin against Ghouta in 2013."

"So did we find 'em?" asked the president as he leaned in to place the photograph on the coffee table.

"According to Admiral Wade, about seventy-two hours ago, a shop owner in Tartus' medina—the old city—approached a patrol of Turkish soldiers and claimed that a house in the neighborhood is being used as part of a facilitation network providing shelter to regime officials. The shop owner said that groups of Alawite men have been coming and going from the house at strange hours. Turkey then passed this information to JSOC's task force at Hama, and NSA is now reporting that a cell phone is operating inside the target house with a prepaid SIM card linked to a batch acquired in Athens five months ago by a former Syrian Air Force Intelligence operative. Now, based on that information and intel provided by local assets in Tartus, Wade believes with some certainty that it's a safe house for a high-value target, possibly Al Mamlouk."

Paulson smiled and looked to his chief of staff, who nodded in agreement. "Awesome. Let's go grab the sucker."

"JSOC is conducting further reconnaissance to get full confirmation, most likely a voice signature, before Wade green-lights the operation," Tanner informed. "The Delta squadron at Hama will then conduct the raid alongside the Turks and the FSA."

"Good."

"Moving on to some better news," Tanner continued, "I'll let Angela talk about Berlin."

Secretary Weisel had spent the better part of two days running between the Ritz-Carlton and the Bundeskanzleramt. She was called to the German capital by Chancellor Theo Haneke to help him mediate a discussion with Ukrainian president Petro Udovenko and Russian foreign minister Uri Popoff on the agreement preventing a full-scale war between them. The Minsk II Protocol was signed almost two years ago after an earlier accord collapsed and now governed the terms of the ceasefire between the Ukrainian Armed Forces and the pro-Russian separatist militias dug in across the east. Monitored by the Organization for Security and Co-operation in Europe (OSCE), the protocol established a seventy-kilometer demilitarized zone between the opposing forces' front lines. It had ensured a tenuous peace, but both sides were prone to human error and miscalculation. The summit in Berlin was meant to keep those wounds from festering.

"Well, I guess all's well that ends well," Weisel said as she placed her coffee cup on the table. "Mostly it was Udovenko who did the complaining. He claimed to have intelligence that some tactical missile systems were hidden in towns around Krasnodon and wanted an answer as to why certain separatist units were massing along the coastal highway leading into Mariupol. Popoff, as usual, denied that Russia had any control over their movements, but…" She shook her head. "It was strange. Popoff called the Kremlin yesterday afternoon, and when he came to dinner, he apologized to Udovenko and said the separatists would pull back. No strings attached." Weisel shrugged. "Last I heard, the OSCE reported that the units had, and DIA verified it. Like I said: all's well."

"Interesting," Paulson noted. "And Angela, how are we with Ambassador Lansing's trip?"

That morning, all eyes in the State Department were fixed on Ambassador Harold Lansing, Weisel's special representative for Middle East peace. Later in the evening he would takeoff from Andrews in a C-17 bound for Damascus with a delegation that had worked for months to secure peace talks between Israel and the newly elected Syrian government. With a bit of plodding and reassurance from Turkey, Lansing finally had a deal in place.

"Everything's good to go," Weisel said happily. "I spoke to Harold just before I came over here, and I'll be in touch with Lisa throughout the day." She referred to Ambassador Lisa Tully, their representative to the United Nations in New York.

Paulson massaged his forearm. "Let's run through it again."

"Sure," she breathed. "By noon, over here, the IDF is due to withdraw the last of their personnel from Shebaa Farms. Once UNIFIL confirms their exit, the Security Council will be informed and pass our resolution stating that the United Nations recognizes the farms as Lebanese territory, not Syrian. Then, when Harold gets to Damascus, Ayyoub will announce that he's accepted our invitation to Annapolis, cut ties with the Iranians, close the border to Hezbollah, and call on them to disarm. Ilan Halevi will be on hand to represent the Israelis."

"And how can we expect Hezbollah to take it?"

"Well they're cut off from their main sponsor—"

"Sir, Hezbollah lost two thousand of its own men in the civil war," Tanner cut in. "All of them, including the men who survived, signed up to fight the Israelis, not die as Praetorians for Hafez Jadid. Hezbollah's leadership has serious problems on their hands. Existential problems. They've put themselves deeply at odds with their base; they've lost the respect of their troops. If the clerics don't clean house now, someone much worse might do it for them."

"I have to agree, Andrew," added Weisel. "It makes sense."

"Okay then." Paulson smiled after a moment's silence. "What's next?"

"Right, moving on." Tanner reached for another folder. "I wanted to touch on this gas deal out of Beijing…"

Nine months earlier, in the full blaze of summer, the Islamic State—known colloquially around the world as *al-Dawla*, ISIS, ISIL or Daesh—saw the borders of its self-proclaimed caliphate recede into a narrow arc along the Euphrates in northeastern Syria. After years of pitched combat, a loose confederation of Iraqi security forces, Kurdish *peshmerga* fighters and Shiite militias loyal to Iran, backed by allied warplanes and special operations forces, retook the northern city of Mosul. Within days of the city's liberation, Sunni tribal leaders in Fallujah and al-Qaim revolted and finally uprooted ISIS from its last foothold in Iraq, chasing the terrorists into the desert. In Syria, their capital, Raqqa, was under siege by the Kurdish People's Protection Units (YPG). ISIS was at a crossroads. That air of invincibility, that mystique which seduced thousands of eager young men and women to the caliphate's call to jihad, was publicly and irrevocably shattered. In response, Abu Malik al-Tikriti, the group's leader, called a rare in-person meeting of his Shura Council, a collection of nine senior advisors, to chart a path forward. The council gathered in the middle of the night at a salt farm across the Euphrates from the Syrian town of Deir ez-Zur. Al-Tikriti's bodyguards jammed cellular signals, but not before a local informant employed by the YPG's intelligence arm slipped away and sent a text message to his Kurdish handlers. Three F/A-18E Super Hornets from the USS *Theodore Roosevelt* were already on patrol over Anbar Province and immediately diverted, breaking the sound barrier as they raced into Syrian airspace. In minutes, a series of explosions shook Deir ez-Zur. Six laser-guided AGM-65 Mavericks slammed into the farm and detonated, painting the night sky with a tremendous fireball that was seen for miles in every direction. The Islamic State was decapitated.

As eulogies for al-Tikriti and his lieutenants flooded onto jihadi chat rooms and social media accounts, ISIS' middle managers started scraping over the detritus like famished vultures. Long-held resentment between the *mujahireen,* the group's legion of foreign fighters, and the old guard from Saddam Hussein's military and intelligence services, boiled over. The provincial governors and emirs of affiliates in Yemen and Libya and the Sinai and Afghanistan cemented authority over their fiefdoms. In besieged Raqqa, fighting broke out in the streets between rival field commanders eager to settle past grudges. Each of them had sworn oaths of allegiance to Abu Malik al-Tikriti, alone—now a pile of scorched bones at the bottom of a crater—and in a short time, the self-destructive tendencies of human nature began tearing the caliphate apart. But one man stood above it.

Abu Usman al-Shishani arrived shortly after the outbreak of civil war in Syria with a band of seasoned jihadists from Chechnya. He was an imposing figure, standing well over six-feet tall with a thick red beard and a pockmarked face. His men garnered a reputation for brutality and prowess on the battlefield. Al-Shishani aligned with ISIS and was placed in charge of the Central Directorate Group, a company of elite shock troops. After the massacre at Deir ez-Zur, while infighting raged around him, al-Shishani launched a bold plot to rally the dispossessed to his side and seize control of the caliphate.

The day was now simply known as "6/6."

On the morning of June 6th four terrorists detonated explosives-laden suitcases in the bustling main concourse of Istanbul's Haydarpasa Terminal. Almost simultaneously, numerous bombs ripped through trams and Metro stations and sent two commuter ferries to the bottom of the Bosphorus. Masked terrorists wrapped in body armor trawled the Grand Bazaar, tossing hand grenades and spraying the crowd with AK-47s. Other men strolled through Taksim Square and visited the plaza outside the Hagia Sophia mosque, where they too became martyrs. In the Levent business district, terrorists barricaded the entrances of the Kanyon Shopping Mall, using

GoPro cameras to broadcast their every step over the Internet, and beheaded each man, woman and child they came across. By noon, when police and responding army units finally gunned down the last terrorist, nearly five hundred people were dead. Abu Usman al-Shishani claimed responsibility "in honor of the fallen princes of the caliphate."

The response was swift. Even before the blood was washed off the streets, Turkey's president, Yusuf Demir, took to the airwaves and made his intentions known. He shamed the Arabs and the Europeans and the Americans and all of mankind for years of apathy, for allowing a wholesale slaughter before its eyes. There would be no paltry display of bombs falling in the desert or quiet commando raids in the night. Turkey would unleash its full military might on Syria. He declared then, for all to see, that the Syrian civil war was coming to an end.

Demir invoked Article 5 of the NATO Charter, a clause stipulating that an armed attack against one alliance member was an attack on all.

On June 8th, the Turkish Second Army—one hundred thousand troops—massed along the Syrian border with an arsenal of M60 main battle tanks and self-propelled howitzers. The vanguard was the 5th and 20th armored brigades and the 28th and 39th mechanized infantry brigades. Their twenty thousand men crossed through a ninety-kilometer section of the border between Azaz and Jarabulus and pushed thirty kilometers into ISIS-held territory by nightfall. The Turkish troops rapidly consolidated their gains and maintained short lines of communication and supply as fixed- and rotary-wing attack aircraft provided cover. Infantry and border patrol units poured in at the rear. The invasion force then advanced on two fronts. From Azaz, an armored column rolled down Highway 214 and assaulted Syrian government lines around Aleppo, relieving the entrenched rebels and capturing the city in less than two weeks. A second front advanced from Jarabulus and followed Highway 4 along the southern bank of Lake Assad toward Raqqa.

It was a medieval scene in the caliphate's capital, encircled by the Turkish Army on the west and YPG fighters on the east. Leishmaniasis, a flesh-eating disease carried by sandflies, had taken hold on the city. The banks of the Euphrates were choked with corpses. The walking dead wandered the streets. As troops entered Raqqa, ISIS unleashed their rage on civilians trapped inside. The jihadists made little attempt to repel the assault; they burned homes, raped and butchered indiscriminately. Much of the foreign *mujahireen,* including al-Shishani, escaped south across the open desert through Jordan and into the isolated, northern frontiers of Saudi Arabia. Others melted into the population and gradually worked their way back to sympathetic enclaves in Europe. Those who stayed behind fought to the last man, until the fever dream of an Islamic caliphate in Syria died for good.

While Aleppo and Raqqa fell, NATO aircraft and warships cleared the way. Syrian MiGs were bombed on the ground before their pilots could reach the runway. Supply depots, air-defense radars and command and control systems were methodically dismantled. In Damascus, President Hafez Jadid watched as Turkish troops captured Idlib and marched south on Hama. Helpless against the onslaught, Jadid mobilized the elite Republican Guard and 4th Armored Division and sent them north, leaving Damascus dangerously undefended. The Syrian opposition saw an opportunity, and struck. Rebel sleeper cells were activated and staged an uprising in Damascus. Within hours, Baath Party headquarters and numerous government ministries were in flames; gun battles raged across the city. A mob advanced on the Presidential Palace atop Mount Mezzeh as the security apparatus around Hafez Jadid melted away. The president, his wife and their three children were trying to flee when the mob spotted them cowering in a shallow ditch. They were all ripped apart, torn limb from limb in a gory spectacle. As the grainy video of their lynching spread online like wildfire, a sense of panic swept from Washington to Tehran. The regime imploded overnight.

At the Iranian embassy in Damascus, Qasem Shateri scrambled to pick up the pieces. His Quds Force had invested billions of dollars and thousands of men from Hezbollah and other Shiite proxies to maintain Jadid's grip. For Shateri, the loss of Syria—the only overland supply route to Lebanon—was an existential threat. In a series of profane cables back to Tehran, he demanded reinforcements and proposed having the IRGC establish a "humanitarian" corridor to Syria through Iraq, essentially cutting the country in half. Yet cooler minds around Ayatollah Khansari—such as Saeed Mofidi—prevailed, and scuttled the assault before it began. Thwarted, Shateri enacted a backup plan. He turned to a group of Syrian generals who still held territory south and west of Damascus and ordered them to fire on Israeli settlements in the Golan Heights. His strategy, borrowed from Saddam Hussein in the Gulf War, was to provoke a military response from the Israelis and sour Arab popular opinion on the invasion.

But the scheme also failed.

Angela Weisel swooped down on Tel Aviv and calmed their tempers while a timely phone call from President Paulson to King Talal II of Jordan opened up a third front. The Syrian forces attacking the Golan Heights were promptly destroyed and the Jordanians secured Damascus before Turkish paratroopers arrived. Qasem Shateri fled on the last Iranian plane out of Syrian airspace.

In Moscow, Mikhail Karetnikov was left dumbfounded. NATO and their Arab puppets had overthrown Russia's key strategic ally in the Middle East.

The Syrian civil war technically ended shortly thereafter.

Much of the regime's political and military leadership were members of the Alawite tribe. When Hafez Jadid was killed many of them shed their uniforms, adopted false identifies and went underground into the protection of a network of facilitators and sympathizers in the coastal cities of Latakia and Tartus and in the an-Nusayriyah Mountains, where the Alawite tribe originated. As for those few indicted on war crimes by the International Criminal Court, they slept with a price on their heads.

A democratically elected government was recently installed in Damascus—to great fanfare before the television cameras. Thousands of Turkish troops still occupied Syria, and the major cities were secure, but disparate militias controlled vast swathes of countryside. All of them held differing visions for Syria's future and their role in creating it. It was a delicate status quo, for the moment guaranteed not by peace, but by sheer exhaustion. Five years of war had left Syria in ruins. Half a million people were dead. Almost nine million were displaced from their homes. Countless more lives were irredeemably scarred. The costs were unquantifiable.

Any resolution, no matter how imperfect or unjust, was welcomed by a civilized world sickened with guilt that it had looked away for so long. They happily accepted that peace—tenuous as it was—and ignored a most famil iar sound. It was undeniable if they listened carefully, beating softly, steadily on the blood-soaked horizon...

War drums.

CHAPTER 6

THE RUSSIAN STARED down the embankment of rotting leaves and twigs toward the bay, his path lit only by the pulsating orange glow of hazard lights. Major Berzin left his Honda Accord and followed a dirt path off Holly Beach Farm Road to the tip of Hackett's Point, a narrow spit sheltering the mouth of Annapolis Harbor from the Chesapeake Bay. Berzin was convinced that he had lost the slightest hint of a tail before he left Washington and was now joined only by the distant calls of Canada geese on the water. The major carefully trudged down through dense brush to the shoreline. As his eyes gradually adjusted to the darkness, he found a small hollow in a tree trunk. Berzin slipped his hand inside the hollow and grasped a rugged USB thumb drive, hidden exactly as he specified in the training the GRU provided long ago. He stowed the thumb drive inside his coat pocket and reached for a thick package under his arm. Within the parcel of heavy-duty black trash bags, tightly wrapped in duct tape, was twenty thousand dollars in cash: a meager offering for services provided to the Kremlin. Berzin stuffed the package in the hollow and clamored back up the embankment, brushing nature's discarded refuse from his clothes, and returned to the Honda.

It was an hour's drive back to Washington on Route 50, which at the time carried only a straggling car or two. Still, Berzin kept a steady gaze on his rear-view mirror, constantly checking for the telltale signs of an FBI surveillance team. After closing twenty miles of lonely blacktop, he pulled the steering wheel hard to the right, swerving clear across three lanes to reach an exit at the last possible moment. As the Honda descended the off-ramp, Berzin stayed focused on his mirrors. Still nothing. He drove aimlessly through the winding residential labyrinth of suburban Maryland. After what seemed like hours, Berzin made a straightaway for the guarded walls of his embassy on Wisconsin Avenue. The information stored on the thumb drive was then transmitted over six thousand miles to a satellite dish on the roof of the vast headquarters complex of the GRU in Moscow's Khodinka neighborhood. The contents were hastily printed and delivered by a lieutenant to the office of the director—hundreds of copied emails and photographed pages of classified memos from the US National Security Council.

Approximately twelve hours after Ambassador Harold Lansing and his delegation departed Joint Base Andrews, the interior lights of the C-17's cavernous cargo bay abruptly went dark over their destination. Beneath his feet, Lansing felt the landing gear extend and lock into place as the aircraft banked sharply and began a quick downward spiral to the ground in a series of tight, controlled turns. The C-17's hold had no windows to view the descent, leaving its weary passengers to sense the drop through the nauseous rolling in their heads. The Air Force pilots in the cockpit had a much better vantage of Damascus silhouetted against the sunset. They arrived at eighteen thousand feet over the city's battered international airport—beyond the range of shoulder-fired SAMs—and approached the runway in a corkscrew maneuver. The pilots had performed the landing hundreds of times in the unfriendly skies over Baghdad and Kabul, and after several turns the aircraft pulled out of the rotation with careful timing and swooped down onto the runway under the cover of darkness. A violent, arresting thud that rattled Lansing's gut, followed by the ear-splitting cry of rubber on concrete, provided the all too familiar sign that he had arrived again in a smoldering battlefield.

With its exterior lights still doused and nearly impossible to spot from beyond the runway, the C-17 taxied to an apron on the south end of the flight line where the delegation began to disembark on the portside aft airstairs. Lansing trailed his security detail off the aircraft. A convoy of twenty blacked-out and armored Chevy Suburbans waited on the apron. Overhead, Lansing heard the heavy chop of a circling Turkish Army AH-1W Super Cobra attack helicopter.

"Ambassador Lansing!" Troy Gillard, the American ambassador in Damascus, struggled to make his voice heard over the whine of the C-17's engines. "It's an honor to welcome you to the new Syria."

"My pleasure, Troy," Lansing responded.

Six men, whose biceps were as large as most men's calves, flanked Gillard, each wearing dark T-shirts under load-bearing vests and toting M4 assault rifles. All were private military contractors from GK Sierra. "I hate to rush things," Gillard informed, "but we shouldn't linger on the flight line. The airport took mortar fire from Tal Maskan just this morning." The ambassador pointed to a cluster of rubble beyond the southeast perimeter fence.

The delegation crammed into the Suburbans within minutes and departed for the Airport Road, speeding down the highway at over a hundred miles per hour. The motorway headed northwest toward central Damascus past the suburbs of al-Ghuzlaniyah and Jaramana. Beyond the three-inch-thick windows, Lansing saw the remains of flattened family homes, and every few hundred feet the convoy swerved to dodge a burnt-out T-72 tank straddling the edge of the highway.

Lansing had spent his life representing the United States in the most unforgiving fringes of the world. He joined the Foreign Service almost fifty years earlier, a week after graduating *summa cum laude* from Harvard, and was first assigned to South Vietnam, in what was then Saigon. Lansing garnered a reputation in the State Department for his sharp-witted and often prophetic cables that quickly became required reading in the White House. He held an instinct for navigating Washington's treacherous sprawl and climbed the ranks through six different administrations and more than a dozen secretaries. Lansing's greatest achievement—the proudest moment of his life, as he prefaced in his memoir—was his role in negotiating the Dayton Accords, which finally put an end to the Bosnian War. Although a Nobel Peace Prize eluded him, his efforts solidified his talent as a diplomatic "closer." Lansing was later dispatched to the United Nations for several years, and then served as ambassador in Baghdad and Kabul after invasion shredded their governments and left their societies on the brink of collapse. Now, after being pulled from a comfortable retirement by Angela Weisel to act as her envoy-at-large in the Middle East, Lansing found himself in Damascus, on the cusp of achieving the unachievable. To aid him in that task, to keep Syria's wounds from bursting open again, an alphabet soup of international organizations and non-profits had descended on the country like locusts.

The United Nations Interim Mission in Syria (UNIMIS), an armed peacekeeping force under the command of an Indian lieutenant general, was responsible for stabilizing and securing the country with the Turkish troops that still remained. With a force of twenty-five thousand observers contributed from a dozen nations, UNIMIS had carved the country into four sectors. Their task was—quite simply—to prevent ethnic cleansing and reprisals, vet the remaining Syrian Armed Forces formations for loyalty to the new government, and combine these units with the standing opposition militias to create a cohesive and competent national military. Also deployed in haste to the region was a nimble but vicious NATO intervention force. NATO's operation in Syria was centered on an Expeditionary Targeting Force stood up by the US Joint Special Operations Command, or JSOC, code-named Task Force OLYMPIA, and was headquartered at Hama Air Base. JSOC kept in-country a package of tier-one special operators mostly drawn from the Navy SEALs and the Army Compartmented Element (popularly known as Delta Force). Rotational deployments of British, French, German and Polish colleagues rounded-out the task force. Working in supporting roles were intelligence, surveillance and reconnaissance (ISR) assets based at RAF Akrotiri, a British airfield in Cyprus, alongside transport and aerial refueling aircraft at Incirlik Air Base in Turkey. Task Force OLYMPIA successfully led the charge over the past nine months to hunt down and capture or kill a rogue's gallery of former regime officials and jihadists.

"I apologize that we had to scrap the arrival ceremony," Gillard craned his neck from the front passenger seat, "but we are still technically in a war zone."

"Never much liked those things anyway," Lansing dismissed. "How's it looking?"

"Good! It's looking real good." Gillard exuded confidence. "The Israeli delegation came in on a chartered flight from Ankara earlier today. We've kept them out of sight in the embassy. Ilan Halevi is leading it, like we thought."

"Any chatter from the Iranians."

"None."

"That's what I like to hear."

Lansing's convoy skirted past the southern spur of Damascus, most of which was still plunged in darkness—public utilities were being rationed to just a few hours each day. It was more apparent there, in neighborhoods closer to government ministries, just what a fierce resistance the Free Syrian Army (FSA) faced when they took the city. Entire side streets were still choked with twisted rebar and crushed concrete. A downed Mil Mi-24 helicopter teetered on the roof of an apartment building. Soon the convoy cleared no fewer than five heavily guarded checkpoints and bounded up the slope of Mount Mezzeh.

On the summit, with a commanding view of the city, was the Presidential Palace, an imposing monolith of polished marble and glass that stretched out over thirty-one thousand square meters. The American delegation stopped in the palace forecourt and was whisked off with little pomp or fanfare to a cold, oversized reception hall. Much work had been done to make the palace functional again, not to say presentable. Bullet holes riddled the walls, the entire north wing had collapsed under heavy shelling and while attempts were made to mask it, the marble in the lesser-travelled corridors was left stained with soot and dried blood. A fitting trophy, Lansing thought.

Not ten minutes had passed into the meeting before the air in the hall came to a stifling degree. Little pleasantries were exchanged between the various camps. At each side of the conference table, official emissaries of

Israel and Syria stared each other down for the first time in twenty years. Speaking for the Syrian camp was the new president, Riad Ayyoub, who during the war served as secretary-general of the National Coalition for Syrian Revolution and Opposition Forces. Ayyoub was a respected Islamist scholar and jurist who spent decades as imam of the Umayyad Mosque in Damascus. Throughout the Turkish invasion and the chaotic days following Hafez Jadid's death, Ayyoub clawed his way to power by striking a complex alliance with the commanders of the FSA and Jaysh al-Islam, a confederation of Islamist and Salafist militias. Yet Ayyoub was no angel. Some opposition leaders who now held seats on his cabinet were accused of committing heinous crimes during the war, but the international community was more than willing to ignore that blemish. Ayyoub was the one individual still alive in Syrian politics who could hold some sway over the militias traipsing about the country. The Gulf Arabs all favored him, and Turkey was willing to tolerate him so long as he kept his house in order. And as for the United States and Europe—they simply wanted to put Syria in their rear-view, wash their hands of the blood, and pretend it all never happened. If Ayyoub could aid their delusions, he was good enough.

Rarely known for humility, Ayyoub proclaimed his role as that of a grand mediator, a vessel through which the Syrian people would begin to rebuild. He recognized his potential pedestal in history. Ayyoub understood that to keep his rivals in the dust, he had to push Syria on an incessant march of progress. He had to build bridges, to cement their place in the wider Middle East. And that was the only reason why he was the greatest advocate for gulping down the bitter pill his country was about to swallow for the world to see.

Ayyoub's unlikely accomplice, who was of a similar mindset and thus sat directly opposite him, was the indispensable right hand and executor of Prime Minister Avi Arad's will. Ilan Halevi's unruly white beard and beady brown eyes, masked by a cheap pair of wire-rimmed glasses, gave him the appearance of a mischievous shopkeeper. He was the national security advisor to the prime minister and his soft voice frequently rang in his boss' ear. Halevi had mustered a delegation of bureaucrats from the Foreign Office in Jerusalem for the covert trip to the capital of a country Israel had technically been at war with since 1967. Pushing them into this historical embrace were the chief negotiators at the ends of the conference table: Lansing and Turkish foreign minister Mehmet Tahir. While the aims and desires of each camp varied greatly, a common enemy had ultimately brought them all to the table: Iran and its extended reach into Lebanon.

Israel's saga of conflict with its archnemesis was well known, but lesser understood was the extent to which Tehran bit the hand that feeds in Syria. In a desperate attempt to prop-up Hafez Jadid's regime, the Iranians sent thousands of fighters from the Revolutionary Guards and Hezbollah to equip and oversee some of the most heinous massacres committed. The stench of the bloated, festering corpses left in their wake hung stubbornly over Syria, and with it, Lansing planned to sever Iran's access to its proxy in Lebanon.

A few hours after his arrival, the United Nations Interim Force in Lebanon (UNIFIL)—the observer mission monitoring the Israel-Lebanon border—reported to the UN Security Council in New York that all IDF personnel had withdrawn from Shebaa Farms. That eight-square-mile stretch of rolling hills and arid soil was a perfect illustration of the impasse consuming the region for more than half a century. Straddling a long and wide ridge, descending from the white slopes of Mount Hermon, the collective of verdant farms backed up to the internationally recognized Lebanon-Syria border in the northeast. On the southwest, the unmarked border followed a dry riverbed called Wadi al-Asal into Israel, where it stopped within a single kilometer of the 1949 Armistice Line. The dispute began in the 1920s when residents of the farms, working their inherited plots of land long before a European bureaucrat drew new lines on a map, regarded themselves as citizens of Lebanon just as their families had for generations. They even paid taxes to the colonial government in Beirut. French diplomats overseeing the mandate were dumfounded as how to divide the land and clearly expressed that its murky status would cause trouble in the future. It did.

During the Six Day War of 1967, the IDF captured this territory from the Syrians along with the entirety of the Golan Heights to the south. In the various diplomatic agreements and UN resolutions that followed, the land was consistently recognized as Syrian territory as it had been administered at the time France ended its colonial mandate over Lebanon. The Lebanese and Syrian governments protested the decision to no avail. And then on June 7th, 2000, Israel brought an end to its costly twenty-two-year occupation of southern Lebanon when the last of its soldiers crossed the UN-mandated "Blue Line," the new demarcation between the two countries. As Shebaa Farms was internationally regarded as de jure Syrian territory, it stayed on the Israeli side of the border as part of the IDF-occupied Golan Heights. Additionally, the IDF held on to Ghajar, an Alawite village two miles west, which was bisected by the new border. These two seemingly insignificant strips of land became crucial to Israel's enemies.

Hezbollah was founded in 1982 as a response to the Israeli invasion of Lebanon—an armed resistance to "stave-off the aggression of the Zionist regime." Key to this tenet of Hezbollah's philosophy was that the resistance would continue so long as a single Jewish soldier remained on Lebanese soil—and to Hezbollah they most certainly did. It was the central reasoning for the enduring Islamic Resistance, the party's military wing, and the long arm of Iran on Israel's northern front. Now, with Israeli troops out of Shebaa Farms, it was Lansing's hope that they would no longer have that reasoning.

As the IDF withdrew, the UN Security Council passed a resolution recognizing the farms as Lebanese territory and placed it under UNIFIL's observer mission. In return, Avi Arad had privately agreed to the arrangement weeks ago, and the UN resolution was meant to provide Arad political cover from the more hawkish elements of his governing coalition. This held the added benefit of the international community recognizing that the IDF had in fact left Lebanon and removed any excuse for Hezbollah to keep its arms. The next step would be realized after a discussion of all the benefits Syria would reap from its cooperation.

The fine details had been arranged earlier in a flurry of phone calls, private visits and delicate negotiations that crawled on for weeks. All that was left was a formality, one last review of the spoils to cement an ironclad understanding of what was now expected of each camp. A package of loans and grants from the World Bank and the International Monetary Fund, totaling sixty billion dollars, was prepared by the State Department to provide much-needed investment in Syria's economy. The seed money provided by European and Gulf Arab states in the immediate aftermath of the civil war had nearly run dry. That fresh injection of capital would be available to the Syrians immediately. To sweeten the deal, the United States Treasury was prepared to add an additional ten billion dollars through a vast series of construction projects designed to reach every corner of the country's devastated infrastructure. Included was a guarantee that Washington would fast-track Syria's membership to the World Trade Organization and provide tax credits to American corporations that did business in Syria. All that was expected of Riad Ayyoub in return was to face the searing lights of television cameras.

Everyone would win who deserved to win, Lansing thought as memoranda were signed and hands were shook across the table. For Syria, the sheer amount of cash to be pumped into its economy was a godsend and would keep the recovery steaming ahead for the foreseeable future. Syria would also have the pleasure of exacting vengeance on a former ally that had turned against the very people on which it so deeply depended. For Israel, the likely concession of the Golan Heights was a fair trade to neuter the Shia army that Iran parked on its northern border. For the United States—more specifically for President Andrew Paulson—it was a crowning second-term policy achievement that would be enshrined in his legacy. But for Harold Lansing, it was just another step in a much grander design to push Tehran's sphere of influence back to its borders and forge a security guarantee for Israel, or what he saw as the key to bringing a meaningful and lasting peace to the Middle East. It was always about peace for Lansing, albeit an inescapable folly—a catalyst for a price he would, one day soon, pay personally.

Ambassador Gillard and the Israelis were hurried out of the palace through a secluded side exit. Gillard rushed back to the embassy and sent an urgent cable to Foggy Bottom detailing the meeting and confirmed that things would proceed as planned. The Israelis went immediately to the airport and would be out of Syrian airspace within minutes of the announcement. It was mutually agreed that the optics of Ayyoub standing shoulder-to-shoulder with Avi Arad's security advisor was not beneficial. Lansing, Ayyoub and Tahir soon stood behind a podium in a makeshift press center in the palace. The press corps in Damascus, which mostly consisted of seasoned war correspondents, was crowded in the small room with haste. The timing of the announcement was also carefully arranged. It would still make the front page of every newspaper and be the lead story the next morning throughout the United States, Europe and the Middle East, allowing the spin masters in Washington and Tel Aviv to sculpt it to their approval.

Ayyoub stepped to the podium first. As the cameras' glare shone harshly on his eyes, it became brutally apparent that he was about to stake the future of his country on just a few carefully chosen words. A red light blinked on in front of him.

"Ladies and gentlemen, good evening," he began in the scholarly tone of Oxford English. "It is my great honor to be joined by two distinguished diplomats: Ambassador Harold Lansing and Foreign Minister Tahir of Turkey." He focused on the teleprompter. "My people have shouldered an unbearable price for their freedom. This much no man can deny. For five years, the world stood by and watched, day by day, as a proud nation was unjustly slaughtered for want of the same rights and liberties taken for granted by civilized nations round the world. Today, with great reverence for the determination and sacrifice of our revolution, we have those freedoms—those freedoms for Syria. Today, we look forward to the future, scarred, but yet determined still to cement peace for our children and for those who survive.

"And so it is with this lasting peace in mind that I announce this evening that the Syrian National Council has agreed to an offer, proposed jointly by the United States and Turkey, to enter into a full and comprehensive dialogue with the State of Israel in order to bring about a final resolution to the differences that have existed between our two peoples for generations."

The press corps stirred.

"I welcome the offer of the United States to host these talks, the first round of which has been set to occur in March in Annapolis, Maryland..."

"You must see this."

Ibrahim al-Din was more than slightly annoyed at the unexpected presence of his brother-in-law and aide-de-camp, Anwar Sabbah, who had stormed unannounced into his sitting room and lifted the television remote. Al-Din brought his youngest daughter off his knee and placed her on the cushion beside him.

"See what?"

"You just... *You must!*" Sabbah was visibly shaken.

The television was changed from a children's show on Al-Manar, a Lebanese satellite channel funded by Hezbollah, and tuned to Al Jazeera, where a breaking news Chyron was plastered across the bottom of the small screen. An interpreter catered the announcement to an Arab viewership.

"How long?" al-Din asked softly.

"Five minutes. Maybe more."

The Arabic voiceover carried above Riad Ayyoub's speech, but the meaning wasn't lost in the slightest. The sickening noise pierced through the protests of his daughter and the patter of foot traffic in the narrow alleyway outside. Soon, al-Din heard nothing else.

"And let the world take note," Ayyoub spoke from Damascus, "that the new Syria is a nation that stands for peace. And we are aware who stood against us in our darkest days. So it is my intent to sever, effective immediately, all diplomatic ties between the Syrian Arab Republic and the Islamic Republic of Iran. Syria accepts the resolution of the United Nations Security Council extending Shebaa Farms as sovereign Lebanese territory and welcomes the quick action on the part of Israel to respect that resolution. Furthermore, we call on Hezbollah to lay down its arms and adopt a policy of nonviolent resistance. We announce this evening that under no circumstances will Syria permit the transfer of illegal arms to Hezbollah, either by Iran or any nation, to occur on its soil..."

Rage flowed through al-Din's veins as he processed it all. His head snapped to the right, where Sabbah stood next to the window, breathless.

Al-Din said nothing. His eyes communicated it all.

CHAPTER 7

DANTE ALIGHIERI DESCRIBED the ninth and deepest pit of hell as an almost gaping void, locked in a perpetual state of suspended animation. It was reserved, in his interpretation, for the great traitors of history who were encapsulated in a lake of ice and contorted in all manner of unnatural positions. Joining them was Satan himself, waist-deep in the lake and beating his six wings in a foolhardy attempt at escape. And in Satan's three mouths, condemned to an eternity of being slowly chewed to bits, were the most treacherous souls imaginable: Brutus, Cassius, and Judas Iscariot. But hell was a very real place on Earth, as Ryan Freeman understood, and at the moment, he was convinced it sat on the top floor of the United States Capitol. There, he was trapped in the icy grips of four blue-faced beasts, his words contorted within their minds in all manner of unnatural positions as he was slowly chewed to bits, deep in the confines of a vaulted room where no one could hear him scream. Dante was wrong. The deepest pit of hell was reserved for the spymasters.

There was a single door to room S-407, tucked away on the isolated fourth floor of the Capitol. Apart from the two uniformed Capitol Police officers who stood guard in the hallway outside, it was nearly indistinguishable in the maze of corridors that connected miscellaneous offices and the private hideaways of various senators. Its only unique feature was a light hanging above the doorway and when flashed red, warned that to enter would constitute a breach of national security. The windowless cavity was a Sensitive Compartmented Information Facility, or SCIF, that was swept daily for electronic listening devices and kept hermetically sealed from the outside world. Sheets of lead sat between the walls, floor and ceiling. Congressional leadership used S-407 to conduct briefings in greater privacy than what was afforded by the committee rooms in the Hart Building and the Capitol Visitor Center.

Seated in front of Freeman, perched high on the dais, were the beasts: the chairmen and ranking-members of the House and Senate intelligence committees. Together they were known as the "Gang of Four." While it didn't exist in statute, there had come to be a generally accepted practice to limit notification of certain intelligence activities to these four members. Gang of Four briefings were typically informal and employed only when the intelligence discussed was believed to be so sensitive in nature that a restricted notification was warranted to reduce the risk of exposure. And Freeman believed that it most certainly was. "To continue from what Geoff has said, I feel that what we're seeing here is not just an attempt to mask the true nature of the facilities' purpose, but a genuine effort to deceive us. Real tradecraft."

Geoffrey Sheridan—the director of national intelligence (DNI)—seated to Freeman's right, already brought the four up to speed on the extent of the Intelligence community's efforts to monitor Picasso and Monet and the activities detected within the secluded valley. In the days since the National Reconnaissance Office first stumbled upon the site in the harsh terrain beside the Haj Ali Gholi dry lake, a veritable army of "squints"—intelligence parlance for imagery analysts—had poured over photographs taken thrice-daily by the KH-13 reconnaissance satellite as it orbited above. The squints were able to glean a few precious nuggets of new information on the ghostly facility, but it hadn't come easily. The analysis from the Directorate of Science and Technology's team of geologists that Freeman had reassigned was still outstanding. CIA and its sister organizations had focused a mighty array of both technological and brain power on the valley, but Freeman's most treasured tool, Saeed Mofidi, hadn't reported back, and until he did, the D/CIA would remain unsatisfied.

"Congressman, does that answer your question?" Freeman smiled through his gritted teeth.

"I just find it disturbing, Director Freeman, that our boys have been watching this place day and night—for how long?—going on a week now, and we are not one bit closer to knowing what in God's name is happening there." Mr. Charles Barrett of Chattanooga, Tennessee, the longtime chairman of the House Intelligence Committee, was prone to impatience and reactionary fits, but Freeman had been advised by his predecessor to occasionally let Mr. Barrett revel in his ignorance, rather than drag him kicking and screaming into the sun.

"Director Freeman, please continue with your briefing," Dawn Singer, the longtime Senate chairman ushered the room back to sanity.

"Thank you, Madam Chair." The D/CIA directed their attention to a recent KH-13 photograph displayed on a television screen to his left. "For reference, this is an overhead shot taken approximately sixteen hours ago. You'll see the lakebed to the north, on the edge of the screen. The valley is centered with the tunnel portal to Monet labeled here, and Picasso is directly below. We've labeled the spoil piles and you can see construction equipment that has been moved beyond the camouflage netting. These are the railcars the DNI described for transporting the spoil out of the tunnel. And it's difficult to see, but we've labeled the access road, which is here in dark blue, leading from the valley and curving out to the west." Freeman was annotating an infrared image shot at night in an attempt to detect heat signatures in the valley.

The National Reconnaissance Office took greater interest in the images they obtained in the evening hours when UFAC analysts correctly judged the site was more active. The birds passing overhead were able to watch construction of Picasso continue unabated. They also pieced together crucial information on the guard patrols that stalked the mountainsides bordering the valley. The patrols appeared on the screen as clustered specks of orange and yellow.

"Pardon me, Director Freeman, but could you explain what those two brighter swirls are near the top of the valley?" asked Mr. Laird, the House ranking-member.

"Of course, Congressman, that's very observant of you. Our analysts believe that to be the infrared signature of an aircraft."

"An aircraft?"

"That's correct. The two 'swirls' the Congressman is referring to match the characteristics of the sort of infrared signature that would be emitted by a light, twin-engine turboprop aircraft. It's likely that our reconnaissance satellite missed this aircraft departing by thirty minutes, perhaps less." Freeman pressed a remote and the screen switched to a second image, covering the same area as the first. The data in the second photograph was run through powerful software programs of the National Geospatial-Intelligence Agency (NGA) and reformed as a "hyperspectral" image.

Hyperspectral imaging collects and processes information across the electromagnetic spectrum of visible and non-visible light. For example, the human eye views light in only three bands: red, green, and blue. Hyperspectral imaging systems divide this spectrum into many more bands, revealing bits of information that would be not be apparent to the human eye under natural conditions. The image Freeman brought on the screen was a kaleidoscope of vivid colors. The mountain ranges bordering the valley shone as a dark, blood red and the softer ground on the valley floor appeared as a lighter pink. Picasso and Monet's tunnel portals were clearly visible in a bright white hue. But on the north side of the valley floor, near the lakebed, was an elongated rectangle, perfectly formed, as if by the hands of man, that covered the location of the two orange swirls on the previous image. It appeared as a heavy blue on the screen, and was covered in thin streaks of neon green.

"This we believe to be a runway, exactly five hundred meters in length," Freeman said flatly. "We judge it to be constructed with concrete pads, installed only a few inches beneath the valley floor and then covered with a thin layer of compacted dirt. This is another example of the efforts to deceive us that the DNI touched upon."

The beasts seemed pleased with the display.

"But to answer your question, Congressman, the infrared signatures you noticed are remnants of heat emitted by the exhaust of an aircraft sitting idle on the runway. This signature from the engines would remain visible to our satellites for up to an hour after takeoff. The green streaks—if you look closely, there are three—represent tire tracks left by the landing gear. Our analysts have taken a look at these tracks and they feel it would match that of a Harbin Y-12, which is a light, twin-engine cargo plane manufactured in China. The IRGC Aerospace Force operates eight such aircraft, three at Mehrabad Airport in Tehran."

"That's just fascinating," Mr. Laird said.

Freeman nodded in agreement.

"Director Freeman," Buzz Turner, ranking-member of the Senate committee, began with a slow drawl, "given all this, how is it that our coverage of these facilities is so limited? Shouldn't we have continuous, twenty-four-hour surveillance on a place like this?"

"Well, Senator, our reconnaissance satellites are very capable," Freeman swallowed, "but are unfortunately limited by the laws of physics. You see, as the distance from the satellite to the ground target increases, the resolution of the image decreases. As the satellite moves farther from the target, factors like humidity, atmosphere pollution, weather, ozone, all come into play. Our KH-13s can take decent images within forty-five degrees of its zenith—the point where the satellite is directly overhead of the ground target. Now, if you were to stand on that valley floor and watch the sky with a telescope, you would see the bird arc from one side of the horizon to the other in fifteen minutes. So that leaves us with a very small viewing window. On top of that, our analysts can view the most amount of detail when the satellite is at its perigee—the lowest point of the orbital path when it's physically closest to the surface of the Earth. With the current alignment of our constellation, these two events overlap once every eight hours. So you can see why our coverage is limited, Senator. For most of the day our screens are either blank or full of static." It was a Hollywood myth, he did not add, that reconnaissance satellites were available at a moment's notice to indefinitely cover any given spot on the planet.

"Would it be possible to retask additional KH-13s to provide a greater window of coverage?" asked Senator Singer.

"The DNI controls the budget, so I feel Geoff would be best suited to answer that question."

Sheridan keyed his microphone. "Madam Chair, the effort to alter the orbital path of one KH-13 reconnaissance satellite, not to mention several, is extremely cost prohibitive and would shorten its expected service life. NRO could not shift the funds in its budget to do so without proper authorization."

"Then why can't you folks just send a drone?" The question was an obvious one to Mr. Barrett.

"The nearest operating base for an RQ-170," the D/CIA responded after a momentary pause, "is Al Dhafra Air Base in the United Arab Emirates. That's eight hundred miles south over some heavily defended desert. If the Iranians have gone to the lengths we've discovered to hide the site, I'm sure they've taken the time to deploy electronic warfare assets. And if they manage to bring one down near the site, our capability to monitor the valley effectively is blown. They'll know we're watching. So no, Congressman, that's not a risk I would recommend taking."

"I just find it absurd that with fifty-five billion dollars at its disposal, our intelligence agencies are unable to say what is going on there. Why are we still sitting here playing guessing games?"

Freeman glanced to Sheridan for backup, but the DNI wanted no part. "Congressman, the men and women working for us are extremely talented at what they do—and they work harder than anyone I've met. But this takes time. It takes time to get it right, not simply report an immature judgment. Our people cannot be expected to divine, out of thin air, what is happening under hundreds of feet of solid rock, not to say read the minds of the people working within. Only another human being on the ground can do that. The quality of our intelligence is not always related to the quantity of cash we throw at it."

Mr. Laird looked down to his briefing papers before reaching for the microphone. "Director Freeman, you and DNI Sheridan have provided a few possibilities of what this place may be: an alternate command facility, missile research and production, chemical or biological weapons storage," he read from the papers. "But both of you, and I notice this is true of the analysis your agencies have produced, seem eager to steer us from the elephant in the room. Why does CIA seem so confident that Picasso and Monet are not nuclear in nature?"

Freeman needed to delve into history and conjure the late name of a fleeting silhouette of a man who had spent his days swallowed up in the pale edifices of the quasi-military-academic institutions that peppered Tehran's northern suburbs. "You'll recall that in 2007, a National Intelligence Estimate was released—"

"I recall, Director Freeman."

"And in a key finding of that NIE, we assessed with high confidence that Iranian military entities *halted* their nuclear weapons program in 2003 for at least several years." The D/CIA pushed his notes aside. His emphasis on the word "halt" was not an accident. It's meaning—distorted either by prejudice or ignorance—pervaded the findings of the 2007 NIE since the day it was published. Freeman had helped draft the estimate and his intended meaning was quite specific. "What the NIE intended to convey through the judgment was that a weapons program was halted, not dismantled. Whether this halt was done temporarily or indefinitely, CIA did not advise then and has not since.

"So in 2003, under the order of Ayatollah Khansari," he continued, "the weapons program, which had been under the auspices of the IRGC since the Gulf War, was discontinued. This program was managed by the Physics Research Center, the PHRC, which operated out of a workshop in the Lavizan neighborhood of Tehran and existed as a parallel effort to the civilian nuclear power program run by the Atomic Energy Organization of Iran. The fate of these programs, as you know, is enumerated in the JCPOA. Back in 2003, when the supreme leader halted development of a bomb, the PHRC was not dismantled, but rather kept intact as a latent capability to resume work on a nuclear weapon if he ever decided to go down that path. And in doing so Iran preserved the ostensibly civilian aspects of its nuclear program—large-scale uranium enrichment—that would allow it to make technical progress toward a bomb capability while hiding evidence of a parallel program that would invite an attack.

"At the time this order came down, the PHRC was headed by a 'Dr. Alireza Fakhrizadeh,' who was a professor of physics at the Imam Hossein University, which is run by the IRGC. If Iran ever did develop a nuclear weapon, this man would have been remembered as their Robert Oppenheimer—he would, undeniably, have been the 'father' of a Persian bomb. In the eighties, Fakhrizadeh was trained by the Soviets at Chelyabinsk-70. His expertise was in weapons design, specifically in crafting the explosive lenses used to compress and detonate the plutonium core of an implosion-type bomb. He was also a recognized expert in methods to reduce the size of a nuclear weapon so that it would fit on a warhead or, say, inside a large suitcase. And so, in 2003, Dr. Fakhrizadeh's workshop in Tehran was razed, the topsoil carted away in dump trucks, and replaced with a public park.

"Fakhrizadeh's staff was relocated to a more secure site at Parchin and took the same processes they were using to perfect detonators for a nuclear bomb and applied it to the manufacture of nanodiamonds. However, in 2007, Fakhrizadeh was killed in car crash—the vehicle he was in slid off an overpass and landed on a highway below. The gas tank ignited and the car was engulfed before emergency responders could reach him. Fakhrizadeh's death was a devastating blow to Iran's nuclear aspirations and set them back years. His removal from the equation was the deciding factor in our judgment that while the Iranians had halted their weapons program, it wouldn't be resumed for several years.

"So, the challenge today for the Intelligence community is determining when, if ever, the supreme leader ordered a resumption of the weapons program. The PHRC has since been renamed—it's now called the 'Organization of Defensive Innovation and Research'—but the team that Fakhrizadeh led is still in place, despite the JCPOA. They go to work every day and continue their research, except instead of a bomb, they think about nanodiamonds."

"But is that true, honest defense conversion or just hedging?" Senator Turned asked. "To me, it sounds like hedging."

"It's both, sir," the D/CIA replied. "Let's look at it from the eyes of an Iranian policymaker. Before the JCPOA, if you were in favor of shuttering the weapons program, you would've likely proposed maintaining the infrastructure for civilian research, if only to divert accusations of being under the thumb of the 'Great Satan' and stunting Iran's scientific destiny. On the other hand, if you were opposed to closing the weapons program, you might favor at least keeping the scientists in place for another day when the debate favored your sensibilities. So, Senator, it's clear how two opposing ideologies may come to the same conclusions for very different reasons. And this is exactly why it's so difficult for our analysts to make a coherent statement about Iran's intentions. It's because their intentions are rarely coherent at all."

Freeman diverted his attention back to Mr. Laird. "CIA is confident that Picasso and Monet are not nuclear in nature because no such order from the supreme leader was ever handed down. As of this moment we have no reason to believe otherwise. And as Khansari continues to recover from his stroke, day-to-day communication with military and intelligence circles has largely been delegated to an adviser in the supreme leader's household. Essentially, this adviser has come to be a key architect of Iranian security policy." While it was well known to US and Israeli intelligence, the supreme leader's debilitating stroke was not public knowledge. The release of this information, they agreed, would greatly destabilize Iran and create a power struggle that would make a delicate situation all the more volatile. "Our asset in Tehran monitors this adviser closely. We'd have sufficient warning of any change." Freeman neglected to add that his asset was the adviser himself.

"And this asset is reliable?"

"The asset's personal integrity with us and within Iran is unquestionable, Congressman."

"May I ask what makes you so certain?"

"Personal trauma."

"Very good. Thank you."

"Well, unless there are any further questions, I think this will be a good place to end our discussion." Senator Singer looked to her fellow beasts, but their appetite was, for the time being, satiated. "Okay then. DNI Sheridan, Mr. Freeman, I thank you both for taking the time to come up here today and brief us on these unsettling developments. I hope to hear from your offices again in the near future. And, *Director* Freeman, it occurs to me that this is the first time you have been with us since your confirmation."

The thought occurred to him much earlier.

"It pleases me to know that a career intelligence officer of such competence and esteem is now at the helm of the Central Intelligence Agency. I know I speak for all of us when I say that I look forward to many gatherings such as this."

The D/CIA forced a smile. "Thank you very much, Madam Chair."

"But before you go, I have just one more question, if you have the time."

"Absolutely, Senator."

"It is my understanding that the request to limit this briefing to chairmen and ranking-members came directly from your office. Now, a man with your lengthy experience in intelligence oversight would certainly understand the connotations that come with a request to exclude the full committee and our respective staff directors from a briefing of this magnitude. It informs me, at least, that the source of the request views the intelligence conveyed in the briefing to be so extraordinary in nature as to constitute a direct threat to national security if the elected representatives of the American people are privy to such a revelation. For the record, Director Freeman, can you confirm that your office was the source of this request?" It was a rhetorical question.

"Senator, I can confirm that the source of the request was, indeed, myself."

"And, Director Freeman, if you'll allow me, I have another question."

The D/CIA nodded.

"You have made quite clear in this briefing, the assurances of the Central Intelligence Agency that Iran has not been deceptive with its intentions. But I would like the assurances, not of the agency you lead, but of you personally. Director Freeman, can you provide us with your personal assurances that the facility in question is not being used by forces of the Islamic Republic of Iran to covertly develop and manufacture a nuclear weapon?"

Freeman was expertly backed into a corner. He looked to the DNI, but there was no solace to be found. Sheridan appeared as if he wanted to come out of his skin. He keyed his microphone. He would do as asked.

"No, Senator, I cannot."

• • •

"Goddamnit, Ryan, what the hell was that?" Sheridan growled as the elevator doors slid open into the ornate Brumidi corridors on the first floor of the Capitol.

"The truth."

The DNI scoffed at the reply. "You sure? From where I sat, it looked like assisted suicide." They went at a hurried pace over the short distance to the Senate carriage entrance, a vaulted archway beneath the Capitol's east front steps. A collection of Chevy Tahoes was arranged in two separate motorcades for the trip back to Virginia. Both sat idle as the moan of their engines echoed down from the vaults.

Freeman maintained his characteristic veneer of stoicism as he navigated the slick marble steps separating him from his car. Doc, the head of his security detail, opened the passenger door and Freeman placed his cracked leather satchel on the floor. Then he turned to the DNI, who persistently hovered over his shoulder. "Don't expect me to lie to these people, Geoff. We should get that straight right now."

"These people deal in lies!" Sheridan pointed back to the towering Capitol above. "It's a game they play with each other. If they think the shadow on the wall is a bird, then tell them it's a bird. They'll call you a genius. Tell them it's a Carolina Wren, they'll call you a lunatic and eat you alive." Sheridan dropped his tone and leaned out of earshot of Freeman's bodyguards. "Play the game and we're all better for it."

Freeman rolled his eyes. "Geoff, that's a game *you* play."

"Ryan, look," Sheridan stopped him. "I'm your friend, and I'm here to protect you, but my friendship is finite. Play the game."

"Well, I feel safer already." Freeman climbed into the heated cabin. "Enjoy the rest of your day."

They came for their messiah and they were not to be disappointed.

A rumor persisted throughout the day that he would appear among them in the flesh. The anticipation bordered on hysteria. Twenty thousand people flooded a thirty-seven-acre public square in Beirut's southern suburbs, packing every inch with the devout and the faithful. There was a plastic chair laid out for nearly all of them. Hats of red, green or white—the Lebanese national colors—to block the sun, were placed on each. A steady stream arrived for hours in snaking convoys of buses, and some had even walked, setting out the day before from towns and villages in Lebanon's southern Shiite heartland. Vendors placed stalls around the perimeter and along the streets leading toward the square, selling snacks and souvenirs, paraphernalia and party memorabilia. Posters bearing the faces of Ayatollah Khansari and martyrs who gave their lives for the Islamic Resistance hung from lampposts. Since the early hours of the morning, martial choirs belted chest-thumping hymns of defiance and revolution. Columns of armed men in uniform, wearing headbands which read in classical Arabic, "O Prophet, we are with thee," marched past the stage that was erected at the top of the square. And as the hour of their deliverance drew near, a more visible security presence gripped the area. Snipers fanned out on rooftops of the drab apartment blocks that lined the square. Stern-looking men in plainclothes walked among the crowd and clutched soft violin cases with the muzzles of sub-machine guns pointing out the front. Radio frequencies and cell phone traffic were combed from a nearby command center for the slightest hint of a threat. But none of these efforts were apparent to the Hezbollah faithful packing the square. They waved thousands of yellow and green party flags and waited for the moment that their messiah—the only man, in their recollection, who fought back against the great injustice that maligned their people, and won—would take center stage. They came to hear a proclamation that was promised for years.

Then it occurred suddenly, without warning from the speakers mounted around the square or preamble from a lesser party cleric. It wasn't necessary. Sheikh Wissam Hamawi, secretary-general of Hezbollah—the "Party of God"—appeared on stage surrounded by bodyguards and stepped to a podium placed behind a wall of blast-proof glass. The crowd frantically surged forward, desperate to get closer to the stage. Sheikh Hamawi was dressed for the part in a fine, silk clerical robe and a black turban atop his head, which implied descent from the Prophet. He waved and smiled, gesturing his hands to them in a calming motion. In return, they cheered madly, and a sea of flags rippled in the wind.

"I seek refuge from God against the accursed Satan—" he spoke plainly into the microphone.

Twenty thousand voices chanted together as one. *"God, God protect Hamawi! God, God protect Hamawi! God, God protect Hamawi!"*

He calmed them again. "—in the name of God, the all-merciful, the all-compassionate; praise be to Almighty God, blessings and peace be upon our prophets, the last of the prophets, Muhammad; his good, righteous, infallible house; his noble companions; and upon all the prophets and messengers."

Hamawi's words of invocation thundered off the apartment blocks around the square as their voices fell silent, subdued and obedient.

"Peace be to you, oh most honest, most righteous and most pure people. Praise be to God who delivered His promise, and rendered our people and Lebanon victorious against our enemy. Thank God who esteemed us, gave us constancy and entrusted us. Thank God, on whom we depend and to whom we turn, who has always been, as He promised: 'best Lord, best disposer of affairs.' Thank God for his aid, support and backing.

"Dear brothers and sisters! Today you astonish the whole world again as you verily prove, and rightfully so, that you are a great people, a steadfast people, a proud people, a loyal and brave people! For days now, a psychological war has been waged on this festival just as one is now being waged against the Resistance.

"They said they will bomb this ground and this rostrum will be destroyed to frighten the people away. Today, by your crowning of this victory celebration, you are more courageous than you were in the July War of aggression. Yes, I stand before you and among you; this puts you and me at risk. However, my heart, my mind and soul did not permit me to address you from afar. I insisted to be with you!

"We are the children of that Imam, who said: 'Is it with death you threaten me? Death to us is normalcy and martyrdom is dignity offered from God!'"

A zealous chorus stirred over the crowd.

"On this day I want to deliver a message that is not new, but final and conclusive to all those who are conspiring and hoping and betting for change. This resistance in Lebanon will survive and you will not be able to defeat it with your psychological, media, political and intelligence wars.

"Not a single army in the world will be able to dismantle our Resistance. No army in the world will be able to make us drop our weapons from our hands. We will never let go of our arms. By the grace of Almighty God, our numbers are increasing day after day, and for those who are betting that our weapons are rusting, we say that our weapons are being renewed! Even now as we gather here in celebration, there are illegal forces just beyond our borders that plot our demise. These forces believe that they can strangle us with heinous edicts. To this, we say woe unto you for your ignorance!" He pounded his fists.

"They scampered into Damascus like rats in the night, their diseased mouths full of blasphemy and false promises to that usurping band of rebel puppets. They thought that we would be divided! They thought that we would be fractured. They thought that we would be cast to the winds! Is there division here this day? Do I see division among this great people?"

And the answer from the people was clear.

"To the people of Syria, our friends, brothers and sisters, we say awake from your slumber and take back what is rightfully yours. Rid yourselves of a band of puppets who make deals and sign papers in the blood of martyrs that do nothing but serve the will of the American administration. The American administration abandons its followers and allies at the first crossroad to search for its interests. Our Arab and Islamic nations should know that the American administration is the enemy and the threat. No government, none at all, which would subject its people to unwarranted and unholy talks with an illegal, occupying and murderous entity, is worthy of your approval. Rise up against this!

"Israel is our enemy. This is an aggressive, illegal and illegitimate entity, which has no future in our land. Its destiny is manifested in our blood and in our motto: 'Death to Israel!'"

And the people cried, *"Al-mawt li-Israel! Al-mawt li-Israel! Al-mawt li-Israel! Al-mawt li-Israel!"*

"And it is the American dogs that are behind Israel. We consider it to be an enemy because it wants to humiliate our governments, our regimes and our peoples. We consider it to be an enemy because it is the greatest plunderer of our treasures, and our oil, and our resources, while millions in our nations suffer. Our motto, as we are not afraid to repeat year after year, is: 'Death to America!'"

And the people cried, *"Al-mawt li-Amreeka! Al-mawt li-Amreeka! Al-mawt li-Amreeka! Al-mawt li-Amreeka!"*

"Some may wonder, is there no end to this hostility?" Yes, there is an end. When the Zionist entity has been smeared from the map, this conflict will come to an end! When the Zionist entity has been swallowed by oblivion, this conflict will come to an end! Only on that blessed day will there be peace. But this latest act of treachery from the pit of hell came only hours after a great victory by the Islamic Resistance. Without exaggeration this is a divine, historic and strategic victory! Dear brothers and sisters! After decades of struggle, after decades of resistance, the liberation of the Shebaa Farms has been realized!"

The crowd erupted with cheers that shook the square.

"And it is to you, oh brave people, oh steadfast and proud people, that this victory is bestowed. Today, we give praise to the martyrs whose blood has forged the liberation of Shebaa Farms. We must acknowledge the grace of the fighting, the resisting and the sacrificing of the people who left their homes, families and universities. It is because of them that we stand here today. It is because of their resistance that this occupation was lifted. After decades of defeat and sustained losses on many fronts—in Lebanon, in Gaza, in Africa—the Zionists realized that if the occupation of Shebaa continued for even another day, it would be a catastrophe. And the Americans ordered this disengagement, not for the women, not for the children of the Lebanese—they stopped this illegal occupation for the sake of Israel. The Zionist entity finds itself besieged on all sides—their cities, and schools, and hospitals, and infrastructure, and military dens—all under an unstoppable blanket of fire, under the weight of fifty thousand rockets! Dear brothers and sisters! Today, we declare victory over our enemy, but our resistance endures stronger and more determined that it ever has. An era of defeats has gone and an era of victories has arrived!"

Sheikh Wissam Hamawi's voice surely sounded prophetic to the masses hanging on his words. But their messiah was bound to disappoint.

• • •

The roar of the propellers sounded as a distant whisper from their perch. A small team of intercept operators—"knob-turners," as they were affectionately known in the JSOC family—clutched heavy noise-canceling headphones to the sides of their skulls and listened closely to the muffled chatter somewhere in the warren of concrete and dust several hundred feet below. They were all native Arabic speakers, recruited by talent spotters on their scours of the US Army personnel database. It was an invaluable trait, allowing them to finesse the delicate nuances of word choice and tone than could only be learned from the banter of relatives, not a textbook. But they were also armed with the technical expertise to snatch nearly every conceivable electronic signal out of thin air.

The Mission Support Activity was the latest bland designation meant to provide an additional layer of operational security to the obscure Fort Belvoir-based unit that shunned the spotlight. In the past twenty years it had known possibly a dozen code names (Centra Spike, Gray Fox and Intrepid Spear, to name a few), but the special operations community usually referred to it as Task Force Orange. TF Orange was just one item on the Joint Special Operations Command's menu, but its specialty lie in signals intelligence (SIGINT) collection and preparation of the battlespace. These were brutally serious men who could install a wiretap on a buried fiber optic cable while holding a small army at bay with precise fire. At its disposal was a fleet of airborne intercept platforms.

The knob-turners of TF Orange sat hunched over a workstation in the confined cabin of an RC-12X Guardrail. It was a twin-engine turboprop aircraft constructed from a Beechcraft Super King Air. That particular build was the newest generation of a platform that saw steady use since the 1970s in Latin America, North Africa and the Arabian Peninsula. The "X" model had been rushed downrange and fielded a new glass cockpit and structural enhancements to house fifty million dollars of sensitive intercept equipment. Summit Aviation of Middletown, Delaware had extended the wingtips of the aircraft to accommodate a package of delicate sensors. Black antennas covered much of the stormy gray fuselage, giving it the outward appearance of a dog that had emerged on the losing end of a fight with a porcupine. While the knob-turners got to work, (the nickname was dated, now they just tapped keyboards and pressed buttons) the pilots of the King Air steadied into a holding pattern at roughly six hundred feet. From this vantage, it orbited in a wide loop over Tartus' medina—the city's medieval core—on Syria's Mediterranean coast. The medina had been built over, within and around a Crusader fortress from the twelfth century.

An array of sensors onboard the King Air was aimed at a squat, cinder block dwelling set back from the outer curtain wall. From the air it looked identical to every other illegally built home in the medina, but the knob-turners had studied it closely and they had little trouble getting ears on target.

With the fall of Damascus, surviving regime figures fled to the relative safety of the an-Nusayriyah Mountains, which ran parallel to the Mediterranean coastline. This hasty retreat to the ancestral home of the Alawite tribe, from which many of the regime's heavyweights descended, spared Syria's coastal cities of Tartus, Latakia and Baniyas from the protracted sieges and stalemates which left the rest of the country in ruins. For that reason, essential utilities such as electrical grids, gas, water and telecommunications infrastructures remained largely intact. This included the GSM mobile phone network of Syriatel.

A typical GSM network like the one operated by Syriatel was made up of a number of base stations, or towers, controlled by a mobile telephone switching office. When a mobile phone was switched on, its transceiver immediately began searching for the nearest tower with the strongest signal. Once the phone established contact with a base station, the tower set up a control link to the phone, along which it transmitted information about its identity so the network could track the phone's location as it moved between towers.

At the heart of the equipment aboard the King Air was a system designed and built by Applied Standard Technology specifically for TF Orange. While classified, its machinery was based on the AST Model 1235 Multi-Channel Digital Receiver System. It was fully computerized and sported sixty independent digital receivers, each of which could switch between the various frequency standards (GSM, 3G, LTE) used by mobile phones. At the press of a button, the knob-turners began a process called "meaconing." Several days earlier, TF Orange had installed a string of malware code onto the target phone's operating system, forcing it to switch on at command, although the screen and all other functions appeared to be off. With the target phone activated, the knob-turners jammed the control link to the nearest tower, forcing the target phone to start scanning the available frequencies for another base station. The knob-turners then established a new counterfeit base station aboard the King Air, which had a much stronger signal than any other tower in the area, attracting the target phone. All outgoing and incoming transmissions to the target phone now passed through the King Air.

With a new control link established between the counterfeit base station and the target phone, the King Air orbited over the medina in wide circles, allowing their computerized direction-finding equipment to triangulate bearings to the target phone from a number of locations and mathematically deduce the precise position of the phone to within a few dozen feet. The knob-turners confirmed that the target was indeed on the second floor of the house they were watching. Using the control link, which was on a different frequency than that used to transmit calls, the knob-turners began to use the target phone as a bug, overhearing and recording anything that was spoken in the phone's immediately vicinity. And in the cramped confines of the old house, voices tended to travel quite far. The knob-turners pressed their headphones closer.

The owner of the target phone—"Subject One" to the knob-turners—was a facilitator and courier to high-ranking regime officials, all HVTs who were now fugitives from The Hague. The facilitator's job was to pass messages between them and provide some semblance of the worldly comforts they enjoyed for decades. His phone was in a coat pocket draped over a chair in the room and used a SIM card from a batch known by NSA to have been purchased by a Syrian intelligence operative in Athens. Subject One hadn't changed the card in weeks and it would prove to be his fatal mistake.

Subject One stood his ground amid a fierce berating by a man the knob-turners designated "Subject Two." The heated and profanity-laced conversation was transcribed automatically on their screens, but the knob-turners still took the time to translate it by hand on yellow legal pads; a fifty-million-dollar computer was still prone to mistakes. The root of the argument, as they could tell, was a box of Honduran cigars that Subject One had just delivered to the safe house. The quality of these cigars, as Subject Two had delicately put it, was "shit." He made it quite clear that nothing short of Cuban Cohibas was worthy of the thick envelopes of cash he regularly paid.

An audio sample of Subject Two's voice was recorded and transmitted to Ayios Nikolaos Station, an outpost of the British Sovereign Base Area in the dusty hills of eastern Cyprus. A fusion cell had been stood up there to support JSOC's Task Force OLYMPIA with members of American, British, French, Turkish and Jordanian intelligence all working in concert. They received the recording of Subject Two and cleaned it of ambient noise. A voice sample of Major General Ali Mamlouk from his last known public appearance was immediately pulled off the servers of Her Majesty's Government Communications Headquarters (GCHQ) at Cheltenham in Gloucestershire, England. The analysts then compared the sample with the recording of Subject Two. In seconds, they had results. The analysts judged with high certainty that the two voices were one and the same. Subject Two was Major General Ali Mamlouk, the former commander of the Syrian National Security Bureau. The findings were sent to the JSOC commander at Hama Air Base where a Delta Force troop was kept on standby.

Smoking was indeed a deadly habit.

CHAPTER 8

TWO FATEFUL QUESTIONS interpret more than eleven hundred years of Russian history: "What is to be done?" and "Who is to blame?" But there was now a third question, a corollary, which speaks to the soul of that nation since the fall and asks: "What is to be done to those who are to blame?"

Andrei Minin sat in the back of his chauffeured Mercedes as it cut through the choking traffic on Moscow's Kutuzovsky Prospekt. He reflected that almost thirty years earlier the boulevard's center lane, guarded by *militsiya* and reserved for high-ranking Communist Party officials, would have shepherded him right out of the city center. But no longer—now it was simply an extra turning lane.

Eventually the patterns of ugly, towering apartment blocks—billowing clouds of golden steam rising from their rooftops—ceased and gave way to the thick birch forests where Marshall Zhukov had stopped the Nazi advance. Many of the Third Reich's soldiers who managed to survive the Soviet counteroffensive were put to work and constructed dachas—small country cottages—for the "classless" society's elite. Now the homes built up along the prestigious highways leading west of Moscow were gathered into gated communities that were hundreds of hectares in size. Russia's *nouveau riche* divided their time between those garish monstrosities, flats in London's Mayfair or Kensington, and estates on the Côte d'Azur or the Costa del Sol. As the Mercedes left the main highway and curved along a twisted lane deep into the trees, Minin came upon a more modest construction

The dacha, a guest house of the *Glavnoe Razvedyvatelnoe Upravlenie*—the Main Intelligence Directorate of the General Staff, or the GRU—was a simple two-story structure clad in red wood paneling with a gray pitched roof that would have looked perfectly at home nestled away in Germany's

Black Forest. The Mercedes came to a stop a few yards from the dacha. Minin emerged from the back seat and noticed, disguised in the twilight, a dozen armed figures stalking the tree line—their faces hidden behind white balaclavas. They were Spetsnaz operators of the 16th Special Purpose Brigade, garrisoned nearby at Chukovo, and kept an airtight perimeter around the dacha.

Minin approached the front door as it gently swung open. *"Privyet, Andruishka.* Come in," a voice beckoned from within.

He kicked the snow from his shoes and entered a small sitting room. It was spartan and dimly lit, with only a few wooden chairs arranged around a table before a roaring fireplace. Heavy red curtains were drawn over the windows.

"Tea?"

"Pozhalujsta."

Colonel-General Vyasheslav Trubnikov placed a spoonful of cherry jam into a porcelain cup and lifted a kettle off the table. "Sit down, *Andruishka,"* he said, pouring the strong black brew over the jam.

Minin was sweating. He loosened his tie before taking the cup from Trubnikov, and eased into a chair beside the flames. "You wanted to talk?" he asked nervously.

"I was curious if you'd made up your mind."

The tea singed Minin's tongue, and he tried to hide the pain. "I hadn't." The cup trembled as it left his lips.

"I think it's time you did, *Andruishka."* Trubnikov crossed his legs, intertwined his fingers and languidly pointed to two red file folders on the table. "And I think you should read those... The one on top first."

A bead of sweat trickled down his brow. Minin wiped it away and reached for the file. He opened the cover and read a banner on the front page, which proclaimed: *Sovershenno Secretno Osoboy Vaznosti* (OB), or "Particularly Important"—the equivalent classification level as "Top Secret" in the United States. Minin shot a glance to Trubnikov and then laid his eyes on the page.

Beneath the banner was a letter of introduction addressed to Karetnikov and humbly presented for his consideration what the authors had labeled Operation ALAGIR. At the bottom, Minin found the signatures of Nikita Porozovsky, minister of defence; General Aleksei Tsekov, chief of the General Staff; Colonel-General Sergei Golovnin, commander of the Western Military District (ZVO); and Trubnikov. Minin read the date; it was signed yesterday.

He turned the page.

Minin dropped the folder in his lap. "You took this?"

"Keep reading." Trubnikov stared at the flames.

It was a plan for the invasion and occupation of eastern Ukraine.

The first section provided a detailed breakdown of the GRU's efforts over recent months to infiltrate special forces and agents into the country, with an emphasis on the eastern port city of Mariupol. Minin learned the true extent to which Trubnikov had built local intelligence networks and coopted the Ukrainian Security Service, the SBU, to the point of incapacitation. There were names of high-placed officers and politicians in Kiev, dozens of them, all of whom clandestinely served Moscow. He read about mysterious units under the GRU's control such as the 2nd Brigade of Separatist Forces and the 1st Army Corps of Novorossiya, and a secret operational headquarters in Donetsk commanded by "Major General Zavizion" who coordinated the deployment of artillery and tactical missiles systems in the Donbass region—all of which, Minin knew, should have been withdrawn long ago under the Minsk II Protocol. He saw orders of battle for the Donetsk People's Militia and the Unified Armed Forces of Novorossiya. That level of infiltration, that dismemberment of the Ukrainian government, was the first stage of Operation ALAGIR, and it was already complete.

Minin nervously sipped his tea.

Upon Karetnikov's order, agents of the GRU would murder the mayor of Mariupol, a widely popular pro-Russian politician and critic of President Petro Udovenko. Her assassination would be orchestrated to frame the Azov Battalion, a nationalist far-right faction of the Ukrainian National Guard. With that act of *maskirovka,* strategic deception, the GRU would have manufactured a crisis, which Russia would then act to resolve, presenting itself as a liberator in the process. With that, Trubnikov would ignite a powder keg.

As Kremlin-sponsored media organizations and "useful idiots" across the world squawked with outrage, the next stage of Operation ALAGIR would begin. *"Vremya Cha"*—Zero Hour—would commence with a crippling blow to Ukraine's command and control infrastructure. Tupolev Blackjack and Backfire bombers, warships of the Black Sea Fleet and the Caspian Flotilla, and artillery barrages from across the border would target runways, highways, railways and bridges; Beriev A-50 "Mainstay" airborne early-warning and control (AEW) aircraft would jam communications; Spetsnaz commandos would emerge from the terrain to seize airfields at Donetsk and Dnipropetrovsk; paratroopers would be flown in under fighter cover, establishing a foothold inside the country; all within the initial hours. Only then would the full invasion commence.

Operation ALAGIR earmarked three hundred thousand troops, thousands of tanks and artillery pieces, and hundreds of combat aircraft—mostly from the ZVO, with reinforcements from the Central Military District (TsVO) and naval infantry of the Baltic Fleet—to be formed into Army Group North and Army Group South. Together, their assault would be relentless.

While the Ukrainian high command reeled from the opening salvo and agents-in-place in Kiev sabotaged any attempt at mustering a meaningful response, both army groups would blitz across the border and destroy regular military and volunteer units as the Russian Air Force quickly took supremacy in the skies. Over the following fourteen days of offensive operations, Army Group North would be reinforced by secondary echelon reserve formations to achieve its strategic goal of reaching the Dnieper River, establishing a five-hundred-kilometer front from Kiev to Dnipropetrovsk and occupying the cities of Kharkiv and Poltava. Meanwhile, Army Group South would blaze through Lugansk and Donetsk, "liberate" Mariupol, and follow the coastline of the Sea of Azov southwest to the Russian-held Crimean Peninsula. After two weeks of combat, the authors of Operation ALAGIR contended, their invasion force would control a quarter of the overall territory of Ukraine…all while NATO argued around a conference table.

The coals hissed and popped in the flames. Minin shut the file and wearily drew his eyes back to Trubnikov. "Is this you?" he asked with a hint of betrayal. "Are you telling me this is going to happen?"

Trubnikov cradled his tea with both hands. He gazed at the fire. "I am merely offering a glimpse of events that may or not come to pass."

"What the fuck is that supposed to mean?" Minin massaged the bridge of his nose.

"That plan sat in my personal safe for years, *Andruishka*. He asked Golovnin and me to dust it off."

"Why?"

"I think you know."

Minin tried not to admit it, tried not see it for himself.

"Mikhail Borisovich has lost his way," Trubnikov said plainly. "He has barricaded himself in a prison of his own making, into a dead end. And he wants the rest of us to pay the consequences."

"It's Syria," Minin muttered.

Trubnikov dipped his chin.

Karetnikov was changed by the bloody climax of the Syrian civil war, Minin knew, and not for the better. The Turkish invasion, the fall of Damascus and the savage demise of Hafez Jadid left him seething, inconsolable with rage. Karetnikov became paranoid and suspicious of anyone who didn't echo his visceral, contemptuous view of the world. He saw conspiracy around every corner, nefarious plots of Western powers determined to usurp him with a mob. Close aides and courtiers, men who'd spent years at his side, had privately confided in Minin how they glimpsed Karetnikov whispering to himself during meetings, as if debating his own shadow. But most of all, Karetnikov despised Andrew Paulson and the "effeminate, godless" Europeans who betrayed him, who lied to him, who schemed with each passing hour to lure Russia to ruin. He wanted them dead—quite literally, Karetnikov wished to murder his counterparts in NATO—and more than once asked Trubnikov to present hypothetical plans on how it might be done, "just to help him sleep." Minin couldn't deny it any longer.

"It's time." Trubnikov set his tea down. "And I know Roman Leonidovich told you the same."

"He did," said Minin. "He's called every night since Tuesday, pleading with me. He talks about his 'vision.'"

"I agree with him."

"You do?" Minin's brow tightened.

Trubnikov dipped his chin again. "Much of mankind would rather live a comfortable illusion than an uncomfortable reality. Our enemies are no different. The notion of American military power is built upon a jerry-rig of presumption. No sheltered boy from Oklahoma is going to die for the Donbass, or the Baltics, or Georgia. It is the greatest Ponzi scheme in history. NATO is utterly meaningless, a string of scarecrows Europe has stuck in the ground so its people can sleep at night. We can strip that lie bare. Lord Ivanov understands this. He understands one does not destroy a superpower by opposing it, but by becoming its greatest ally. And we can't while Mikhail Borisovich still rules."

Minin hesitated. "And what then?"

Trubnikov grabbed the second file resting on the table. "Our Washington *rezidentura* sent this in yesterday. The quality's poor, and it hasn't been translated, but I don't think that'll slow you down." He handed the file to Minin.

He opened the cover and found a stack of photographed pages snapped hastily under the glare of a desk lamp. The shadow of a slender forearm ran along the frame. Minin squinted to read the words, but then he noticed a familiar seal, and his eyes widened. It was a five-page-memo printed on the letterhead of the newly minted director of the CIA. The memo was addressed to members of the IC/EXCOM—the Intelligence Community Executive Committee—and included in its distribution list the chairman of the National Intelligence Council (NIC), Dr. Eli Tanner, and various staffers throughout Langley. In it, as Minin read, Ryan Freeman went into great detail about reservations he had regarding a draft Special National Intelligence Estimate. The draft, which was authored by the NIC and circulated for comment, attempted to provide an authoritative assessment of the toll that the Syrian civil war exacted on Hezbollah's military readiness and the degree of dissent within the party's ranks. The NIC was of the opinion that Syria's reorientation toward the West left Hezbollah in a state of crisis, and that they would certainly lay down their arms to preserve their standing among the Lebanese public. Freeman countered in the memo that while CIA believed the disillusionment of Hezbollah's members was quite real, it was not directed at the party's mission of resistance, but rather at its leadership. The ranks were not looking for a change in mission, Freeman argued, but a change in the leadership that had failed them in Syria. If an alternative were to emerge, he warned, the Hezbollah faithful might be eager to engineer that change.

"I met Ryan Freeman once. Years ago. In Berlin. He was a young man then, not unlike you," Trubnikov added as Minin finished reading the memo, and slowly cracked a prideful grin. "But I tempered him."

"I don't understand." Minin placed the file on the table.

"He's absolutely right."

"About Hezbollah?"

Trubnikov nodded. "That's where we'd start."

"How?"

"The American."

Minin shook his head. "He disgusts me."

A spark shot out from the embers. "He doesn't care."

Minin thought of the charred baroque façade of Château Bartholoni and flames dancing on Lake Geneva in the night. "I can't stop thinking about it," he said. "I can't even imagine."

Trubnikov looked away. "It's done."

"Did you know? Did you know how?"

"No, I—"

"There was smoke in his lungs, *Slava*. He was still alive...when he burned."

"You'd do well to stop."

"But he didn't deserve that. No one does"

Trubnikov became irritated. "You made the damned phone call, *Andruishka*. Did you forget that? You asked *me*. You told me that he was a problem, that Ivanov wanted him gone, that it would please Mikhail Borisovich, and I obliged. Arseni Sokoloff is dead, and you have your arrangement with the Chinese." He shrugged. "The American gave you a gift."

"And you trust him?" Minin's voice quivered.

"I point. He bites. He returns. He has for years... And if you ask, it'll be the same with Mikhail Borisovich.'"

Minin brushed his hair back. "How would he do it?" He cleared his throat. "The American. How would he do it?"

Trubnikov thought for a moment. "I'll tell you Mikhail Borisovich is considering attacking Ukraine in April. If so, he'll have to order it in the next two weeks so Golovnin and I can prepare. It has to be before then. Once his authorization starts moving through the chain of command, it'll be unstoppable. Too many are aware as it is."

Minin's hands trembled. "I thought there'd be more time."

"There's not," Trubnikov asserted.

"I know he cleared his schedule next week. He was supposed to visit an industrial fair in Omsk, but he cancelled it. There was no explanation. He's spending three days at Dolgiye Borodny. He leaves Tuesday night."

Karetnikov maintained twenty palaces and villas spread across the vast Russian interior. One of his favorites was the Dolgiye Borodny estate on the shore of Lake Valdai, a one-hour flight from Moscow.

"He's deciding on Ukraine," Trubnikov nodded. "Is Volodnin going with him? He has to, otherwise nothing will change."

"I think so."

"It'll happen then. Lavrov will take his place, and you're in a perfect position to guide him as we need."

"Okay…" Minin relented with a grieved sigh.

"Do not go see him. Promise me."

"I can't look at him anymore."

Trubnikov leaned forward and touched his hand. "Please don't be sorry," he consoled. "That man has failed you, just as he has failed all of us. There is no other way."

The flames reflected in Minin's eyes. "I have to go."

"Fine," Trubnikov pulled away. "We'll talk when it's over."

Minin went to his Mercedes without saying another word.

What is to be done to those who are to blame? The answer to that question was the American's art—and he was about to sculpt his masterpiece.

CHAPTER 9

"TIME ON TARGET, one minute," the helo pilot breathed dispassionately into his radio and pointed a single finger out the cockpit door to ensure his passengers perched on the skids copied the message over the roaring engines and the howling wind.

Chief Petty Officer Robert Harris received the signal and checked the safety lanyard pinned to his back for what must have been the tenth time since dust off. It was now past one in the morning and Harris found himself with the familiar vantage he had night after night: working the vampire shift, watching the Syrian coastline breeze beneath him at seventy miles-per-hour. He and the three other operators on the helo rode on pods, or benches, bolted to the sides of the MH-6M Little Bird, a light helicopter with a distinctive oval-shaped airframe. The operators with Harris were from C Squadron of ACE, and that fact made him more than a bit out of sorts. Harris was an operator from the Naval Special Warfare Development Group (DEVGRU), which was commonly known to the public as the vaunted SEAL Team Six. A month ago, during a raid in Baniyas, several Delta operators were critically wounded in a helo crash. JSOC put out a request for additional assaulters to its Special Mission Units and Harris volunteered, placing him in Syria until permanent replacements from Delta could be sent in to finish out the squadron's deployment.

The city lights of Tartus were gaining on the horizon as the Little Birds banked sharply to hook around the port and approached the target house from the south. Harris watched the second Little Bird flying in formation off their right flank. They were the roof team and would swoop down on the target house from above and assault down while the ground team, backed-up by the FSA and Turkish mechanized infantry, would drive in, breach the first floor and assault up, meeting in the middle.

A Delta operator Harris had quickly befriended, Staff Sergeant Jon

Rooker, sat on the bench of the opposite helo and calmly flipped Harris his middle finger. Harris returned the gesture.

The Little Birds dropped altitude over the harbor and passed a few feet over the rusting hull of a capsized cargo ship, now just another relic of civil war. Soon, the outer walls of the Crusader fortress, Tartus' medina, emerged from behind a row of disused gantry cranes.

"Thirty seconds."

The Little Birds completed the hook around the port and swiftly closed in on the fortress. Harris flipped down his night vision goggles (NVGs) from the mount on his cranial helmet and switched the system on, cloaking the air around him in a crisp, green ambient light. The Ground Panoramic Night Vision Goggle (GPNVG-18) was manufactured by L-3 Warrior Systems and featured four image intensifier tubes, enabling use of his peripheral vision; the view through a standard pair of NVGs was akin to looking through two toilet paper tubes, not ideal for a close quarters firefight. Next, Harris tightened the sling attached to his Heckler & Koch 416 carbine, which he had customized with a ten-inch barrel for maneuverability indoors, an infrared laser sight and an AAC sound suppressor.

He looked down. The skids of the Little Birds dangled mere inches over medina's curtain wall. Drawing his eyes forward, Harris saw the copilot pointing a laser at the roof of the target house. The helo pilots were all seasoned pros from the 160th Special Operations Aviation Regiment, the "Night Stalkers." Quite simply, they were the best in the business. They had performed thousands of textbook raids such as this, and never failed to navigate to the exact rooftop in an endless sea of cinder block and plaster.

Through his NVGs, Harris had a clear view of the labyrinth below. Millennia of conflict and change had mutilated the medina beyond recognition. Two- and three-story family homes, many with small balconies, had been built over, around and within massive structures of ancient masonry like wasp nests in an abandoned barn.

"Ten seconds."

Harris released the safety lanyard and chambered a round into his 416.

The rotor wash from the helos battered clotheslines and satellite dishes, and unrolled a dust cloud as the helos steadied over the target house. Both Little Birds came to a controlled hover and the pilots executed a lip landing, gently placing the skids down on the rooftop. In moments, the team jumped from the skids to the roof and the Little Birds were gone.

"Roof team deployed. Dagger Two-One, exiting Alpha Oscar," Harris' earpiece crackled.

The swirling clouds of dust and thrashing rotor wash gave way to a deceptive calm as Harris and the seven Delta operators formed up in a stack without uttering a word. Harris was first on the roof door. He pressed his body against an adjacent wall while the team gathered on his six. Rooker was directly behind him and squeezed Harris' right shoulder, signaling his presence. The door was made of sturdy wood and protected on the exterior by a wrought iron gate. A quick shake of the handle revealed to Harris that the gate was bolted from inside.

"Breacher," he whispered.

A Delta operator rushed to the front of the stack and placed a long, thin strip of plastic explosive along the length of the door, then stepped back in formation. "Set."

Harris pressed two fingers to the microphone pad strapped to his throat. "Breaching the roof in five, four, three, two… *Execute!"*

The Delta operator squeezed the detonator, triggering a bright yellow flash, echoed by a muffled thud that wrestled Harris' gut. The blast consumed the hinges and sent the gate crashing inward with the splintered remains of the door. Harris held the 416 tightly in the pit of his arm and steadied the barrel toward a blackened stairwell. The team had studied the face of their HVT closely—Ali Mamlouk—and they would recognize him in an instant. With the distraction of the first blast, they had only several seconds to wait until, on queue, they heard the sound of the second breaching charge on the first floor, followed by the unmistakable clap of automatic gunfire.

Harris started down the stairs when he felt a tight squeeze on his shoulder. He realized why, and his heart plunged into his stomach.

"We're on the wrong fucking roof!" Rooker barked.

"Back out, back out!" Harris ordered. The stack retreated through the doorway and gathered at a corner of the roof. They looked to the adjoining house and saw successive bursts of light through the windows, accompanied by the sustained rattle of Kalashnikov fire.

"Son of a bitch!" Rooker exclaimed. The 160th had finally made a mistake. From the air, the houses looked identical, but someone somewhere botched the pre-op planning and the Little Birds had overflown the target house by a single roof. They had approached from the south and landed one too far. Now the correct target, the house directly south, erupted with the clamor of chaos. Worse, the ground team was in there alone without the backup they were expecting to charge down the stairs.

"We're not worth jack shit up here." Harris looked over the edge of the roof. A large courtyard sat adjacent to the houses. At the opposite end, Harris spotted a three-story cinder block structure. If the team could get on top of it they would have a platform to cover down, across the courtyard, at the target house. "We need to get on that roof over there and provide overwatch," he pointed.

"We can take the alley," a Delta operator shouted over a small explosion coming from the target house.

Rooker keyed his radio and updated the assault commander as the team rushed down to street level. Outside, they formed up again behind Harris and observed their surroundings. The alley was dark, choked with discarded trash, and no more than fifteen feet wide—a tactical nightmare. Awakened by the gunfire, locals began to peer out of lighted windows and gather on their rooftops. The stack started moving deliberately down the alley. Harris kept the barrel of his 416 trained on the heads dotting up above. Any of them with a grudge could pull a weapon and rake them with lead.

They heard an interpreter plea over a bullhorn in hurried Arabic in the distance. "A security operation is underway! Go back! Back, back in your homes!"

The stack cleared a corner in the alleyway in seconds and advanced parallel to the courtyard. Harris watched the entrance to the house materialize in the green glow of his NVGs.

"We've got an eagle down! I say again—eagle down," the distressed voice of a Delta operator cried over the radio. The ground team had taken a casualty. "Be advised," the Delta operator struggled to speak over the gunfire, "there are multiple hostiles barricaded on the second floor of the target structure. Hostiles are laying down suppressive fire with small arms and tossing frags down the stairwell. Negative ID on the HVT. That is a *negative* ID on HVT Calypso. Ground team is pulling back and requesting additional resources, over."

The stack in the alley ran to the three-story house and formed up at each side of the entrance. "Harris, kick that fucking door in!" Rooker ordered.

Harris thrust the sole of his right boot just above the lock, splintering the wood and violently throwing the door back on its hinges. Rooker was first through the threshold at a run and saw four bodies recoiling in shock. *"Erfaa' yadayk! Erfaa' yadayk!* Get the fuck down!" he roared. The frightened family complied and shouted in panicked confusion. They were flexi-cuffed and placed on their knees before a wall. A pair of Delta operators watched over them. The remainder of the team went to clear each room and rushed topside.

Harris went prone on the rooftop with a clear view facing west to the target house and steadied the barrel of his 416 on a ledge. Part of the ground team had fanned out into the courtyard and found cover in a series of cramped, stone alcoves. Harris saw the green trails of their infrared lasers scanning the window frames for targets. They arrived at a stalemate with the regime loyalists holed up on the second floor. It was tactically impossible for the ground team to fight their way up the stairs against a barrage of Kalashnikov fire and exploding grenades. But the fighters in the house showed no sign of relenting. With each passing minute, one of the fighters—Harris guessed there were at least six—would brandish an AK-47 out of a window, lay on the trigger, and empty a thirty-round magazine.

The operators in the courtyard drew their fire while the remainder of the ground team swept the first floor of the target house. Soon, the call broke through the radio chatter in Harris' earpiece. "Calypso. I say again: Calypso. HVT is in custody. Moving now for extract, over."

Ali Mamlouk had somehow been captured alive and was quickly being whisked away from the site. Harris was relieved at the news. Delta had gotten its prize. Now they just had to wipe up the mess. The next radio calls were to a Turkish mechanized infantry unit holding the perimeter a few hundred yards away. "Send up an ACV!" his earpiece squawked. Harris watched the Delta operators in the courtyard systematically break cover with a few bursts of suppressive fire and pull back to safety. It was standard operating procedure to have multiple rings of security around a target to keep anything in or out. Deployed with Delta on the operation, was the Fastaqim Kama Umirt unit of the FSA and a battalion of the Turkish Army's 28th Mechanized Infantry Brigade, which fielded the ACV-300, an infantry fighting vehicle armed with a twenty-five-millimeter cannon.

Harris heard the bellicose rumble of a diesel engine and the chomp of tank treads approaching the site. Without preamble, the ACV revved its motors and burst through a wall that had stood for centuries, littering the courtyard with limestone bricks and crumbled mortar. Kalashnikov rounds ricocheted off its armor plating. The ACV pulled atop a mound of rubble and rotated its turret with a mechanical scream to aim directly at the side of the target house. A column of flame leapt from the turret. A short burst of incendiary rounds ripped through the second-floor wall, tearing wide gashes in sections of the concrete. Shooting from the house stopped and the acrid stench of cordite stifled the air. The ACV reversed off the mound, and the assault commander—a captain from Delta—stormed into the courtyard, clearly exposing himself to fire.

"No, no, no!" he climbed effortlessly onto the turret and shouted down to the ACV commander through the open hatch. "You are to demolish the top floor," he reiterated, hurling down beads of spit. "The entire second floor, fucking level it. *Level it!*" The captain jumped from the turret and vanished from Harris' line of sight. A moment later, the ACV lurched back atop the mound.

The regime loyalists shouted out from within the house and emptied several magazines at the turret.

The next barrage from the ACV shook the whole medina and crashed into the target house with successive explosions. A fire erupted on a corner of the second floor. Thick black smoke billowed up from the holes in the concrete. But the patter of gunfire continued.

And then Harris saw it in his iron sights. A man emerged from behind what was left of the wall. His torso and left arm were covered in bright orange flames. In his right arm was an AK-47, which he discharged wildly into the courtyard. Harris could see his eyes. They were hazel—like his own—and filled with pain and desperation. He knew he was going to die, Harris reasoned. How could he not? The seconds stalled to a trickle. Harris raised his 416, placing the laser sight squarely on the man's forehead. Harris held his breath, though his heart was pounding, and pulled the trigger twice. The double tap soared over the courtyard and shattered the man's skull in a cloud of pink mist, dropping him back in the fire.

No more pain, he justified.

Rooker raced to his side. "You pop one of 'em?"

"Yeah. He was burning."

"You sure?"

"Pretty sure."

"Nice, bro!"

The ACV's cannon went dry as a section of the roof collapsed, stirring up a whirl of glowing embers. The gunfire stopped.

The assault team knew the house contained useful intelligence that would point JSOC's hunters to their next target. The fire was quickly doused and a crew was sent in to sift through the rubble for anything useful.

Forty minutes passed and the sun had slowly begun to rise over Tartus. Harris rested against a wall in the alley and held his helmet under his arm. After shaking beads of sweat from his blond hair, he tugged at his Camel-Bak hose and squirted a blast of cold water on his face.

"Yo, Harris, get your ass up here and see this," Rooker called on the radio.

"Wilco."

Harris trudged up the stairs where the ground team had been pinned. The single casualty from the operation, Harris learned, took a round to the thigh. A few others were peppered with shrapnel, but it was all relatively minor. Ali Mamlouk, astonishingly, was discovered wedged in a cavity between two interior walls on the first floor. It was a small miracle that he was captured alive.

Harris climbed up to what was left of the second floor and saw a vision of hell. They had all met ghastly ends. At his feet was a body matching the physical description of Mamlouk's facilitator—Subject One from the intercepts. An ACV round literally ripped the man in two, leaving only a head, arms and an upper torso intact. The remaining bits of skin on the man's face, Harris saw, had turned a pale gray-white from the sudden, massive loss of blood, which now canopied the nearest wall with a grizzly red and black splatter.

"You hear how they bagged the general?" Rooker appeared and drew Harris' attention. The display hardly seemed to faze him. "Bastard didn't even stand up and fight."

Harris shook his head.

"Hey, beer's on us next time we see those helo pilots! Get a gander at this." Rooker led him to the side of the floor that was left untouched by the fire. "We've only found four bodies. *Four* assholes lasted that long! You've gotta give 'em credit."

"Yep…" Harris looked around at the devastation, including the body he had put there. They stepped over a severed leg, into the hallway leading to the door that opened onto the roof. Crates of ammunition and hand grenades lined the walls. Without the ACV coming to the rescue, the cache would have been enough to hold off the assault team for hours.

"Intel royally fucked us on this one," Rooker continued, "but I'm not complaining."

At the end of the hall, facing the door, Harris saw a wall of sandbags stacked eight-high. Mounted on them was a PKM, a Russian belt-fed general-purpose machine gun, attached to a bipod. Harris jerked his head around to the remains of the facilitator and the charred body of the man whose skull he shattered. Then he looked back to the PKM.

"You were first through the door, bro," Rooker said. "You would've walked right into that."

CHAPTER 10

AL-EMIR, AL-HADI AND *al-Sayyed* were the three titles written in flowing Arabic that first struck visitors to Hezbollah's private dominion. They adorned banners spanning the concrete canyons of the *dahieh*. *"Al-Emir"*—the Commander—was Ayatollah Ruhollah Khomeini, the late founder of the Islamic Republic of Iran and the spiritual figurehead of the revolution he sparked; *"al-Hadi"*—the Guide—was Ayatollah Ali Mostafa Khansari, the current supreme leader of Iran and Khomeini's successor; *"al-Sayyed"*—the Master—was Sheikh Wissam Hamawi, the secretary-general of Hezbollah. Such was the extent of the Party of God's pantheon, in that rigid order; a shepherding credo to lead the Hezbollah faithful in times light and dark. But that credo would soon be tested, and it would reveal what little weight it truly held to a party under siege from without and within.

The *dahieh* was a collection of suburbs at the southern extremity of Beirut's urban sprawl. Like the Beqaa Valley to the east, or the Shiite heartlands near the fortified Israeli border, the *dahieh* was a Hezbollah stronghold, a vacuum and a state within a state where the Lebanese government held no sovereignty and knew better than to try and exercise it. Thousands of party members lived there. At the heart of the *dahieh* was the "Security Quarter"—*al-Murabba' al-Amni*—Hezbollah's headquarters and home to its central offices and senior leadership. That nondescript cluster of drab, concrete apartment blocks was a walled compound, secured by heavy steel sliding gates and watched by a massive surveillance system—both revealed and hidden. Hundreds of cameras screened the surrounding streets and alleyways. Plainclothes militiamen would detain and interrogate anyone who appeared out of place. The *dahieh* was a pressure cooker encased in concrete, steel and the ordained laws of political and spiritual oppression. As Ibrahim al-Din surveyed the neighborhood from behind tinted glass, he had the striking suspicion that the seal on that pressure cooker had shown its first cracks, and might soon boil over.

He was driven to the main gate of the Security Quarter by Anwar Sabbah, his aide-de-camp and brother-in-law, and was stopped by a pair of armed guards in black uniforms and berets. Kalashnikovs were slung over their shoulders. The guards checked Sabbah's papers as the trunk was searched and an inspection mirror scoured the underside of their Isuzu Trooper. Once cleared, the SUV was directed to the ground-floor garage of a tall apartment building at the center of the compound.

"Wait here, this shouldn't take long." Al-Din rose from the SUV.

Members of Hamawi's security detail met al-Din at the car and waved a magnetometer over his body before escorting him to an elevator. As they ascended in silence, al-Din was compelled to ponder if Hamawi's protectors realized the nature of their company. He asked himself if they knew what acts he committed and of what he was still capable. Surely they did—his name was a synonym for terror—but did they recognize him? Al-Din had undergone several rounds of plastic surgery in the late eighties and had since existed as a ghost. He was sought by Western intelligence agencies for thirty years, but in Ouzai, the coastal Beirut slum where he was born, he walked the streets freely with only an assumed name and face to mask his identity. Just his eyes remained the same, the pale green orbs. That much would never change.

The elevator doors opened and al-Din was ushered to a comfortable antechamber on the fourth floor. Gaudy Louis XV armchairs and sofas filled the room and thick velvet drapes covered the windows. On the walls, al-Din saw a collection of vanity photographs: Hamawi posing with Ayatollah Khansari, Iranian politicians, or addressing thousands in a public square not far from where he stood. Prominently displayed was one framed picture of the secretary-general with the late Hafez Jadid whose foolish bloodletting, al-Din mused, had likely brought him here. He heard muffled voices beyond a pair of wooden doors at the far side of the antechamber. Once deemed a liability to Iran's quest for empire, he had been cast out of Hezbollah's inner circle, but stupid he was not. Al-Din maintained a network of informants reaching deep into the Security Quarter and he knew full well the reason for his summons.

Ten minutes had passed when the muffled voices beyond the doors grew quiet. Al-Din stood at a window and pulled the drapes aside to look out over the compound. The doors swung open at his back. Instinctively, al-Din turned to look over his right shoulder and saw, emerging through the doorway, a man he instantly recognized. It was Colonel Samir Basri, commander of the *Bureau d'information,* the intelligence wing of the Lebanese Internal Security Forces (ISF). He had the fit frame of a veteran soldier, was in his mid-forties, and wore an expensive Italian suit, which was far beyond the reach of his government salary. There was a distinctive liveliness to Colonel Basri's gait, al-Din noted, as he turned his head and tracked the soldier through the antechamber.

But Basri looked back. Their eyes met for only a second, maybe less. In that ripple in time, Basri slowed his step and his face went flush at the sight of the green-eyed man.

Al-Din turned his head to the left and focused again on the window, cursing himself in his mind. He watched Basri in his periphery.

The colonel stopped in his tracks, and stared.

Another second crawled past. Al-Din kept his head turned and his eyes fixed out the window. Finally, there was a relieving shift in the air. The colonel dismissively breezed out of the room, and was gone.

He continued his gaze when from behind him called a voice known to millions in the Arab world. "Abu Dokhan... Please."

Wissam Hamawi stood on the threshold of the double doors and out-stretched an arm to welcome the master terrorist into his office. Al-Din followed—begrudgingly—and took a seat before an antique desk. Secluded in a corner of the office and waiting in silence was Dr. Hussein Khalil, the secretary-general's trusted political adviser and a member of Hezbollah's governing Shura Council. Hamawi sunk behind the desk and released a tired exhale. He was dressed in his iconic uniform of fine black clerical robes and a tightly wrapped turban that feigned descent from the Prophet, but the specter al-Din watched with muted glee was more shade than sol-dier. Gone was the boisterous colossus of defiance that stood, not a day earlier, before twenty thousand people and proclaimed that victory was in their grasp. That was a lie. Victory had never been more illusive, and they only had him to blame.

That voice had garnered an ill repute and fateful trust among Israelis, foretelling consequences and dictating assurances, which rarely bode well for the Jewish state. Even senior IDF officers admitted behind closed doors their grudging and wary respect for Hamawi. Yet those passionate out-bursts, more sermon than political prose, were only for public consumption and part of a carefully crafted veneer. In private—far from the wellspring of adoring audiences that hung on every word of his fiery rhetoric—he exuded a mild-mannered awkwardness, polite, soft-spoken and burdened with a lisp since childhood. For that congregation, he would cake his face with beige foundation to mask his imperfections and convey the impression of youth-ful vitality, which had long since faded. But the face al-Din watched that morning was marred with the weight of lies and broken promises. His beard had turned a steely gray and his skin, sheltered behind the walls of *al-Murabba' al-Amni,* had become pallid. Stress had withered his pudgy cheeks to two well-defined streaks of bone. Al-Din saw that Hamawi's face had finally transformed to reveal the truth of his character that had been hidden within. It was the face of a man who knew he was hunted.

"Abu Dokhan, there is no easy way to say this..."

"Then perhaps you should just say it." Al-Din examined the back of his hand with the bored demeanor of a tawdry pimp.

"The outcome of the war in Syria was not what any of us had hoped," Hamawi delved into the rehearsed lines of the *mea culpa* he would deliver to many that day. "This leaves us with certain tactical and strategic realities to consider."

But al-Din was more interested in the pattern of wrinkles on his hand.

"Early this morning, the Shura Council came to a decision about the future of the party and the mission of the Islamic Resistance to come. As you are aware, the agreement the rebels have reached with the United States, while unfortunate, makes it nearly impossible to rearm our forces. This automatically puts us at a supreme disadvantage against the Zionists. Any losses inflicted upon us in battle would be all the more painful, and we would not be able to recover," Hamawi lectured on. "So it is with these bitter realities in mind that the Shura Council ruled this morning to dissolve the Islamic Resistance and integrate with the Lebanese Armed Forces, pending a resolution between Syria and the Zionists which addresses the occupation of the Golan Heights."

Suddenly al-Din's hand was no longer the center of his world.

"I have already contacted the representatives of His Excellency in Tehran, including the Iranian ambassador here in Beirut and Colonel Basri of the ISF. Later today, our bloc in parliament will make an official announcement. Please know that this is not what I wanted."

"No, just what you've sown."

Hamawi stared at his lap. "There is also the matter of your outstanding arrest warrants abroad." Here was the leverage with which Hamawi hoped to contain al-Din. "Your contribution to our struggle is one of legend to the *mujahedeen* and we are all appreciative of your service. We see no cause to betray that service and so the party will provide a secure shelter in Lebanon—your home—for the rest of your natural life."

"That's too kind."

"However, you will never again use Hezbollah as a flag of convenience for either your own endeavors or those of any client. And I want your word that Lebanese soil will not be used to plan and organize. Should you violate this agreement, you will quickly find that there is no shelter to be found in Lebanon. Do you understand?" Hamawi sat back in his chair and waited, but the pale green orbs seemed unfazed. "Well, are you going to respond?"

"Oh, I think I'll respond in my own good time," al-Din smiled. "You do what you need to do to survive. Keep scratching your ragged claws at the rocks and the dirt just to stay upright; keep searching for solid ground, and I'll keep digging the earth out from under you." Then something shifted behind those orbs. "I have to say, Wissam, I much rather prefer you this way. It makes such a good show."

• • •

Major General Qasem Shateri was as hot as an ember. He stopped abruptly in his report to wipe the sweat from his forehead and survey his surroundings. It was the last place he wanted to be that morning—the office of Saeed Mofidi, a man for whom he had little time. Nonetheless, Mofidi was gatekeeper to the supreme leader and without the consent of *"vali-e faghih,"* nothing could be done—or so it was on paper. *"Baradar,* I must protest. To report on a matter of this urgency in the presence of anyone but His Excellency is not only incredibly unorthodox, it is unacceptable! I cannot—"

"His Excellency is at rest," Mofidi stopped the general in his tracks, "and with regrets, is unable to join us." He slipped on a pair of reading glasses. Khansari was oblivious that a meeting was even taking place; Mofidi called on Shateri for his own agenda. "But, please, continue."

"Of course, I pray that His Excellency is of the utmost health."

Mofidi nodded for the general to continue the postmortem.

"At approximately seven this morning, I was notified of an urgent phone call from the secretary-general. We had already spoken at least five times yesterday, so I took the call in my office, at which point he told me that Hezbollah's Shura Council unanimously voted to dissolve the Islamic Resistance, pending negotiations between Syria and the Zionist regime. I made clear my frustrations that this decision was made without consulting either the supreme leader or myself. Sheikh Hamawi was apologetic but insisted that Hezbollah could not endure in Lebanon as a viable political entity unless it took substantial measures to distance itself from us. He reiterated his staunch commitment to the struggle against the Zionist regime and promised to seek guidance from the supreme leader on issues concerning Lebanon in the future. I assured him that we would speak again soon. Our conversation then ended. At that point, I immediately contacted my field commander in Beirut, who is still reporting on the situation from our embassy, and asked what he knew. Incredibly, he was totally unaware of what had happened. I'm afraid Hezbollah made this decision entirely on their own."

The stillness in Mofidi's office underscored what an unmitigated disaster this was for the Islamic Republic of Iran. With its chief ally in the Middle East fought to a slow, protracted defeat and its proxy on Israel's northern border left isolated and vilified, Iran was pushed back almost a thousand miles to its natural borders; its snaking tentacles cleaved from the whole and left to wither and rot in the detritus of its own hubris. The lowly hung heads around Tehran that morning were hardly in denial of that, but neither did they sink into some accepted fate. They simply had to craft a new strategy. For an architect of that strategy, all eyes looked to Shateri, including Mofidi's friends across the Atlantic.

Major General Qasem Shateri was the feared commander of the Islamic

Revolutionary Guard Corps' Quds Force, the hub of Iran's global force projection network. He lorded over a carefully tended flock of terrorist movements, militias and nomadic guns-for-hire spanning from Sudan, through the Sinai Peninsula to Gaza and the West Bank, into the sweltering slums of Baghdad, across the Shiite enclaves of the Gulf emirates, to the lawless tribal frontiers of Afghanistan and Yemen. In maintaining such a network of proxies and clients through sustained covert transfers of arms, cash and trainings, Iran sought to build a sort of strategic deterrent to protect the regime from external threats—to ensure that an attack on Iran would be a costly endeavor for any foe, not the least, the United States and Israel.

As Mofidi watched the regime's top enforcer, he thought about an even deadlier deterrent. With the virtual surrender of Hezbollah, the regime's hardliners would naturally seek another way to project its will. Mofidi had one option in mind. If any imagination was responsible for the ongoing construction at Picasso and Monet, it was likely that of the man seated before him.

"His Excellency specifically asked about the status of the weapon systems we've deployed to Lebanon. Will those systems remain active? Will we attempt to recover them? Or are they simply lost?"

Shateri thought that was a strangely amateur question and stranger still to come from the supreme leader. But he would entertain it. "Hezbollah still holds hundreds of long-range missile systems of our design and manufacture: Zelzals, Fajrs and a limited number of Fateh-110s. We no longer count Katuyshas, there are too many, but they reach above fifty thousand. These are stored in secure bunker complexes in the northern Beqaa Valley, mostly, with some deployed to urban areas near Beirut and Jezzine. We, of course, are quite familiar with these complexes—we helped construct them—but if we were to physically remove them, we would have to risk doing so by sea, an action I would not recommend. Unfortunately, without an air bridge from Syria, removing the systems is beyond our capability, at least plausibly. They will have to remain in Lebanon for the time being."

"And how does *al-Quds* intend to recover this unexpected loss?"

Shateri shook his head. "This is much more than a loss in footing, this is a severe blow to our ability to assert ourselves globally. If the Americans or the Zionists were to attack this very day, we could do little beyond close the Strait of Hormuz. *Baradar,* I cannot stress how exposed this leaves us."

"You intend to do *what* about this, is my question," Mofidi interrupted.

"Well, if I had my way, we'd storm the *dahieh* and install someone with a spine."

"I'd caution you against such language. His Excellency was quite clear in his belief that if Hezbollah is to be of any use to us, it must first be a Lebanese political party for the people of Lebanon."

Shateri dialed himself back. "Of course I do not pretend to match the wisdom and divine guidance of His Excellency. I simply seek to understand why."

"And in time, I have no doubt you will," Mofidi smiled.

"Right." Qasem Shateri despised Mofidi. "It is my intent to increase tenfold our assistance to the resistance groups on the southern front of occupied Palestine—Hamas and Islamic Jihad. These brothers remain popular among the Arabs and personally assured me of their continued loyalty. I feel that whatever strategic depth we lose in Syria and Lebanon, we could eventually recover in Gaza and Sinai. I've taken it upon myself to phone the Sudanese ambassador and he signals that his capital sees no reason to amend our previous arrangements."

"His Excellency should be pleased."

"And so to reaffirm our commitment to our brothers in Gaza, I intend to provide Islamic Jihad with a goodwill package under the cover of our agricultural concerns." Shateri recited from memory: "Twenty thousand rifles, two million rounds, three thousand kilos of high explosives, detonators, body armor, and Type 72 anti-tank mines—given His Excellency's consent."

Mofidi swallowed hard, unable to show his true emotions. His friends across the Atlantic would have to get word. "I will inform His Excellency."

"We have arranged for a vessel under Liberian flag—which has not been used in past operations. The shipment departs Bandar Abbas in the morning and will make port at Bur Sudan. Our local partners will handle matters from there."

"Of course," Mofidi allowed. Now he had to take a leap of faith and stab aimlessly in the dark. He couldn't miss. It was merely an assumption that Shateri would have the answers he needed. Mofidi could be horribly mistaken. He had to choose his next words carefully. If he was wrong, they could very well put him before a firing squad that same day.

Omid. Mofidi tried not to dwell on that. His friends were counting on him.

"Since we find ourselves on the topic of deterrence—and I have to confess, this confused me until His Excellency clarified—I was asked to inquire on the progress at Haj Ali Gholi."

Shateri's eyes narrowed and he cocked his head slightly to the right. He had been genuinely broadsided, and Mofidi could immediately tell he hit a nerve—just what nerve, he did not know. Shateri parsed those words for a moment before responding.

"His Excellency inquired about *that?*"

"He did."

"Project 260?"

"Correct."

"Curious." Shateri pursed his lips and spoke flatly, "I would be honored to inform His Excellency that Dr. Fakhrizadeh has extracted fifty kilograms of plutonium-239 and the appropriate amount of tritium. God willing, he intends to assemble and test a device in the summer."

And Saeed Mofidi's world was shattered.

Shateri gathered his papers. "As I have no doubt you are aware, today is quite busy. If you have no other inquiries, I should be on my way."

"No, I think that will be all, thank you," Mofidi fought to hide the tremble in his voice.

"Good."

Mofidi stayed in his office until seven o'clock that evening, expecting at any moment for Shateri's thugs to burst through the door and throw a black hood over his head. But they never came. Beit Rahbari was now largely dark and empty, apart from the regular foot patrols of IRGC sentries. Outside, floodlights flashed on and illuminated the tall pines trees dotting the courtyard. It had taken just two sentences to rewrite all that he thought he knew about Iran's jilted love affair with the atom: *fifty kilograms of plutonium-239; assemble and test a device in the summer.* And he had two names: "Project 260" and "Dr. Fakhrizadeh," who was supposed to be dead, Mofidi did not need reminding. There could be no other meaning to Shateri's words, no discernible ambiguity to his intent, no possible, remotely comprehensible alternate explanation but to reveal one fatal finality—the Islamic Republic of Iran would be a nuclear power in a matter of months.

Mofidi draped his coat over his shoulders and slipped each aging arm through the sleeves. His secretary in the anteroom outside called the garage to arrange for his staff car. It was waiting with Babak behind the wheel as he exited the building. Twenty minutes later, through the usual checkpoints on Pasteur Street and the miles of choking traffic, he was alone behind the walls of his villa on Ammar Street. He checked the time and retreated to his bedroom, drawing his curtains shut before lighting a candle in the center window. He sat at his desk with a stack of water-soluble paper, a pen steady in his hand, and scratched out a revelation that could seal his country's fate.

A lime green taxi stopped in front of the Tehran office of the Arab Banking Corporation at 17 Haghani Highway on just the second wave. *Not bad,* Jack Galloway thought to himself as he collapsed onto the back seat.

"Where are you going?" asked the cabbie, an elderly woman whose hair was hidden beneath a black *hijab.*

"Hashemi Street in Jamaran," he replied in flawless Persian with a re-hearsed accent to match his cover.

"You German?"

"Swiss," Jack lied.

"My cousin, he moved to Geneva."

"Very nice. You don't think you could take Ammar Street, could you?"

"Cost you more."

"That's fine, I'll pay." Jack eased his back onto the microfiber upholstery as the cab pulled away from the curb and vanished within the sprawl. After what seemed like an unacceptably long period of painful conversation, Jack saw the shuttered storefronts of Tajrish Square, near the mosque were CITADEL prayed daily. The cabbie then eased around the square and onto Ammar Street, lined by shade trees and dignified homes, all with entrances secured by wrought iron—not unlike parts of Washington, Jack often thought. On his left, through the shade trees, emerged a white stone villa surrounded by walls and manicured gardens. Jacked craned his neck to see up over the walls and caught the soft yellow glow of a candle burning on the top floor. It was the subtlest of signals that, come morning, Jack's asset would make contact.

Mofidi had easily covered ten pages in coarse black ink by the time he finished his report. With each stroke of his pen, he detailed how dangerously the Islamic Republic of Iran had fallen astray. He touched on everything: Ayatollah Khansari's waning health, Qasem Shateri's eagerness to dictate policy from the field, the arms shipment to Palestinian Islamic Jihad and then finally, the disturbing answer to the question that had filled the incandescent screens at Langley for days. At the end of the report, CITADEL included an apology to his faithful handlers. He couldn't help but feel that he failed them.

He read through the report one last time and made sure everything was included. Satisfied, he laid the pages out on his desk in order. Next, he removed a fourteen-megapixel digital camera and snapped a clear photo of each page. The photos were recorded on a thirty-two-gigabyte memory card, which he placed in the inner pocket of the suit jacket he would wear the next day. He then drifted to his bathroom and dissolved the pages in the sink. Mofidi wanted to look up in the mirror for one last glance before he slunk off to bed, but the view would have been much too frightening.

CHAPTER 11

AT THE MOMENT she hated everyone and everything. Nina Davenport forced the brakes of her white Volvo to a sudden halt in the alleyway. The engine idled over the crack of exploding fireworks in the darkness above. Nina released the safety on her Glock and pressed the muzzle into the dashboard. She scanned the shadows, yet TOPSAIL was a no-show.

Just beyond the alleyway and the shadows before her, Rue Gouraud was a world apart. The street was the main, albeit narrow thoroughfare through the bustling Gemmayze neighborhood of East Beirut. Past sundown, it became a haven for the glamorous youth and the inhibited, indulgent dregs of the south, where anything was acceptable so long as it was done with good taste. Since mid-morning, Gemmayze, like the other Christian and Sunni areas of Beirut, was mobbed by the cheering and reveling opponents of the Party of God. They poured into the streets within seconds of Wissam Hamawi's tired and defeated visage appearing on their television screens to announce an end to Lebanon's indentured servitude to the mullahs in Tehran. Now, that jubilant and frantic mob occupied the pubs and cafés that littered Gemmayze, and Rue Gouraud was awash with a chorus of drunken howls and blaring car horns.

Nina Davenport had no time for any of it.

She cast her glare up the side of an elegant stone building that dated back to the Ottoman era and was recently converted into luxury flats. One of the flats, which occupied a large section of the top floor and held a view over the Mediterranean, was owned by TOPSAIL—a fact known only to Nina and his loyal security detail, not his wife. Three nights a week, he would disappear into the flat with the freshest in an endless procession of girls plucked off the streets of Beirut. The arrangement not only served his needs, but allowed for his security detail—their cooperation did not go unrewarded—to turn a blind eye as TOPSAIL slipped their watch and escaped through a service exit, only to inexplicably reappear in the flat thirty minutes later. The lights were off on the top floor, but Nina knew damn well he was up there, and her patience was growing thin. She reached for the radio concealed in the Volvo's middle console and called her backup, a heavily armed team of ex-special forces contractors waiting in a silver Mitsubishi Pajero stopped along Rue Gouraud. "He has thirty seconds to get his rocks off or I'm going up there and dragging him down those god-damn stairs, myself." She threw the radio on the passenger seat.

"Please don't do that," Ortega, the team leader, reasoned, although he discovered long ago that it was essentially pointless with her.

"Thirty seconds and I start busting guns." Nina was only half serious. She watched and waited as the seconds drew on and her frustration boiled. The muzzle of her Glock forced an indentation on the leather dashboard. Then, just as she slapped her hand on the gearshift to speed off, her eyes caught a gentle wave through the shadows.

She reached over the middle console and popped open the rear passenger door before slipping the Volvo into gear and letting it drift down the alleyway. As the car rolled past the building's service exit, TOPSAIL slid through the open door and laid flat on the seat.

"Got 'em," Nina radioed her backup. She pressed her foot on the gas pedal and sank into the masses on Rue Gouraud.

"Roger. Eyes on." In her rear-view mirror, she saw the Mitsubishi gently pull off the curb and follow a short distance behind.

Now she had business to attend to. "Jesus, where the *fuck* were you, Samir?" she roared to the prone lump on the backseat. "I thought you were burned! I came *this* close to pulling—"

"It is Valentina's fault, not mine," smiled Colonel Samir Basri, the dapper commander of the ISF's *Bureau d'information,* who was also known to a select few in northern Virginia as simply, "TOPSAIL."

"Really?" Nina threw daggers off the rear-view mirror. "Valentina? Is that her name? Valentina?"

"I think so. Why do you care?"

Nina brought her eyes back to the road. "We deposited another fifty thousand in your account. So what do you have for me?" The account she referred to was a burgeoning stockpile of funds safely held in escrow by the steady hands at the Geneva branch of Lombard Odier & Cie—and by "we," Nina meant the Central Intelligence Agency.

"The good secretary-general thinks he's found a lead—or a scapegoat, however you wish to see it." Basri sat upright.

Nina had contributed to a report in the President's Daily Brief, based on TOPSAIL's intelligence, entitled *"Hezbollah Scours Source of Lost IRGC Aid Funds."* In the report, Nina claimed that Hezbollah's capable intelligence apparatus, Unit 910, had launched an investigation into the fate of an estimated two million US dollars in aid money provided by the Revolutionary Guards that vanished in the chaos that followed the hasty climax of the Syrian civil war. Secretary-General Wissam Hamawi, the report revealed, was personally orchestrating the investigation and no corner of Hezbollah's vast politico-military behemoth was being spared scrutiny. In light of the sea change that had swept over the Party of God that morning, Nina found that it suddenly made sense: The reliable spigot of cash that flowed from Tehran for thirty years was now welded shut, and Hezbollah hadn't a penny to waste. Nina's colorful prose had always generated traction among the analysts and staff operations officers at Langley, but her latest dispatch from the field garnered an unwelcome bit of attention from Tel Aviv. The Israelis were demanding access to TOPSAIL intelligence and unless she could pull fresh fruit from the source, she may have to share the entire tree.

Yet Colonel Samir Basri was the clearest vision of a protean figure if there ever was one. Indefatigably shrewd and bursting with native wit—despite his corrupting and condemnable demons—Basri was the only indispensable ingredient in Lebanon's hopelessly complex blend of sectarian wrangling. He had a knack for navigating the sprawl, the tangled web of factions that delineated a most complex cast of characters: Shiites, Sunnis, Druze, Maronite Christians, moderates, radicals and the bundle of suicidal, homicidal maniacs—all of them respected Colonel Samir Basri's word. That trust, a voice that all could stomach, had led Basri to become a valuable mediator between the Lebanese security services and Hezbollah. The access TOPSAIL willingly provided to CIA made his hefty fee of fifty thousand dollars per meeting a bargain.

"Who?" Nina asked.

"Not who, but where. Hamawi told me that party officers raided the Western Beqaa branch of the Jihad al-Binna Foundation in Machgara."

"And you believe him?" Nina looked through the rear-view mirror.

"No, but because I like you, I had the *bureau* check with our local assets in Machgara. This morning the area around the office was sealed-off and men claiming to be Hezbollah carted away boxes of files. So Hamawi wasn't lying."

The Jihad al-Binna Foundation was Hezbollah's in-house construction arm. In the aftermath of the 2006 war with Israel, the *dahieh* and large swaths of southern Lebanon and the Beqaa Valley were left a smoldering ruin. Mere hours after the bombs stopped falling, Hezbollah officers descended on the flattened houses and shattered apartment buildings armed, not with AK-47s, but sacks brimming with crisp American dollars, and wasted no time in freely distributing fistfuls to families whose homes were flattened. It was an unbeatable public relations coup and it was all made possible by the Revolutionary Guards; the cash was airlifted from Iran. After endearing itself to the people of Lebanon, Hezbollah, not the government, took the initiative to rebuild all that was destroyed. Now in Hezbollah's strongholds there was little to suggest that war ever visited.

"The good secretary-general didn't mention it to me at our meeting, but I think it's only a matter of time before Walid Rada is arrested," Basri continued. "Even if he wasn't personally involved, it happened under his watch, in his office." Walid Rada was the director of Jihad al-Binna's Western Beqaa branch.

"Thank you, Samir, that's very helpful." Nina now had something solid to report back to Langley. She drove aimlessly around Gemmayze for the duration of the meeting and made her way back to Rue Gouraud and Basri's flat. "What did Hamawi say about disarming the Resistance?"

"Basically what he said on television. If America can bring the Israelis and the Syrians to an amicable agreement that settles the Golan Heights, then Hezbollah will lay down its arms. It's very simple. Until then, the Islamic Resistance is in a state of suspended animation, so to speak. Of course, I'll believe it when I see it, but Hamawi has no other choice and he knows that. His only goal is self-preservation at this point. And Iran's days of empire in this part of the world are over. Mark my words."

"Right," Nina frowned. She knew it would be more complicated.

There was a moment of silence before Basri cut the air. "I shouldn't even tell you this."

"Tell me what?"

"No, it's the oddest thing."

"Don't fucking jerk me off, Samir. Tell me what?" Nina had her daggers out again.

"It happened when I was leaving Hamawi's office..." Basri paused.

"And what?"

"Well, I saw a man. He was standing, with his back turned to me, gazing at something out the window. And I hardly even noticed him at first, but then he turned. I saw him for only a moment. Our eyes met for less than a second, but there was something there. It was so familiar."

"That's it?"

"No, I've been thinking about it all day. It was those eyes, those green eyes. I know those eyes. And then I realized it. I had seen something so," Basri searched for the right word, "momentous... I saw Ibrahim al-Din."

Nina glared at Basri through the mirror, entranced by what he had just told her. The wail of a car horn snapped her back to earth. She had drifted over the center lane into traffic. Nina gripped the wheel and veered back over, not a second before impact. "That's impossible."

"I know what I saw!" Basri pleaded. "I saw Ibrahim al-Din."

"Samir, there hasn't been a confirmed sighting of him in twenty-four years."

"Then reset that clock to zero, because I know what I saw! Abu Dokhan was there—alive—in Wissam Hamawi's office, in the Security Quarter, this morning, standing not ten feet from me. Ibrahim al-Din is alive and he is here in Beirut."

Nina pulled the Volvo into the alleyway behind Basri's flat and stopped in front of the service exit. "Samir, I appreciate all of your help. Check under my seat. I scrounged up a little spending money for your trouble."

Basri removed a thick envelope of cash and counted its contents.

"As long as you keep me informed and your mouth shut, I could not care less about your personal life. I didn't get in this business expecting to work with saints. But you need to lay off the teenagers." Nina kept her eyes forward. "That's not what we pay you for. Think about your own daughters. Those girls have fathers, too."

Samir Basri stuffed the envelope in his jacket and reached for the door handle. *"Had.* You meant 'had.'"

Nina's stomach turned as she watched TOPSAIL disappear into the alley. She made her way back to the American embassy in the hills above Beirut and, for now, remained in denial.

Under different circumstances, the harsh tone of Hebrew would have been an unwelcome sound to Mehdi Vaziri. But the circumstances were extraordinary, and that rattle of grating Semitic consonants was surprisingly poetic. To Vaziri it was nothing less than the voice of freedom, a freedom beyond the gated prison of his home, and a freedom far from his suffering countrymen—whom he had hastily abandoned in the dead of night.

He was seated aft in the cabin of a pristine white Gulfstream IV, adjacent to a window that looked out on a heat mirage dancing over the flight line. Sharjah International Airport had a single runway, rimmed by windswept sand dunes on one side and a flat sea of free trade warehouses on the opposite. The city was distinctly less glamorous than its neighbor, Dubai, the shimmering global business hub. But with the mundane came anonymity and Sharjah was a mere eighty miles across the Persian Gulf from the Iranian port of Bandar Lengeh. Vaziri had made that journey overnight in the hold of a wooden fishing dhow.

The Gulfstream's Israeli crew completed their checklists and manned the cockpit while the security team pulled back from the discrete perimeter they had established around the jet. Chocks were pulled from the undercarriage. A moment later he watched the wingtip beyond his window shudder forward as the plane began a bated crawl to the runway.

To his left, his wife, Fatemeh, kept her eyes hidden behind a handkerchief. They had not been dry for hours.

As the Gulfstream sped down the runway and thrust itself into the morning sky, Vaziri watched the northern horizon. He knew that at some undefined point far out there, the swelling expanse of teal before him abutted an end. Beyond that end was his home.

And he searched for it.

He knew alarms were sounding in Tehran by now and in due time an army of the ayatollah's thugs would descend on anyone he had spoken to in the past ten years. But still, he searched, and as he soared higher, he noticed the faintest apparition.

At that place where the swelling expanse met its ultimate finality, there was a hideous beige smear streaking along the horizon. It was little more than a blemish on the face of the earth.

As the Gulfstream banked to the south and lurched its wing up toward the sun, Mehdi Vaziri felt his heart sink and he suspected that it was the last glimpse of home that would ever grace his eyes.

And he was right.

Mofidi was awoken with a phone call at dawn. At the other end was the distressed voice of Hojjatoleslam Hossein Taeb, commander of the IRGC Intelligence Unit, the *Etelaat-e-Sepah*. Some hours ago, Mehdi Vaziri—undoubtedly with assistance—broke his house arrest and was nowhere to be found. His associates around the country were in the process of being rounded up and tossed into the darkest hole the regime could muster. The supreme leader had to take action, which meant Mofidi had to moonlight as God's earthy lieutenant.

After a quick shower, prayers and a modest breakfast, he stood waiting under the bare trees in the garden that fronted his villa. Babak arrived promptly behind the wheel of the armored Peugeot, and after the usual pleasantries, they were bound for Beit Rahbari on Pasteur Street. A cool air had swept down from the mountains overnight and chased away the noxious smog clouds, but he knew they would return, as always. The Peugeot pulled into Tajrish Square, which was already packed with cabbies, transit buses and merchants scampering to open their stalls that lined the sidewalk.

"Stop here," Mofidi announced, pointing to a particular stall, "I want to grab a paper."

Babak pulled the Peugeot along the curb, diverting the traffic behind into the adjacent lane, and waited as Mofidi sprung out of the car. Babak couldn't quite understand how a man with such unrestricted access as Mofidi would bother to waste his time and money on a rag. Mofidi would know first-hand that nearly all of the paper's contents were canned and spoon-fed to the country's restricted and monitored press. But Babak didn't care to ask.

"*Salam!* I'll take a copy of *Hamshahri*," Mofidi told the vendor, who immediately produced that day's issue. He looked at the cover and frowned—

further approved and sterilized coverage denouncing the nightmare ensuing in Syria and Lebanon. Mofidi shook his head, "Rubbish. No, let me have today's *Kayhan*," which was a much more conservative paper. He reached inside his pocket and slid a few thousand rials in the folded copy of *Hamshahri* and smiled at the vendor. It was much more than the paper's modest cost.

"*Merci!*" the vendor, Akbar, beamed and quickly pocketed the extra rials—and the memory card Mofidi included.

Akbar watched the older, well-dressed man return to the Peugeot and drift away with the heavy traffic. He did not know the man's name—he was strongly advised not to care—but they just so happened to pray at the same mosque, Masjid Giahi, which was just up the street. Yet each time the man visited the stall, he always paid more than was required of him—and whomever the man was working with paid even better. Akbar was the father to a young family of five, all of whom had mouths to feed and rapidly growing bodies to clothe. The extra income was welcomed, and as long as the cash came steadily, his silence was guaranteed.

Several hours passed and Akbar managed to sell a meager portion of his wares when another familiar face appeared before his stall. The man was younger, and much fitter than his usual customers, but he exuded a guarded demeanor. Dark sunglasses shielded his eyes and a few inches of cropped brown hair sat atop his head. He shaved, which was unusual for an Iranian, but his appearance didn't suggest he was one at all. He looked much more European than Persian, and yet spoke the language as a native. But if one thing was certain, the man had his armor on, and kept everything around him at bay.

"A copy of *Hamshahri*, please," the man asked and placed a fifty-thousand-rial banknote on the counter. "You wouldn't happen to have change?"

"*Baleh!*" Akbar replied and reached into his pocket, tucking the change and the memory card into a folded copy of that day's *Hamshahri*.

"*Merci,*" Jack Galloway forced a smile, and drifted away with the crowd.

He strolled two blocks west before hailing a cab and ordered it to an address in central Tehran that he had picked at random in his planning the night before. His head was on a swivel, looking for any kind of pattern. Nothing. After navigating the streets, the cab stopped on the side of Enghelab Avenue, a major thoroughfare that bisected the city, east to west. Jack stepped to the curb and passed quickly through a side gate of Tehran University. He checked his watch as a stream of students poured out of the class buildings from every direction. It was timed perfectly. Through the mob of students, he kept under cover all the way through campus until he exited a second gate on the opposite end of the university, and quickly flagged another cab.

"Hashemi Street in Jamaran," he ordered.

Jack took yet another glance for a tail and caught nothing. He was trained to act on instinct, but there was a thrill involved in each pass that always stayed with him. CITADEL reports were an absolute top priority at Langley and there was zero room for failure. At the moment, it was Jack's mission in life to ensure they got there safely and without delay. The messages that Jack conveyed from Tehran were Washington's light in the dark abyss of Iran's deception, and they alone had informed policy countless times. Yet there was always a sense of dread, and Jack understood the possibility that some day he may deliver the trigger that would spark a war.

The Arab Banking Corporation was not expecting him until noon and he returned to his home in an affluent neighborhood of North Tehran. The house was a decent size at Western standards and had the appearance of where a Swiss expat might live. As the front door swung open, Jack eyed each corner for anything out of place—also an instinct. In his bedroom, he closed the drapes and removed a Toshiba laptop from a cavity in the floorboards. Sitting next to it were three bundles of five thousand euros, each wrapped in cellophane, a Canadian passport filled with numerous counterfeit visas and entry stamps, an LST-5C SATCOM radio and a Walther P99 handgun with four spare clips of nine-millimeter ammunition. So far, he hadn't the need for any of it. After the laptop booted up, he inserted the camera's memory card and brought up each picture as a JPEG file. Thankfully, CITADEL had numbered each page in corresponding order and he knew where to start his translation.

Jack opened a blank Word document and started reading through the report. "Fuck, me," he muttered and began furiously typing. After each page was converted from Persian to English, he printed the new document, double-sided on five sheets of "flash paper." The sheets were a form of nitrocellulose, which burned quickly without any trace of smoke or ash. It could be lit with a cigarette and would disintegrate completely within seconds. The memory card was snapped in half between his fingers and flushed down the toilet, before the laptop's hard drive was wiped clean with several passes of random data. The five sheets were folded neatly and placed inside an envelope addressed to a post office box in Dubai. Jack took the envelope with him and went for a jog through the quiet residential streets around his home. It took the better part of an hour, but when he was comfortable that not a soul was watching, he dropped the letter into a random mailbox.

"Rossiya" was clearly displayed in painted Cyrillic letters midway down the white fuselage. A red-and-blue stripe stretched the length of the aircraft and its two wings each swept out ninety feet, both carrying dual Pratt & Whit-

ney PW2337 Turbofan engines. It was the prized creation of the Voronezh Aviation Factory and was officially designated an Ilyushin IL-96PU—the PU stood for "Command Point" in the Russian Cyrillic alphabet. The plane rested gracefully inside a secure hangar at Vnukovo-2, a government terminal within the larger Vnukovo International Airport, seventeen miles south of Moscow. The interior, designed and furnished by the British firm Diamonite, was fitted with leather upholstery and gold leaf, much of which carried the coat of arms of the president of the Russian Federation.

A maintenance crew huddled beneath the cockpit and gazed up into the mechanical innards of the aircraft. It was scheduled to depart in four hours for a routine flight to Mikhail Karetnikov's estate on Lake Valdai. Before that could happen, everything needed to be checked and rechecked multiple times. The avionics package had just passed inspection when a small cavalcade of military vehicles   UAZ jeeps and a KAMAZ truck—sped through the open hangar doors and charged at the plane, stopping just inches in front of the airstairs. A grimacing man, whose chest bulged out of the pressed uniform of a Russian Air Force major, leapt down from the passenger seat of the lead jeep. "Who is in command here?"

The crew chief, a sergeant, sheepishly stepped forward.

"You are to end your shift immediately and return to the terminal! The hangar is to be evacuated of all unauthorized personnel and sealed until further notice. This is direct from the Federal Protective Service." The major flashed his identification for no less than a second and slapped out his massive arm, revealing the printed and signed orders. "This truck will transport you and your men. Leave your tools and equipment."

The crew chief hastily read the orders and looked back with a confused gaze. "Sir, I do not understand. My crew was just dispatched and we have hardly completed our inspection. It would be appreciated if there were—"

"That sounds distinctly like a sergeant perilously questioning the direct orders of a senior officer," the major barked. "You may phone command yourself if you are so unconvinced of the nature of your duties."

The crew chief stood in silence for a moment, then clicked his heels at attention and saluted sharply. "At once!"

"I may yet be kind in any reports that are produced on this matter. You are relieved, Sergeant."

"Yes, sir!" The crew chief and his men were quickly whisked away in the KAMAZ.

With the hangar empty and secure, the major—that, he was not—and his cohorts were alone with the aircraft of President Mikhail Karetnikov. They disembarked from the jeeps and rushed to work. Time was scarce.

• • •

Sajid Bata was just a day short of fourteen, and he inhaled deeply. He felt the burn first, then the familiar itch along the back of his throat. He fought to force it down like his brother showed him, but the burning was more than his uninitiated lungs could weather. Sajid doubled over and launched into a coughing fit, letting loose an acrid plume of pungent smoke.

His brother, Zyed, cackled with delight and reached for the hand-rolled cigarette that was stuffed with the finest Moroccan hashish that one could find in their miserable corner of the world. "What a little faggot!" Zyed exclaimed as he watched his brother wipe tears from his eyes and slump almost lifeless onto the worn and grimy sofa.

"Tell me about your day, Sajid," asked Badi Haddad, who enabled it all. He handed Sajid a chipped glass filled to the brim with crudely distilled vodka. Sajid sipped from the glass and winced. It, too, was a taste he was keen to acquire. "Madame Boullée is a whore! Do you believe she wants my *redoublement* for the entire year if I fail this exam?"

"Fuck Madame Boullée! Shit, who would want to?" Zyed laughed. "I must have cheated my way through that entire course!"

"I am sure that if Allah wills it, all will work out in the end," Haddad reassured. "You know, Allah is the hope to all our troubles. There is nothing that cannot be done without Him."

"True shit." Sajid took the cigarette back from his brother, and again tried in vain to prove himself, and again doubled over in a fit.

"Come closer, Sajid," Haddad beckoned. "There is something I want to share with the both of you."

The walls of Badi Haddad's flat seemed razor-thin. At any given time of day, or night, there was a parade of foot traffic in the dimly lit hall outside the bolted door and shouting was audible in the units above, below and to the sides. But such was the nature of subsistence in the blighted *banlieue* of Clichy-sous-Bois, an impoverished suburb twenty kilometers north of Paris. Without any major roads or rail lines passing through, Clichy was isolated from the larger metropolis. The majority of the *banlieue's* residents had emigrated from the former French colonial outposts in northern and equatorial Africa. Institutional racism and right-wing xenophobia kept them largely confined to public estates, which were little more than clusters of towering, dilapidated and graffiti-strewn housing blocks like La Forestière, where Haddad stayed and the Bata brothers lived with their grandmother in the neighboring tower. However, Haddad and the Batas were Arabs, a minority within a minority. The brothers arrived only months earlier from rural Syria—refugees, and orphaned. The French culture and language hadn't come easily since then. The boys were alienated and alone, and whenever they found anything, or anyone, that reminded them of home, they latched on with hunger in their hearts like a baited fish, impaling its scaly mouth on a barbed hook.

"We are brothers, aren't we? Us three?" Haddad grinned, like a carnival barker trying to lure passersby into a sideshow.

Sajid pondered for a moment. "Sure."

"I mean, *you* two are brothers, obviously. But *we three,* we can be brothers. And brothers cannot truly be brothers unless they have secrets, no?"

Zyed took a drag on the cigarette and offered up the unlit end to Haddad, who politely shook his head. "You don't want a hit?" Zyed asked.

"But you bought it!" Sajid exclaimed.

"For you to enjoy. Sajid, you and your brother have secrets that you both keep for each other, don't you?"

"Yes."

"Like the fact that he is still a virgin! I keep that secret... Oh wait!"

"Shut up, Zyed! You are a virgin, too!"

Haddad smiled again and brought them back to the point. "Sajid, that is something to be proud of, not ashamed. Allah tells us that purity and chastity are beautiful, beautiful things. Do you know what else Allah says is beautiful? And this can be the first secret I share with you. Do you know what that secret is?"

"No," Sajid replied.

"That to die in His service is the most beautiful act that any man, woman—or child, can commit. Did you know that?"

The boys were silent before he continued.

"And I'll tell you another secret. Would you like to hear?"

"Yes." Sajid drew the hook in further.

"I am a lieutenant in a great army."

And the boys were silent still.

"This army you know. This army has brought damnation, and jihad, to the Zionists and the enemies of Islam for more than thirty years. Now that is a very long time, is it not?"

"Hezbollah?" Sajid mumbled.

Haddad nodded. "And like we three, this army is also a brotherhood—a brotherhood of *shaheed.* A brotherhood of martyrs." He paused. "Sajid, would you and your brother like to see something cool?"

Sajid spun his head around and looked to Zyed, who shrugged his shoulders. "Yes!" Sajid turned back and gasped.

Haddad placed a laptop on the bare floor and brought up a video file. It began to play. "Watch this."

The laptop's screen showed the grainy image of a teenage boy with a round, youthful face and tanned olive skin wading up to his knees in a clear stream. A grove of cedar trees stood on the bank behind him. Without any narration or preamble from the boy, he cupped his hands together, plunged them deep into the flowing stream, and splashed the water over his face and bald scalp.

"This was Ali Saffedine," Haddad explained, "and we were once brothers. But now, he is known to my army as '*al-Shaheed al-Ammar.*'"

The video shifted. Now the frame was centered on Saffedine's boyish face, which lent him his macabre *nom de guerre*. He was dressed in camouflage fatigues, a green bandana was wrapped around his head and he sat with his legs crossed under him. An AK-47 rested on his lap. The flag of the Islamic Resistance hung on the wall at his back. Saffedine looked directly into the camera and read a prepared statement. Through the rough audio, Sajid and Zyed could hear the boy pronounce his last will and testament. After offering his body to God, he detailed his final wishes for his family and dictated how his remains were to be prepared and buried. Finally, he gave a warning to the invaders that occupied his country, and promised that more like him would follow.

Again, the video shifted to the vantage from a rooftop, which looked onto a dusty road that weaved a path down a hill to a rural valley below. The frame of the camera was moving rapidly, scanning the hillside, until it settled upon two Israeli M113 armored personnel carriers parked on either side of the road. A group of soldiers milled around the APCs. The date stamp on the far right corner of the screen read, "29 May 1996."

"This is Rubb Talatheen. We grew up not far from here."

A moment later, an old Mercedes sedan rolled into the frame and rattled its way down the road toward the Israeli APCs. The soldiers quickly saw it and tried to signal it to come to a halt.

The Mercedes accelerated.

Panic ensued. The soldiers opened up with a volley of automatic gunfire at the windshield and the engine block.

But the Mercedes didn't stop.

The soldiers dove for cover wherever they could find it as the Mercedes rolled between the armored vehicles. A brilliant flash of light filled the screen and the Mercedes, the APCs and the soldiers, disappeared into a mountainous cloud of smoke and dust.

Over the microphone, the camera operator launched into a hysterical chant. *"Allahu Akbar! Allahu Akbar!"*

Haddad stopped the video and moved his eyes over Zyed, and then Sajid. Their reaction was just as he hoped. "Isn't that cool?"

At dusk, Mikhail Karetnikov climbed the airstairs of the Ilyushin IL-96 on the apron at Vnukovo-2. A copy of the plan outlining Operation ALAGIR was locked inside his attaché case. Valery Volodnin and much of the great man's senior staff boarded after him. In minutes, the Ilyushin glided off the runway, set a course due west, into the shrouded horizon and the waiting embrace of the American.

CHAPTER 12

THE FACELESS AMERICAN was tossed to the floor of the SUV like trash.

"Drive!" Anwar Sabbah commanded. He peered over the seat and examined the hooded specter lying inert in the trunk, its legs and arms tightly bound. In twenty minutes, it hadn't flinched a muscle or uttered a sound. Sabbah almost wondered if it was still breathing. But he couldn't pull his eyes away. Where there should have been a face—a face with life, a face with emotion, a face with pain, or even a hint of love—there was only a black shroud.

A growing storm blanketed western Russia. In the previous twelve hours, a low-pressure system had blown in from the Gulf of Finland and clashed with a pocket of frigid air from the icy recesses of the Article Circle above the Kola Peninsula. The result at Borisovky-Khotilovo Air Base, near Karetnikov's dacha at Dolgiye Borodny on Lake Valdai, was sustained headwinds of thirty knots and visibility dropping by the second.

Forty minutes out.

Sabbah was fixated on his cargo, watching for a sliver of humanity. But through the shroud, Sabbah would find none of it. Behind that frayed and soiled black fabric there was something uninhabited, uncompromising, unflinching and unforgiving. Whatever he sought to find, it simply was not there.

But Sabbah kept watch as the SUV rattled over pockmarked roads, turning indiscriminately through the concrete and rusted tin gorges of Ouzai. The dense slum was once a sleepy fishing village, but after years of illegal construction it became engulfed in the larger sprawl and now sat forgotten in the narrow void between Beirut's Airport Road and the Mediterranean. Social services, policing and other demonstrations of sovereignty by the Lebanese government were a fantasy. Armed militias, who flew the flag of Hezbollah yet answered only to Ibrahim al-Din, transformed the slum into a fortress, and nothing moved without their knowledge.

The Ilyushin began its descent into the storm and was immediately racked by rising and falling currents of frigid air. The pilot, a colonel in the Russian Air Force, gripped the throttle steadily. Beyond the cockpit was a swirling mass of ice and snow that appeared just inches through the darkness. Having near zero visibility, the pilot switched the aircraft into autopilot and gifted their safe arrival to its sophisticated avionics package, which was the standard—and predictable—procedure. His first officer was given the responsibility to regulate its descent down to the airfield. Several spaces aft, Mikhail Karetnikov watched the weather deteriorate from a window in his gilded cabin and remained, for now, ignorant.

Twenty minutes out.

The bonds around the faceless American's ankles were cut and Sabbah's clenched hand gripped the shirt on its back. "Out! Get out!" he barked.

It moved, slowly, and lifted itself without hesitation or resistance off the floor of the SUV's trunk and stood calmly on the pavement. Plastic cable ties were still wrapped around its wrists and the shroud remained.

Sabbah grabbed the back of its collar and pressed the muzzle of a nine-millimeter Makarov pistol into its spine, forcing it deeper into a blind alleyway hidden in the heart of Ouzai. Three other militiamen, all armed with Kalashnikovs, poured from the SUV and followed with their barrels trained on the black shroud. At the end of the alleyway, Sabbah turned the faceless American to the right and through the open doorway of a squat, cinder block home. They came through a cluttered kitchen that reeked of burnt meat. A woman, covered from head to toe in an Iranian-style *chador,* huddled with a group of young children in a corner. Sabbah led the faceless American up a creaking flight of stairs to the second floor and rounded another corner into a spartan and dusty room.

Ibrahim al-Din stood patiently, eyeing his new guest with curiosity.

Sabbah kicked at its knees and forced it hard to the floor. Again, there was not a word of protest. The militiamen entered next and surrounded it with their fingers steady on the trigger. After an approving nod from al-Din, Sabbah grabbed the top of the shroud and ripped the veil from the faceless American.

Behind that frayed and soiled black fabric was a man with the most unprepossessing features that the likes of God or any other entity might possibly think to design. Stiff stalks of cropped, graying hair sprouted from the man's scalp and the dark pupils on the surface of his unblinking eyes moved frantically over each and every object in the arc of his sight. His high cheekbones were starkly pronounced from under his pale, gaunt skin. There was not a single thing, Sabbah noticed, that indicated decent health of the mind, body, or spirit.

Without invitation, the faceless American spoke for first time. "I've been watching you," he told al-Din, his voice unnervingly soft and steady.

"I know." Al-Din slightly tilted his head and tried to understand. "Walk the streets of the *dahieh* and speak my name long enough, and eventually I hear it. Why are you here?"

"I am your humble servant." His eyes shifted constantly.

Al-Din blinked. "And why are you here?"

The faceless American's sight narrowed and focused squarely on al-Din. "Because sometimes you bargain with God and the devil answers."

At three minutes out, things began to happen.

On a bearing of 299 degrees northwest, with an airspeed of 221 knots and a dropping elevation of two thousand feet, the pilot received clearance from the control tower to make an immediate landing at Borisovsky Air Base. Visibility from the cockpit was still pitiful and made it nearly impossible for a human eye to land an aircraft of that size, or any, under those conditions. Tied into the Ilyushin's avionics package was an array of sensors installed along the belly of the fuselage that would enable the aircraft to glide safely to the runway. The system was called a radio altimeter, and Karetnikov's plane was equipped with only one. On the first officer's primary flight display, a screen showed the current altitude between the fuselage and the ground below. As the altitude changed with their descent, the data generated by the sensors was fed into the aircraft's autothrottle, which in turn regulated the amount of thrust required by the engines. Working in concert, the system calculated the exact speed and varying altitude to bring the aircraft down to Earth and stop on the runway without the clear field of vision required by a human eye. Yet, as was so often true with human beings, machines were also prone to corruption.

Borisovsky, as a decaying outpost of the Soviet Air Defense Forces, was not fitted with the instrument landing system that had became common on airfields around the world, leaving the controllers in the tower with no further source of data beyond what the pilots radioed to them.

The screen before the first officer now read an altitude of 1,500 feet—a measure that was horribly wrong. The sensitive circuitry of the radio altimeter was reprogrammed to show on the flight display as a hundred feet less than their actual evaluation. With each passing second, the aircraft was slipping further down a trajectory to bring them in far short of the runway. But the pilots realized none of it.

Ten seconds out—but it was too late.

The howling winds and the swirling mass of ice and snow dissipated before them, and all that remained was solid ground.

"Shoot him," al-Din breathed dispassionately.

Sabbah raised his weapon.

"Guns won't save you," the faceless American kept his narrow gaze. "Death finds us all in the end."

One of al-Din's men chuckled in a distinctly mocking tone.

The faceless American tilted his head down to the floor and hunched his shoulders forward. His left hand, still bound by the cable tie, began to violently spasm. "When I was a boy…" he paused, and then, this time slower, "When I was a boy, one night, it was cold. Again, it was always cold. And we, consumed, our portion of wood for the stove we had between the dozen of us. That was all we had. That wood was all we had. My father… Well, my mother, cast me out…into the cold; the cold that I knew. She cast me out to find more. And so I took the ax, the ax that sat by our stove. And I left into the cold. And it was dark. And I staggered, through the snow, as I knew, and as I always had. It came naturally to me, as did other curious things. Around, there was a field, and beyond that, woods—miles of woods, and trees, and animals. So I staggered—through the snow, through the cold, to the woods, to the tree line at the edge of the woods. And as I came closer to the edge of the woods, as I staggered, there I first saw him: a silhouette, a vague outline. I staggered closer. And I saw it. I saw him. There my father had fallen, fallen to his knees, his shoulders hunched forward. His clothes were drenched, dripping into the snow. I smelt kerosene. And in his hands, his cold hands, I saw a book of matches in his fingers. Then I knew. His sin consumed him—his unforgivable sin; the sin of being my father; the sin of thrusting me, unasked, into life. He came to escape the same fate to which I was doomed; he came to cleanse himself in the snow and cold that I knew. There was no pain from him, never any pain. But he looked up at me with those pathetic animal's eyes. But he couldn't do it. He was a coward. So I took the matches into my hands, my cold hands. I tore one off, and—like an angel of mercy—I lit the match. And…"

The faceless American shifted his focus back to al-Din. The spasms in his hand suddenly stopped. "Now, shall we begin?"

• • •

President Mikhail Karetnikov was seated at his desk when the end came. A deafening roar, with a kind of furious intensity that he could never attempt to imagine, erupted from the forward section of the aircraft. Above the roar, he heard the first screams. He was thrown from his desk and slammed against a window on the bulkhead and saw the very surface of the Earth rising up to claim him. Karetnikov forced his eyes shut and wrapped his trembling arms around the metal base of his chair. Gravity betrayed him and was hardly relative. He felt the searing heat and saw a wave of fire wash over the window frame. He heard more screams—this time softer—then a low, wrenching metallic groan from beneath his feet. A bright flash of sparks and a rapid staccato of electrical cables streaming down from above assaulted his senses. And he felt the wind, the howling, cold wind that he knew, and then a rupture, and a deathly shriek. He gripped harder at the base of the chair and felt the steel tear into his hands. The pressure of the cabin shifted and his inner ear canal popped. From behind his eyelids that he clenched shut, Karetnikov saw a brilliant glow, and he felt the winds. He opened his eyes and saw the night sky before him, the swirling mass of ice and snow, and a surging tide of flames.

"I represent a particular faction of the Russian government," the faceless American remained on his knees, "and this faction finds itself at odds with—I should say, former—President Karetnikov and his unwillingness to aid their pursuits of empire over the world's energy reserves." He rolled his eyes. "And so, the reason I am here, is to render the world that they seek by offering my services, and demanding yours."

Al-Din sighed. "Why would I ever—"

"Because I know what *you* seek!" the faceless American snapped, a gentle spasm in his left hand. "You seek war…the last war, a war that will run Israel back under the sea from whence it came. I can, and will, give you that war, for a small price. You, with my assistance, will draw the United States into attacking your old masters in Iran—the same masters who abandoned you here to rot. In exchange, I will take Hezbollah from those spineless clerics, and hand it, to you."

"And how do you intend to do that?"

"By making you and your band a nuclear power."

Al-Din stared down his guest. "And you? What do you seek?"

The faceless American hissed, *"Chaos."*

A gaping fissure split open at Karetnikov's feet. A whole section of the aircraft, stretching from his cabin to the tail, broke free and careened forward, plowing through dirt and snow, and snapping the trunks of heavy fir trees like twigs. It veered sideways, the tail turning toward him, and rolled uncontrollably—sparks, insulation, baggage and bodies, all hurled from the plane and tossed through the sky.

He clamped himself tighter around the chair. If he could hold on and face the winds and fire that desperately pulled at his feet, he could cheat the nothingness before him.

A trunk tore the starboard wing in two, setting free a torrent of jet fuel. It ignited and blew back at the twisting and tumbling section of the plane, swallowing it whole. The fire lapped at the bottom of his shoes and the winds screamed in his ears. The chair rattled loose. If Karetnikov could just hold on, for even a few seconds more…

But the flames grew higher; and the winds, stronger; and the howling, softer; and the lights, dimmer; and then, black.

"Do you have a name?" al-Din asked, as Sabbah cut the cable tie around his wrists.

The faceless American rose to his feet. "My name is David Kazanoff."

The world's once and future master terrorist grinned and offered up his hand. "And I am Ibrahim."

CHAPTER 13

THE AMERICAN EMBASSY in Moscow is situated at No. 8 Bolshoy Devi-atinsky Pereulok in a towering glass and stone edifice that took some twen-ty-seven tortured years to complete. In 1985, during the final act of the Cold War, counterintelligence uncovered that the KGB had honeycombed the chancery building's steel skeleton with listening devices to such a degree that it essentially rendered the half-built embassy unusable. A quarter-century of head-scratching and diplomatic gridlock later, the top two floors of the embassy were dissembled brick-by-brick and replaced with four new floors, constructed to the most stringent security standards. Although their present adversaries now operated under a different alphabet soup of three-letter acronyms, the elements of the US Intelligence community in Moscow had considerably turned the tables on their host.

Atop the flat roof of the completed embassy building, an array of anten-nas led down through steel conduits to radio receivers of remarkable design and sophistication. These receivers were, in turn, plugged into banks of servers collectively processing petabytes of data in real time. Together, it created a giant ear pressed to the thoughts, whispers and secrets slingshot-ted through the Moscow air. At the system's helm, inside a windowless vault on the eighth floor, were a dozen Russian linguists in the employ of the Special Collection Service, known within the vast hierarchy of the Na-tional Security Agency as "F6." The linguists, a blend of active-duty military personnel and civilian contractors, worked in continuous shifts and collect-ed nearly the entire spectrum of electronic signals released within a hundred miles of the embassy walls. On that particular night, the secrets floating in the chilled air of the Russian capital were largely routine and mundane. But that ended abruptly.

"Whoa, whoa, whoa..." One of the linguists pressed the earphones closer to his head and blinked erratically at the screen before him. He turned back to his superior. "El-tee, I'm getting some serious chatter here!"

"What is it?" an Army lieutenant rolled her chair to his workstation.

"Some sort of explosion in Tver Oblast. Borisovsky Air Base. Sounds like a plane went down short of the runway. Weather's been an issue out there all night."

"MiG?"

"Negative, it's much bigger. Hold on, I'm hearing the tail number." The linguist hastily scribbled the numbers coming over the airwaves. "Romeo Alpha niner-six-zero-one-two. An Ilyushin niner-six. EMERCOM search and rescue units just landed at the crash site. Lots of bodies."

"Stay with it," the lieutenant ordered, and then shouted to another across the room. "Run that tail number!"

After a few pecks on the keyboard, the room went still. "El-tee, that aircraft is registered to Rossiya Airlines! VIP transport!"

"Keep listening," she told the linguist and flew back on her chair to an STE secure telephone. She lifted the receiver and pressed "#" on the keypad, immediately routing her to the National Security Operations Center, located deep in the heart of NSA headquarters on the grounds of Fort Meade, Maryland. A duty officer answered on the first ring.

"NSOC Watch," said a disembodied male voice.

"This is Station Moscow. We're getting reports of a downed military aircraft approximately an hour west of the city. Staff ran the tail number and it matches an IL-96 used for presidential and VIP transport." After relaying further information over the next ten minutes, the duty officer reached for a dedicated line connecting him to the White House Situation Room.

"So the good news is, she's down to Stanford and Yale." First Lady Melissa Paulson stabbed her fork into a filet of Alaskan halibut. "And I know she really likes the program at Stanford, but I think the distance scares her."

President Paulson shook his head. "I keep telling her she needs to get out of the bubble, cut the cord, go live your life while you can."

"Well, you know she's stubborn, Andrew. I can't imagine where she gets that from."

"Not my side."

They were seated in the dining room of the 1789 Restaurant on the corner of Prospect and 36th streets in Georgetown. Apart from the intermittent flash from a smartphone camera on the sidewalk, the entourage of armed Secret Service agents monitoring the kitchen staff, or the humming motorcade backed into the alley behind Wisemiller's Grocery, everything was as normal as it could be when the first couple came to dinner with only a few minutes notice.

"So which do you think she'll choose?" the president asked.

"My money's on Yale., like her dad But I could be wrong."

"As long as she's happy."

"That's what I keep telling her."

Paulson noticed the special agent in charge of his detail emerging from behind the kitchen's swinging aluminum door. With a sour look on his face, he slowly approached the president's table and bent down to whisper in his ear. "I beg your pardon, sir, but there's an urgent call for you. It's Dr. Tanner."

That name told the president all he needed to hear. "Alright." He looked to his wife and took the napkin from his lap. "I'll be back."

"Take your time." The first lady kept her eyes on her plate.

Paulson stood and followed the agent through the kitchen and into a small storage room that had been cleared for the essential communications equipment that followed the president wherever he went. A Cisco 7975 telephone connected to the Executive VoIP network sat on a table. Paulson placed the handset to his ear. "Eli?"

"Mr. President," the national security advisor stood in the buzzing Watch Center of the White House Situation Room in the basement of the West Wing, "I'm terribly sorry to interrupt your dinner, and please extend my apologies to the first lady."

"What's up, Eli?"

"I've received a CRITIC from NSA. A few minutes ago the Special Collection Element at our embassy in Moscow intercepted traffic from the Russian General Staff mobilizing a large force for a search and rescue operation around an airfield near Karetnikov's estate an hour northwest of Moscow. At this time, it appears that an aircraft carrying VIPs crashed upon landing in a snowstorm."

Paulson felt the blood drain from his face. "Was Karetnikov on board?"

"We don't know, sir. Concurrently, there has been a noticeable increase in force protection posture around the missile fields at Kozelsk and Tatischevo, the strategic bomber base at Engels-2 and the Northern Fleet's SSBN pens on the Kola Peninsula. NMCC sent a message over the hotline inquiring about the situation. The Russians immediately responded, claiming it was an exercise involving the Interior Ministry. We replied, asking about the boost in security around their strategic weapons facilities. That message was ignored."

"There's been no increase in the operational readiness of those forces?"

"That's right, sir. We've only seen an increase in perimeter security."

"So what's your opinion, Eli?"

"Mr. President, I feel that President Karetnikov was either killed in that crash or is still missing. Until they know for sure what has transpired, the Russians are merely ensuring the security of their nuclear stockpile."

Paulson looked down at his shoes. "Okay, I'm on my way in."

"We'll be ready, sir."

The president hung up the phone and made the long walk back to the table. Melissa was one step ahead him; their dinners waited in take-out boxes. "Well," she smiled, "is the world ending?"

Andrei Minin found himself in the throes of a nightmare. It was a nightmare of his creation, and he now understood that there would be no waking. For the past three hours he sat—numb and unable to speak more than a few words—around a heavy oak conference table just off what was Karetnikov's ceremonial office in the Kremlin Senate building. Around him were all the familiar faces—the sunken, lost and desperate faces—ministers Nikita Porozovsky and Uri Popoff, the ministers of emergency situations and the internal affairs, the directors of the FSB and the FSO, and General Tsekov of the General Staff. All of them, Minin reminded himself, were on the list of names that Vyasheslav Trubnikov judged untrustworthy. In the coming months, all of them would have to go, one way or another.

Finally, at the head of the table, with the wide eyes of a small, defenseless animal awaiting the oncoming grille of a semi, sat Dmitri Lavrov, the new president of the Russian Federation. Lavrov had staked his claim to life as a functionary of the Communist Party of the Soviet Union, and when that imploded, a federal tax inspector. But Lavrov's most endearing quality was loyalty—to Mikhail Karetnikov—and that was the only reason he, as Karetnikov's appointed prime minister, now sat in his master's chair as one of the most powerful men on Earth: a sheep whose shepherd lay slaughtered in the field.

Yet Karetnikov kept good company, and surrounded himself with a corps of seasoned and trusted advisers that stretched back to his reign over the Saint Petersburg mayor's office. But Minin was part of a dying breed; many of them were scattered in the woods near Borisovsky Air Base. Now Lavrov would be forced to seek new counsel, and Minin was more than willing to step to the fore.

Minin's attention was hardly focused on the meeting unfolding around him. Like a moth drawn to the fire, his eyes strayed beyond the polycarbonate-coated windows nearest his chair to the ghostly sentries patrolling the courtyard amid the amber electric haze and falling snow. And then he remembered the dacha in the birch forests west of Moscow where just a few short days ago this all began; where Mikhail Karetnikov, whom he loved, had been condemned to the fetishes of a madman; and where yet they still asked themselves the question, "What is to be done to those who are to blame?"

Now the American had answered.

President Karetnikov's remains were found cradled in the branches of a burning tree. The EMERCOM search and rescue units were the first to find him, and had done so with enough time to remove the body of their commander-in-chief before it had been rendered to bits of bone and flakes of carbon. The plane's wreckage was scattered over several hectares like flaming jigsaw pieces. At the center of it all was a charred gash of toppled trees and pulverized dirt cut hundreds of feet through the forest before the runway. At the end of the macabre rainbow were the mangled and crushed remains of the cockpit and the melted forward section of the fuselage. The wings had largely disintegrated in the explosion and the only evidence to suggest that they were ever there was the nozzle of a jet engine protruding up from beneath the snow-covered ground. The aft section of the fuselage, which broke away seconds after impact, rolled over on its side and was lodged in an unnatural, contorted position. Lastly, there was an image that had scorched a special place in Minin's conscience. High atop the tail of Karetnikov's plane, the tricolor white, blue and red flag of the Russian Federation survived. Driven across it, were heavy streaks of soot and the dried blood of his countrymen.

If Andrei Minin needed any assurances of the caliber of demon that he had conjured up from below, there it was in the starkest contrast.

And the American's answer was unmistakable.

CHAPTER 14

SHE HAD BEEN awake through the night, sometimes pacing, sometimes staring at the walls, sometimes seeing nothing but the blackness of her palms pressed to her face, sometimes watching the sea and waiting for something tangible in the deep, blue abyss—but all the while searching, all the while hunting.

Nina smelled blood.

It was nearly six in the morning and the first rays of light peaked over the Awkar hills, projecting down onto the pink swells of the Mediterranean. Pressed against her balcony railing, she had a clear vantage over the Marine Security Guards standing watch on the roof of the Baaklini annex, past the razor wire and concrete barricades, and beyond the luxury flats and resort hotels along the coastal highway, to the sea. From there, her eyes could trace the rocky shoreline ten kilometers though the heavy morning haze to downtown Beirut on the edge of a peninsula, where charmless glass and steel high-rises towered over French mandate villas, next to family homes pockmarked by the echoes of bullets and mortars. And then, prompt to the second, came the emotive cry of the *muezzin's* call to prayer from a nearby mosque amid the faint chime of church bells. Around her, the compound slowly stirred to life.

The US embassy in Beirut occupied an eighteen-acre tract of hillside in the predominantly Christian hamlet of Awkar, located approximately twenty minutes north of the city. It was the second site of the American diplomatic mission to Lebanon. In April of 1983, a truck bomb pancaked the central façade of the first embassy in Ibrahim al-Din's grand entrance to the stage of international terror. And again in September of 1984, another truck bomb—sent by al-Din—inflicted massive damage to the Baaklini annex, which served as a daily reminder to Nina that he was still out there, lurking, somewhere in that warren of concrete and haze along the sea. The current embassy managed to survive for over thirty years and existed as a crowded hodgepodge of prefabricated modular structures set among a handful of stone villas. The size and arrangement of the compound far outlived its usefulness and had become notoriously overcrowded and functionally obsolete. A new embassy complex was supposedly in the pipeline, but the State Department, citing various budgetary and bureaucratic constraints, dragged its feet for years. Nina's home for the past seven months was one of the eighteen rooms of the Tango Inn, the embassy lodging for temporary duty personnel. It resembled any decent Western three-star hotel room with a comfortable-enough bed, acceptable furniture and a new television connected to the offerings of AETN, the American Embassy TV Network. And of course, through the sliding glass door, was the balcony with a sweeping view of the Med. Yet since Nina moved in, the room came to resemble a cross between a frat house in May and a paper factory in the eye of a hurricane. She had been there for the better part of a year, but the embassy and the agency's station still considered her "temporary personnel." It had taken her that long to even start to rebuild, and for the first time, she thought she had something remotely real, something tangible, something to hunt.

Nina Davenport grew up in the foothills of western North Carolina's Brushy Mountains, in an isolated and homogenous town where, in a desperate bid for entertainment, most of the high school spent their Friday nights loitering in a Walmart parking lot. She shunned from her memory the majority of those years and she'd be the first to mock the archaic social norms of that dying world, but if anyone else dared join her, she'd be the first to put them on the floor. She was the first of her five siblings to attend college—Harvard—almost exclusively on grants, and came out *summa cum laude* with an AB in Near Eastern Languages and Civilizations. From Harvard, she was selected as a Marshall Scholar and read Philosophy, Politics and Economics at University College, Oxford. A month after returning from the United Kingdom, she found herself in a mosquito-infested marsh along the south bank of the York River outside Williamsburg, Virginia at Camp Peary, known officially within the Central Intelligence Agency as the Kisevalter Center for Advanced Studies, or more simply, "the Farm."

At the Farm, she spent a year being gradually initiated into all things clandestine: escape and evasion, wiretapping, defensive driving, hand-to-hand combat, weapons and explosives, surveillance and countersurveillance, selecting and loading dead-drops, brush passes, car tosses, photography, covert communications, body language analysis, and the full gamut of dark deception and trickery. But the ability to handle a sports car during a chase through a foreign city while simultaneously pleasuring your unlikely spying cohort was, unfortunately for those in the business, not the daily occupational hazard that popular cultural so often, frustratingly, portrayed. Rather, the most valuable skill imparted to Nina was to take her patience and fine attention to life's little details, her ability to examine the hidden motives and connections that so often became lost in the maddening morass of purposeful deceit—traits that came naturally to her—and turn them into a weapon. And that, quite simply, was what made Nina Davenport dangerous.

Her job title was "targeting officer," which meant Nina often traded the fluorescent-lit cubicles at Langley for some of the most inhospitable places on Earth to track a specific terrorist group or personality. Thus far in her career, she had been deployed to Camp Lemonnier in Djibouti on the Horn of Africa, and to the various remote forward operating bases in the mountainous hinterland of the Afghanistan-Pakistan border. There, her action arm was the ninjas of JSOC, who kicked in doors and squeezed triggers at the precise date, time and coordinates of her choosing. The nature of warfare in the twenty-first century, where the primary targets were clandestine networks interspersed among a civilian populace rather than tank divisions laid out on the plains of Central Europe, required precise "targeting packages" collected from a range of sources to generate high value, actionable intelligence to fuel the insatiable appetite of the "find, fix, finish" machine which America's special operations forces had become. Nina had a knack for fueling that engine: an innate talent to pull the right threads and follow the proper crumbs; to sit and wait for months—years, if necessary—toiling over the operational minutia; stitching together the dates, relationships, motives and shared desires; revealing the wider sprawl, not through one particular source, intercept or interrogation, but through them all; collating, quantifying, and striking. Her career had prepared her, and led her, by way of bewildering stupidity, to Lebanon, where she finally caught the first scent of a target that had no equal.

When she first heard the story—the full story, unvarnished by the station's personnel—she swore that one day when she was an instructor at the Farm, she would hold it up as a shining example of what to do if your goal was to get each and every asset working for you ripped off the streets and summarily executed. Nina had used a smorgasbord of four-letter words to describe it, but now she was here to rebuild. A little over a year ago, CIA's Beirut Station had a sizable network of paid informants—agents, or assets—within Hezbollah who regularly reported back to their handlers—operations officers, all Americans with diplomatic immunity, such as Nina—on a range of information concerning the group: party gossip, relations with Iran and the Lebanese governments, fund-raising and outreach, details of operations abroad, the organization and readiness of the Islamic Resistance, deployments of offensive weapons, and essentially anything that the assets could learn without arousing suspicion. In order for these assets to communicate with their handlers, they were provided with prepaid mobile phones of the kind that could be purchased nearly anywhere in Beirut. These informants would travel to a prearranged location in the city and place a call to their handlers, lasting only a matter of seconds, to schedule in-person meetings. The informants would only use these mobile phones to contact their American handlers and for nothing else. In theory, the system worked rather well. However, Hezbollah was quite smarter than it appeared.

Hezbollah's capable counterintelligence apparatus had begun monitoring the full spectrum of telecommunications signals originating within Lebanon. Using sophisticated software provided to them by the Iranians, they were able to trawl massive quantities of metadata and sift out suspicious anomalies. In doing so, they quickly identified specific mobile phones that were used rarely, or from certain locations and only for an unusually short amount of time. From there, it was a matter of discerning which party members in those specific areas, at those specific times, possessed any information worth selling to a foreign intelligence agency. And in an act that further amazed Nina, the agency's handlers used the code word "Pizza" to instruct their agents to meet at a local Beirut Pizza Hut. Hezbollah's counterintelligence officers immediately put every pizza restaurant in Beirut under surveillance—there weren't many—and quickly identified a dozen spies within their ranks. In short order, the entire network was rolled up, the informants were never heard from again, and their handlers were flown back to Washington in disgrace. With just a few simple steps, the world's foremost intelligence agency had effectively been put out of business in Lebanon, and left blind to the inner workings of the world's most capable terrorist organization.

Nina was pulled off the spines of the Hindu Kush and dispatched to Beirut by CIA's Counterterrorism Center with the mission to rebuild the agency's decimated operation against Hezbollah. It was no easy task. Terrorist organizations are, by nature, fanatical. No one volunteers to strap a bomb to their waist because they are wavering in their beliefs. But that sense of duty and fanaticism is doubly so when the cause for which one is fantastically committing suicide is widely accepted by a huge swath of the Middle East, and indeed the world, as a legitimate resistance against an illegal and oppressive force—that being Israel. For that reason, penetrating Hezbollah was notoriously difficult despite the near-bottomless pockets of the Central Intelligence Agency. In recent months that sense of venerated prestige had greatly diminished thanks to Hezbollah's disastrous foray into the Syrian civil war, yet the party's rank and file were not queuing up to offer their services to the highest bidding intelligence officer; their dismay was directed at their leadership, while their resolve remained iron-clad.

So Nina waited, patiently toiling away at the threads and the crumbs as she always had. Colonel Samir Basri—TOPSAIL—was an invaluable asset to her, as could be seen by the absurd fistfuls of cash she threw at him. His recruitment was the first development worthy of writing home. He had direct access to the party leadership, face-to-face meetings with the secretary-general; not nearly an insider, but a respected interlocutor, a mediator needed by all sides to sustain the peace that had been suspended over Lebanon by tenterhooks. And now, with little more than a fleeting glance in an office anteroom, Basri laid eyes on a ghost, and Nina knew what that meant.

There was no sweeter glory, no greater prize, no more dangerous game, no more worthy foe than Ibrahim al-Din. And she wanted him. She wanted him because he was unattainable. She wanted him because he breathed the same air as her. She wanted him for the thrill of the chase. She wanted him more than anything that ever passed before her grasp. She wanted blood.

Another hour dragged by and her view of the heaving sea hadn't changed. She took a deep drag on a cigarette, pushed the smoke from her lungs, and stared onward. It was a nervous tic Nina had since college, nor her fondest, not that she cared, but it was the most reliable tell that her composure wasn't long to hold. If she lit up, run. She checked her watch. Her friend up the hill wouldn't have that luxury. Nina tossed the cigarette off the balcony and turned into her room. In a matter of minutes, she stormed the maze of stairs and ramps leading to the upper reaches of the embassy. On the northern edge of the compound, next to the helipad, sat the chancery, a stone villa with a terracotta roof. In addition to the embassy's executive offices, it housed the more secure facilities that couldn't be placed in a modular trailer. That included CIA's Beirut Station. Hidden behind an unmarked, cypher-locked door, the station had a small communications center, a conference room and a collection of workstations, many collecting dust. Her eyes rapidly scanned the empty space and she found her unwitting target in an adjacent office.

"What is it?" Nina demanded, having zero time for pleasantries.

Tom Stessel, the chief of station (COS), looked up from the cable he was reading, initially confused, but understanding once he saw her. "'Hello, Tom, how are you this morning?'" he said sarcastically. "'I'm fine, Nina, and you? That's great to hear. What can I do for you?' See, that's how normal people greet each other. Now you try."

"Fuck off," she said flatly. "And good morning to you. What is it?"

"What is what?" Stessel blinked.

"What we talked about yesterday. Have you thought about it? I've been waiting for hours."

"Don't tell me you've been—"

"That doesn't matter."

Stessel sighed. "Me needing to think about something would imply that my immediate decision was somehow not clear enough," he condescended.

Nina bit her lip. "Tom," she breathed, "I am merely asking for your permission to ask for permission to ask TOPSAIL to follow it further."

"Well, when I can make sense of that—"

"Don't fucking patronize me, you know damn well what I mean."

Stessel knew exactly what she meant. Since Colonel Basri told Nina that he saw a man who, in passing, resembled Ibrahim al-Din outside Wissam Hamawi's office, she spoke and thought about nothing else. It was becoming an obsession and Stessel knew it. She wanted—demanded—that Stessel report it to Langley and allow her to have her agent investigate deeper. However, the evidence, if one could even call it that, to suggest that al-Din might have been in the Security Quarter was so circumstantial, so unlikely, so absurd, that even pondering if it might be true was asking for career-ending ridicule. Moreover, the United States had just achieved the impossible in getting Syria and Israel to agree to face each other at the negotiating table. In doing so, they had at least to appear to be an impartial mediator. An offensive operation against Hezbollah in the streets of Beirut would endanger that carefully crafted image, and Stessel refused to be the one to suggest it. "You want me to believe that your asset, a child molester—let's not forget that—whose 'shag pad' you are funding, *maybe* saw a guy who has not been spotted in public for twenty years? You want me to stake my credibility, and yours, on that?"

"Yeah, that's about right."

"Then you're crazy."

"Tom, we're not talking about 'Abu Dipshit' and his terrorist pals sitting in a cave somewhere finding teenagers dumb enough to shove a bomb up their ass. We're talking about the Henry Ford of terrorism. The man practically *invented* the suicide bomber. And you want to squander the first shot in two decades—"

"Nina!"

"Fuck, we don't even know what he looks like!"

"Exactly."

She fell silent.

"No, Nina. My answer was and is *no*. This is not some tribal shithole in Afghanistan—"

"You're right, it's a tribal shithole in Lebanon."

"Be that as it may," he winced, "this is a sovereign shithole and it has laws and an elected government, at which our country is not at war. You can't just come here and buzz around in choppers, playing 'cowboys and Indians' with your SOF buddies. I won't allow it. As long as you are in Lebanon, you will operate by my rules, and they are not simply your rules."

Nina tensed her shoulders. Her face went flush. She was brimming with rage and Stessel knew it. "And the Iranian aid money that's missing?"

"Follow it."

"Fine." She turned and started for the door. "We'll see."

• • •

"Harold!" The chairman of the Palestine Liberation Organization (PLO) and president of Fatah, Hanna Sayigh, was a rare, jovial sight that afternoon.

"*Salam,* Hanna." Harold Lansing stood from the cushioned chair where he had been waiting.

"*Wa'alaykum as-Salam.* Come inside, please." Sayigh beckoned Lansing to his inner sanctum. A large portrait of Yasser Arafat hung proudly on the wall and the flag of the Arab Revolt flanked his desk. Outside, beyond the tall windows, a column of Palestinian National Security Forces soldiers marched through the courtyard of the Muqataa, the PLO's administrative complex at the center of Ramallah in the West Bank. They sat opposite each other, a tray of tea was placed on the table between them, and they looked on in silence for a moment as old friends, or wary acquaintances, often do, unsure of what to say.

Sayigh broke the spell. "How are you?"

"I'm all right."

"You've been busy."

"We've been lucky."

"Yes. Yes, you have," Sayigh nodded. "Quite to the point." He turned toward the low winter sun shining through the windows. "But luck often belies our better senses, does it not? Clouds…when one might expect it to reassure."

"How do you mean?" Lansing smiled, and reached for his cup.

"I don't want you think that your recent adventure in Damascus is the cure for all the ailments in this region. Believe it or not, some enjoy the sickness. But that's another discussion for another day. What can I do for you?"

Lansing pulled the tail of his suit jacket out from under him. "I don't think it's the cure, but I'll be honest: I intend to find it. I'm merely here to feel the waters and gauge opinions. What can I do to get you and Avi Arad sitting across from one another, just like we are now?"

Sayigh snorted into his teacup and placed it back on the table. The Israeli prime minister was Sayigh's nemesis for the better part of a decade and he had been a party to this exact exchange multiple times, and at every encounter the result was exactly the same: deadlock. And for it, Palestine suffered. In an effort to relieve that agony, Sayigh had worked to bring his party, Fatah, which ruled the West Bank, into a unity coalition with Hamas, a terrorist organization, which ruled Gaza Strip—to the considerable ire of Avi Arad and the Israeli political class. But the United States was always the bearer of lofty and flourishing words of peace, reassurances to the world that somehow, someway this time was different. It never was. Sayigh knew why, and Lansing did, too, but they didn't voice it. It was too maddening.

There were forces at work in the Middle East for which peace was impossible. For those forces, the only acceptable end game was death, for themselves and everyone around them. But maybe this time really was different. Sayigh would bite. "You usually don't come around here unless your staff has cooked something up. Or is one Nobel Prize not enough for President Paulson?"

Lansing scoffed at the veiled insult. "Hanna, I consider you to be a serious person, and a friend. We've begun to settle the Golan; I'd like the West Bank to be next. Help me help you."

"And where might Gaza fit in there?"

"Let's not get ahead of ourselves." Lansing reached for his tea again.

"What do you propose?"

"I'd like to engineer a prisoner exchange—one thousand for one. In return, you and Arad agree to talks. Just talks."

Eight years ago, Moshe Adler was a corporal in the IDF Armor Corps, stationed at the Kerem Shalom crossing along the border with Gaza. At dawn on a placid Sunday in late June, a squad of militants from the Iranian-backed Palestinian Islamic Jihad (PIJ) burrowed three hundred meters into Israel and emerged under the camouflage of shade trees. Supported by mortars and anti-tank rockets from Gaza, the militants split into three units and unleashed a barrage of RPG and small arms fire on three targets: a watchtower, an armored personnel carrier and a Merkava Mark III tank. As the first two units created a diversion, the third advanced on the Merkava and fired an RPG at the rear access door. The explosion wounded several crewmembers and caused the engine to erupt in flames, crippling the tank's ventilation system. The interior filled with smoke and in a panic the crew went to escape, but the militants were waiting for them. As the Merkava commander threw open the access hatch on the turret, a round struck him in the temple. The militants then leapt atop the turret and tossed a grenade into the hatch, killing two more crew members. A second RPG was fired at the rear access hatch, blowing it open. The Merkava's only surviving crew member, a nineteen-year-old tank gunner—Moshe Adler—was forced out at gunpoint and whisked away to Gaza as the other two units covered their escape. By the time the IDF's Southern Command could mobilize an adequate response, Adler was long gone, disappeared into the rambling slums on Gaza's fringe. He had remained there for eight long years.

The principle of repatriating Israel's missing soldiers or their remains was sacrosanct in the Israeli conscience. In Jewish law, the *Halakha,* it is called *"Pidyon Shuvyim,"* or "Redemption of Captives," which made it a religious commandment from God to recover any Jew held by gentiles. Occupying a juncture somewhere between the living and the dead, Israel's POWs and MIAs were an illustration of a national ethos when that nation found itself under a perpetual state of siege. There was always a shred of hope that one day they would return home and life would resume as normal, just as there was always a shred of hope that Israel would find peace and the siege would be lifted. More simply, in a society where nearly every household had a member serving in the armed forces, it was rather easy to squeeze oneself into the other shoe. Moshe Adler's unfortunate case was no different. For eight years, he remained in Israeli hearts and minds, the subject of countless vigils and debates, and endless backbreaking intelligence work, which yielded its share of aborted rescue attempts. Adler was a symbol, a rallying cry, and for Harold Lansing, a useful tool.

"There's only one Israeli worth a thousand Palestinians," Sayigh muttered, reaching for his tea again.

"I want Adler released," Lansing pressed. "You must think it's time?"

"Don't make me answer that."

"Can you help?"

"Perhaps, so long as your expectations remain in line. I wouldn't say I'm popular with *al-Muqawama al-Shabiyya.*" Sayigh referred to the Popular Resistance Committees, a coalition of armed Palestinian factions in Gaza who were opposed to the PLO's conciliatory approach to Israel, while they sought only to wipe it from the face of the earth. Among their ranks were members of Hamas, PIJ and the al-Aqsa Martyrs' Brigades. Behind them were the arms and financing of the Iranian Revolutionary Guards and, until recently, Hezbollah. "The biggest problem with your proposal is that, from what I hear, Adler does not belong to any Palestinian. He belongs to the Iranians... One, in particular."

"Who?"

"Rasoul Gharib Abadi, their ambassador to Sudan. But 'ambassador' is a misnomer; Mr. Abadi is an officer of the Quds Force. I'm sure your CIA knows this." Sayigh finished his tea. "His brief is the whole of North Africa. The smuggling networks that run along the Nile, to the Sinai and under the wire into Gaza are his doing. The Persian-speaking men running around Somalia, and Libya, and Mali, and Niger like they own the place are his doing. The transformation of Hamas and PIJ from roving packs of teenagers throwing rocks to a capable military force is his doing. And I've no doubt that he'd love to assassinate me, if ever he had the chance."

Lansing cracked an uneasy smile. "Let's hope it never comes to that."

"Right, but when you triumphantly defanged Hezbollah, you left Abadi as the only field commander Iran has on the front of their mortal enemy. You've increased his stock exponentially."

Lansing became agitated with his friend. "Hanna, can you help me get Adler freed, or not? Do you want to help me? That's the better question."

Sayigh sat back in his chair. "No, the better question is: How can I help you when all you've done is hamper my ability to do so?"

"Hanna, you know what Adler's release would mean. You know what a shock that would be. If you had a role to play in that, any role at all, Arad would have no choice but to sit down and talk with you. That's all I want."

"When I said that luck often belies our better senses, this is what I meant. What's the expression you Americans have? 'Spike the turf?'"

"Spike the ball."

"That's it! That's what you've done. You've rolled into Damascus, Iran's home court, and spat in their faces. You've snipped the pride right from between their legs. Your luck has clouded your better senses, my friend. It has caused you to miss the fact that there are people in this diseased corner of the world who enjoy the sickness, people for whom the only order is disorder. You've spat in their faces. And Harold—I'm saying this as a friend—there *will* be consequences. Iran will not look at what you've done and drift off into the sunset like Dean Martin."

"John Wayne."

"My point is that Iran's revolution hangs over this part of the world like a stifling haze. And now that you've crippled their proxy to Israel's north, their eye is set solely on the south—at Gaza—with Hamas, Islamic Jihad and the bandits in the Sinai—people who would like to see my corpse dragged through the street. And then you expect me to be in a position to help you?"

"Hanna—"

"No listen, Harold. If you want peace, if you want anything more than a nice photo of Arad and I, you need to get back in your jet, go straight to the White House, and you need to tell your president that it is impossible until Iran has been totally removed from the equation. Until then, peace is a myth. They will not allow it."

Lansing gently nodded in acceptance. He was masterfully upstaged. "Alright, Hanna. I understand. Just give me something to tell Arad."

"When are you seeing him?"

"Paris. Thursday night."

"Tell him that I will do what I can to get his boy back."

"Thank you, Hanna." Lansing stood and offered his hand.

Sayigh did the same and pulled him close. "But remember what I said. The diseased never forget. And neither should you."

"I'll be in touch."

"I know. Good luck, my friend. You'll need it."

Lansing was escorted by his security detail to a pair of Suburbans waiting in the courtyard. The convoy took Highway 60, was ushered around traffic at the Qalandiya Checkpoint, and arrived in Jerusalem by late afternoon. At the consulate-general on Agron Street, Lansing prepared a detailed cable to Angela Weisel—careful to include all that Hanna Sayigh had told him.

• • •

The mental tests were always worse than the physical tests. He figured that out on day one, the moment he stepped off the bus at BUD/S (Basic Underwater Demolition/SEAL) Training in Coronado. He learned that the frigid waters of the Pacific could always hurl one more breaker, the training cadre could order one more climb up a sixty-foot cargo net, or one more swim through the pool with his arms and legs bound; but there was always an end justifying their torturous means, and that end resided in the mind. To survive, he placed all his strength into reaching the next meal. It didn't matter if his legs were about to give way beneath him or if the tips of his fingers had turned a pale blue. If he could drag himself to chow, then, for now, he survived. To devour the whale in a single bite was suicide. The torture would end—he always knew it would—and until it did, he would repeat that cycle three times a day, every day. It had been fourteen years since he stepped off that bus, nineteen and still every bit a child, naïve and exuding a romantic fantasy of the life he chose for himself. In many respects, Chief Petty Officer Robert Harris knew that child was still in there, not quite dead yet. It survived, as he did, one bite at a time.

Harris pulled aside the camouflage poncho liner that hung over his bunk and squinted into the diffused light. The sun was nearing the end of its sprint to the horizon, which meant his day was just beginning. JSOC's ninjas were nocturnal creatures. He'd slept well enough thanks largely to an Ambien, but the grogginess was slow to fade. And he wasn't alone; snores still rumbled around the hut. Harris swung his burning and fatigued legs out from the bunk and rose quietly. A Gatorade bottle full of urine sat on a table within reach. They were in the overflow housing on the compound, so the row of chemical latrines—heads, as he knew them—were roughly a hundred yards away—much too far to bother staggering over in his sleep. His procedure was more practical. At the end of the bunk in a wooden rack, his "kit"—gear—and his weapons were squared away and ready for action, and his uniforms were folded next to a few pairs of boots. The previous morning, he made sure that the batteries on his NVGs and sights were fresh and that his radios were charged. His load-bearing vest, which held two ballistic plates and an assortment of Velcro pouches for ammo and equipment, also hung on the rack. Harris brought several weapons with him to Syria. His primary weapon, which he used nightly, was a Heckler & Koch 416 assault rifle based on the famous M4 family. He had equipped it with a ten-inch barrel for maneuverability, an EOTech optical red dot sight with a 3x magnifier, and an AAC sound suppressor. For missions where stealth was a priority, he brought a suppressed HKMP7 submachine gun. It didn't have the stopping power of the 416's 5.56 round, but it could easily take out a room full of jihadis without waking their friends next door. For backup, he had the standard Navy-issue SIG Sauer P226 and an HK45C. On each of his weapons, the expert armorers at DEVGRU had taken care to customize the triggers and grips to his precise specifications. Suspended to the rack by a pushpin was a photo of his wife, Sandra, and their five-year-old son, Ben. Another child was due at the end of spring, but they didn't know if it would be a boy or a girl. Sandra was waiting for him to find out. He would be with them soon, one bite at a time.

He dressed himself and reluctantly walked out of the hut and into the daylight. Outside, Hama Air Base buzzed with life. The air base formerly housed three squadrons of Syrian MiGs, but that wreckage had since been swept away. Now, on the northern side of the runway was the primary logistics base of the United Nations Interim Mission in Syria's Sector West, which covered the governates of Idlib, Latakia, Tartus and Hama—some of the most restive parts of the country. Everything south of the runway belonged to JSOC's Task Force OLYMPIA, and was the launch pad for operations throughout Syria's coastal cities and the an-Nusayriyah Mountains. JSOC's enclave on the base featured its own gym, chow hall, a tactical operations center and rows of plywood huts for housing. The compound also hosted a prison, surrounded by multiple rings of razor wire, where JSOC and CIA interrogators drained captured regime officials of any scrap of intelligence before handing them off to the International Criminal Court in The Hague. Ali Mamlouk was inside somewhere, grappling with the cold certainty that awaited him.

Harris tried to purge it from memory, but the raid that captured Mamlouk stayed with him. It wasn't the image of the burning regime loyalist, his eyes filled with agony as he fired wildly into the courtyard that haunted him. He had been desensitized to those sights long ago. Killing was part of his job. Harris had probably taken twelve lives since he earned his Trident, although the exact number was a bit hazy. All of them would have gladly taken his own, if he allowed it. "Proud" wasn't quite the appropriate word to describe his feelings on that, but he never lost sleep over one of them. Yet he was losing sleep over this.

Harris hadn't admitted it to himself yet, but that raid was the closest he came to death in fourteen years of serving in Naval Special Warfare. The only reason he stood there, the afternoon sun warming his face, was due to a mistake—a common error that could only be attributed to an imperfect human soul. Had the 160th not botched the pre-op planning and put the Little Bird directly on the target house, instead of overflying it by a single roof, Harris would've breached the door and waltzed straight into a machine gun nest. The PKM that the regime loyalists had placed in the hallway would've cut him in half; he had no delusions about that. Worse yet: No amount of training could have prepared him. No amount of intelligence would have warned him. No amount of armor and technological wizardry might have saved him. It was dumb luck that kept him on this earth. It was a mistake that under any other circumstance he and his teammates would've come back to base and bitched about. Yet that mistake ensured that he would live to see his wife and little boy one more time—and that his next child wouldn't grow up without a father. For that, he was grateful.

Robert Harris, the warrior, didn't really know how to process that. Robert Harris, the father and the husband, didn't really care. He had never faced a mental test quite so severe, and the strategy of one bite at a time wasn't sufficient. It was just too exacting, dumb luck—too random, too unforgiving, too cold.

An operations officer assigned to the Dubai listening post of CIA's Iran Operations Division left the al-Thanawiya Post Office in Deira and walked the short distance to the corniche along the Dubai Creek, where he hailed the first passing cab. He directed the driver to Terminal 3 at the airport. In his possession was a letter that had just arrived from Tehran. The return address was never used twice, but the officer understood that the sender was always the same. The letter, as usual, was printed on thin sheets of nitrocellulose-based paper, and with the proper amount of heat would disintegrate without the telltale signs of smoke or ash. This particular letter was thicker than most of the others—five pages, double-sided—but that was none of his concern. He removed the letter from its envelope, folded it tightly, and placed it inside a titanium cigarette case that was fitted with a small pyrotechnic charge. If the case was opened incorrectly, the charge would ignite, incinerating the contents. At the terminal, the officer bypassed security with a confident flash of his diplomatic passport and was soon seated in business class aboard a Boeing 777. Right on schedule at five-thirty in the evening, Emirates Flight 205 began rolling on the tarmac. There wouldn't be a wink of sleep for him, but in fourteen long hours, he would land in Washington, and CITADEL's words would shake the city to its core.

CHAPTER 15

HIS LORDSHIP'S ESTATE rose gracefully in the misty twilight over the gray-green crowns of Buckinghamshire. It sat at an idyllic bend in the river Thames—thirty miles west of Central London—hoisted atop a forty-meter chalk cliff covered by trees that dangled precariously upon the rise. Over that rise, the estate opened to nearly four hundred acres of formal gardens, rolling woodlands and a tended parterre, giving the estate its name: Cliveden House, meaning, "valley among cliffs." From the parterre, there was a magnificent vista over the lands to the south, holding a steady vantage on the plains and the downs of Surrey and Berkshire, and on a clear day even the higher parapets of Windsor Castle. Cliveden had stood on the grounds in some form for over three hundred years and was once home to the highest rungs of aristocracy, counting the 1st Earl of Orkney and three of his mistresses; Frederick, Prince of Wales; the 2nd Duke of Buckingham, the 2nd Duke of Sutherland, the 1st Duke of Westminster and the Viscounts Astor. The previous two houses were both destroyed in fires, but the current estate had stood since 1849 without yet meeting a similar fate. The new Cliveden was sprawling. The estate was centered around a ten-bedroom Italianate mansion, designed to echo the rich ornamental tastes of the Renaissance with the blended architectural styles of the English Palladian and the Roman Cinquecento. At its base was a four-hundred-foot brick terrace, which dated from the seventeenth century and faced south, toward the Thames. The mansion's exterior was rendered in cement and fitted with terracotta capitals, keystones and finials, rising three stories to a flat, balustraded roofline. Flanking the mansion on either side were single-story wings that ran to the east and west, reaching out around the courtyard at the front of the house, forming a symmetrical *cour d'honneur*. Rising above the western Garden Wing was a thirty-meter clock tower, featuring four faces framed by gilded surrounds, topped with a copy of Auguste Dumont's colossal winged male figure, *Le Génie de la Liberté*, the original of which stood atop the July Column at Place de la Bastille in Paris.

As the thick shelf of clouds above the estate's damp acres dimmed from a dreary gray to a pitched black, the soft, refracted glow from the chandeliers in the state rooms on the ground floor gradually twinkled on like stage lights, swinging back the curtains for the next act of a great opera. In a way, Cliveden had always been a theater, brimming with the machinations of pleasure, politics, power, and common greed.

As guests arrived at the estate that evening, they were met by members of His Lordship's private security detail and armed officers of Scotland Yard's Diplomatic Protection Group at the gatehouse on Cliveden Road. Once cleared, they were directed onward down the Grand Avenue, past the Fountain of Love, carved in marble and volcanic rock, and led to the stone portico above the main entrance on the north side of the mansion. From there a pair of footmen, dressed in exquisite waistcoats, escorted them through the Great Hall, before announcing their arrival into the heated air of the Drawing Room.

His Lordship had acquired the freehold to the entirety of the Cliveden estate from the National Trust in 1984 and immediately contracted the Parisian firm, Maison Jansen, to restore Cliveden exactly as it was at the turn of the century, save for a few new touches of his own. Laid out on the ground floor of the mansion were the state rooms, which had been designed to resemble an Italian palazzo—matching the exterior—and housed the majority of His Lordship's art collection, the most vast and well-curated in Europe not held by a museum or royalty. Through the main entrance off the courtyard, past the footmen, was the expansive Great Hall, furnished with walls paneled in fine English oak; the three *Art de la guerre* tapestries: *Attaque, Campement* and *Embuscade,* each woven in Brussels by Le Clere & Van der Borch in the early-eighteenth century; Corinthian columns and pilasters with swags of carved flowers; and suits of Gothic plate armor, dating from the Holy Roman Empire. As part of the restoration, the old flagstone floor had been removed and the original Minton encaustic tiles tracked down and replaced precisely as they were once laid. At the right end of the hall, leading to His Lordship's private apartment, was a wooden grand staircase with the newel posts intricately carved to represent the numerous historical figures in Cliveden's past. A fresco covered the staircase's ceiling, portraying the Duchess of Sutherland's children as the four seasons. At the opposite end of the hall sat a sixteenth-century stone chimneypiece taken from the Burgundian Château d'Arnay-le-Duc when it was pulled down. Connected to the Great Hall by a set of wide double doors was the French Dining Room, overlooking the terrace. The room took its name from the gilded, rococo paneling—wainscots and overdoors, painted in muted green with carvings of hares, pheasants, hunting dogs and rifles that covered the walls; the mirrors and swirling, marble chimneypiece; and the molded plasterwork ceilings, which had all been taken from the Château d'Asnières, the hunting lodge of Louis XV's mistress, the Marquise de Pompadour, and reconstructed at Cliveden. The console tables and buffet were painstakingly designed and custom built to match the room, which could comfortably seat sixty for dinner. Adjacent to the French Dining Room, through the library, was the Drawing Room. In daylight it held a remarkable view of the terrace and the parterre, gazing out over the cliffs to the Thames through six sets of French doors. The terracotta-colored walls of the room were adorned with a range of paintings covering the Renaissance, Baroque, and Neoclassical eras—notable among them, El Greco's *Christ Driving the Money Changers from the Temple,* and Peter Paul Ruben's *Massacre of the Innocents.* In a corner, near the windows, a string quartet—two violinists, a violist and a cellist—from the Academy of St Martin in the Fields, played a rendition of Maurice Ravel's *Pavane pour une infante défunte.* Another marble chimneypiece, flanked by bookcases, sat at the head of the room, and three Bohemian crystal chandeliers hung from the ceiling.

His Lordship had taken a special interest in that ceiling. He commissioned a team of artists from the Royal Academy who spent over a year crafting a magnificent fresco across its entirety. It depicted the cosmos: Saturn and its moons, Venus, Jupiter, Mars and the constellations, all ordered into the undeniable alignment of the whole. Now His Lordship could rightfully take his place under the adoring heavens. Yet the fresco reflected his own—unspoken—personal motto, taken directly from the pages of the Bible and, as he had naturally found it imperfect, altered it by a single word: *"The earth is His Lordship's, and the fullness thereof; the world, and they that dwell therein."*

Receptions were hosted at Cliveden at least once a month, and although the excuses for the little gatherings varied greatly, they were often called to bolster the coffers of the *en vogue* charity or cause of the week, and in so doing inflate the colossal ego of the self-crowned benefactor or patron, with whom His Lordship more often than not had good business, and whose opinions might be swayed with the help of the benevolent hearts of the friends of His Lordship. It was in the backhanded tradition of *noblesse oblige* that they pried open their fat wallets, to do their utmost—for all their peers to see—to reach down (figuratively) into whatever maligned hive of molecular life they all fawned over at the moment and aid those poor, wretched husks in humanoid form in what small way they could, before scanning the Drawing Room for the nearest glass of vintage '96 Bollinger *Grande Année.* Once the heated air of the room embraced his guests, parting them of their money was an easy task—most were simply left in awe. An invitation to Cliveden was universally a cause for celebration, an indication that one had finally "arrived," a chance to revel for even a minute in the sacred presence of His Lordship, which was the true reason they made the short trek out from London or the hop over the Channel. A few had been coming to Cliveden for years, but the full guest list often fluctuated with His Lordship's business interests. There were more flushed Asian and Slavic faces in the drawing room than in *soirées* past. In all, there were nearly sixty lured into the room, each tended to by a domestic household staff that was so attentive in their hospitality and expansive in scope as to be second only to that of the Sovereign.

His Lordship surrounded himself with the most fascinating and nauseating company that any man could hope to keep. A cursory examination of the Drawing Room quickly resembled a dissection of some ghastly, maligned creature, slowly rotting away from within—ignorant of the encroaching cancer as it gleefully constructed card towers of Babel to the sky. They buzzed like blue flies at the splendid gathering at the home of His Lordship. There was the Comte de Paris, the *Orléanist* pretender to the French throne; the Margrave of Baden; the Aga Khan, the imam of Nizari Ismailism, a denomination of Shia Islam with fifteen million adherents worldwide; the chief executive of the Hong Kong Monetary Authority; the lord mayor of the City of London; a retired air chief marshal and the most recent chief of the Defence Staff, the professional head of the British Armed Forces; the governor of the Bank of England; the chancellor of Oxford University; the president of the European Court of Justice; and a South African mining baron engaged in polite conversation with the chairman of one of the world's largest investment banks, a Danish shipping magnate whose conglomerate controlled a massive percentage of trade over the seas, and the chief executive of a vertically-integrated oil and gas "supermajor" which held exploration and production rights on all seven continents. Coincidently, the host of that marvelous gathering was the single largest shareholder in all of their corporations. But they were just a few friends of His Lordship, all of them disfigured by the grotesque leprosy of illusion and deceit.

Not exempt from this damnation was the guest of honor that evening, the vessel for the colossal ego which was to be stoked: His Royal Highness, Prince Farid bin Abdulaziz al-Saud, minister of petroleum and mineral resources of the Kingdom of Saudi Arabia. Prince Farid circuited the drawing room—aided by the first secretary of their embassy in Mayfair, who discreetly whispered an appropriate name and title in the prince's ear—offering up limp handshakes (with his right hand and only to the men) and mumbled words of gratitude to the buzzing blue flies as he passed. With his left hand he held together the embroidered gold lapels of a *bisht,* a flowing, black wool cloak, over a *thaub,* an ankle-length white cotton tunic. Most of his face was kept hidden from view by a *ghutrah,* a white headdress suspended by an *agal,* a threaded black cord. Only his most principal features were displayed, and they had been carefully prepared by a battery of creams and moisturizers meant to belie the aging, fibrous flesh stretched over his brittle bones like cheap leather. But the blue flies were more than happy to make his acquaintance. Prince Farid held the keys to the vast hydrocarbon deposits locked beneath the shifting sands of Arabia, the grease that kept the wheels of the global economy spinning in tandem. With the kingdom's two hundred and sixty billion barrels of proven crude reserves under his management, he was the undisputed master of OPEC—the Organization of the Petroleum Exporting Countries—and he alone held the influence necessary to force a consensus among the cartel's members to set production levels, and thus drive the price of crude up or down as he saw fit. And his word carried no less weight inside the kingdom. Prince Farid was the king's older half-brother and the reigning patriarch of a faction within the royal family known unofficially as the "Sudairi Seven," a group of sons born to Hassa bint Ahmed al-Sudairi, the favorite wife of King Abdulaziz, the founder of Saudi Arabia. Only four of the brothers were still living, and all were well into their eighties, but their power had not waned in the slightest. Over the past fifty years the brothers systematically took control over the primary cogs in the family business: the ministries of Defense and the Interior, the National Guard, the governorship of Riyadh and the petroleum sector, while their sons were appointed to key posts in the armed forces and dispatched as ambassadors to major allies. Farid and his full brothers were the very definition of the "old guard." Yet, somehow, the prince still found room in his heart for charity—when it suited him.

Prince Farid was a trustee and a patron of the King Abdulaziz Foundation, one of the largest private charities in the world. "Driven by the interests and passions of the House of Saud," the foundation held an endowment of twenty billion US dollars and funded countless aid and development projects in the Middle East, the Horn of Africa and Central Asia. Their current flagship undertaking, which was lauded as a miracle for Islamic culture and antiquity, was a bid to finance the reconstruction of the Old City of Aleppo, a UNESCO World Heritage Site ravaged by years of fighting in the Syrian civil war. And it was with this worthy cause that His Lordship planned to appeal to the prince's ego and pass the largest bribe in recorded history. Cliveden was the theater for the opera, but first, His Lordship had to arrive on stage.

The "Oracle of St James's"—His Lordship's affectionate *nom de guerre*— was delayed in his departure from Paris earlier that afternoon, as his private secretary apologetically explained to the blue flies, but as of half-an-hour ago had "crossed the Channel and was somewhere over East Sussex." But fueled by a stream of Bollinger to loosen their mouths and their wallets, the blue flies hardly seemed pressed for time. They simply stood around, admiring each other, and waited for the financial titan of Eurasia.

His Lordship headed a private investment firm that managed seven trillion dollars in assets, which placed it as the largest shareholder in one in four corporations in Europe, with steady gains in Asia. This gave him enormous influence to wield over international markets, on par with, and even surpassing, many central bank governors, finance ministers and heads of state. His Lordship was all too aware of that influence and made liberal use of it, collecting banks and pipelines like some collected stamps. Yet it was never about money. The aim was control, a prize that no amount of cash could buy. But even still, it was never enough, nor would it be.

And then, as promised, he entered to center stage. The blue flies' attention was directed to the chandeliers suspended from the drawing room's frescoed ceiling. The Bohemian crystals rattled gently with the low chop of rotor blades overhead. Their heads turned to the glow of floodlights on the parterre. Descending in the darkness, through the glare on the French doors, was the airframe of a pearl white Airbus H175 helicopter. It hovered for a moment before the landing gear touched the wet grass. The rotors whined to a stop. Security officers fanned out around the parterre as a man emerged from the cabin, backed by a small entourage, and made for the stairs up to the terrace. Now the footmen took their place on opposite sides of a French door. One held it open as the man approached. The other proudly announced into the heated air of the drawing room: "The Lord Ivanov!" His Lordship, Roman Leonidovich Ivanov—Baron Ivanov of Taplow, Knight of the Most Noble Order of the Garter, Knight of Obedience of the Sovereign Military Order of Malta, *grand-croix de la Ordre national de la Légion d'honneur,* and so forth—smiled widely to his audience with the shit-eating grin of a master conman. He was perfectly dressed for the part in a bespoke dinner jacket and tie from Henry Poole & Co on Savile Row. His imperfections were, of course, masked behind artificially tanned skin and feathery white hair combed strategically over his balding scalp.

The blue flies were still, frozen in his rapture.

Ivanov clasped his manicured hands together in prayer like an altar boy. "Ladies and gentlemen, *mesdames et messieurs, mea maxima culpa.*" He took a few steps deeper into the drawing room, trailed by bodyguards. "You see, I was delayed, but detained might also be an appropriate way to describe my plight." He scratched behind his ear with one hand and placed the other in his trouser pocket. "It's the most amusing story; I must share it. As you may know, at Davos a few weeks back I was part of a discussion on stage, and in passing I apparently questioned the value of US Treasury bonds. To tell you the truth, I hardly recall it. Yet in the front row was my friend, Mr. Wa Qishan, the Chinese vice premier for finance." Ivanov smiled again. "And as you can imagine, my remarks didn't sit well with some people. Truly, this queer predicament was quite distressing at the time. So, yesterday evening, I hosted a little supper for my colleagues in the Bilderberg Steering Committee at my *pied-à-terre* in Paris to support the candidacy of my dear friend, the Viscount Picqué, for president of the European Commission." He gestured to his friend standing in the drawing room.

His Lordship was being modest. Ivanov's Parisian *"pied-à-terre"* was the Hôtel Lambert, a grand mansion townhouse once owned by Voltaire on the tip of the Île Saint-Louis, an island in the Seine. And his "dear friend," the Viscount Gérard Picqué, was a Belgian minister of state, former prime minister, and current chairman of GDF Suez, a massive French multinational concerned with natural gas and electricity distribution. His bid for president of the European Commission had the backing of both Berlin and Paris—not to mention Ivanov—and was entirely assured. But, His Lordship digressed.

"I remained in Paris overnight and received a call earlier this morning from the chairman of the Federal Reserve. It appears he was in Basel for a meeting of the Bank for International Settlements and simply *could not* run back across the Atlantic before popping in to visit. Much to my dismay, I spent the remainder of the day in my salon, whilst he assured me of the important role Treasury bonds play in liquidity and stability, etcetera, etcetera and whatnot. I likewise assured him of my participation at the next auction and said I would ring Beijing at the nearest opportunity and urge them to do the same." Ivanov laughed slightly. "So it seems someone will finance the great American debt for another year!"

The blue flies politely found it hysterical.

"But, thankfully, that matter is water passed under the bridge, and I can now be where my heart lingered all day...with you dear people." Ivanov confidently floated toward the roaring fireplace and rested an elbow on the marble mantelpiece. "Now, *where* is His Royal Highness?"

Prince Farid came forward with a languid gait, clutching his *bisht*. "Roman, you must be thanked for your generosity and hospitality—"

"The prince and I were schoolmates at Le Rosey during the war," Ivanov boomed to his audience. "Some of my fondest memories of youth are with His Highness. When was that one winter in particular? Forty-four? Forty-five?"

"Forty-five."

"Ah, yes! Winter, forty-five. We had moved to the Gstaad campus, and of course by then most of the boys had been summoned home, or to what was left of it. But," he leaned closer to the prince, "your father was off dealing with Mr. Roosevelt and my father was busy scampering around Geneva, trying to secure my inheritance, so we were essentially left to our own devices, weren't we?"

The prince gently nodded.

"That *gemütlich* little town was empty, mind, so we had the run of the place—lorded over the chalet like kings, we did. Not even the headmaster, *Monsieur* Carnal, bless him, gave it a second thought. Hardly any class time;

frittered the whole day on the slopes." His Lordship cracked a whimsical smile. "Fond memories, indeed. Now look at us...bloody geriatrics, we are."

But Ivanov, given his polite and modest sense of taste, omitted the story from that winter of how Prince Farid's bodyguard—a retired inspector of the Bern *Polizei*—had been kind enough to bolster the fourteen-year-olds' privacy upon what was already afforded by the small, empty and lonely campus, as the two occasionally explored the deeper facts of life. But that was quite a long time ago, and some truths ought never be unearthed, especially given the Wahabist zeal of the House of Saud—modern sensibilities be damned.

"At any rate, that's ancient history—water passed under the bridge. Let's get down to the splendid cause that brings us together this evening." Not a sound beyond Ivanov's voice was audible in the drawing room, not a cough, a whisper, nor the clink of a champagne glass. Nothing. They were still, as he wanted them. Silent and obedient. "The King Abdulaziz Foundation carries out its crucial work in the name of His Majesty's legacy: to alleviate disease and poverty the world-over and preserve the vibrant cultural heritage of Islamic antiquity." His Lordship spoke mostly from the cuff, spinning the details as he went. "Today, on the very doorstep of our continent, we bear witness to a caliber of human suffering previously thought to be rendered by our international systems as a distasteful relic of the past: a half-million souls lost, nine million displaced from their homes, genocide, wholesale slaughter, the use of weapons declared *abhorrent* by civilized people, children gassed in their beds, writhing in agony on our television screens." Ivanov brushed his hair to the side as he thought up the next bit... He had it. "And we watched until the bitter end. We waited until intervention was not just unavoidable, but crucial for our own security, and only then did we not avert our gaze from that horrid chapter of history.

"Ladies and gentlemen, *mesdames et messieurs,* the people of Syria are tired of waiting—they languish, whilst we thrive... But no more. Out of their benevolent and full hearts, the House of Saud has launched an unprecedented effort to alleviate their suffering and bring some modicum of hope into their lives. In the past year alone, the King Abdulaziz Foundation has partnered with the UNHCR and *Médecins Sans Frontières* to supply twenty-five thousand chemical toilets, drill numerous wells and deliver three field hospitals to the Zaatari and Mrajeeb al-Fhood refugee camps in Jordan. However, their work will continue into the foreseeable future as civilized people clean up the mess from the single greatest humanitarian catastrophe of our time. Their latest endeavor, in concert with the German Technical Cooperation and UNESCO, is to restore the Old City of Aleppo brick-by-brick, exactly as it was before the first shot was fired. Your gifts this evening will go directly to that effort, ensuring that this crucial work to preserve a vital and an earliest piece of our collective past continues without delay."

Ivanov paused and moved his hand into his inner jacket pocket.

The blue flies hadn't uttered a sound. This was it.

"And to demonstrate my solidarity with the foundation's cause and my belief in their mission, please allow me to make the first contribution." He removed a cheque and handed it to the prince. "One billion pounds."

Their silence held for a moment, processing it all, before the blue flies let loose a gasp, and then thunderous applause. Prince Farid was genuinely taken aback, his *ghutrah* had damn near slid off his head in the rush to smack his arthritic hands together. Their applause continued for what seemed like an eternity, but Ivanov kept his place next to the fire, letting it bleed into his pores. He had set the bar rather high. The blue flies' state was becoming a bit awkward and Ivanov checked his watch—there was still business to attend to and he needed those people out of his house.

"Ladies and gentlemen, please," he put his hands out to calm them. "Please, I beg you." And they gradually complied again, into silence. "I'm told my household has been good enough to prepare dinner. An *Amuse-bouche,* game *consommé* and braised venison?" he asked to the butler standing in a corner, who nodded. "Delightful," Ivanov looked the blue flies in the eyes, "I can only speak for myself, but I'm famished. Ladies and gentlemen, my man will come 'round with cards on which you may record your gift. In the meantime, please help yourself to more champagne."

The blue flies stirred as one amorphous mass toward the nearest glass of Bollinger, as was predictable. But Ivanov remained by the fire and watched them for a moment, brooding over a vast creation of his own grand design like the eyes of God.

Dinner was well-received—typically—and after another hour drifted past, the blue flies—as the script read—buttoned their overcoats, covered the bare shoulders of their glittering evening gowns from the elements, dipped into their chauffeured cars and went back from whence they came, leaving Ivanov and Prince Farid to handle the real business of the night— alone—in the library.

The library was wedged between the Drawing and French Dining rooms and paneled in rich cedar wood; Nancy Astor had taken to calling it the "cigar box" in her day. Anchoring the room in a corner was another carved marble fireplace, around which the two sat in high-back leather chairs. Three paintings were displayed in the library, and they were some of Ivanov's most prized possessions. On the far wall, shared with the Drawing Room, hung *Ivan the Terrible and His Son Ivan on November 16, 1581* by Ilya Repin. The work depicted the notorious emperor, his face fraught with ter-ror, as his bloodied son died quietly in his arms after he had lashed out in a fit of rage. On the opposite wall, shared with the dining room, was *Ruins After the Fire* by Paul Sandby, a watercolor showing the charred and gutted remains of Cliveden in the eighteenth century. And lastly, shown proudly over the fireplace, was a Versailles version of Jacques-Louis David's *Napoleon Crossing the Alps*—His Lordship made sure everyone saw it. The shelves were full of various rare editions he had collected at auction. Large sections were dedicated to the Classics, history, military strategy and economics, with special attention given to the greats of Russian literature: Tolstoy, Dostoyevsky, Turgenev, Bulgakov, Gogol, and Mayakovsky. Sitting on a table, near a window facing out over the parterre, was a first edition of Tolstoy's *What Is to Be Done?*, which sharply critiques Russian society in the late-nineteenth century. In fact, Ivanov saw himself as something of an expert in Russian literature, but it was little more than a desperate claim to a heritage which was never really his own. The truth being, Ivanov was hardly more Russian than Farid.

He was born in Neuilly-sur-Seine, 1931, to a member of the former tsarist aristocracy who had fled the Bolsheviks with his family as a teenager, and a daughter of a Swiss banking dynasty that reached back to the fourteenth century. His family fled Paris for Geneva when the Nazis invaded Holland—his mother's relatives were Jewish—where they remained even after the war. Ivanov, for his part, was educated at Le Rosey, the most uptight and privileged boarding school in the hemisphere, and later at Oxford. He then used the family business as a launch pad to found his investment firm, the Ivanov Group, and build the largest financial empire ever seen in private hands. When the question as to why he was a lifelong bachelor was inevitably posed, he would simply reply that he was married to business. And it was the truth: the two had a sweeping affair that spanned the decades. But there was little "Russian" about him, and to show for it he spent most of the Cold War with the KGB tracking his every move. Yet still, he saw those people as his own, and dreamed of a Russia that was "good for business;" not the chaos capitalism of Yeltsin's era, or the state-controlled, feudal oligarchies and brutism of Karetnikov's reign, but something much more agreeable, something much more Western—progressive, even. Ivanov felt it in his marrow that the Russians deserved salvation, and he was keen to be their savior.

"You've done an incredible thing for the people of Syria, Roman," the prince noted.

Ivanov took a Davidoff cigarette from the box sitting near his chair and lit it. "That warms my heart." He expelled a cloud from his lungs and flicked the ashes into the fire. "Are you staying the night?"

"No," Farid stroked the lapels of his *bisht*. "No, I don't think that will be possible."

"Pity," he sipped from a glass of Cognac *cuvée*. "Tell me, how is life in His Majesty's court? Is your brother stable? Happy in his work?"

"My brother has the disposition of a wrecking ball."

"Sometimes that's a relief."

"Clearly you haven't met my family." The prince cleared his throat. "My brother is fine. But our neighbors across the gulf have been making a noisy ruckus. And no one likes bad neighbors."

"We certainly don't." Ivanov took another drag and breathed, "Would you like to be king?"

The prince smiled uncomfortably. "I'm much too old—"

"I didn't ask if you could, I asked if you wanted."

Farid crossed his hands in his lap, subconsciously guarding himself. "Roman, what the hell was with the theatrics over that cheque? And when have you *ever* given a damn about Syria? Do you find me to be some common idiot?"

Ivanov tossed the cigarette into the flames. "I think it's time your noisy neighbors had their reckoning." Then he stood, looking the prince over. "Now don't you move a muscle." He went to the table where the copy of *What Is to Be Done?* sat, flipped to a particular page, and removed a few pieces of fine paper folded in thirds and tucked into the spine. "I do for you, and you do for me; that's how it used to work, anyway," Ivanov took his seat.

"What is that?"

Ivanov held the papers to his chest. "Before I give this to you, I need to provide some context."

"Please."

"I'm old, Farid, and I'm not long for this world. Neither of us is. But before I leave, I intend to shape the century."

"What are you—"

"Just listen. All I ask is that you listen. In my hands is a letter that I received this morning via urgent diplomatic pouch from the Russian embassy in Paris. The sender was Andrei Minin, an aide to Karetnikov." Ivanov lied through his teeth. "Andrei, the young chap, is a sort of protégé of mine. Tomorrow, he will be named as President Lavrov's new chief of staff and be granted oversight of the country's energy sector. You understand this had to be decided quietly, it being a period of national mourning, and all."

Prince Farid frowned. "That was awful, what happened to Karetnikov last night. Do send my sympathies."

"Yes, terrible tragedy that was," Ivanov blinked. "Listen, a momentous change is coming to Russia."

"What kind of change?"

"Karetnikov's thuggery is over; the mindless support of mass murderers for the sake of opposing the West is over; the detestable homophobic rhetoric, which serves no purpose, is over; the jailings, persecutions, and mysterious deaths are over. In their place: just good business." Ivanov passed the letter.

Prince Farid pressed the folds flat and began to read. It was handwritten and signed by Minin, and what it offered was nothing short of extraordinary.

"Moscow intends to join OPEC at the next meeting in Vienna, and Andrei would like His Majesty's blessing. In exchange, you will receive Russia's complete and total diplomatic abandonment of the Islamic Republic of Iran."

Farid stopped reading and looked up to Ivanov. The papers in his hands were trembling.

Ivanov snatched the papers back and threw them into the flames. His Lordship watched them burn and turn to ash before his eyes, floating lifelessly into the smoke. "Tell me, my old friend… Can you do me this one last favor?"

CHAPTER 16

"FUCK STESSEL," NINA resolved. She crushed the cigarette under her boot heel, burst into the villa on the north end of the embassy compound, and stormed down to the agency's vaulted offices. The station was nearly empty and only a few essential personnel remained, the rest having gone back to their apartments for the night.

As normal people do, Nina's better judgment scolded.

She retrieved the report from the safe by her desk and made a beeline for the communications room, quietly shutting the door behind her.

Sean Strickland, one of the station's comms officers, looked up behind him and breathed a pained sigh at what he saw. *"What...?"*

Nina held out the report. "I need this sent." She saw the time. "Now."

Strickland sighed again and took the report from her hand. He gave the page a glance, careful to divert his eyes from the content, even though he held all the proper clearances—it was a matter of principle. At the computer terminal before him he had full access to Intelink-TS, the secure intranet of the US Intelligence community, which was hosted on JWICS, the Joint Worldwide Intelligence Communications System. Intelink-TS was the most sensitive part of the network and was cleared to facilitate the sharing of intelligence products up to the Top Secret/Sensitive Compartmented Information (TS/SCI) level. Beyond that, there was nothing higher. "Uh, Stessel's initials aren't on here."

"I know that...and now you know that."

The Beirut station chief was a fierce micromanager and defender of his turf; nothing left the borders of his fiefdom without his approval, and that even went for the personnel not directly under his control, like Nina. Stessel refused to allow the "hearsay" that was TOPSAIL's story of Ibrahim al-Din roaming around Hezbollah's Security Quarter to reach Langley.

But Nina was done arguing with him.

"I can't send this. Here, take it. I never saw it, I never touched it!" Strickland tried to shove it back in her hand.

"Hey, just do it, okay?"

"This is going to C/CTC?"

"Yep."

He paused. "You're gonna get me in trouble again."

Nina slowly came forward and sat on his desk. "I'll make it up to you."

He looked up at her. "No, you won't."

"No, I mean it this time."

"Really?"

"Obviously." She rolled her eyes.

Another pained sigh. "Fine."

She jumped from the desk. "Thanks, cutie, you're the best!"

They called him "the Ferryman"—an allusion to the ancient Greek daemon that transported souls across the river Styx into the Underworld. It was only ever spoken out of earshot as they huddled in their cubicles, but he still knew. Yet it didn't bother him in the slightest. In fact, he found it flattering.

It was from his windowless office in the bowels of Langley that he dragged thousands of jihadi dead from this world to the next. On-demand, he watched the spectacles unfold on the television screen suspended to the far wall; and with each new smoke tendril that rose from a wooded valley in Pakistan, a desolate dirt road in Yemen, or an isolated camp in Syria, he would simply strike another from the list. It never seemed to shorten, but that wasn't his intention—he only sought to burn away the unsightly over-growth. And all the while, as he calmly watched them meet their end, he clutched a string of prayer beads, letting the tiny ivory globes slip through his fingers as he recited in his mind the ninety-nine names of God.

Roger Mathis, the chief of the CIA's Counterterrorism Center (C/CTC), was a scruffy and brooding figure in his late-fifties who wore a wardrobe made up almost exclusively of black suits from Sears. He had a personality like sandpaper, as many colleagues and subordinates would say; surly and irascible, but imbued with an unshakeable charisma, a fine attention to op-erational detail and a network of contacts that made him more indispensa-ble than any of the mid-level juju men at Langley. His first overseas assign-ments were in Africa, where he met a local woman, converted to Islam, married her, and later divorced her. The continent in those days had little to no interference from headquarters, and it acted as an incubator for Mathis to operate unrestrained, developing an encyclopedic knowledge of insur-gencies, tribal warfare and politics. After several decades in the field, he im-ported that mentality to the cube farms of suburban Virginia and ruthlessly carved out a subterranean empire for himself in the CTC. The advent of drones raining death on terrorists around the world was a product of that mentality. Mathis gave birth to the idea, nursed it through infancy, and looked on with pride as the terrorist networks he dedicated his life to decimating crumbled like dirt in his fist. He forced his enemies to choose between absent leaders or dead leaders, and neither option was ideal. Along the way he made his share of enemies throughout the Intelligence community, but found wary allies in dozens more. One, who gleefully latched on to his style, was Nina Davenport. Mathis not only brought Nina under his wing, eager to see her take his place one day, but forged their relationship into a formidable "bad cop/bad cop" tag team, with Mathis reigning in Langley, and her blazing through the field to, in her words, "convert heathens by the sword."

His office was stripped of any sign of a personal life. When he moved in seven years earlier his predecessor took away the plaques and vanity photographs, leaving the walls bare. Mathis kept it that way. His only addition was a large topographic map of the Syria-Iraq border and a hideaway bed jammed into a closet. Anything else would merely be a distraction. The object of his focus, often through the night and into the creeping dawn, was a trio of computer monitors atop his desk which were connected to "pizza boxes"—a stack of five rectangular hard drives corresponding to the various databases of the NSA, DIA, FBI, NGA and NRO. He sat still at his desk—one of the rare occasions that day—and combed through the mass of operational cables and analytical reports that streamed in from disparate outposts around the planet and a host of office buildings lodged between Baltimore and Norfolk. A system of filters and auto-indexing helped Mathis make sense of it all, and each new message announced its arrival onto the preview pane of IBM Notes with a bright red banner.

A new dispatch from Beirut snagged his attention.

He opened the cable and read it over four times for clarity, faster with each pass. A second later, with a click of his mouse, two copies of the cable materialized on one of three printers in his office, which was labeled orange for handling TS/SCI information. He reached for the nearest manila folder within arm's length and dashed from his office.

Outside, the Counterterrorism Center was plagued with the weary pandemonium of a casino floor at dawn: never peaking, nor truly subsiding. The main hall was a wide, cavernous room bursting with cubicles that dominated most of the floor space in the basement of the New Headquarters Building (NHB). There were no windows or references to the world beyond (such luxuries were a security risk) and the entire hall was perpetually drenched in a synthetic, fluorescent glow. In the maze of cubicles, it had become difficult to locate colleagues as little as a few feet away. Rather, the landmarks for the legion of analysts, operational managers, and support staff who made the room a second home were numerous street signs directing the way to exotic destinations such as, "Zawahiri Way," or "Haqqani Highway," and "ISIS Aisle." As Mathis expertly breezed through the maze, he caught in the corner of his eye a quiet, neglected cluster of cubicles, over which rose a sign that read, "Al-Din Drive."

NHB, the newer of the two main buildings on campus, consisted of two six-story glass office towers connected by a large central atrium. An elevator brought Mathis up four levels to the surface. He went through the atrium, past the courtyard and the cafeteria, to the Old Headquarters Building (OHB). A second elevator delivered him directly to the wood-paneled corridors of the seventh floor. With a flash of his badge to security—although it wasn't necessary with his reputation—he rounded a corner into the office of Grace Shaw, the deputy director for operations (DDO) and his immediate superior. She looked up from her desk, chewing on the temple of her reading glasses.

"Boss in?"

"Yeah."

"Need to see him."

"Why?"

Mathis pointed to the manila folder under his arm. "Nina Davenport says TOPSAIL possibly had eyes on Ibrahim al-Din."

"Let's go." Shaw sprang from her chair and bounded into the corridor with Mathis in tow. She took a copy of the cable and read it through. They waved themselves around the pair of secretaries, past the director's conference and dining rooms, and straight into the D/CIA's office.

Ryan Freeman looked up, chewing on the temple of his reading glasses.

Shaw gave the introduction. "Nina Davenport says TOPSAIL possibly had eyes on Ibrahim al-Din."

Freeman planted his face in his palms. "Jesus Christ, this day won't end." In the twenty-four hours since Mikhail Karetnikov's death, eighteen were spent shuttling between his desk and the conference room, four at the White House and only two at home to shower and not quite sleep, but rather slip below the threshold of what could be considered consciousness. "To the couch."

They went to the sofa and chairs set around a coffee table where Freeman found himself doing most of his work.

"This just came in, sir," said Mathis, taking a seat opposite the director. "I haven't even had time to tell the branch chiefs."

"We could call and send them up," Shaw added.

"No, that's fine. Just let me see." Freeman took the second copy of the cable and read it to himself, drowning out their commentary in his mind. It flowed in the typical style of reporting to come from Beirut since Nina's arrival. Her fingerprints were all over it.

EYES ONLY C/CTC FROM CTC/BEIRUT
LATEST MEETING WITH ASSET AM/TOPSAIL
1. ASSET HAD URGENT NEWS ON HEZB PULLBACK, ISLAMIC RE-SISTANCE DISARMAMENT. CONFIRMED ADDITIONAL COMINT/HUMINT/OSINT REPORTS THAT SG HAMAWI WILL HONOR AGREEMENT TO INTEGRATE ISLAMIC RESISTANCE WITH LAF PENDING OUTCOME OF ISRAELI/SYRIAN NEGOTIATIONS. CONFIDENT THAT HEZB PRIORITY IS PRESERVATION/CREDIBILITY IN PUBLIC EYE. PREDICTED MINIMAL IRANIAN INTERFERENCE IN LEBANON.
2. ASSET REPORTS SUSPECT OF HEZB INT INVESTIGATION RE MISSING IRGC AID FUNDS IS WITH JIHAD AL-BINNA FOUNDA-TION WESTERN BEQAA BRANCH. CONFIRMED THAT TWO DAYS PRIOR, ARMED HEZB CI FORCES SEALED AREA AROUND BRANCH OFFICE IN MACHGARA, REMOVED HARD DRIVES, FILES. ASSET PREDICTS WALID RADA, BRANCH DIRECTOR, IS FOCUS OF INT INVESTIGATION AND MAY BE ARRESTED.
3. ASSET WAS HESITANT BUT REVEALED SPOTTING A MAN IN HEZB SECURITY QUARTER OF DAHIEH, BEIRUT, TWO DAYS PRI-OR, MATCHING LAST-KNOWN PHYSICAL DESCRIPTION OF IBRAHIM AL-DIN, COMMANDER OF HEZB ISLAMIC JIHAD ORGANIZATION. ASSET WAS ADAMANT OF THIS. IF CONFIRMED WOULD BE FIRST SIGHTING OF AL-DIN IN TWENTY-THREE YEARS.
4. REQUEST THAT WALID RADA BE CONSIDERED A POTENTIAL RECRUITMENT TARGET. REQUEST THAT ASSET BE ALLOWED TO INVESTIGATE POSSIBILITY OF IBRAHIM AL-DIN PRESENCE IN SOUTH BEIRUT.
5. FORTY THOUSAND PAID TO ASSET.

Freeman dropped the folder on the table and furiously massaged the bridge of his nose. "Hold on, start with the aid money. We're talking—what?—two million?"

Mathis nodded. "Two million US and change, sir. Cash."

Shaw leaned in. "We're talking about the same funds once flown in regularly from Tehran to Damascus in a diplomatic pouch, and then disbursed directly to Hezbollah's aid organizations on the ground. The money rarely, if ever, passed through party command and control."

"That's why it's taking them so long to audit."

Freeman was a bit calmer. "And this cash went missing last month?"

"Approximately," said Mathis.

"So, let's say, hypothetically, Walid Rada buried this cash under some field in the Beqaa Valley for a rainy day. Why would *our* money make him more agreeable?"

"We can give him a better umbrella," C/CTC said flatly.

Freeman grinned. "Okay, let's stop there. Now the Elvis sighting."

Shaw could only shrug her shoulders. "Ryan, we have the commander of the Internal Security Forces' Intelligence Bureau swearing up and down that he saw—first hand—Ibrahim al-Din in the Security Quarter. That's a pretty damn good Elvis. And what have we had? For twenty-three years, what have we had?"

"Director Freeman, what the cable didn't say, for OPSEC, was that TOPSAIL was walking out of Wissam Hamawi's office when he saw this guy."

Freeman nodded and crossed his legs, pressing back into the cushions. "I agree—with all of it. We should recruit Walid Rada, if only to say we did it. We should dust off al-Din's file, because what the hell else have we had? But here's the problem—with all of it: It's in Lebanon. And right next to Lebanon is Syria, and right below it is Israel. And that's where it'll stop."

"Sir—"

"Hear me out, Roger," he said, jabbing the folder. "I'll take this to the White House because I think it's worth a try, but we already know the answer."

Mathis and Shaw did know, although they let Freeman say it.

"While Israel and Syria are at the table, there is no appetite to let us run around Beirut and pick people off the streets. We're mediators, not agitators—until such time as that changes, anyway. I'll get us an audience with Tanner, hopefully tomorrow, to discuss this. In the meantime, Roger, get your people on this and let's make sure we got it down. Cable Nina Davenport back and tell her she's in a holding pattern. Okay?"

"That's fine, sir."

"Thank you, Roger," Freeman nodded as C/CTC left the way he came.

Shaw shut the door behind Mathis and went back to the chair opposite her boss. "I know this must be hard for you."

"Bullshit's an acquired taste."

Shaw smirked. "Go home. I got it here."

"You should, too."

"Eh, I got a few more things."

"What's the word on Mehdi Vaziri?"

"Paris COS is getting transcripts of the debriefings—unredacted; P.S., you're welcome—he should get the first batch in the morning."

"Good."

Shaw looked down to her lap and twiddled her thumbs. "Courier's coming in from Dubai with CITADEL's report around midnight. I'll wait here for it."

Freeman sighed and went for his coat. "If he says anything other than, 'The ayatollah wishes to go to Disney,' I'll blow an aneurism. Call me."

"Sure thing. Bye, boss."

• • •

Emirates Flight 205 came in low over the farm fields of Loudoun County. On schedule, at eleven-thirty, the Boeing 777 was cleared for landing on runway 1C at Dulles and skidded to a controlled halt before taxiing to its allotted gate at Concourse A. Persia House's operations officer, one of the few bodies still alert after fourteen hours locked in a pressurized can, stood and stretched his legs as business class began to clear out. Tucked away in his jacket pocket, the titanium cigarette case remained out of sight for the duration of the flight. He grabbed his bag from the overhead compartment and joined the slow procession up the jetway into the terminal. With a confident wave of his diplomatic passport, he bypassed the herd at customs and continued on to the terminal's entrance, where he hopped a shuttle to the blue economy parking lot. A nondescript Chevy Impala with a key taped in the wheel well had been left for him.

The officer merged onto the Dulles Toll Road, a wide corridor lined with lifeless office towers, and took Exit 19B for Dolley Madison Boulevard. At Langley's gatehouse, he presented the pass placed in the glove box and parked in a space near the front entrance of the Old Headquarters Building. He strode over the large granite agency seal inlaid on the main lobby floor and slid through the row of electronic gates. The officer made his way to Corridor C and stopped at a heavy, cypher-locked door up a slight ramp. Behind it was the Iran Operations Division. He navigated through the rows of empty cubicles and found the office of the division chief, Peter Stavros, and placed the message in his hands. After forty-eight hours in transit, CITADEL's words were finally home.

Freeman checked the time on no fewer than three-dozen occasions in the last hour. Still, the ticking hands of the grandfather clock in their library were grating. He tried to distract himself but he noticed few avenues of escape. His wife, Mary, sat near him, but her focus was on the stack of midterm papers in her lap. He already read the *Times* and the *Post* cover-to-cover, and naturally had a decent idea of what they might say tomorrow. The D/CIA fidgeted in his chair like a toddler. "How's class?"

Mary Freeman knew exactly what she signed up for when she agreed to marry an intelligence officer. She didn't feel deceived in the slightest, nor did she let it show that it bothered her. But it bothered her. Her husband had been gone for an entire day—and she knew why—but, like a mobster, any talk of business at home was strictly off-limits. It wasn't illegal, just a state secret. That left her and her husband talking exclusively about *her* business. Mary was an assistant professor and the Villani Chair in Economics at Georgetown College. She taught two classes that semester, a freshman-level international trade class and a PhD seminar. She sighed, drowning a defenseless cover page in red ink, "I think we need some work. But, if you're at Georgetown and confuse 'your' and 'you're'—on every page—I think it has more to do with your parents' bank account than your SAT scores."

"Did Val get a call-back for the part?" Their only child, Valerie, was in her final year at Juilliard in New York and was desperately auditioning to play Desdemona in a production of *Othello* at the Lincoln Center that summer.

"I think she hears next week. You know, I've been wondering about how we'll manage her apartment. Queens is sorta affordable—"

Just then a monotone chirping flooded the room. They both stared for a moment at the STE secure telephone squawking on a corner table.

"Are you gonna let it ring?" She watched her husband answer and place his hand on his flushed forehead.

"Okay—okay," she heard him say. "I'm coming in now." Ryan slowly put the phone down and gazed at the floor. He looked like was about to be sick.

"Go," she allowed. "I'll be here when you get back. I always will."

CHAPTER 17

HE WASN'T TOLD much. He didn't need to be. He already knew.

The slow ascent from the executive parking garage to the seventh floor was agonizing. Freeman closed his eyes and breathed as he listened to the cables hoist him up toward the truth. It was the only rest he would have for hours. Then, with a polite chime, the doors slid open, and his sanctuary was gone.

Shaw waited for him with the bitter expression of a failed surgeon. She broke the news. "Iran is building a bomb."

"That had better be a fucking joke." Before the words even left his mouth, he realized how hollow they were.

"Come on," she beckoned him through the doors. "Pete's in my office."

Peter Stavros, chief of the Iran Operations Division (C/IOD), spun his head around as Freeman slammed the door behind them and tossed his coat over a chair. He watched the D/CIA pace for a moment.

"What did he say?" Freeman asked.

Shaw passed him a folder bordered in red- and white-striped tape. It was one of three copies she had made herself. The original nitrocellulose pages that Jack Galloway had printed in Tehran now sat as confetti inside a burn bag on Stavros's desk and were bound for the incinerator.

Raw CITADEL information, straight from the pen of Saeed Mofidi, was classified as Special Intelligence/Eyes Only-Σ. Only six individuals in the agency were cleared for Σ data. Beyond the three in the room, they were limited to Jack Galloway, who handled Mofidi and processed all of his messages; the deputy director for intelligence (DD/I); and the head of the Office of Iran Analysis, who were both charged with digesting Mofidi's words into the larger trawl of secrets that the CIA gleaned from Iran. The intelligence obtained from CITADEL had a slightly wider audience and was categorized under the digraph "SD," which denoted Iranian collection operations, and was assigned a code word, or "crypt," which changed monthly. It was currently MONARCH. Still, the number of individuals with access to SD/MONARCH information remained under one hundred—remarkably small for the mammoth US Intelligence community. The reasoning for the stringent classification was not to hoard the intelligence itself, but to defend the source and keep him alive. It was said that there are many old or bold spies, but not both. Saeed Mofidi was a magnificently rare exception to that rule. For that reason, that fearful inevitability, Freeman viciously guarded access to the elite Σ fraternity. Even the DNI or the national security advisor did not have the slightest clue of CITADEL's identity, nor did they care to find out. Freeman's intransigence was not a byproduct of distrust. Rather, they were better off not knowing all the sources and methods; they had no need to lay their eyes on the crown jewels.

Dispatches from the jewel in the agency's crown always sounded with a familiar overture. Just as Milton began *Paradise Lost* with an invocation of the Heavenly Muse, so too did CITADEL seek divine guidance on his mission. Freeman's eyes glided effortlessly over the words, and as with each message, he found himself taken aback by Saeed Mofidi's pure gall and determination, forged by the meltdown of a father's broken heart.

In the name of Almighty God, the Most Gracious and Merciful, Freeman read, *I eagerly await the day when judgment is brought upon the individuals who have, for so long, thrived on the torment of others; the individuals who, by callous indifference, destroyed what I loved most in this world with one hand, and asked me to serve with the other. So what outlet is afforded to my grief? By what means may I execute the sin of vengeance? I find our enduring friendship to be the most appropriate weapon. And although under political law our friendship is labeled treason, under natural law—the law of Almighty God—it can be deemed none other than long-overdue atonement. Either by my hands, our hands, or some unknown X, I can only have faith in the long arc of Almighty God's will that it will be done— and through Him, realized. And on that day, I can do little more but pray that my own sins; my years of accomplice, my years of feigned ignorance and servitude; can yet be forgiven, and my soul saved. After all, my friends, nothing lasts forever. But in the meantime, I have found an unsound answer to your question...*

Mofidi described it all without reservation: Ayatollah Khansari's waning health, Iran's reaction to Hezbollah's disarmament, the coming talks with Syria, and the exposed state in which it left Iran; the disappearance of Mehdi Vaziri and the growing manhunt to track him down; the meeting with Qasem Shateri and his eagerness to dictate policy from the field; the Quds Force's plan to double support to Hamas and PIJ, and the massive arms shipment that was currently bound for Sudan. Finally, Mofidi laid out Shateri's response to a direct question about the progress at Haj Ali Gholi: Dr. Fakhrizadeh had extracted fifty kilograms of plutonium-239 and was planning to construct and test a device in the summer. It didn't take an expert mind to discern what that device would be.

Freeman dropped the file on Shaw's desk. "Dr. Fakhrizadeh?"

"That's what it says," Shaw replied.

"Dr. *Alireza* Fakhrizadeh?"

"There's only one we know of, sir," said Stavros.

"He's dead. I saw the goddamn pictures!"

Shaw wiped her brow. "Apparently not, Ryan."

"Sir, we need to seriously consider the facts," Stavros stood. "If the IRGC has extracted enough plutonium for a crude atomic weapon—"

"Five, by my count, Pete!"

"Then, sir, it would stand to reason that Monet would likely comprise a twenty-megawatt reactor—perhaps of the Magnox design, like at Yongbyon—alongside a reprocessing facility of some size and fabrication workshops. Picasso, meanwhile, is likely a test site…for their first device. The construction we've observed at both sites, the rock overburden and geology, would all support that assertion. The evidence fits."

"And Fakhrizadeh was their man to accomplish all of this," said Shaw."

"*Is,*" Freeman corrected, and slumped into the chair behind her desk. He stared at some undetermined point for a moment before snapping back to reality. "We need to get an advisory about that arms shipment to our liaison at CENTCOM J2, now."

"It's done, Ryan."

Freeman reached for the file and began to read again, assuring himself that it was real. "This changes everything. Absolutely everything." He slowly shook his head in disbelief. "Let's make some calls."

At 1:16 A.M., Freeman reached Geoffrey Sheridan, the director of national intelligence; by 1:52, senior analysts and branch chiefs from Persia House, the Counterproliferation Center, and the Weapons Intelligence, Nonproliferation and Arms Control Center (WINPAC) began to fill the empty parking lots that radiated out from the Old Headquarters Building while similar procedures were underway at Fort Meade, Chantilly, Tysons Corner, Fort Belvoir, Bolling Air Force Base, Foggy Bottom and the Pentagon; at approximately three o'clock, a secure conference call was initiated by the DNI with members of IC/EXCOM—the Intelligence Community Executive Committee—which consisted of Freeman, the directors of the NSA, DIA, NGA, NRO, and their relevant underlings; at 4:23, Eli Tanner, the national security advisor, was awoken at his home along the Chesapeake Bay; by five o'clock, items on President Paulson's schedule were being hastily canceled and rearranged as the secretaries of state and defense were notified; at 5:15, a Secret Service agent knocked on the president's bedroom door; and by seven that morning, with the first rays of sunlight hidden behind the clouds, a fleet of armored, black Suburbans were wedged between the gates at opposite ends of West Executive Drive like Tetris tiles.

The walls of the main briefing area in the White House Situation Room were covered in off-white fabric and polished cherry wood molding, resembling the offices of a quaint Midwest law firm. Six flat-panel monitors were mounted on the far wall, which displayed the latest overhead imagery of Monet and Picasso complemented by annotated graphics. Freeman kept his head down and continuously reread his notes like the awkward "new kid" in a school cafeteria. Around him, the regulars at the table made small talk and, for now, allowed the D/CIA to keep his lunch money. Freeman had been in senior positions at the agency long enough for their mystique to fade; they were no longer just talking heads on his television screen, as most in the country knew them, but actual sentient beings who, when assembled, were inarguably some of the most powerful people in recorded history. But Freeman didn't quite feel comfortable enough to label them as colleagues. Vice President Brandon Jacobs—easily the loudest voice in the room—sat near the head of the table, just to the right of where his boss would soon appear. Descending from that point, the chieftains gradually faded in seniority, which in that room was extremely relative. Secretary of State Angela Weisel, the president's favorite disciple and a national celebrity in her own right, came next. Her blond hair was still damp, as Freeman could see, but her pantsuit was immaculately pressed and she allowed herself only short responses to Jacobs' pointless banter. Out of the bunch, Freeman easily respected her the most—and woe betide the soul that dared cross her. Third highest in the political pantheon came Henry Rusk, the secretary of defense, who unfortunately for him, was left grounded by a blizzard at his ranch in Telluride, Colorado. His face appeared on one of the monitors, wearing an open-collar Oxford shirt and sipping from an oversized coffee mug. In the secretary's designated chair sat the chairman of the Joint Chiefs of Staff, Admiral Lloyd Benson, a career naval aviator whose blue service dress uniform carried a small constellation of stars. Opposite the admiral was Geoffrey Sheridan, and to the right of him sat Freeman, who was slightly more than midway down the table: not fully accepted into the rarified stratosphere, yet not relegated to the lesser caste around the bottom half. Reaching to the end of the table was the deputy chief of staff for operations, the national security advisor to the vice president, and the White House counsel.

Freeman silently rehearsed his lines as Sheridan leaned closer to his shoulder.

"Do you have this? I need you to have this," the DNI whispered.

"Well, I don't intend to projectile vomit or say anything overtly racist, so, yes, I think I 'have this.'"

"Fine."

"Fine."

Just then, the senior watch officer opened the door and announced, "Ladies and gentlemen, the president."

On the most primal, muscle instinct—as a flinch or a sneeze—everyone around the table immediately stood. Andrew Paulson confidently breezed in, trailed by Eli Tanner and Larry Dawson, his chief of staff. "Please have a seat." And they did, while the president took his familiar perch at the head. "Thank you, everyone, for coming in so early and on such short notice. I'd rather we dispense with the nonsense and just get to it." Paulson opened a leather portfolio and glanced over the contents before drawing his eyes up. "Who's first?"

Tanner, who now sat at the president's left, cleared his throat. "Uh, sir, we'll start with Dr. Sheridan, who will bring us up to speed from your previous briefing, and then move to Director Freeman who can inform us on this morning's developments."

"Sounds good," the president shot his gaze down the table. "Geoff, go."

Freeman noticed Sheridan drop his voice register down slightly from its natural place. "Mr. President, as you are aware, early last week, a reconnaissance satellite detected signs of a previously unknown subterranean facility bordering the Haj Ali Gholi dry lakebed in Semnan Province, approximately two hundred miles east of Tehran. The latest overhead shots of the facility are on the forward screen. The facility itself is contained within a valley just off the lakebed, and the primary observable features are two northern and southern tunnel portals which we have designated Monet and Picasso, respectively. The Monet portal, as you can see, is fabricated with poured concrete and steel rebar. A manned guard post sits at the entrance, and there is a paved road leading into the tunnel. These key features, in addition to vehicle traffic which we have positively identified during evening hours, leads us to judge with high confidence that Monet has been complete and fully operational for some time." Sheridan paused to turn a page in his prepared notes. "Now as for Picasso, situated about one kilometer south of Monet, we see more observable features." The image on the screen zoomed to the appropriate portal. "It is still clearly a construction site. The two brownish ovals you see are spoil piles—mounds of excavated earth—which cover some five hundred square meters and likely, our analysts judge, contain approximately one thousand cubic-meters of crushed rock. This leads us to believe, based on the level of activity we've observed, that construction of Picasso began late last year, sometime between October and December. Interestingly, construction at Picasso, as well as activity at Monet, happens exclusively at night; the entire facility seems to suspend operations during the day, which makes any quantifiable surveillance rather tricky. Construction equipment at Picasso is stored under this camouflage netting *here.* Also, leading into the tunnel is a small rail line for mining carts, which transport the spoil material from the mountain.

"Since discovery of the site, our analysts have been largely puzzled as to its mission. We briefly considered the possibility that we're looking at an alternate command post, but the lack of aboveground support infrastructure and perimeter security would not aid that conclusion. Likewise, the geography of the mountain and the type of construction underway would not suggest an additional enrichment plant. We also looked at the possibility that it could be a missile development and explosives testing site, but the relative isolation from other primary R&D facilities—Parchin, Simorgh, Tabriz—made that a stretch. Most puzzling to us is the fact that the facility appears to be staffed by a skeleton crew. A single cargo aircraft, likely from Mehrabad Airport in Tehran, supplies the site. Of course, this suggests a very tight compartmentalization, which would naturally lead us to believe that more nefarious activities are underway inside the mountain. And, with that, I will hand it over to Director Freeman."

Now it was Freeman's turn to fall face-first into the fire. Up the table, the president and his loftiest disciples hadn't made a sound. If they had nothing to say, he thought, that would change very soon. "Thank you, Dr. Sheridan. Um, Mr. President, just to build upon something that the DNI said, what led us to discover the site was the construction, at Picasso, however what drew us in, what piqued our interest—excuse me," Freeman coughed, "from an analytical standpoint, was the tradecraft that we observed, the very clear and deliberate efforts to camouflage against our surveillance. CIA's in-house imagery experts have been poring over every scrap of overhead data that we could get, twenty-four hours straight, since we ID'd it. I had several task forces reassigned just for that purpose. We passed it around to DIA, NGA, the J2 directorates at STRATCOM, DTRA, JSOC, and CENTCOM for a second opinion—nothing. We were stumped. So, after my second briefing on the site, which I believe was seventy-two hours after discovery, we tasked our primary HUMINT asset in Tehran to see what might fall out if we shook the tree a bit, if you will. As you know, sir, that's not a decision I make lightly. This is an asset we use quite sparingly, and typically we wait for the asset to contact us, rather than pass requirement after requirement just to fill every collection gap we have. The reason being is, we don't want to place the asset in an unnecessary, compromising position."

"So what happened?" the president asked.

"Right, sir. Five days later, the asset made contact with our handler in Tehran and the report entered the courier chain to make its way to us. Security constraints force us to rely on a system of cut-outs and couriers—it's slow, but it's safer than any method of transmitting electronically. And it arrived this morning, just after midnight." Freeman lifted a thin stack of papers and passed it to Sheridan who took one and had it circulate around the table. "Coming around to you is a one-page summary of the MONARCH report we received." It was a bullet-pointed version of CITADEL's lengthy letter, stripped of any personal qualities and rewritten in dry, sterile English.

Jacobs, who either finished reading first, or simply could not keep quiet, slapped the page on the table. "Christ, Andrew!" he crossed his arms.

"Let's just listen," Paulson assured. "Director Freeman, please continue."

"Quite admirably," Freeman breathed, realizing he crossed the point of no return, "our asset raised the topic during a discussion with a very senior officer of the Revolutionary Guards. Our asset posed the question presumably on behalf of a higher official as to avoid suspicion. The wording—the exact framing of the question as reported back—was to 'inquire on the progress at Haj Ali Gholi.' That was all our asset said, no further prodding. The senior IRGC officer responded with a question: 'Project 260?' which we interpret to be the operation's cover designation. Now, the direct response from this senior officer, who our asset reported seemed flustered and surprised by this question was, as written to us: 'I would be honored to inform'—the higher official; name redacted—'that Dr. Fakhrizadeh has extracted fifty kilograms of plutonium-239 and the appropriate amount of tritium. God willing, he intends to assemble and test a device in the summer.' That was it. No further information was offered to our asset, who likewise did not pursue it. The meeting, as reported to us, ended almost immediately thereafter."

"And that's all we have?" said the president.

"Well yes, sir," Freeman reluctantly nodded, "but from those two sentences we can deduce an incredible amount of detail."

"Please elaborate."

"Of course, sir. The keywords here being: 'Project 260, Dr. Fakhrizadeh, fifty kilos of plutonium-239, and tritium.' That alone provides a huge window in which to analyze. So, Mr. President, unless there are any immediate questions, I would like to first explain what we could infer from the scientific and technical side, and then provide detail on the individual who, we believe, was mentioned by this senior IRGC official."

Paulson consented with a wave of his hand.

"Mr. President, CIA is prepared to hypothesize that the facility in question, specifically the Monet portal, houses a nuclear reactor to reprocess plutonium from spent uranium fuel rods, a facility to conduct reprocessing using the PUREX procedure, and a fabrication workshop; the Picasso portal, in all likelihood, is an incomplete underground test site."

"Is this definitive, Ryan?" asked Weisel.

"No, ma'am," he assured. "Our findings, as of yet, are by no means conclusive, but our analysts—given the source and what we can see on the ground—are pretty confident. I trust their opinion, and I would not share it with you all this morning unless I did. So, to get into the technical side of things, what we believe we have here is a 'natural uranium, graphite-moderated, carbon dioxide cooled-reactor,' with a power capacity of approximately twenty megawatts. We've seen a reactor of this same design used to extract plutonium at North Korea's Yongbyon center and the Syrian government's attempted project at al-Kibar. Both reactors were based on declassified blueprints of the Calder Hall Magnox design, and we believe that the same is true here. How this reactor operates is fairly straightforward: the fuel rods are natural uranium-238—that's unenriched, so the centrifuge issue wouldn't necessarily apply here, past what they've already demonstrated—containing point-five percent aluminum and clad in a magnesium canister, containing point-five percent zirconium. Surrounding each fuel rod is what's called a 'graphite moderator,' which has to be constructed to a very high and specific purity—not easily obtained. Connected to the reactor vessel is a 'heat exchanger'—this design would feature two—which injects cool water and then disposes the energy produced by operation in the form of hot water. The reactor core itself would be located inside a steel canister, further placed within a thick cement encasement. Located directly adjacent to the reactor hall would be a reprocessing facility, utilizing 'hot cells,' which are shielded radiation containment chambers. Irradiated fuel from the reactor would be brought here, where the rods are essentially chopped apart and dissolved in nitric acid. From that process, plutonium-239, enriched to at least ninety-five percent purity, is extracted." Freeman stopped reading for a moment. "Is everyone still with me, so far?"

And there were nods all around.

"Okay," the D/CIA continued. "A reactor of this size, if operated efficiently, would produce roughly ten kilograms of plutonium-239 each year, enough for a crude, improvised nuclear device with a yield of maybe one kiloton. Assuming the information given to our asset is current and accurate, given fifty kilograms, this reactor would have been operational for about five years, and Iran would presently hold the fissile material for four, possibly five such weapons."

"May I stop you right there, Ryan?" Tanner raised his hand.

"Yeah, please. What's your question?"

"I'm a little amazed here. They built this inside a mountain? A reactor? A reactor with radiation, and incredible levels of heat, and gases, and nasty chemicals—I mean, nitric acid? And what about the support infrastructure? Water, air filtration, all of that. It's a desert we're staring at."

"No, that's a great point. We've observed attempts to reduce the size of this reactor design before—the Syrians with al-Kibar is a prime example—but none have placed it underground, until now. Uh, let me try and briefly illustrate how such a facility would look if we carved that mountain away:

Essentially, the entire reactor facility could be placed within a concrete box fifty-by-fifty meters in length. Inside that box you would have the reactor, the two heat exchangers, and a spent fuel pond. That's just the reactor hall. The processing plant, workshops, dormitories, and other support structures would add to the scope, but not by much. Carving out a chamber of that size within a mountain, while difficult, is far from impossible. The real technical achievement is getting the materials to such an isolated site undetected."

Admiral Benson chimed in, looking up at the image on the screen. "They must've hauled in the cement by the spoonful."

"That's right, sir," the D/CIA agreed. "If you take a look at the geology report we've prepared," he held up a copy, "and I should add that the findings have been seconded by AFTAC and Los Alamos—you'll see that located some distance beneath this general region is a fairly large aquifer. It wouldn't be a stretch to surmise the existence of a pumping station in the facility which draws water up to the reactor and discharges it back into the aquifer. This would solve the problem of a lack of surface water at the site, while making detection extraordinarily difficult. And as for air filtration, as the national security advisor mentioned, reactors require ventilation to carry away radioactive gasses emitted from the reactor core. In a conventional design, this is accomplished with a smoke stack—easily spotted by our recon birds. However, it would be possible to use a system of filters and intakes to disperse these gases into the atmosphere through a series of vents which could be installed covertly—say, a false boulder—throughout the mountain. All of this has been accomplished before, and while it is certainly impressive, it is no technical feat. As we know, what is the work of geniuses the first time is the work of tinsmiths the second."

"Okay," the president nodded, digesting it all. "Okay."

"So, if I may, I'll continue."

"Go right ahead."

"The next item I wanted to touch upon," Freeman shifted his notes, "was the individual—'Dr. Fakhrizadeh'—mentioned by the senior IRGC officer. CIA suspects, unless there are two, and that's not quite possible, that the officer was referring to Alireza Fakhrizadeh, who until his supposed death in 2007, was the director of the Physics Research Center. The PHRC, as you may recall, sir, has since be renamed the 'Organization of Defensive Innovation and Research,' or SPND; which is the parallel branch of Iran's nuclear program tasked with developing a weapon. However, since 2003, all of their research, that we've been able to see, has been concerned with 'dual-use' technologies, which have both civil and military functions. Essentially, it's an excuse to keep their scientists working until the day comes when they decide to restart their weapons program."

"Which has already come and gone, you're saying," Jacobs interrupted.

"It's not quite so simple, Mr. Vice President. The Israelis are the authority on Fakhrizadeh's background, and even they don't know much. We believe he was born sometime in the early 1960s, was educated by the Soviets at Chelyabinsk-70, was an IRGC officer, and held a teaching position at Imam Hossein University in Tehran. His expertise—and this always disturbed us—was in shaping the high-explosive lenses that are placed around a plutonium core in an implosion-type nuclear weapon. To quickly jump back into the technical side, this design utilizes an explosive tamper—the lenses—detonated at the exact same time to compress the plutonium core inward—an implosion—to produce a critical mass and a fission chain reaction. These lenses are notoriously difficult to fabricate, as to achieve full critical mass they have to be sculpted to such a fine exactness in angle—much like eyeglasses, or nanodiamonds, which the SPND researches today. However, Fakhrizadeh's focus in the years prior to the nuclear program being shelved was the development of a neutron generator. That's the thing you need to make a nuke explode. Essentially, it's installed in the pit at the center of a plutonium core. When the explosive lenses detonate, it ionizes a wafer of deuterium." Freeman was relying entirely on his notes now; his comfort zone was tradecraft, not physics. "The blast forces the deuterium to bombard a target of tritium—this is all happening over a millisecond within the plutonium core. This produces a surge of neutrons, creating a chain reaction inside the core, starting a self-sustaining critical mass. The next thing you get is a mushroom cloud." Freeman looked up and saw them all watching him intently. He slowed down for the next part. "Basically, a neutron generator, the explosive lenses, they allow you to cause a nuclear explosion with less fissile material—plutonium—and would thus enable the construction of a physically smaller bomb. That was Alireza Fakhrizadeh's life work. He wanted to build a nuke that could fit inside a suitcase."

"And you are saying, Director Freeman, that this Alireza Fakhrizadeh did not meet his end in 2007?" the president asked.

"Unless there are somehow, miraculously, two Dr. Fakhrizadehs working at senior levels in the nuclear program under the IRGC, then, yes, that's exactly what I'm saying."

"And how did he die—the first time—if I may ask?"

Freeman didn't need notes to explain; he had been personally involved.

"Prior to 2007, Fakhrizadeh was on everyone's radar. He was subject to a travel ban and sanctions by the UN Security Council, the EU and the Treasury. The IAEA had asked to interview him several times on their trips to Tehran but couldn't get near him. Then in 2006, Mossad was trailing a Syrian *mukhabarat* officer who checked into the Lanesborough hotel in London. The Syrian went shopping at Harrods and stupidly left his laptop in the suite. Mossad broke in and mirrored the hard drive. On the drive, they found numerous pictures and schematics of an unfinished reactor complex in Syria at a place called al-Kibar, along the Euphrates. One of the pictures," Freeman reached into a file and removed a glossy photograph, "was this."

The photograph showed three middle-aged men standing side-by-side in front of a beige industrial façade. "This one on the left," Freeman pointed, "is Chon Chibu, director of the Yongbyon Nuclear Scientific Research Center; in the middle is the late director-general of the Syrian Atomic Energy Commission, Ibrahim Othmani; and on the right is our man, Dr. Alireza Fakhrizadeh." Freeman placed the photo back in the file.

"Of course," Freeman continued, "this intelligence culminated in Operation Orchard, September 2007, when the Israeli Air Force bombed the reactor at al-Kibar. For the Israelis, Fakhrizadeh's involvement in the project was the last straw. The prime minister ordered his assassination. A month later, before Mossad could complete the mission, Fakhrizadeh's Peugeot slid off an overpass onto the Hemmat Expressway in Tehran. The Peugeot caught fire and Fakhrizadeh was supposedly killed along with his driver and bodyguard. His death was one of the primary factors that led us to judge in our NIE that Iran's weapons program was shelved and would not be restarted in the near future."

"So he faked his death?" the Paulson asked.

"Think about it, sir. If someone is out to kill you, what better way to stop them than to beat them to it? And what better way to complete your work in peace and quiet than to make everyone believe you're dead? After al-Kibar was bombed, it's likely that he faked his death to get us off his tail, picked up the pieces, and started over again with his own copy of the reactor—this time under a mountain so we couldn't see it. The timing for construction and operation of the reactor to this point would fit that assessment. He would've had ample time by now to finish what he started. And I think that's what we're seeing, sir."

Paulson pressed himself back in the chair. "Okay, guys, what do we do?"

"Clearly we need to act," Jacobs yelped unpleasantly.

"Act how?" Weisel countered.

"Act to get rid of it. Now. Before this goes on any longer. I mean, how else are we supposed to interpret this? They lied to you, Angela. They sat there and they lied to you. They've lied to all of us!"

"Admiral?" Paulson looked down the table.

"Mr. President," Benson responded.

"If I asked your people to take this place out, how would you do it?"

The Joint Chiefs chairman studied the overhead image on the screen. "Sir, we could kill everyone in that place tomorrow if you ordered it. It's buried under six hundred feet of rock. That's a hard target. We could forward deploy a pair of B-2s from Whiteman to RAF Fairford. Hypothetically, the first aircraft would pass over the Med and Turkey, evade their air defenses, and drop a couple two-thousand-pounders on each portal. The warheads would suck the air out of the tunnels and set it on fire; no personnel could survive that. The second aircraft would follow in and drop a few GBU-57s—that's our Massive Ordnance Penetrator. They'd easily collapse both tunnels and bury anything inside. However, sir, without more concrete information," he turned to Freeman, "I cannot promise that the site would be completely unsalvageable."

"Sir," Secretary Rusk's voice came through the speakers, "with all due respect to the vice president, what we're talking about here is a massive contingency operation that would take months to properly plan and prepare—not to mention lay the groundwork diplomatically. You can't just fly in and out in a matter of hours. We're not the Israelis."

Freeman was relieved to hear Rusk speak sensibly.

"That's exactly right, Al," Weisel agreed.

"But they *lied* to you, Angela!" Jacobs persisted.

"In all likelihood, sir," Freeman heard himself say, "no, they didn't."

The vice president craned his neck to see the desolate reaches of the table. "And how's that, Director Freeman? You say Iran is building a bomb. They say they're not. Either you are wrong, or they are lying. Which is it?"

"It's neither, sir. Madam Secretary, Iran's foreign minister sat there in Lausanne and promised you no uranium enrichment past twenty percent, and they've done that; they promised the majority of centrifuges at Natanz and Fordow would be made inoperable, and they are; they promised no fuel would be transferred to the heavy water reactor at Arak, it hasn't; they allowed the IAEA daily access to Natanz and Fordow, and we all read the inspectors' reports. All of these points are verifiable and we continue to verify them. Madam Secretary, no one has lied to you. *Iran*—in the sense of that country's civilian policymakers, the people who would decide to restart a weapons program—is not building a nuclear bomb; Alireza Fakhrizadeh and someone over him in the Revolutionary Guards *are* building a bomb. And that is what we desperately need to find. You can't lie about something you have no knowledge of."

"That doesn't make sense, Ryan," Tanner disagreed. "How is it that Iran's leadership has no knowledge of this program? And how is it that your asset, if he in such a position to monitor the supreme leader, was totally unaware of this program until just a few days ago?

"Our asset first approached us in 2008, but was not in the post he currently occupies until 2010. That wouldn't put him in a position to be aware of this program until after it was authorized. Given Ayatollah Khansari's medical state, it wouldn't have come back across his desk until we tasked him to inquire about it. And I'm not comfortable saying much more."

"So, I'm getting that there's a lot more we need to know before we act?"

said the president.

"Andrew," the vice president resolved, "we are going to lose control of this, and we are going to lose control of it fast."

"Director Freeman," Paulson ignored him, "what can your people do?"

The D/CIA spoke before he could fully process what was about to leave his mouth. He needed to impress the president. He needed to make his mark or the coming deluge would wash the moment right from his hands.

"I can get us inside."

Sheridan turned to Freeman with a look of shock and disbelief.

Freeman awkwardly found himself in agreement with the DNI. The deluge had swept him away, too. Now he had to swim or drown.

"You get can us inside *there,*" the president pointed to the screen.

"Yes, sir," Freeman fought to keep his head above water. "I can get us inside. I'll need time and I'll need resources, but we can do it."

"Okay, do it," Paulson allowed. "Put a plan together and I'll look at." The president scanned the room. "Is that all?"

"Just one more thing, sir," Tanner raised his hand and looked down the table to Freeman. "At the beginning of your briefing, you said that 'Project 260' was one of the keywords your asset reported back, but you never told us why. What is Project 260?"

"We believe that to be the program's cover designation."

"And why is that important? What does it tell you?"

Freeman felt the sickness return to his stomach. "In Twelver Shiism, the year 260—874 AD in the Roman calendar—was when Muhammad al-Mahdi, the Twelfth Imam, disappeared, or was 'concealed from mankind by God.' His reappearance, Shiite eschatology says, will usher in the apocalypse."

"Right, let's leave it there," Paulson sighed. "Director Freeman, have your people put a proposal together. When I get back from Moscow—Karetnikov's funeral—I'd like to see something preliminary. Henry," the president spoke to the screen, "Admiral Benson, put together some options for me. Until then, thank you all for coming."

As Paulson stood, they rose as well. Jacobs was second out the door on the president's heals. Freeman gathered his notes while the usual suspects exchanged the familiar pleasantries. He caught up to Tanner in the Watch Center, just outside the conference room.

"Eli, can we go upstairs and talk for a second?"

"Unless you're gonna tell me someone's driving around Manhattan with a nuke in their trunk, this needs to wait."

"Well, no," Freeman cracked an uneasy smile.

"I have some time tomorrow morning at eight."

"That's fine."

• • •

Freeman arrived back at Langley thirty minutes later and went straight to his office without saying much of anything, exhausted and dismayed. He braced himself before lifting the phone to summon Shaw and Stavros. As he slumped into his desk chair, his secretary knocked and crept in with a handwritten message. Angela Weisel wanted him back downtown for coffee that afternoon.

CHAPTER 18

MOFIDI HAD SENT the supreme leader away for good measure. He had come to an agreement with both Ayatollah Khansari's personal physician and his eldest son—a rising seminarian in Qom—that it would benefit His Excellency to leave Tehran for a week or two. The ayatollah's medical team was partial to peculiar prognoses: caviar and trout from the Lar River was a favorite remedy; for what, Mofidi didn't entirely understand. Their latest finding was that the air quality in Tehran was much too poor. Which it was, Mofidi would agree. The solution, therefore, was to ship the supreme leader up to his sprawling Malek Abad estate in Mashad, in the northeast corner of the country and coincidently, Khansari's hometown. The drier air, his doctors assured, would purge the capillaries in his brain of impurities, blunt the dementia symptoms, and make the ayatollah more lucid. Essentially, slow the inevitable. Mofidi consented for his own reasons. With the supreme leader out of Tehran, his defense adviser could speak and act with more authority. He hoped—*hoped*—he could rein in the madness.

Three days had passed since Mehdi Vaziri, the leader of the Green Movement and the regime's most feared critic, had broken his house arrest and vanished into the night. Vaziri and his wife were confined to their home for nearly four years and kept sealed-off from the outside world—unable to organize and communicate with the other opposition figures; unable to incite the millions of Iranians who sympathized with his message to rise up against the regime. But all that could change at any moment. The regime's security forces lost their control over him and by now Vaziri could have been anywhere: hiding with like-minded dissident groups, or worse, in the protective custody of a foreign intelligence service. And Mofidi saw how terrified the regime's unshakable enforcers were of just the latest catastrophe that had befallen them in the last week. But this one was different, Mofidi knew. Hezbollah was just another proxy, and Iran had plenty of those. Yet the only weapon a man like Mehdi Vaziri needed to spark a revolution in Iran was an Internet connection.

Mehdi Vaziri's home was located along a narrow lane, just off one of the major boulevards in North Tehran. When the IRGC placed him under house arrest, they erected tall metal gates at either end of the lane and installed thick bars over the windows, effectively creating a personal prison. The rare visitors they allowed were limited to immediate family members, who were all thoroughly searched before they could get near Vaziri. Yet incredibly, through the ring of steel the IRGC had placed him in, Mehdi Vaziri and his wife managed to slip away. On the morning of their escape, the IRGC discovered a false floor in the bathroom, under which was a tunnel, carved with hand tools, leading to an abandoned house approximately three hundred meters away. It would have taken weeks to dig, and *someone* must have been in communication with Vaziri, which was another feat, entirely.

Every one of the IRGC officers charged with guarding the house, even those not on duty that night, were swiftly rounded up for interrogation. Likewise, Vaziri's extended family members and associates still in the country were now populating the empty cells at Prison 59, a detention center run by the IRGC's Intelligence Unit—the *Etelaat-e-Sepah.* The unit's commander, Hossein Taeb, sat before Mofidi in his office with Major General Qasem Shateri, commander of the IRGC's Quds Force. The former attempted to explain to Mofidi—and by proxy, the supreme leader—how such an outrage was possible; while the latter, Mofidi expected, was going to tell—not request—what the regime's most dreaded enforcers planned to do about it.

"Brother Saeed," Taeb continued, "based on our interrogation of the crew, we can confirm that the fishing dhow made landfall in Sharjah at about five A.M." Hossein Taeb was a *hojjatoleslam,* a mid-ranking cleric. His fat white turban must have been wrapped in haste that morning, Mofidi observed; it kept sliding down his forehead, and Mofidi couldn't help but notice how ridiculous he looked.

The dhow and its crew from Bandar Lengeh, a sleepy fishing village on the Persian Gulf, was the breakthrough in the *Etelaat's* search for Vaziri. A jealous fisherman from the town informed the local police that members of another crew were paid fifty thousand US dollars to transport a small group of fit, foreign-looking men and two trunks, each about six feet in length, across the gulf to Sharjah, in the United Arab Emirates. The crew was handed over to the *Etelaat,* and after some slight "convincing," made full confessions and would be quietly shot before the day was over.

"Following the Emirates connection," Taeb pushed the turban back atop his head, "we discovered that a Gulfstream IV, tail number: HS-J8T, departed Sharjah at exactly six that morning. We've been unable to obtain the manifest or the flight plan. However, we can inform that an import-export firm registered in Thailand owns a Gulfstream with that tail number. Our agents in Bangkok tracked down the address listed with the registry and found an empty office."

That was bad news for the regime's enforcers, Mofidi knew. Only a foreign intelligence service could bring those resources to bear. It was the revelation they were looking for: Mehdi Vaziri had defected into the arms of the regime's sworn enemies. That likewise put Mofidi in an excellent position to understand Vaziri's mindset, not that he could explain it to the pair before him. Yet that, too, was bad news for Vaziri. When it came to a man like him, the regime would never let him go without a fight. And that was equally true for Saeed Mofidi.

"Several hours after departure from Sharjah, this Gulfstream arrived at Bolzano Airport," Taeb struggled with the pronunciation, "at Alto Adige, in the Italian Alps, near the Austrian border. From there, the trail evaporates, I'm disappointed to say."

"Hmm," Mofidi shifted in his chair and smiled, "perhaps he just needed a ski holiday?"

The pair before him saw no humor in the joke.

"So," Mofidi ended the awkward pause, "what are we doing about it?"

Taeb jumped at the opportunity to prove his worth. "Brother Saeed, at my precise instructions, *every single one* of our operatives in Europe have been tasked to direct all of their efforts into finding this traitorous rat! Assuming that he remains on the continent, I urge you to assure His Excellency that he will not stay at large for long." Then he corrected his turban.

Qasem Shateri rubbed the gray beard girding his cut jawline. "It should be noted that a key focus of our recovery operation—" the Quds Force commander curiously labeled it a recovery, yet Mofidi knew the only thing he intended to recover was a scalp, "—is to monitor the other *monafiqeen* groups in Europe." *Monafiqeen* was a Persian term that loosely translated as "hypocrites," and was used as a blanket label for Iranian dissidents and other enemies of the Islamic Revolution. "Even if he has been taken in by a foreign service, it would be safe to assume that he will attempt to contact his followers on the continent, and we must be watching if and when he does."

"And you've taken the necessary steps to do so?" Mofidi asked.

"I have." Shateri offered nothing further.

"It may reassure His Excellency if I were able to provide more—"

"Then, Brother Saeed, you may inform His Excellency that I have deployed Unit 400 to our embassy in Vienna."

"...I see."

And that told Mofidi all he needed to hear. Unit 400 was a small detachment of the Quds Force specializing in assassinations, kidnappings and other violent operations. Wherever they went, the bodies of the regime's enemies appeared in their wake.

Shateri was visibly annoyed that he, again, had to justify himself to Mofidi. "Brother Saeed, it should go without explanation that such insubordination on the part of our people simply cannot be tolerated. The authority of our revolution rests on the principle that individuals such as Mehdi Vaziri will not go unpunished for their misdoings. It is very simple: When you betray our revolution, you forfeit your right to exist."

"And if Mehdi Vaziri is under the protection of a foreign intelligence service in a European capital, then what? How then will you...punish him?"

The answer was obvious to Shateri. "Anyone who comes to the aid of our enemies equally forfeits their existence. Brother Saeed, you should know by now that I do not discriminate."

It was a pleasant thing to behold the light, as Mehdi Vaziri discovered.

Initially, his optic nerves had deemed it little more than a discordant haze, devoid of meaning: blinding, terrifying, and inescapable. With time, the firing electrical currents that dazzled the synapses subsided, the light faded, and the only lingering memory of the morass was something altogether attractive, something meaningful. Only then, for the first moment in his existence, did he see the truth, beating ceaselessly against the retreating fog. He was recalled to life.

But the fog was still present on the horizon.

In the meantime, Vaziri grew accustomed to his new view of the dazzling French capital. From the sitting room, he passed the hours locked in a dead stare over the bare tops of chestnut trees on the Tuileries Garden. The vantage extended from the baroque pavilions of the Louvre to the left, down Rue de Rivoli, to the Egyptian obelisk on Place de la Concorde to the right. During rare reprieves in the torrential downpour that afternoon, he could see across to the left bank of the Seine and glimpse the Palais Bourbon and the Musée d'Orsay. Occasionally his wife, Fatemeh, would emerge from the bedroom, a haggard wreck, wipe the tears from her bloodshot eyes, and sit with him. The two would sip tea in abject silence for a short while before the memories of their children and the reality of their treason would consume Fatemeh's thoughts. And then she would drop the cup, sometimes missing the table and shattering on the parquet floor, let slip an agonized shriek—Vaziri had grown numb to the sound—and retreat back to the cave of self-loathing she made for herself under the cold sheets.

The Vaziris were just the latest in a string of banished undesirables to take refuge in the Hôtel Meurice. In 1931, after his ouster in a coup, King Alfonso XIII of Spain established his government-in-exile at Le Meurice; and once the general-manager was forced to obtain a court order compelling Dutch courtesan and German spy, Mata Hari, to settle an outstanding debt. The surrealist painter, Salvador Dalí, took residence in the hotel for one month every year, and famously paraded a herd of sheep into his suite. Now Mehdi and Fatemeh Vaziri were added to that dismal list, and suite 102/103 was where they would hide from the world. Their hosts worked diligently to make their surely miserable stay as comfortable as possible. The floors were laid with wool-and-silk rugs, and each room was painstakingly decorated with antique Louis XVI furniture. They had three hundred eighty square-meters of space to avoid each other. Two additional suites had been adjoined to the main apartment, adding an extra sitting room and two bedrooms, which ran down the Rue de Rivoli façade, wrapping around the southwest corner of the hotel to Rue de Castiglione.

One of the bedrooms was cleared out to house the French National Police's *Service de la protection* (SDLP), which posted plainclothes officers in the halls and the lobby. The cover story told to the concierge and cleaning staff was that a Brazilian sugar baron had booked an extended stay in suite 102/103 and demanded absolute privacy. It was hardly an outrageous request for the veteran staff and they gave it little thought. So, the Vaziris were effectively left alone to shower themselves with hatred. The French security men mostly kept to themselves in their command post down the hall and hardly cared about their domestic disputes.

But the Israeli visitors were a different matter.

The small contingent of Mossad field officers—*katsas*—came from the embassy twice each day, usually timed with breakfast and lunch. Their battery of questions for Vaziri was seemingly endless. Nothing that could possibly come from his mouth disinterested them. They too would sit with him, but unlike Fatemeh, they hung on his every syllable. And when Vaziri didn't care to speak, they would encourage him. Usually the common refrain was that theirs was a common enemy, and only together could they inflict lasting damage. Just that morning, when Vaziri's appetite for conversation had soured, a *katsa* named Ezra played for him a recorded phone conversation of two "senior Iranian intelligence officers." Who exactly they were or how the Israelis obtained the recording, Vaziri did not care, but it filled him with equal parts exhilaration and dread. Vaziri listened to the two Iranians shouting at each other, condemning each other with every sort of foul obscenity for this catastrophe that each was convinced the other had allowed. That catastrophe was Mehdi Vaziri's defection. Their common enemy was turning on itself, Ezra gleefully explained. Would he stand with them to press the attack?

He would, but Vaziri had no choice.

Mehdi Vaziri and the contents of his mind were now the official property of the Israeli foreign intelligence service and their generous colleagues in the French *Direction générale de la Sécurité extérieure*—the General Directorate for External Security, or DGSE. From the moment the Mossad lifted the oxygen mask from his face, brought him out from under the sedatives, and pulled him from the trunk—opening his eyes to the full blaze of the desert sun—Vaziri's fate was sealed. That discordant haze had faded and in the clarity he could see the life to which he was recalled, designed and engineered by an architect other than himself. Mehdi Vaziri was now a strategic commodity to be exploited to the fullest and tossed away.

Freeman studied the photographs placed on the credenza. They were usually an accurate indicator of one's priorities, an insight to where a person placed the most value. None of the high-powered heads of state or military leaders who paraded through the office on a daily basis were displayed. Instead, Freeman saw the Pope, the Dalai Lama, an Afghan women's rights advocate, and a rock star who raised millions for AIDS and malaria research. They hinted at a value that was much more human.

He had been left in the secretary's office on the seventh floor of the Harry Truman Building, the State Department's headquarters in Foggy Bottom, for a little over fifteen minutes. The wait just gave Freeman's mind more time to wander. That he could recall, Ryan had never been alone in a room with her, and the thought that his time had come was slightly intimidating. He couldn't decide what she wanted with him, although he figured it involved what transpired at the White House that morning. Whether she intended to congratulate or condemn him, Freeman had no idea. Angela Weisel was a force of nature, an unrelenting energy that could make or break a person with a few choice words.

She blew through the doors without warning.

"So sorry, Ryan!" Weisel glided across the room to a sofa covered in blue floral upholstery, flopping a large Dior tote bag on the cushion.

"Not a problem."

"Come sit." Weisel beckoned him to a high-back armchair adjacent to the sofa. "Help yourself to coffee," she pointed at the china set on the table. "If you're hungry, I can have something sent up."

"Coffee's fine, thanks," Freeman took a seat.

Weisel loosened a yellow Hermès scarf around her neck. "Committee hearing ran long. Congresscritters have their panties in a wad about Russia."

Freeman poured a cup. "They have nothing to worry about."

"But you know the routine. Unless they see someone rocketed out of Uncle Sam's ass on the back of a bald eagle, they cry conspiracy."

He took the first sip and swallowed. "Madam Secretary—"

"No, no," she stopped him with a playful smile, pouring one for herself. "First names among principals."

"Uh, Angela," he forced himself to say, "if my comments at the White House this morning were in any way out of line, or off-putting, then I apologize. I only hoped to—"

"What? No!" Weisel interrupted again, laughing. "Actually," she wiped the lipstick off the rim of her cup with a napkin, "I should apologize. That display from Eli and the vice president was out of line, not you."

Freeman felt relieved.

"Listen, Ryan, my door is closed. It's just us. I don't want you to feel any sort of obligation to regurgitate the same popular points from down the street. On the contrary, I want you to tell me something unpopular."

He placed his coffee on the table. "If that door's closed, Eli's a prick."

"Eli doesn't like your trade. A drone can't get compromised and tarnish the president's good name."

Freeman's eyes rolled toward her. "I beg your pardon, but it can."

"Hmm," she sipped, *"touché...* But regardless, Eli *is* a prick, and everyone who needs to know, does."

"Except his boss."

"Oh, but he does," Weisel admitted with her playful smile. "I called Harry from the car this morning. He'd be here too if he wasn't snowbound in the Rockies—shame for him. We're both fans."

Freeman was confused. "Fans of what?"

"Fans of you, Ryan. Anyway, the secretary of defense and I have an unwritten—let's call it a suicide pact. We came in together and we intend to leave together. If that were under duress, then, well, they'd have to take the both of us. We run defense and offense for each other when it's needed. It works rather well, let's us say and do things other cabinet members can't. They know we'd write books, and that wouldn't end well for anyone...

"And we were thinking our club could squeeze in another," she said. "The Intelligence community—at least at the top—is full of assholes. It would help to have someone with a brain playing for our team."

The D/CIA took a particularly long sip.

"Of course," Weisel kept on, "it's entirely up to you. If it seems like something too sticky, then we would understand. No hard feelings."

"No, that's not it at all... I'd love to."

"Good," she smiled. "Now we can talk." Weisel topped off his cup. "You're familiar with Harold Lansing's meeting in Ramallah a few days back?"

"I read the cable."

"You read the cable sent to the collective, not the cable sent to me."

"I wasn't aware there was a discrepancy."

"There usually is. In that meeting, Hanna Sayigh, our illustrious PLO chairman, basically threatened Lansing—that was only in the cable to me."

"About?"

"He said we're backing the Iranians into a corner. He said we went too far in Syria—'spiked the ball,' he said. He said eventually they're going to lash out."

"Anything concrete, or just conjecture?"

"Oh, no, he had nothing specific, just a warning. A gut feeling."

"Gut feelings go a long way in intelligence assessments…"

"I beg your pardon, but they do."

"Touché," Freeman placed his coffee on the table.

"Anyway, Harold is trying to get Sayigh and Avi Arad at a table together, hopefully after Annapolis next month. In the meantime, he's persuaded Sayigh to do what he can to get Moshe Adler released."

"Islamic Jihad is holding him in Gaza. Rafah, somewhere."

"So, the Quds Force is holding him?" Weisel added.

"Basically," the D/CIA admitted.

"Do you see how backing Iran into a corner any further bothers me?"

Freeman nodded. "I do."

"Harold is of the belief, as am I, that there cannot be a solution between Israel and Palestine before Tel Aviv has a security guarantee. We can debate how merited that demand is until Israel is overrun, but they have a point and it's what they want, so we have to deal with it. Problem is, and this is where I think you'll agree, we can't guarantee Israel's security until Iran is out of the equation."

Freeman shook his head. "You're not talking about regime change?"

"No, absolutely not. In fact, that's the last thing I'm talking about. I'm talking about getting Iran out of the Palestinian cause, which is the most counterfeited franchise in history. I'm talking about engaging with Iran directly, without any pretenses or preconditions. I'm talking about offering Iran a deal that will finally bring them into the community of responsible nations, and quite possibly marginalize those zealots in the IRGC who are responsible for whatever's happening under that mountain your people found. I'm talking about making that mountain unnecessary. Do you follow me?"

Freeman nodded again.

"Now," Weisel continued, removing the scarf from her neck, "I can't count on the Russians to mediate between us. Maybe that'll change after they put ole' bear wrangler in the ground, but I'm not betting on it. So, I need a new backchannel in Tehran. I need someone who can get to the supreme leader, or at least speak for him, and bypass the IRGC, who will scuttle the whole process. And I think you already have someone who fits that description."

Freeman placed his cup on the cable and forced himself back in the chair, rubbing the bridge of his nose. "Angela, I didn't come here to—"

"Your sourcing behind all the MONARCH reports? It's one man, isn't it?"

Freeman hunched over and gripped his knees. "Madam Secretary," he reverted to saying, "I am not comfortable—"

"Your asset is Saeed Mofidi."

The prolonged silence gave her the answer.

"I told you, my door is closed." She paused, letting the moment resonate. "Ryan, you need to be congratulated. The United States has not had a better asset overseas since Oleg Penkovsky."

Freeman shot up. There was a hint of moisture over his eyes. "Then you know why I will use every ounce of my power to keep him alive."

"As will I."

"Angela, there are only six people on Earth who know that."

"Now there are seven. I told you, we're on the same team."

"My staff is constrained in how we handle him."

"I understand that. Harold is meeting Avi Arad in Paris tomorrow afternoon. He only needs to assure Arad that we're working with trustworthy people in Tehran. That's it. That's step one."

"Step two?"

"The president's support. In Moscow, likely on the way back, I'll have the chance to see him alone. He's quite malleable when Eli's not around. I'll convince him that we need to consider a new offer to Tehran that'll take the wind out of the IRGC's sails. The president is really thinking about his legacy now. He wants tangible progress between Israel and Palestine. I think he'll listen."

"What do you want me to do?"

"Go back to Langley and make sure that bomb doesn't go off in our faces. After that, no matter what we said, thought, or did—wouldn't do a damn."

Freeman heeded Weisel's advice. He returned to Langley and got back to work. His suite on the southeast corner of the OHB held the finest view on campus. He lingered by the windows, watching in one instance, everything in sight and yet nothing at all. The light above dimmed with the seconds as rush hour began to spin alive in its earliest throes. Freeman caught a glimpse through the stockade of bare branches to the traffic flow on the George Washington Parkway. At first he heard the muted whine of sirens, and then he saw the panicked, pulsating lights. A Virginia State Police cruiser whisked by—six of them—and a fire engine and an ambulance, surging southbound with the current toward Arlington and the tangled mess of highway spurs sprawled around the Pentagon.

And then Freeman heard a knock at the door.

"Sir?" his secretary asked. "Ms. Shaw and Mr. Stavros are here."

"Sure, send them in."

The two appeared in the doorway and made for the sofas.

"How was your hot date with *Madame* Secretary," Shaw crooned.

"What's she like in real life? Was she everything you hoped she'd be and more?"

Freeman smirked and took a seat opposite them. "The wing nut blogs are surprisingly accurate: a harmonious blend of Chairman Mao and Herr Hitler, if ever that was possible," he joked.

"But no fangs?" said Stavros.

"Not that I saw," the D/CIA nodded. "…What's up?"

"Pete's people have been busy downstairs."

Stavros laid out a stack of folders and briefing books from the analysts and operations staff in Persia House. Freeman had volunteered the agency to penetrate Picasso and Monet to the president, and it now fell on Stavros' team to deliver. It was safe to say that the director was not the popular toast in the cubicles off Corridor C. "I cabled Jack," he began. "He'll get the one-time pad in place to transmit back to CITADEL. We'll instruct him that we've received his message and are looking at its contents; stay put, keep your head down."

Freeman cleared his throat. "We need to modify his cov-comm plan. That courier chain through the mail is too vulnerable if the Iranians get spooked."

Shaw turned to Stavros. "Yeah, we've talked about that."

"A few months ago," Stavros said, "Jack made contact with a Bank Melli auditor who runs the regular pilgrimage to the Dubai branch."

"Does he have kids?" Freeman asked.

"Five. By our count."

"Then he can use the cash."

"That's what we said," Shaw admitted.

"Okay," the D/CIA agreed. "Have Jack reestablish contact and let's get the funds in his account."

Stavros shuffled his papers. "I spoke with our liaison in Tampa."

"Regarding the arms shipment?" Freeman asked. In CITADEL's report, Qasem Shateri detailed the Quds Force's plan to redouble support for Islamic Jihad and Hamas in Gaza. Their first act was to transfer a large weapons consignment through their smuggling network in Sudan.

"Yeah. NAVCENT is attempting to track a merchant vessel transiting the Gulf of Aden as we speak. We think it's the one."

Stavros placed a few glossy photographs on the table in front of the D/CIA. They showed the rusting hull of a bulk freighter, roughly one hundred meters in length, pulled alongside a pier. The pictures were evidently taken in a hurried manner by a digital camera, likely concealed in a bag.

"The *Catarina A,* registered in Liberia," he pointed to the block letters displayed on the ship's stern, "owned by the Marshallese 'Blacksea Shipping and Trading Company Limited.' She originally departed Mumbai with a load of cement, and then, three days ago, arrived in Bandar Abbas. While in port there, we know she took on ten, unmarked, forty-foot shipping containers. We know the containers were pre-sealed before they reached the dock. Now we can't exactly confirm this, but our asset reports the containers were physically loaded onto the ship by the Jahan Darya Shipping Agency, which just happens to be Blacksea's exclusive port agent in Iran."

"Oh…" Freeman raised his eyebrows, "that's convenient." Jahan Darya was known to be the IRGC's local front company in the port.

"The manifest we obtained lists the contents of those containers as agricultural equipment bound for Sudan, which matches up nicely with CITADEL's report. You can take that as you wish. She left Bandar Abbas shortly after the containers came aboard and arrived this afternoon in Salalah, Oman, where a longshoreman snapped these," Stavros pointed to the photos. "She took on two more containers in Oman and switched off her AIS transponders once she hit international waters. As soon as we reestablish contact, the Navy will hand the operation off to NATO. The Brits have a destroyer on station to conduct the boarding."

"What's up with the crew?"

"The longshoreman heard Persian around the dock."

"We'll have results early this morning," added Shaw.

"Good, let's touch on that first thing tomorrow," Freeman handed a photograph back to Stavros. "What's new on Fakhrizadeh?"

"Honestly," he reshuffled his papers, "not much. Our reporting from the crash is pretty cut-and-dry. Of course, since then we've had nothing. It would be helpful to get a second look at the autopsy report, but only Mossad has the operational support on the ground in Tehran to get it. I could make the ask."

"No, that's a bad idea," Freeman shook his head.

"Why? If they can get it—"

"We can't go to Mossad through the normal channels and say: 'That Iranian nuclear scientist you were trying to assassinate years ago, the one who died before you could kill him, can we have his autopsy report?' They'll immediately ask why we need it. We'll lie, but they'll find out anyway because they're like that. And then Arad will put F-15s on the runway, and then we'll have World War III. We're not asking them."

"So how can we get it?" Shaw asked.

Freeman thought on that for a moment. It would be a stretch.

"We'll make a trade," he stated. "CTC's asset in Beirut—TOPSAIL—the one who's saying he saw Ibrahim al-Din in the Security Quarter?"

"That's Nina Davenport's grab."

"Okay," Freeman looked to Shaw, "last week, the Israelis asked to be read-in on TOPSAIL's reports. We politely told them to fuck off. Let's change that."

"I don't follow you, sir," Stavros said.

"I'll go over there—to Tel Aviv—and meet with Benny Isaac, personal-ly."

Binyamin Isaac was the notorious director-general of the Mossad who held an iron grip over the Israeli intelligence service for thirty-seven years. Freeman saw him in the same high esteem of a childhood hero.

"I'll meet with Isaac and offer him that trade," he continued. "I'll say we had a VW who dropped a nugget about Alireza Fakhrizadeh working in Parchin, or something." Freeman referred to a virtual walk-in, an anony-mous source who submitted information to the CIA over the agency's pub-lic website. In denied areas like Iran, it was often their best bet for a source of any value. But, like most things over the Internet, the offers were often bogus. "That'll explain why we're interested. I'll ask Isaac to keep this be-tween us—he will because he's old-fashioned. Mossad will get us the autop-sy report and then we'll kill the VW in cable traffic to cover our tracks. We'll say we looked at the web server behind the email and it had a MAC address linked to IRGC Intelligence. We'll put out a notice labeling the VW as deception—generate a lot of noise so Mossad will see it—and write it off as a dangle."

"So, we'll get the report and keep Mossad off our asses," Stavros agreed.

"That's not bad," Shaw followed. "I'll get Info Ops on it."

"Let's drop the crumbs and let them sit a few days before I talk to him. Mathis and I have a meeting with Tanner tomorrow, I'll be sure to run it by His Highness when I see him," Freeman said. "Pete, what's your thinking on penetrating Picasso and Monet?"

Stavros gathered his papers. "We're dusting off some old contingency plans with the Covert Action Staff. There's a few ideas being tossed around, but until we firm it up, I'd like to keep it close to the chest, if that's fine."

"Understandable. If you need any elbows thrown around, let me know."

"Will do, boss." Stavros paused for a moment. "Actually—any favors you can call in at JSOC?"

Freeman smiled. "A few."

CHAPTER 19

SAJID BATA CHARGED up the pitch and left his brother behind. With his
ankles locked and his toes in an alternating point to the wet grass, he tapped
the soccer ball with his laces and moved forward in quick bursts of energy.
Sajid was unstoppable now. The cheering resonated in his ears and the
lights glinted over the whites of his eyes. Just a few more meters to the end,
a few more kicks, a few more seconds to glory. His calves ached and the
cold night air singed his lungs. But none of it mattered. For that one moment, Sajid Bata was invincible and the entire world was laid out before
him. For that one fleeting ripple in time, he could feel happiness. And
more—he could smile.

Sajid drew his leg up, hurled it back to earth, and watched the ball fly.

It rocketed through the rusted posts and smashed against the net.

"Goooaaalll!" He threw out his arms and screamed, running in a triumphant circle. In his mind's eye he saw the frantic, cheering masses leap to
their feet and cry out his name. For that one moment, the stars and planets
orbited only Sajid.

And perhaps, in the next life, they really would.

"Sajid, damnit!" Zyed Bata gasped out at his back.

"Fuck you, you lose!" Sajid made a victory lap around the field.

"I can't breathe." Zyed fell to his knees and gripped his heaving chest,
panting for each ounce of air.

"It's that shit you smoke," Sajid ducked under the net to grab the soccer
ball. "It's too much. Shreds up your lungs. That's what they say."

"Let's go home. Please." Zyed pushed himself up and staggered forward.

"Okay, brother," Sajid wedged the ball under his arm. "Let's go home."

In an earlier incarnation of life, home was a stone house in a field on the
outskirts of Nubl, a Shiite town that straddled the road between Aleppo and
the Turkish border, until the Syrian opposition besieged the town and left it

a smoking pyre. In the ensuing weeks and months, home was the war-torn, bloodied alleys of Aleppo—a blemish on the map where men went to die. And now, looking around, the boys' home was little more than the grim walls and crammed windows of tower blocks looming in on all sides. But La Forestière, one of the desolate housing projects in Clichy-sous-Bois on Paris' northern fringe, was the shallowest substitute for that word. The truth was, the boys had no home; no home would have them.

"I keep telling you—one day, al-Ittihad's star forward is right here," Sajid pointed to his chest, "and *all* Aleppo Stadium just goes mad."

Zyed frowned and kept his eyes to the grass. "Aleppo Stadium is a crater."

"Well," Sajid shrugged, "maybe Man City? Barça?"

"You're full of shit."

The downpours from earlier that afternoon subsided, but the pitch behind Gymnase Henri Barbusse—the project's sports center—was saturated. The pitch sat adjacent to La Forestière's parking lot, separated only by a short fence and a drainage ditch that swelled over its sides. Normally, as they had done countless times, the boys would stumble through the ditch and hop the fence, but their tired legs were already smeared with mud and grass stains. They gave the obstacle a cursory glance and opted to take the long way around, back to what they called home, for lack of a better alternative.

A diffused orange glow projected upon the clouds lit the way. The boys stepped off the pitch and continued past the gym to the gate, which was never shut. On the gym's side was a string of graffiti that appeared months ago and read, *"A bas l'état, les flics et les patrons!"* Down with the state, the coppers and the bosses! It was a common slogan for the disaffected class of African and Arab immigrants that populated the projects of Clichy-sous-Bois. But the boys gave little mind to politics.

They walked through the open gate and turned left, facing down the narrow street that led back to La Forestière. The unmistakable low rumble of rap music radiating out from an open car window and the rough patois of urban French hit their ears. The stench of hash smoke hung in the damp air. A few meters down the street the boys saw a half-dozen young black men—most were nineteen, Zyed's age—standing around a battered Renault sedan, laughing and carrying on. One of them, standing six inches taller than the rest, was called Fabrice, a recent refugee from the fighting in Cameroon. The others congregated around him like spokes to a hub.

The boys took stock of the gauntlet before them.

"Let's go the other way," Sajid tugged at his brother's arm.

"Fuck that," Zyed stared ahead.

"Please! Before they see, let's just go around."

"I am not walking through that ditch, Sajid," Zyed resolved.

But it was too late. The boys were spotted.

"Oi! Arabs!" Fabrice shouted. "Faggot Arabs!"

A beer bottle shattered on the pavement.

"Fuck off back where you came from!" Fabrice's deep voice boomed.

Zyed took the first step. "We're walking."

Reluctantly, yet as he had since birth, Sajid followed. They managed a few more paces before the volley ensued.

Fabrice and the others spread out, covering the width of the street. They jeered at the oncoming pair and threw up signs with their hands. A second bottle was tossed and landed in shards just next to the boys.

"Ta mère suce des bites en enfer!" Fabrice shouted.

"Casse-toi! Casse-toi!" another cried.

The boys inched closer. Sajid's stomach was tied in knots. His face had gone flush and a bead of sweat trailed down his brow. He felt sick. He wanted to turn around and run, charge back to the field and over the fence to safety—to home. But Zyed refused. His face was a stoic slab of granite. He had to be strong for the both of them. Sajid had no choice but to follow, headfirst, into whatever or whomever stood before them. They had to do it together.

Fabrice came forward from the gang in a cocky strut. "I told you to fuck off, faggot Arabs!" He stopped dead in their tracks, all six-foot, seven-inches of solid muscle and bone lodged defiantly before the boys.

"We just want to go home," Sajid's voice quivered in the little broken French he knew.

"Go home?" Fabrice's nostrils flared. "Fuck your home!"

"Please," Sajid muttered.

"Please," Fabrice shrieked in a mocking tone. "Oi," he turned to the others behind him, "look at this little fucking cunt. Look at him."

Zyed stewed in silent agony beside his brother. He wanted to kill Fabrice. Zyed wanted to watch him bleed out like a pig. It was the feeling of rage that consumed him when he was forced to admit how truly powerless he was. Zyed felt it before. He felt it the day a stray artillery shell hit the side of their home in Nubl. He felt it when the concussion blew his father to pieces and the shrapnel sheered his mother's legs off. Zyed knew it then: the feeling of being powerless. And Zyed felt it now.

"You want to go home, cunt?" Fabrice roared. "Fuck you, cunt! How 'bout I go home with your fucking mum?"

Sajid whimpered—powerless.

"You want to go home?"

Fabrice pulled a dull knife from his pocket.

"How 'bout I stick this blade in your fucking gut?"

A clenched fist tore into the side of Fabrice's jaw.

Fabrice recoiled and gripped his face. The knife flung from his hand and landed somewhere on the dark pavement.

Zyed realized the gravity of what he had done in that moment. But he hardly cared. If he was destined to die on that street, so be it.

"Run!" Zyed screamed to his frozen brother.

The word scarcely left his mouth before Fabrice recovered and launched a hook backed by all the force his right arm could muster that slammed into Zyed's left cheekbone with a sharp crunch.

Sajid watched his brother drop to the ground. His feet instinctively took flight. He shot down the street toward La Forestière, gasping and wheezing with each breath. Behind him, the gang descended on his brother in a loose circle.

The first kick came from Fabrice; but the second, third, fourth, fifth— Zyed wasn't certain. They came in rapid succession, a sustained barrage of agony. He pulled himself in a ball, his knees as near to his chest as he could manage and his forearms locked together in front of his face. He felt the pain surround him: over his ribs and shins, his arms and the top of his skull. Each blow seemed to rain down harsher than the last. Their soles cut into his skin and rattled his bones to the breaking point. And with each, he hated them more.

Sajid burst into the tower block and bounded up the stairs as fast as his legs would take him. He headed where his instinct demanded, to the only person who cared enough to help. Sajid reached the ninth floor, barely able to remain standing, but leapt into the hallway at a sprint. He kept running until he found the right door, the only place where he and his brother were welcome.

"Badi!" he pounded his fists on the wood. "Badi! Badi, help!"

The door swung open and Sajid stumbled into the flat.

"What? Sajid, what?" Badi Haddad anxiously asked.

"Zyed!" the boy doubled over in a hysteric wheeze. "He's—"

Haddad crouched down and grabbed Sajid's chin, looking the boy squarely in his petrified eyes. "Sajid, look at me," he said calmly. *"Look* at me. Where is your brother? Where is Zyed?"

"Outside!" he gasped. "Fabrice." And a single tear rolled down his cheek. "They'll kill him."

Without another word, Haddad moved to the kitchen and reached in a drawer. He retrieved a small, nine-millimeter Makarov pistol and chambered a round. Haddad turned back to Sajid, stuffing the pistol in his waist. "Where?"

As Zyed lay in the street, gazing blankly at the death that called out to him, he felt nothing within the range of qualifiable human emotions that could be labeled as fear. Death frightens because it is unfamiliar. But Zyed Bata had seen so much death that it was more familiar to him than life, itself. And suddenly, it wasn't so frightening. For most lives, including his own, it was welcomed.

And he remembered, as a heavy sole crashed into his gut, the video Badi Haddad showed them of Ali Saffedine—the martyr who committed his body to a great army called Hezbollah. Zyed remembered the car as it rolled down the hill, the Israeli soldiers loosing a salvo of gunfire, and the thud that rattled the camera before a rising cloud of smoke. Ali Saffedine took that rage and hopelessness, the feeling of being powerless that consumed him, and harnessed it to his will. Zyed Bata wanted the power to shape, not just his own life, but the lives of countless others—even the power to end them. It was in that hopeless, powerless moment, as the barrage of agony consumed him, that he realized: he wanted to murder as many people as possible.

Badi Haddad stormed down the street in wide, deliberate paces.

"You have a gun?" Sajid exclaimed at his back. "Why do you have a gun? Badi!" The boy's pleas became more desperate. "Badi, where did you get a gun?"

"Shut up," he said flatly.

The gang moved away to watch. Fabrice was poised over Zyed on his knees, hurling one furious blow after another. Haddad came from behind.

"Please, don't do this!" Sajid cried. *"Please,* just— No! No! No!"

Haddad pulled the Makarov and leveled it at Fabrice's skull.

The gang saw the pistol and jumped back, shouting to Fabrice.

Haddad squeezed the trigger. A round sprang from the barrel, zipped past Fabrice's head, and struck the pavement with a bright spark.

Fabrice flinched wildly and spun around to his feet.

Two more shots, then a third and a fourth rattled the pavement mere inches from where Fabrice stood.

Haddad clenched his left hand around Fabrice's jugular, and with the Makarov in his right, slammed the butt against his nose. Fabrice yelped and tumbled to the ground. Haddad followed him down and grabbed his head, squeezing it between his palms, and battered it repeatedly against the pavement. Fabrice wailed as the others watched on in disbelief. Haddad took the Makarov and wedged it behind his earlobe.

"Touch him again and I'll saw your fucking head off!" he hissed.

Haddad rose to his feet, waving the Makarov at the others. "And if *any* of you utter one fucking word!" He didn't need to finish the promise.

Sajid rushed to his brother and lifted the beaten pulp from the ground. He hoisted Zyed up and dragged his brother's right arm over his shoulder. Wide gashes cut into his eyebrow and the bridge of his nose. The front of his shirt was smeared with blood. "Are you okay?" Sajid asked.

But Zyed could only manage a pained moan.

Haddad placed the Makarov in his waist and turned to Zyed, offering a bloodied hand. "Let's go home."

• • •

The tan Isuzu Trooper's headlights were doused and it jounced up the shallow ravine in near-total darkness. Anwar Sabbah gripped the wheel in his hands and squinted over the dashboard at the dirt road appearing inches before the grille. From the passenger seat, Ibrahim al-Din spotted the perimeter force silhouetted against the night sky atop the ridgeline—three of them, all Russians—standing motionless in the inky void, watching through trained rifle sights. They were part of the platoon (thirty men, or so, in total) his new friend had flown in from Cyprus and Athens on falsified passports over the last forty-eight hours. Al-Din provided them with a handful of smaller safe houses throughout Beirut, but it was from here that his new friend, the American, intended to conduct their operations.

When the American first explained the sheer scope of his designs and the firepower that he would place at al-Din's fingertips, he could scarcely breathe. As he watched the darkness pass beyond his window, he felt the same flutter in his lungs. To orchestrate these designs, al-Din's friend demanded to be alone. And al-Din had found the perfect location. They were thirty-five miles northeast of Beirut in the rugged hills that lined the western edge of the Beqaa Valley. Sabbah turned off the last paved road a few kilometers back in the village of Zarayeb and followed a rutted dirt trail. Al-Din knew they were close; the Russians watching from the ridge was the first sign. They had passed the precipice.

The sky was clear near the top of the hill. As the Isuzu made a sharp turn, al-Din saw the gray-blue valley floor sprawled out a thousand meters below, covered by acres of cannabis and poppy fields, and patrolled by the private militias of feudal drug lords who paid the military and Internal Security Forces to keep a wide berth. The lights in Baalbek glinted just to the south, and on the far edge of the valley rose the snow-capped crests of the Anti-Lebanon Mountains, beyond which was the smoldering carnage known as Syria. Al-Din chose wisely.

Sabbah rounded another turn into the final rise toward the hilltop. In that moment al-Din saw the buildings materialize beyond the windshield and the black shapes in human form orbiting around it. The main structure was a plain cinder block house of the sort that littered the Middle East, rising two levels to a flat roof. Al-Din knew it had sat empty for years. A dozen meters left of the house was a windowless barn, also made of cinder blocks. Off to the right, at a slightly higher elevation, were the remains of the original house occupying the hilltop. The roof had long since caved in, leaving only the crumbling limestone walls rising up from the ground. Two off-road trucks were parked between the house and the barn. A third sat covered in camouflage netting by the ruins. By the bed of each truck, al-Din counted five tall, fit-looking men with tanned faces and beards hauling wooden crates into the house—weapons, ammunition, explosives, field rations and combat gear smuggled over the Syrian border. Sabbah stopped the Isuzu and al-Din stepped down from the passenger side. They spoke a blend of Russian and Chechen—terse and purposeful words directing each other about with a quiet sense of urgency. Although al-Din couldn't understand them, their inner meaning was conveyed with clarity: these men who washed over the hilltop under the cover of darkness were professionals, and vastly more capable than anyone Hezbollah could field. Al-Din had heard of them before, and in fact they were so capable, so relentless, that Moscow would not have them. His new friend recruited them to assist with the simple objective of lighting the Middle East ablaze.

"Wait here," al-Din told Sabbah, who remained in the driver's seat. He approached a pair of soldiers who were wheeling an electric generator around the house. One turned to al-Din, and to his surprise, spoke perfect Arabic.

"He is in the ruins."

Al-Din nodded and began walking in that direction, letting his eyes adjust to the darkness. Over the short rise, he came to the gray, weathered walls and exposed foundations. And then al-Din saw him standing alone—motionless—beyond the open threshold.

David Kazanoff faced away from al-Din, dragging his gaze over the wall. A brief moment passed before he allowed any acknowledgement of the person behind him. It was as if he didn't care. He held his chin up slightly, looking perhaps at the top of the wall. The rest of him didn't move.

And then he muttered, "Come with me."

It was the familiar voice al-Din heard in his home: that monotone sigh; a register that never rose or fell; a voice that failed to derive any sign of decipherable life, a voice that allowed the notion of a presence, yet denied the signature of an affable existence.

Kazanoff walked by and out of the threshold. Al-Din trailed several paces behind, moving toward the barn. They had passed the house when Kazanoff, still walking, pointed to a slope beside the road leading down to the valley.

"I'll place land mines there." He pointed to another slope, "And there."

"You are quite safe here," al-Din assured.

Kazanoff didn't respond.

They approached the barn. Al-Din heard the howl of welding torches coming from within. Rolls of plastic sheeting, coiled aluminum ventilation hoses, and bags of cement sat beside it. Kazanoff stopped at the corrugated metal door and rapped twice with his fist. A Spetsnaz soldier, with a respirator strapped over his nose and mouth, opened it just enough to slide out. Amid a cascade of yellow sparks and a thick cloud of smoke, al-Din spotted a crew working atop metal scaffolding, their faces hidden behind tinted, black helmets. Four iron posts were sunk into freshly poured concrete on the barn's floor. On the scaffolding, the crew now worked to weld trusses to each post, creating a large square frame that filled the barn's interior. The Spetsnaz soldier shut the door, blunting the noise, and removed his respirator.

Kazanoff was silent still.

The soldier lodged the mask under his arm. Like the other, he spoke flawless Arabic. *"As-salamu 'alaykum,* Commander al-Din," he offered his hand, "I am Ruslan Baranov."

"Salam," al-Din took it and motioned to the barn. "Is this for the—"

"Yes," Baranov answered. "When we recover it, it will come here."

Al-Din could feel it in his lungs. "Why this construction, then? If it is intact and operational, as you say, why is this necessary?"

"Physics is a fickle friend, Commander. It has been hidden within a basement foundation for nearly twenty-six years—safe from the elements, yes, but it is not external factors that concern me, it is the unstoppable processes inside."

"I don't understand," al-Din shook his head.

"The device's core continuously emits heat—half-life decay, of course— which can damage electrical components. The explosive lenses and plastics give off very small amounts of hydrogen, oxygen: water vapor, which causes oxidation and corrosion. These are issues we need to prepare for."

"So you are not certain if it will even function?"

"Oh, no, Commander," Baranov's eyes widened. "My unit operated these weapons. It was our job to place them and ensure that they would still detonate when the orders came. They were engineered to have redundancies. And they were—*are*—quite rugged, much more so than you may imagine. It will work, Commander. My task is to have it explode with as high a yield as possible. The core is surrounded by explosive lenses of very exact specifications, all which must fire within the same millisecond to compress the core into the size of a walnut. Only then do we have a critical chain reaction, one event cascading seamlessly after another. It is possible that corrosion may have cracked several of the lenses, so we will have to repair them."

"And you can do that here, in a barn?"

"Repairing the lenses is not as complicated as it seems. This can be done with the same instruments used to manufacture eyeglasses, which we can find in Beirut. The difficult task is to do this in a sanitized location. That's what we're building, Commander. A fabrication lab. When the trusses are complete, we'll lay weather-sealed plastic sheeting over the sides and install ventilation to remove dust and humidity. Of course, none of this may be necessary. It may be in perfect condition. We simply won't know until we retrieve it."

"And you will do that? Personally?" al-Din asked.

"When the time is right, I will lead a team to Germany and bring it back."

Al-Din nodded and looked to Kazanoff, who hadn't flinched.

"It will work, Commander," Baranov continued. "Even if we have a partial detonation, you will have still orchestrated the most sensational raid in history. At that level of devastation, the minutia does not quite matter."

CHAPTER 20

THEY WHIRLED TOGETHER in an umbilical embrace, charging ceaselessly toward the blue haze on the curved horizon—partners in a boundless vacuum. Seven hundred miles below, lightning flashes peppered the anvil-shaped cloud structures over the jungles of Central Africa as the pair screamed eastward at sixteen thousand miles per hour toward the Indian Ocean. Their gaze swept across a wide arc that stretched from the prime meridian to the Maldives, and nothing that moved on the waters between escaped their notice.

INTRUDER 9A and 9B circled together in low Earth orbit at a sixty-four-degree inclination to the plane of the equator. Both were the latest third generation additions to the Naval Ocean Surveillance System, a global constellation of SIGINT satellites that monitored the thousands of vessels underway on the world's seas. They orbited in a tight formation—one trailing the other by a distance of approximately fifty kilometers—and analyzed radio operating frequencies and transmission patterns to determine the locations and headings of maritime traffic.

As the pair moved over the Horn of Africa, a set of tasking orders uploaded by the Program Operations Coordination Group at NSA came into effect. An array of passive infrared scanners and millimeter wave radiometers on the satellites' bus trawled the cloud of electronic signals hovering over the Gulf of Aden. The signals originated on dozens of vessels transiting the waters between Yemen and Somalia: tankers laden with crude oil and liquid natural gas bound for Europe and North America; freighters hauling raw materials mined in India and stacked shipping containers packed with consumer goods from China; roll-on/roll-off ships carrying automobiles assembled in Japan and Korea; local fishing dhows and private yachts—all of which operated bridge-to-bridge radios and navigation radars. Each of those systems emitted a constant stream of data that bled up to the stars, where INTRUDER 9A and 9B lurked in the abyss.

The satellites' arrays intercepted the data and processed it through their onboard computers. They hunted for the unique signature of a navigation radar system originally detected off the coast of Salalah, Oman. The merchant vessel operating the radar, the *Catarina A,* switched off its transponder when it hit international waters and attempted to transit the gulf anonymously without broadcasting her course, speed and heading. Once the satellites detected signatures from each vessel within an area of two-and-a-half million square-miles, they got to work. The satellites cross-referenced the known signature from the *Catarina A* with every shred of data floating on the black expanse below. Within a millisecond, they had a match. Next, 9A and 9B separately calculated the time it took for the radar signal to reach each satellite. Hyperbolic lines drawn from both satellites then estimated the point of origin for the radar signal. At the spot where the lines intersected, the satellites located their prey.

Five thousand feet over the Gulf of Aden, beneath a starry, crystalline sky, a P-3C Orion attached to Combined Joint Task Force-Horn of Africa out of Camp Lemonnier, Djibouti rushed to the coordinates sent by the INTRUDER satellites. An MX-20 electro-optical/infrared camera swiveled between the surveillance plane's retracted landing gear and scanned the heaving darkness. After a few passes over the search grid, the camera acquired a target.

"Mark, mark, mark," the Orion's tactical coordinator announced at her workstation along the port side of the fuselage.

Centered in the reticles on the screen was a silky, grayscale FLIR image of an old freighter, stretching a full hundred meters from bow to stern, as it wallowed in six-foot seas. The *Catarina A*'s deck was cold, appearing on the screen just slightly lighter than the frigid, black water around her. Her superstructure was situated well aft and shown as bright white, the exhaust funnel emitting the most concentrated heat signature. A pair of large cargo hatches dominated the forward two-thirds of the deck. Between the hatches, in the narrow space over the winch housing, sat the V-shaped remnants of a crane. The booms appeared to have been cleaved off with thermal lances, leaving the iron stubs to rise over the deck like the product of a botched amputation. *Catarina* labored no less awkwardly through the water at eighteen knots, a decent clip that undoubtedly pushed the diesel engines to their limit. Her bow listed dangerously lower than her stern, and with each swell that passed under her keel she pitched sharply before smacking down on the waves. It was a clear indicator to the Orion's tactical coordinator that the cargo was unevenly distributed, which was in itself a greater hint that something nefarious sat in the holds.

Beyond the ship's grim external appearance, her curious movements suggested that whoever stood at the helm was either blatantly inviting a pirate attack or was determined to mask their presence from warships patrolling the gulf. *Catarina* was underway a mere twenty-five nautical miles off the Somali coastline, far south of the Internationally Recommended Transit Corridor (IRTC), a narrow shipping lane established by NATO and the European Union to coalesce and defend merchant vessels. Normal marine traffic simply kept as far from Somalia as possible. To inflame the situation, her running lights were extinguished, the shipping company neglected to register the vessel with UK Maritime Trade Operations in Dubai, and attempts to raise her bridge on channel sixteen VHF radio were ignored. It was indicative that either the captain was woefully incompetent to navigate those waters, or, as intelligence suggested, the *Catarina A* transported weapons bound for Gaza. Both scenarios demanded a response.

"Yep," the tactical coordinator exhaled through her teeth, "that's the one." She keyed her radio. *"Dauntless,* this is Black Gull Six."

Inside the dimly lit operations room of the HMS *Dauntless,* a Royal Navy Type 45 destroyer, the principal warfare officer (PWO) bent over his console and viewed the Orion's live feed. "Black Gull Six, *Dauntless.* Read you Lima Charlie. Go ahead, over."

"Dauntless, please confirm you copy IR visual of motor vessel *Catarina A.* Suspect vessel underway west-northwest, bearing two-seven-six degrees; speed, eighteen knots."

"Roger, Black Gull Six. *Dauntless* confirms your mark. Suspect vessel is underway west-northwest, bearing two-seven-six degrees; speed, eighteen knots. Thanks for the data, over."

"Dauntless, we're almost to bingo. Need to RTB and refuel. Can we get you anything out here?"

"How's about a pint of your finest ale?"

The Orion's tactical coordinator smiled. "Will do, *Dauntless.* Happy hunting. Black Gull Six, out."

Captain Haywood scanned the scabrous, rusting hull on the northwesterly horizon. It sat a little over one kilometer off the HMS *Dauntless'* bow, toiling through the rolling surf with a clear course toward the Bab el-Mandeb strait, the narrow mouth of the Red Sea. During the past hour, the staff below in the Ops Room checked the P-3 Orion's IR visual against the *Catarina A*'s hull and superstructure data published in the *Lloyd's Register of Shipping* and found a conclusive match. Billions worth of aerospace, passive signals intercept and electro-optical technology still required verification from the trustworthy "Mark 1 Eyeball." He lowered the binoculars to his chest. Now *Dauntless* would close in for the kill.

Haywood radioed an update to Allied Maritime Command, the central command of all NATO naval assets, based at Northwood Headquarters outside London. As *Dauntless'* commanding officer, Haywood was dual-hatted as commander of Combined Task Force 508, which was the NATO formation stood-up to support the alliance's anti-piracy mission in the Indian Ocean.

For his flagship, Captain Haywood had one of the most capable warships the Royal Navy ever fielded: the HMS *Dauntless*. She was the second ship of the Type 45 air-defense destroyers and sat rather low in the water with a sharp, angular profile designed to minimize her radar cross-section so that it resembled something like a small fishing boat, which is exactly what the *Catarina A*'s bridge crew would have seen on their scopes, not an eighty-five thousand-ton destroyer creeping up from behind.

However, the faint orange tint that previously sat far to the east had risen to a brightening yellow smear on the horizon. Dawn was only two hours away, and anyone who looked off *Catarina*'s stern would easily spot the massive warship closing in. Her crew certainly knew *Dauntless* was there, Haywood reasoned, yet they showed no sign of a reaction. But that could change in an instant, and at any moment the crew could start dumping arms over the side and make a turn for Somalia. It was a favored tactic by smugglers to position their ship at the edge of an unfriendly country's territorial waters. If detected—and they were—the ship could simply run for the coast. Once *Catarina A* passed that imaginary line in the sea, *Dauntless* could not pursue, and the weapons suspected to be onboard would vanish forever. Captain Haywood needed to act fast if he were to prevent that.

He stepped back from the bridge windows. A screen recessed into the console before him indicated a distance of eight hundred meters to the old freighter. Haywood turned to the helmsman and called out an order.

"Come left, two-five-zero degrees."

The helmsman chirped back, "Come left, sir, two-five-zero degrees, aye!"

The captain saw *Dauntless'* bow begin turning slightly to port. He mouthed a second order.

"All ahead full."

"All ahead full, aye!" echoed the lee helmsman, who lifted a phone and relayed the order to the Ship's Control Center, where a few extra turns of power were placed on the screws.

Dauntless propelled herself forward at twenty-nine knots—the swells battering against her sleek, gray hull—and gradually inched into position abaft the beam on *Catarina A*'s leeward quarter. Putting it plainly, Captain Haywood sought to put his ship between *Catarina* and the Somali coast, denying any avenue of escape. The warship had wrestled total control over its target's movement, and it could now make its intentions known.

Haywood confidently stretched his arms behind his back. "Right, let's give them a rouse. Sound horns. And call Lieutenant Alford to the bridge."

A deep, bellowing din boomed over the waves. *Dauntless* was equipped with two horns, one on either side of the bridge, and both shattered the still, pre-dawn air with the force necessary to launch any souls in a five-mile radius from their beds. Everyone aboard the MV *Catarina A* was now wide-awake—Captain Haywood could be certain of that—which meant *someone* ought to answer his radio hails. He brought the binoculars back to his eyes and focused on the freighter's drab superstructure.

A man dressed in a dirty white shirt and a dark vest stood on the *Catarina's* port bridge wing, his hand shading his brow from the sunrise, and looked back in bewilderment at the *Dauntless*. The man remained frozen for a moment before darting back in through the open hatch.

That someone better have answers, Haywood thought.

He pulled a radio headset over his ears and adjusted the microphone in front of his mouth. "PWO, this is the captain."

Below the bridge in Ops Room, the principal warfare officer sat ready. "Captain, this is PWO. Read you Lima Charlie and awaiting orders, over."

"PWO, captain. At this time, you are cleared to establish comms with the suspect vessel, over."

"Captain, aye. Establishing comms with suspect vessel, over."

Haywood's order was verbally passed to the communications officer seated along the Ops Room's far wall. She handled the *Dauntless'* secure SATCOM and VHF radios, linking the warship back to Britain, to US Fifth Fleet headquarters in Bahrain, and to the numerous commercial and naval vessels in the region. By law, all merchant ships were required to continuously monitor marine band radio channel sixteen. Thus far, the *Catarina A* had failed to respond to numerous hails. The benign scenario was that her radio was broken, which did occasionally happen; yet more likely, as Haywood suspected, her crew was just ignoring them, and praying that they could reach Sudan unnoticed. But that was no longer possible—*Dauntless* would seize her cargo, or it would send her to the bottom of the gulf.

The hail was spoken in English by a female junior rate, politely, but with a firm voice. Haywood heard the call through his headset.

"Motor vessel *Catarina A,* this is coalition warship Delta Three-Three. Request you state your port of origin, your flag, registry, international call sign, your cargo, your last port of call, next port of call and final destination, over."

Based on data published in the *Lloyd's Register* and intelligence handed down from the Americans, *Dauntless* already had those answers. But, it was protocol in interrogations such as these to start off slow, with a non-confrontational demeanor, draw the illusion of a routine contact, and not show their cards too early: give the *Catarina's* crew a chance to lead themselves into a trap. *Dauntless* wasn't without cause to stop her. After all, the freighter *was* operating suspiciously, far south of established shipping lanes near the coastline of a failed state. She could be in distress, hijacked by pirates—or simply transporting illegal arms from a widely recognized sponsor of terrorists to a known proxy militia in flagrant disregard of multiple international conventions. Either way, the politeness was not an open-ended offer.

In the captain's peripheral, a man came to an abrupt stop a few paces away, allowed a sharp salute, and announced himself with a Scottish brogue.

Haywood turned to see Lieutenant Alford, the detachment commander from Fleet Standby Rifle Troop, the Royal Marines unit dedicated to boarding and searching suspect vessels at sea.

"Captain, the boarding party and top cover teams are good to go in the hangar and standing by for final briefing," Alford said.

"Wonderful. We've just established radio comms with the *Catarina A.* There's our little menace off the bow."

"Ignored?"

"No luck…yet," the captain frowned and passed Alford the binoculars.

"I've just got off the line with MARCOM," Haywood continued. "The preferred course of action is to have *Catarina* divert under escort to Djibouti. However, as on-scene commander is it my call to determine if that is possible."

The captain let Alford scan the freighter for a moment. "What do you see?"

"The deck clutter is concerning," said the lieutenant, with the binoculars raised to his eyes. He saw a series of high-pressure fire hoses dangling over the hull like dead, yellow snakes. They took in seawater and could shoot it back out over the sides with enough force to knock off any pirates—or marines—attempting to climb aboard. "The crane booms and cable housings would make for a nasty ambush. Nor do I care for the fire hoses. It might be a safer bet to wait until the sun is fully up." Alford handed the binoculars back.

"I'd agree—but I'm not keen to give the crew any more time to dispose of the cargo. They already know we're here and they've been uncooperative to this point. And we don't have the manpower to cover her for a few hours. It's not something I'm willing to risk."

"Aye, sir."

"So what's your recommendation, tactically?"

Alford gave the freighter a second scan before looking back to the captain. "We deploy the Merlin for top cover support over the seaboats—five men in the cab, five in each boat. The top cover team does an initial pass and then fast-ropes to the forecastle, securing the main deck and those cable housings; the second team climbs aboard amidships, secures the bridge, superstructure, and the crew; the third team goes below and sweeps the engineering spaces and the holds."

"That should do just fine." Haywood keyed his radio mic. "PWO, Captain. Any response to our hail, over?"

The PWO's voice came back in his ear. "Captain, PWO. Negative, over."

Haywood shook his head and smirked at Alford. "PWO, Captain. Inform the suspect vessel that she will divert under escort or make herself subject to boarding, over."

A few seconds later, Haywood heard the same firm voice of the female junior rate, minus the politeness.

"Motor vessel *Catarina A,* this is coalition warship Delta Three-Three. It is believed that you are carrying illicit cargo that is subject to interception under United Nations Security Council Resolution 1747, and you will not be allowed to proceed. You may, however, decide to return to your port of origin at this time. If you do not decide to turn back, you will be directed to proceed under escort to Djibouti where this cargo will be taken into custody. Coalition warship intends no harm to your ship, your cargo, or your crew. Master and crew will be free to leave as soon as your vessel has reached its new destination. Please do not resist. Cooperate in this action so that we can avoid any damage or injury and ensure the safety of the crew. Failure to comply with this order will subject your vessel to boarding, your cargo to seizure, and your crew to criminal prosecution. Indicate your intent to comply immediately. Over."

"Let's step outside," Haywood said and opened a watertight hatch leading to *Dauntless'* starboard bridge wing. They filed out onto the narrow walkway and took in a clearer view of the *Catarina.* It moved forward, unrelenting, across a five hundred-meter patch of white-capped swells, stoked by the searing desert winds blowing from the north. The captain looked through his binoculars again, peering over the freighter's portholes, ladders and hatches, hoping to see another sign of activity. "This doesn't need to be difficult," the captain mouthed aloud, as if they could hear him across the waves.

Yet the old freighter charged ahead in silent defiance, a column of surging seawater flowing from her stern. She was testing Haywood's patience.

"Captain, PWO," he heard in his earpiece.

"PWO, Captain. Go ahead, over," he replied.

"Negative response to our hail, sir."

"Standby," Haywood lifted a finger from his mic. He turned to Alford, who offered a single, confident nod without a moment's hesitation.

"PWO, Captain," he keyed his mic and spoke with a tinge of annoyance. "I will not play games with these people. Lay a four-inch round across the bow of the suspect vessel. You have batteries released, over."

There was a short pause before the reply came. "Captain, this is PWO. Aye—lay a four-inch round across the bow of the suspect vessel. I understand I have batteries released, over."

Mounted on *Dauntless'* forecastle was a 4.5-inch Mark 8 Mod 1 deck gun. Without preamble, it sprang alive with a mechanical moan and pivoted ninety degrees to starboard. Its large-bore barrel locked on to *Catarina's* superstructure with exact precision and hung suspended in the air, calculating minute adjustments for the target's pitch and speed. Then it spun back, thirty degrees to port, before it recoiled into its boxy housing and thrust forth a steel projectile with a flash and a thud, snapping the sound barrier with ease. The shell smacked through the sea forty meters off the *Catarina's* bow, launching a high column of spray that fell lifelessly upon the swells.

A black cloud of smoke washed over *Dauntless'* bridge and vanished with the wind. Not a moment later, the call sounded in Haywood's ear:

"Captain, PWO. Uh, sir—apparently the captain of motor vessel *Catarina A* has rediscovered his voice. It seems there are limited English speakers aboard his vessel and it took some time for him to find the way from his cabin to the bridge. He's quite apologetic, over."

Haywood rolled his eyes. "PWO, Captain. And I've no doubt he is. Please enquire if the good captain will be so kind as to heave to and drop anchor, over."

He turned to Lieutenant Alford, who had a smile ingrained on his face from ear to ear. "You should head aft while I get this bit sorted."

MV *Catarina A* was promptly advised to prepare for the boarding party. The instructions, as relayed to her captain by an interpreter in *Dauntless'* Ops Room, were to come to a dead stop at her current heading, energize all interior and exterior lights, assemble the crew on the bridge, and to have the ship's paperwork and crew IDs readily available. All of this was done without much hassle. The Mark 8 deck gun, as it turned out, was quite persuasive. Yet the *Catarina's* captain still held some capacity to keep his mouth shut, insisting that the containers sitting in the holds carried only agricultural equipment and cement, exactly as the manifest listed—nothing more. It was likely that he told the truth, at least as much as he understood. The IRGC and their proxies rarely brought the shipping crews into the fold. Even their contracted smuggling groups in Sudan and Egypt knew little of what they transported, and were simply met with cash once they reached Gaza.

While Captain Haywood and his staff conducted the secondary interrogations, Lieutenant Alford prepared to get his men aboard to open the containers and lay eyes on whatever sat inside. He gathered his detachment of marines in the hangar. The ship's helicopter, a Merlin HM1, was pushed out to the flight deck, which dominated *Dauntless'* stern section, leaving a cavernous space for the marines to ready their kit and run through the normal briefings. They stood in a loose circle, all fifteen, around a table covered with photographs of the freighter. Their gear was sorted in piles behind them. As they carefully strapped on body armor and webbing equipment over their digital camouflage uniforms, Alford brought them up to speed.

"We're working off a tip from our American cousins," said the lieutenant, his Scottish accent bouncing off the hangar walls. "Roughly seventy-two hours prior, the vessel across the way there departed Iran with a registered cargo of cement and farming equipment. The freighter's final destination is Sudan. Specifically, we are searching for ten, forty-foot shipping containers loaded in Iran. The Americans believe that she carries—hold on," Alford read, "twenty thousand assorted small arms, ten million rounds, three thousand kilos of unspecified explosives, and an unknown quantity of Type 72 AT mines. Americans say the recipient is Palestinian Islamic Jihad."

"What's the crew situation?" asked one of his men, Corporal Foley.

"Her CO reports seventeen personnel. That puts us right on par. All locals, as we can tell—Persian and Arabic speakers, very little English—so we need to take it slow, keep it courteous, and use our terps."

"Aye, sir."

The lieutenant drew his finger to a photograph and placed it over the *Catarina*'s forecastle. "Right, so here's how we'll do this... Foley, Simms, Halloran, Derby, and myself will deploy in the helo with the sniper team—we're Alpha One-Zero on the net—and do the initial overwatch pass—make sure everything is straight. The rest of you—that's Bravo and Charlie One-Zero—will head over in the seaboats and come alongside amidships at port. Her crew is putting down a ladder. Alpha will fast-rope to the forecastle, secure the forward deck and cover the bridge whilst Bravo and Charlie come aboard. At that point, Bravo advances to the bridge and liaises with the captain, IDs the crew and escorts them to the fantail. Alpha and Charlie head below and sweep the engineering spaces and the holds. Her cargo is loaded into Conex boxes, so we'll check as many as we can reach—hopefully locate the arms—and search the rest once we reach port. I can't stress this enough: document *everything*, that's photos, video; take down as many serial numbers as you can see. CMC at Northwood is keyed in on this personally, so it has to be right... Aye?"

"Aye!" was the united response.

"Brilliant," replied Alford. "Mates, this should be fairly simple. Let's head over, do our job, and get back for a proper breakfast."

Twenty minutes later authorization came on high from Northwood.

The Merlin's rotor blades began to churn with a deliberate pull. Alford clipped himself into the helo's safety harness attached to the fuselage behind him and brought his knees tight against his chest. His primary weapon was wedged upright between his legs. It was an L22A1 carbine, standard-issue for the marines in his detachment, outfitted with a vertical front grip and a torch fixed beneath the barrel. Secured in Alford's thigh holster was a nine-millimeter Browning Hi-Power, also standard-issue for the Royal Marines. Foley, Simms, Halloran, and Derby sat on the benches around the lieutenant, their gear and weapons squared away as his own. Alford watched the pilots run through the pre-flight checklists. Mounted to the Merlin's starboard cabin door, the gunner loaded an ammunition belt into the L7A2 general-purpose machine gun (GPMG). To port, the two-man Maritime Sniper Team adjusted the scopes on their fifty-caliber AW50 rifles. Above, the helo's engines gave a pitched whine. Forward on the *Dauntless,* the two additional teams gathered in a pair of Pacific 24 rigid inflatable boats and were gently lowered over the side and released into the swells.

Alford stuck two fingers inside the Gecko protective helmet strapped to his head and adjusted the built-in earpiece.

He keyed his radio. "Bravo One-Zero, Alpha One-Zero, comms check."

"Solid copy, Alpha," his earpiece reported.

"Charlie One-Zero, Alpha One-Zero, comms check."

"Good to go, Alpha."

"Right," Alford spoke to the helo pilot, who craned his head back from the cockpit, "let's do this."

The Merlin lifted from the flight deck and stirred a swarm of sea spray. It eased back off the *Dauntless'* fantail and steadied over the water before it turned to starboard and gained altitude. Alford watched his ship shrink beneath him, her gray hull slightly blending with the roiling expanse around her. On the waves, the seaboats skimmed toward the *Catarina* at fifty knots. The helo closed the gap to the merchant ship in approximately thirty seconds, approaching from her stern. Bravo and Charlie were still en route, battling the swells, but would hold back until the helo could loop around and get a better look.

Alford inched closer to the cabin door to see the wallowing mass below. She came to a full stop, as ordered, and dropped a ladder over the side amidships at port. It was marked with a light, as the pilot reported and the lieutenant could see, and there was no one standing near it. That was a good sign; the crew may have finally decided to cooperate. The pilot pulled on the cyclic grip and forced the Merlin into a hard bank to the right, hooking past the amputated crane booms and over *Catarina's* bow toward her starboard side. They dropped a few feet in altitude and slowed, the snipers poring over the deck and superstructure with their high-powered scopes.

"I count three on the bridge, over," a sniper spoke through the radio. "That is three personnel ID'd on the bridge."

Alford knew that wasn't right.

Catarina's captain was specifically told to assemble his entire crew on the bridge—and they supposedly had a full house of seventeen aboard.

Haywood, watching the Merlin through binoculars on *Dauntless'* bridge, immediately caught the discrepancy. "Tiger One, this is *Dauntless*," he called to the helo, "please verify again your count. Suspect vessel is reported to have seventeen crewmembers. That is one-seven personnel, over."

"*Dauntless,* Tiger One. I copy. Verifying now, over."

Alford watched the sniper blink and press his eye back against the scope. It seemed like an eternity for the response.

"*Dauntless,* Tiger One. Negative. I count three personnel on the bridge."

"Shit," Alford said under the engine's roar.

"Tiger One, *Dauntless*," Haywood's voice replied after a moment. "Roger on your count. We are reestablishing comms with the suspect vessel. Alpha One-Zero, proceed with overwatch and insertion, over."

"Alpha One-Zero copies," Alford sighed. "Over."

The Merlin banked over *Catarina's* stern for the final pass. Below, the seaboats gradually pulled alongside at port and held in formation to board.

Haywood was livid. The captain on that rusting bathtub across the way was intent on making his life difficult since *Dauntless'* very first radio hail. Haywood had enough of it. He would personally see to it that the captain and every one of his crew were made into an example. He reported the situation back to Northwood, which essentially told him to handle it.

"PWO, Captain," he barked into his mic. "Patch me through directly to the captain of motor vessel *Catarina A,* over."

"Captain, PWO. Roger. Standby."

The Merlin hovered fifty feet over *Catarina's* forecastle.

Alford watched the early morning light appear as the rear ramp lowered into place with a slow, hydraulic grunt. The crew chief trudged down and braced himself in the precipice, fracturing the glint. He signaled to the pilot with a raised thumb, released a seventy-foot braided rope attached to the mount bar that spanned the overhead space just aft of the rear ramp, tossed the coil, and let it fall with a dead wobble to the deck. He shouted over the intercom, "Rope out!"

The five marines released themselves from their harness and stood.

Bravo One-Zero's Pacific 24 eased alongside the ladder dropped at *Catarina's* port side as the coxswain fought the swells battering the hull. Charlie rolled idle at their stern. Both readied their guns for the signal and the climb.

On the Merlin, Alpha One-Zero faced the black rope in a single line: Foley in front, Alford at the rear to moderate the insertion.

"*Go!*" Alford cried.

Haywood snapped at the captain across the waves. "*Catarina A,* this is the commander of coalition warship. Under the UN Convention on the

Law of the Sea, this behaviour is totally unacceptable! You were instructed—"

An unmistakable pop sounded in Haywood's headset. A gunshot.

Corporal Foley took the rope in his hands and turned his body ninety
degrees clear of the helo, suspended fifty feet over the metal deck.

The first marine on the boat gripped the ladder and began to scale the
rusting hull.

Haywood flinched. "Tiger One, *Dauntless*. Was that your people?"

The sniper caught the muzzle flash inside the bridge, then a quick burst
of red mist. "Shots fired. Shots fired on the bridge." Something moved in
the reticles. A man darted outside to the bridge wing. The sniper swung his
rifle to catch him. But it was too late.

"RPG! RPG in the open!"

It was a slender tube with a bulbous end. The sighting bar was up and a
single human eye sat behind it, fixed on the Merlin's tail rotor.

A thin blast of smoke appeared behind the launcher pipe.

The sniper squeezed the trigger and watched a fifty-caliber round hollow
the man's chest. He dropped in just under a second.

But the RPG's bulbous end had launched itself free and whistled between the crane booms.

Rifle rounds spidered the cockpit windscreen. The pilot shoved the cyclic against the console and dropped the helo's nose toward the deck, veering the tail skyward and out of the RPG's path. A violent jolt shook the
fuselage.

The rope slipped from Foley's gloves. He reached forward in a desperate
spasm—but his hands grasped only air.

Alford watched Foley plunge from sight.

Catarina's fire hoses—the dead yellow snakes—came alive and cast a
tremendous curtain of water over the hull, hurling the marines from the
ladder and splashing them into the sea. The Pacific 24s sitting alongside
began to flood. Bravo and Charlie's coxswains swerved their boats hard to
the left, free of the deluge while the marines made a panicked swim back to
them.

"Fuck!" Alford screamed in horror once Foley fell. He heard gunfire
sounding against the fuselage and hysterical calls from Haywood in his radio. But he ignored them. His team's training took over. The Merlin leveled
out and Halloran, next in line behind Foley, steadied the rope in his arms
and descended to the deck. It took only seconds for Simms and Derby to
follow. Alford took the rope last, held it tightly against his gloves, and
pulled his legs clear of the ramp. He looked down. There Foley lay, motionless on his back, clouded in the dust. His team members had fanned out
around him and were all down on one knee—in full combat stance—firing
at the bridge through their iron sights.

Alford slid down the rope to the forecastle, using only his hands to brake.

The Merlin took sustained small arms fire from *Catarina*'s bridge. In the helo's starboard cabin door, the gunner tried to acquire a specific target but the muzzle flashes reflected against the windows like a yellow sheet. The only option was to strafe indiscriminately and hope he hit something. And he did just that—laying on the GPMG's trigger, allowing a good portion of the ammo belt to disappear into the feeding tray. The recoil rattled his shoulder and the flash dazzled his eyes. A volley ranged over the deck and exploded the bridge windows inward in tiny shards. The shooting stopped, but only for a moment, and began again, distinctly less intense.

The soles of Alford's boots touched the forecastle as a steady hail of smoking cartridge casings clinked on the metal deck. Rotor wash screamed in his ears and the sand and grit stung his exposed skin. He swung his L22 carbine around on the sling, readied it in his hands, and immediately made for Foley. The corporal was still motionless, knocked unconscious by the fall. Alford checked his pulse—still beating—and the back of his skull—their helmets were worth the price. He looked down to Foley's legs. The bloodied and jagged end of his left femur pierced out through his uniform.

Halloran took Alford's shoulder and shouted in his ear, "Sir, his leg is shattered! I tried to check his spine but I'm afraid to move him."

Alford came back against Halloran's ear, "I need you to pull him behind that cable housing. Stay there and stabilize him. We can't move him very far on our own. We need to clear the bridge and call for CASEVAC."

Halloran looked dismayed. "Bravo and Charlie bugged out. We need to stay put until the helo can bring them over."

"Negative, we have to move." Alford shook his head.

"What?"

"I don't know who the fuck these lads are, but they're not putting up this fight over some rusty AKs. We need to clear the ship and get below before they scuttle the whole fucking boat. This cannot wait. We are on our own now, do you understand?"

"Aye, sir," Halloran nodded.

"Brilliant," Alford patted his shoulder. "Now let's move him."

They pulled Foley from the line of fire before Alford keyed his radio. *"Dauntless,* this is Alpha One-Zero. Come back, over."

Captain Haywood's reply was nearly instant. "Alpha, *Dauntless.* What the hell is happening over there?"

"Dauntless, they opened up on us with RPG and small arms fire from the bridge. Corporal Foley is down. I say again, Corporal Foley is down. He fell from the helo during insertion. He is alive, but he has a broken femur and a possible spinal injury, over."

"Copy, Alpha. Bravo and Charlie One-Zero were forced to pull back.

They cannot come aboard until those fire hoses are switched off and we cannot deploy CASEVAC until the vessel's topside is secure. Do you copy? Over."

"Roger, *Dauntless*. Alpha copies. Request permission to push aft and clear the bridge, over."

There was a short pause, which irritated Alford. "Alpha One-Zero, *Dauntless*. You are authorized to advance on the bridge and switch off those fire hoses at this time. Hold that position until reinforcements arrive. Is that clear?"

"Roger, *Dauntless*. Alpha will advance on the bridge and hold for reinforcements, over." Halloran tended to Foley. Over the noise, Alford signaled for Simms and Derby to move closer to him. "Tiger One, this is Alpha One-Zero," he called through his mic.

"Go, Alpha," the helo pilot's voice replied.

"Tiger One, Alpha is moving to seize the bridge and allow reinforcements to come aboard. We will move aft on the deck along the vessel's port side. Request you provide overwatch on the bridge until we have reached the superstructure."

The Merlin pilot's voice squawked over the airwaves. "Roger, Alpha. We'll have you boys covered, over."

"Cheers, Tiger One. Out." He turned to Simms and Derby. "We'll push up the ladders to the bridge and shut down the hoses; the helo will cover our advance. Keep a tight stack. I'll take point. Derby, watch the bridge wings; Simms, cover our flank and get any hostiles moving past the cargo hatches... This is what we train for. Aye?"

"Aye, sir," said Simms.

"Roger," Derby replied.

"Right, mates, let's go."

The marines crouched behind a deck fitting and waited for the onslaught.

Alford reached for his radio. "Tiger One, light them up!"

Not a second later, a furious crack from the GMPG sounded over their heads in quick, sustained bursts. The rounds ripped into the metal around *Catarina*'s bridge and blew in sections of the windows still in the frames.

"Now!" Alford cried.

The marines jumped down from the forecastle and fell in behind the lieutenant before charging up the deck toward the superstructure. Their knees were slightly bent and they held their rifles tightly under their arms, scanning for anything moving toward them. They pushed past the cargo hatches and the crane, reaching the ladders without resistance. Above, the GPMG expelled the last of its thousand rounds into the bridge and fell silent. The marines pressed themselves against the superstructure.

Alford looked up. He saw an open stairwell rising three decks to the bridge with a landing on each level. Most merchant ships had padlocked iron grates blocking access to each deck; thankfully, *Catarina* wasn't so well equipped. Tactically, stairwells were the stuff of nightmares. There were a multitude of angles and blind spots, each of which had to be covered. Worse still was ascending up, *without* the high ground.

Alford gripped Derby's shoulder and pointed with four fingers to the first landing. Derby turned with his rifle and swung the muzzle around to cover the position. Next, he pointed to Simms, and then to the second flight leading toward the landing. Simms covered that angle. Alford put his right eye squarely behind the sights and moved on the balls of his feet up the stairs. He hit the landing and crouched, aiming up to the next landing, and waited for his men to fall into the same position.

As he waited, he heard a flurry of quick pops from somewhere in the superstructure. They had to get inside.

The marines swiftly cleared up to the third deck. Alford signaled for his team to press against the bulkhead. Before them was the port bridge wing. In front of him laid the RPG, next to it, the corpse of the man who fired it. A gaping hole tore though his sternum and a pool of blood swelled out from under him. The rest was splattered against the rusting white paint. The man wore a simple T-shirt and a dirty pair of jeans under a load-bearing vest covered with ammunition pouches. An AK-47 rested next to the RPG launcher tube at his side. Alford hadn't an inkling who these men were, but they were certainly professionals—trained—not crewmembers with a grudge. Alford tightened his jaw.

More faint shots echoed from inside. He moved faster.

Bits of glass crunched under their boots. The open hatch leading to the bridge sat directly ahead. Alford fought to slow his breathing. The marines instinctively stacked up on the right side of the hatch. Alford listened for any sign of movement on the bridge, but heard nothing.

He turned to Derby and Simms and whispered, "Clear on three."

They nodded...

"One."

...and placed their fingers on the trigger.

"Two."

Alford swallowed hard.

"Three."

He burst through the hatch and made for the right corner. His eye caught movement at the opposite side of the bridge. A man leapt up from behind a console and aimed an AK barrel at Alford, squeezing off three rounds. Alford spun his body around as the bullet zipped not an inch from his ear. He put the man in his sights and fired twice, watching two holes appear on the man's neck. Derby ran in behind Alford, advancing on the left, and got off one shot that disappeared into the man's torso. Simms swept in next, directly behind Derby, and fired, shattering the man's forehead and dropping him to the floor.

"Search!" Alford exhaled.

They scanned the room. *Catarina*'s bridge was fairly small, with a single main console at the center. Dark red blood covered the floor, sprinkled with shattered glass and cartridge casings. Bullet holes chewed up the walls and most of the computer screens in the console were smashed. The marines counted six bodies, including the one they just killed.

"Clear left!"

"Clear right!"

"Simms, switch the hoses off."

"Aye," he said, and began searching for the right panel.

Five of the men were dressed similarly in load-bearing vests—all shredded by the GPMG. But one caught Alford's attention. Lying by the ship's radio was a man who appeared distinctly older than the others, wearing a simple white shirt and dark vest. He had taken a single shot to the back of his head. Alford knew it was the captain, executed.

Derby came toward the lieutenant and motioned with his rifle to a body at their feet. "Sir, who are these guys?"

"Hell if I know," Alford sighed and turned the man's head with his boot, "but whatever's below, they don't want us to have it."

"Got it!" Simms called as the hoses over the hull fell dead once more.

"Cheers!" Alford went for his radio. *"Dauntless,* Alpha One-Zero."

"Go, Alpha."

"Dauntless, bridge is secure and fire hoses are deactivated. I say again, bridge secure and fire hoses are deactivated. Sir, the hostiles onboard do not appear to be members of the crew. Hostiles have AK-47s and tactical gear. It further appears that the captain was executed, over."

It took a moment for the reply. "Alpha One-Zero, *Dauntless.* Brilliant work. Reinforcements are coming aboard shortly. Hold your position."

"Dauntless, Alpha—" Suddenly the lamps overhead flickered out and the functioning screens went black. The marines scrambled behind the console and trained their rifles toward the lime green door that opened onto the superstructure's only stairwell.

Alford dropped his voice, almost to a whisper. "Uh, *Dauntless,* we've just lost electrical power over here." A battery-operated emergency light activated, throwing a dim red glow throughout the bridge.

"Alpha One-Zero, copy that. What's your status?" Haywood asked.

Engine room, Simms mouthed to Alford, who nodded.

"Dauntless, we've taken a defensive posture on the bridge but cannot guarantee our security or the integrity of the vessel. Sir, request permission to sweep the two decks immediately below our position, over."

There was no pause from Haywood. "Alpha One-Zero, you are authorized to take any necessary action to secure that vessel, over."

"Roger, *Dauntless*. Moving now, out."

The bridge was located on the third and uppermost level of the *Catarina A*'s superstructure. Directly below was "B" deck, and beneath that lay "A" deck. Situated farther down, not inside the superstructure, but within the hull of the vessel herself, was a pair of corridors running to the aft and forward cargo holds and the engineering spaces. A single stairwell connected all of it, and the marines had no choice but to push down it if they were to secure the ship.

"On the door," Alford whispered.

The marines came around the console and formed up at the frame. Judging by the absence of hinges, they could tell that the door opened outward, into the stairwell—a tactical advantage for them. Alford let his L22 carbine fall on the sling and removed his Browning Hi-Power from its holster. He placed his right hand on the knob, pressed down, and swung the door fully open.

"Torches," he breathed, switching back to the rifle.

Three beams of radiant white light from beneath their carbine barrels flooded the stairwell. They swept down the narrow flight to the next level, stacking up again at a door labeled "B Deck." Alford breached first and the two others followed in at his back.

"Hold." Alford held a clenched fist, and the stack paused, pinning themselves against the bulkhead.

They were at the end of a blackened corridor that stretched to the superstructure's port side. He counted eight doors in total, four on each side; all were open. It was utterly silent, and the air was unnervingly still. Worse, there wasn't a solitary sign of life. Looking forward, with his rifle aimed down the hall, he whispered back to his men, "Eight compartments, fairly small. Simms, you and I take them one at a time. Derby, cover our six."

Alford felt a grip on his shoulder, signaling that they understood.

The entire deck was berthing space for the crew. Yet as the marines searched, they found none of them, only signs of their passing. There were two crammed bunks per compartment, and on each they saw that the bedding had been ripped away and strewn on the floor, as if in haste, or even by force. Alford and Simms quickly cleared the final compartment and came back to Derby, who was crouched down in the corridor.

"We got sweet fuck-all here," said the lieutenant. "Let's keep moving."

Down the next flight of stairs they came upon "A" deck and swept out into an identical, blackened, corridor. Only something was different—the smell, and one all too familiar to them. It was the acidic stench of burnt gunpowder. Alford knew they had crept further into the cave.

There were six compartments on this deck. Alford pointed to the nearest door to their left. The marines stacked up and started counting as the smell surged stronger. *"Three."* Alford burst into the compartment first and made for the corner straight ahead. He realized they were in the ship's mess. Then he stopped, turned with his rifle, pulling the light with him, and was instantly struck with horror.

Sixteen people—*Catarina*'s entire crew—lay heaped upon one another in a bloodied mass of flesh, all of them raked with gunfire.

"Jesus," he gasped.

Simms dropped his carbine on the sling and inched toward the heap. "Sir, what the fuck is this?"

"At least we know where they went." Alford felt his heart stir in his chest. "Cavalry should be here any second," he started for the door. "I'll call it in. Let's get the last compartments." They stacked up again behind Alford, who turned cautiously into the corridor, dragging the light.

A single man stood at the corridor's end, breaking the beam.

"Help me," he muttered, squinting in the light.

Alford put the man's head in his sights. "Show your hands!" he roared.

"Help me."

His clothes appeared bulkier than normal and he trembled uncontrollably like a wet dog. Alford could barely make out his face in the glare, seeing mostly a shivering black shadow projected on the wall. "Show your *fucking* hands!"

"Help me," he moaned with a heavy accent.

Simms barked the order in Arabic. *"Raweenee edeek! Raweenee edeek!"*

"Help me." But the man wasn't speaking to them.

"Show me your fucking hands! Now!"

The shadow's arms slowly began to rise. His left arm was slumped slightly and his fingers were curled over his palm in a loose fist.

Alford came forward a step.

The trembling stopped and the man began speaking in Arabic, at first in a whisper, and then gradually louder. *"La 'ilaha 'il 'Allah, Muhammadun rasu-lu-llah."* He closed his eyes, brought his fingers away from his palm, and revealed a detonator switch.

Simms grabbed Alford's vest, heaving him back into the ship's mess.

The bomb's pressure wave rolled upward, ripping the man apart at his neck bones and lower jaw, the body's weakest point. There was a short, bright flash that was abruptly consumed by a dense cloud and a hail of tiny shrapnel. *Catarina* buckled with a deafening rumble, collapsing the decks where the man stood and blowing out a section of the portside superstructure into the sea. The marines dove to the floor in the mess, which remained intact on *Catarina*'s starboard end. Smoke flooded into the room. Fire alarms wailed overhead and sprinklers in the ceiling showered them with stagnant water. Alford gripped his ears and languidly rolled on his back, checking if he could feel each limb. And then he heard gunfire.

"Contact right!" It was Derby, yelling somewhere in the smoke.

Alford saw two flashes and their reports over the klaxons. He rolled to his side and drew the Browning from its holster. Derby was on his feet. A man with an AK-47 dropped dead by the door. A second charged in. Alford raised his pistol toward the doorway and squeezed the trigger, getting off five rounds. The second fell atop the first. He saw Derby turn again, his eyes so wide they nearly swallowed his forehead. "Get down!"

Bullet holes ripped through the bulkhead in front of Alford in wide, indiscriminate streaks. Bits of vermiculite panels flew through the air like confetti. The rounds whizzed over their heads and ricocheted off the metal bulkhead behind them. "Jesus-fucking-Christ!" he heard Derby scream. The barrage kept up, ripping larger holes in the bulkhead. Alford grasped at the drenched floor around him for his rifle. He caught it and took it in his arms, rolled flat on his back, and emptied the magazine into the bulkhead. The shooting stopped, giving way again to the alarms and the downpour from the ceiling.

"Down the stairs, it's just one!" Derby cried.

Alford came to his feet and felt sick. He hadn't heard from Simms.

"Simms!" he shouted, scanning the carnage.

"Here!"

Alford moved through the smoke and the rain toward the sound, coming to his knees when he saw it. "Oh my god."

Simms's right side was shredded like ground meat. Bits of shrapnel protruded from below his arm where their vests had no coverage. He squirmed on the floor, visibly in pain. "I'm fine," he panted. "I think I'm all right."

Alford leaned closer to Simms and a rage fell over him. "Stay here, okay?" his voice trembled. "Stay here, and I'll come for you."

Derby came over and spotted them. "Fuck!"

"How many?" Alford asked.

"Uh…sir…just one. He ran down the stairs."

Alford turned to Simms. "I'll fix this."

The two marines bounded into the corridor and saw the morning sun flood through the gaping hole in the superstructure. They charged down the final flight of stairs and came upon the entrance for the aft cargo hold. They tucked their rifles against their shoulders and aimed through the open hatch, casting the light from the torches inside.

It was a labyrinth of shadows drenched in gloom. Rows of shipping containers were laid out before them in high canyons of corrugated steel. There were five rows stacked closely together, forming a maze of narrow passageways. Alford played his torch beam into the darkness, counting maybe thirty containers in all. Whatever they weren't supposed to have was in here; so too, he realized, was whoever didn't want them to have it. They had reached the cave's end.

Something rapped in the darkness, followed by a scraping sound.

Alford gestured in the noise's direction and whispered to Derby, "Slow."

Their boots gave a low patter on the deck plates as they advanced forward, coming around the starboard corner of the first container, low on their knees and moving purposefully, swinging their muzzles from left to right in slow, exact arcs against the shadows.

Another noise sounded in the gloom—a slight bang—this time closer.

They covered the distance up the row of containers and paused, assessing their surroundings. A five-foot void sat between the end of the first row and the second line of containers, forming a tight aisle that opened onto the other passageways in a T-shaped intersection heading left and right. Alford gripped Derby's shoulder and pointed left, and then he touched his own chest and pointed right. Derby nodded, swung around the corner, and halted.

"Sir!"

Alford spun on his heels and shot his light down the corridor.

A man stood motionless at the end, his back to a container and both hands raised high in the air. An AK-47 sat on the deck before him and he kicked it forward with his foot.

It occurred to Alford that all he had to do was throw the man to the ground and restrain him; his clothes clung too tightly to conceal a bomb, and he had willing kicked his weapon away. But that would have been too easy. Alford's eyes stung and the rage returned. That would have muddied his purpose.

And that was when it all began to reel. Alford stepped closer, narrowing the beam around the man. He didn't speak; neither of them did. Alford swore the man was laughing, but there was no sound, only the glare dancing on his face. The lieutenant planted his feet on the deck. He could feel the sweat gathering on his brow and a pounding resound deep within his skull, the veins throbbing beneath his skin. He saw the light, the light that he cast. It was burning; he couldn't stand it anymore. The light cast off the steel behind the man and slashed at Alford's eyes like a blade. And the sweat dripped from his brow and over his eyelids, blinding him with a curtain of salt. He felt the cymbals of light pulsing through his head. The ship carried up a dense, fiery breath and it seemed like the hull had split open from one end to the other and unleashed, not water, but hell itself. Alford's entire being tensed and he squeezed the rifle. The trigger gave; and there, in that noise, sharp and deafening at a single ripple in time...

One shot pierced the man's left eye, throwing him back on the steel.

Derby ran ahead. Alford walked, wiping the sweat from his brow.

Blood and brain matter coated the shipping container. In his death throes, the man uncontrollably twitched and convulsed. Derby was frozen. Alford stepped forward, trained his rifle only inches from the man's chest and fired twice, slamming his body against the deck until it fell motionless.

The lieutenant wiped his brow with his sleeve again and cast the light down the side of the container. A canvas bag rested on the floor. He came up to the bag and nudged it open with his foot. Four rounded blocks of Semtex plastic explosive sat inside, disconnected from the priming assemblies. Alford judged that it weighed about ten kilograms, more than enough to send the *Catarina A* to the bottom of the gulf.

They came around to the container doors. Alford grasped the latching handle, pulled it into the upright position, and swung the doors open. Derby shone his light inside, illuminating, at the container's entrance, an olive green, airtight hatch marked with Russian lettering. A porthole in the hatch allowed the marines to look inside.

Footsteps from their reinforcements echoed in the distance.

Alford squinted. He saw two high-back chairs bolted to the ground before a small workstation. Recessed into the console were two computer screens and a satellite radio.

Derby eased back from the container. "What the hell is that?"

Alford sighed. "What they didn't want us to find."

CHAPTER 21

"THERE WERE TEN. We think they boarded on a container loaded in Oman." Roger Mathis opened the file and passed a photograph over the table.

Eli Tanner took it in his manicured hands and examined the scene from behind the polished lenses of his Burberry eyeglasses. It showed the interior of a shipping container in *Catarina A*'s forward cargo hold, drenched in camera flash. The floor was strewn with candy bar wrappers, empty tuna fish cans, water jugs and loose 7.62-millimeter rounds. A bucket filled with urine sat by the corrugated steel wall.

"The Brits were kind enough to scan the prints," Mathis continued. "Their names pinged right away, all known Islamic Jihad OGs. Shin Bet has tracked some of these guys for years. We're lucky to be rid of them." C/CTC passed another photo to the national security advisor. It was taken on the bridge and displayed more carnage than Tanner would have preferred to see so early in the morning. "Abdel-Rahim Jaara, Nassem Jabari, and Ali Yusuf al-Reyashi were all popped on the bridge; not sure who the other three are yet." Mathis handed a picture of the ship's mess, showing the crew in a bloodied heap and the bulkhead torn apart like Swiss cheese. "Two more went down here."

Tanner cleared his throat and passed them back.

"The guy who, uh…" Mathis sipped his coffee and pretended to press a detonator switch in his hand. "They're still mopping his DNA off the ceiling, but I'd bet money that's Shadi Abu Zeid. I heard he always wanted to try it." He placed the mug on the table and dug through the file in his lap. "Here's one." Mathis pulled another image from the middle and offered it up. Tanner hesitated a moment before accepting. "Mr. GQ right here"— the picture displayed the terrorist who took a round through his eye; a pink *pâté* of brain matter canopied the container behind where he fell—"is Sami

213

Salim Ishaq. They caught him priming a satchel charge in the hold. His big brother blew up a shawarma joint in Tel Aviv about six years ago. Nice family."

Tanner gave a slight, contemptuous frown and slid the photo back with his index finger. "I see."

Mathis closed the file. "We're still getting the details in from NATO, but our working theory right now is that the PIJ operatives came aboard in Oman as a security element to escort the ship to Sudan before the Iranians could take over. When the Brits intercepted her, well, these guys did their job—took out the captain, the crew, damn near scuttled the cargo, too. Of course," he waved his hand, "she should reach Djibouti by nightfall. My local people will meet her at the dock. FBI is sending a forensics team down from Baghdad, too."

"Yes, about the cargo," the national security advisor picked the lint from his cashmere sweater and pointed to a binder on the table, "explain to me again, just what is that thing?"

"That *thing,*" Ryan Freeman breathed, "is troublesome."

The D/CIA opened the binder and placed a diagram on the table.

There were other items on the agenda that Freeman needed to discuss before Tanner left with the president for Moscow that afternoon: the Israelis, Alireza Fakhrizadeh and Hezbollah; but this issue had so mercilessly thrust itself to the foreground. He set a photo next to the diagram. It showed the shipping container found in the *Catarina*'s aft cargo hold, a section of the container's starboard side was cut away with a welding torch. Freeman placed another photo beside the first, detailing what sat inside. Illuminated by the lurid flash, Tanner saw four large tubes connected to a pair of hydraulic pistons. He looked back to the diagram. It was a perfect match.

"We've seen these before," Freeman said, "but only as a prototype. A Russian defense contractor, Concern Morinfornsystem-Agat, has shopped this design around for a few years. It's called 'Club-K.' It was first revealed at the MAKS Airshow in Moscow and has ginned up hype at every arms expo since. As far as we've seen, it's only existed as marketing material, a proof-of-concept to a potential investor with disposable capital. But they've never found a buyer to come along and pay for development."

Tanner picked up the diagram and examined it closer.

"Essentially," Freeman continued, "the idea is to conceal a satellite-guided missile system inside an ordinary shipping container, making it virtually indistinguishable from the millions of other containers moving on ships, rail, highways. Inside each of those four tubes is a Soumar cruise missile—basically a reverse engineered Iranian copy of a Russian Kh-55. You'll see on the diagram that the top of the container lifts back and those pistons raise the launcher tubes upright, into firing position. The front section of the container is the command module, where the targeting and comms systems are operated."

Tanner held up the diagram and jabbed it with his finger. "This isn't a mockup, they actually built this?"

"I'm afraid so," Freeman lowered his head.

"The Russians?"

"No. This," he pointed to the photos, *"this* is not a Russian design. The Soumars, of course, are domestically produced. Most of the electronics appear to be Frankensteined from the export versions of various Russian SAM systems. But I have to give them credit, they've done an excellent job."

Tanner pushed his glasses onto his forehead and rubbed his eyes. "And they wanted to deploy this goddamn thing in Gaza?"

"No, sir, not exactly," Mathis shook his head. "You couldn't smuggle this past the Israelis, and the Pasdaran wouldn't trust PIJ with it anyway. My guess? They're trying to recoup the forward-based tactical missiles around Israel's periphery that they lost when we cut off Hezbollah. The IRGC has lost Syria, and now Lebanon; Sudan is the next logical choice."

"Who would've likely taken control of it, if it reached Sudan?"

"Colonel Rasoul Gharib Abadi," Mathis said flatly, "their ambassador in Khartoum, but that's only a diplomatic cover. He runs the Quds Force's Division 6000, responsible for operations in North Africa and Gaza; he's also the handler for Azzam al-Nakhalah, PIJ's military chief. Their secretary-general, Ramadan Shallah, is just a political figurehead in Tehran. Colonel Abadi, through his buddy, Azzam, calls the shots."

"And they could hit Israel from there? What's the range on these things?"

"Two thousand kilometers," Freeman stated.

"Christ."

"Sir, this container has 'asymmetric' written all over it," said Mathis. "You could put it on a ship, park it off Tel Aviv, and they'd barely have time for their lips to reach their ass."

Tanner sunk in his chair and tightened his jaw. "That's colorful."

"Eli, I have to stress again that we keep the circle around this small."

"You mean shut out the Israelis?"

"If you'd like to put it that way…"

Tanner removed his glasses and tapped them on the table. "They already know we've found something. And they've asked for their defense attaché in Djibouti to meet the ship when it arrives. You'd like me to tell them no?"

"I'd like you to stall them until we can frame it appropriately."

"Frame it how?"

"That we've captured the only known operational system and that it's not a threat to them." Freeman was getting rather adept at this dance.

"One call from Arad to the Oval," Tanner pointed to the hallway beyond his office door, "and that won't hold."

"Well, that's your arena, not mine," Freeman sourly admitted.

"I'll talk to him on the plane," Tanner allowed. There was a moment of tense silence before the national security advisor sighed, "Okay, what dragged you out here in the first place?"

Freeman shifted his eyes to Mathis, who began.

"Sir, you'll recall early last week that there was an article in the PDB from my lead officer in Beirut, entitled, *'Hezbollah Scours Source of Lost IRGC Aid Funds'?*"

"Yes, I passed it on to Ilan Halevi in Arad's office."

Freeman frowned at his lap.

"Right, sir, and they sent us a request to be read-in on the source—"

"Which I denied," Freeman added.

Tanner shot a look to the D/CIA and turned back to Mathis. "What's your point, Roger?"

Mathis handed over a copy of Nina Davenport's most recent cable. "I received that from my officer late Wednesday night. If you look at paragraph two, it details a meeting she had with her asset—TOPSAIL—during which she was informed that Hezbollah's investigation is focusing on its construction arm, the Jihad al-Binna Foundation's Western Beqaa branch, and specifically its director, a man named Walid Rada."

"How much is missing?"

"Two million US and change, sir," Mathis said. "This is the same cash we saw Hezbollah distributing directly to locals in Beirut and the south after Israel attacked in '06. For that reason, the funds never went through the party's central accounts, making their audit rather difficult."

"And TOPSAIL says that they suspect Walid Rada of embezzlement?"

"You could say that, sir."

Tanner ran his finger over the report and paused. "Wait, what the hell is this? Paragraph three?" He read aloud, "'Asset was hesitant but revealed spotting a man in Security Quarter of Beirut, matching last-known physical description of—"

"Hold on, Eli," Freeman interrupted.

"—*Ibrahim al-Din?'*" Tanner's eyes widened. "You can't be serious?"

"Eli," the D/CIA assured, "I find that to be conjecture, and we are not considering that entirely plausible without corroborating information. I brought this to you specifically because of Hezbollah's investigation." He paused for a moment. "After the issue with Picasso and Monet at the NSC meeting yesterday, my staff dusted off everything we have on Alireza Fakhrizadeh, trying to establish what we do know and what we do not know. You can imagine it's not much. As we draw up plans for penetrating the Haj Ali Gholi site, it would be extraordinarily helpful to be as well versed on the site's presumed director as possible. However, Mossad is the recognized authority on Fakhrizadeh. Normally, we would simply ask the liaison here for their files, but as you can also imagine, we cannot exactly tell them why, if our interest is to prevent immediate airstrikes against Iran. For that reason, I proposed going to Tel Aviv and meeting with Benny Isaac to make a trade for Fakhrizadeh's autopsy report under the guise of a cover story."

Tanner pushed back in his chair. "What's your plan?"

"The Israelis have demonstrated an interested in TOPSAIL. I would show this report to Isaac and offer full access to TOPSAIL's reporting, allow them to recruit Walid Rada as their own, and conduct his debriefing together after extraction. In exchange, I would ask them to retrieve Fakhrizadeh's autopsy report from Tehran and give us anything else they have on him."

"And Isaac wouldn't be suspicious about this at all?"

Freeman nodded. "He very well may, but if he is, I doubt he'll say anything. Isaac is old fashioned, gentlemen's rules and all. It's hard to explain unless you know him. The cover story I'll use is that we had a virtual walk-in drop information about Fakhrizadeh working in Parchin. That'll explain our sudden interest. A day or so after we get the files from Mossad, we'll say we traced the webserver behind the VW and found it connected to IRGC Intelligence—write it off as a dangle. And then we'll loudly kill the whole thing in cable traffic so we know Mossad will see it as genuine. IOD and Info Ops have talked it out and they think it's a good legend."

"One concern—"

Freeman was waiting for him and had a counterattack prepared. "No, Eli, we will not be running an offensive intelligence operation in the streets of Beirut. This is entirely an Israeli affair, if Mossad chooses. Roger's officer in Beirut will be there solely to advise and run TOPSAIL, nothing more. Our position as an impartial mediator between Israel and the Syrians will not be effected in the slightest."

Tanner cracked an entertained smirk. "Fine. I'll have to run it by him on the plane first, before you do anything, but that's fine."

Freeman uncoiled a notch and breathed.

"Oh," Tanner continued, "let me take these files with me. In case he asks questions, I'd like to have the answers right in front me."

That struck Freeman as an incredibly amateur thing to say. Tanner was supposed to be a font of wisdom on every facet of foreign policy and national security—all of it at the president's disposal. He was, in his own way. After ten years running the Council on Foreign Relations, shuttling between parties in New York and Washington, there wasn't a room in either that he couldn't work, nor a testy head of state he couldn't woo with a well-timed phone call. But he wouldn't last an hour on an operation, Freeman knew. In that realm, Tanner was a rarefied dilettante; the type of person who could waltz down the meat aisle of a supermarket and assume everything simply materialized on the shelf in neat, colorful packages.

Tanner checked his watch. "I have to run back to the house before I head over to Andrews." The national security advisor and his wife lived on a plantation along the Chesapeake in Saint Michaels, Maryland. She inherited millions from her late father's diverse holdings in tech, aviation, entertainment and shipping stocks. He gathered the files and slid on his glasses. "We're done here."

Ten minutes later, a pair of agency Tahoes cut down Constitution Avenue toward Arlington. Freeman stared aimlessly out his window to the bare trees on the National Mall zipping by like a haze. It was bitterly cold that morning. The Tidal Basin had frozen over in the night, and the paths that wove around the monuments were desolate beyond a few zealous joggers. Freeman hadn't spoken since they stepped in the car.

"You shot down the al-Din line pretty fast," Mathis broke the silence.

Freeman kept staring. "Waste of time."

"You don't think we can find him?"

The D/CIA turned from the passing haze. "No."

"Why?"

He gazed back into the haze. "Because the only shot in hell we have to find a man like Ibrahim al-Din is to drop on our knees and pray that one day he staggers out of his cave and decides to come for us."

Not another word was said. The Tahoes crossed the Potomac, taking the George Washington Parkway to Langley. Freeman went to his office and slumped onto the sofa; Grace Shaw appeared a moment later. In minutes, a call was placed to an old gray man with a serial number tattooed on his forearm in a nondescript building in the dry suburbs of Tel Aviv.

He wrote lists. They never kept to a rigid style or order, and mostly they just rambled. He wrote lists of his favorite sports teams, of the people who lived in his town, of classmates or of objects in his home. He wrote lists of the way things were in his old life for when his memory stole them away. And he drew pictures. He wasn't quite good at it, not that anyone ever saw them. He drew pictures of birds, mostly, and sometimes he sketched bears, goats, or elephants. He drew the faces of the people he loved, although their features were fading. When they allowed, he also played games, rolling his socks into balls and tossing them into a wastebasket.

During the first month of captivity, Corporal Moshe Adler was moved by the hour in an endless scramble to keep out of sight of the Israeli drones and helicopter gunships that loitered constantly overhead. He rarely saw daylight during that time and his captors were under strict orders not to have any interaction with him. That time was the most taxing. He remembered the stories from his childhood of the IDF airman who was shot down over Lebanon and simply vanished into the hills, never to return. Adler feared the same would happen to him, that he would be forgotten. He feared that more than death.

As the glare on Adler's kidnapping faded, the movements gradually became routine and his captors grew more familiar, even friendly. On a few occasions, different armed men would burst into his room, shouting. They would throw a hood over his head and stuff a gag in his mouth, shove him into a car and speed off into the night. For the next several days, Adler would languish in a tunnel or at the bottom of a well in abject darkness. Those spells terrified him, and at any moment he expected gunfire and explosions to erupt around him, or for one of the guards to storm in and put a bullet through his temple. But those spells would inevitably cease; whatever spooked his captors would subside, and he would return to one of the crammed flats where the years drifted by, melding into one, harrowing odyssey.

Once, not too long after his kidnapping, a rather powerful man came to see him, surrounded by bodyguards. The man had a trimmed gray beard and wore a high-buttoned collarless shirt—an Iranian. He gave Adler a bouquet of bright red carnations out of respect and introduced himself as a general. The general sat on the floor next to Adler and asked him, in flawless Hebrew, about his family. Adler told him at length about his parents, his brothers and his sisters. And then, the general calmly lowered his voice and told Adler to forget them, as he had slipped into the blackest crevices of their minds. Adler, he said, was a ghost.

But today, Moshe Adler's captivity would ultimately end.

He sat on a cushion inside a locked room in a flat along a wretched street that dead-ended in a large mound of earth, stone blocks and rubble. The sunny beaches that swept down into the Mediterranean were only a hundred meters west, and the barricade of steel and cement that demarcated Gaza's border with Egypt sat opposite a short stretch of fields to the south. Outside the room, his guards—all seasoned Palestinian Islamic Jihad fighters—crowded around a radio broadcasting a soccer game from Cairo.

Adler heard car doors slam over the announcer's cries.

The guards stirred in the other room and switched off the radio. Footsteps sounded on the creaking stairs below. Locks tumbled in the door. It swung open, casting daylight into the darkness. Adler squinted, and saw Azzam al-Nakhalah standing in the frame.

CHAPTER 22

A STREAM OF tractor-trailers and passenger cars slowed against the howling winds over the bay. Tanner kept his eyes on the BlackBerry in his lap or straight ahead through the windshield; he refused to look down. He sat in the back of a Suburban driven by a US Army NCO of the White House Transportation Agency in the right lane of the Chesapeake Bay Bridge's eastbound span. The bridge held two narrow lanes of whizzing traffic, stretching four miles to Kent Island. There were no shoulders, and at either end the only bulwark from the icy water was a three-foot Jersey barrier. From the Suburban's high perch that bulwark virtually disappeared. Tanner looked ahead as they arched over the main channel.

And then it happened in a singular moment.

Fifty feet ahead in the right lane, a white Mercedes slammed the brakes and screeched to a dead halt. The cars behind swerved erratically to avoid it. Traffic stopped with a blare of horns and smoking brake pads.

A woman lurched from the Mercedes and crawled atop the hood.

She was barefoot and wore a dark red evening gown that stirred fiercely with the wind. Her long white hair fluttered out and blanketed her face. A diamond necklace glinted in the sun. Tanner leaned forward in his seat. Two people from the car directly behind jumped out and ran toward her, shouting.

But it happened so fast.

She toed the precipice and turned her back to the open bay. The pair nearest to her screamed and grasped out. The woman splayed her arms into the wind and let go. Gravity took her over the side. She fell back and doubled over, her arms and legs pointed to the sky. And then she vanished from Tanner's sight; dropping ceaselessly, willing, and eager, toward the madness.

• • •

Roger Mathis cabled Beirut immediately upon returning from the White House. The news was exactly as Nina feared: she would have to share TOP-SAIL's reporting with Mossad. Still, it wasn't quite the apocalypse she initially envisioned after C/CTC's earlier messages. Colonel Samir Basri would strictly be her asset, only the information gleaned from him would be used in direct support of an offensive Israeli intelligence operation in Lebanon—of which Nina would ensure that he remained ignorant. Basri was no cheerleader of the Israelis. If Basri knew that he provided tacit support to lure a mid-level Hezbollah officer to defect, he might very well collect his winnings and pull back from the Central Intelligence Agency's teat. Nina understood that would be her primary role in whatever came of the director's meeting in Tel Aviv—to keep TOPSAIL onboard at any cost. She couldn't afford to lose him, despite his glaring vices. Then she would be blind again.

Nina hadn't risen from her desk in hours; her focus that morning was drawn to the MV *Catarina A*'s seizure. The reports poured in every thirty minutes with a red notification banner on her computer screen. There was a media blackout on the raid, although the more adept journalists in Washington and London had posted some rumblings to Twitter. The next day, after the ship docked in Djibouti and Combined Joint Task Force-Horn of Africa took custody of the weapons found aboard, NATO would hold a press conference and direct the world's attention to the caliber of firepower Iran was pumping into Sudan and Gaza. It wasn't exactly Nina's brief, but she worked the Horn of Africa before, and she had an encyclopedic knowledge of the various smuggling rings and Sudanese intelligence networks that the IRGC used to exert its will in that desolate part of the world. As she saw it, those Iranian proxies were just more cogs in the wheel, and what happened down there could ripple through the Levant.

She scrolled down the panes on her screen as a shadow tilted over her.

"A word, please." It was Tom Stessel, the Beirut station chief, and he was not asking.

Nina paused and rolled her eyes to the right, where he stood.

"Now," Stessel hissed, "...please."

She shifted her eyes back, locked the screen, and stood. Stessel was already midway to his office across the room. Nina followed and shut the door behind her.

Stessel was poised behind his desk and brandished a piece of paper. "Do you know what this is?"

Nina shrugged. "Can I use my imagination?"

"It's from the chief of the Near East Division. Do you know what it says?"

"Again, may I be creative?"

His nostrils flared and he slapped the paper on the desk. "It's a cable—to *me*—asking why Grace-*fucking*-Shaw is telling *him* that the director is flying to Tel Aviv to plan an op in Beirut based on intel from *your* fucking source. Naturally, he wants to know what the fuck is unfolding here that would warrant his fucking boss coming and telling him what's happening on the ground on *his* turf. Meanwhile, his fucking senior officer in the country hasn't told him jack-shit about any of this. Do you see what happens when the shit flows backwards?"

"Yes," Nina admitted, "I can picture there being a minor quandary."

Stessel dropped his volume a notch. "Nina. I cannot do my job in this country if I am not told what we are doing within its borders."

She sat in one of the chairs by his desk. "Tom, I'm being as straight with you as I can—whether or not you believe that, I don't really care—but I had nothing to do with whatever they've cooked up at headquarters."

"Nothing?"

"*Nothing*. My panties are just as chafed as yours. I don't want to share TOPSAIL with Mossad, and you know damn well if he knew what they're doing with him, he'd walk. You know this."

Stessel sat as well.

"You told me," Nina continued, "that you had no objections to sending TOPSAIL's report about Hezbollah probing Walid Rada back to CTC. I did that. Did I suggest him as a possible recruitment target? You're damn right I did. Rada is in a shit position, he's weak and we can turn him. That's why I'm here, Tom, to penetrate Hezbollah because your people fucked it up."

Nina pressed back in the chair and crossed her legs.

"Why are they doing this?"

"What are you talking about?

"Why are they trading some Hezb bureaucrat who bit off more than he can chew and will probably get exactly what he deserves?"

"Tom, I have no idea," she shook her head. "I've asked, but no one at headquarters will talk. I know there's some new special-access program with the Iran Ops people. The director personally runs it. And whatever it is, he thought our little source here played such an important role that he took it to the White House. But—and I say this with respect, Tom—it's not your goddamn problem anymore. The director wants something and he thinks trading Walid Rada to the Israelis will get it for him. If Benny Isaac wants Rada, then he'll send his people up here and they'll get their man, one way or another. Our only concern is making sure TOPSAIL stays onboard with us. I need him. *You* need him."

Stessel calmed. "Nina, we don't have to do this. We don't have to be constantly at each other's throats. And I don't know about you, but I can't work like this, you know, if this keeps up. If Mathis won't send you home, then I'll fucking resign. I'm serious. I've served my time, I sure as hell don't need this shit."

"Tom," Nina cocked her head to the side and smiled, "that's sweet."

"Can you please just utter one fucking syllable without an iota of sarcasm and condescension?" he grunted.

She smirked. "I have a hard time speaking in a non-condescending way to people who should absolutely be condescended to."

"Oh, for fuck's sake."

"But seeing as we're a couple now and we don't have secrets," she offered, "you should know that I'm meeting with TOPSAIL tonight."

"I want to know exactly what happens in the morning."

"You will," she nodded.

"Good," he reached over the desk and extended his hand. "Truce?"

Nina accepted with a modest grin. "For now."

The painting arrived timely that morning via courier from Roman Ivanov. As inscribed on the attached card, it was purely a gift to convey the Oracle of St James's most sincere congratulations to his young protégé on his new appointment, made official in a press release the previous day. Yet as with every act by Ivanov, there wasn't the damnedest bit of sincerity about it. Beneath the veneer, woven into the oil-stained fibers of the canvass, laid a sinister message and an admission of accomplice to mass murder that they would display in the Kremlin for all to see. Andrei Ilyich Minin placed the card on the mantel—it was written in Russian calligraphy, and clearly not by Ivanov; he could hardly speak the language fluently, much less write it with such grace—and admired the painting that was propped beside the fireplace. It was an 1890 work by Nikolai Ge, one of Russia's great artists, and was inspired by the Gospel of John, chapter eighteen, verse thirty-eight. The work depicted a moment during the trial of Christ in *praetorium* before Pontius Pilate. Ge painted a brooding Christ, pushed into the shadows against the backdrop of a monolithic wall, standing motionless like a tree trunk with the ends of his robe flowing to the floor like roots. Opposite Christ, across a bright field of light, stood Pilate, cloaked in the sun like a Pagan god. In the scripture, Christ responds to Pilate's questioning and declares, "I came into the world to bear witness about the truth." To that, Pilate countered with indifference, *"Quod est veritas?"* What is truth?

Minin drew his eyes down the canvass to the letters stamped into the gold plate at the bottom of the frame and read the painting's title: *Quod Est Veritas?* The message conveyed was rather clear if one understood Roman Ivanov's thinking as Minin did.

Ivanov long considered himself a student of philosophy. During the protracted dialogues leading to their pact to eliminate Mikhail Karetnikov and launch their little enterprise in the Middle East, Ivanov regularly invoked the "Problem of Truth." It was a metaphysical subject that philosophers had debated for millennia, encompassing what truths are and what, if anything, gives them form and makes them valid. Truth was not a singular construct, he would argue, but a narrow spectrum, a line divided into segments. At the most rarified, phosphorescent terminus of that line was an understanding of the intelligible: an absolute knowledge attained only by the intellect. Ivanov called it the Realm of Being. And then, at the farthest contrast of that spectrum, disjointed from the light and plunged fully into darkness, sat the Realm of Becoming: a world of mere shadows and reflections of physical and spiritual truths—illusions projected upon a wall. This realm, uncoupled from the absolute, is not fixed by any enduring reality, but decided by a group or individual for themselves or some other, manufactured and eternally changing. Ivanov explained that these false "charades" of truths are opinions with which the minds of ordinary people are brimming.

Minin studied the image of Christ shoved into the darkness juxtaposed to a false idol bathed in light. "Truth," he recalled Ivanov declare, "is what we damn well say it is."

Nikolai Ge's painting was destined to loom over the fireplace of Minin's new office in the Kremlin Senate building. It occupied a spacious suite on the first floor, overlooking a triangular square dotted with bare trees and crisscrossed by cobblestone walkways. The office was traditionally reserved for the head of the Presidential Administration, which Minin was appointed to not twenty-four hours earlier. His predecessor, Valery Volodnin had been burned alive at Borisovsky Air Base.

Wrapped in a single package, Minin would serve as gatekeeper, confidant and aide-de-camp to President Dmitri Lavrov. He now managed the president's executive office, the vital organ used to exercise control over the state's various ministries and agencies; coordinated the formation of foreign and domestic policy, relations with the Federal Assembly and the courts, press and communications strategy; and he directed the president's security and logistical arrangements. Minin could now strangle Lavrov in his guiding embrace. His new staff was spread over two buildings inside the Kremlin walls: the Senate, where he operated with the president's other executive aides, and the Arsenal, which garrisoned the Presidential Regiment, an elite unit that ensured the compound's security and guarded senior state officials. Minin also controlled offices a few blocks east at 4 Staraya Square, once headquarters to the CPSU's Central Committee. Supplementing his new responsibility, Minin would also be named chairman of both Gazprom and Rosneft. If all then went according to plan, those positions would give Minin a seat at the OPEC board of governors. But, he reminded himself, all could still—easily—crumble to pieces.

Minin's office wasn't quite his own yet. A work crew moved about the suite, gathering up Volodnin's effects and packing them in the stepped mounds of boxes that had materialized in the corridor over the past few days, marking the offices of Karetnikov's advisers like nameless headstones.

He gave the painting a final glance, left the workers to their task, and stepped into the wide hall. His heels pattered gently on the parquet floor as he whistled past the graveyard.

Just four hundred yards away, in St. George Hall of the Grand Kremlin Palace, Mikhail Karetnikov's remains lay in state inside a flag-draped casket guarded by a detachment of the Presidential Regiment. Over the past two days, thousands from around the country filed in to pay their respects. They waited for hours in the biting cold in a queue that snaked over a mile through the Borovitskaya gate, up Manezhnaya Ulitsa, and back around into Red Square. Minin saw their chapped faces in the blowing snow when his motorcade charged past earlier that morning. There was nothing quite like it in the country's history, certainly not since Stalin died, he thought. The Russian people were not accustomed to such a wrenching, visceral period of collective agony. Never had they had such a hero to grieve. The old party ceremonies to ferry the Politburo's dour old men into whatever unknown fate awaited them were just as dry and artificial as the embalming fluid that made their corpses presentable to the working masses. Of course, after the fall, there was Yeltsin, but his legacy was so tattered by the bitter memories of the systematic pillaging of state assets that his demise was largely a relief. But lastly, there was Mikhail Borisovich Karetnikov, a man for whom his supporters and detractors alike had to look back to the tsars to find any equal.

His rise from the KGB, to the Saint Petersburg bureaucracy, and finally to the Kremlin was so meteoric that the people hardly had time to become acquainted before Karetnikov cemented his rule over the country. In the sixteen years since, he was the one man who pulled them from the utter national humiliation of the nineties. Karetnikov promised them that Russia would—not could—be a global, universally respected, feared power once more. And he made it so. He shoved the oligarchs into their rightful place, free to go forth and reap their fortunes so long as they did not cross him. He initiated a slow creep back toward a multipolar world order, divested from the unchallenged hegemony of the United States. He expanded Russia's territory by force, annexing Crimea and effectively snapping off puppet enclaves in Georgia and Moldova, reviving the nostalgic idea of *"Novorossiya."* And for it, his people loved him. That would be, Minin reflected, Mikhail Karetnikov's most enduring legacy: reinvigorating the Russian people's appetite for conquest. It would be his own legacy, Minin resolved some time ago, to satisfy their hunger.

Karetnikov would take his place in the lofty pantheon of Russian national icons. Minin would see to it. But back on earth—in the Realm of Becoming—Minin's immediate task in the coming weeks was to sweep away any vestiges of loyalty to what would soon be the old order of business: people for whom the man was more important than the mission. After fourteen years of Karetnikov's unchallenged reign, they infested Moscow like cockroaches.

Minin would start with his immediate staff in the Presidential Administration by sacking the various main directorate chiefs and functionaries whom he could not trust. Next, Minin would turn to the Federal Assembly, which Karetnikov had spent more than a decade magnificently transforming into his personal echo chamber. Minin had to ensure the backing, or at least the abstinence, of the chairmen of the State Duma and the Federation Council, as well as the leader of the United Russia party. However, the greatest threat to Minin and his co-conspirators were Karetnikov's most loyal servants: Foreign Minister Uri Popoff, Defence Minister Nikita Porozovsky and General Aleksei Tsekov. Minin would deal with them last.

But for the time being, Andrei Minin had the most important ally of all, a man with whose protection he could rise above the law, and with whose voice and signature he could blind a superpower and strangle it in his embrace.

President Dmitri Lavrov found some small measure of protection behind the massive oak desk at the far end of his office. He was almost cowering, Minin thought as he bowled past the secretaries and through the double doors, spotting the president's slim, wrinkled frame jutting out from the chair. It was as if he tried to make sense of it all, slowly in his mind, how a man so undeserving, so unprepared could be thrust into a place of unbridled power and responsibility. Minin knew it from inception: Lavrov did not stand a chance.

"I hope I'm not disturbing you, sir," Minin stepped closer.

Lavrov stirred in the chair. "No, not at all, Andrei Ilyich, I was just…" The wrinkles on his forehead became more pronounced. "It doesn't matter."

Minin stopped within three feet of the president and towered over him. "It should please you to know, sir, that I've received word from Roman Leonidovich. He tells me Prince Farid visited the king in Riyadh yesterday and discussed our offer. Ivanov reports that His Majesty is rather receptive to the idea."

"Good," Lavrov nodded and looked at his lap, "that's very good."

Minin did not add that the cheque Ivanov cut for no less than one billion pounds undoubtedly made Saudi Arabia's monarch more supple. The deal was tipped—at least on the surface—overwhelmingly in favor of the Saudis. The terms were rather simple: At the next OPEC board of governors meeting in Vienna, Saudi Arabia would sponsor Russia's application for membership into the cartel. It would be the most sensational development to hit energy markets since the embargo of the 1970s, dramatically boosting the cartel's clout and sway over the global price of crude oil. The Saudis had numerous reasons to welcome Moscow with open arms. Over the past decade, OPEC watched the influence of its production quotas—the cartel's primary tool over the market—wane as a revolution in shale oil exploration swept over North America, OPEC's largest importer. That meant the cartel's share of global oil production hovered stagnantly around forty percent, the lowest in its history. However, with the addition of Moscow to the board of governors, OPEC would again control well over half of the world's crude oil deposits, making their influence over the markets all the more potent.

The Saudis would justify sponsoring Moscow by asserting that Russian membership would make production cuts less traumatic globally. Moreover, the deal would drastically enhance the security and stability of energy markets. OPEC was able to respond to crises and avert what would otherwise be cataclysmic economic meltdowns because of its ability to produce more oil than it currently exported. This spare production capacity functioned like an elastic waistband around the energy market's bloated gut, able to expand and contract as necessary. The cartel endured by its ability to meet unexpected losses in production, whether by the hands of social strife, natural disaster or terrorism. Without that assurance, the cartel would collapse and the global economy would spiral into a flaming heap. As it stood, Saudi Arabia was the only OPEC member able to actually produce more crude oil than it currently exported; it was the only member with capacity to spare, the other members were all pushed to their limit by the developed world's insatiable thirst for petroleum. That fact alone gave Riyadh hegemony over the cartel's members.

Yet it just so happened that there was only one other nation with the same ability to produce more oil than it exported: the Russian Federation. So with Moscow sitting at the table, the Saudis could sleep soundly with the assurance that if some catastrophe were to befall them, another member was ready to take control of the cartel and keep markets stable.

Minin would work diligently to manufacture that catastrophe.

To assuage the kingdom's political and diplomatic anxieties, Minin also prepared to effectively castrate the Saudis' "noisy neighbor" across the Persian Gulf, the Islamic Republic of Iran. That was the quid pro quo of the arrangement. In exchange for Saudi Arabia sponsoring Russia, and inevitably provoking the ire of Washington, Minin would guarantee Russia's full and total diplomatic abandonment of Iran—withdrawing its ambassador and shuttering its embassy in Tehran, expelling Iran's diplomatic staff from Moscow and dissolving all standing economic and military relationships, including Russian backing for the Bushehr Nuclear Power Plant. Further, Minin would give Riyadh veto power over Russian arms exports to the Middle East via a classified memorandum between the GRU and its Saudi counterpart, the General Intelligence Presidency. It was an offer Riyadh could not refuse: give Russia a seat in their exclusive club and neutralize their sworn nemesis as a strategic threat in the region. But of course, there was a complication. In order to join OPEC, Russia needed the unanimous consent of the cartel's four founding members, of which Iran was one. Clearly then, Minin would have to wait until membership was secured before pulling the rug out from under Tehran. The Saudis naturally understood this.

And yet there was another obstacle. Moscow could not appear to simply "wake up" one day and decide to abandon one of their longest and most valuable allies; that much was obvious. There had to be an irrefutable impetus for such a momentous shift in the Kremlin's policy. First, Iran must be framed for an act so heinous that no other nation could possibly stand at its side, even Russia.

The planning for that heinous act was already well underway in Lebanon, in the hands of a psychopath that Minin and General Trubnikov had unleashed.

Minin eased himself into a chair opposite Lavrov's desk, purging those dark musings from his mind. "But we need to confront the problem posed by the Americans."

"We do," Lavrov agreed.

"They will not take this offer lightly. One phone call from the White House could scare the Saudis off and scuttle this entire deal. We need to be proactive in how we handle them," he said decisively.

"Handle the Americans?"

"Yes, sir. We need to get in front of them. Tell them first. We aren't doing this to harm their interests and they need to know that." Minin leaned in closer. "We need to be honest, sir," and he uttered the next words with a smile and not a hint of irony, "because we have nothing to hide."

"The other ministers will disagree…"

"No, of course they will," Minin pulled back and snapped, "but their shepherd is gone and it's time they accustom themselves to that reality."

He froze for a moment, hearing what he just said. Lavrov looked confused. Minin breathed and submerged those dangerous, revealing thoughts.

"I beg your pardon, sir, that was unbecoming."

"No, it's alright. It's alright," Lavrov assured. "Tell me what to do."

"Meet with Paulson," Minin said flatly. "We needn't make awkward glances across the cathedral at each other like schoolboys. Meet with him, sir. Invite him and his staff to breakfast the morning after the funeral. We can talk like adults." He leaned in again. "Tell him our truth, sir… We have nothing to hide."

Angela Weisel emerged from an armored Cadillac DTS limousine into the frigid air that swirled over the tarmac at Joint Base Andrews. The painted blue and white fuselage of the Boeing VC-25A—not yet possessing its call sign, "Air Force One"—towered nearly six stories ahead. Staffers and bodyguards poured out of the SUVs and minivans that snaked behind the limousine and followed a few deliberate paces behind her. The secretary clutched her overcoat's lapels as she began closing the hundred feet to the plane. She'd better get used to it, she reasoned; it would be no warmer where they were headed.

Weisel ascended the aft airstairs and pushed her sunglasses over her bangs as she stepped aboard. She bypassed the press pool, seated near the tail, and made her way forward, down a corridor along the port side of the fuselage, past the conference room, to the senior staff cabin near the plane's nose. Eli Tanner was sunk into one of four plush leather chairs, a thick briefing book splayed over his lap. They exchanged pleasantries, but Weisel noticed that Tanner seemed distant, even disturbed by something.

A female voice rose over the VC-25's public address system. "Attention onboard the aircraft: We have a departure. The president is ten minutes out."

They had fifteen minutes to takeoff, and another ten hours to Moscow.

The White House was being crucified in the press and on Capitol Hill for not dispatching some lesser delegation to Karetnikov's funeral. The prevailing argument was that the departed Russian strongman was a ruthless thug who suppressed any shred of opposition in his own country, trampled over his neighbors with flagrant disregard for international law, propped-up a genocidal regime in Syria and directly challenged American leadership in the world. Sending the president to Moscow, they cried over the airwaves, was essentially turning a blind eye to Mikhail Karetnikov's detestable reign. Privately, most of Paulson's national security team begged the president not to attend, warning him of the media feeding frenzy that would ensue. Weisel was one of the few dissenting voices, telling him flat-out that not going was unspeakably idiotic. But the babbling pundits and breathless bloggers failed to understand that scantly anyone sitting in that cathedral the next morning would shed a tear at the sight of Karetnikov's casket. The only people who would mourn the man—apart from the grieving masses whose opinions were sculpted by the state-owned press—were the chosen few who would stand to lose out, economically or politically, because of his demise.

The storm that guided Karetnikov's plane into ground was one of the greatest gifts the White House could have received. Angela Weisel recognized that. By forcing President Paulson to weather the temporary media and congressional scorn, she was positioning the United States to fill the vacuum that would inevitably consume the Kremlin. Whoever emerged victorious had to be an ally. Adversity between the two great powers served no purpose. Her mission once they touched down in Moscow was not to lament a dictator, but to find a partner willing to wash away the detritus and steer Russia back toward the light. Weisel would find that partner. But in due time, the tragedy and conflict of Karetnikov's reign would seem like a pleasant memory.

Jack Galloway bent and stretched his legs, craning his neck to either side and taking a final scan over the trail. Again, he was black—free of surveillance. The switchbacks on the upper extremity of Jamshidieh Park, itself on the lower slopes of the Alborz Mountains, were empty at this time of day; locals hardly ventured far from home after sundown. It was a double-edged sword for Jack: with fewer people on the streets, it was markedly more difficult for a surveillance team to stalk him undetected, but it also stripped Jack of any useful cover. Tehran wasn't safe after dark. In the inquisitive eyes of the roaming police officers in their distinctive bottle green uniforms, anyone walking the streets at night was a thief, a fornicator, or worse—a spy. That meant Jack had a finite period to do his job and get back behind closed doors.

He reached for the familiar rock just off the trail, the one smoother and darker than the others, and moved it to the side before brushing clear a patch of dirt. An eight-inch spike, waterproof and hollow, emerged from the ground with a tug of the attached string. Jack unscrewed the top, then reached down his leg and popped open a cavity concealed in the heel of his right tennis shoe. He removed a small piece of paper wrapped in tinfoil and thumbed it down to the bottom of the spike, screwed the top on, and shoved it back in the earth where he found it. Only a few seconds passed; Jack had performed the maneuver countless times. He sprang back to his feet and casually returned to a brisk jog, this time down the slope, toward the sulfurous noise at the mountain's base.

Now that the dead-drop was loaded, a short sequence of events would commence. Early the next morning, just as the suspicious glare of the police would fade with the rising sun, a cut-out in Jack's small network, Akbar— the street vendor who operated a news stand in Tajrish Square, and coincidently attended the same mosque as Saeed Mofidi—would enter Jamshidieh Park and retrieve the dead-drop's contents, a one-time pad necessary to decode a shortwave radio transmission broadcast by CIA from Camp Arifjan in Kuwait. Meanwhile, an underpaid worker of the Tehran Sanitation Department would deftly place a small chalk mark on a lamppost opposite a walled villa on Ammar Street—also, coincidently, Mofidi's home. The chalk mark would signal to Mofidi that a message would be transmitted that evening. When he left Ayatollah Khansari's compound later in the afternoon, he would direct the driver to Masjid Giahi, his regular mosque, for afternoon prayers. As Mofidi exited the mosque, he would switch his own shoes with an identical pair left by Akbar. Concealed within would be the one-time pad to decode his new instructions. It was the typical mechanics of tradecraft, albeit slower and less technologically advanced than was the new standard. But it was safer, not as prone to interception and compromise, and could possibly extend the shelf life of the CIA's most valuable asset. Saeed Mofidi's eyes and ears yielded the only useful senses the United States had possessed in Iran for decades.

For the Central Intelligence Agency, peering into Iran was often done from the periphery, like casting sonar waves into the darkness to discern some semblance of form, but never details. Often the returns were dead ends and false promises. Under Peter Stavros' leadership, the Iran Operations Division—"Persia House"—ringed Iran with a network of listening posts in Frankfurt, Herat, Dubai, Istanbul, Baku and Erbil. These outposts were often embedded with the agency's station in the local US embassy or consulate, almost always sparring for space, resources and autonomy. The case officers assigned to them spent countless hours meticulously sifting the sands, waiting to see what might become lodged in the grate. Occasionally a few pebbles revealed themselves. For example, an officer may watch a hotel in the hopes of cold-pitching an Iranian on holiday who was known to have contacts back home worthy of exploit; or an officer in Dubai operating under commercial cover may lure an Iranian businessman into a tempting, bogus investment opportunity. Persia House also curated a running list of Iranian scientists that it continuously tracked and updated. They monitored every Persian name that was connected to PhD programs at European universities, every Iranian that lent their hand to a published academic journal or attended a conference, and every purchasing agent that crossed an international border to snatch up laboratory or computer equipment to ship back home—all of them were pinging lights on Langley's radar. However, the Iranians weren't stupid—far from it—and they knew their best and brightest had a price on their scalps. The ones who were truly a prize—the elite few connected to the nuclear program—hardly ever left the country, and when they did they kept the company of several minders from the Ministry of Intelligence. Now, the going wisdom at Langley was that if one of those precious few were spotted alone, they were most likely a dangle and it was better to steer far clear.

And that left Jack in denied, unforgiving territory to guide and protect the one friend the United States possessed in Tehran. That was the nature of Jack's existence, the burden he carried—to live surrounded, and yet utterly alone.

It was a tangible, physical sensation that signified its presence, maddeningly indescribable but undeniably real, like an itch or a quiver burrowed somewhere in his mind; the gentle drum of anxiety. It was the rock and the insecurity that anchored him down in the quicksand of reality—the quiet agony we all suffer. Maybe one day it would fade, and maybe one day he would accept that it did not have to be this way, that this indescribable, undeniable reality was avoidable, controllable, and malleable. Maybe one day he would no longer be afraid to seek the life he desired; and maybe one day he would no longer believe that he didn't deserve it. Maybe one day someone would show him how.

But until that day, that was the inescapable truth of Jack's existence, the purpose and the force that pulled him up each day: that we crave what we've lost, and we covet what we've never known.

The Kerem Shalom Crossing rose like a mirage from the fields around it—a haze of concrete walls, razor wire, surveillance cameras, loudspeakers and watchful Israeli armored personnel carriers. Nearly four kilometers in the distance, over the 1950 armistice line and beyond a cratered no-man's land, sat Gaza and its southernmost town of Rafah. For the strip's two million inhabitants, Kerem Shalom was their outlet to the rest of the world and the chokepoint through which all their imports and exports flowed, regulated and inspected by the Israel Airports Authority. There was no direct contact between the Israeli customs officers and the Hamas members that managed the Gaza side of the crossing from a post down the road in Rafah. Aid shipments into the strip were driven by the Israelis to a paved clearing just over the armistice line and later picked up by the Shaiber Company, a Palestinian shipping firm licensed by the IDF to access the crossing. Exports shipped out of Gaza were handled in the same manner: the Shaiber Company drove trucks to the clearing and abandoned the cargo, allowing the Israeli inspectors to clear the goods and transport them over the border. The process was rigorous and took the inspectors approximately forty-five minutes to clear each shipment coming out of Israel, and nearly twice as long for loads coming in.

But the day drew to a close, and the sun slipped further behind the Mediterranean. Kerem Shalom shut down at night; the crossing wasn't equipped with lights, which would have only exposed the Israeli inspectors to sniper fire from across the border. There was one final shipment to clear before the job was done—a load of red carnations headed out of Gaza and bound for a market in Amsterdam. The flowers, grown proudly by struggling Palestinian farmers, were one of the few exports Israel allowed to leave the strip, having worked out an agreement with the Dutch government. It would be Valentine's Day soon and the flowers were in high demand, fetching a premium price for the farmers.

An Isuzu refrigerator truck was parked on the clearing. A team of Israeli inspectors approached it and first ran a mirror along the undercarriage. No explosives. One inspector clicked on a flashlight and looked inside the cab.

Nothing unusual. They moved down to the roller doors and copied the serial number on the seal before snapping it off with a wire cutter. They struggled with the handle for a moment, but it gave, and they heaved the door up on the tracks.

The stench of rotting flesh was overwhelming.

The inspectors recoiled and guarded their noses. They shined the light inside and, in the blackness, found pallets neatly filled with bright red carnations, doused in dried blood.

An inspector hoisted himself inside and trained the beam on the pallets. Wedged between two of them, in a coagulated, maroon pool, the inspector saw the form of a man's body dressed in an olive green uniform. He inched closer, guided by the light. The light ran up the man's legs, over his back and his shoulders to his neck. A bullet wound punctured the back of the man's skull, leading through to his shattered forehead. The inspector felt his stomach churn as he eased closer. He could make out the patch on the man's arm.

It was Corporal Moshe Adler—after eight years—finally home.

CHAPTER 23

HAROLD LANSING WAITED before the tall windows overlooking the garden of the Hôtel de Marigny. He idled for no less than twenty minutes in the Salon Rouge, amid tired Louis XVI furniture and gilded wood paneling, while the man he came to see, the man who brought him to Paris, finished up a late dinner with the French president, René Laniel, across the street in the Palais de l'Élysée. Ambassador Lansing was not invited—nor did that snub bother him in the slightest. He had come to see himself as a traveling physician, parachuting in with his bottomless bowling bag to save the willfully ignorant natives from their own poor habits. As he stood there in that vast, dated room—watching the minutes pass—he began to suspect that his next patient wasn't too eager to take his medicine. Lansing remembered what Hanna Sayigh told him in Ramallah: "Some enjoy the sickness."

Footsteps sounded in the foyer beyond. Lansing turned and saw a colossus appear in the threshold, rising no less than six-foot-six in a tailored Brioni suit; a shock of gray hair strategically combed over his retreating hairline.

"Magnificent night, isn't it?" Prime Minister Avigdor Arad clasped his hands behind his back and cracked a wry smile. "Hello, Harold."

"How are you, Avi?" said Lansing.

But the prime minister didn't answer. He strolled toward the windows, almost floating, and stopped within a few inches of Lansing, looking out over the garden; his hands still tightly held behind his back. "Let's take a walk."

The Hôtel de Marigny sat in Paris' 8th arrondissement, where Rue du Faubourg Saint-Honoré meets Place Beauvau. In its current form, the building dated back to 1872 when Baron Gustave de Rothschild merged two smaller townhouses into one sprawling mansion at the city's heart. In the early-nineteen seventies, the French government purchased the *hôtel particulier* to house visiting heads of state. The garden stretched out from the main façade with symmetrical gravel pathways edged in stone, empty flow-erbeds and tightly trimmed hedges under a canopy of bare chestnut trees. A high stone wall provided modest insulation from the humming taxis, coach-es and mopeds surging through the evening rush. The pair ambled past a marble fountain—dry for the winter—and moved deeper into the garden, making small talk until they were well out of earshot of the prime minister's bodyguards. Just then, the unmistakable pulse of an ambulance siren charg-ing toward Champs-Élysées forced them to pause.

Lansing took the opening as his cue to begin. "I may have something for you," he shouted as the siren subsided.

"I damn well hope so," said Arad, glancing to the Shin Bet officers watching him from the parterre, near the fountain. "Let's sit," he gestured to a marble bench beside them.

"I spoke with Sayigh in Ramallah—"

"Yes, I know you did. Sounds riveting."

Lansing ignored the obnoxious jab. "I think he wants to help."

"Does he now?"

"Fatah's negotiations with Hamas are by no means final."

Arad raised an eyebrow. "Is that what he told you? That man," he scoffed. "That's not what I've heard."

"What'd you hear?"

"Let's just say the Muqataa's walls are riddled with holes—literally and figuratively," he grinned. "Hamas looks at Israel—all the time looking at Israel—and they see us abandoning Shebaa Farms, they see us flying into Damascus and striking deals, they see us talking to our enemies and they think, 'Oh, gee, if the mouse is getting cookies...'"

"Avi—"

"They think, 'What can I get, too?' So they want us to loosen restrictions on Kerem Shalom, they want us to get the Egyptians to back off the Rafah Crossing, they want their people to get more cabinet positions in the Pales-tinian Authority; and because Hanna Sayigh and his fellow autocrats in Fa-tah are so desperate not to be burned in effigy in Gaza City, they play along. Sayigh wants *you* to get *me* to help him. That's what he wants."

Lansing realized long ago that Avi Arad was not the easiest man to talk to. Watching him debate a point, simply listening to him talk, was to have a view of a master artist at work. Arad did it so effortlessly, so deftly that if one let him speak for only a few moments without rebuttal, the man had already crafted an argument so logically and emotionally bulletproof that it was nearly impossible to persuade him otherwise. Heads of state and for-eign ministers equally loathed his phone calls for that very reason: they of-ten had no choice but to sit back and take whatever barrage Arad felt like unleashing their way. For Lansing and Angela Weisel, getting him to strong-arm his cabinet into ceding Shebaa Farms to Lebanon was a *pièce de résistance* of statesmanship, requiring countless calls and flights between the Syrians, the Lebanese, the Turks and the United Nations. The return on giving up that slice of verdant farmland on Israel's northern border was rather large— forcing Hezbollah to disarm and bringing the Syrians to peace talks next month in Annapolis—but as if that wasn't enough, Lansing wanted to bring his plate back for seconds. He wanted Avi Arad at a table for negotiations with Hanna Sayigh and the Palestinian Authority. Lansing was not quite so bold as to think something useful could come of those talks, but as old men at twilight look back upon their life, they begin to see the voids, the blemishes that cried out for healing. It was a play Lansing had to make.

He saw the hurdles before him. Hamas, pushed away from the Iranians by their stance in the Syrian civil war, had edged nearer to Fatah, their traditional rival led by Hanna Sayigh. The result was a kind of rapprochement between the two; the first chance in nearly a decade to reconcile the differences that emerged after contested election results erupted in gunfire, ending with Fatah controlling the West Bank and Hamas in Gaza. But Arad asserted himself at the first opportunity, condemning the rapprochement and declaring that any Palestinian coalition which included Hamas—a terrorist organization bent on destroying Israel—would not be recognized by Israel. And so, as Hamas leaned further toward Fatah, the Israelis leaned further away. Meanwhile, the Iranians, not to be outdone and keen to regain their influence in Gaza, had doubled their backing to the second-largest militant group in the strip, Palestinian Islamic Jihad. Weisel and Lansing unwittingly complicated the situation. In giving Hezbollah no strategic alternative but to disarm, and thus driving Iran from Lebanon, the sights of the IRGC's shadowy mastermind—Qasem Shateri—were now fixed totally on Israel's southern border, with Gaza and his new proxy, PIJ, and searching for the first opening to exact revenge for being shoved in a corner. It was just as Sayigh had warned him. That reality was the very definition of blowback.

But Lansing thought he had a more valuable card to play. He thought he had the one bit of leverage that could leave the confident and lecturing Avi Arad utterly speechless. He thought he could get Moshe Adler released.

He thought.

Lansing had a counter. "Avi, you and Hanna Sayigh—as well as I—are all part of the same hypocrisy. Let's not pretend we must remain blind to that."

"Oh, but my friend," said Arad, "you are mistaken. I am not so hypocritical to preach peace, and reconciliation, and the need for this ridiculous 'togetherness' while posturing myself next to a terrorist group that fires rockets into Israel, and instills fanaticism in its children, and acts as if it has no control over a kidnapped Israeli soldier being held on its own soil. That hypocrisy belongs to Hanna Sayigh and him alone."

He was just too good, Lansing admitted and fell silent for a moment.

"Listen, Harold," Arad offered, "my job, my service to the Israeli people is to maintain a sustainable quiet." That was a favorite term Avi Arad used whenever he was given the chance, and sometimes even when he wasn't. The "sustainable quiet." It was a vague term, and purposefully so, which essentially meant that his government was willing to tolerate violence up to a certain level; that Israel could accept a limited number of rocket launches from Gaza, so long as they did not cause serious damage on the ground, certainly so long as they did not harm Israelis, and so long as they did not require a large response by the IDF. It boiled down to the optics of Israel's familiar *status quo ante*—the situation it repeatedly faced after its occasional throwdowns with the Palestinians. Arad used the perpetual Hamas boogeyman to energize his conservative base, while Hamas used rage against the Zionists to turn Gazans' eyes from the unmitigated squalor that engulfed them. The two used each other for their own political purposes.

Arad was indeed a hypocrite—just capable with rhetoric.

"Israel's will and Israel's ability to sustain that quiet," he continued, "is continuously threatened. I trust you heard about that business in the Gulf of Aden this morning?"

Lansing had read the cables. "Yes, I did."

"Do you know what the Royal Marines found on that ship?" It was a rhetorical question. "Four Russian cruise missiles fitted inside a standard shipping container. Do you know the range on each of those missiles? Two *thousand* kilometers. Do you know why the Iranians were basing them in Sudan? To strike Israel. Do you know what four of those warheads targeting the Kirya could do? They could decapitate the IDF in a single blow—flatten the middle of Tel Aviv. Do you know who shot at the Royal Marines to protect those missiles? Terrorists—Harold—terrorists from Palestinian Islamic Jihad. Do you know who allows Islamic Jihad to operate in Gaza? Hamas does. Do you know who wants a closer relationship with Hamas? Hanna Sayigh. Do you know who wants me to sit down and talk to Hanna Sayigh like old pals? You do, Harold, you do."

Arad breathed in through his nose, pausing before making his final point. "The Iranians are like water, Harold; they find their own course, filter through the cracks and seep in at the weakest point. That ship is proof that they are over-compensating for losses that you helped inflict. And when you compensate, you often go much too far. This is the threat Israel faces, from all sides, without end."

Lansing had enough. It was time to show his cards. "Avi, I don't need the lecture. Really, I don't. I'm not some dim-witted kid on a Birthright tour. You're so smart and calculating, think this through..."

He could see Arad rush for a response.

"If you want to marginalize the Iranians, then pulling Hamas toward Fatah should be the first thing that pops into that thick skull of yours every waking moment. And if Sayigh wants to bring them into his coalition, then you should move every rock and stone that you possibly can to make it happen. Suck it up, tuck away your pride, and legitimize him. Give Hanna Sayigh the political capital he needs to force Hamas to rein in Islamic Jihad—and then you'll have driven Iran from your borders for good. Watch the Knesset criticize that!"

Arad's Achilles heel was actually situated on his right flank. He governed his country through a precarious bloc representing the conservative end of Israel's political spectrum: the Likud, Yisrael Beiteinu, and Jewish Home parties. His own party, Likud, did not have a clear majority in the Knesset, Israel's unicameral parliament. Because of that, Arad had to constantly appeal to the right wing of his bloc or risk losing his mandate to rule. This forced Arad to be managerial and risk-averse, not a bold visionary as he so wanted, and sensitive to pressure from the right. Therefore, shaking hands with Hanna Sayigh and sitting at a table that included members of Hamas was tantamount to political suicide for Arad. Lansing understood this, but he thought he could offer the prime minister something much bigger, something that would provide unbreakable cover.

He thought.

"Secretary Weisel and I have considered this approach for some time," he continued, "and after we saw how you handled Shebaa Farms, we thought now may be our opportunity—"

"What are you talking about?"

"When I met with Hanna Sayigh, I gave a proposal that I could guarantee your place at renewed negotiations if he could urge Hamas to pressure PIJ into releasing Moshe Adler. There would be an exchange, of course: one thousand Palestinian prisoners, and they won't all be choirboys."

Avi Arad was finally speechless. He stirred on the bench, breathless.

"I spoke with Hanna again this morning."

"What did he say?"

"Well, it looks promising. He talked to Hamas and they didn't balk at the idea. They would bring it to Azzam al-Nakhalah in Islamic Jihad. Of course, Avi, I'd hoped to have more for you, but that's all I can do for now. If that were to happen, if we could get Adler released, would that bring you to the table? Would that steady your base? Would you stand with me?"

"Harold, I want that boy back—by any means," said Arad.

"I want him back, too, Avi," he smiled. He thought he was winning.

In the corner of his eye, Arad caught movement on the parterre, back toward the *hôtel*. The head of his protection detail spoke into his jacket sleeve. Ilan Halevi, his national security advisor, appeared next to the dry fountain with a grim look set behind his cheap wire-rimmed glasses. Something was wrong.

"Excuse me a moment," he told Lansing.

Arad stood and walked toward the fountain. Lansing saw Halevi put his arm over the prime minister's shoulder and pull him close. He couldn't hear them. Whatever Arad was being told, it didn't take long for the effects to settle in. Lansing saw Arad's legs tremble and his body double over for a moment. And then Lansing started to worry. He saw Arad wipe his eyes, speak a final word to Halevi, and turn back toward him. The prime minister walked much slower this time, with his head hung low on his shoulders; his entire frame seemed to melt into the gravel. Now Arad was only a few steps away.

"Is everything alright?" Lansing asked.

"Oh, yes," he grinned, "it's fine... You were saying? About the boy?"

"Well, Avi, not to mention what a huge moral victory Moshe Adler's return would be for the IDF and what closure it would bring to his family, it allows the support you need in the media, in the Knesset, and in your cabinet to negotiate with Hanna Sayigh. It would show the conservatives in your country that one can make real gains while working with the Palestinians in good faith."

"You think so?" Arad asked dryly, staring at the ground.

"Avi," Lansing smiled, "I'm convinced."

Arad drew his head up and glared at Lansing with two sunken, bloodshot eyes. "Then you should know that Moshe Adler is dead."

"What?" his face went flush.

"I said Moshe Adler...is dead. He was just found—executed—in a truck at the Kerem Shalom Crossing."

"Oh my god," Lansing gasped and put his head in his hands.

Arad loomed—all six-foot-six of him—over Lansing like a monolith of rage. "Listen to me, Harold."

"Avi. I had—"

"Shut the fuck up and listen!" Arad barked. "This is what happens when you think animals can be made to act like human beings. This is what happens when you treat a war like one of your political games."

"Please, Avi—"

"This is a war, Harold! A war!" he spat. "And because of your failure to accept it, that boy is gone. Now I have to call his family before the press gets hold of this. You and I are finished. Do you understand? Go back and tell that disgusting bitch in the State Department that I'll gladly sit down with Hanna Sayigh in hell!"

•   •   •

Her bare ass shown in the dim light bleeding through from the street: a sprawl of pale flesh and brown hair facedown on the cotton sheets. Her name was irrelevant; there were countless more just like her dotting the corniche and the alleyways beside Beirut's clubs and bars or the parking lots of the glamorous new nightlife emporiums up the coast in Jounieh. Most of them appeared in Lebanon to escape the civil war that consumed Syria. The girls poured across the border with no family, no money, not a friend in the world—and for men like Colonel Samir Basri, they were ripe for the picking.

Basri viewed himself in the bedroom mirror, adjusted his collar stays and started to pull his right arm through his jacket sleeve. They always seemed so timid the first time around, and this one was no different. He learned to spot the pros—the girls who had been at it for a while, the ones who took pride in their work. They were few and far between. Most, like her, only wanted it to end, and that piqued his insecurities. He tried to remember her age. Sixteen? Seventeen? Certainly no older, otherwise he wouldn't have paid as much as he did. She probably wasn't even sleeping, just lying sedate with her eyes clenched shut until he left for however long and she could relax. Come morning, he'd drop her back in the pond and throw out his lure for the next catch. He brought his left arm through the sleeve. Basri's dates—that's what he called them—were arranged by a club owner in Jounieh who recently ran afoul of the Internal Security Forces and now let Basri break in his newest stock as a kind of tribute. Sometimes he struck gold, other times just rock. But he had no interest in seeing this one again. He would have his security tell the club owner to find another with a different personality, one more outgoing and energetic.

And then he thought of Nina, with her flowing auburn hair, her fair skin, and that slight backwater drawl in her voice that she stubbornly fought to subdue. She was so enticingly flawed. He wondered what it would be like to have her, too. Basri checked his watch—time to go meet her.

In the alley behind his flat, Nina sat restlessly as rain pelted the Volvo's roof and charted a course down the windshield. She eyed the service exit submerged in the shadows ahead. TOPSAIL would come through the door at any moment. She thumbed the trigger guard of the Glock in her hand, digging the muzzle into the dashboard. There was a delicate balance she had to strike. Nina needed to pull from her agent as much information on Walid Rada as she could, without revealing to Basri that every word he said would support an Israeli intelligence operation inside Lebanon. Nor did she have much time. She suspected that Hezbollah was already sizing the noose around Rada's neck. Nina needed to know how close they were to arresting him. Mossad would have to move fast—which they could, she knew. They would first have to make contact with Rada, persuade him to leave behind his home, his entire life, and flee the country with a foreign intelligence service. It was a gamble, but she needed them to make it work.

"We're clear in the street," Ortega said through the radio in the center console. He was the head of her security detail from the Global Response Staff, the team of ex-SOF contractors CIA hired to protect its officers in the field, calling from a Mitsubishi Pajero waiting along Rue Gouraud.

"Roger," she replied into her mic.

And then there was that other grating issue burning a hole through Nina's mind: Ibrahim al-Din. TOPSAIL reported what was quite likely the first credible sighting of the master terrorist in twenty-three years—and the chieftains at Langley and the White House essentially ignored it. How could she explain that? She couldn't; it was insane to willingly let al-Din walk the streets for even one more day. But Nina had no choice. She had to justify it. She had to keep Samir Basri onboard.

The service exit swung open and a silhouette emerged into the rain. Nina reached back and popped open the rear passenger door, put the Volvo in drive and let it ease down the alleyway. As it rolled past the exit, Basri slid into the back and went prone on the seat. She gave the Volvo some gas and turned out onto Rue Gouraud. "I got 'em," Nina radioed.

"Copy that. Eyes on."

The Pajero inched off the curb and followed several cars behind. Nina sank into the late-night traffic and made for the hills on the eastern fringe of the city.

"I wanted you to hear this from me first," she said. "Moshe Adler was executed today... Islamic Jihad dumped his body at the border."

As they gained a bit of speed, Basri sat upright with a groan. "I'm devastated by that."

"You don't need to be a dick."

"So will they start bombing hospitals and schools, or what?"

"I don't know," she glanced in the mirror. And after a brief silence, she continued, "Your spending money's under the seat, the rest is in your account."

"Too kind, as always," he bent down and grabbed the envelope.

"Samir, this is getting serious. The director was impressed by your last report and took it to the White House."

"Ryan Freeman knows who I am?" Basri asked skeptically.

"Of course he does." Nina embellished the truth. Freeman had little idea who Samir Basri really was. As far as he was concerned, TOPSAIL was no more than an anonymous cryptonym at the top of a cable. But Nina knew it would push Basri along if she inflated his importance. That was part of her job, to be whatever her asset need her to be: a friend, a mother, a confidant, a lover—whatever it took to exploit Basri to the fullest, she would do. Nina would identify and target his weaknesses, and Samir Basri had two: his fetish for young women and his ego. "I—Director Freeman," she corrected herself, "needs to know exactly what's happening down in Machgara with Walid Rada."

"It's looking grim for our friend. I put a surveillance unit on his house and his office. That was Tuesday, after our last meeting. Wednesday morning, the head of the Judicial Police got a call from someone in the Security Quarter, someone close to the secretary-general, politely asking for ISF to remain five kilometers outside the Machgara city limits. There was no option, I pulled my men."

"Shit," Nina smacked the steering wheel.

"That's about as much as I know."

"So for forty-eight hours, you've had no presence in Machgara? For all you know, Rada could be in some basement getting his teeth yanked with pliers."

"'Fraid so."

"Jesus…"

"Whatever you're going to do, do it fast. It's only a matter of time before they arrest him," Basri calmly said.

"Thanks for the pep talk."

Nina saw him lean forward a bit between the two front seats. She gently flinched, not that he could see, and remembered the Glock at her side.

"You didn't ask me about *him.*"

"Who?" Nina fixed one eye on Basri and the other on the road.

"Al-Din. What did your director say about al-Din?"

"Samir, I'm sorry. You know I have full confidence in you."

Basri dropped back on his seat with an incredulous scoff.

"Samir, nobody wants to hear about that right now," Nina exclaimed, glaring back in her mirror. "There are bigger agendas at play here, okay? There are much more powerful people who are trying to build a new Middle East, and they have no desire to dig up old skeletons." Nina was disgusted with herself.

Basri rested his head in his hand and gazed out the window. "You people are so fucking naïve…"

"Samir—"

"No, Nina!" he cried. "I have no fucking shred of doubt at what I saw. Ibrahim al-Din still walks this earth and he is here in Beirut. Goddamnit, I walked right past him—I watched him with my own eyes. He is here!"

"I believe you, Samir. I believe you! I tried. There is nothing I can do."

"But *they* don't."

"No," she resigned, turning back to see him, "they don't. And I'm sorry."

Basri shook his head. "You Americans think you can come here, plant your flag and declare victory and all your enemies will step back and say, 'Okay, you win this time.' It doesn't work that way! When Wissam Hamawi, when the secretary-general, goes on television and says Hezbollah will disarm, Hezbollah will hand over its weapons to the state, do you people truly believe he speaks for all of Hezbollah? Do you think Iran, which gave him those weapons, will allow him to do that? The Iranians will do everything in their power to take Hezbollah back. And when Hamawi and the sheikhs are dragged from the Security Quarter and shot in the streets, who do you think will lead the charge?"

Nina could not bring herself to disagree with him.

"Mark my words," Basri continued, "when Iran has exhausted itself in Gaza, and with Islamic Jihad, it will come back here to Lebanon and it will call on Ibrahim al-Din to take back what is theirs. He will burn this country to the ground!"

Nina kept her eyes on the road; she couldn't bear to look at him. Every word of it was true. But she was powerless. "I know he will," she muttered.

They spoke no more after that. Nina made a loose circuit through Beirut's eastern suburbs and turned back toward Basri's flat in Gemmayze where they pulled into the alleyway off Rue Gouraud fifteen, tense, minutes later. The Volvo's engine idled over the rain. Nina put the car in park and turned around in the seat. She needed him.

"Samir, I need you to know this... You are the United States of America's eyes and ears in Beirut. We trust you, we value you, and we want you to be safe. I need you to understand that."

Basri didn't respond.

Nina exhaled. "Have your men stay away from Machgara."

"Anything you say," he grumbled.

"Samir, some things are going to happen soon—and it is imperative that when they do you are as far from Walid Rada as humanly possible. I'm telling you this for your safety."

"Whatever it is you people are planning, I don't want to know. As long as no one dies in Lebanon, I don't care."

Nina put her hand on his knee. "I promise. No one dies."

Air Force One touched down on the runway of Vnukovo Airport at nine-fifteen in the morning, Moscow time. In the ten hours since the president's delegation departed Andrews it seemed as if the entire world had come undone. Word of Adler's execution first reached Eli Tanner in the form of a phone call from the White House Situation Room, which was responding to a CRITIC report from NSA—generated via means best left unspoken. President Paulson's small brain trust gathered in the plane's conference room and hashed out what little hard details they could discover. Avi Arad was in the air over southern Greece and thus unreachable. Weisel did manage to raise her counterparts from Turkey, Qatar and Egypt—most were also en route to Moscow—and demanded they figure out exactly who on the ground in Gaza made such an asinine decision. Secretary Rusk was tele-conferenced in from the Pentagon. The Israeli Air Force's 69 Squadron, operating F-15Is out of Hatzerim Air Base, appeared to be mobilizing. He couldn't say more; the situation was just too fluid.

Meanwhile, another call came to Angela Weisel from the US ambassador in Moscow. The Kremlin requested the pleasure of hosting President Paulson and his staff for breakfast the next morning at Dmitri Lavrov's country residence in Barvikha, west of Moscow. Cordial as the offer was, it sent a cold shockwave through the plane, possibly more so than Adler's execution. The United States—Paulson, specifically—was supposedly the instrument of a waning unipolar world order; the mastermind of intricate Russophobic plots and conspiracies to dismantle that great, unique civilization and subju-gate its people to disdainful, neo-fascist Western norms. But now, even be-fore he was properly buried, Mikhail Karetnikov's successor wanted to host Paulson for breakfast? It struck the president and his staff as completely bewildering. There was a short, heated debate on whether they should ac-cept. Would the gathering be an opportunity for Lavrov to lecture Paulson on the long history of American deceptions and evils? If so, the president's time was much too valuable to be wasted. Weisel, for her part, made her feelings quite known: Yes, damnit, go! And as was often the case, she got her way. Now, even before they landed, the Secret Service was bending over backwards to handle the logistical ballet that necessitated the president of the United States spending the night in a foreign capital. There wasn't nearly enough time for his advance team and protective detail to book three full stories of a major hotel and sweep every corner of the property and the adjacent blocks. The only viable alternative was Spaso House, the ambassa-dor's palatial residence in the Arbat District. Details of the offer were pre-dictably leaked to the press pool perched aft, who were all essentially froth-ing at the mouth.

Understandably, Paulson and his people were exhausted.

As the delegation decamped from Air Force One, they made for the two-dozen vehicles lined up on the tarmac, unloaded from three mammoth C-17 cargo transports that arrived earlier in the morning. Blacked-out Sub-urbans were clustered around the president's two identical Cadillac limou-sines and carried his immediate security detail, military aides and Secret Ser-vice Counter Assault Team. One Suburban, which featured two collinear antennas mounted on the roof, was dedicated to electronic countermeas-ures designed to defeat guided attacks from RPGs, improvised explosive devices and anti-tank missiles. Another was nicknamed the "Roadrunner" and provided encrypted communications via the Defense Satellite Commu-nications System constellation. A small fleet of rented vans for staff, a press bus and an ambulance rounded out the rear of the motorcade. Paulson was welcomed at the bottom of the airstairs by his ambassador and the head of the Kremlin's protocol directorate. In ten minutes the motorcade was loaded and took off behind a loose phalanx of *politsiya* motorbikes on the M3 highway, north, toward Moscow.

The president sat with Weisel, Tanner and Larry Dawson—his chief of staff—in the hermetically sealed cabin, surrounded by six inches of armor plating. As they faced each other, they all collectively began to wonder how it came to this.

"So let me get this straight," Paulson said, "Lansing was *with* Avi when he found out? Physically next to him?"

Weisel gave a reluctant nod. "That's what Harold told me. They were in the garden, he was actually getting through to Avi, and that's when he heard. He stormed out of the meeting and that was the end of it."

"Ain't that some luck." The president fumed at the randomness, at the cruelty, at the impossibly foul nature of the entire ordeal. "And he blames us? He thinks we got that boy killed?"

"Sir, you have to understand his mindset," Tanner reasoned.

"I've been trying for seven years," Paulson snapped. "Do enlighten me."

Tanner shut his mouth.

"This is retaliation for that arms seizure off Somalia," Weisel breathed.

"So, Iran ordered it?" the president asked dryly.

"Yeah, you could say that."

Paulson gripped the bridge of his nose. "Okay, let's get this clear: whoever did this, whoever shot that boy—Hamas, Islamic Jihad; whoever—they will pay dearly. I want that known."

Dawson stirred from his place next to the president. He was always one of the last to speak. "We need to say something, even if it's just a condemnation."

"Right," Paulson agreed. "Take this down," he told Dawson. "'On behalf of the American people, I extend my deepest and heartfelt condolences to the family of Corporal Moshe Adler. As a father, I cannot imagine the indescribable pain the parents of that brave soldier are suffering. The United States condemns in the strongest possible terms this senseless and unprovoked act of terror. I offer our full support to Israel and the Palestinian authorities in Gaza'—make sure it's stated that way—'to find the perpetrators of this crime and bring them to justice. I urge all parties to refrain from steps that could further destabilize the situation. As the Israeli people deal with this tragedy, they have the full support and friendship of the United States.' Fill in the blanks."

"That's good," Tanner said.

"Angela, can you have the embassy release this just before the funeral starts?" Dawson finished writing.

"Yeah." Weisel brushed a strand of hair from her face and read aloud off her BlackBerry screen. "Okay, getting this from the ambassador in Tel Aviv: 'Arad's plane landed forty minutes ago at Ben Gurion and the Security Cabinet is currently meeting in emergency session at the Kirya. The prime minister's office has instructed the Israel Broadcasting Authority to clear prime-time programming for an address by the prime minister. There is heavy border police and IDF presence in East Jerusalem.'"

"They're bombing," Paulson declared.

"Now, Mr. President," Tanner offered, "we don't know that."

"Everyone useful I could talk to is in that meeting." Weisel slid her phone into her coat pocket. "Until they get out, we're dead in the water."

"By then they could have already hit Gaza," Dawson added.

"I should call Avi," the president nodded.

Tanner shot a wary glance to Weisel. "With respect, sir, you're probably the last person he wants to hear."

"He's right, Andrew," she conceded.

"And, Angela, you're a close second."

Paulson became agitated again. "Why do we bother with this diplomacy bullshit if no one will even talk to us?"

"The Russians will," Weisel realized.

"What?" the president blurted.

"The timing here is impeccable," she quickly laughed in amazement. "This is likely blowback for capturing Iranian cruise missiles copied from Russian designs...and where are we?" Weisel pointed out the window. "Lavrov wants to talk, Andrew, he's demonstrated that. Maybe this is a blessing in disguise."

Moscow is a city constructed by human hands on an inhuman scale. The motorcade swept up Leninsky Avenue, one of the many grand boulevards of granite so wide that one can only cross beneath in dimly lit passages accessed by narrow stairs cut like fissures in the soot-laden snowbanks. As they sped toward its core, the city gradually pealed back its layers and conveyed no illusions of its past and future. On the outer edges of Moscow, in districts like Lomonosovsky and Yasenevo, glimmering new apartment blocks of steel, glass and concrete towered like gnawed ribs stabbed in the frozen dirt: the dregs of capitalism and foreign investment. Drawing nearer to the Kremlin, past the Third Ring Road, in the districts of Yakimanka and Tagansky, Moscow offered signs of its schizophrenic history: restored nineteenth-century edifices, once rambling mansions of the tsarist merchant class, now offices and *pieds-à-terre* of oligarchs, the chosen few who sliced up Soviet state assets among themselves; amid the dour, gray high-rises of stucco and masonry, once commissioned by Stalin himself, as brooding temples to the dream of World Socialism—ghosts of a promised new world order felled by hubris.

Past the Garden Ring, the city's innermost rind, Moscow resembled a military occupation zone depopulated of civilian life. Twelve thousand soldiers from the Internal Troops of the Ministry of Internal Affairs and the Western Military District were deployed to seal off central Moscow and protect the funeral venue, the Cathedral of Christ the Saviour. Checkpoints reinforced by T-90 main battle tanks and BTR armored personnel carriers had been established at critical intersections and on the bridges leading over the Moskva River. Masked snipers dotted rooftops and fighter jets patrolled overhead between clumped snow clouds. Residents living inside the security area, many of them wealthy, were encouraged to go to their country dachas for the weekend, and given the eerie emptiness on the streets, most if not all complied.

Russia is a country that spans nine time zones, and in each of them — from Kaliningrad to Vladivostok—life had fallen to a standstill. Karetnikov's interment was televised for all his people to see; for them all to arrive at the final, anguished truth that their collective nightmare was real; for them to say goodbye. A row of network uplink vans topped by huge satellite dishes lined Gogolevsky Boulevard, near the cathedral, and transmitted a live feed of the proceedings to millions around the globe. Naturally, the sort of commentary provided on their television screens varied greatly by geography. Television cameras were fitted on booms and mounted on raised platforms along the edges of the nave. Leading up to the altar, the cathedral brimmed with the nation's political elite and a corps of foreign dignitaries that indicated where Karetnikov's deepest friendships had once lain. The Chinese sent a rather high-ranking delegation, led by their president, Han Jing, with his foreign minister and state councilor. Also present, and seated as far from the Americans as possible, was a group of bearded men wearing their telltale black suits and collarless white shirts—diplomats of the Islamic Republic of Iran, led by Javad Zanjani. Relatively few heads of state from NATO countries were present in the cathedral. The German chancellor Theo Haneke was seated several rows behind Paulson, not far from the British foreign secretary; France had dispatched its foreign minister, as had Turkey and Italy. Russia's former client states in Eastern Europe had all sent representation at the ambassadorial level. There were no traces of the Baltic countries, Ukraine or Georgia—whose leaders most likely watched on TV and popped champagne. The rest was a bizarre hodgepodge of eclectic dictators from Central Asia and military strongmen from Africa, pseudo-democratic socialists from South America, and a small group of obscure faces from Southeast Asia. None showed much remorse.

Precisely at ten in the morning, a procession of white-robed priests with large, unruly beards and gilded miters atop their heads started down the nave behind a golden cross, brandished by Patriarch Pimen II. Behind the priests were ten non-commissioned officers of the Presidential Regiment's 1st Cavalry Squadron carrying Karetnikov's flag-draped casket. The coffin was carefully laid under the cathedral's magnificent dome. And then it began with Pimen's pained exhortation to the heavens. "Holy God, Holy Mighty, Holy and immortal, have mercy on us."

They stood throughout the funeral, as was customary for the Russian Orthodox Church. Paulson had never seen anything quite like it. It drew on for over an hour, the patriarch and priests chanting in unison through the Divine Liturgy, at once indescribably beautiful and unspeakably haunting. They moved together in various rituals around the cedar box holding Karetnikov's charred remains, swinging a censer forward and back, unleashing a cloud of aromatic black smoke toward the casket. President Lavrov was standing in the front, next to Lyudmila Karetnikova whose eyes appeared like sunken red holes in their sockets. Next to them both, Paulson examined a younger man with neat blond hair and a boyish face. He was the most distraught of them all. Lyudmila rested her head on his shoulder in an attempt to console him, but the young man was lost in whatever dark shadow enveloped him. His face was buried in his hands; his moaning sobs warbling over the priests' emotive chants.

Paulson leaned toward Weisel and whispered in her ear, "Angela, who's that man crying up there?"

"Who?" she scanned the front row.

He tried to point with his chin. "Next to Lavrov, with the blond hair. Karetnikov's ex-wife has her head on his shoulder."

"Oh," Weisel noticed him, "that's Andrei Minin; been with Karetnikov for years. Since Saint Petersburg, I think. He's Lavrov's chief of staff now."

Paulson turned his eyes from the anguished spectacle.

After the priests concluded their liturgy, Karetnikov's cavalry escort slowly carried the casket down the nave and out the doors to a waiting gun carriage for the procession to Novodevichy Cemetery, where the once-mortal tsar would sit and rot for the remainder of eternity.

As Paulson watched the procession empty out from the cathedral, a lucid realization crept into his mind. It was a terrible thought, but undeniably and unavoidably true: Mikhail Borisovich Karetnikov was now justly in hell.

CHAPTER 24

SANDRA HARRIS HAD been here before. Quite a few times, actually. The first was still a vivid memory. She had gone with his parents and sister to see him off to recruit training in Illinois. He was ready to leave, to get as far away from California as possible. They weren't engaged yet, but Sandra already knew in her heart that he was the one. The near-endless stream of letters shot between them for those seven, arduous weeks only further solidified that premonition. A year later, he was accepted to BUD/S in San Diego. As he left for the airport Sandra could tell he was frightened, not so much by the infamously grueling nature of the training, but by nearly the year they would spend apart. Sandra knew he couldn't bear the thought of losing her; he hadn't ever been with anyone else. And so to her amazement, he dropped down on his knee right there and proposed. She understood then—as she blurted an emphatic, "Yes!"—what their life together would entail. It was a predictable cycle: eighteen months of training around the country with short periods of leave thrown in, followed by six months of deployment. How often they could speak varied widely by the mission. Occasionally they exchanged regular texts, emails and phone calls, and other times she could spend weeks without hearing from him. His first operational deployment—to Afghanistan—was the most taxing for them both. Those days leading toward it were a long goodbye, and they each struggled in their own way to prepare. Once he finally left, Sandra discovered what she called "the three firsts," the three most difficult realizations that always haunted her immediately after he left no matter how many times she had confronted them before: the first night alone, the first morning waking up to a half-empty bed, and the first time coming home from work to a house without a husband. But Sandra was not one to sit around feeling sorry for herself. She discovered that her husband's deployments had a few veiled perks: she no longer had to wash her hair or shave her legs each day, which was certainly welcomed; she donned his old PT shorts like a cape, unilaterally invaded the yard and conquered the lawnmower. Sandra learned to adapt to whatever came their way; she learned that she was strong enough to cope.

And then, in every way imaginable, the most beautiful thing that could have possibly happened forced them to question just how capable they truly were.

All of their values, everything they ever thought was important or meaningful, were irreversibly changed by having a child who so desperately needed them with each labored, victorious breath. The birth of their son, Ben, turned their lives upside down. Were it not for their health insurance through Tricare, which provided for the innumerable surgeries and treatments necessary to keep their son alive against impossible odds, Sandra knew her husband would have left the Navy the very night Ben was born and rushed into emergency cardiac surgery. He emerged through those dark hours a drastically different man. Becoming a father was equally the happiest and most terrifying moment her husband had experienced, doubly so than any firefight. After fourteen years of service to Naval Special Warfare, fourteen years of her husband's fickle mortality—and now another five years of their son's—hanging over her neck like a guillotine blade, Sandra thought the predictable cycle was drawing to a close. It was the most difficult thing she had ever endured, but like her son, and in many ways like her husband, each new breath was a victory. For that simple reason, Sandra and her husband carefully chose their battles, working past the trivial arguments and enjoying the happiness they shared together, because they knew all too well that their time as a family could be cut short at any moment.

She looked down to her pregnant belly as she waited for him to appear through the automatic doors. Sandra Harris had been here before—and she hoped this time would be the last.

The sun was low that morning, shielded by the bronze fog that unfurled over Hampton Roads in the night. She peered through the condensation streaks on the windshield of their Subaru Forester, tinkering with the defrost dial to see any glimpse of him past the protective steel bollards ahead, while Boomer, their black Labrador, panted impatiently from a blanket draped over the backseat.

About fifteen minutes prior, Sandra watched the white 767 land on the runway of Chambers Field at Naval Station Norfolk and taxi toward the squat Air Mobility Command terminal. Now she could see the plane's stabilizer edge up from behind the fencing. Exactly when and how her husband left Syria was classified, but she knew from their emails that he'd managed to squeeze a spot on a Space-A flight out of Incirlik Air Base in Turkey to Sigonella, Sicily, and then board a regular AMC charter through the Mediterranean and across the Atlantic to Virginia. In all, he'd probably been in transit for the better part of eighteen hours. Her eyes were fixed on the terminal ahead; she was starting to get anxious. The glass doors slid open, and a familiar face stepped onto the sidewalk.

Chief Petty Officer Robert Harris started through the bollards and into the parking lot under the load of an oversized canvas rucksack strapped to his back and a massive olive Pelican case in each hand. He briefly paused to scan the cars and shuddered in the cold, wearing only a tan field jacket, a maroon V-neck T-shirt and jeans. Standing six feet tall and weighing one hundred seventy pounds soaking wet—not thick, but lean like a swimmer— Harris was noticeably smaller than most in his unit. He spotted their car and kept walking.

"Boomer, look," Sandra reached behind her seat and scratched at the dog's neck. "Look, it's Daddy." She emerged from the Forester, filling the cabin with an electric chime.

Her husband saw her and shot a beaming, goofy smile from ear to ear.

"Hi!" she waved as he came closer.

"I'm cold!"

"Yeah, it's February, dork!"

Harris closed the distance to her, set the Pelican cases on the ground, and took her in his arms. They kissed and held each other for a few minutes. Boomer barked from the car.

"I brought a friend," she pulled back and cleared the mist from her eyes.

"Boomer!" Harris rushed over and threw open the rear passenger door. He crouched down and hugged the dog tight, digging his knuckles behind Boomer's flappy ears. "Hey, buddy!" Boomer whined and beat his tail on the seat as Harris kissed the side of his face. "I don't care about Mommy, I missed you most."

"Whatever," Sandra chuckled.

Harris noticed the empty car seat next to Boomer's blanket. "Little man's at school?" he stood and went to lift the hatch.

"Yup."

"How's he doing?" he placed his rucksack in the back.

"Great. There're four other kids in his class. Miss Sprouse is amazing."

"Good." Harris came back around for the two Pelican cases. "Whoa!" he stopped and pointed at Sandra's stomach, "Look at *that;* I didn't even notice."

"Hope you're happy," she smiled.

Harris leaned in and kissed her again. "Very."

He placed the cases in the back and then sat in the passenger seat, rubbing his hands together for warmth. "Quick, crank the heat up."

"Give it a minute." She eased out of the parking space. "Oh, that's clearly not for me, by the way," Sandra gestured to the large coffee in the cup holder.

"You're amazing." He pealed back the lid and took a sip. "Baby's good?"

"I've felt a little nauseous the past couple mornings, but the doctor says it's normal—not nearly as bad as the first time around. We have an ultrasound appointment. Should be the one." Sandra was seventeen weeks in, but they wanted to be together to hear the news.

"What are you thinking?" Harris asked.

"I think it's a girl," she glowed.

"That's it? That's your verdict?"

"Yep, I can feel it. I think you're getting your little girl this time."

Harris smiled.

Sandra left the naval base through Gate 22 and made for Interstate 64 eastbound toward Virginia Beach. The usual morning rush had already subsided and the lanes were mostly clear. "How was the flight?"

"Bumpy through Turkey," he drew the cup from his lips, "but it smoothed out once I switched birds in Sicily. Those damn C-130s are a death trap."

"Are you going in today?"

"For a bit. I need to check in with the chief and get everything unloaded. The guns are cleaned, I just don't want them sitting in the house overnight. And something's up with the 416 trigger—pressure's off—I want them to take a look before I get it on the range again. I won't be long."

"Okay." She spoke up again after a pause, "Z has a new girlfriend."

Harris laughed. "Of course he does. You meet her?"

"No, I saw her on Facebook. Little twentysomething from Lynnhaven."

"So Ben likes the new school? Do you like the new school?"

"Robert, it's amazing," she blinked. "The stuff his teacher and her aides do with those kids is incredible."

"Really?"

"Yeah, he's only been there three weeks and I can already tell that he's so much more calm, he's able to articulate things better. Oh, and they set him up with a tablet. There's an app on it for him to build sentences from pictures and it speaks the words for him. You have to see this thing, he knows his way around it better than I do."

"How are the fits? Has he tried to hit himself?"

"Um," she nodded, "he still gets frustrated, his mind wraps around something and it sets him off. But his teacher told me they're trying to show him better ways to express himself, and I've definitely seen that at home."

"Well, that's good."

Sandra took an exit off the interstate onto a wide avenue lined with box stores, chain restaurants and strip malls. It was always the clearest sign to Harris that he was home—and in many ways of what he fought for, oddly enough.

"Does he know I'm back?"

"I told him this morning, 'Daddy's coming home!' and you know, in his own way, I think he understands."

Harris raked his blond hair over to the side and itched the sparse scruff on his face. Boomer eased his head between the seats and nudged his damp nose in Harris's ear. "Jeez," he flinched and reached back to pet his dog, "Hi, pal."

They stopped at a red light. He saw his wife's hand resting on the gearshift. Harris took it in his and lifted it slowly, placing his lips on her skin, and held it for a moment. "'Sup?" he nodded.

She grinned and nodded back. "'Sup?"

Sandra parked along the curb in front of their house on Minneapolis Drive in Midway Manor, a military housing development in Virginia Beach. It was a modest three-bedroom home with a garage, white vinyl and red brick siding, and backed up to a row of tall pines before the adjacent apartment complex. Leaving his gear in the Forester, Harris opened the car for Boomer who bolted to the front door. They went inside and Harris felt like he could breathe safely for the first time in a month. The floors were mostly hardwood, peppered here and there with toys, and the refrigerator in the kitchen was canvassed by Batman drawings. Ben was fixated on the superhero and his room upstairs was decked-out with any sort of related paraphernalia his parents could find. Harris carried a photo in his wallet taken last Halloween; it showed Ben, hoisted up in Harris's arms as the Dark Knight, and his dad as Robin—or, as Harris saw it, Ben was dressed as his hero, but Harris was holding his.

He took a long, hot shower, washing away the grime instilled on the flight, and changed into a warmer set of clothes. When he descended back down the stairs thirty minutes later, he found Sandra milling about in the kitchen.

"You're off all day?" he asked.

"Yup. All day."

She worked as a receptionist at a nearby animal hospital where they had come across Boomer as a puppy. The job afforded her the considerable time needed to care for Ben, especially when Harris was deployed.

"When's the munchkin getting home?"

Sandra leaned against the counter. "Bus has been dropping him off around three-thirty."

Harris moved over and pulled her toward him. "I'll be back by then."

"What do you want for dinner?"

"Whatever you want," he kissed her. "Just no MREs."

"You got it."

He started walking to the door. "'Back soon. Love you, mean it!"

"You better!" Sandra yelled.

Outside, Harris heaved open the garage door, revealing a spotless 1985 rally blue Jeep CJ-7, a predecessor to the Wrangler. Harris moved the rucksack and the two Pelican cases from the Forester into the Jeep. Backing out of the driveway, he plugged in his phone and brought up a playlist loaded with a few of his favorites, David Bowie and Creedence Clearwater Revival. It took about twenty minutes to reach the base, although his personal best was twelve.

Dam Neck Annex, itself a detachment of the massive Naval Air Station Oceana, hosted a wide array of tenant commands: various Navy and Marine Corps training units, a Coast Guard intelligence fusion center, and the main processing facility for the underwater hydrophone network monitoring Russian submarine activity in the North Atlantic. However, most notable among the tenants was one of JSOC's two primary counterterrorism units, the Naval Special Warfare Development Group (DEVGRU), or commonly known in the media as "SEAL Team Six." DEVGRU, along with its counterpart at Fort Bragg, the Army Compartmented Element (ACE)—often called "Delta Force"—constituted the National Missions Force, the elite tip of the US military's spear, charged with conducting unconventional warfare, special reconnaissance and kinetic targeted killings in denied territory or other areas where an overt American presence on the ground was neither feasible nor advisable. Nearly fifteen years under the continuous burden of terrorism and insurgencies in the Middle East acted as a crucible for the units and their parent, the Joint Special Operations Command, forging its tight-knit group of operators into an oiled machine specifically designed to hand deliver death upon the doorsteps of those who plotted against the United States. It was a self-churning storm that propelled men such as Robert Harris to force those like ISIS to keep their focus on extending their own lives rather than shortening the lives of Americans. But Harris had been consumed by that storm for most of his adult life, he missed so much of his family, and with Ben's condition he could never bet how much longer they would have together. He wondered, as he passed through the gate leading to the annex, if it was time for that good fight to be fought by someone else.

Harris drove up Regulus Avenue, the main thoroughfare on base, to a segregated compound of beige, mostly windowless offices and warehouses set on an isthmus of dunes between Lake Redwing and the Atlantic at the north side of the annex. As he flashed his ID at the second and final checkpoint, Harris was reminded that theirs was a fight without end. Everything the command did was geared toward preparing for war. DEVGRU squadrons trained constantly when not deployed and signs of that preparation were evident from the moment he approached the gate. The calm air blowing off the sea was continuously broken by the rattle of gunfire from the ranges farther up the beach, or by the muffled thud of a breaching charge detonating in one of the kill houses secluded away in the marsh, and it was not uncommon to see operators moving around the compound in full combat kit with rifles resting on slings at their chests. Those men knew all too well that the United States was and would continue to be at war, and it was their burden, their professional undertaking to see it through to whatever theoretical climax that might one day come.

He parked by the "head shed"—the command's headquarters building—and hauled his gear up to the second deck, where the unit kept its heart. DEVGRU was split into six assault squadrons: Gold, Silver, Blue, Gray, Black and Red. Each squadron was led by a commander, and was in turn divided into several troops led by a lieutenant commander (the exact number fluctuated by rotational deployments and availability). Within each troop were several teams consisting of maybe six operators led by a senior enlisted SEAL. Every squadron was further outfitted with support and intelligence personnel who worked closely with the command's staff. All of the squadrons kept their team rooms, their Holy of Holies, on the second deck—or the second floor—of DEVGRU's headquarters building. Harris had spent his entire career in Red Squadron and quickly found himself up the stairs and at home.

His squadron's team room resembled a cross between a frat house living room and high-tech command center. It was a large space with a stocked bar and a kitchen, four conference tables, and second-hand sofas. Offices for the commander and master chief, as well as a separate room for operational briefings, were located off one wall, and on the opposite hung a massive flag of a white and black American Indian head—the squadron's mascot—against a blood red background. Harris would never forget the first time he set foot inside. It was just after selection, when new recruits were drafted into a squadron. The SEAL community was small, and each recruit was preceded by their reputation from their previous "regular" team in either Virginia Beach or Coronado. Some reputations were better than others, yet if one made it to the second deck, it was no accident: they had earned their place among the elite of the elite. Formalities of rank and the stringent regulations of the broader Navy were swept away; an operator's ability to perform in combat was far more valuable to the command than the insignia on his uniform. Such was true for Harris. On that day, he came to Red Squadron bearing an offering of Corona, as was customary for new arrivals. Standing before him and the other recruits was a stockade of burly senior guys with long hair and beards and a patchwork of tattoos incised on their arms. Right away Harris questioned if this was a good idea. He looked nothing like them; if Harris were to wear a short sleeve white shirt and a black tie, he could have easily passed as a Mormon missionary. On the exterior he resembled their polar opposite, not bursting with any sort of testosterone and machismo—growing out a full beard was a chore for Harris. But on the interior, as standing there proved, he had the same storm that propelled men like that forward into war.

They asked his name, but as soon as Harris answered, his voice was cut down by a chorus of boos. "Shut the fuck up, nobody cares!" They ritually did that to each of the recruits. But once it was done, it was done for good. Now Harris was equally part of the family. No one had time for petty bullshit.

Six years of countless trainings and deployments spanning the globe had passed since that day. And whatever debt he thought he owed, Harris was slowly beginning to consider it paid.

He went down an adjacent hallway to his cage; every DEVGRU operator had one. It was an order of magnitude larger than a walk-in closet and rectangular in shape. The two parallel walls were lined with metal shelving and the back wall featured a rod for hanging his dress whites and service blues—they were rarely worn—with several MultiCam uniforms and Massif ACU combat shirts. Apart from deployments and trainings, the uniforms often just hung on the rod. DEVGRU operators traveled and came into work on a daily basis in civvies as to minimize any undue attention. In fact, it was a joke that the only time Harris ever polished his gold buttons was because someone either died or was receiving a medal. There was no middle ground with his profession.

Sorted on the shelves were several large duffle bags, color-coded and stocked for the different types of missions his unit could be called upon to execute. One bag contained his jump kit to perform HAHO (High Altitude, High Opening) and HALO (High Altitude, Low Opening) drops from aircraft and helicopters, namely, an oxygen mask, a parachute and cold weather gear; and another was loaded with his dive kit for combat swimmer and ship-boarding operations, including a wetsuit, fins, and a Dräger LAV-7 rebreather that recycled carbon dioxide into healthy oxygen and prevented mission-compromising air bubbles from floating to the surface. There was also a third bag for CQC (close-quarters combat) equipment that carried a fire-resistant Nomex assault suit and ballistic armor plates for his vest.

He cracked open the Pelican cases and began methodically unpacking the weapons he brought downrange to Syria. One case carried his Heckler & Koch 416, equipped with a ten-inch barrel and a sound suppressor, set snuggly in the foam insert beside an HKMP7 submachine gun. The second case carried his two side arms and night vision goggles. Harris left several other weapons behind when he deployed: two Colt M4s—one with a fourteen-inch barrel, the other with a ten. Both were suppressed, although the fourteen-inch version was configured for long-range shooting with a

mounted 2.5X10 scope; and the ten-inch was geared toward night operations with a clip-on thermal sight and an infrared laser. Lastly, Harris owned
an HK416C, a smaller variant with a sliding collapsible buttstock. He used
it sparingly, but it could easily sit concealed on a sling under a jacket, and
with the considerable stopping power of its 5.56 round, it was perfect for
the close protection details DEVGRU occasionally operated. Harris set the
guns back on their rack, checking for safety's sake that the chambers were
clear, when he heard a delightful, familiar howl coming from behind.

"Holy fuck!" a handsome, broad-chested man in camouflage spun into
his cage like a tornado. "I knew I saw that piece of shit out front." Chief
Petty Officer Wilmer Zapata swallowed Harris up in a clunky bear hug,
forced him down into a headlock, and furiously rubbed his knuckles against
Harris's scalp. "There's my Robby Boy," Zapata let Harris out of the hold
and lightly slapped his cheek. "Let me see that face!"

Harris recovered and brushed his hair back over. His face was bright
red. "Christ. Nice to see you too, Z," he smiled.

Wilmer Zapata—exclusively known as "Z" since the age of two—had
skipped out on his high school graduation to enlist in the Navy. He then
spent a year brawling with his shipmates on the USS *Bataan* to escape bore-
dom before his master chief implored him to take that angst and put it to
good use with the SEALs. Z and Harris served in the same boat crew at
BUD/S, Class 235, and were essentially welded together at the hip ever
since.

"When'd you get in? Just now?" he asked with a ubiquitous grin stamped
on his face.

"This morning. Five hours on a C-130 over the Med, dude."

"*Shoo,*" Z whistled, "your ass has gotta be sore." He leaned by the gun
rack while Harris returned to work on the remainder of his kit. "How was it
out there?"

"Solid guys at Delta, but it's a fucking mess," Harris looked up from his
radios. "The UN and NATO are running around like decapitated chickens
to keep the new guys in Damascus from becoming decapitated chickens.
Meanwhile, we're running around trying to decapitate the people who
would do the decapitating before they get the chance."

"At least they didn't ship you to Raqqa with those goddamn savages."

"I definitely don't need that shit," Harris agreed.

"Fuck them, you're here now," Z crossed his arms. "So what's next?"

"Back in the squadron, I guess. I was gonna check in with the chief, but
I don't see him or anybody else around."

"Shipped down to Harvey Point for the day. Some exercise."

"Explains that."

"You know," Z pondered aloud, "if the CO's cool with it—and if he
just volunteered you to the JSOC brass, I don't see why he wouldn't—you

could hang out with me in Green Team for a bit; babysit the FNGs, see if it's for you."

Green Team was the qualification course for all potential DEVGRU recruits, the FNGs, or the "Fuckin' New Guys." Candidates from the east and west coast teams were run through a brutal, nine-month battery of obstacles that demanded absolute perfection for a chance to join the command. Z was pulled out of Red Squadron some time ago to fill an empty slot in the training cadre. The first three months of the course were dedicated to CQC and located mostly at Fort Story, a few miles up the coast by the mouth of the Chesapeake Bay. Z and the other instructors were beginning to watch constantly for the weak links in the class, and would easily ship them back off to their home teams.

"No offense, but that sounds like a rung above staff duty."

"It's not, dude," Z shook his head. "Come out to the range next week and check it out. We'll show you a good time."

"Maybe. I've thought about waiting until the baby's born and then putting in my papers. I can't keep running off on Sandy, not with Ben getting older."

"Honestly, that's fucking stupid."

"Why?" Harris sounded defensive.

Z unhooked his arms and came closer. "Because you're going to retire, and then what the hell are you gonna do? You're thirty-three, you're an E-7 pulling in forty grand a year, you've got one-point-five kids, and you've done nothing but sling a gun for most of your life. Again…what are you gonna do?"

Harris didn't have an answer that would satisfy him, or Z.

"Listen," Z said, "wait it out a couple years. Come over to Green Team where you'll be home each night, where you're certainly—probably—not getting shot at, and relax for a while. You'll make master chief, guaranteed, and then retire on that pension with your benefits. That's cake, dude."

"I guess."

"Hell, Constellis would snatch you up on the spot. And those fuckers drop six figures on their guys like it's nothing. You know I went down to Moyock a couple weeks ago and scoped out their ranges? Shit's a dream."

"No," Harris said flatly. "I'm not trying to accidentally pop a twelve-year-old in a market and then find myself getting ass raped in some Pakistani prison."

"Nah, fuck that," Z scoffed, "that's what emergency exfil's for. Plus, I'd pay to see some toothless hadji try and ass rape you."

"Whatever."

"Oh!" Z exclaimed. "You have to meet Maggie! She's incredible."

"Yeah, congrats, Sandy told me you were spoken for again."

"Thanks, man. Peeped her at Central one night with some of the crew.

She was all over me and that was the end of it." He paused for a moment. "Maybe it has something to do with getting paid to kill terrorists?"

"You think?"

"Anyway, she's awesome. She might even be that special woman to douse the inferno raging right here," Z pointed to his chest.

Harris smiled. "I'm happy for you, Z. Really."

"Well," he slapped the gun rack and gestured to Harris's kit, "I'll leave you to this. I'd offer to help, but I know how psycho OCD you are."

"Later, man," Harris went to shake his hand.

"Wait!" Z pulled back. "Burgers and booze at your earliest convenience. Bring your lady friend and I'll bring mine. I know I'll have to slap some veggie dogs on the grill for junior, but you get the idea."

"I do, asshole. What about tomorrow? Sandy already got a sitter."

"Negative, Chief, I'm driving home tonight for my niece's *quinceañera.*"

"Which one?" Harris grinned.

"Dude, I don't even remember. I'm bringing Maggie to meet them all, too, bro. Shit's gonna be real!"

Harris laughed. "Good luck with that."

"I'll need it," Z shook Harris's hand and started to walk. "See you Monday. Come check out the ranges with us, dipshit!"

"Roger, boss."

Harris finished up his business and headed out. There wasn't much else to accomplish with the squadron down in North Carolina for the day. Z had a point. Maybe it was too soon to give up the only life he had ever known. He left base and pulled the Jeep into their driveway at Midway Manor just in time to greet his hero who had endured through his own short life against all odds.

The yellow school van from Windsor Woods Elementary arrived right on schedule at three-thirty. Harris and Sandra came down to the curb as the van flashed its amber lights. The doors folded back and the bus aide helped him to the stairs. Ben looked down with each step and didn't quite realize what loomed before him. Harris squatted down at the curb and splayed his arms out. Then Ben looked up, nearing the final step, and saw him, unleashing a luminous smile that flooded Harris with light.

"Hey, little man, your dad's home." He scooped Ben off the last step and rose with a grunt, holding his son close. Harris brushed back Ben's shaggy blond hair and planted a kiss on his forehead.

Sandra waved to the bus as the three turned and walked inside.

When Ben was born, the doctors gave him six months to live. Six months later, that prognosis was generously upped to a year. Five years in, his heart was still beating. It was a mistake, a fluke—a miracle—that Ben

Harris was still alive.

He was autistic and verbally incapable of speech, only able to articulate sounds and bits of words that had been repeatedly etched in his memory. Ben's brain processed language a nanosecond slower than it should, causing his world to resemble a poorly dubbed film in a foreign language. Yet what condemned the boy to spend life teetering on the edge of mortality was a congenital heart defect, an anomaly in the wiring of his heart that could abruptly choke off the blood flow to his vital organs. His life was a war that was only won so long as it did not end.

On the night Ben arrived two months premature—and on many nights to follow—Harris was utterly devastated, but he dared not show it. He looked into the future with dread, not only toward the financial and emotional hardships that would burden him and his wife, but also toward the muddied, murky existence his first and only child was forced to bear. What kind of life would Ben lead? How long would that life be? It was unfair, he thought, and ironic, that a man whose work demanded absolute perfection in every facet of life, could give life to a boy who—on a black and white, medical scale—was so tragically flawed. In the deepest, most selfish reaches of Harris's mind he craved what was "normal." But after one hundred thirty-six agonizing days, when Ben finally emerged from the NICU and Harris could take his son in his arms, he learned that what he craved was relative.

It was astonishing to discover that a fragment of his soul now existed beyond his body. It was the paradox of fatherhood. And "normal," he learned, was merely the common reality that a person has experienced. This was the only life, the only son he ever knew and the only son he ever craved; and so, to him, Ben was impossibly perfect—he was normal—and Harris would not have him any other way. He realized, from the cold hand fate had dealt, that Ben loved unconditionally. It was his gift to the world.

What kind of life would Ben lead and how long would it last? It didn't matter. Ben's life would be the happiest, longest and most meaningful that his father could possibly hope to provide.

And Harris would be there, fighting, to see it outstretch his own, so long as fate could be enticed to spare him. He resolved that he would never speak another word of that raid in Tartus on the night he was dropped, by fate, on the wrong roof and kept from walking into a machine gun nest. After fourteen years, he had been saved from the jaws of those beasts who would take him from his normal life by none other than fate: fate, that had brought Robert Harris home safely to his family before; fate, that would pull him away from them again.

CHAPTER 25

SAEED MOFIDI GREW bored of these tirades, poetic as they were.

"Palestine is a beating heart whose blood runs through the veins of mankind to present a new humanity at any time. Palestine gifts welfare to the world; it shakes the conscience and wakes nations from their deep sleep. Palestine in this period of time is between right and wrong, justice and injustice, the oppressor and the oppressed."

Qasem Shateri's long, angular face and arched eyebrows were mangled with rage as he beat his fists on the table. There was a hint of shameless *schadenfreude* disguised in Mofidi's grin while he watched the fearsome Quds Force commander squirm. Shateri was like an animal, Mofidi thought, ensnared in a trap—only Mofidi couldn't tell if he was preparing to yelp or bite.

"Rather than criticize and question as *Baradar* Saeed has done," Shateri railed on, "he should give praise to Allah for the commanders who will not compromise and submit to pressure and not retreat against the conspiracies of submission. Brother Saeed should thank God for and exalt the brave *mujahedeen* of al-Qassam Brigades, al-Aqsa Martyrs' Brigade, al-Nasser Salah al-Deen Brigades, the political *shura* of Hamas, Islamic Jihad and all the resistance groups. The painful scenes in Palestine break our hearts and cover our chests with grief, a grief that in its essence has a deep wrath, a wrath that at the appropriate time will be poured on the heads of the criminal Zionists."

Mofidi looked beside him to the stoic and dignified face of *Hojjatoleslam* Behrouz Rostani, the president of Iran, whom Mofidi had called in to mediate what was assured to be a screaming match, swiftly devolving into a muddied slush of raving diatribes and attestations of paranoid plots against the Islamic Revolution. It was not that Mofidi sought to avoid such a display, but rather he wanted Rostani to see it first-hand, he wanted the president to witness Shateri's mania and to understand the danger Mofidi was left to contend with on his own in the supreme leader's absence. Better yet: grown men do not shed all semblance of coherency and shout at the top of their lungs if their charges are unfounded. To see the venerable Qasem Shateri shriek at the slightest hint of accusation, Mofidi knew he asked the right questions; he knew he was winning.

"God damn any oppressor who has wronged Palestine and continues to do so," Shateri cried. "God damn any oppressor who defended and defends this criminal regime. God damn anyone who slams the doors of relief to Palestine and who is a partner to the Zionists in their crimes. Before almighty God, we three in this room took an oath with the martyrs that we will remain bound to and not change, just as we are and have been in doing our religious duty in supporting the resistance. We cry that we continue to insist on their victory until the ground, the sky, and the sea turn into hell for the Zionists. The murderers and mercenaries must know that for not even one moment will we stop our defense and support of the resistance—so help us God!"

A sharp rap of Shateri's knuckles on the wood told Mofidi that, perhaps, it was over for now. "Are you finished?" he asked.

Shateri leaned in and hissed through his teeth, "Not by half."

"The issue before us, as seen by my vantage," Rostani splayed his fingers across his chest, "is a vast disconnect between deeds and presumed intentions."

That statement annoyed Mofidi. There were no disconnects, no misunderstandings, only bald-faced lies uttered by a narcissistic opportunist. And Rostani was supposed to be wise enough to recognize them.

"At one side, we have *Baradar* Qasem's actions, undoubtedly done with a full heart to support our friends in Palestine—his deeds," Rostani outstretched his hands like a scale. "And on the opposite, we have *Baradar* Saeed's understanding of the nature of these deeds, which in reality manifest themselves in far greater terms than, perhaps, they were conveyed in his mind—his presumed intentions." Rostani tipped one end of the scale. "Thus we do not have equality, and in the supreme leader's absence, we certainly need to find it. Now, *Baradar* Qasem, can you see how today's deeds in Gaza and in the Gulf of Aden could be cause for great alarm, not only for Brother Saeed, but for myself and others?"

"I can see how they may be cause for great rejoicing," Shateri said.

Mofidi scoffed. The man's skull was damn near impenetrable.

"Allow me to run through this again, Mr. President," Mofidi stated emphatically, turning to Shateri. "A week ago, you sat right here in my office and told me that in response to Hezbollah laying down its weapons, *al-Quds* would increase—ten-fold—its support to resistance groups fighting on the Zionists' southern front. I, and the supreme leader, agreed with these measures—"

Shateri was incredulous. "Have I not delivered by an order of twenty?"

"You delivered, and you lied!" Mofidi snapped.

"In the face of your weakness and inaction!"

"You knowingly deceived me, and therefore you knowingly deceived Ayatollah Khansari!" Mofidi felt the blood simmer beneath his skin. "And I can prove it, *baradar*. A week ago, you informed me that a Liberian vessel, the *Catarina A*, was shipping—and I quote—'twenty thousand automatic rifles, two million rounds of ammunition—"

"You wrote that down?"

"—three thousand kilos of high explosives, and Type-72 anti-tank mines.'"

"Why would you *ever* write that down, you pitiful bastard?"

"Nothing of the sort was found on that vessel, *Baradar* Qasem. Not once did you mention anything to me of what was actually found: ten shipping containers, each laden with four Soumar cruise missiles, which, to my knowledge, have not been authorized for export by the supreme leader or the defense ministry. Was any of this brought to your attention, Mr. President?"

"It was not," Rostani replied.

"Not once," Mofidi continued, "did *Baradar* Qasem mention anything of an Islamic Jihad unit being brought aboard in Oman to escort these arms to Sudan; the same unit which murdered the ship's crew, critically wounded several British marines, and tried to scuttle the ship."

"And all are being greeted in Paradise—"

"After inviting the third Zionist assault on Gaza in as many years!" Mofidi turned back to Rostani, "Mr. President, this all speaks to a gross and dangerous recklessness by *Baradar* Qasem and *al-Quds*. He is charged with orchestrating our support to the resistance and so he must ultimately be held responsible for their actions. A Zionist soldier has been executed without the supreme leader's consent on the direct orders of his *subordinate* in Khartoum. *Baradar* Qasem sees nothing wrong with that! He has been allowed to dictate this country's foreign policy from the field for too long, and it must stop."

Shateri managed a wry grin for the first time that afternoon. "But, Mr. President, this is where *Baradar* Saeed falls into the pit of hopeless ideas. This is a war without end. It will never stop."

"It will stop, God damn you!" Mofidi spat. "These actions, which are reckless and entirely without sanction, will stop, and they must before you drag this country into a war it is neither strategically nor tactically positioned to fight."

Mofidi saw Shateri push back in his chair and cock his head inquisitively to the side, just as he had a week before when he begrudgingly revealed the truth to Mofidi about the tunnels at Haj Ali Gholi and the project under Dr. Fakhrizadeh's control. Shateri narrowed his eyes, and with his next words uttered something so terrifying that, as with the last time, Mofidi would write about it to his friends at Langley.

"The battlefield is mankind's lost Paradise," Shateri declared, "the paradise in which morality and human conduct are at their highest. One type of paradise that men imagine is about streams, beautiful maidens, and lush landscape. But there is another kind of paradise…the battlefield."

Mofidi still had work to do. At six-thirty, he slumped into the back of the Peugeot and allowed his driver, Babak, to whisk him away from Beit Rahbari as quickly as traffic would permit. Earlier that morning Mofidi noticed the chalk mark etched by the bin men on the lamppost across from his home. He knew that at midnight a message from the Americans would float through the airwaves in the form of coded numbers breathed dispassionately by a computerized voice. Mofidi hadn't heard from his friends across the Atlantic since he answered their question about Haj Ali Gholi. A week had passed without a response and the anxiety swelled inside him. He couldn't predict how the Americans would respond—nor could they, to be fair. And yet, he thought, a bomb hadn't fallen through his office ceiling, which was always a welcomed sign. If Mofidi learned anything from his relationship with the Americans, it was that they all too often felt compelled to use military force due to their own insecurities, due to fear and anger instilled every time by a deficit of information, never a surplus. That was Mofidi's job, as he saw it: to keep the colossus informed as best he could, to keep the bombs from raining through his ceiling for as long as possible. And he knew there was still much work to do.

But first, Mofidi needed to pray.

Babak cut through the traffic to Masjid Giahi off Tajrish Square in North Tehran. The Peugeot idled while Mofidi slipped through the mosque's wide doors, appearing again thirty minutes later, this time wearing a pair of loafers he switched inside with Akbar. With a few quiet words and a nod, Mofidi directed Babak to his villa on Ammar Street.

Safely behind the walls, he changed, ate what he could stomach, and removed the one-time pad from the cavity in his heel. Like the dozens he received before, it was a small sheet of digits written in fifty-six groups of five, which was needed to decode the message that would broadcast at midnight from Camp Arifjan in Kuwait. Mofidi still had four hours to wait, but his mind buzzed. Before he even heard what the Americans had to say, he knew what he needed to tell them. He needed to write.

Mofidi lit a candle in his bedroom window to signal to Jack that he would make contact in the morning. He pulled the curtains, doused the lights, save for one at his small desk, and gathered a few pages of the water-soluble paper the Americans provided. He told them everything.

During prayers, as he prostrated himself toward the *qiblah* wall, he felt ashamed—his thoughts kept straying from God to that false prophet, Shateri. Mofidi would start there.

"Hajj" Qasem, as his Arabs subjects called him, was a man so easily misunderstood by the people who needed to understand him the most. Religion, or some delusion of a God who loved exclusively His creations which thought like him, did not drive Shateri; rather, it was zealous nationalism and a love of the fight. He was a pragmatist, not an ideologue; and, perhaps most crucial to cracking his motivations, he was not a diabolical mastermind with a grand strategy, but a keen opportunist who grasped out and manipulated events as they occurred. That, alone, was how Shateri constructed a wide axis of resistance that stretched from Cyprus to Afghanistan. And perhaps by some slight of cosmic justice, it was through disparate events beyond prediction that his axis had begun to crumble around him. Mofidi knew that what he had seen over the past twenty-four hours in Gaza, Sudan and the Gulf of Aden—and even inside those tunnels at Haj Ali Gholi—was a mad attempt by Shateri to keep that axis, his Frankenstein, clinging to life.

On Ayatollah Khansari's orders, Shateri took control of the IRGC's Quds Force twelve years ago and was given the mandate to crush any force in the Middle East that threatened the Islamic Revolution. At the time still reeling from his son's execution, Mofidi was posted as the Iranian defense attaché in Baghdad. In the aftermath of America's invasion and occupation of Iraq, Mofidi had a prime vantage to watch how quickly Shateri moved. His men swooped into the embassy, elbowed Mofidi aside and mobilized Iraq's Shiite militias against the Americans. Mofidi then watched Shateri systematically turn Iran's once sworn nemesis into a puppet, buying each new politician in Baghdad and assassinating the ones not for sale. It was breathtaking to watch. While stationed in Baghdad, Mofidi first established his relationship with CIA and began routinely reporting on the threat Shateri posed. Returning to Tehran a few years later, Mofidi was closer to Shateri and could tell the Americans even more.

Ironically enough, it was Shateri who concluded that Ibrahim al-Din was a liability and ordered Hezbollah's leadership to force him into an early retirement. Shateri preferred to manage the party's military wing more directly. He instituted the run of trainings and massive arms shipments through Syria that rebuilt Hezbollah after its conflict with Israel in 2006 and shaped it into a machine even more powerful than the Lebanese Armed Forces. He did the same in Gaza with Hamas and Islamic Jihad, placing one of his own as the ambassador in Sudan to manage logistics and operational planning. By the time Mofidi was chosen as the supreme leader's military advisor—to

Langley's rejoicing and Shateri's scorn—*al-Qud's* had largely realized its great axis of proxies and terrorist networks throughout the Middle East. And Shateri, for his part, had positioned himself as the largest and most venomous spider in the web.

But then came the Syrian civil war.

Initially, Shateri dismissed the opposition in Syria as a disorganized mob attempting to march on the Bastille—and for quite some time he was right—before realizing what that mob from history was able to accomplish. For Shateri, the loss of Syria was rightfully seen as an existential threat, and the defense of his allies in Damascus became a point of pride. He brought Hezbollah over the border from Lebanon to prop up the Syrian military and created irregular Alawite and Shiite militias that massacred scores of civilians around the country. Could his connection have been unequivocally proven, Shateri could easily be tried *in absentia* at The Hague. Yet the viciousness he exhibited in supporting Damascus ultimately helped give rise to ISIS—a ravenous band of orcs marauding through the desert—who invaded Iraq, causing his puppet government in Baghdad to implode, and creating a threat so monstrous that the West was finally compelled to intervene in Syria, eventually leading Damascus to fall and propelling the disorganized mob to victory.

Qasem Shateri, like numerous great men before him, had fallen victim to his own untenable hubris. Not a few months back, Mofidi openly posited in a report to Langley that Shateri was suicidal. Unfortunately, that never came to pass; Shateri was not so cowardly, or even brave, as one might see it. If he were to consign himself to death, Shateri was the sort to drag everyone with him—and perhaps that's just what he was planning.

Mofidi jotted that down.

The execution of Corporal Moshe Adler at the hands of Islamic Jihad was ultimately Qasem Shateri's work, he wrote to the Americans; the firefight on the *Catarina A* and the attempted basing of cruise missiles in Sudan was certainly Qasem Shateri's work; and all of it is what happens when you present an opportunist with no further opportunities.

Mofidi wasn't afraid to admonish his friends.

A man who only calls his shots as the game rages on has inherently flawed foresight, which makes him inherently dangerous. It was all tied together for Mofidi: the construction of a nuclear weapon at Haj Ali Gholi; provoking a conflict with the Israelis—again—in Gaza; deploying his hit squad, Unit 400, to Vienna to hunt down Mehdi Vaziri by stalking any dissidents he may contact; it was a strategy joined only by its fractured nature. Qasem Shateri had no idea what move he would make next, he hadn't thought ahead on the chessboard in his mind, and he seemed to care little for how his opponents might counter. Shateri will do something drastic, Mofidi concluded, before scratching in beside it, *"he already has."*

Mofidi wrote slowly by hand; it was nearly midnight when he finished. He readied the one-time pad and tuned his shortwave radio to the right frequency. Shortly, he heard three consecutive beeps and a disembodied female voice announce his call sign.

"Five-one-niner. Five-one-niner. Five-one-niner."

"Okay, here's confirmation—the Israelis just hit eighteen targets in Gaza, but the Pentagon's getting word that we'll see at least twenty-five more strike sorties before dawn," Tanner flipped through his briefing book.

"Good," President Paulson sawed into a pork chop, momentarily diverting his eyes from CNN.

After Karetnikov's funeral, the president's entourage had descended on Spaso House, the neoclassical residence of the American ambassador in Moscow, Patrick Berne. Paulson's stay in the city was entirely improvised; the embassy was in a scramble throughout the day to find hotels for White House and State Department staffers, Secret Service agents and the press pool. In the interim, Ambassador Berne suffered the indignity of seeing his home turned into an outpost of the West Wing. A television was brought down from the family quarters and placed in the library, where Paulson huddled with Tanner, Dawson and Berne, while Weisel barricaded herself upstairs in the latter's study to work the phones.

It was the fourth time by Paulson's count that he and his staff had watched this identical scene unfold. And, for now, he could scarcely do more.

CNN's senior international correspondent was in a live shot from the balcony of the al-Deira Hotel in Gaza, explaining the developing situation to the anchor back in New York. Every few minutes the muffled clap of exploding ordnance rocked the hotel. A massive fireball erupted behind the concrete silhouettes in the background. The sound of Red Crescent ambulance sirens wailed through the streets. Predictably, the anchor would plead with his correspondent to "stay safe" before cutting to commercials.

"Turn this off," Paulson said.

Berne leveled a remote and the TV fell silent.

Tanner crossed his legs and read off the details forwarded to him from Washington. "It's a slew of real-estate targets, sir: Qassam launching positions, unmanned outposts, ammunitions depots and rocket production facilities. F-15s from Hatzerim toppled al-Aqsa TV's antenna array in Gaza City; they're off the air, for now. Offices belonging to the Shaiber Company—that's the shipping firm that dumped Adler's body at the border—have also been hit. NSA is hearing reports that Hamas' police chief may have been killed in one of the strikes, but they can't immediately verify that. Casualty estimates are in the dozens."

"Wait, was the police chief targeted?" asked Dawson.

"Doubtful. If he was, it wouldn't mesh with what Angela's heard. He was probably in the wrong place at the wrong time."

"But I still don't understand," the president started sawing into his pork chop again, "is Avi going after Hamas, just Islamic Jihad, or both? What's the scope of this operation? He didn't say anything about it in the speech and no one over there has said anything to us."

"He's probably keeping his options open," Dawson offered. "Wouldn't you? At least, that's how I'd advise you. If he draws the parameters too narrow, before their intelligence picture is fully developed, and they have to go deeper into Gaza, he'll get nailed for mission creep."

Paulson dropped his fork on the plate. "I do not want ground forces going over the armistice line. I do not want a repeat of last summer, and the number of strikes they're getting off on the opening night worries me."

"Sir, expect their operations tempo to slow in the next few days," Tanner shook his head. "The IDF will burn through Shin Bet's initial target deck and then they'll have to work off real-time ISR. That's when you'll see mistakes made and collateral stack up."

"And any sympathy Avi has right now will evaporate," Paulson huffed.

Heels sounded on the staircase, gaining nearer to the library. They turned their heads as Angela Weisel blew into the room, clearing the bangs from her face, and dropped next to the president on the sofa. "You'll like this, Andrew," the secretary of state assured.

"Talk to me."

She smiled. "I just got off the phone with Cairo and Zohry wants nothing to do with this. He sees Iran trying to put cruise missiles in Sudan as just as big a threat to Egypt as it is to Israel. He's pulling back his ambassadors in Tehran and Khartoum for consultations. So, privately, they're rooting for Israel, but I'm told that if any UN facilities are hit—accidentally or not—that will change quickly."

"And what about the smugglers Iran's using?" Tanner asked.

"We'll see an uptick in raids across the Sinai as soon as tomorrow."

"Fantastic," Paulson nodded.

"I had Lansing call Hanna Sayigh," she went on. "He's very apologetic—actually, both were. Anyway, Fatah is demanding that Hamas address Islamic Jihad's actions before they'll offer to mediate."

"They're panicking," Dawson declared.

"It's the same story in the Gulf," Weisel added. "Hamas leadership in Doha tried, and failed, to get an audience with the emir. They've called around to anyone who'll listen in Oman, the Emirates, Kuwait; they're all telling Hamas the same thing: rein in Islamic Jihad before we'll help. And that's exactly what the Israelis want."

"You got through to them?" Paulson asked.

"Well, the foreign minister was finally kind enough to return my call—eight hours later. It's a mess in Tel Aviv. The only people Avi wants to speak to right now are his generals. A few cabinet members are pushing for the IDF to recapture Rafah and wipe out Islamic Jihad for good. They're ordering up twenty thousand reservists in the morning."

Paulson was about to come out of his skin.

"But don't worry," Weisel stopped him, "that won't happen. The IDF wants to drive a wedge between Hamas and PIJ. And, right now, it's working."

"How so?"

"No one wants this war—and I mean *no one,* especially not Hamas. Gaza has just started to rebuild from the last showdown and now this happens. Politically, this is suicide. Nobody will want to see their house leveled for the hundredth time because some thugs got trigger-happy and shot an Israeli soldier. So, it puts Hamas in an awkward position. They can fight back with little outside support and see Gaza destroyed again, or they can force out Islamic Jihad and the Quds Force. Ultimately, I'm told, that's what the Israelis are hoping for—that Hamas will hand over the people who killed Adler and no one else has to die needlessly. Tel Aviv knows that Hamas has to shoot back, at least initially, and they're willing to absorb a few rocket strikes. But they want to see immediate movement toward a settlement. That's why no senior Hamas members have been targeted tonight. They need them alive to negotiate."

The president frowned. "You're saying we should sit this one out?"

"I'm telling you we should let it run its course."

Paulson took stock of it all, running the options in his mind. "I want someone to go over there in person and make damn sure this strategy holds."

"If I brought a plane in from Germany, I could leave tonight," she offered.

"No, I need you with me when I see Lavrov tomorrow."

Tanner broke in. "Ryan Freeman's heading to Tel Aviv to meet with Mossad's director-general. He's leaving at the end of the week, I think."

"Fine. But tell him to go as soon as possible," the president ordered.

"From what I understand, sir, the timing of their meeting is contingent with an operation CIA is mounting to recruit a Hezbollah member. We talked about it on the flight over? The specifics are a bit complicated."

Paulson shrugged. "Then his people need to adapt accordingly."

"Angela, where are the Russians on this?" Dawson asked.

"Not a peep," she breathed.

"How so?"

"I've asked that question to everyone I've spoken to today, *and* tried myself, and no one up the street will answer the phones. Moscow is MIA."

Paulson had almost forgotten that the best person he could speak to sat directly opposite him—in fact, they had commandeered his house. "Patrick," the president asked, "do you find that strange?"

The ambassador pondered for a moment. "Actually, sir, given what I've watched in the past few days, it isn't strange at all." Berne looked down at the floor. "On my first day here, I went to the Kremlin and presented my credentials to Karetnikov. He just stared me down and said, 'We know your embassy is working with the opposition to undermine me.' It took me a second to realize what he was talking about. And I said to him, 'Mr. President, what do you mean?' He kept glaring at me with this determined, 'we-will-prevail' look and said, 'We know this.' And that was the end of the meeting, that was my first encounter with him…"

"That man was nuts," Dawson scoffed.

"No, I don't think so," Berne shook his head. "Karetnikov always thought that at the end of the day, American power has some practical purpose. He wasn't a crackpot. But I really struggled with that. You know, he swore to the moment he died that Langley orchestrated ISIS' attack on Istanbul? Seriously, that's what he went around telling people. So, was he just trying to psych us out and appeal to the lowest common denominator? Or was he actually breathing in his own fumes? I don't think we'll ever know."

There was a pause, a moment of punctuation before Berne continued.

"It's hard to swallow the idea that removing just one man can so drastically alter the landscape of an entire country; like a chemical compound, take out one molecule and its whole nature is altered. But, in this case, I think it's true."

Berne shifted in his chair. None of them could interrupt.

"Russia, now—with all Karetnikov's bluster about its vastness, its exceptionalism, its unique moral paradigm—has become, not so much a country or a place on the map, but a state of mind that is totally alien to anything understood by the postmodern West. That wouldn't have happened without Mikhail Karetnikov, and now that he's gone, I don't think it's a state of mind that can be sustained. That one, critical molecule has been removed."

"So, what now?" Weisel asked. "Do you think Russians will get together and sing 'Kumbaya,' join NATO, and let gays marry?"

"Maybe," Berne smiled, and his answer took them as a slight shock.

"Last month," he continued, "I ran into Roman Ivanov at Davos. He really is quite a brilliant man if you just listen to him talk. Anyway, Channel One—state TV here—had just run this hit piece on me, playing a soundbite of me speaking on human rights, and one of their 'commentators' asked if I was a pedophile and suggested that I had a role in funding the Contras; never mind that I was in high school when that happened. FSB agents were showing up outside my kids' school. Ivanov came up to me and started profusely apologizing for what his country had become. He and Karetnikov both believed that Russia is a truly great civilization, but they radically differed on how to keep it there. Maybe that's why they hated each other so much. But it was strange, he just kept going on—eloquently—about how Russia deserves so much better, and how it can happen so easily if only 'that Chekist dictator'—that's what he called Karetnikov—was gone. Kind of poetic, isn't it? A few weeks later, Ivanov got his wish."

"So Russia is a liberal democracy now?" Paulson asked.

"Not quite, sir. There's a lot of work to be done. But I don't find it strange that the Russians haven't made a statement on Gaza. And I'll tell you why. Andrei Minin—you'll all meet him tomorrow—is a known protégé of Ivanov, and he just took over as Dmitri Lavrov's chief of staff. That's why you were invited to breakfast tomorrow morning, Mr. President: because Lavrov, through Andrei Minin, wants a fresh start with the United States. None of the power ministers in Karetnikov's old cabinet have even once been spotted in the Kremlin since the night he died. That speaks volumes."

Berne shook his head, letting it sink in.

"Something very special, and very rare, is happening up the street."

There was a palpable silence in the library, a spine-tingling feeling lodged somewhere between curiosity and dread.

Berne let out a resigned sigh. "The course of human history was altered when Karetnikov's plane went into the ground, and I don't think we've even begun to realize just how different it will be."

Major Berzin waited almost two days for them to call off the search.

An old woman had leapt from the bridge—driven her Mercedes midspan, stopped dead in traffic and threw herself over the side. The 186-foot drop would have killed her before the frigid water had the chance, and the search was only meant to recover her remains. For nearly forty-eight hours, the Coast Guard and Maryland State Police had scoured the icy, gray shoreline and yielded no results. The current in that narrow reach of the bay was notorious and likely submerged her body deep beneath the surface, dragging her downstream.

And that gave Berzin an opening to unload his dead-drop.

Darkness and a vicious early-morning chill provided cover. The dead-drop's isolation and utter loneliness along the bay assured him that the only human souls Berzin might encounter were the FBI, and he'd lost the smallest hint of them back near an apartment complex in Prince George's County. Sufficiently clear of surveillance, he left his Honda Accord and followed a dirt path off Holly Beach Farm Road toward the tip of Hackett's Point, a narrow spit by the mouth of Annapolis Harbor. Berzin walked almost to the edge, near the fractured shards of ice and rotting leaves packed along the shore. Three kilometers ahead he saw the pulsing red glow of aircraft warning lights atop the Chesapeake Bay Bridge. He stopped when he found the usual tree. It had changed since his last visit; its branches were mangled in suspended animation by the driving winds.

Berzin reached up to the trunk's small hollow and stuck his hand in the cavity. He ran his fingers around the bark and quickly felt the tough, rubber exterior of a thumb drive. He smiled and exchanged it with an identical, clean drive from his pocket. Next, Berzin removed a black trash bag, tightly wrapped in duct tape, from inside his jacket and stuffed it down the hollow: twenty thousand dollars in cash—a pittance for services rendered to the GRU.

Five minutes later, he emerged from the trail, casually zipping up his fly. He turned the Honda's lights back on when he reached a main road. A mile onward, Berzin made a hard serve off Route 50, running a countersurveillance route through the back woods of Howard and Montgomery counties, and arrived at the Russian embassy in Washington before daybreak.

CHAPTER 26

JACK WAS ABOUT to throw out the whole damned routine.

It didn't bother him much, and he'd figured it was only a matter of time until Langley passed the order. At the very least, it gave him something else to do beyond peer over his shoulder, waiting for the regime's white blood cells to detect him floating through their veins.

The variables were calculated in his mind like a machine as he waded through the morning bustle on Tajrish Square. Peter Stavros in Persia House instructed him to modify CITADEL's covert communications plan by extending his courier chain. The current plan called for Jack to scrub Mofidi's identifiable voice and translate the message by hand, and then anonymously post it to a box number in Dubai where an officer would retrieve it and fly the message to Washington in a diplomatic bag. It had worked flawlessly for nearly two years, but there was a marked vulnerability in relying on Iran's postal service, and Langley wanted to be rid of it. For their new plan, Jack would reactivate an asset in Tehran he established some time ago. Mr. Nourizadeh, as Jack called him, was an auditor for Bank Melli who ran a weekly trip across the Persian Gulf to Dubai—a perfect legend to smuggle CITADEL's messages out of Iran. Mr. Nourizadeh also had five children to feed and was thankful for the extra cash, but Jack knew it wasn't the true reason he offered up his services to the Central Intelligence Agency. As Jack long understood, many more people were willing to betray their country than one might realize, and for the exact same reason that compelled some to line up and pay money to jump out of a plane, or stick needles into their arms. For some, the chance to break the cast of mundanity in their lives was just too enticing. And, for them, Jack was more than willing to oblige.

The candle in Mofidi's bedroom window the previous night came as a surprise to Jack, not to mention a slight annoyance. He didn't expect a response from his agent so soon, and the message Langley had transmitted from Kuwait only instructed Mofidi to keep his head down and wait. *This* was not an example of keeping one's head down. Jack had implored Mofidi before: Do not contact us unless absolutely necessary. Do not take unnecessary risks. Do not let them take away your life.

But Saeed Mofidi was one of the wisest men Jack had ever encountered. *If he had something to say,* he thought, *we had better listen.*

Jack edged his way through the stalls along Tajrish Square to the same vendor he found himself greeting every morning after CITADEL made contact. He approached, his eyes shielded behind sunglasses, and his armor ready. "A copy of *Hamshahri,* please?"

If Mikhail Borisovich Karetnikov was—until quite recently—the guiding heart of a resurgent, neo-imperialist Russia, Colonel-General Vyasheslav Arkadyevich Trubnikov was destined to be its cold, exacting brain. It was off the artificially lit corridors like the one he patrolled that morning, past the cypher locks and placards drenched with Cyrillic acronyms, in the gray edifice of concrete and glass surrounded by crumbling warehouses and shiny apartment blocks in northern Moscow, where Trubnikov had taken the Kremlin's feverish fantasies of resurgence and reckoning and refined them into the operational plans which deftly knocked Russia's opponents off kilter.

There was a name for his strategy. It was an old moniker favored by the Soviet special services, encompassing all endeavors to weaken and humiliate the United States in the eyes of its allies; to sow discord among NATO members; to prepare the battlefield for an inescapable, destined, and necessary war.

Trubnikov called it "active measures."

With the Kremlin's backing and protection, Trubnikov transformed his own pocket empire, the GRU, into a clearinghouse for his brand of non-linear warfare, blending outright force, disinformation, political and economic sabotage and covert operations. Over the past year, he watched their fantasies turn to reality in the form of thin summaries delivered each morning to his desk. They illustrated vivid portraits of the separatists fighting in eastern Ukraine, offensive intelligence operations in the Baltics, clandestine donations made to far-right European politicians, propaganda planted with Western press agencies, and new efforts to manipulate Russian-speaking minority groups throughout Central Asia. He brought the summaries to meetings with Karetnikov right up to the day he died and argued what those two souls knew all along: that Western civilization had reached its zenith, where only economic comforts matter, and that it hadn't an ounce of will to defend its spoils. Of course, they understood that NATO was still undeniably stronger in conventional military terms, but Trubnikov mastered the art of prying open his enemies' divisions, executing deniable operations far afield with disposable third-party combatants, striking against strategic locations and personalities. With active measures, Trubnikov demonstrated that it hardly mattered whose tanks and fighter planes were better built. Better yet, he proved to the Kremlin, and himself, that in the twenty-first century—with just a smattering of subversive agents and the proper dosage of surgical violence—a great power like the Russian Federation could still rip its neighbors in two with nary a consequence.

And now, with the guiding heart gouged out, the calculating brain was free to play out that special brand of warfare on a global stage.

But first a few sections of his house needed cleaning. General Trubnikov emerged from the depths of the GRU's Situational Centre, feeling thoroughly disgusted with himself, like a starved animal eating one of its young to spare the litter; unpleasant, but necessary. He had sent five Spetsnaz teams backed by airpower and artillery to conduct a series of overnight raids in the Donetsk and Lugansk regions of eastern Ukraine. That much was routine. Making things explode across the border was now a daily event for Trubnikov, but the targets last night were all firmly inside rebel-held territory. And with the president of the United States in Moscow, it would certainly cause a stir, as was his intention. With his men back in the safety of Russian airspace, Trubnikov returned to his office and found a ream of papers sitting on his desk. He sat down as a smile eased on his face. Then Trubnikov began to dig.

It was the latest trove from Agent SIRIUS, the GRU's prized asset in the United States. As was typical for the agent's reporting, there was no thematic thread or political commentary provided, no overture offered, nothing to link the disparate array of American state secrets given to Moscow every few weeks. SIRIUS simply made a wholesale document dump comprising anything and everything the agent was fortunate enough to come across. As messy and unfocused as it often was, SIRIUS' reports were critical in the GRU's efforts to patch the holes in the Russian intelligence community's understanding of Washington's innermost thoughts. For that reason, Trubnikov viciously guarded his asset from his jealous rivals in the SVR and FSB. SIRIUS' access was just too good; it was not uncommon for Trubnikov to read President Paulson's handwriting sprawled beneath White House letterhead.

There were around two hundred pages this time, all poorly lit photographs snapped in the dead of night. Trubnikov scanned the lot: they captured emails shot between National Security Council staffers and senior officials at the State Department and the Pentagon, a few background reports produced by analysts at CIA and several shorthand accounts of Oval Office meetings. Trubnikov could pick through it all later. His attention shifted for the moment to a file set aside from the rest. It had been pulled by Trubnikov's deputy and contained every scrap of information from the haul which pertained to Iran, Lebanon, Hezbollah, and Israeli Mossad operations in the region: all the valuable bits that would go straight to Kazanoff.

Trubnikov opened the file and read the first few lines of an article from the President's Daily Brief penned by a CIA officer in Beirut. *"Hezbollah Scours Source of Lost IRGC Aid Funds."* He stopped there and flipped to the next document: a cable from the same CIA officer detailing a meeting with her asset, TOPSAIL; Hezbollah was closing in on Walid Rada, a bureaucrat in the party's construction company; TOPSAIL was also confident that he'd spotted outside Wissam Hamawi's office—Trubnikov paused to ensure he hadn't misread—*Ibrahim al-Din.* Trubnikov froze. But he had to keep reading. He turned to the next document, learning that Mehdi Vaziri had indeed defected to Mossad and was being debriefed at the Hôtel Meurice in Paris under the cover of a Brazilian sugar baron. He breathlessly pored over the next document, detailing the reverse-engineered Soumar cruise missiles NATO had discovered aboard the *Catarina A* and the ingenious delivery system they were packed inside. Trubnikov came to the middle of the file. The latter half—twenty-pages stamped "TOPSECRET//SI//ORCON"— was a draft executive summary prepared for Congressional leadership by CIA's Iran Operations Division on the Picasso and Monet bunker network at Haj Ali Gholi. Trubnikov felt overwhelmed. He had to lock this down immediately; absolutely no one else could see what he just read.

His arm sprung toward his phone and in minutes Colonel Konstantin Zelenko of the GRU's Second Directorate—responsible for agent intelligence in the Western Hemisphere—appeared through the door and saluted.

"Who else has seen this?" Trubnikov held up the file.

Zelenko stood at attention, not looking his superior directly in the eyes. "Major Berzin in the Washington *rezidentura,* myself and you, General—as per your instructions."

"Sit down."

Zelenko lowered into a chair before the general's desk. White exhaust clouds unfurled beyond the windows. Trubnikov relaxed a bit, hoping it might be contagious. "How long have we been together, *Kostya?"*

"Since Berlin, General."

"And as we've been together since Berlin, surely you've come to understand when a matter does not entirely seem 'in order?'"

"Yes, General."

"And as you understand when a matter isn't entirely in order, surely you've come to understand how such matters require the utmost discretion?"

"Yes, General."

"Then surely you understand me when I say that, effective immediately, any and all reports from Agent SIRIUS are to bypass the normal channels and be transmitted by Major Berzin directly to this desk, circumventing the eyes of everyone in your directorate, including yourself?"

"Yes, General."

"Then I've trained you well. Dismissed, Colonel."

Zelenko rose, saluted, and left the way he came.

After waiting a few moments, Trubnikov got up and locked the door. He then pulled a laptop from his desk drawer and powered it on. As Trubnikov also instructed, Zelenko had placed the documents from the separate file on a thumb drive. The general plugged the drive into the laptop and encrypted each document using the signature of a 256-bit PGP encryption key held only by Kazanoff in Lebanon. Next, Trubnikov used a program called Steghide to compress each document into a single pixel within a stock photograph of a city park. He then logged into a Proton Mail account, an encrypted email service hosted on servers in Switzerland, and attached the altered photograph to a new message and saved it as a draft, ensuring that no scrap of data would cross the open, monitored channels of the Internet. Trubnikov shut off the laptop, removed the thumb drive and dropped it in a glass of water sitting on his desk. Finally, he placed the hard copies in his personal safe, locking away the only evidence that he or the GRU had any shred of involvement in what would come.

This was the second time in less than twelve hours that Tanner had to dole out the gritty details. Bombs had fallen in a wholly different part of the world, but unlike Gaza, this time he hadn't the slightest warning.

"Around three-thirty, local time, four Russian MiGs pinged a Ukrainian radar station at Bashkyrivka, near Kharkiv," Tanner exhaled in the vacuum of Paulson's limousine as it sped into the birch forests west of Moscow. "The jets were observed turning south, where they hit several targets around Donetsk, including an electrical substation, which knocked out power to the area."

He stopped reading and cleared his throat. "Now it gets weird."

But the president gave no reaction, focusing instead on the passing protesters assembled along the highway.

"Behind the MiGs," Tanner went on, "a group of helos entered Ukrainian airspace, dropped altitude and vanished off the scopes. For the next three hours, local assets behind rebel lines reported explosions and sustained gunfire in and around Lugansk, Horlivka and Krasnodon."

"Those towns are held by the rebels?" asked Larry Dawson.

"They're all miles from the frontline; outside Kiev's control for months," he answered. "Shooting stopped just before dawn. The separatists supposedly took heavy losses and NSA has reason to suspect that their command structure is in disarray."

"Udovenko and the NSDC are screaming about the airspace violation," Weisel added.

"Beyond that, we don't know much else, sir," said Tanner. "SHAPE and EUCOM are watching for developments on their end."

"So was this Lavrov's play all along, Angela?" Paulson asked.

"Too early to say."

"Why would he attack the separatists? His own men?" he pressed.

"It's too early, Andrew."

"Shit," the president bit his lip.

"Lavrov didn't raise that army, Karetnikov did," Weisel said. "Those aren't his men in Ukraine. And maybe it's become good for business to see them swept aside."

There was a short, tense silence in the limousine.

"Someone had to say it."

"What time is it in DC?" said Paulson.

Tanner checked his watch. "Two-thirty."

The president turned to Dawson. "Larry, have Brandon call Udovenko first thing; they have a good rapport. Angela, can your people keep the lines with Kiev open until then?"

"Yeah."

"Eli, put together a VTC with Geoff Sheridan and Ryan Freeman as soon as we get back on the plane."

"Done, sir."

"This whole thing," Paulson shook his head, "—it's just so goddamn strange. Since the funeral yesterday, I felt like I've been walking on Mars."

"Why the hell else do you think they wanted us here, Andrew?" Weisel smiled. The answer was obvious to her.

There was no one in the president's inner circle who could be so frank with him and not expect an inch of reprisal. Dawson and Tanner accepted it long ago, and even the first lady had learned that it was better not to try and drill into Paulson's head; its core could be denser than diamonds. But Weisel was different. She knew full well how smart he was, and she wasn't afraid to tell Paulson when he wasn't using the brain that put him inside that armored limo, twice.

"I don't know, Angela, you tell me," he countered.

"Look, apart from assassinating Karetnikov, the Russians couldn't have arranged a better situation. They're not stupid. They see their economy in the tank, they watch crude prices dropping through the floor, they see the ruble about as valuable as toilet paper. Sure, they can go on state TV and talk a big game all they want, but the Russians—the sane ones, anyway— know they screwed up. They have real problems to deal with, and it's just like Berne said last night: Mikhail Karetnikov was the single, oblong piece of shit clogging the pipes."

"That's nice," Tanner smirked.

"I'm paraphrasing, but it's true," she continued. "How do they get their country moving again? How do they flush out the shit? What did Berne say?" The questions were rhetorical. "The sane Russians keep the crazy Russians out of the Kremlin, now they cut the separatists off at the knees, and next they ask our forgiveness. Dmitri Lavrov—or some whisper in his ear—is an actor who we've criminally underestimated. Why are we here, Andrew? The answer's pretty clear to me. Right or wrong, in a few minutes, we'll know."

Paulson's motorcade followed the Rublyovka-Uspenskoye Highway beyond Moscow's western fringe into Barvikha, one of the relatively new "millionaires' ghettos" that had been carved into estates arranged like giant Lego blocks for oligarchs and government officials, proximity to Karetnikov being the principal marker of one's feudal worth. And for that proximity, many were subject to sanctions, severing access to bank accounts and seizing property holdings in the West—a harsh consequence of sycophancy.

The *politsiya* escorts ushered the motorcade past impenetrable mounds of blackened snow and ice and even higher walls of stone and iron spikes to a squat gatehouse manned by uniformed FSO officers. It slowed to maneuver around concrete chicanes and continued down a long drive leading deeper into the woods. Rounding a bend, the dacha came firmly into view.

Gorki-9, Dmitri Lavrov's country estate, seemed to reflect up from the surrounding snow. It was a white, two-story mansion topped with a golden dome and was typical of the various assaulting architectural tastes favored by the country's elite whose interests had long surpassed aesthetics. Paulson's limousine crawled to a stop under the front portico, and as his Secret Service detail fanned into position, he peered through the armored windows. There would be no cavalry escort, no tangled flags in the wind, no ceremonial fuss to bother with; only a lone protocol officer, the same one who met him on the tarmac the previous morning, stood in the cold to greet him. The message was clear: Despite the mysterious overtures, in the face of all the hope brought on by Mikhail Karetnikov's demise, this was no social call.

Ambassador Berne stormed out from the dacha and under the portico. He had been at Gorki-9 since dawn, huddled with his staff and the White House advance team as they attempted to sketch out a loose agenda with the Russians. Typically, meetings between heads of state required weeks of preparation, but Berne was tasked with piecing it all together in just a few hours. The stress showed. He marched to the limousine, a stack of folders under his arm and strands of damp hair dangling in his eyes.

"I'm sorry, sir," he called to the president as a Secret Service agent pulled open the rear door. "I should've reached you earlier, but I couldn't get out."

"What's wrong, Patrick?"

Berne rested an arm on the limousine's roof and hunched into the cabin. "Lavrov sent all his men away about ten minutes ago. Popoff and the Foreign Ministry sherpas, the Kremlin aides; he just up and told them all to get out."

"What? Why?" Weisel gasped.

"I can't get anyone to tell me anything," Berne shrugged.

Paulson cast a grim look to his advisers. "He's playing with me."

"We should've never put you in this position, sir," Tanner said.

"Did you bring up Ukraine?" Dawson asked Berne.

"'For security purposes,'" he parroted, "'all discussion of current military operations on foreign soil will be out of bounds.'"

"Out of bounds, my ass," Paulson barked and glanced to the press photographers assembling along the driveway. "He's still inside, Patrick?"

"It's just Lavrov and Andrei Minin, alone. But they're in there. And they want to see you."

The president turned to Weisel. "Lavrov's playing with me, Angela."

"So did the guy before him," she said. "Get in there and play, too."

Paulson emerged from the limousine into a spasm of camera flashes. He went to the waiting protocol officer who switched on an artificial smile and sang, "President Paulson, on behalf of the Russian Federation, it is my distinct honor to welcome you—"

"I'm sure it is," Paulson cut him off. "Please show me to President Lavrov, we have urgent business and I don't want to wait."

The smile collapsed. "Right this way, Mr. President."

Paulson and his team were escorted into an entry foyer and through a pair of wide oak doors to a dining room smothered with gold plating and mirrors that overlooked Gorki-9's snow-covered lawns. There he saw them; no aides, no honor guard, no security, no press, no hangers-on: just the only two people in all of Russia who mattered. Lavrov looked different up close—far worse, if Paulson was being honest. His gut sagged lazily below his waist, the bottom two buttons of his shirt desperately clung to their threads; and he was shorter than the cameras made him appear, standing no taller than five-and-a-half feet. Mostly, he looked tired, Paulson noticed, like he wanted to crumble back into the dirt from whence he came—not the usual appearance of a man who controlled a nuclear arsenal.

At Lavrov's side was Minin, whom Paulson remembered sobbing uncontrollably into Lyudmila Karetnikova's shoulder. Not a day later, his grief was washed away. Carved into his round, boyish face was the assured grin of a teenager who'd just gotten laid.

"Gospodin Prezident," Lavrov lurched forward and offered his hand, *"jeto*

prijatno, nakonec, vstretit'sja s vami."

Lavrov spoke no English, Paulson reminded himself, just as Minin cut in to translate: "Mr. President, it is a pleasure to finally make your acquaintance." Minin paused as Lavrov continued, before trailing in as he finished. "Although I wish this meeting could have occurred under better circumstances, it is my sincerest wish that through Mikhail Borisovich's passing, our two nations may once more foster a strengthening of our similarities and a respect of our differences."

Paulson looked in Lavrov's eyes. There was none of the quiet confidence or the menace of Karetnikov's; they exuded the vitality of a dead fish.

"President Lavrov, I thank you for the kind words. And while I share in these very high sentiments, I remain deeply troubled by the realities of our relationship. It is my understanding that early this morning there was an unannounced incursion by your armed forces into the sovereign territory of Ukraine. Your predecessor's actions have levied a high price on your people. While I, too, wish to move past that in our new dialogue, there must be an immediate accounting for this military operation or I'm afraid this meeting will end before it begins. I am not one for adolescent tests of will, sir, and I hope neither are you."

Minin immediately began translating. Lavrov listened intently to every word, giving a few quick nods, and then smiled.

"Sadites'. Pozhalujsta."

"Please. Sit," Minin echoed.

On one side of the table were five places set for breakfast: for Paulson, Weisel, Dawson, Tanner and Berne; and on the other, just two. They took their seats, with Lavrov slowly slipping into a chair opposite Paulson. Berne, a fluent Russian speaker, placed a yellow notepad in front of him and began furiously taking his own account of everything that transpired. The others could do little more than watch.

"Andruishka..." Lavrov cued Minin.

Starting in flawless Oxford English, Minin spoke as if he had been rehearsing his lines for weeks. Unknown to any of them, he had. "At two this morning, Moscow time, and on the orders of President Lavrov, five teams of Special Purpose Forces under operational command of the General Staff Main Intelligence Directorate, crossed into Ukrainian airspace via helicopter and proceeded to their designated objectives. Their mission was two-fold: The first, to conduct a thorough search of the villages surrounding Horlivka, Krasnodon and Lugansk for heavy weapons stockpiled in violation of the Minsk II Protocol. It is my pleasure to inform you, Mr. President, that our forces did recover components for the Tornado-S, Uragan, Smerch and Tochka tactical missile systems, which should have been removed from the theater weeks ago. These illegal weapons were marked with strobes and struck by overhead fighter aircraft. Other caches were prepped with explosives and destroyed on-scene."

Paulson looked down the table. Berne had stopped writing. The others were floored.

"Secondly," Minin continued, "our forces were instructed to capture and recover the following separatist personalities: Vladimir Konov, commander of the Unified Armed Forces of Novorossiya; Igor Strelkov, a Russian citizen with known ties to separatist intelligence organs; Igor Besler, a regional commander of the Donbass People's Militia; Nikolai Kozitsyn, the leader of a Cossak volunteer regiment; and Alexander Zakharchenko, prime minister of the Donetsk People's Republic. As you know, all five men have been indicted by Dutch authorities for their role in downing Malaysia Airlines Flight 17. These men have been taken into custody and returned to Russian soil, and we will soon contact the Dutch embassy to begin extradition proceedings. In the execution of these objectives, our forces met steep resistance and in order to safely recover our personnel, the use of close air support was authorized with care taken to avoid civilian causalities. All Russian forces have since returned back across the border."

Minin let reality settle. He watched the president of the United States' face turn red with embarrassment. He saw Angela Weisel, who normally could not keep her mouth shut for longer than five minutes, at a total loss for words. *Strangle them in your embrace,* he thought.

"President Lavrov," Paulson found the will to speak, "if these developments are true, they are most welcome. And I thank you for your support. But I hope you are not offended if I do not take your word on faith alone."

Minin interrupted, not bothering to translate for his boss. He'd taken the driver's seat days ago. "Naturally, the OSCE, the UN, and anybody else who's curious are more than welcome to go in and inspect. They'll find exactly what I—we—told you. We've nothing to hide," he smiled.

Paulson stared Minin down. "Then, Andrei, please tell your president that's very encouraging."

The two chatted briefly in Russian before Minin returned his gaze. "Mr. President," he cleared his throat, "Mikhail Borisovich Karetnikov is dead." Minin thought that was obvious enough, but always worth reiterating. "I—we—cannot atone for his sins, only the Almighty can do that. But we can erect something new, something good atop the ruins. Let that begin today."

Paulson gently nodded. "Dmitri, if I may—if your actions and your words are true, then you have an equal partner in me."

Paulson was ignoring Minin on purpose and that irritated him to death. Even still, Minin dutifully translated. And then he turned back, speaking on his own. He thought up the next bit on the night Karetnikov's plane hit the ground.

"De Tocqueville once concluded of our nations: 'Their point of departure is different, their paths are varied; nonetheless, each one of them seems called by a secret design of Providence to hold in its hands one day the destinies of half the world...' We think this day is now."

Minin continued. "Sitting here, in this room, are the commanders of the two most powerful militaries in history, each with the capability to destroy this planet multiple times over. In our hands, quite literally, is the fate of all mankind. We take this responsibility seriously."

"As do I," Paulson acknowledged Minin.

Minin quickly mumbled something in Russian. "Violent as it may have been, please take our actions this morning as a gesture of goodwill. We would like to propose an annex to the Minsk Protocol. Of course, the following should receive the full vetting of all parties involved, but we think it best if you hear our terms first."

Berne and Weisel grabbed their pens and started tearing down a page.

"President Lavrov is prepared to publicly call upon the separatists in Ukraine to lay down their arms as early as—why not today? In exchange, we would like the *Verkhovna Rada* and President Udovenko to make good on their promises and expedite legislation granting full legal immunity to all Russian-speaking Ukrainian citizens for any actions taken against the state. This immunity must extend to their ability to hold public office; we consider that item non-negotiable. Now, Mr. President, as you've made clear, you believe Ukraine should be free to choose its own destiny. We agree. We also feel that this sentiment must not only apply to the Kiev government, but to all Ukrainian peoples. And so, within six months of this annex being signed, we would like to see new municipal elections in the east on a referendum granting increased autonomy to the oblasts. These elections should be free and fair and absolutely open to international observation, and you will have our word that we will not interfere in their outcome. Crimea, unfortunately, is finished. While President Lavrov isn't proud of the way in which it was taken, historically and ethnically it is Russian territory. If we can come to an agreement that honors the spirit of these terms, then we will have an end to the conflict in Ukraine. And we can finally put this dreadful period behind us...because, after all, there is so much more we seek to accomplish."

"Well, that does sound promising," Paulson leaned back. "Angela?"

Weisel placed her reading glasses on the table and rubbed her eyes. "In principle, I see no major pitfalls. I think the allies will be open to consideration, with consultations. The return of those men sought by the Netherlands will be an important first step. I am concerned about Crimea. I'd hope to have more discussions on that. Also, there's the matter of a full and thorough investigation by the UN for atrocities perpetrated by both sides— we must account for that. And then there's the issue of reparations."

"Oh, of course, Madam Secretary," Minin exclaimed and translated to his boss. He and Lavrov laughed. "That is my mistake. Apologies. Naturally, we will not solve the world's problems over breakfast! There should and there must be a fair exchange of ideas to come."

"Naturally," Weisel smiled uneasily.

"Mr. President," Minin's expression turned serious again, "We are not ones for 'adolescent tests of will.' We do not see Ukraine, the Baltics, Georgia, Syria, the Arctic, as boundaries, we see them as bridges; we do not see them as flashpoints or as frozen conflict zones of the nineteenth and twentieth centuries, we see them as opportunities for lasting peace. Mikhail Borisovich regretfully declared the end of the Cold War as a 'tragedy.' We see it as a squandered opportunity to finally achieve what your Francis Fukuyama called, 'The End of History.' We are eager to make good on lost time, sir. We seek a new alliance between Russia and America to bridge humanity's last great divide: between East and West; we seek a partnership to stamp out our species' great ills."

The scale of it all was staggering, Paulson thought. He had come to Moscow expecting a familiar lecture. Instead, he'd been handed the greatest victory of his presidency. They would carve out a special spot on Mount Rushmore when this was over, they would tear down the Washington Monument and put up a monolith of his own. And yet, he couldn't possibly know, he was bearing witness to the most convincing string of lies he'd ever heard.

"And we would welcome the Kremlin with open arms." The words compulsively slipped off Paulson's tongue.

"We mean to join OPEC—"

Tanner launched into a coughing fit. His body seized in the chair as he hastily reached for a water glass.

"Are you alright?" Minin's eyes shifted down the table.

"Yes, fine," replied Tanner after a gulp. "Excuse me."

"We mean to join OPEC," Minin reiterated without a second thought, "at the conference in Vienna early next month."

"We've heard nothing about this until just now," Weisel said with more than a hint of incredulity. "And this flies against every one of your policies; Russia's always hedged against the cartel's production quotas to your advantage. Why change course so radically in under a week?"

Minin turned to Lavrov. Both let off a mumble and a shrug. And then Minin turned back. "Well, Madam Secretary, there was a change of policymakers. And I'd certainly hope you've heard nothing about it. It was, after all, a state secret until just now," he politely laughed.

Minin's bluntness smacked them as an unpleasant surprise, like a well-choreographed dance of humility and hostility—at one moment building them up, so in the next he could tear them back down.

"I shouldn't be so frank," he retreated.

"I believe what concerns Secretary Weisel," Paulson offered, "is exactly how you came to this decision. Surely, you wouldn't propose to join OPEC without being assured admission, which means you must have already approached the Saudis. And they've said nothing to us." For a brief moment, Paulson realized that he had forgotten Lavrov was even in the room, sitting directly opposite him. But in that moment he also knew he'd discovered the whisper in Lavrov's ear—the one so criminally underestimated by them all.

"Yes, we apologize for the secrecy, Mr. President," Minin grinned and shifted in his seat. "These cloak-and-dagger methods are unbecoming. At President Lavrov's direction, I asked if Roman Ivanov would convey a message from us to Prince Farid bin Abdulaziz, who was recently a guest at his home. Prince Farid brought this message to his brother, King Abdul. The purpose of this message, naturally, was to determine if the House of Saud would object to Russia pursuing membership in the cartel. His Majesty does not object, and on the contrary, offered to sponsor us. I, myself, was surprised...as were we all."

"And you offered them what in return?" Weisel asked.

Minin first translated for Lavrov. "We see certain benefits in a unipolar world: Security. Safety. Stability," he began. "None of this messy business that comes when forces are stretched to either extreme. Such is the old way of business," Minin dismissed with a swat. "The Middle East is the greatest consequence of this unfortunate to and fro. And in return, we see the chaos sowed by the Islamic State throughout Iraq and Syria. And as we speak, we see renewed chaos in Gaza by the detestable actions of Palestinian Islamic Jihad and their supporters..."

Weisel's ears perked.

"Such savages have no role to play in the dialogue between nations; they are a scourge upon mankind and they must be exterminated. There will be no middle ground. We feel that this also must apply to countries that support and enable such savagery. Countries like Iran."

Paulson wanted to vomit.

"So what did we offer the Saudis?" Minin asked. "We offered that the Russian Federation would sever diplomatic and military ties with the Islamic Republic of Iran. This extends to any support we provide to their nuclear program."

The dining room doors opened and a host of servers entered with silver trays bearing breakfast.

"As you are all no doubt aware," he continued, "membership in OPEC requires the consent of all five founding states, of which Iran is one. This puts us in a rather awkward position."

A server placed breakfast in front of Minin. He placed a napkin on his lap. "Mr. President, we have been totally forthright with you this morning, more so, perhaps, than in the last sixty years of our shared history. You see that we have nothing to hide. We ask that you extend the same courtesy to us and keep this strategy in strict confidence among the few in this room. It should not leave these four walls."

Paulson nodded.

"Once our place in OPEC is secured, we see no reason that our relationship with Tehran should continue." Minin took his fork and smiled wide. "I think you will find, sir, that we can be the very best of friends."

CHAPTER 27

MOVSAR GELAYEV—WHO, in a previous life, raped and murdered an eighty-year-old woman in the Chechen village of Alkhan-Yurt when she tried to stop his unit from burning her house—slid his BMW motorcycle into an empty space along the Beirut corniche where Avenue de Paris meets Rue Ibn Sina, traded his helmet for a nondescript baseball cap, and felt for the Tokarev pistol concealed against his rib cage. He scanned the sidewalk through passing strollers, chic young things and hawker stands, spotted a lit sign for the Café Younes, and made for a gap in traffic.

Inside, the café was largely divided into two camps: packs of teenagers, chatting between glances at their smartphones, and mute old men sharing drags on twisted waterpipes. Each tried to deny the existence of the other. Some gathered around a TV mounted to the wall and watched two Al Jazeera commentators spar over the Israeli airstrikes that rocked Gaza in the night. In the stir, Gelayev was roundly disregarded as he walked through the open door and ordered a coffee, which was just how he wanted it.

He placed a few liras on the counter and took his cup, inspecting the crowd as he turned. In the back corner, sitting at a chipped wooden table, was a man whose face was hidden behind the day's edition of *an-Nahar*. Gelayev looked closer. The upper right corner of the front page was dog-eared. He went for the empty adjacent table and sat, taking care not to look at the man. Over roughly the next ten minutes, Gelayev interrogated the world around him. He kept a weather eye on his bike outside, making certain that none of the cars he'd spotted on the drive over curiously reappeared. He watched the faces in the café. None were too familiar. Over a grating Nancy Ajram pop song, he overhead bits of their conversations transition seamlessly from Arabic, to French, to English and back around again, often in the same sentence. None were even remotely interesting. All the while, the man sitting beside him did the same.

Once an unspoken sense of security was settled, the man folded his newspaper into thirds, stood, and went through the door, never making eye contact. As he left, Gelayev budged an inch toward the empty table, reached for the paper and slid it under his arm. He sat for another minute or two with his coffee, filtering out the sunken grinds with his teeth. He scrutinized the café one last time, checking their faces, their whispers, where their attention had fallen. And then, in one smooth motion, Gelayev lifted the paper, letting a thumb drive tumble from the folds into his hand, and made for the street.

Gelayev timed his trip back to coincide with the afternoon rush, when the capital disgorges a half-million vehicles into a handful of narrow, poorly maintained roads. On his motorcycle, Gelayev zipped between the riotous, frozen fabric of horns and radio stations along the Elias el-Hrawi Highway into the foothills of the Mount Lebanon range. He sped ahead at nearly a hundred kilometers-per-hour, cutting between lanes and weaving around cars, constantly pushing forward and making any surveillance effort impossible to mount from the ground alone. As he reached Baabda, the traffic thinned and Gelayev was forced to take greater care, spinning his head back at any given moment or searching the sky above. But Gelayev was free, without the smallest hint of a tail. He followed the highway through the hills until it opened up again into the flat plains of the Beqaa Valley, taking an exit near Zahlé, toward Baalbek.

Just then, all light began to fade.

He turned north down increasingly deserted roads and skirted Zarayeb. Moving deeper, into sprawling cannabis and poppy fields, the terrain started to rise again. His tires fought for traction in the dirt as he came up the ridge. In the twilight, Gelayev noticed that the perimeter force was invisible and likely hidden under ghillie suits; and by the time Gelayev arrived, they would have already radioed ahead. Coming up the final rise to the barren hilltop, Gelayev stopped the motorcycle before the cinder-block house. There were no visible lights inside and the few trucks and SUVs parked in the clearing were covered with camouflage nets.

Gelayev entered and passed a sentry just inside the door—another Russian whom he'd served with for years—and came into a small room lit only by candles arranged on the floor. On the walls were maps marking numerous oil and gas facilities strewn throughout the desolate recesses of Saudi Arabia's Eastern Province. Standing beside them, in the dim light, was David Kazanoff.

• • •

The scaffold was in place. Four iron posts were stabbed into the ground and joined by an equal number of trusses welded to the corners, essentially forming a large box that dominated the barn's interior. Industrial drum fans worked to solidify the concrete floor. That in itself was an achievement; there needed to be a perfectly level platform to perform any maintenance on the device, if that was even necessary. Once the floor was finished— under darkness or heavy cloud cover—a crew would lay weather-sealed plastic sheeting over the sides and thread aluminum ventilation hoses through the roof. That would be finished in a matter of days. Then Ruslan Baranov would move to the next, greater problem: deciding how to best filter out trace amounts of plutonium before it could escape the barn and be detected by any, hypothetical, surveillance. He was supposed to have months to solve these issues before moving against their target.

Baranov rolled open the barn's metal door and stepped outside, pulling it shut behind him. He heard a motorcycle engine roar off into the valley. A violent gust buffeted the hilltop as he placed a cigarette between his lips and reached for a lighter. He threw his thumb down the wheel, unleashing a dull spark that fluttered and extinguished in the wind. Baranov turned his body toward the barn and cupped the lighter with his hand, striking the wheel again, and again, only to the same result. He shivered in the familiar cold and, defeated, tossed the cigarette to the dirt. As he looked up, he spotted a morose shadow advancing on him from the house below. Baranov recognized the stooped gait and shuffled steps that seemed at once motionless and unstoppable. As the shadow inched closer, he heard Kazanoff call to him, scarcely piercing the wind.

"It's time."

A camouflage net was pulled off a gray Nissan Patrol and in moments Baranov found himself in the back, beside Kazanoff, bound for Beirut. In a folder on his lap were the majority of the thumb drive's contents—the latest haul of American secrets sent from General Trubnikov in Moscow. Kazanoff hadn't spoken since they left the hilltop but Baranov knew that something forced his hand. As he struggled to read the pages in the dark, he began piecing together the likely cause. In his hands was a copy of CIA's executive summary detailing their assessment of the Iranian bunker network at Haj Ali Gholi. The report covered it all: the approximate technical specifications, their maddening theories on how Dr. Alireza Fakhrizadeh could have escaped death at the hands of Mossad, and their troubling finding that Iran's Revolutionary Guards may have a small, functional nuclear weapon in a matter of months—possibly the size of a large suitcase. Then Baranov understood, even if a small part of him wished he didn't.

"You're sending me to Germany?" he asked.

"Yes. The Americans have a prophecy and it's time we fulfill it."

Baranov backed away from the subject, wading deeper into the file.

"They're mounting an operation in Lebanon," Baranov added with a hint of alarm, before reading further. Hezbollah tightened the noose around a bureaucrat named Walid Rada for suspected embezzlement. The information came from an asset known as TOPSAIL, who also claimed to have spotted Ibrahim al-Din in the Security Quarter some days ago. "Are we warning him?"

"No," Kazanoff breathed to Baranov's surprise, "we'll tell him nothing until the last moment. Right now, Langley is deciding whether they want Mossad to recruit Walid Rada for their own. Eventually, they'll allow it. Tomorrow, I'll dispatch a team to Machgara to watch Rada and wait for them to show. 'TOPSAIL,' the source behind it all, is Colonel Samir Basri, head of the ISF's Intelligence Bureau, and his American handler," Kazanoff turned to look at Baranov, "is a woman."

Baranov quickly scanned the cables, but none of what Kazanoff said was anywhere to be found.

"We will tell al-Din not a word of this," he reiterated. "And I'll address them in my own way… Keep reading; there's more."

Baranov forced his eyes down to the pages and discovered that Mossad officers had extricated Mehdi Vaziri from Iran and were debriefing him inside the Hôtel Meurice in Paris. By the time his eyes rose again, the SUV slowly pulled through a dark side street somewhere in Ouzai. They stopped in a blind alley. Kazanoff stepped out, carrying the folder, and idly shuffled past two plain-clothed militiamen armed with AK-47s. Baranov followed him through a door and up a flight of stairs, hearing the unmistakable sound of a children's program ahead. They climbed to the top and rounded a corner, entering a cluttered living room lit by the dull, electric glow of a television screen.

Al-Din sat on a tattered sofa wearing a simple cloth tunic that fell to his ankles. Stretched over his lap, absorbed in the cartoon playing on the TV, was a small girl no older than three with plump cheeks and curly black hair. She gave them no mind.

"You have something for me?" al-Din briefly drew his eyes from the glow.

Kazanoff stared at the girl and offered a few photographs from the folder. "This was found on that Iranian freighter off Somalia…"

Al-Din placed the girl on the cushion next to him and reached for the photographs. "Qasem Shateri is growing restless—and reckless," he said, sliding on a pair of glasses.

"As I told you he would."

Al-Din leafed through the carnage displayed on the *Catarina A*'s bridge to a photo of the shipping containers in the hold. He turned one photograph to the side and froze, recognizing the four Soumar cruise missile tubes attached to hydraulic lifts. "A coincidence," he said."

"A useful one."

"Fine," al-Din nodded, handing the photos back, "do it."

"I'm sending my men to Germany in the coming days," Kazanoff added and took a seat on the sofa, sandwiching the girl between him and al-Din. He wouldn't give him Langley's report on Haj Ali Gholi; al-Din didn't understand English. "Qasem Shateri is also building a bomb. Did you know this?"

"No."

"It's time," Kazanoff replied and reached over the girl to place a hand on al-Din's knee, "to do all the things I promised you we would. This is my gift."

Al-Din glanced at Kazanoff's hand.

"In order to learn this about Qasem Shateri, the Americans must have someone very close to him," Baranov heard Kazanoff say, again not understanding how he could possibly know. "I will find this person."

Al-Din felt the pressure inch up his thigh.

"I'm also sending my men to Paris."

"What is in Paris?"

"Mehdi Vaziri...whom you will publicly slaughter for me."

Still four hours from Washington, Air Force One flew southwest into an endless sunset. Cape Farewell, the southernmost point of Greenland—an inhospitable dagger of black granite headlands, yawning fjords and sweeping glaciers that split the North Atlantic from the Labrador Sea—passed thirty thousand feet below. From her leather swivel chair in the senior staff cabin, Angela Weisel watched the pink smear on the horizon sink farther behind the starboard wing and waited patiently for the snores beside her to grow more frequent.

Tanner had pulled his legs up into a loose ball and his head was bent precariously against the contours of his chair; a bit of drool glistened on the corner of his mouth. He looked extraordinarily uncomfortable, she thought, and helpless in an endearing sort of way. Better yet, he hadn't spoken in nearly an hour. Another snore rumbled from the lump. Weisel might have finally found her opportunity.

She pressed down on the armrests and slowly rose to her feat, creeping to the portside corridor. Weisel craned her neck left, looking aft to the staff section beyond the conference room. She spotted Dawson, facing away from her, in spirited conversation with the White House press secretary. Her two obstacles were either distracted or unconscious. Then she turned right and her eyes fell on the entrance to Paulson's suite located in the VC-

25A's nose, under the cockpit. A lone Secret Service agent guarded the door, but she could take him.

Weisel made her move. She bowled to the agent with a confidant stride and stopped abruptly, feigning a hint of annoyance. "Is the president available? I need to see him."

The agent stood without expression and gave two gentle knocks. "Sir, the secretary of state is here for you."

"Yeah, sure," Paulson's voice replied.

The agent yielded and opened the door.

"Thanks, Joshua," Paulson said as Weisel came in.

"Sir," the agent nodded and closed it behind her.

The president was stretched out on a folding sofa along the starboard fuselage, wearing a Yale sweatshirt and faded jeans. A beer bottle balanced on his stomach and an old *South Park* episode his body man had DVR'd played on a television on the aft bulkhead.

"The shit they say on this goddamn show cracks me up," he swigged. "Especially the fat kid."

"Andrew, I need to talk to you."

"You know," he groaned, switched off the TV and sat upright, "when you told me I had to go to that funeral myself and not just send Berne and a press release, I thought for sure you'd lost it."

"Me, too."

"But I think—and it's crazy that I'm saying this—I needed to see Karetnikov dead, or at least in a box. That made it real. In the back of my mind, I always assumed he would live to see me put in the ground."

"Fate begged to differ." Weisel helped herself to the cushion beside him.

"What the hell happened back there?"

She shrugged. "Lot's of talk."

"No, that wasn't—"

"Moscow's played us before," Weisel interrupted. "Putting down the separatists was a mercy killing; it cost them almost nothing and they had everything to gain. But cutting off Iran to appease the Saudis? That's different. And I'll believe it when I see it. Lavrov still has an election hanging over his head."

"But no one could challenge him," he reasoned.

"We'll see. Moscow is still full of Karetnikov's old flock and ninety days is a long time to hold a consensus. Some will try and carve out a piece of the empire, but I think it'll be resolved before the end. There may be a few bodies in the process, Lavrov will stay in the Kremlin."

"I like him."

"Lavrov's a good man. Odd, but decent."

"No. Minin." Paulson shook his head. "He's just...familiar."

"He can talk the talk. Which is either very good or very bad." Weisel leaned over, pressed her knees, and took a deep breath.

Paulson grew worried. "What did you want to tell me?"

She straightened her back and brushed her hair away. "I've been considering this for a while, but the past few days put it all into perspective: Gaza flaring up again, and the Russians having their 'come to Jesus' moment."

"Angela, what is it?"

"Last week, when Harold Lansing met Sayigh in Ramallah, he asked if Hamas could pressure Islamic Jihad into releasing Moshe Adler before the Annapolis conference next month. The hope was to give Avi a victory he can present to his base as proof that he can get concessions from the Palestinians while negotiating with them. Our thought process was that if the Israelis and the Syrians make progress over the Golan Heights at Annapolis, we could get Avi to put the West Bank on the table next."

"Right, I know all of this."

Weisel bit down on her lip. "And so, because of us, Adler is dead."

The president shook his head. "That boy was killed because we intercepted weapons that Islamic Jihad wanted smuggled through Sudan. They needed to retaliate and they knew executing Adler would hurt the most."

"No, he was killed so that the Israelis would be forced to attack Gaza again. The Iranians don't want Israel and Syria to reach a peace agreement, they don't wants the Palestinians involved in any sort of negotiations, and they definitely don't want the status quo we've fought to establish over the past nine months to hold. Agents of the IRGC murdered Moshe Adler, and Avi Arad played right into their hands.

"Listen," she pressed on, "the hardliners in the Revolutionary Guards have been left with almost nothing. The Syrian regime collapsed overnight, and we performed a miracle by putting rational people in Damascus, and now that country sees some hope for the first time in five years. We took that victory in Syria and used it to force Hezbollah to lay down its arms if it wants to have any political future in Lebanon. Now we have the Russians running toward the West again and they're willing to cut Iran loose to do so. That's the tipping point."

"How do you mean? A tipping point for what?"

"Trying to put cruise missiles in Sudan and executing an Israeli soldier was just the beginning," she said gravely. "But Lavrov severing diplomatic relations with Iran to please the Saudis will plunge Tehran into an existential crisis the likes of which they've never imagined. Total war with Iraq in the eighties will look tame in comparison. I promise you, they won't idly sit by and watch their revolution collapse. We need to be prepared to deal with the consequences. They will blame us for this and they will come after us in every way possible. And let's not forget that all of this magically coincides with the strong likelihood that the IRGC is building a nuclear bomb right under the ayatollah's nose."

The president massaged his eyelids, took his fingers away and blinked, revealing two red pits filled with exhaustion. "Did you just come here to give me a headache, or was there some other point?"

Weisel frowned. "Harold is of the opinion, as am I, that it's impossible to solve the Israel-Palestine issue until Iran is removed from the equation. We cannot guarantee Israel's security while the Revolutionary Guards are working overtime to destroy it. Obviously, bombing them out of the picture would be disastrous for everyone involved, so they must be enticed in some other way. I've had something in mind, but if what we were told today pans out, then our position is much better than I'd hoped."

Paulson finished his beer. "How so?"

"You and I have always privately known that our end game with the Iranians, short of war, is forcing an international embargo of their oil exports. That would mean blockading their coastline and seizing the reserves we know they've hidden offshore. Now, if Russia joins OPEC they'd easily be able to fill the supply shortage and take pressure off the Saudis. And if Lavrov severs ties with Tehran, then getting this through the Security Council would be much easier; without the Russians, China would likely abstain rather than stand alone."

"But," the president countered, "we'd cause the collapse of the regime and then be forced to deal with whatever chaos comes after"

"Yeah, that's where the plan get's messy," admitted Weisel.

"So surely you're going to offer an alternative…"

"Andrew, before CIA manages to prove that the Revolutionary Guards are building a nuclear bomb—and we're forced to make some life and death decisions—we need to negotiate with Iran one last time. The problem when it comes to talking to the Iranians is that the brain is never really sure what the hands are doing. I flew back and forth to Switzerland for months trying to make a deal with these people, we did, and the whole time a faction of the IRGC had an alternate nuclear program that no one—including the Iranian negotiating team—knew about. So I'm saying that we need to go around the bureaucracy, around all the 'factions,' and communicate directly with the supreme leader. But Khansari is isolated and sick, he has very little involvement in forming policy, he only signs off on them. We need to open a backchannel with someone who can get to him, someone we know and trust, someone we control."

"And who the hell would that be?"

Weisel eased a wry grin. "Langley's MONARCH intelligence, the sourcing behind whatever we think is happening with that bomb, it's all one man."

"Jesus Christ," Paulson said as the blood drained from his face. "Who?"

"For your sake, that's as much as you should know."

"Of course," he nodded.

"Ryan told me his source's authority and reputation inside the regime are unquestionable," Weisel continued. "He can get to Khansari, alone, and make sure any offer we pass through a third party gets the supreme leader's approval. All we need is the ayatollah's tacit blessing to restart negotiations and the hardliners will have nothing to run with."

"Okay," Paulson said, "then what? What could we possibly offer them that hasn't been on the table already?"

"You're going to send Khansari a letter detailing three points that we're willing to discuss. We'll demand full reciprocity; for each point, the Iranians must give up something equal in return. This is going to hurt, Andrew. And your last year in the White House will not be pleasant for it. But I promise, if you make this deal with Iran, you will marginalize the hardliners and make that bomb they're building unnecessary. And if Lavrov cuts Iran off, they'll have no choice but to fold. Then we can guarantee Israel's security, and instead of Iran antagonizing the peace process, we'll have them at the table as mediators."

"Congress won't impeach me for this, will they?"

"No," she scoffed. "And put Brandon in the Oval early? Please!"

Paulson smiled. "Alright, Ange, what's your play?"

"To start, we give them Iraq..."

Air Force One landed shortly before midnight. After Paulson was whisked to Marine One for the last leg of the trip, the rest aboard the plane were free to disembark. Weisel casually stepped down the aft airstairs to her motorcade waiting on the tarmac. Once inside the heated cabin of the armored Suburban, she reached into her purse, pulled out her BlackBerry, and fired off a quick email to Ryan Freeman, telling him to call the next morning.

CHAPTER 28

AN ELECTRIC BLUE glow cast back on Freeman's glasses. For the past several minutes, their lenses had been covered with a glossy sheen of parading maps and reconnaissance photos marking highway checkpoints and armed desert encampments, graphic overlays and PowerPoint charts revealing known and suspected hierarchies and relationships. Most of it was review, both to him and the two-dozen agency employees scattered around the room. But before they could argue their case, they had to weave in the tangled realities on the ground. The stakes were high, Freeman knew; if he couldn't convince his guest that morning, they would be forced to scrap the entire operation before it even began.

Since discovering Project 260 and the bunker complex, Picasso and Monet, which masked it, Peter Stavros created a special-access program within the Iran Operations Division—Persia House—to manage and control all further intelligence trickling in regarding the project and its presumed director, Alireza Fakhrizadeh. The security compartment around it was tight, consisting of approximately fifty people in the Beltway who knew of the program's existence. Inside that was a smaller, more restricted task force, led by Stavros, and manned with imagery experts and politico-military analysts, geologists and physicists, psychologists and operational planners. All hand-picked. Casting a wider net to draw in the necessary talent presented its own problems. The ones not from Persia House came from offices spread around Langley, and in those offices were colleagues working on other projects who surely would not welcome their absence. Questions would be asked and answers would be invented; people would talk, as they are wont to do. Freeman knew that time was not on their side, nor did he appreciate how many had come aboard, although Shaw and Stavros routinely assured him that they were working with a skeleton crew. Still, he rolled over each morning and picked his phone off the nightstand with dread that some eager reporter would cement their career at his expense. But this was all his own doing, Freeman reminded himself. This was the result of opening his mouth to the president and declaring that CIA could penetrate the Revolutionary Guard's holiest of holies. Now before Freeman could present a plan, he had to secure the muscle that would go into Iran and execute it on the ground.

Most of the task force was squeezed into a darkened lecture hall, rising up at Freeman's back in rows of pitched seats. Shaw sat directly behind him with Stavros. Roger Mathis hid somewhere further back in the shadows. Representatives had also come in from the Special Activities Division and the Covert Action Staff, both of which had opened their contingency plans to Stavros. Also scattered throughout the hall were officers of the JSOC Intelligence Brigade, who'd shipped up from Fort Bragg in the last twenty-four hours to carve out a chunk of territory in Persia House. Yet Freeman's focus was entirely fixed on the man next to him—the only opinion that mattered at the moment—the commander of the Joint Special Operations Command, Vice Admiral Eric Wade.

Originally from Lowell, Massachusetts and one of nine children, Wade was once the subject of a SEAL recruitment poster; a literal vision of perfection as the Navy wanted their elite to be seen. Thirty years later, that image hardly faded. He had the squared jaw of a Rottweiler and the compact frame of an Olympic swimmer, and somehow possessed the capacity to be at once disarming and intimidating to anyone he came across. It was an image that largely belied his personality. Wade was an unmistakable introvert. He shunned the media—the days after bin Laden's assassination were excruciating for him—and he lived not unlike a monk, eating one meal a day and sleeping four hours a night, allowing the time to devote himself entirely to the men at his command and the mission they were given. He took that charge as seriously as a commandment from God. In the immediate aftermath of the Syrian civil war, as Pentagon machinery flooded in-country to extinguish the chaos, Wade forward deployed his entire staff to Damascus, eating MREs and sleeping in tents with his troops. For it, Wade's men—a motley, strong-willed group of soldiers, sailors, airmen and marines—loved him and affectionately called him their "Pope." That respect spilled over into the White House. His intolerance for their bureaucracy was well known and he had a direct line to Eli Tanner, who usually wouldn't dare contradict his advice to the president. That was ultimately what made Wade so valuable to Freeman. He was one of the few reliable voices who couldn't be ignored. And if Freeman could convert him to CIA's thinking, not only would Freeman have the operators needed to go into Iran and execute their plan, he would have a powerful ally to push it through the National Security Council. Without Wade, Freeman's ship was sunk before it set sail.

And so while those around him listened, Freeman kept turning his head to watch Wade in quick glances, deciphering every blink and nod for a sign.

Leading the briefing—or sales pitch, as one might see it—was Marcia Lath, Stavros's deputy, and a rare holdover from the Soviet desk who'd reinvented herself countless times. Her latest fields of expertise were the Iranian security services and the schoolyard brawl often called Iraqi tribal affairs. She navigated the winding, warring cliques with ease.

Each time Lath pressed the remote clutched in her palm, the projection screen on the wall would seamlessly transition to another map or overhead photograph further illustrating the strategic situation in northern Iraq, which was crucial to confronting CIA's greater issue across the border in Iran. Following ISIS' expulsion from Iraq nine months ago, a host of fractured militias and rebel groups now dominated territory stretching from Baghdad up to the Turkish border. The conflict that raged for over a year had left their armories bursting with heavy weapons and left thousands of battle-hardened veterans among their ranks. With their common enemy driven underground, the one unifying threat that kept the various factions from turning their guns on each other was gone. Worse still, most were merely the personal playthings of foreign masters, each determined to claim a pound of flesh and dictate the country's future on their terms. Iraq was a live grenade, and Freeman had a good idea who was waiting to come along and pull the pin: *Hajj* Qasem Shateri.

When ISIS blitzed into Iraq from Syria and captured huge swaths of the country without resistance, eventually stopping a few kilometers from downtown Baghdad, a group of Shiite clerics issued a *fatwa* ordering "righteous jihad" against the terrorists and compelled all able-bodied Shiites to take up arms. Numerous existing militias—most created by Iran to resist the former American occupation—answered the call and were placed under an umbrella organization named "Hashid Shaabi," or, the Popular Mobilisation Units. The militias were intended to operate under direction from Baghdad and within the legal framework of the Interior Ministry. But, as often happens with hired guns, their loyalties remained with the highest bidder, the Quds Force. On the battlefield, the militias' capabilities far exceeded the Iraqi Army and proved decisive in retaking several cities, ultimately setting the stage for ISIS's defeat. With the last war consigned to history, the militias were supposed to disband and melt back into the population. That never happened. Hashid Shaabi and its largest subsidiaries—the Badr Organization, Kata'ib Hezbollah, Asa'ib Ahl al-Haq and Saraya al-Khorasani—now controlled four provinces and exercised great influence over a fifth.

Lath provided commentary on a map showing the current balance of power. Using a network of old US forward operating bases, Hashid Shaabi overtly deployed forces throughout the Baghdad suburbs and reached as far south as Karbala and as far west as Samarra, along the Tigris. Their intentions around the capital, while denied, were well known.

During the battle with ISIS, the militias indiscriminately shelled the 124-mile agricultural belt around Baghdad. Their expressed goal was to prevent the terrorists from finding a safe haven among sympathetic Sunni villages that could be used to mount an assault on the city. Eighty-three thousand people, most with no ISIS affiliation, fled the onslaught. With the army's tacit support, the militias swept in to fill the vacuum and refused to allow civilians to return, leaving dozens of burned-out towns and cratered farmland dotted with bloated, purple bodies festering in the sun. Effectively, Hashid Shaabi had purged Sunnis from Baghdad's periphery and irreversibly altered Iraq's demography. Farther north, the militias embarked on a similar campaign. The Badr Organization, Hashid Shaabi's most powerful group, occupied Diyala Province and raided numerous villages, summarily executing suspected ISIS collaborators and bulldozing their family's homes. As Lath explained, the Badr Organization's advance halted at Tuz Khormato, a town about fifty-five miles south of the Kurdish-occupied oil fields rimming Kirkuk. The militia had promised not to move into new territory, but that was only valid so long as the Quds Force pulling the strings did not decide otherwise.

Opposite that short gap of open highway, from Kirkuk all the way north to Zakho on the Turkish border was Iraqi Kurdistan, whose people had been granted the right to self-rule in 2003 and did so competently. During the civil war, Kurdish *peshmerga* forces—literally meaning "one who confronts death"—proved themselves adroit in tackling ISIS. Supported by allied airpower and counseled by Wade's discreet advisers on the ground, the Kurds quickly banded together to repel a series of attacks on their capital of Erbil, helped break a siege around Mount Sinjar, and later contributed almost half of the force that wrestled Mosul from the terrorists' grip. But their cooperation had not always been so assured—nor would it be again.

The wider Kurdish diaspora, which reached into pockets of Turkey, Iran and Syria, campaigned over forty years for their independence. After generations of fighting and with thousands dead, the Kurds had something tangible to show for their efforts, but the dream of forging one unified country was still just that. It didn't help that most of those forty years had been consumed by infighting. In Iraqi Kurdistan, the political landscape was concerned with a delicate balance between two dominant secular parties: the Kurdistan Democratic Party (KDP) and the Patriotic Union of Kurdistan (PUK). Both had a fifty-fifty coalition, forming the Kurdistan Regional Government (KRG) and ensuring that neither held supremacy over the other. It was a careful arrangement; changes in leadership often ignited a game of musical chairs in the KRG and Iraqi national positions reserved for the Kurds, which could quickly escalate to more deadly squabbles. The KDP, headquartered in Erbil and led by Ezzedine Barzani, was organized around disparate clans and familial ties, much like a mafia outfit. The PUK, based farther south in Sulemaniyah and led by Barham Mustafa, was more an umbrella group of diverse personalities and interests, typically sympathetic to Iran. Outlying this power struggle was the pair of rebel groups that saw themselves as the true vanguard of Kurdish nationalism.

Sheltered on Mount Qandil, a series of forested valleys and gray spines straddling the Iranian border, were approximately three thousand fighters of the Kurdistan Workers' Party (PKK), which had waged a low-level insurgency against Turkey for years. They sat in canvas tents and cinder block huts, oiling rusty Kalashnikovs and counting ammunition while the greater movement around them determined the next front in the war for Kurdish independence. Based in separate camps from the PKK was the armed wing of the Party for a Free Life in Kurdistan. PJAK was the Iranian offshoot of the Kurdistan Workers' Party, committed to achieving the same goals over the mountains in Iran. Their specialty lay in hit-and-run assaults with small arms and grenades to explicitly avenge the deaths of Kurdish activists and civilians by Iranian security forces, often resulting in their own being killed or captured and brutally tortured by the Revolutionary Guards. But PJAK thought it had at last found its moment. As Kurds caught their breath from the blowback of the Syrian civil war, they took stock of what was won and what was lost, and they considered their future. While their movement had earned great gains with autonomy in Iraq and Syria, and reconciliation with Turkey, absolutely no progress was made inside Iran. Moreover, they eyed savage Shiite militias seizing ground not an hour's drive south—an Iranian stain bleeding into the fabric of Iraq. Most quietly admitted that it was time to bring the fight to Iran. The Kurds earned their right to independence and the horror of ISIS stripped away any lingering fear of death. Some, like the KDP and PUK, just argued.

But one man already went back to war.

Lath hit the remote again. The screen suspended overhead flashed white and instantly switched to a photograph. It depicted a towering beast of a man dressed in camouflage fatigues, rising six-foot-five and striking a triumphant pose. He stood amid a wild patch of purple thistles—their flowers and barbed leaves washed with drying blood—and stared off toward the burning horizon. His eyes glimmered, as if to be delighted at the carnage, and his muscular arms were pressed to the horned hilts of two daggers strapped to his belt. The man had coarse black hair flowing from his scalp like a mane and a long beard tied with thread into three prongs. An M4 hung from a sling on his right shoulder. "Major General Jamil Gorani," Lath declared, "the 'Dark Lion' of Kurdistan."

In the corner of his eye, Freeman watched a smirk form on Wade's face.

"No doubt you've seen this picture before, Admiral," she said. Lath was right; almost a year ago, the portrait made headlines around the world and the *Agence France-Presse* journalist who snapped it was awarded a Pulitzer. It captured the aftermath of an ISIS assault on Gorani's peshmerga fighters dug-in atop Bashiqah, a treeless promontory overlooking the northeastern outskirts of Mosul. Twenty suicide bombers backed by mortars charged up the slopes. Gorani ordered his snipers to target the terrorists' explosive vests. The outcome, as the picture showed, had showered the hillside, watering the thistles.

"This was taken about six weeks before the Nineveh offensive began," Lath added, referring to the operation to retake Mosul, "and it's the last known photograph of Gorani, as far as we're aware."

Wade nodded in approval. "That man is as hard as they come."

"Just to provide a quick overview," she tapped the remote, changing to a PowerPoint slide, "Gorani is either sixty-two or sixty-four, depending on the DOB. He's from Bardarash, Iraqi Kurdistan, and his father was one of the leading tribesmen. Almost nothing is known of his early life. In 1968, we know he joined the KDP as a bodyguard to Ezzedine Barzani and the two remained close friends until their supposed falling-out. He's seen combat in every Kurdish engagement over the last forty years, from insurrections against Baghdad to internal struggles with the PUK. Eventually, he landed the rank of major general and was given command of a KDP peshmerga brigade in his hometown. His garrison's location, about twenty-five miles from Mosul, proved quite valuable in the civil war. After the siege of Mount Sinjar, Gorani received permission from Barzani to establish a training camp for Sinjari militants and other volunteers from Nineveh Province dislocated by the fighting."

"That whole area was hot," said Wade. "I know a few thousand refugees came out of Tal Afar, alone. The peshmerga wouldn't have locked down Dohuk without Gorani capturing Highway 2. He held their entire western flank all by himself until Baghdad got its act together."

"You've met him?" asked Freeman.

"Never had the pleasure. But the JOC in Erbil couldn't say enough— about him and his 'sons.'"

Lath addressed her audience. "Gorani took in some men whose families were killed in the retreat from ISIS and adopted them as his own. We believe he's adopted ten in all. Their tribal and religious identities vary. Some are Yazidis, some Christian, and most Muslim, but all are loyal to Gorani first and Kurdistan second. This has been a point of contention; there's evidence to suggest that in the Bardarash camp the men swore a personal oath of allegiance to Gorani, not to the KDP or Ezzedine Barzani. Naturally, this was not received well in Erbil."

"He built a private army," Freeman summed it up for the admiral.

"Like the Lost Boys in *Peter Pan,*" Wade grinned.

"After the liberation of Mosul," Lath continued, "Gorani faced calls from both Barzani and Baghdad to disband his militia and return to his old command in the KDP. Gorani refused, stating that these men were rightfully a part of his family. Barham Mustafa and PUK then forced a decree through the Kurdish parliament, also ordering the militia to disband. Again, Gorani refused, and essentially dared the peshmerga to enforce the decree. Meanwhile, the Kurdistan Workers' Party and PJAK negotiated a deal with Erbil allowing them to return to Mount Qandil, albeit behind a peshmerga buffer zone—widely seen to appease Turkey and Iran."

Lath clicked to another slide. "This occurred as the Interior Ministry allowed the Badr Organization to hold its forces in Diyala Province. In an interview with the Kurdish newspaper, *Hawlati,* Gorani was asked for his response and called on Kurds across the diaspora to turn their resistance against Iran. He said something to the effect that Qasem Shateri had his hand up Barham Mustafa's rear end to use as a puppet."

A short burst of restrained laughter ran through the room.

"Sources in Erbil reported that Barzani was incensed. A week later, five gunmen attacked Gorani's home in the middle of the night. His wife, Nasrin, and eldest son by birth, Arjen, were both killed. Our analysts initially thought the assassins may have been from Barzani's personal bodyguard, however we later deduced from SIGINT collects that the culprit was likely the Badr Organization. Gorani, for his part, believes that the two conspired. He condemned Barzani, renounced any affiliation to the KDP or the peshmerga, and took his militia—calling themselves 'the Sons of Gorani'— and headed east, vowing revenge against Iran and Qasem Shateri. Their last confirmed location was the PJAK camp on Mount Qandil, three months ago. So, with that bringing us up to speed, Admiral, I'll now hand it over to Peter Stavros, our chief of the IOD."

Wade leaned toward Freeman's ear. "I see your play here, Ryan."

The D/CIA froze. Wade seemed receptive.

Stavros came down the center aisle from the row behind them and took Lath's place at the head of the room. "Thank you, Marcia," he said as she filled an empty seat. "Admiral Wade, I know I speak for the whole task force when I say it's an honor to have our colleagues from JSOC here today..."

He summoned a map on the screen above. Its focus was on Iran's West Azerbaijan and Kurdistan provinces, collectively dubbed *"Rojhelat"* by PJAK and the ragtag fighters on Mount Qandil. Key towns, highways and geographic landmarks were featured, and the Iraqi border snaked a jagged, black path down the left edge of the screen. Five red dots were laid throughout the provinces, each marking the site of an Iranian officer's execution.

"Before you, Admiral, are the primary Kurdish areas of northwestern Iran, most of which have seen unrest over the last six weeks following the suicide of Farinaz Katani." Stavros spoke of a maid at the Tara Hotel in West Azerbaijan's capital, Mahabad, who flung herself from a fourth-floor window to escape being raped by an Intelligence Ministry official. Hundreds had taken to the streets and demanded justice, although none would be done, at least not by the state. "While we don't expect much to come of the demonstrations, we've observed an interesting rash of assassinations in the same area, all set just a few miles from the Iraqi border. Internal media coverage of the murders has been suppressed, and regional and international outlets have focused exclusively on the protests, so it's been quite difficult for us to piece together a complete accounting."

"Your man?" Wade interjected.

"We see his hand," Stavros admitted. "These five markers," he pointed overhead, "each represent an assassination. The first was discovered three days after Katani's suicide. Here, seven miles from the Penjwin border crossing, a logistics officer for the Badr Organization was found in the reeds along Lake Zarivar. A truck driver noticed the vultures. Three shots, small caliber, right to the sternum; nobody saw a thing. His car is still missing, as far as we know."

Wade allowed a slight, pleased nod.

"The second and third occurred in Piranshahr, a hundred miles north. Both were captains in the IRGC's Saberin Unit and had recently returned from Diyala Province and, again, were affiliated with the Badr Organization. The two were eating outside a restaurant in the city and were targeted by sniper fire. A round struck each of them in their chairs, simultaneously. The fourth took place along a stretch of Highway 46, west of Sanandaj. An SUV overtook a vehicle carrying the assistant defence attaché of the Iranian consulate in Erbil. Men in the SUV opened up on the attaché's car and killed him. Now, we find the fifth and latest assassination to be the most concerning. Two weeks ago, the aide-de-camp to Abu Mahdi al-Mohandis—whom you'll know as Qasem Shateri's personal envoy to Hashid Shaabi in Baghdad—was stopped at an intersection right in the center of Mahabad. At ten a.m., in broad daylight, two men on a motorcycle pulled alongside his staff car, attached a magnetic IED to the rear passenger door and sped off. The explosion also killed the aide's bodyguard and his driver; injured maybe three additional bystanders."

"This concerns you?" Wade's eyes narrowed.

"There's been a natural progression in violence. But this most recent attacks strikes us as incredibly bold. As the Iranians take obvious steps to increase the security of their personnel returning from Iraq, we worry that the individuals responsible will likewise overcompensate and expose themselves to unnecessary risk. We feel they need proper counsel. On the ground, Admiral."

"Whoa, whoa, whoa," Wade laughed and pressed out his hands, "Let us assume for discussion's sake that Gorani is behind the killings. That is your assumption, yes?"

"Correct, sir."

"Okay, so working off that belief alone, what inspires confidence in you that Gorani is remotely capable of achieving some sort of victory—strategic, tactical, or personal—against the IRGC and their proxies in Iraq?" Wade turned to Freeman, "Seeing as my own men are likely to do the counseling."

Freeman began to sweat. But he knew Stavros could hold his own.

"Right, Admiral, that's an excellent question." Stavros kicked the ground with the tip of his shoe. "Our confidence is inspired by nothing other than the proven anxieties of the IRGC and Hashid Shaabi, as illuminated in SIGINT collects, that an individual, whom they also deduce is Jamil Gorani, is highly adept at killing valuable personnel—personnel who aren't easily replaced. That's what attracts us to him."

Freeman relaxed a notch.

"We're attracted by the skillset," Stavros continued, "and the professional-grade tradecraft necessary to target these five individuals, maintain persistent surveillance on each over a defended international border, and to conduct kinetic strikes in denied territory. All of these indicators are quite promising to us, more so than any other insurgent force operating within Iran over the last twenty years. It presents an opportunity we'd be foolish to ignore, Admiral."

Wade agreed. "Yes. Yes, it does."

"To put it simply: If Gorani and his sons want to murder IRGC officers, we would like to help and suggest one of particular value. And that's Dr. Alireza Fakhrizadeh."

"But in order to help him, we need JSOC's help first," Freeman added.

"Okay." Wade showed little emotion.

"We think Gorani is tied into PJAK's intelligence net, which hasn't been penetrated by the Quds Force to the same extant as the PUK and *Asayish*," said Stavros, referring to Iraqi Kurdistan's fledgling security service. "Based on our limited knowledge of Gorani's time in the PJAK camp on Mount Qandil, we tasked a local asset to place an RFID tag on the clothing of a courier inside the camp. As expected, we observed the courier passing from Qandil, over the border, and traveling fifty-four kilometers north to the Ushnu-Sulduz Valley. The courier arrived here…" Stavros pressed the remote and a Global Hawk reconnaissance image flashed on the screen overhead.

Wade studied it. A long cluster of earth-colored mud houses made a steep climb up both sides of a rocky gorge divided by a shallow stream that washed over a bed of gray stones. The village was stepped, as in a series of terraces stretching the full height of the gorge, with the flat roof of each house providing the front yard of the house above it.

"...in Palanjar," Stavros said, "a Kurdish town of maybe thirty. To give a sense of orientation, the village sits at thirty-seven degrees, two minutes north; forty-four degrees, fifty-six minutes east. That's the Gadar River running down the middle. It's only five kilometers from the Iraqi border and seventy-six kilometers from Mahabad. And there is no reason for that PJAK courier to come here other than to meet Gorani."

"Why there?" Wade asked.

"It ticks all the boxes," said Stavros plainly. "We know from census data that there's been quite a population drain in recent years; most young people have left. Only a few old shepherding families remain. And the tribe takes guest right quite seriously. If Gorani and his sons did arrive, the elders would shelter them without much second thought. It's as far off the grid as one can get."

"So you think CIA's really found Gorani, Ryan?"

"Eric, I wouldn't have dragged you up here if I didn't."

"Admiral," Stavros said, "our task force judges with high confidence that Major General Jamil Gorani and his sons are using Palanjar as a base in Iranian Kurdistan to execute IRGC officers connected to Shiite militias in Iraq. My request to Director Freeman is that IOD is given command over a team of four operators from a JSOC Special Mission Unit to clandestinely enter this village and make contact with Gorani so that we may determine the tactical situation of his men. Sir, we have to reach Gorani before the Iranians do."

Wade made his decision at that moment. "If you go in and find him and you determine his men are ready to fight, then what?"

Stavros hit the remote again. "We're calling it Operation PACER."

Another twenty minutes passed and the task force funneled through a cypher-locked door and into the hallway. Freeman and Wade left together—the two had come to an understanding.

"I'm leaving for Israel tonight," Freeman said. "The president thinks Isaac can help smooth things over with Arad. I'll ask him for Fakhrizadeh's autopsy report. The NSC's meeting when I get back to figure this all out. Weisel has some other plan in motion at State; they're the carrot, we're the stick."

"Ryan, you need to understand, this is pure risk."

"That's why I called, Eric. I just need four of your best. We'll give them back in one piece. Promise."

Wade looked away. "I already have one in mind."

CHAPTER 29

A BREATH OF burnt gunpowder rose to his nose and a string of muzzle flashes battered his eyes. Harris fought to match their pace as they pressed up the narrow corridor, putting down each target enticingly dangled before them. Watching from the network of catwalks overhead that spidered out through the cavernous facility, the four Green Team candidates moved like clockwork—each keeping their rifle trained on the targets sliding through their arcs, snapping off a double-tap to the chest and a third "security round" to the head lest the sheets of paper spring back to life. Zapata orchestrated it all on a tablet giving him total control over that section of the kill house, from the lighting and the street sounds booming off the speakers, to the life-size targets that zipped deftly along recessed tracks. Naval Special Warfare's close-quarters combat (CQC) range at Fort Story was the most advanced on the east coast. It spread out across twenty-five thousand square feet and fifty-two reconfigurable rooms. To absorb live ammunition, the walls were made of half-inch steel plates and ballistic rubber with a top layer of Styrofoam painted to match any real-world setting the instructors could conjure. Z had the corridor resemble a back alley in some nameless Middle Eastern city. Harris kept his distance behind Z and the five other instructors who scrutinized the candidates' every step. They had a job to do, and he didn't want to interfere.

Green Team candidates came from one of the ten "regular" SEAL teams based in Virginia Beach and Coronado. After several combat tours, some operatives elected to try for DEVGRU's qualification course and reach the pinnacle of their profession in a JSOC Special Mission Unit. Few made the cut. In Green Team, it was no longer acceptable to just be a SEAL, one had to perform perfectly– without fail—at each and every juncture. The first three of the nine-month-course were dedicated to CQC, and while each candidate had ample shooting experience from past trainings and deployments, their old habits needed rewiring. In the kill house, candidates expelled untold numbers of live rounds at hundreds of targets, and each pull of the trigger had to hit its mark. All of the candidates could clear a room full of bad guys—even dumb infantry could do that—but massacring nameless terrorists wasn't DEVGRU's mission; they were the scalpel, not the sledge. To practice that mantra, instructors would later divide the candidates into two groups and make one play the hostages, while the second had to breach the room and knock down paper captors, firing mere inches over their friends' fragile skulls. On that day alone, a third would quit. Guaranteed. The goal for instructors like Z in those early stages was to create levels of stress that could break even the hardest man, to see who plainly did not want to be there. Simply passing was failing and second place was the first casualty.

Z and the instructors ahead stopped and focused their inquisitive gaze below. Harris came closer. The candidates cleared the corridor and formed up at a door leading to an adjacent room.

Harris could see over the partition wall. There were no targets hung in the next room, only a table tipped on its side and several plastic deck chairs. The first SEAL on the door—a petty officer from Coronado—pushed it open with the back of his gloved hand and paused at the threshold, searching for a target. Seeing the room was empty, he stepped in and floated to the left wall, stopping midway. At the same time, the second SEAL in the stack instinctively slid toward the right wall to cover his teammate.

"Moving," the second said, and stopped roughly parallel to the first.

Harris heard a grumble between the instructors. Z pecked at the tablet.

A spring released in the floor, releasing a target from behind the table.

"Contact!" the first SEAL cried, swung his rifle right and loosed a volley.

"Clear right," reported the second SEAL.

"Clear left," echoed the first.

"Safe 'em, let 'em hang," said Z.

Fans hidden in the rafters activated and cleansed the air. The smoke faded, revealing a paper jihadist dressed in quintessential black robes clutching a little girl with bright red curls. The terrorist was clearly dead—eight bullet holes ran from his neck down to where the girl's left eye should have been.

Harris removed his earplugs and cringed.

The candidates safed their rifles and let them drop on their slings, some wiping large beads of sweat from their eyes. The first SEAL recognized his error and turned a ghostly white.

"Couple problems," Z began plainly. "Did we miss your move call?" he asked to the petty officer from Coronado.

The first SEAL shook his head and looked to the floor. He knew Z hadn't missed it, that was merely the instructors' way of being kind and not completely embarrassing him in front of his teammates. He failed.

"Not telling the operator behind you that you're about to clear your arc is a safety violation to boot," Z added. "But you also didn't clear the full length of your wall. If you had, you would've seen Abu Yahoo pressing a piece to Shirley Temple's temple. It wouldn't have gotten the drop on you and you wouldn't have panicked and laid on the trigger. Copy?"

"Check," the petty officer muttered.

"Clear your whole arc. Always." Z let them see his disappointment. There was no bargaining, either. If the instructor said a candidate was wrong, they were wrong. Z wasn't out to get them, in fact he saw himself as quite merciful. Mistakes were bound to happen, but that was inexcusable. The petty officer from Coronado would be dismissed by dinner and on a flight home by morning.

"We have to do better than that," Z concluded. "Ladder climbs. Go.

Later, Harris tussled with his car keys in the parking lot.

"Could you see yourself doing that?" Z leaned against his silver Mustang.

"Sort of," Harris answered with a demure grin.

"Fuck you. Yes, you could." Z glanced at his phone and popped the car door open. "Farah and Whitford are already there."

"I've never met them."

"You will now," he bowed into the driver's seat. "Solid guys."

"Wait, where are we going?"

"Lynnhaven Pub."

"Right behind you."

Harris followed Z through Gate 6 and turned onto Route 60, accelerating past frozen cypress groves and scrub pines. The thought of joining Green Team's training cadre wasn't so unpleasant. *I could do that,* he thought...*maybe.* Still, he would wait a while longer before making a decision. He already knew what Sandra's opinion would be and Z's persistent nagging didn't exactly make him an unbiased fountain of advice. *Give it a week,* Harris reasoned. Why not? He would be home, every night, with the people he loved; he could watch his children grow up. It was a respectable way out, his more cautious side urged, a path to avoid the unavoidable mistakes that would put him in a casket. It was an escape—a chance to live. *Give it a week,* he resolved, *and do it.*

The drive took less than five minutes. He turned left at an intersection and followed Z into the fissured lot of a strip mall where the Lynnhaven Pub sat sandwiched between a plumber's shop and a hair salon. They walked to the entrance just as a cold drizzle began falling. It was a welcoming dive. The entire establishment was no wider than twelve feet, and a well-worn bar stretched from the door, back approximately half the pub's length where it opened up around a billiards table. A large Virginia Tech logo was plastered over the front window and an autographed photo of

Ron Jeremy hung proudly over the register. Harris noticed the bar was empty save for two men perched on tattered stools. One was tall and built like a tank with tattoo-covered biceps as round as a typical man's calf and a four-inch beard so flawlessly maintained that he could've equally passed for an Afghan tribesman or a Brooklyn hipster. The other was shorter and lean—like Harris—with pale green eyes, olive skin and unkempt black hair. Both had a notable repute in the command and Z was keen to make the necessary introductions.

"Chief Harris," Z strolled ahead and drummed on the bearded man's back, "may I present Petty Officer First Class Bryce Whitford."

"How's it going?" Whitford turned to meet Harris' hand.

"Hi. Robert."

"And," Z squeezed the lean man's shoulders, "Petty Officer First Class Jamie Farah. I'd do battle with these two any day."

"Nice to meet you," he greeted Farah and took the stool next to Z.

The bartender drew her eyes up from the well. "What are you drinking?"

"Jameson. On the rocks," Harris told her.

Z flopped his wallet down. "Something hoppy. I'll let you pick."

"Hungry?" Farah asked. "Brisket here's like thermite for your mouth."

"I'm good, thanks," Harris said.

"Yeah, this guy's a vegetarian," Z revealed.

Z didn't even have one drink in him, Harris thought, and that asshole was already tearing his life apart. Harris never wanted to talk about himself. He hated it. And he loathed diving into the awkward truths that revealed just how much he was unlike the rest of his teammates: truths like being a vegetarian, or his boyish looks—or a truth like his son.

"No shit," Whitford barked.

"Yup," he raked his hair to the side. The bartender came with his whiskey. Harris slid the glass toward him and stabbed the ice with a cocktail straw.

She placed a snifter glass in front of Z. It was filled to the brim with some mysterious dark brew that resembled congealing blood. "Down more than three of these and you'll be on the deck."

"Got it," Z gave a quick salute.

"So you eat no meat?" Farah wondered. "None?"

Harris struggled on the first sip. "Not since I was eight. Not willingly."

"You saw some furry thing get disemboweled?" Whitford laughed.

"No," he said. "I don't like the taste. Never did. I've had it a few times on deployments, when I could eat it or starve, but I never liked it. Why kill something when I don't have to?"

Farah cocked his head and raised a bottle to his lips. "Got us there."

Z leaned his chest over the bar. "I'm trying to get Robby Boy here in on the cadre."

"Not a bad gig," Whitford said. "Got a family?"

"A five-year-old. Another on the way."

"No, sir. You don't wanna be out there claiming scalps."

Harris knew from reputation that both were in a position to know: they had been claiming scalps longer than most. Farah and Whitford were attached to Black Squadron. Initially formed as DEVGRU's sniper unit, Black Squadron was rebuilt after September 11th by the team's CO, Eric Wade, to conduct "advance force operations" (AFO) in denied enemy territory and supply actionable intelligence ahead of a larger military engagement. Both had spent the greater part of their careers in Afghanistan, running agents with Langley across the border in Pakistani tribal areas and operating mobile listening stations out of the region's ubiquitous, colorful "jingle" trucks for NSA. The two were chameleons—in appearance and personality—and could melt into their terrain, going months with minimal support from the larger JSOC apparatus. Farah, for his part, was part of a rare breed valued by the military. He was half Lebanese from his father's side—Irish on his mother's—and spoke Arabic natively. The region's myriad of languages and cultures came easily to him; the Navy had picked up his tuition to master Persian, Pashto, Urdu and Kurdish. Whitford even once caused a small diplomatic incident when he was forced to decline an offer to marry the daughter of a notorious Pashtun warlord. They perfectly filled their roles, and they were exactly what Harris did not want to be: absent, and alone.

"That's what I keep telling him," Z swigged his beer. "We need instructors who've been around long enough to know what the fuck they're talking about but aren't about to cash in."

"That's the truth," Farah agreed.

"Guys today age out of active duty and they want to go private, making six figures to stop a bullet for some billionaire. They want a book deal."

"I could use six figures." Harris grinned and crushed an ice cube between his molars.

"You could kiss my ass, is what you could do," Z quipped.

Harris downed his whiskey and signaled for another. "Give me a week."

Z shot a doubtful look down the bar. "You hear that bullshit?"

Freeman was sunk into a plump armchair in a corner of the VIP lounge at Andrews. A squall moving over Washington pushed back his departure by forty minutes. He passed the time staring at his phone and ran through no fewer than a dozen levels in Angry Birds. To look up at CNN only invited dread. The Pentagon confirmed that the IDF would begin another round of strike sorties against PIJ and Hamas depots throughout Gaza in the night. His security detail was uncomfortable with the arrangement. The flight into

Tel Aviv was scheduled to last eleven hours with a refueling stop at Shannon Airport in Ireland. Given the time difference, that put Freeman's plane arriving at Ben Gurion just as the operation got underway. Naturally, CIA's Office of Security didn't want their boss dropping into an active combat zone. A conference call had just ended between Doc—the head of Freeman's detail—their pilot for the trip, and the regional security officer at the embassy in Tel Aviv, who could only report that the Israelis swore to the integrity of their airspace. The IDF's message was clear enough: deal with the situation as is or scrap the visit. Freeman couldn't afford that, leaving his bodyguards no other option than to hope for the best.

He could see the apron from his chair. A C-37A—the military conversion of a Gulfstream V—in blue and white livery sat on the concrete pad, and airmen from the 99th Airlift Squadron worked through the rain, running down the necessary pre-flight checklists to ensure the bird didn't drop into the Atlantic. The delay gave Freeman's mind time to wander. He only met Binyamin Isaac, the legendary director-general of the Mossad, on one occasion. A year ago, Freeman was dispatched to represent the agency at a meeting of Western intelligence chiefs in Brussels to discuss ISIS and the coming endgame of the Syrian civil war. He had just been brought out of the Directorate of Operations and made acting deputy director while the D/CIA at the time—now his predecessor—was embroiled in a sex scandal and subject to a federal subpoena. The summit was Freeman's big audition, his moment not to make an ass of himself. During a reception at NATO Headquarters, Isaac was the first to approach him. Freeman's initial thought upon seeing the slanted, gray old man was of the Jedi master, Yoda, from *Star Wars*. He masked his intentions behind tiny round spectacles and walked with a cane and the support of leg braces—a thwarted Iraqi assassin left his right side partially paralyzed. Isaac snatched Freeman's hand, pulled him down to his lips, and whispered, "High time that fucker's cock got the best of him, eh?" giggled, and shuffled off. Freeman was stunned.

In hindsight, Freeman couldn't have asked for a truer introduction. Once his predecessor resigned as part of a plea bargain to avoid trial, and Freeman was named to take over the agency, Isaac shipped two-dozen white roses and a sympathy card to Freeman's wife. The man, the legend, was a paragon of spymasters the world-over. He was unstoppable, and some even suspected immortal. Isaac was the original of his species, and Freeman knew that they could all but hope to be flawed imitations.

Forty minutes passed and, as promised, the C-37's engines started turning. Freeman was led into the rain and climbed the airstairs. He chose a seat with a decent view along the portside fuselage and placed his cracked leather satchel at his feet. Once clearance came from the tower, the jet began a slow taxi to the slick runway and was soon airborne. Freeman watched the ground yield to dreary whiffs of cloud over the Chesapeake Bay, and he worried what the view would reveal when he glided back to Earth.

Wars often begin with the purest intentions.

Nothing was more hatefully apparent to him. The television placed on an end table near the executive assistant's desk was split into four muted screens, each relaying a different news network's reporting on the latest round of airstrikes that would hit Gaza come nightfall. Their endless loops of stock footage showed Israeli fighters taxiing to a runway and panicked Palestinians rushing bloodied bodies into hospitals; their glaring Chyron graphics trumpeted, "Hamas Leaders In Hiding," and "Arad Vows Revenge." All of it was taunting, a reminder of his failure, of his grand naïveté that cost lives. He fixed his eyes on the sheets of rain drifting beyond the window. Someone had to pay the price, and it ought to be him.

Harold Lansing decided as much on the long walk from the little townhouse he kept on Olive Street in Georgetown. His socks and pant cuffs were soggy from the rain lashing beneath his umbrella, although he hardly cared. Lansing undid the latch on his briefcase and found a sealed envelope next to an Amtrak ticket home. He placed the envelope in his lap and pressed his fingers to the linen paper. Goading the Israelis and the Syrians into talks, purging Iranian influence from Lebanon, bringing a sense of stability and closure after years of conflict in the Middle East—it all seemed right. But he overreached. And his optimism would leave scores dead. The guilt devoured him. In Kabul, a roadside bomb meant for him had once killed a dozen soldiers, but he swore this was worse. He felt the envelope. It wasn't supposed to end like this.

"Harold?" a voice called.

He sprung from his daze. Angela Weisel loomed in the doorway ahead. "Come on."

Lansing forced his lunch back down his throat and stood, fastening his jacket button. He took the briefcase in one hand, the envelope in the other, and stepped into her office. Weisel shut the door behind them. His shoes were welded to the carpet.

"You can sit," she said with a hint of confusion at his demeanor and went for the blue floral-upholstered sofa.

Lansing chose the high-back chair.

"Coffee?"

"No. Um, Madam Secretary, I—"

Weisel's BlackBerry began chirping out of site. "Christ. Hold on." She rolled her eyes and dug through her purse, silencing it after a few rings. "If my husband keeps calling every ten minutes, I'll file a damn restraining order." She took a breath and pressed her hands to her knees. "What's new?"

It struck Lansing that Weisel had no idea why he came to see her. How could she not? He expected her to drag him into her office the minute he returned from Paris. Lansing had been sent to convey a message from the president to a crucial American ally and instead waltzed into a catastrophe of his own making. But shockingly, none of that seemed to matter to her. It was business as usual. Yet Lansing had to pay the price. He offered the envelope. "Madam Secretary, I am ashamed of my failure with Prime Minister Arad. Truly, if I even remotely suspected that Islamic Jihad would've reacted so harshly and butchered that poor boy, I would have never thought to reach out to the Palestinians…"

Weisel sliced open the envelope and removed a typewritten letter.

"I miscalculated. For that, I must apologize, and tender my resignation."

The secretary of state read the first few lines, tightened her lips, and tore the letter to shreds. She handed it back like it was drenched with venom. "Burn that shit before someone sees it."

Lansing was speechless.

"We have work to do," she said determinedly.

"Ma'am, I don't understand," his voice raced. "I'm in no position to try and repair the damage done with Israel. Someone else needs—"

"I don't give two fucks about Avi Arad's feelings," Weisel declared. "Eli gets paid to worry about that nonsense, not me. Yes, his soldier was executed, and it's a tragedy, but what Arad said to you is right: this is a war. And many more of his soldiers will die before it's done. It's time we recognize that."

Lansing still couldn't bring himself to look her in the eye.

"What happened to Moshe Adler is not your fault, these airstrikes are not your fault, and what happened in Paris was completely outside your control. Qasem Shateri and his minions played a flawless hand. They've lost Hezbollah and they need the Palestinians to take up arms for their cause. Avi is far too predictable. Hell, it wouldn't surprise me if those missiles we seized heading to Sudan were bait." Weisel glanced at the rain before continuing. "We need to accept that there are people in Tehran who intend to win, who are working against the wishes of the supreme leader, and who have actively undermined our efforts, in good faith, to resolve their nuclear program. Beyond that, I can't say more. But trust me, I've never seen anything like it."

"Okay," he said with trepidation.

"Tonight the IDF will try and eliminate as much of its target deck as it can. These are real estate targets: launching positions, depots, stationary assets that they've had in the crosshairs for months. Islamic Jihad will suffer the most, by design. Hamas won't entirely be spared; the IDF can't miss an opening to degrade those capabilities while it has the chance. Their objective is to pressure Hamas into handing over Azzam al-Nakhalah—Shateri's man in Gaza—and anyone else in PIJ with a role in Adler's execution. Avi wants their heads on spikes."

"Hamas won't budge that easily."

"No, they won't. And they can't unless they want to be the laughingstock of the Middle East. That's the problem. Arad's generals don't want another war with Hamas; I can't say the same for him. So, to keep this fight under control, I'm told that the deputy head of Qatari State Security is with Fawzi Abu Musameh right now, in Gaza, to make sure Hamas doesn't do anything to force a larger Israeli response—also to keep Musameh from 'accidentally' getting hit. Shateri is betting on it. But unless Hamas caves soon and arrests al-Nakhalah, the IDF will exhaust their deck and have to target in real-time. And we both know the struggle of separating civilians from armed terrorists," she ended with a grim tone.

Lansing shook his head in disbelief. "I really thought we had this one."

"We lost this round, but we'll get our hits in," Weisel dismissed. "The Israelis and the Syrians are still coming to Annapolis, Hezbollah is still disarming, and ISIS is not returning any time soon. If anything, you've been vindicated."

He really didn't see how she could come to that conclusion.

"You've argued for years, Harold," she continued, "that we cannot resolve Israel's place in the Middle East while Iran is part of the equation. What happened with Moshe Adler only proves that. The very same faction that's working behind our backs on the nuclear issue will never allow peace. Their survival in the regime depends on it. Gaza will burn itself out—these situations always do—and we'll find ourselves back where we started."

Lansing believed her, but his faith in finding a solution was exhausted.

"Harold, I need you. I need you with me for what's to come."

"What's next?" he asked, reluctant to hear her answer.

Weisel pressed back into the sofa. "The president's asked me to contact Ayatollah Khansari and offer to restart negotiations right where we left off when Damascus fell. Langley's stumbled upon some very troubling information and we think if we act now, with a proposal the mullahs wouldn't dare reject, we might be able to head off Shateri and his friends who've created this mess."

"Good luck reaching Khansari."

"Exactly," she smiled. "We can't get to him. The Revolutionary Guards control every shred of information that comes near the man. We need a detour, a way around the Pasdaran, someone who can guarantee the ayatollah's consent. CIA has an individual who fits the bill."

"Who?"

"It's best if you don't know." She leaned in, as if the walls were listening. "This is where I need you. Find a third party, maybe in Europe, someone off the grid who can travel to Tehran without attracting suspicion and deliver our terms. That's it. Langley will take over from there."

Lansing turned away and nodded. "I have no idea who could do that, but I know who does. Morteza Ghanbari. He's at Princeton; also runs the American Iranian Council. We go back twenty years. The man's contacts are unbeatable; if anyone can pull it off, he knows them."

"Good," Weisel leaned back. "Don't reach out to him just yet. The NSC is going to talk this over. I'll ask the president to have you read-in. I want you there. If the boss says the word, you'll be on your way."

Lansing stepped through the turnstiles and exited onto C Street, the soaked limestone of the Harry Truman Building rising at his back. He still didn't fully comprehend what the hell happened inside, nor did he expect to for some time. But it didn't matter. He put up his umbrella against the rain and walked.

Navid Nourizadeh had a particular item in mind. He made a detour on his way home from Bank Melli's head office on Ferdowsi Avenue and came to the Tajrish Bazaar in North Tehran. If what he needed could be found anywhere in the city, it would be here. A recent renovation washed away most of the old shabbiness, but a stubborn hint of grunge remained. Slender passages lined with shops niched into the sandy brick walls connected cavernous vaults crowded with stalls of nuts, spices and fruits. Packs of women engulfed in *chadors* floated by, as if levitating over the paving stones. Bright neon signs of twisted Persian letters announced goods and prices in the off chance the shrieking hawkers standing beneath them failed to make their offerings perfectly clear. The market continued the tradition of Tehran's place at the epicenter of the Silk Road; everything was for sale. Cell phones and miniature satellite dishes practically burst from the stalls; coiled shisha pipes hung from hooks in the ceiling; ornate pots, rugs and jewelry packed the shelves. A few shops even had spaces tucked behind the clutter, often no larger than a closet, stuffed with goods the regime had banned. While the hawkers weren't eager to force them on the passing crowds, with the right connections and an even better price, they could still be bought.

But Mr. Nourizadeh had no mind for any of that. He was looking to buy his wife a gift before he left on a business trip for the remainder of the week. Nourizadeh was an auditor for Bank Melli Iran, the country's largest, and made frequent visits across the gulf to the branches in Dubai, Abu Dhabi, Sharjah and Muscat. Travel was easy enough. As the bank was government-owned, Nourizadeh was issued an official passport, which placed him above scrutiny by customs officers, and the Intelligence Ministry determined he wasn't a risk, letting him move abroad unsupervised. Yet his prolonged absence did take its toll, not only on his wife and their three children, but also on himself. He hadn't always remained faithful on his trips. It was a fair trade, he reasoned, to keep his family living the life to which they had grown accustomed. His salary was sufficient, but with so many to support, it could have been better—a problem he sought to remedy in his own way. Everything had its price. He thought this gift might just serve as a necessary reminder.

Nourizadeh spotted a sign etched into the bricks and froze, the crowd channeling around him like water. The shop before him displayed vivid bolts of cloth in every conceivable color. Scarves, shawls and veils decorated with gold and silver threads draped from rings. It was precisely what he'd come to find. He stepped into the narrow alcove and eyed the selection.

A merchant eased around a small counter and announced with a sunny disposition, *"Khosh amadid!* Could I help you find something?"

Nourizadeh dipped his head to avoid the merchant's gaze. "My friend from Isfahan suggested I come by; said you had the finest shawls in the bazaar."

"Oh," the merchant's voice fluttered with apprehension. "Are you after anything in particular?"

"Well," said Nourizadeh as he waved a hand over the fabrics, "something wool. Something pashmina."

"Perhaps indigo?" the merchant asked, holding for the correct response.

"With silver stitching."

"We don't keep that out front," said the merchant, "but if you'll come in the back, I can show you something you may find suitable."

Mr. Nourizadeh followed the merchant around the counter and through a locked door. He was shown into a storage room lit with a red fluorescent bulb. Styrofoam packaging and cardboard boxes were stacked against the walls, upon one of which sat Jack Galloway. The merchant, wanting nothing to do with what would follow, said nothing and locked the door as he left.

"Thank you for doing this again, Navid," Jack said.

Nourizadeh shrugged. "I need the money and I trust you."

"How are the kids?"

"Spoiled."

"The wife?"

"A bitch."

Jack crossed his arms. "Well, we can help you there."

"How much?" Nourizadeh twitched.

"Ten. Half now," he drew a fat envelope from inside his coat, "half when we confirm receipt."

Nourizadeh nodded and took the cash.

"And your flight arrangements?" Jack asked.

"Emirates 976. Departs at six tomorrow morning from Imam Khomeini and lands in Dubai by seven-thirty."

"Okay," Jack nodded, "get on the Metro at Terminal 3, then walk half-way down the platform until you see a man sitting on a bench wearing a black blazer and khaki pants. He'll have a Burberry shopping bag on the spot to his left. He knows what you look like. When he sees you, he'll place the bag at his foot. Sit next to him, drop this in the bag." Jack offered a pack of Davidoff cigarettes. Hidden beneath the pack's tinfoil wrapper was a miniature SD memory card containing an encrypted transcript of CITA-DEL's latest report. "Don't lose that," Jack added as Nourizadeh took it. "Get on the next train and you're done."

"Will I have to do this every time?"

"You don't *have* to do anything," Jack corrected. "But we take care of our friends. And if you ever feel unsafe, if you feel some undue attention, just let me know—or better yet: don't. I'll get the hint."

Nourizadeh slipped the cigarettes in his coat.

Jack knocked twice on the door and then placed his hand on Nouriza-deh's shoulder. "I'm happy we can be friends." The lock tumbled into place. "You go first."

Nourizadeh went to leave as the merchant cracked the door.

"Oh," Jack remembered and pulled a few rials from his pocket. "Buy her one. On me. Bitches like shawls, too."

After paying the merchant for his services, Jack ran a long countersurveil-lance route, using the night as cover, and arrived at his home on Hashemi Street in Jamaran. He sat for several hours, disquieted by the silence and unnerved by the windows. An anxious hum in his skull drew him toward the blackness outside, but he tried to fight, to resist the urge to turn his eyes on the inky glass. He shot up, panting, and stormed through the house, pulling the drapes one by one. But it didn't help. The hum lingered—and he couldn't bear the thought of having to face it alone. A clock in the kitchen showed it was nearly three in the morning. His eyelids drew heavy and his mind dull.

Jack switched off the lights and climbed in bed. A pall fell over his room that carried the same taint of misery lurking beyond the windows. Next came a chill, the familiar cold that dragged him away for as long as he could remember. He fought to stay awake, to prop himself up into consciousness. But it was a vain attempt. Jack sensed a force pull him deeper into the bed, a power as formidable and effortless as gravity. It was so easy, so simple, he knew, to just let go. Soon his mouth was cemented shut—he couldn't speak, nor did he care to. The farther he fell, the colder he became, like ice water surged through his veins. Although paralyzed, his limbs bolted to the bed, Jack was alert; his eyes recognized every object in the room just as they existed in reality, but with all his might he could not lift a finger.

Gravity strangled him in its loving embrace.

He felt the hair on his arms and legs bristle, and Jack knew it was close. A vibration swelled from the depths of his mind, building from a sweet treble to an awful, consuming quake that seemed to pummel the earth.

And then, expectedly, Jack heard their screams.

There were tens of thousands, layered and in unison, but each striking a solitary chord in his ears. They wailed, moaned and howled in unimaginable agony. He heard flames rising from one great furnace to meet them, towers falling and bones crumbling to ash. Their cries grew more anguished until, at once, it stopped, as if a cold wind had descended and swept them away.

Jack became jealous, even angry. Something gave them peace.

The vibrations shook him and white noise flooded his ears. From an infinitely small point on the wall, a morose shadow emerged like a flat object in three dimensions, gaining form into the featureless silhouette of a man. It was blacker than the darkest night and towered over his bed. Its lanky arms fell down to its knees and its fingers were splayed out—its left hand wracked in violent spasms. It stared without eyes.

Jack knew it and it knew him. Long ago it told him a name—the Black Emperor—and it vowed to come for him at the moment he was ready to die. And Jack believed it. He believed all its soaring promises. It gave those wailing thousands peace, saved them from a wretched life for which they did not ask. All it asked in return was to follow it, to let it carry him into the void.

It moved with a disjointed gait beyond the foot of Jack's bed, observing him with intense curiosity. Its left hand twitched and convulsed. Every hint of light in the room bent around it as it crept closer and seemed to vanish within. The vibrations grew overwhelming and radiated from it.

Jack wondered if this was the moment. Was this his time to die? He still had a choice—he held on to that much—but it called out for him. It wanted him to choose. It wanted Jack to accept its gift.

It calmly approached to within a hair's breadth and loomed beside Jack's face. The blackness lapped at his flesh, but suddenly— It pulled away as the vibrations subsided.

Not yet.

CHAPTER 30

ELEVEN HOURS AFTER departing Washington, Freeman's C-37A crossed the Israeli coastline and began a steep descent to Ben Gurion Airport. While the IDF's air-control center on Baal-Hazor Hill assured them of a clear approach vector, his security detail remained on edge. They were each pressed against a cabin porthole, watching the horizon for the smoking tail of an incoming surface-to-air missile arcing up to shoot them out of the sky. Freeman pitched in and took one of the windows. Tel Aviv spread out from the wingtip like circuitry: thousands of shimmering yellow, orange, green and white lights crawling on for miles, their advance halted only by the sea. He saw the portside flaps extend and felt the landing gear drop into place beneath him. The Gulfstream bled altitude, swooping over fields until it passed the airport's perimeter fence and hung meters, then feet, over the runway. It struggled for traction, jolting Freeman forward, and gradually came to a crawl before taxiing to the military terminal on the eastern edge of the airfield.

Freeman counted five armored Chevy Suburbans with an escort of police cruisers waiting for him at an isolated apron. The C-37 stopped and chocks were wedged against the wheels. In minutes, the airstairs were deployed and Freeman shadowed Doc to the tarmac. Ten plain-clothed officers from Shin Bet—Israel's internal security service—draped in body armor with FN P90 submachine guns and Tavor assault rifles resting on their chests, stood to greet him. CIA's Tel Aviv station chief came forward from the group with an outstretched hand.

"Director Freeman," the station chief said as the C-37's engines powered down, "it's a pleasure to welcome you to Israel. Shame it couldn't be under better circumstances."

"That's okay, I go where the work takes me," the D/CIA grinned.

"Sir," announced a Shin Bet officer with a booming voice and a thick accent, "we need to move you into a vehicle. It is not safe here."

Freeman heeded the advice. "Let's go then."

They loaded into the convoy and left the airport through a service exit, making for Highway 1 westbound toward Tel Aviv. A clock in the Suburban's dashboard told him it was ten minutes past three in the morning. The roads were deserted.

"We're heading up the coast to Netanya," the station chief informed. "Mossad's arranged use of a safe house there. It's more private than a hotel. You're meeting Isaac in his office at nine, so you can get some sleep."

"Okay," Freeman conceded, sensing jet lag take hold.

The Suburban's radio barked something in Hebrew. A Shin Bet officer behind the wheel unclipped the handset from the dashboard, fired back a terse reply and craned his neck toward the windshield, ominously searching the night sky. "We're holding up here."

"Why?" Doc asked.

"Hamas rocket fire," the officer informed with cool composure. "The launch trajectory has it striking a kibbutz only a few kilometers from here. We'll hold until its intercepted. No need to worry."

The convoy approached the Gannot Interchange, a tangled web of ramps and spurs surrounded by open fields. It pulled alongside the shoulder beneath an overpass. Shin Bet officers poured from the escort vehicles, guns ready, and established a tight perimeter around Freeman's Suburban. Air-raid sirens pulsed from the nearest town.

"Sir, you should lay flat between the seats," Doc urged, but Freeman ignored it. He wanted to see the show for himself.

Freeman saw through the concrete pylons supporting the interchange's upper deck and behind a pair of electrical transmission towers into the clear skies over Palmachim Air Force Base, sitting less than ten miles southwest. He scoured the horizon and spotted a single Qassam rocket. It streaked northward in the air as a radiant white orb piercing the darkness.

A yellow flash erupted beyond the fields and drew Freeman's attention back to the ground. He heard a deep rushing noise boom over the sirens. A second orb, a Tamir interceptor—red and strikingly more vivid—launched skyward with a trail of fiery orange smoke. It climbed hundreds of feet and set a suicide course for the incoming rocket.

Freeman watched the Tamir automatically adjust its path, gaining speed and altitude with every moment. It surged ahead and burst against the Qassam, detonating the rocket's payload with a thunderous clap that echoed for miles over the fields.

"That Iron Dome's worth every penny," he observed as the Shin Bet officers lowered their weapons and retreated to the Suburbans.

"Mosquitos," his driver dismissed.

It took half an hour to reach Netanya, a resort town thirty kilometers north of Tel Aviv in Israel's Sharon plain. When the convoy stopped, Freeman hopped down from the Suburban and discovered a stack of concrete, glass and steel looming over the dunes. The condominium was aptly named SeaView and sat alone on the town's rim. Freeman heard the Mediterranean rolling in several hundred yards away and spotted a handful of half-finished façades farther down the beach, still cloaked in the night. The Shin Bet officers led him inside.

Freeman was brought to a penthouse occupying the seventeenth floor. As the elevator doors slid open, he found a sleek, sparsely furnished white box sprawling over five hundred square-meters with floor-to-ceiling windows on all sides. He was shown through the living room and the library to the master suite on the building's north front, itself the size of a decent apartment. Freeman looked down to the bed and tried to remember a time when he was happier to see one. Yet a part of him wasn't quite ready to surrender. He helped himself through the sliding glass door and stepped out onto the balcony.

Pressed against the railing, he could taste the salt, feel the damp breeze and hear the surf pummel the beach. But nothing was out there—only blackness. It crushed him. He wanted to see, to set his eyes on what he knew in his heart was so plainly obvious, to disprove that glaring void. But nothing was there.

He could do little more but stare into the gathering night.

"He's here."

Freeman was thrust back into consciousness. His head leapt from the pillow and spun toward the sound, his legs writhing between the sheets. Blinking erratically, he spotted one of his bodyguards filling the doorframe. "What?" he gasped.

"He's here," the bodyguard repeated.

"Jesus," Freeman clasped his forehead. "Who? Who is here?"

"Isaac."

"Fuck!" He dove for his phone on the nightstand. "What time is it?"

"Six-thirty. Your meeting isn't for three hours."

Freeman propped himself up on his elbow, questioning if he was truly awake.

"He's out there," his bodyguard shrugged.

"Wait," the D/CIA rubbed the grit from his eyes, "why?"

The bodyguard held his shrug. "A car pulled up and the guys downstairs told us he was in the elevator. Should I ask him to leave, sir?"

"No, it's alright," he sighed. "Give me a minute."

The bodyguard shut the door and Freeman gathered his wits. He sniffed an armpit for good measure and slid on a pair of flannel pajama pants from the suitcase he hadn't bothered to unpack. A faded gray T-shirt, damp with sweat, clung to his shoulders. It wasn't how he envisioned a private audience with the vaunted Israeli spymaster even in his wildest imagination. Accepting the bizarre hand that fate had dealt, he slipped into the hallway.

The Mediterranean sprawled beyond the soaring windows, matching the sky with an identical shade of sapphire, erasing the horizon and bathing the entire penthouse in its afterglow. Freeman's bare feet pattered through the empty library, past white lacquer walls, flowing white draperies and sharp-angled white furniture. He came into the living room and heard a disembodied voice call from the kitchen. It was slow and deliberate and sung like a steaming teakettle—the very same voice that whispered to him years before.

"You ought to have a word with your man, Ryan," the voice simmered. "I told him to let you rest, but he'd hear none of it."

Freeman rounded a corner into the kitchen. Binyamin Isaac—director-general of the Institute for Intelligence and Special Operations, better known as Mossad—leaned over the countertop with his right hand gripped on the marble for support. A hooked cane rested within reach. Isaac rose scarcely over five feet and carried a gentle face slack with wrinkles. He was slim, but hardly gaunt. Just as Freeman remembered, wire-rimmed spectacles sheltered his beady blue eyes and much of his scalp was bald, leaving a feathery gray semicircle of hair that resembled a monastic crown. Isaac retained little control over the right side of his body from the waist down. His trousers revealed the outline of carbon fiber leg braces. If it was painful to stand, he seemed to will the sensation numb.

The old man knew his way around the kitchen. Isaac hobbled to the island and dug through a grocery bag, removing and methodically staging a carton of eggs, butter, tomatoes and cucumbers, a sleeve of coffee beans and a crusty loaf of Russian black bread. Water rolled in a pot on the range beside an antique stovetop coffee percolator.

Freeman grappled with the appalling strangeness of it all. "Mr. Isaac—"

"Benny."

Freeman still wasn't accustomed to the club of first names. "Okay. Benny, this is all *very* nice of you, but could I maybe shower?"

"You're forty-nine." Isaac brought an old, manual grinder out from the bag and spooned in a heap of beans.

"Yes," Freeman answered, although it wasn't a question.

"So was I." He wrapped his fingers around the crank and began turning with a slight wince. "Do you take it black?"

"Black's fine," Freeman muttered.

"You don't. I should've gotten milk," the old man caught the lie. "Oh well, you'd better like it," he smiled with a chuckle. "I eat this each and every morning and I won't make an exception for the likes of you."

As Isaac ground the beans into a coarse powder, Freeman saw discomfort in the man's eyes and noticed his inflamed, swollen joints. With a deeper glance, he spotted the faded, six-digit serial number—141688—tattooed in thin black ink inside Isaac's forearm. Freeman looked over the counter at the fresh food Isaac brought and around at the magnificent apartment Isaac arranged for him to rest. The old man was shrewder than Freeman could hope to imagine, and he knew the stress, the unfathomable weight they carried. Isaac understood that they shouldered the burden together. Freeman was once told a few crucial details of Isaac's personal life, which due to government sensors were not public knowledge. He knew Isaac's wife of nearly five decades succumbed to breast cancer fifteen years earlier, and that Isaac had come to work the day of her funeral and since hardly spoke of her. He knew they never had children- the rumor was that Isaac was incapable of fathering them, and that he was too consumed by his post to consider adoption.

Freeman connected the dots.

Isaac had no need to do any of this, no need to arrive at the crack of dawn and make Freeman something as simple as breakfast. But the old man did nothing without calculated cause. He wanted to gauge Freeman as two men sitting at a table with more in common than one of them was wise enough to realize; he wanted to do what he could to stitch the lacerations left by that familiar weight on Freeman's back, as his own had long since clotted into scars. And as Freeman watched the subdued pain on Isaac's face, it struck him. This was Isaac's daily routine and it brought him suffering with every moment, but he endured, he kept grinding those beans to dust. This was Isaac's meditation, his protest. The enormity of his small gesture—his act of surrogate fatherhood—washed over Freeman, filling him with guilt. Freeman's eyes swelled and he quickly wiped away the tears before they could be seen. Now he understood.

Benny Isaac was an old man who wanted someone to talk to, marooned in life with far too much left to say, and—despite his well of quiet dignity—today he did not want to face it alone.

"Can I do anything to help? Anything at all?"

Isaac dumped the ground beans into the percolator with the scalding water from the pot and ran his mangled fingers under the sink. "No, your company is help enough."

"Really," Freeman insisted. "I want to."

The old man took a butcher knife from the counter, pointed it at Freeman's chest and silently drew it toward a metal stool on the opposite side of the island.

Freeman took the seat. "Thank you."

Isaac left the coffee to brew and strained himself to reach into a high cabinet, pulling out a cutting board. "I was scheduled to drop by the *Kirya* before our meeting, but after all that ruckus last night, I think I'd rather pluck my eyeballs out with fishhooks. Truth be told, we don't need those idiots, anyway. So I figured, why not pop in for breakfast? I sent my driver to the market and came 'round." He set the board on the island and frowned. "I was really hoping to surprise you."

"You did, don't worry," Freeman smiled and felt more relaxed. "But what happened with the airstrikes? I haven't had a chance to—"

"As I was saying," Isaac took the blade and began dicing a tomato, "I was also forty-nine when Menachem Begin—may the louse rest in peace—asked me to serve as *memune.*" He spoke of his honorific and revered title, a Hebrew word meaning "first among equals," that was bestowed upon each of Mossad's directors-general. Before Isaac there had only been five worthy of the name. "That was the fourth of November, 1979, and the very same day those bearded jackals stole your embassy in Tehran, if you'd believe." He slid the tiny tomato cubes into a bowl, rinsed the pale red fluid from his cutting board, and restarted the process with a cucumber. "The learning curve was minimal. I'd been with the Institute since Ben-Gurion signed the charter, was attached to all the big operations up to that point, and watched each of my predecessors do the job before me...some not so well. And the PMs of the day," he scoffed, "are a shekel a dozen. There's a reason they're called prime ministers *'of the day.'*"

"Avi seems to be staying put."

Isaac looked up with a hint of intrigue behind his spectacles and purred, "Realities change," and kept slicing the cucumber. "Of course, you didn't quite have the luxury I did, Ryan. You were a company man right from university, yes. All smarts. Good on you. First posting in London for only six months—that must've been rough starting out at CIA's retirement home—then Bonn and East Berlin. I heard about that awful business there."

"Yeah," Freeman admitted and dipped his head to the marble countertop.

"Next they brought you home and chained you to a desk until you could screw your head on straight again. Honestly, I'm surprised you weren't sent away to stud at the Farm and get picked apart by swamp flies. After you'd said your vows, to a lovely young woman I might add, and brought a beautiful daughter into the world, they shipped you off to Africa, to the sphincter of society. But Africa was quite different for a spook back then. You could be left to your devices and hone those smarts. Then, lo and behold, a different group of bearded jackals knocked some very tall buildings down and your smarts became very valuable to some very important people... And here we are."

"Here we are."

Isaac placed the cucumber bits into the same bowl. "No, sir, you did not have it as good as me. I had time to learn from my predecessor. Yours ran out the door with his pants around his ankles." The old man cackled at the cleverness of his own joke. "And before him, the seventh floor was a carrousel of dim-witted politicians, believe me. Then you waltzed into an acutely egocentric White House with all its entrenched potentates and seem to be faring fine."

"Thanks. Thank you, Benny."

Isaac took two mugs from a cabinet, filled them both with coffee, and hobbled back to the island, passing one to his guest. "But no matter if it's a president, a prime minister, or a king," he sipped, "they never understand."

"I don't follow." Freeman rested his elbows on the counter.

"The decisions we make," the old man said. "We make the unpleasant decisions that sanitize their own. I've spent eighty-two years on this rock and I've been forced to make them for longer than any man should. These decisions are rarely questions of war and peace, they're primal questions of life and death. That's the currency we trade. That's why you and I are here this morning: to barter with another's life, to deal in the gainful commerce of death. We scrape away the filth so that when our contemporary kings are reduced to murder, they can rest their heads with some frail guarantee of who will live and who will die and for what purpose. Yet when kings kill it's romantic, it's poetry. No one writes poems about slitting a defector's throat in a storm drain. No one writes poems about shredding a toddler to bits at a wedding because her uncle funneled money to terrorists. That's our business, the business of the Reaper. But without us," Isaac drank, "history's proven that kings have a hard time keeping those heads."

Processing the barrage, Freeman could only lift the mug to his lips.

"No one will ever tell you that, Ryan," said Isaac, "but it's what we are. We're glorified bin men." He placed both hands on the countertop and spread apart his knotted, swollen fingers. "These damned things have never taken a life—then again, they can barely wipe my own ass—but I'm still a murderer. Oh yes, I've killed men, and women. Children, too. I've killed them with my words, with pens and phones, even a nod. It's all the same. Death is death and what happens after matters only to the unlucky many left behind. And before your tale is told, Ryan, you'll do the same—you'll make those unpleasant decisions so that your king can sleep at night. And the day will come much sooner than you'd suspect."

As Isaac moved back to the stove, Freeman thought he'd discovered the old man's second truth, his darker reality. Isaac had been a constant for longer than anyone could compare, he weathered eleven changes of government, so much chaos and turmoil—wars, insurgencies, coups, assassinations, treasons—that he had become welded to the machine, fused to the planks of his ship. Isaac was Mossad's fearless captain for thirty-seven years, a living entombment of institutional memory. As he saw it, the politicians, the diplomats and the military men, their brief shelf lives did not allow them to hold a grudge against Israel's enemies. But while they came and went, Isaac remained, and he remembered. He was a man whose entire purpose was centered on a clock and a list. Isaac knew his time grew thin, and he was hell-bent on making his enemies suffer once more before the end. Freeman watched the old man. He feared he had a glaring view of his own stark future—and he hoped, pleaded, that he was wrong.

Two eggs were cracked into a skillet and placed over medium heat. Isaac took a spatula and began edging the whites toward the yolk. After an uneasy silence, he said, "I can count the number of people who know what I'm about to tell you on one hand, Ryan."

"Guess it's good that I'm paid to keep secrets, huh?" Freeman's attempt at levity fell flat. Isaac kept his back turned and gave no reaction.

"My earliest memory," Isaac began, facing the skillet, "is of standing outside a synagogue in my hometown, Munkacs, in eastern Czechoslovakia. I was with my father, Yaakov Batzdorff—which was my name too at the time—and I was helping him sell copies of this yellow book that I'm pretty sure was *Das Kapital.* Anyway, the rabbi came out on the steps, chased us away and said we were 'worse than rats.' I think I remember it so well because it was the first time I learned that someone I didn't know, and who didn't know me, could be so cruel. That was my entire childhood, we were always being chased somewhere. But the rabbi was right about one thing: my father *was* worse than a rat. All the rabbis hated him. He belonged to the local Comintern branch, they held meetings in our flat, and they all clung to this fantasy that Karl Marx would descend from the clouds and rescue us, maybe in the form of Stalin's tanks. I remember them going on about how 'Opium is the opiate of the opium addicts,' or whatever that other bearded jackal said."

Freeman smiled again. "It went something like that."

"The man was a dyed-in-the-wool leftist," Isaac continued. "And godless. My older brother, Shlomo, and my two younger sisters, we never understood why at Hanukkah, and Passover, and Rosh Hashanah all the other kids could celebrate, but not us. We were Jews, like them. Fast-forward a few years to March 1939. I was eight. I woke up and saw that my grandparents were in our flat, listening to our radio, and crying. Our part of Czechoslovakia declared independence during the Nazi annexation and Hungary invaded to stop it. For the next several months, the Hungarians mostly left us alone, but my father couldn't work and I still don't know how he kept the flat. One night I heard a commotion, I went into my parent's room and saw a Gestapo officer holding them at gunpoint. He kept shouting, '*Aufwachen. Aufwachen.*' I'd never seen a gun before, and I later realized what happened to my mother was rape. My father did nothing to stop it. They'd have shot him, but still."

Freeman listened on with the same trepidation of watching a person's leg about to break. He knew nothing good was coming, but couldn't turn away. He wanted to keep listening, if only to prove that he could hold on to the end.

"That night we were taken to the Terezin ghetto. It was home for the next two years. We lived together in one room of a shared flat, but we struggled to get by. Starvation and disease were everywhere. Most of the ghetto's Jewish council came from Munkacs, and they didn't make our lives easier. I quickly realized that if we needed something, no one was going to hand it to us; I taught myself to survive, I fought constantly with the other boys and stole extra food to bring back to the flat. My father always encouraged me to keep stealing, but he would never go out and do it himself. And Shlomo was too frightened to leave his mattress for weeks on end. That was the first time I recall feeling truly ashamed of my father. By 1943, the lot of us were rounded up and put on cattle cars to make room for more Jews from Denmark. Shlomo broke way from us in the crowd and I still don't know what happened to him. I had no idea where we were going."

Isaac eased the fried eggs out from the skillet and onto a plate. He set it aside and cracked two more over the pan. "How's your coffee? Need more?"

"I'm good, thanks."

"No, you can tell me it's shit."

"Really, Benny, it's fine."

"When the cattle cars opened again at Auschwitz, I believed we'd gone to the spaceship from *The War of the Worlds*. It was dark, we'd been locked inside for days, and all we could see were flashlights in our eyes. I heard dogs barking. And the stench, Ryan. It was real, this acidic black dust that you could see and taste and feel prick your skin. The guards ordered us out in so many words and started forming two lines. An SS doctor came and inspected us. If you were over a certain age, and appeared healthy, he put you in the left line. Anyone else got sent to the right. I was thirteen when I arrived, but I'd kept my strength in the ghetto, and I was in very good shape for my age. So, we're waiting in this parade of thousands, and my father ran ahead in line. Just, off. I'd no clue why. When he came back, he made my mother swear to give my sisters to my grandparents and to lie and tell the doctor she was a nurse. She did as told. My sisters and grandparents went in the right line; we went in the left. A few hours later, she turned frantic and asked a guard where they'd gone. He pointed to the smokestacks."

Isaac turned from the stove and raised his forearm to Freeman. "And then they gave me this." He went back to the crackling eggs. "The next day, my mother threw herself in front of a truck. I don't blame her for opting out, but I can't blame my father either. He made an unpleasant decision. He could've lost his wife *and* his daughters, or he could've sacrificed two of his children to save her. It was an act of love, really. There was no way for me to say it then, but I know I was proud of him. We were placed in Section B2B, the Czech family camp, and worked in a sewing shop. What I taught myself in the ghetto saved me: as long as I kept my strength, I would live. I volunteered to move boulders from one end of camp to the other. I played football on a little patch of grass near the crematorium. I made do with a hopeless reality. Five months later, they told us B2B was being moved to a labor camp in Germany, but before we left, we needed hot showers and fresh uniforms. So as we marched to the showers, I heard from the little *Deutsch* I'd picked up that something was *'kaput.'* That something was the gas chamber, which must have malfunctioned minutes earlier. We marched back. Three days went by and we marched again. This time, a train happened to arrive with ten thousand Jews from Belarus. The guards were furious. They'd nowhere to put them so we marched back and they managed to gas all ten thousand that same day. But the next day, there was no escape. I had to pick a god to save me. By this point, we all knew we were going to die. We were starving, and helpless, but not stupid. As we stopped at the showers, I saw the camp foreman and a group of SS officers pulling men to dig trenches. I was picked. My father was not."

Isaac slid the last two eggs onto another plate and carried them both to the island where he laid a spoonful of the diced tomatoes and cucumbers beside them. He took the black bread and sliced a few thick pieces. "I didn't know a person could get so hysterical," he said, taking his plate around to the stool next to Freeman. "My father, I mean."

"Right," Freeman sighed.

Isaac swallowed after his first bite. "He fell to his knees, begging, howling at the guards to let me, his son, back in line for the gas chamber. I've struggled to see what ran through his mind for seventy years. But he knew he was going to die. And he knew I was going to live, at least for now. He could not fathom the reality of dying alone, this godless man who spent his life lecturing on the sheer vanity of how others chose to confront their mortality, could not confront it himself. He snapped. And the bastard expected me to go down with him."

"What did the guards do?"

The old man raised his eyebrows. "They asked me if he really was my father and I said I'd never laid eyes on him before. So they executed him."

Freeman exhaled through his nose. "I'm sorry."

"Why? You didn't put a round in his head."

Freeman jabbed at his eggs.

"I made an unpleasant decision. I denied my own father. I killed him, but not with my hands. Our section was liquidated, and thirteen hundred people, everyone I had left in the world, died that day. But I survived. I stayed at Auschwitz until June 1944. Five hundred of us were sent to the Schwartz Heiden labor camp outside Dresden to repair a coal-gasoline conversion plant your air force bombed. There was nothing we could do. Come spring of forty-five, the plant was rubble, so they made us march into Austria. We set out with three thousand, but after a few weeks, only two hundred of us were left. We buried most along the roads. By May, the SS put us on cattle cars, but the rails were so damaged it took ages to move anywhere. Then one day, as we were locked in the cars, someone noticed that the SS had fled. The war was over. We forced open the doors and walked down the tracks a few kilometers until we reached the next town. It was Terezin, my ghetto. I weighed thirty-three kilos that day."

Freeman shook his head in disbelief. "That's amazing, Benny."

"The Czech Red Cross helped me get to Prague. I recovered, but then went right back to the only thing I knew, really—the streets. It seemed natural. I lived under bridges and in sewer tunnels for about a year." Isaac paused. "Then I met Otto. I usually broke into homes before and after holidays; there was always something good to steal. I remember it was Christmas Eve. It was cold and snowing, and I hadn't eaten in days. I burgled the townhouse of a doctor, Otto Isaac. As I tore through his cupboards, he caught me."

Isaac had to pause again, and Freeman could sense that what came next was far more painful.

"And he cooked me breakfast—as much as I could eat."

Freeman set his fork down.

"He owed me absolutely nothing. I wronged him. And he could've phoned the police, he could've beaten me, sent me back into the cold, but he didn't. He fed me, and he clothed me, and gave me a safe place to rest for as long I wanted. And when I woke that morning he didn't send me away." Isaac cleared a tear from his eye. "With all the armor I'd built up, it didn't save me. He did. A stranger saved me that night. He gave me back my dignity. And he taught me that I wasn't worse than a rat, that I was a human being. I stayed with him the next night and the night after. He introduced me to God and claimed me as his son. I took his name as my own. But Comrade Stalin and his tanks were coming, so we bought our way onto an *Aliyah Bet* ship sailing from Venice and landed in Haifa that summer. He wanted me to go to rabbinical school, but I wanted to fight. So in 1948 I joined Haganah's intelligence branch, and sixty years later, here we are," Isaac smiled. "You know, when Otto said he wanted me to become a rabbi, I suspect, in a way, this is what he meant all along."

The two finished eating. Freeman volunteered to handle the dirty dishes but Isaac insisted that he should not lift a finger. Eventually, the D/CIA yielded and let the stubborn old man have his way. Another pot of coffee was brewed and they moved to the dining room table set alongside the windows. It was nearly seven, but the sea and the sky hadn't yet split on the horizon. Freeman was eager to start talking business, but Isaac still had more to say.

"How's Mary? *Doctor* Freeman, I should add," said Isaac.

"The wife's great."

"She's still at Georgetown, yes?"

"Yeah," Freeman nodded, "she just got a big promotion about six months ago. She's chair of the Economics Department."

"Did she like the flowers I sent?"

"That was too nice of you," he laughed. "The sympathy card worried me a bit, but Mary was flattered to say the least. At our house, in the sitting room, we have a big picture window that faces the street; she put the vase right there so everybody in Silver Spring could see."

"And your daughter? Valerie isn't it?"

He beamed with pride. "Val's just killing it right now. She's finishing up at Juilliard this semester, in New York—I swear, she's never coming home. And actually the week after her commencement, she's playing an understudy for *Othello* at the Lincoln Center. So we'll drive up for the premier, tour backstage and all. But she wants to get an apartment in Brooklyn with her boyfriend for the summer, so I don't know how her mom and I are scrounging up the cash for that. It's exciting, though. I'm proud of her."

"It shows, Ryan."

Freeman saw an opening. "You know, Benny, I'm thrilled we got together like this—it's opened my eyes—and I hope we can do it again soon. But there's a lot of machinery on both sides of the world waiting for the two of us to make some moves. If I fly back to DC without good news, my ass is toast."

"Yes," Isaac nodded, "you are absolutely right. You've indulged me long enough. Fire away."

Freeman polished off his second round of coffee. "What went down in Gaza last night? I haven't had a chance to check for myself. The White House's priority is to keep Annapolis on track, and they're worried that Arad is dragging Israel into another stalemate. But he's not talking to any of us right now."

"Hamas launched forty rockets last night," said Isaac.

"Christ," the D/CIA clenched his teeth.

"Iron Dome picked off most, and the handful that got through didn't cause much damage. A bus stop in Ashkelon had its windows blown out, but we can fix that. Of course, the Qataris babysitting Fawzi Abu Musameh were supposed to prevent this. But we're starting to learn that Hamas leadership probably didn't order the launches."

"Then who did?"

"Those forty rockets were all fired by IDQB's Northern Gaza Division."

Isaac spoke of the Izz ad-Din al-Qassam Brigades, the armed wing of Hamas that fielded five divisions, each assigned a section of the Strip. A veteran jihadist, Khader Issa—known by the *nom de guerre* "Abu Tariq"—led the IDQB. On paper, Issa answered to Hamas' prime minister in Gaza, Abu Musameh. "But we know from their radio chatter," he continued, "that no launch instructions came from Issa or anyone in IDQB's headquarters. So the division's commander, Bassam Sinwar, must've acted on his own or taken orders from another."

"Like the Quds Force."

Isaac raised his hands, happy to let Freeman make the conclusion.

"Shit," Freeman groaned and rubbed his eyes.

"Qasem Shateri is a very resourceful man, he wants nothing more than to lure us into Gaza again. He seems to know Arad better than Arad knows himself," Isaac sighed. "But anyone responsible for Moshe Adler's murder must die—Israel can't afford to tolerate it. And this is a point where there cannot be any daylight between us, Ryan."

"Oh, there isn't," Freeman shook his head. "Hammer the bastards."

"I intend to," Isaac admitted with confidence. "Azzam al-Nakhalah and Rasoul Abadi top my list right now. I'll get them, soon enough."

Freeman knew of Colonel Rasoul Gharib Abadi as the chief of the Quds Force's Division 6000, Iran's ambassador to the Sudan and Shateri's lieutenant for North Africa. Syria's collapse and Hezbollah's subsequent decision to face reality and disarm catapulted Abadi into the spotlight. He became the Quds Force's sole field commander on Israel's southern border and made his charge to funnel arms and cash into Gaza, to Palestinian Islamic Jihad and Azzam al-Nakhalah, a strategic necessity. If Shateri was the architect of Adler's murder and the chaos to follow, Abadi was the engineer, and al-Nakhalah was the foreman. Isaac would let none go unpunished.

"One day, I'd love to meet whatever asset you have in Tehran," Isaac said, giving Freeman pause. "If the *Catarina A* reached Sudan with those cruise missiles, we would've had a catastrophe on our hands. We owe him a debt."

"We learned of that shipment through a few sources," Freeman lied, he hoped convincingly, "but I didn't believe it at first. No one at Langley had ever seen an operational Club-K before, just the Russian sales mock-ups."

"Either way we look at it, basing tactical missiles in Sudan was a logical move on their part. Shateri's desperate: first Damascus goes, then Beirut. We've watched the Quds Force stockpile small arms and explosives in Sudan for a while now. They're using an Iraqi airline to fly into Khartoum, but the manifests are forged. We think a convoy moves the cargo to a staging area about an hour's drive north of the city. From there, what's bound for Gaza is passed to the Bedouin smuggling rings who bribe the Egyptian border guards, drive across the Sinai and under the few tunnels we haven't destroyed."

"You've found this place?" Freeman asked.

"A village along the Nile called Wad Ramli," said Isaac. "Iran's managed an agricultural project there since the mid-nineties. We know from over-heads of their compound and a contact who visits relatives in the area that the project hasn't supported local farmers in at least a year. But, the village gossip is that there's now a second compound in Wad Ramli, not visible from the main road, that's bursting with Pasdaran. Around the same time Damascus fell, the compound sprouted four huge Quonset huts, practically overnight. We paid a shepherd to steer his flock right up to the fence and a bearded man in fatigues politely shooed him away. Why? We can assume."

"CIA's had our own problem in regard to the IRGC," Freeman cleared his throat and donned the most convincing guise he could muster. "Frank-ly, it's stumped us. We don't want to brush it aside, because if true, it'd be a golden opportunity to look inside their operations. I'd like to see if you could help."

Isaac nodded—a curt signal that Freeman had the old man's attention.

"I need to get my bag." Freeman shuffled back to the bedroom, return-ing a moment later with his cracked leather satchel. He removed a manila folder fronted by a Top Secret cover sheet and placed it on the table. "Our Information Operations Center noticed an unsolicited email to CIA's public website with some pretty interesting details." Freeman opened the folder and slid a page toward Isaac. "This virtual walk-in claims to work for the SPND at Parchin. Doing what? We don't know. However, the VW's email used some pretty technical jargon, and this schematic was attached," he pointed. "You can't forge that."

But the schematic was forged, and expertly so, by Peter Stavros and his minions in Persia House. It was part of the elaborate cover story they'd concocted to deceive Isaac and Mossad into stealing Alireza Fakhrizadeh's autopsy report—without sparking a third world war in the process.

Isaac inspected it for a minute, then asked, "Is this a—"

"A fast rise-time oscillograph," Freeman answered. "Very good."

The instrument was of a rare sort that could be used to calculate the immensely small electrical currents pulsing through a neutron generator at the heart of an implosion-type nuclear bomb. Stavros figured it was obscure enough to pique Isaac's attention without sparking panic. Mossad routinely monitored, and often sabotaged, Iran's attempts to procure such specialized equipment. Exports and re-transfers of dual-use technology—hardware with both civilian and military purposes—was controlled by a multinational consortium known as the Nuclear Suppliers Group. To bypass those re-strictions, the IRGC operated a dizzying web of fronts and dubious brokers to purchase and smuggle the equipment with layers of artifice. However, the Israelis kept several brokers on their payroll. Before the equipment reached Iran, Mossad's skilled operatives would break into warehouses in cities like Dubai, Karachi or Ashgabat and tamper with it ever so slightly. Once the equipment was installed in the workshops of the SPND or one of the country's quasi-military universities, it would function properly, but its readings would be skewed just enough to avoid notice. After months and even years of using this faulty equipment, their research would be immeasurably flawed, and Iran's scientists would be no closer to a bomb.

"But look at this here," Freeman eased in beside Isaac. "Our analysts say these are alterations; this shouldn't be on any oscillograph you got off the shelf. We can't explain that. And that's why we think the VW's bona fides are legit. Benny, did your people make these alterations?"

Isaac was silent for what seemed like an eternity. "I don't know."

Freeman persisted, showing his concern to hold the guise. "But you're saying your people *might* have done this?"

"Ryan, I really couldn't say," he dismissed with a passive shrug. "Maybe. I'd have to check with my people. But if not us, or you, it could've been MI6."

"No, the Brits didn't touch this."

"The French?"

"Definitely not."

The old man blinked. "Then I suppose it must've been us, if your analysts claim its been tampered with. I'll tell you the Iranians would have an oscillograph like that at Parchin. So, congratulations, you have a prospective source inside. What does this mystery man expect from the Americans?"

"The email didn't say, just offered more if we wanted," he lied. "But that's not even the most interesting part."

Isaac looked down his nose at Freeman and smiled. "Are you going to tell me the Iranians already have a bomb?"

Freeman allowed an uneasy chuckle, although he reeled inside. "The email claimed that Dr. Alireza Fakhrizadeh is still working at Parchin."

"That's not a name I expected to hear again," Isaac said, visibly unnerved. "How many people have seen this email?"

"Info Ops, our analysts in Persia House and WINPAC; couple others at ODNI. I'll admit, it sounds like bullshit to us too, but we wanted to do our due diligence and check it out. This VW may very well be deceptive." Freeman had to place the groundwork that CIA would later use to cover their tracks. "I wanted to go back over what happened in '07."

In his first life, Alireza Fakhrizadeh was a professor at Imam Hossein University in Tehran and director of the IRGC's Physics Research Center. Trained by the Soviets at Chelyabinsk-70, Fakhrizadeh studied methods to shrink the explosive lenses used to trigger the plutonium core of a nuclear weapon. His specialty lay in building a bomb physically smaller, to the extent that it could fit inside a suitcase. At the Physic's Research Center, Fakhrizadeh led Iran's classified weapons project, working parallel to the avowed civilian energy program. After Ayatollah Khansari shuttered the project in 2007, his team was renamed the SPND—or, the Organization of Defensive Innovation and Research—and put to use researching dual-use equipment until an order came to restart work on a nuclear bomb. It never did, at least from the supreme leader, and in that same year, Fakhrizadeh was killed in a fiery car crash—before Mossad managed to do the deed itself.

He was consigned to history until Saeed Mofidi learned, from the mouth of Qasem Shateri himself, that a "Doctor Fakhrizadeh" was still very much alive and only months from finishing his life's work. Before CIA could confirm it, they had to discover how he managed to cheat death.

"Ryan, the after action report we shared with Langley was the truth," Isaac shook his head. "Once we pulled his photo off that Syrian's hard drive in London and linked him with al-Kibar, he went right on my list. The PM signed off and the job went to Kidon." Isaac referred to Mossad's in-house death squad, a secretive unit based in the Negev desert that carried out assassinations around the world on the direct orders of the Israeli prime minister. "Our advance team went to Tehran to set up surveillance. We established his routines; his movement patterns from the university, out to Parchin and to his home; we gauged his security; we mapped every detail of the man's life. And then, about a week out from the hit, we watched his car slide off that bridge onto the highway."

Isaac pursed his lips before adding, "Grizzly. He suffered. Shame we couldn't have the pleasure of making it worse."

Freeman crossed his arms on the table. "Benny, what's your network like in Tehran right now?"

"Better than yours. Otherwise you wouldn't be here."

"Have anybody in the city's mortuary?"

"Probably," Isaac considered. "If not, I can."

"Can you get Fakhrizadeh's autopsy report?"

Isaac grinned. "We can try."

Freeman took another folder from his satchel and passed it to Isaac. "That's a report from a targeting officer in our Beirut station. A partial version made it into the President's Daily Brief about two weeks ago. It's yours."

Isaac opened it and read the title: *Hezbollah Scours Source of Lost IRGC Aid Funds*. "To what do I owe the honor?" he said, reading it over.

"At the time, Ilan Halevi asked to be read-in on the sourcing."

"Speaking of bearded jackals..."

"We told him to go fuck himself."

"As you should've."

"But, Benny, if you can get us that autopsy report, we'd reconsider."

Isaac slowly closed the folder with one of his knotted fingers and scanned Freeman with suspicion. "Ryan—my boy—why is Langley so desperate to confirm a string of anonymous words sent over the Internet?"

Freeman thought fast and opted for the jugular; something that he knew Isaac would appreciate. "Because Alireza Fakhrizadeh needs to stay dead."

The old man cracked a wry smile that exuded pride. "Okay."

"Since the report came out," Freeman continued, "we've learned that Hezbollah's found a key suspect for embezzling those funds."

"How much is missing? Approximately?"

"Two million, US. The guy's guilty, Hezbollah knows it, and he's a prime candidate to defect. I'll give him to you."

"Who?"

Freeman brought his hand over the table and stared Isaac down. "Get me Fakhrizadeh's autopsy report."

Isaac accepted Freeman's hand. "Done."

"Walid Rada, head of the Jihad al-Binna Foundation's Western Beqaa branch. The guy's been involved in building every one of Hezbollah's bunkers in the south and you want what he knows."

"I do," Isaac confessed, looking to the sea. "What's his situation?"

"Not well, or so we gather," said Freeman. "Our source claims Jihad al-Binna's office in Machgara was raided and Hezbollah's counterintelligence unit took everything not nailed down. ISF had Rada under surveillance for a while, but the Judicial Police got a request from Wissam Hamawi to withdraw five kilometers from the town. So they did." He shrugged, "And people say Lebanon's a sovereign country."

"Fewer bodies in our way," Isaac thought aloud.

"So this is how I see it working," Freeman shifted in his chair. "You send up a team to coordinate with our targeting officer, and we'll use our source on the ground to plan the operation. But we have to move fast; Rada could be arrested any day. Your team will pitch him, turn him, and get him out of Dodge. He's your prize. We'll share the debriefing."

"CIA doesn't want to risk a standoff with Hezbollah on their own turf?"

"The White House," Freeman corrected, "doesn't want to jeopardize its role as a mediator for the Annapolis talks by running an offensive intelligence operation in Lebanon."

"But the Syrians have more right to be disgusted with Hezbollah than anyone. They drew out their misery for years."

"I don't make policy."

"No, you don't," Isaac agreed. "We'll do it, but I'll ask just one more favor in return. Consider it payback for breakfast."

"Okay," he uneasily accepted.

"JSOC is holding Ali Mamlouk at Hama Air Base, are they not?"

"I think so. Why?" It took Freeman a moment to remember the name. Ali Mamlouk was the director of the Syrian National Security Bureau and a member of President Hafez Jadid's inner circle. Once Damascus fell and the regime imploded, Mamlouk went underground until a random tip and SIGINT intercepts led JSOC to his front door in Tartus. After a firefight with his guards, Mamlouk was pulled from inside a wall and whisked to the cells at Hama Air Base.

"He was our asset and we'd like to speak to him before he's carted off to The Hague," Isaac said matter-of-factly.

It took Freeman by surprise, and also slightly annoyed him that Langley was never told Mossad had planted a spy right at Hafez Jadid's side. Then again, Isaac knew nothing of Saeed Mofidi. "Ali Mamlouk was yours?"

"Life is full of contradictions and strange things, Ryan."

"But gassing the rebels was practically his idea?"

"That's why we'd like to talk to him. Actually, he first contacted us about three years into the war through mutual friends in Istanbul. Several of the generals he'd been allied with were executed for speaking out against Shateri's influence with the president. He was tired of being an Iranian stooge and wanted to stop the train from careening off the cliff. Mamlouk thought if he brought them Jadid's head, he could parlay with the rebels and sue for peace. Never happened, of course. Shateri got word and put him under house arrest. We lost contact."

"So you just want to wish him well?" Freeman wondered.

"No, hardly," said Isaac. "There's anywhere between five to ten tons of sarin precursor agents that we need to confirm were destroyed. Granted, it isn't much—but it's enough."

"Benny," Freeman shook his head in disbelief, "this has been disproven about a dozen times by the UN, the Russians, the EU; everybody. The OPCW hauled thirteen hundred tons of chemicals through an active war zone. Obviously every number we have isn't going to match. But we've combed through each of their production and storage facilities multiple times and they're empty, picked clean down to the last inch of copper wire."

"That's what worries me," Isaac countered.

Freeman hated that he'd fallen for the trap. "Okay," he surrendered, "I'll talk to Admiral Wade and see what we can do. But I want to keep getting the transcripts of Mehdi Vaziri's debriefings—unredacted."

"Oh, that's no problem," Isaac assured.

"How's he doing?"

The old man's face signaled disappointment. Mossad had freed the Iranian opposition leader from house arrest and spirited him over the Persian Gulf in a fishing dhow. Vaziri and his wife were now holed up in an opulent suite at the Hôtel Meurice in Paris, struggling to collect their shattered lives. Meanwhile, their rescuers came to realize just how little intelligence value they possessed.

"Well, Fatemeh spends the entire day hopped up on anti-depressants and sleeping pills. I'm told Mehdi isn't far behind her," Isaac shrugged. "Honestly, I'm beginning to regret pulling them out of Tehran. The debriefings have just shown us how crushed the Green Movement's become. Vaziri knows nothing, and I'm not sure what we're going to do with him. The French don't want to give them asylum and he refuses to come here on moral grounds. But he doesn't have much of a choice, does he? I think it'll end up that I have to go and convince him to come to Israel myself. But, if you want the transcripts, they're yours."

Freeman pushed back from the table, satisfied that he'd accomplished his mission. CIA would get Fakhrizadeh's autopsy report and Israel would be none the wiser of just how close their mortal enemy was to completing a nuclear weapon—at least not yet. "Alright, one more thing. What am I telling the president about this mess in Gaza?"

Isaac gave a long exhale and thought it over. "Tell Paulson to let Arad stamp his feet for a while. He'll burn himself out; I've seen it before. Trying to stop him only makes the tantrum worse. And let me settle the score with *Hajj* Qasem. Once I've removed his minions, the fighting will stop."

"No ground troops?"

"None."

"When can we get this thing moving in Lebanon?"

"I can have an officer in Beirut as soon as tonight."

"Alright," said Freeman, "I'll cable the embassy when we're done."

Isaac pressed on his cane and hoisted himself upright, staring at some undetermined point on the emerging horizon. "I wonder, in the meantime, if we'll shake Ibrahim al-Din from the trees as well? He's still out there."

"I wouldn't bet on it," Freeman resigned.

"Oh, but I would. I'd bet anything," the gray old man smiled. "That's one unpleasant decision I'd love to make."

Dense fog rolled off the Atlantic, smothering the cliffs and marshes of Ireland's west coast, forcing the C-37A to divert from Shannon and refuel at RAF Lakenheath before attempting the seven-hour crossing. England was no less dreary. Mist tamped the flat East Anglia countryside like a straitjacket, cloaking the sodium lamps over the tarmac in a dull orange haze. An R-11 Refueler truck was parked by the Gulfstream's starboard side, pushing over a thousand pounds of JP-8 into its wings. Freeman sat along the port fuselage, nursing a Heineken bottle and picking through a bowl of cashews with a secure telephone held to his ear.

"Looks like the old man bought it, Pete. Nice job," he said.

Shaw and Stavros huddled over the desk phone in her office on Langley's seventh floor. "Hey, that was your idea, boss. I just executed."

"Well, whatever the hell it was, it worked."

"Ryan, when can we expect to see this damn thing?" Shaw asked.

"Isaac's tasking the Collections Department and their station in Doha will handle it remotely inside Tehran. Mossad has a few assets in the local police, so my guess is that's how they'd penetrate the mortuary. I'd like us to have the autopsy report by the end of the month. Isaac also wanted access to Ali Mamlouk before JSOC hands him over to The Hague. He's on some kick about not all of the sarin precursors being accounted for, so I tossed that in as part of the deal. Why not? The theory's bullshit and Mamlouk's worth nothing to us."

Freeman practically sensed their eyes roll an ocean away.

"How about the Gaza fallout?" she pressed.

"Neither side is nearly as committed to this thing as they say in front of the TV cameras. And I'm starting to think Shateri's doing it for his own amusement. But Isaac promised no ground troops and said I could take it to the president."

Shaw adopted a solemn tone. "Our friend had a few choice things to tell us about Shateri." The courier's flight from Dubai arrived at Dulles several hours earlier with CITADEL's latest message. It did not bode well.

"What'd he say?" Freeman asked, unnerved to hear the answer.

"We'll talk about it tomorrow. He's frightened by the Quds Force; says Shateri's dictating policy from the field and nobody knows his endgame. Rostani's useless and IRGC Intelligence is tearing apart Europe to find Vaziri."

Freeman swigged from the Heineken bottle and anxiously rubbed the bridge of his nose. "Are we ready to pitch PACER to the NSC?"

Shaw looked across her desk to Stavros.

"Roger that, sir," he said. "Persia House is good to go."

"Did your people decide how they're contacting Gorani?"

"Erbil's on it," Stavros replied. "They've tapped a reliable asset who works one of the alcohol smuggling rings along the border. Once we get the green light, they'll give him an encrypted sat phone with our number and let him take it to Palanjar. If Gorani's there—hopefully—he'll give us a call. All the guy wanted for payment was a battery-operated space heater."

"I'll take that deal," Freeman chewed a handful of cashews. "You're coming with me to the White House, right?"

"Let's do it, sir."

"Grace, are we cleared to move on Walid Rada?"

"All prepped, Ryan," she said. "I went down to CTC earlier and had a nice chat with the Hezbollah Desk—they're excited, to say the least. Mathis briefed Nina Davenport and," she checked her watch, "if I'm not screwing up the time difference, she should be meeting that Mossad officer as we speak."

"Awesome," Freeman sipped as the Refueler backed away.

"Ryan," Shaw added, "hate to break it to you, but you sound like shit."

"I'm just tired," he breathed.

"Get some sleep on the flight and come in tomorrow when you're ready."

"Yeah, boss," said Stavros, "don't worry about a thing. We've got it all under control here."

The Gulfstream started moving to the runway and Freeman fastened his seatbelt. "That's what I'm afraid of," he laughed. "See you soon."

CHAPTER 31

As NINA DAVENPORT flipped down the sun visor and stared into the vanity mirror, she saw a glaring reflection of all she loathed. Her face resembled a thin layer of plasticine molded to the fine contours of her skull, coated with foundation, lipstick and eyeliner. Each strand of her auburn hair was shoved under a beige cap stretched over her scalp. Duct tape supported her breasts and the rest of her was squeezed into a red, long-sleeve dress that fell to her knees like a sausage casing. Nina thought she looked like a doll melting in a fire. Many would have taken one glance and called her stunning, but she just frowned in disgust. It was a mask, and for her purposes, a fitting disguise. She took a blond wig from the passenger seat and pulled it taught over the cap, teasing apart the bangs with her applied fingernails. Across the parking lot, a queue stretched out from the bouncers guarding the entrance to Mad, one of Beirut's most popular nightspots when the beaches and rooftops were still too cold. The club sat inside a converted warehouse on the city's northeastern edge, opposite a landfill and a rusted tank farm: a world apart from the dusty suburbs just a few miles south, where Hezbollah's gunmen roamed the streets.

She forced a final look of contempt in the mirror. It was time to move. She lifted the radio from the center console and called the Global Response Staff unit watching her from a nearby SUV. "I'm heading up."

On half-inch heels, she strode down a wide tunnel wrapped with hundreds of dazzling LEDs, shifting in patterns from blue to green and yellow to purple. The tunnel's mouth opened ahead into a cavernous abyss wracked with the chaotic buzz and mounting roar of techno music. Nina entered as the bass dropped. A rhombus-shaped halo of multicolored lights mounted on the ceiling blazed in sync with the electronic rhythm; lasers flittered in the darkness; ethereal videos projected on screens canopied the walls; scantily clad women danced on raised platforms; and waitresses weaved through the crowd with sparkling Balthazar champagne bottles held over their heads.

Somewhere within it all was the man Nina came to meet.

She waded through the pulsing throng of Lebanon's immaculate glitterati and eased alongside the club's main bar. A bartender—who'd been told to look for a woman matching Nina's description—quickly came up to her before any of his coworkers had an opportunity.

"I'll take a Negroni," she struggled to say over the blaring, computerized beats. "Double the gin, easy on the vermouth and very little garnish." Nina drew a fifty-dollar bill from her wristlet and passed it to him with a wink. "And a shot for each of us. Pick your poison."

The bartender smiled and went off, returning a minute later with her drink and two shot glasses filled with top-shelf vodka. They downed their shots together and smacked the empty glasses on the bar. He then took Nina's change, covered it with his hand, and casually slid it over in one, smooth motion.

"*Merci, habibi,*" she crooned, taking the coins and a small, flesh-colored wireless earpiece.

Nina then cut a path to the outdoor terrace off the dance floor, overlooking the strangely alluring industrial decay. The music was softer here, and the horde not nearly as dense. She walked past a few chatting smokers arrayed on sofas to a quiet corner of the terrace. A cluster of gasometers rose across the street, and beyond that was the Mediterranean. Looking south, she saw the lit gantry cranes fronting Saint George Bay, and sitting north were the Awkar hills where the American embassy was perched. Nina sipped from the glass and tucked the radio into her ear canal.

"Who's the bartender?" she breathed into the night.

"One of ours," a man's voice answered through the radio. The same music playing inside echoed in the background.

Nina couldn't help but smile. She knew that voice all too well, and it was one she often thought she'd never hear again.

"I like your dress," said the voice.

Nina looked down at herself with scorn. "I look like I've joined the slutty lollipop guild," she shot back. "And my tits have enough duct tape on them to strap down a pudgy five-year-old."

There was a resigned pause on the other end before the voice replied, "I just thought you looked nice."

"I miss you," she said, only realizing it once the words rolled into the air. Nina froze, dying for him to say it too—but there was only a trace of static and the resonate noise booming off the club's speakers. Her heart sank for a moment, knowing she wouldn't hear it. But she recovered. "You should've seen my face when I heard you were coming up here."

"Oh, I see it every day."

Nina bit her lip. "How're we doing this thing?"

"What's your situation on the ground?"

"Not good," she answered with a slight drawl. "You're gonna have to run this one fast. For all I know he's already been pinched."

Nina felt a hand touch her hip. A sweaty man with permed hair whose breath reeked of liquor and cigarettes pressed his waist against the small of her back and hissed, "What's your name, gorgeous?"

Without flinching, Nina dug her heel into the top of his foot and smiled as she heard him shriek.

"Bitch!" he spat and stormed away.

The voice laughed in her ear.

Nina knew he must be close. "When can I see you?"

After another pause the voice answered, "How's dinner tomorrow?"

"When and where?"

"Six. I'm up in Batroun. There's a little church called Saint Stephen's right by the harbor. Follow the alley behind it to the last house before the seawall. It's got a red door."

A breeze caught her wig. "What should I bring?"

"Just you," he said. "None of that other stuff."

Nina stretched her arms on the railing. "I think I can find it."

"Yeah, I know you can."

Harris watched a grainy image appear on the computer monitor. Initially it revealed only a vague outline, but soon he saw hints of arms and legs—the beginnings of a tiny person. Glimpsing his child for the first time, Harris stirred with pride. Sandra reclined on the exam table in their OB/GYN's office and craned her neck, gazing at the ultrasound scanner.

The sonographer carefully moved a plastic transducer through the clear gel spread over her swollen abdomen. "There's your baby," she said as the picture came into view and pointed a cursor at a trembling gray patch on the screen.

"Is that the heartbeat?" Sandra beamed.

"Yup, it's a little bigger now," the sonographer answered.

"Can we hear it?"

"Sure." The sonographer turned a dial and yellow EKG lines zigzagged across the monitor with a low, rhythmic warble. "BPM's 158, which is great."

Sandra locked eyes with Harris and smiled

The sonographer inched the transducer down her stomach. "How far along are you today?"

"I'm supposed to be at seventeen weeks, but at my first ultrasound I was a bit further along than I should've been."

"You were off by five days," Harris added.

"That's interesting," the sonographer read the monitor. "It does look like you're ahead of schedule. Eight ounces is the weight right now and overall measurements are eighteen weeks and three days."

"Oh wow," Sandra exclaimed. "Does that change the due date?"

"Not really," she replied. "You're still on target for May 27th."

"Okay," Harris nodded.

"Can you tell the gender yet?"

"Maybe," said the sonographer. "It's still pretty skeletal, not much fat and skin, but let me try." She ran the transducer back up Sandra's abdomen. "The feet keep kicking and the ankles are crossed, so I'm not sure." The sonographer prodded for a moment until she found a better angle. "Wait, there it is."

Harris leaned in closer to the monitor.

The sonographer pointed to the screen. "See it right there? Congratulations, Dad, you're having a daughter."

Harris smiled and felt Sandra squeeze his hand.

"Everything looks normal," the sonographer turned to them. "You have yourselves a healthy, beautiful baby girl."

Harris kept her hand in his and bent down to kiss his wife's forehead.

Sandra's face gave way to tears of joy.

Nina skirted her security detail and drove almost sixty kilometers up the coastal highway into Lebanon's predominantly Christian north. Tom Stessel would surely be annoyed that she left post without an escort, but she mostly lived these days to ruffle his feathers. Besides, Nina had to face this alone.

Saint Stephen's was impossible to miss. The church's soaring neoclassical façade was designed by a nineteenth-century Italian architect using a distinct hodgepodge of Byzantine, Roman and Gothic arts, and sat like an anchor in Batroun's center. Across the quay at her back was a sheltered harbor dotted with fishing skiffs gently jostling against the encroaching tide. She found the alley behind the church and followed it toward the sea. Paved with cobbles and lined with narrow homes honeycombed amid the ancient stones, it was more a blind passageway than a street and could barely fit a compact car. As Nina came to the end, she found a billowing palm just before the alley sloped into the tidal basin. Sheltered under its fronds was a sandstone house with a red door.

Nina rapped her knuckles on the fraying paint and waited. Her hands were clammy and her knees felt like hot rubber. She had to face it, despite her better judgment. Not for the mission, or for the agency, but for herself.

The door opened, and waiting behind it was the face her mind, and her heart, had pegged to that familiar voice—and one her conscience mourned.

She sighed and cast out her arms. "Hey, stranger…"

Nathan Cohen held her for what seemed like hours to Nina. Nothing about him had changed: not his calming scent, or the warmth of his cheek pressed to hers, nor the lure of his hands against her back. He was exactly as she remembered.

Cohen pulled away. "How long's it been?"

"Twelve years," she answered with a tinge of shame.

He exhaled and shook his head. "Come inside."

Cohen took her coat and Nina followed him into a sitting room rimmed by more sandstone bricks and appointed with mismatched secondhand furniture packed with loose cushions. A row of windows occupied the far wall and a balcony hung over the tidal basin. Shallow pools, rising and falling on the surf, stretched a few yards to the seawall. The Phoenicians had constructed it from petrified sand dunes, gradually eroded by human hands and nature into a battered monolith of rock and salt that stood forty meters high and over two hundred meters long. A receding storm had churned the Mediterranean into a fury; white-capped breakers charged on the wind and shattered against the wall, hurling spray effortlessly into the basin.

"This doesn't suck," Nina observed.

"No, it does not," he said, moving into the kitchen where fish and rice simmered on the stove. "Wine?"

"Obviously," she helped herself to the sofa. "So what are you telling people that you're doing here?"

"I'm a Canadian freelance filmmaker hired by a studio in Toronto to do a piece on the Syrian refugee crisis," Cohen called from out of view. "But they've only asked at passport control." He appeared with a bottle of Château Kefraya merlot. "Local swill," he smiled.

"It's booze, right?"

He uncorked the bottle, poured two glasses and went back to the kitchen.

"Where are the others?"

"My 'film crew?'" he asked. "They're flying in tomorrow and activating a few safe houses around Beirut. We'll link up then."

"And the story with this place?"

"I was told that a sympathetic Lebanese shipping broker in Antwerp bought this house a while ago and never visits. He lets us use it. Whether or not that's true, I don't know."

Nathan Cohen was of a rare sort. He was one of only thirty to thirty-five *katsas*—or case officers—deployed by Mossad around the world. While its counterparts at Langley often posted dozens of officers and support staff to its dispersed stations, Mossad managed with a skeleton crew of no more than six. But for what the Israeli intelligence service lacked in numbers, it compensated by magnitudes in the devotion of the people it was sworn to defend. Utilizing the global Jewish diaspora, Mossad tapped a bottomless well of support. *Sayanim*—Hebrew for "assistants"—were Jews living outside Israel who volunteered to aid operations when called upon. In a city like Paris alone, Mossad counted two thousand in active service with another five thousand lying dormant. *Sayanim* went about their lives, but when a *katsa* approached, they furnished whatever support was most easily attainable. For example, a *sayan* working in a rental agency could provide vehicles without the necessary paperwork; a landlord or a hotel manager could arrange safe houses and hide sites; and a doctor could mend a bullet wound without alerting the local police. The possibilities were unlimited. It was the *sayanim's* abundance of loyalty that allowed Mossad to pass unseen over the earth, striking and disappearing as needed. Cohen valued their devotion and knew it well; his own had brought him to Israel.

Cohen was born in Vancouver. His father was a successful Jewish real estate developer and his mother was an Anglican schoolteacher. At thirteen, his mother converted to Judaism and the family moved to Tel Aviv. After completing his compulsory military service in the Golani Infantry Brigade of the IDF's Northern Command, he left Israel to study history at University College London, where he became involved in the Drama Society and briefly considered acting for a career. However, others back home noticed his talent to immerse himself in a role and convinced him to put it to good use. Cohen's international background, language skills and appearance—he took his mother's traits and looked nothing like a typical Israeli—made him a valuable target for Mossad. His first assignment in the Bitzur Division—which was responsible for preventing terrorist attacks against foreign Jewish communities—was to Buenos Aires, where he monitored the financial networks and support cells linked to Hezbollah. Later, he collected intelligence on Hezbollah activities in sub-Saharan Africa. His next assignment, with the Tevel Division, was to Washington, where he served as a liaison. After proving himself to Benny Isaac, Cohen was recalled to Tel Aviv and placed in the Caesarea Division—Mossad's special operations unit—to serve under non-official cover as a counterterrorism officer-at-large, advising and directing intelligence efforts against Hezbollah wherever the old man needed him.

Cohen set two dinner plates on the shabby coffee table.

"Oh my god," she blurted, genuinely shocked.

"What?"

"Nothing, I just get really excited when people can cook."

He folded his legs and sat opposite her on the floor. "So what do you eat?"

"I dunno," Nina gulped her wine. "Fries?"

Cohen brushed it aside. "Why don't you tell me what's going on here. Isaac explained a bit, but I got the sense there's not much concrete information."

"I've been in-country about six months," Nina began, "working to fix that fucking travesty I'm sure you know all about."

He closed his eyes and gave a few slight nods.

"Well, overtime I've developed a new asset in the ISF—"

"Who?"

"Not a chance, baby boy," she reached for her glass. "His reporting's always been reliable, real gripping stuff. We cross-check it against the station's few other agents and it works out; nothing's been open source, and if its been conjecture, it confirms itself in a few days. He's wonderful."

"Right…"

"I've followed this rumor that Hezbollah's lost track of about two million in Pasdaran aid funds—the same cash they shoveled out around the south during reconstruction. Word was that the secretary-general's handling the investigation himself. So about two weeks back, right around the time the party announces it's going to disarm, my asset reports that they've found a prime suspect. Hamawi's furious, of course. With Iran's wallet closed, he needs every dime he can get if Hezbollah's going to survive."

"And that suspect's Walid Rada?" Cohen asked.

"Exactly. Chief of the Western Beqaa branch of the Jihad al-Binna Foundation; he's directed every one of their construction projects in the valley. It makes sense, right? My asset also tells me that Hezbollah sealed off the branch office in Machgara and carted away boxes."

"Seems like the guy's screwed," he remarked.

"Which is great for us," she added. "Later, I get a report that Hezbollah asked the Judicial Police to keep the ISF five kilometers outside Machgara."

"When was this?" Cohen sounded concerned.

"Four days ago."

"Damn," he looked away.

Nina shrugged. "So we might be too late."

"Is your asset in a position to know if Rada was arrested?"

"Yeah," she considered, "unless they just shot him in a field."

"And you have no SIGINT collects on him?"

Nina shook her head. "White House won't let us."

Cohen wiped his upper lip and thought for a moment. "First thing we need to do is trawl his phone calls, text messages, emails, Internet searches; we need to get inside Rada's mind. I can have our people handle that. Then we need to get boots on the ground in Machgara and physically put eyes on this guy. What's his family situation?"

"He's married," she said, "they have a daughter. I think she's four."

"Okay," Cohen nodded, "there's an incentive. Once we piece his life together a bit, we'll approach him. It's very simple, as I see it. Why should he have any loyalty to Hezbollah? And whatever animosity he has for us will pale against a death sentence. We'll appeal to his survival instincts. We'll get him, his wife and his kid new passports and we'll get them out."

Nina downed her wine. "The sooner the better. Honestly, we needed this done yesterday."

"What's the hold up?" he asked, pouring her another glass.

She shrugged again. "Politics."

"I can't make any promises." He looked up at her from the floor. "I've learned that people in dangerous situations are often dumber than they should be, but I think we can bring Rada over."

Nina purposely took another hard gulp, steeling herself. "You know what else my asset said?"

"No, but I think you're about to tell me."

She brought the glass down and smiled at him. "He said Ibrahim al-Din was spotted in the Security Quarter."

Cohen couldn't help but laugh. He slapped his hand over his mouth to keep the wine from spilling out. "Wow," he coughed. "I don't know, are you sure this guy's trustworthy?"

"Absolutely," she answered without a second's hesitation.

"Nina—"

"That's why I came here, Nathan," her voice smoldered, "to find him. I wanted to handle it like we did in AfPak. I wanted to set up picket lines in the suburbs, run static surveillance on his old associates, use our leverage in the ISF to kick in doors and get this done. And I've only vetted bullshit."

"That's how you get a firefight on your hands."

"But if Hezbollah's sheltering him, they're not beholden to Iran anymore; and if they're disarming, they're in no state to fight as it is. I don't know why we're so afraid of them."

"Like you said, it's politics."

Nina rolled her eyes. "I feel like Captain Ahab sniffing the waves."

Cohen squinted. "Remember how that book ends?"

She remembered, only she chose not to dwell on it.

"Who knows?" he grabbed the bottle and topped off their glasses. "Maybe when we snatch Rada, you'll spot your white whale."

Cohen brought a map of Lebanon downstairs and spread it over the table. Over the next thirty minutes they discussed the tactical situation in the Beqaa Valley, marking known Hezbollah positions, points of access and egress, and areas they knew should be avoided at all cost. Nina downed two more glasses of wine in short order and felt a sufficient buzz. She sat across from him on the floor. Despite her better judgment, she could contain herself no longer.

"What happened? With you, I mean."

The question caught Cohen off guard. He stumbled for a moment before answering, "Life happened."

"Are you with someone?" the alcohol begged.

"I got married over the summer. You'd like her. Her name's Daliah; she works for a marketing firm in Tel Aviv. And we actually had a little girl last month; we named her Violet. If I had a picture I'd show you, but she's beautiful. They both are."

Nina was devastated, but she could only smile. "Nathan, that's great."

"You?"

"What you see is pretty much it," she admitted with a trace of embarrassment, and drank. "I can basically count the times I've been home in the last eight years on one hand. I like the work, I do—I'd have nothing without it. It's hard, though. But you know that."

"Do you still talk to anyone from London?"

"No. No, I do not," she shook her head. "I don't bother to stay in touch with many people, and many people don't bother to stay in touch with me."

Nathan began to feel sorry for her. "When I was in DC, I tried to look you up, just to say 'hey.' They said you were in Kabul."

"Probably. When in doubt, I was probably in Kabul."

"Have you had anyone? Since?"

"A few," Nina said, "but I wouldn't say I *had* them. When I'm home there's usually a new flavor, and then after a few days I get sick of someone hanging on me. Mostly they don't get it anyway."

"That surprises me."

"I'm no catch," she said, "I'm utterly alone and completely crazy, and I'm not sure which caused the other," and laughed, forcing back tears.

"It doesn't have to be that way."

Nina placed her glass on the floor. "What happened? With us."

Cohen shifted his legs. "Well... I watched you disappear into that crowd at Heathrow, expecting a call seven hours later. I sat up that night, waiting. After twelve years, I think I still am."

Nina went abroad for her junior year of college. She left Harvard in the fall and spent that semester at the American University in Cairo, studying Arabic. In the spring, she went to the University of London's School of Oriental and African Studies to attend their Islamic history program. On her first day in the city, a friend she made in class convinced her to walk down the street to the Bloomsbury Theatre, where UCL's Drama Society was performing *Romeo and Juliet*. She had a seat in the front row and Nathan Cohen caught her eye. That weekend she attended a party at the same friend's flat, and the boy she noticed up on stage clumsily spilt a bottle of rum down her back—and that was the end of it.

And now she couldn't bring herself to face him. Nina stared at the wooden planks beneath her and brushed the hair from her eyes. "Nathan, I'm sorry."

"Why?" he asked with a playful chuckle.

"What?" she drew her eyes up.

"Why should you be sorry?"

"I abandoned you," her voice cracked.

"Nina, I was in a dark place when we met. And at first, I didn't understand why you were being so nice to me. Maybe, I don't know, I had just never thought about myself that way. I didn't see why anyone should care that much, but you showed me that someone did." He pursed his lips and sighed. "You know, I still think about you far more often than I should. Before Daliah, there was no one else but you. I didn't want there to be—because they weren't Nina Davenport... You ruined me for other women."

She took a moment to collect herself. "What was that play you were in?"

"Romeo and Juliet."

"Shit, I should know that," she breathed.

Cohen grinned. "'Love goes toward love, as schoolboys from their books; but love goes from love, toward school with heavy looks.'"

Nina rubbed her eyelids. "I got sick this morning thinking about coming up here. All these years, I thought you hated me."

"I couldn't hate you if I tried," Cohen said.

"Were you in love with me?"

"I like to think I was. For you, I want to. I'd never experienced anything like that, and to be honest, I haven't since. You know, I often wondered what would've happened if you stayed, but it doesn't matter. People enter our lives for a reason. And people leave our lives for a reason. You taught me that. But even still, I wanted nothing more than to spend mine with you." Cohen shivered. "I wished for that more than you can imagine.

A single tear fell down her face. "But my life was in Boston, and—"

"Nina, I would have followed you anywhere. You were the one worth throwing it all away. And you know that."

"Why?"

"Because you made me smile. For the first time in a long time, you made me smile. You gave me peace. We had our time together, and I couldn't ask for even a minute more. You and I are always meant to say goodbye. And I can't thank you enough for the happiness you gave me, because even to this day, I have no idea why someone like you wasted a minute on someone like me."

Nina covered her face.

"It doesn't matter if I have you. Knowing that you exist is enough for me."

She sprung forward and kissed him, pulling away a few seconds later, her fingers trembling against his chest. "I'm sorry... I'm so sorry. I need to go."

• • •

Nina sped down the coastal highway toward Beirut without passing another car for miles. The Volvo's headlights illuminated the snaking shoreline. She fought to hold herself together, but as she drove, the cracks in the dam crumbled into a sweeping deluge. Nina slammed the breaks, stirring a cloud of dust behind her, and swerved onto an overlook looming above the sea. She broke down into anguished sobs, clenched her fists and pummeled the steering wheel, screaming into her hands.

"Fuck, fuck, fuck!"

CHAPTER 32

"WHEN WAS THE last time you came to one of these?" asked Freeman, stepping down from the Suburban onto West Executive Drive, sandwiched between the White House and the Eisenhower Building.

"Not since the JCPOA," Stavros remembered, wrangling with a stack of binders and briefing books under his arm.

"Never gets any less weird." The D/CIA slid on his glasses. "I half-expect them to shackle an intern to the table and start ripping out entrails."

"What about senior intelligence officers?"

Freeman gave a quick appraisal and dismissed, "Too old."

They passed under an awning into the ground floor lobby of the West Wing. After Freeman signed them in with a uniformed Secret Service officer and checked their phones with the receptionist, they turned down a short corridor that descended into the Situation Room. Weisel appeared as they rounded the corner, nearly smacking into them. She seemed cross.

"Good, you made it," the secretary anxiously observed.

"What's up?"

Weisel scanned the corridor. "Come in here." She took them inside the Ward Room, a wood-paneled dining room reserved for cabinet members and top officials adjacent to the Navy's White House Mess. Harold Lansing sat alone at an empty table. She looked to the open doors. "Okay, we only have a minute."

"Angela, what's wrong?" Freeman demanded.

Her eyes met his and she swallowed. "Ryan, I have it on good authority that Eli and the vice president were in the family quarters until eleven-thirty last night. They want Paulson to go public with Haj Ali Gholi at the UN."

"No," he stuttered and shook his head. "No, they can't do that." Freeman shot a panicked glance to Stavros. "Is he?"

"It's an option that the president is considering."

"That's a death sentence for our asset."

"I know." Weisel touched his arm. "And you need to just relax before we go in there. I am handling it. But I thought you should know."

"Thanks, Angela," he breathed. "Did you talk to Paulson?"

"I called Dawson earlier this morning. He's privately counseled the president against it."

"Where's the president now?"

"The Oval."

"With Eli?"

Weisel nodded.

"Shit." Freeman gripped his hair.

"It's going to be fine, Ryan." She waved Lansing over. "I'm not sure if you've met Harold Lansing, my special rep for the Mid East."

"Ambassador," Freeman shook Lansing's hand.

"Nice to finally meet you, Director Freeman," Lansing said.

"Uh," the D/CIA motioned to Stavros, "this is Peter Stavros, chief of our Iran Operations Division. Pete, if you don't know who this lady is, you're fired," he joked.

"Hi, Pete," Weisel smiled. "Are you two ready on your end?"

"Good to go, Madam Secretary." Stavros patted his binders.

"Awesome," she said, "Harold and I have our proposal drawn out that compliments your operation. I ran it by the president on the flight back from Moscow; he's open to it."

"What about Eli?" Freeman asked.

"Fuck Eli."

Weisel led them through the Watch Center and into the Situation Room's main briefing area. Freeman and Stavros were the last to arrive; the D/CIA sat to the right of Geoffrey Sheridan, the director of national intelligence, and Stavros took a chair against the wall directly behind his boss. Freeman sized up the crowd—the principals of the National Security Council and their relevant underlings stirred around the conference table like overgrown fish in a bowl. Vice President Jacobs sat beside the president's chief of staff, Larry Dawson. Several Pentagon staffers accompanied Secretary Rusk and Joint Chiefs chairman, Admiral Lloyd Benson, including one Freeman knew from countless phone calls: Colonel Dominic Pohl, commander of the Air Force Technical Applications Center, or AFTAC. Weisel brought two of her lieutenants from Foggy Bottom: the under secretary for political affairs, Samuel Heidt and the assistant secretary for arms control, verification and compliance, Dr. Alaina Teplitz. Both had spent months shuttling between Geneva, Lausanne and Vienna, managing the US negotiating team that produced the Joint Comprehensive Plan of Action with Iranian diplomats. The sprawling agreement was supposed to make it scientifically impossible for the Islamic Republic of Iran to manufacture a nuclear weapon. In exchange, international sanctions would have been gradually lifted over eight years, freeing hundreds of billions in seized assets and allowing Iranian banks to access the global financial system. Both sides believed they had negotiated in good faith, and both sides had been deceived. What the Intelligence community discovered beside that lakebed at Haj Ali Gholi two weeks ago illustrated the maddening reality that indeed the Iranian mind was not aware of what its hands were doing. Shateri and his supporters in the Revolutionary Guards played Weisel, Paulson and their contemporaries in Tehran for fools. Freeman was a witness to Shateri's burgeoning influence through a web of plots and counterplots that spanned the world. He considered that fact, recalling Isaac's lessons, and he knew that *Hajj* Qasem with a personal nuclear arsenal was an unparalleled nightmare.

The senior watch officer came through the door and gave his usual refrain. "Ladies and gentlemen, the president."

Freeman rose with the others as Paulson entered with Tanner, sitting once the president took his place at the head of the table.

"Okay," Paulson opened a leather folio, "it seems Geoff is first."

"Yes, sir," Tanner offered.

"Go ahead, Geoff."

The DNI cleared his throat. "Mr. President, I'd like to give you an update on the IC's analysis of Haj Ali Gholi. Our estimate of the site remains mostly unchanged. Excavation of the southern tunnel portal, Picasso, continues on its normal pace, and we've observed the same routine activities throughout the site, again, mostly at night. ODNI has taken on the task of red-teaming CIA's assessments and we continue to posit a number of alternatives to the site's purpose, namely a missile production facility or a hardened, alternate command post of some sort. However, after exhaustive analysis, the IC cannot conclusively judge—given our current intelligence— whether Haj Ali Gholi is or is not the location of a clandestine nuclear research laboratory. Therefore, sir, my recommendation at this time is to allow the task force at CIA to continue its work so that we may confirm, one way or another, the scope of Iran's deception. Seeing as our developments in this area are lighter than I'd hoped, I've asked Colonel Dominic Pohl of AFTAC to come and give a briefing on how a hypothetical nuclear test at Haj Ali Gholi might be hidden from international monitoring."

Paulson peered down the table over the top of his reading glasses. "Okay, thanks, Geoff. Colonel, the room's all yours."

The Air Force Technical Applications Center, based at Patrick Air Force Base in Florida, operated the US Atomic Energy Detection System (AEDS), which was a global network of space-based, ground, aerial and hydro-acoustic sensors to identify evidence of nuclear detonations and accidents. AFTAC's scientists and analysts then used that data to determine which events were man-made—an explosion in the desert—or natural—an earthquake—in order to monitor compliance to the host of international nonproliferation treaties.

"Mr. President, it's a privilege to be with you this morning," Colonel Pohl began. "Since discovery of this site, approximately eighteen days ago, AFTAC has been working closely with our partners in the Intelligence community to both clarify our overhead reconnaissance and either verify or dismiss the claims of its nature. While this work continues, I thought it would be helpful for policymakers to have a greater understanding on the concepts of evasive testing, which I believe may explain the purpose of the southern portal."

As Pohl opened a bound report, Freeman noticed that Tanner was furiously scribbling notes on a yellow legal pad. The national security advisor did that constantly at meetings, dictating their words almost verbatim, and Freeman was always curious to know what eventually became of those notes.

"As you're no doubt aware," Pohl said, "the CTBTO Preparatory Commission operates five hundred seismograph stations around the world, of which our sensors are a part. These stations exist to monitor, pinpoint and analyze earthquake activity, as the minute geologic tremors they emit allow us to conclude whether this activity is natural or artificial. Essentially, how we make this determination is through an analysis of wave patterns. In an earthquake, the ground starts slowly shaking as plates slide against each other, and then seismic activity gradually increases as the ground begins to move." Pohl flattened his hands and carefully rubbed the sides of his index fingers together. "However, in an explosion, the initial blast is extremely powerful," he grated his fingers, "and the subsequent shaking of the ground grows progressively less severe. Now, there are methods of evasive testing that are intended to reduce the specific types of signals from a nuclear blast, which we look for. Most work to mask or disguise these signals by combining them with the benign signals of a non-nuclear source, such as chemical explosions used in mining. One such method is called 'cavity decoupling.'"

Freeman turned his head back to Stavros. Both knew what troubling notion the colonel was about to place on the table; the two had already reached it themselves.

"As the name suggests," Pohl continued, "cavity decoupling makes it theoretically possible to 'hide' a nuclear blast by detonating the device in a tremendous underground cavity." The colonel swept his hands in a circle to illustrate his point. "This decreases notable effects on the ground because the blast's thermal output—the energy it releases—is used to compress the gases in the cavity."

Paulson looked a tad confused.

"Okay," said the colonel, "let's imagine a tunnel is bored straight into the side of a mountain and a crude nuclear weapon fabricated with ten kilograms of plutonium-239 is placed at the center. A detonation of that much fissile material, barring a failure of the explosive lenses, would have a yield of roughly one kiloton, which would in turn produce a ground disturbance equivalent to a four-point-two magnitude earthquake. This is called a tamped explosion. The bomb's thermal output is expended into non-elastic processes such as melting and crushing rock, thus creating strong, irregular signals that every seismograph station within a thousand miles would register.

"Now let's imagine that before this test, a massive cave is excavated at the center of this same mountain, all of the spoil is carted away and the space is empty apart from oxygen, methane, hydrogen; all naturally-occurring. That's our cavity. Next, that same one-kiloton nuclear device is installed on a platform inside that cavity and detonated. Instead of the bomb's thermal output being expended into the rock, it's used to compress the gasses—essentially, air—inside that cavity, an empty space, causing a minimal seismic disturbance. Rather than a four-point-two magnitude earthquake, we'd have something on the order of a one-point-five, which could occur right now under our feet and we wouldn't be able to notice. Does that help, Mr. President?"

"A bit, Colonel," Paulson said. "But you'll have to excuse me, I made sure I was stoned for my freshman-year physics class."

"Right, sir," Pohl smiled. "Think of it this way: Person A stands inside of a large, empty room and screams; Person B, waiting outside the room, easily hears it. Now pack the same room with a thousand people, all are talking; Person A screams again, makes the same amount of noise, but Person B doesn't perceive a thing. It's a bad example, but it fits."

"Colonel Pohl," Jacobs stirred, "how does this method affect atmospheric testing? Wouldn't an explosion of that size still release radiation into the air, which we could detect?"

"It may, sir," Pohl admitted. "What you're talking about is called containment failure. After an underground nuclear blast, once heat and steam dissipates, the pressure inside the cavity falls below the level needed to support the rock overburden; the cavity then collapses, creating a rubble chimney—easily visible to every reconnaissance satellite overhead—and releases radioactive particles into the atmosphere. That's called venting. What we would search for after such an incident, let's say to prove our seismic data, is any amount of ionizing radiation, specifically various xenon isotopes, the proper ratio of which isn't found in nature and only indicative of a nuclear test."

"Could the mountain at Haj Ali Gholi support such a detonation?" asked Secretary Rusk.

"I'm guessing, but I believe a one-kiloton shot needs an overburden of

ninety meters for the cavity to stay fully-contained. If it were, it'd be difficult to prove an explosion. And correct me if I'm wrong, Dr. Sheridan, but
that mountain could support a twenty- to forty-kiloton shot?"

Sheridan nodded.

Paulson's eyes narrowed. "This is what you believe the southern portal is
for. Is that correct?"

"Yes, Mr. President," answered Pohl. "If the IRGC has attained fifty
kilograms of fissile material and intends to conduct a test this summer, like
CIA's intelligence suggests, then that's really the only logical use for a new
tunnel at the site. Picasso, I would say, provides access to this cavity they're
currently excavating. The amount of spoil material we see on the ground,
and their work pace, would support that theory. And, I'll add, this test
would also serve to destroy evidence of any research facility that's also inside that mountain."

Freeman saw their faces sour at the head of the table. The vice president, especially, seemed to break against his reactionary instinct.

"Andrew, we've gone beyond the point that we can stay silent about
this," Jacobs urged. "Enough damage has already been done to our credibility with the Arabs and the Israelis. How long are we supposed to sit on this
information? How long are we supposed to delay action on this blatant violation of trust?"

"Brandon, this has nothing to do with trust," said Paulson. "Never did I
trust the Iranians; never did I believe that every faction in Tehran was
onboard with our agreement. This deal was based on verification and proof.
Proof, Brandon; that's what we're trying to find before we hurl ourselves
into a situation we don't fully understand."

Freeman hadn't voted for Paulson, but in that instant he wished he did.

Jacobs took the hint and pressed back into his chair. The president
looked to his agenda. "Angela. What've you got?"

"Okay," she sighed and shuffled through her papers. "We've pulled together the negotiating team we had in Vienna to pick over the JCPOA
word-by-word and see which tenants have been violated and what options
we have available to us. The good news is that we've discovered this site
only nine months after signing the agreement, so none of our unilateral
sanctions have expired, and neither have many of the Europeans'. Also, our
statutory sanctions focused on Iran's support for terrorism, human rights
abuses and missile activities remain in effect; we don't need to take any action in that regard." Weisel's tone shifted. "However, I see two core issues
we must confront: how we handle the internationally-binding UN Security
Council sanctions, which have expired; and the question of how we address
this problem, short of military action."

Weisel tapped her pen against the table. "As for the Security Council,
those asset freezes and travel bans were lifted when the council adopted the

JCPOA. We cannot simply snap them back with an executive order. On the surface," she said, "Iran's avowed, civilian nuclear program still adheres to the agreement: Iran keeps its number of IR-1 centrifuges below six thousand, it's given up its IR-2 centrifuges, Fordow is being converted to an R&D facility, and it still possesses fewer than seven hundred pounds of low-enriched uranium. We have to bear in mind that the facility CIA has uncovered at Haj Ali Gholi is not, in any way, related to Iran's avowed nuclear program, which we've severely constrained. What we're seeing here is a separate, parallel weapons development project run by the Revolutionary Guards, and meant solely to produce a bomb. That's it," Weisel stated. "And so while the IAEA hasn't reached its broader conclusion that all nuclear material in Iran remains in peaceful activities, it has no reason to charge otherwise without our intelligence."

"So we should tell them," the vice president added.

"No," her eyes rolled toward Jacobs. "Mr. President, I'd strongly caution you against that. Until the Intelligence community has had ample time to build a complete picture and protect the lives of its sources, we should do no such thing. Once we've gathered our evidence and are ready to go public, we have means under the JCPOA to refer a complaint to the Joint Commission that Iran isn't holding its end of the bargain, and we're freed from our commitments. Thirty days following, all of the UN sanctions which were lifted will drop right back into force without a vote in the Security Council, bypassing a Chinese veto—this also assumes that the Russians are with us by that time."

Weisel paused and realized that only a few in that room knew of the trump card they'd been given in Moscow. "Mr. President, for discussion's sake, can we explain what the Russians told us?"

Paulson thought for a moment and then ordered, "What Angela's about to say does not leave these walls."

She nodded. "The day after Karetnikov's funeral, the president, Larry, Eli and myself were invited to Dmitri Lavrov's home. Over breakfast, Lavrov and his chief of staff, Andrei Minin, told us that in addition to resolving the conflict in Ukraine, Russia was prepared to shift its orientation toward the West. This includes a bid to join OPEC next month. To gain Saudi support, Lavrov's promised to sever relations with the Iranians after the vote's taken place." Weisel let the shockwave echo around the table and then she shrugged. "So, there's that."

Freeman couldn't decide how to react. He'd seen it coming—every one of the reports from Moscow Station suggested it: Karetnikov's old allies across the country were either diving for cover or bending to the new order. But this was something else, entirely. Lavrov cutting Iran loose to save himself had the potential to remake, not just the Middle East, but the world. It should have been a cause for celebration, but Freeman knew better. Qasem

Shateri was already a desperate man, Mofidi had said as much, but this would drop him into a tailspin—with an atomic bomb in tow.

"Something's bothered me over the last couple days," said Weisel. "I keep thinking back to the moment I sat across that table from Zanjani, and we finally came to a deal." She spoke of Javad Zanjani, Iran's foreign minister and a key moderate in the regime. "But I need to know if he lied to me. I've asked myself that a lot, and I don't think I was. President Rostani and Javad Zanjani are both good and decent men. I believe that. And I know that Qasem Shateri, the Quds Force and those factions in the IRGC are just as big a threat to them and the Iranian people as they are to us. Rostani was elected to better the lives of ordinary Iranians, and that's why he took great risk in defying the hardliners to make this deal. We need to remember that as we go forward."

Weisel turned around and took a folder from Under Secretary Heidt. "So where do we go from here? I can think of a few courses of action. In keeping with that line of thought, any action we take must work directly to cripple the rogue actors behind Haj Ali Gholi. The sanctions we had in place before the JCPOA clearly did not stop the IRGC from getting a bomb and there's no reason to think bringing them back will magically change that. On the contrary, that move would only decimate any economic gains Iran's managed over the past nine months and turn Rostani's base against him. We need to ensure that whatever we do empowers the moderate forces in Tehran to reel in the IRGC. State's worked closely with the Office of Terrorism and Financial Intelligence at Treasury to draw up a plan that enforces standing sanctions by targeting entities specifically linked to the Quds Force's cash flow. We've identified forty-two companies publicly traded on the Tehran Stock Exchange and 218 smaller firms directly controlled by three IRGC holding companies, giving us a total of 1,073 managers who can be subjected to travel bans and asset freezes. First in line should be companies owned by the IRGC Cooperative Foundation, or the *Bonyad-e Taavon Sepah*. Intelligence has suggested for some time that this foundation is closely linked to the Basra oil syndicates run by Qasem Shateri in southern Iraq. The smuggling operation nets the Quds Force approximately twenty million dollars a day; shutting down that source of revenue would weaken Shateri's ability to fund his proxies overseas and bribe the political class in Tehran."

"Angela, how would we rationalize that?" Tanner asked.

"Beg your pardon?"

"How would we explain to the rest of Congress and our allies why we got up one day and decided to go on the offensive against the Iranians when we're trying to implement our agreement with them?"

"Well," she considered, "implementation of the JCPOA is up to the IAEA now. We have very little to do with it, actually. But any of these new sanctions can be tied into Gaza and Islamic Jihad's execution of Moshe Adler—which I think we'll all agree, the evidence of Shateri's involvement is overwhelming."

The president stretched back. "There's more, Angela…"

"There is," she said. "As we know, after the JCPOA was signed, we undertook a staunch effort to build a new relationship with the Iranians. There were five rounds of negotiations in Geneva over those months, and I really thought we were making progress. Zanjani did, too. And then Turkey invaded Syria and Damascus fell overnight. The Iranians packed up and left, and we've had no official contact with them since. I thought, as did many others," Weisel motioned to Lansing, "that the end of Jadid's regime would cripple hardliners like Shateri. In some ways it did: Hezbollah is disarming and in a few weeks we'll have the leaders of Israel and Syria sitting down together. In some ways it didn't: look at Gaza and this other mess we have. So, I took it upon myself to discuss with the president ways that we could redouble our efforts to bring Iran into the community of responsible nations and sideline their extremists."

Tanner lifted his head from his notes.

"I'm proposing that the president sends a letter to Ayatollah Khansari detailing a proposal which, if honored, could normalize relations between us," Weisel continued. "Once this letter's received in Tehran, CIA's asset near Khansari can ensure that it makes it to the supreme leader and gets a fair appraisal, cutting the Revolutionary Guards out of the equation. Likewise, Ambassador Lansing has a contact who can suggest an intermediary to travel to Tehran with this letter. I'll let the ambassador explain."

Lansing crossed his arms on the table and looked to Paulson. "Sir, I've known Professor Morteza Ghanbari for twenty years. He chairs the History Department at Princeton and is on the board of the American Iranian Council."

The president nodded. "They do good work."

"Morteza's contacts in Iran are second to none," Lansing added. "He's well respected by the mullahs. I'm sure that he can get this letter to Khansari."

"And what exactly would we offer them?" Jacobs asked.

Weisel answered. "The president's letter would outline three points: First, the US will recognize that Iran has a right to intimate, but stabilizing involvement in Iraqi affairs and in the Persian Gulf, the same way the US claims the Western Hemisphere in the Monroe Doctrine. In exchange, Iran pledges active support for Iraqi stabilization, including disbanding the Shiite militia groups formed to fight ISIS. Second, Iran promises an end to material support for armed Palestinian opposition groups, commits to supporting a two-state solution with Israel, and supports Hezbollah's transition to a peaceful political party in Lebanon. In exchange, the US will call upon Israel to abolish its nuclear weapons and support establishing a WMD-free zone in the Middle East. Third, the US will lift its sanctions ahead of the JCPOA provisions and begin the process of normalizing relations if Iran disbands the Revolutionary Guards and dissolves their activities abroad."

"Andrew…" the vice president insisted.

Paulson winced and held up his index finger.

"Andrew, this is crazy—"

"Not now. We will get there. But not now," he said. "Ryan?"

"Yes, sir," answered Freeman.

"I'm told Langley has a plan to deal with this mess."

Freeman opened a binder outlining Operation PACER. "Pete Stavros, who's sitting behind me, is the chief of our Iran Operations Division. Since our last meeting on the topic, he and his staff have worked tirelessly to identify, as we see it, the core intelligence gaps in our understanding of Haj Ali Gholi. Pete's met with our partners in the IC and the Pentagon, dusted off a few contingencies, and I think has put together a cohesive covert action plan, which I wholeheartedly endorse. I think this operation enables us to build a full picture of the greater problem, and may allow us to sabotage this program before the IRGC's been able to finish its work." The D/CIA gave an overview of the strategic situation in Iraq, the influence of Qasem Shateri's militias, how it led to Jamil Gorani taking his "sons" into Iranian Kurdistan, and the mysterious rash of dead IRGC officers that followed. "Our Erbil Station has tasked a local asset in a smuggling ring that trades alcohol and gasoline over the border to bring a secure, pre-programmed satellite phone to Palanjar," he continued. "If Gorani has based his militia in the village, it's our hope that we'll have a conversation with him."

Tanner shook his head. "And you want to put troops in Iran?"

"No, not exactly," Freeman responded. "This plan would take four officers of a JSOC Special Mission Unit and place them under CIA's Title 50 authority. IOD and the Special Activities Division would jointly run this operation from inside Langley, not Fort Bragg or Virginia Beach. Overall command would be given to the officer we currently have in Tehran under non-official cover. As for JSOC's men, they would be temporarily taken off active duty and essentially put on loan to us. There'd be no American combat troops in Iran."

"Director Freeman, why do you need JSOC's men?" asked Dawson.

"We need people who can shoot their way out of the country. If it comes to that." Freeman wished he could've phrased it more delicately.

"*Will* it come to that?"

"I certainly hope not."

Paulson crossed his legs. "Okay, so if all goes to plan and this Gorani fellow calls you back, then what?"

"JSOC's embedded some of their staff within IOD, so we have a seamless relationship in regards to planning. Once we hear from Gorani, the operator JSOC's selected to lead their element would come up and we'd piece together insertion, escape and evasion routes, comms and supplies. Right now, we're considering a High Altitude, High Opening drop over Iraqi airspace and the team would glide over the border into Iran. After they've reached Palanjar, their first objective would be to gauge the readiness of Gorani's militia. If we find that they're serious about taking the fight to the IRGC, we'd train them in surveillance and mount an operation to track down Dr. Alireza Fakhrizadeh. The details of his supposed death in 2007 are still unclear, but we're going back over every shred of information we can find to see what we missed."

"Ryan, does Mossad seem aware of this operation at all?" said Tanner.

"No. I spoke to Benny Isaac for several hours. We had our bases covered, but not once did he seem suspicious about Fakhrizadeh."

"Go on, Ryan," the president said.

"Once we identify Fakhrizadeh and confirm if he's still alive and, as our source claims, directing Project 260, we have a few options. We could attempt to coerce a defection, which isn't likely at all; we could allow him to remain in place, and unwittingly provide us information; or we could remove him."

"You mean kill him?" Jacobs added.

"That's right, sir," Freeman said. "If Fakhrizadeh's managing this program for the IRGC, then we could assume that his expertise is critical to producing a functional bomb. Take him out before the bomb's completed and the dream dies with him."

"What's to say another doesn't pick up where he left off one, two years down the road?" Jacobs pressed.

"Nothing," Freeman conceded. "Until we know the extent of this program and the nature of Fakhrizadeh's involvement—if he is involved—then I can't answer that, sir. First we have to find him, and then we'll see."

"Larry," the president turned to his chief of staff, "any roadblocks here?"

"Nothing major," Dawson said. "Director Freeman's right, this is firmly within their Title 50 authority. A covert action finding will have to be provided to Congressional leadership, but that's no problem. They've been in the loop from the beginning. If it came to a targeted killing of Fakhrizadeh, or any others on the ground, the DOJ would be brought in, but—as you know—we can do it."

"Okay, thank you." Paulson was silent for a moment, considering the deluge of information dumped before him. "Ryan, I want to ask you something because I know you're a smart guy—I wouldn't have appointed you if I didn't," the president said after another minute and gestured to Jacobs and Tanner at either side. "These two kept me up pretty late last night. They want me to send Angela to New York, rally our allies and blow the lid on this catastro-fuck right now. Why shouldn't I?"

Freeman stared down the president of the United States and answered. "Sir, we're only sitting here today because our source put his life in danger to bring us this information. He didn't have to do it, we asked him to. In the eight years he's worked for us, not once has he accepted a dime, not once has he misled us, and not once has he said it couldn't be done. I told this to Angela, and now I'll tell you, Mr. President: the United States has not had a better source overseas in fifty years. He's a stranger to all of you, myself included, but I know this much—he has endured more pain in one lifetime than any man should. And he does not deserve to die. Do that, sir, and he will. I promise you."

"He's right, Andrew," Weisel quietly admitted from her chair.

Paulson held Freeman's gaze and then turned his attention down the table. "Admiral Benson?"

"Sir?"

"We're gonna need to cover our asses. What's our standing force posture in the Middle East?"

"Mr. President, as it stands today, we have five hundred SOF advisers remaining in Baghdad and Erbil; another twenty-five hundred support personnel on the ground in Kuwait. In Qatar, the 379th Wing at al-Udeid hosts several B-1 bombers, KC-135 refuelers and an assortment of ISR aircraft. At Al Dhafra Air Base in the UAE, the 380th Wing has KC-10s and Global Hawks. In the Arabian Sea, we have the *Stennis* Strike Group with its full complement of F-18s. Also, the *Nimitz* just left Pearl Harbor. She has another port call in Singapore, but is scheduled to enter CENTCOM's area of responsibility by mid-March."

"If I may add," Secretary Rusk cut in, "I'd recommend increasing our maritime security assets in the region. If Russia does cut ties with Tehran we could see blowback on Gulf shipping."

"What are our options there?"

Benson answered. "The *Bataan* Amphibious Ready Group is in the middle of its pre-deployment workup. We could cut that training short and push up their departure date. The 22nd Marine Expeditionary Unit is embarked with it. Stationing the *Bataan* with the *Nimitz* in the Persian Gulf would cover us with any contingencies.

"Okay, let's get that moving ASAP," Paulson nodded. "I think I'm done on this. Angela and Harold, draft a letter to Khansari so I can read it. Eli and Larry, see that we get an executive ordered prepped on those additional sanctions. Director Freeman—Ryan—standby; I'll sleep on your proposal and get back to you tomorrow. That does it," he gathered his folio and rose. "Thanks for coming." The president left with Jacobs and Eli in hot pursuit.

Passing the Ward Room, Freeman pulled Weisel aside. "What the hell was that? What happened in there?"

She was just as stunned as him. "Ryan, you were fantastic."

"How?" he blurted in disbelief. "What did I say?"

Weisel shrugged.

"Angela, what was that?"

"I don't think I've ever seen him that decisive."

"That was a little more than decisive."

"Oh, you wanted a twenty-minute diatribe from Brandon?"

"Right," Freeman admitted. "So what now?"

Weisel ran her fingers through her hair and sighed. "Harold and I go back and starting writing a letter to a man who can barely read... And you wait."

"Sir, for what it's worth," Stavros offered, "I'm pretty happy."

"Yeah, you're front and center now," said Freeman. "What about Eli?"

"What about him?" Weisel blinked.

"He and the vice president just bend over?"

"No," she said matter-of-factly and smiled. "But I told you I had this under control. You just need to start trusting me."

CHAPTER 33

ZYED BATA CAME to the only place that would have him. He rapped at the door on the ninth story of the tower block at La Forestière, anxiously waiting to get out of the hall. A junkie slumped lifelessly in the landing of the far stairwell and in the opposite flat an argument seeped through the crumbling plaster. Zyed knocked again. This time the door opened, revealing Badi Haddad, who for a moment strained to recognize the boy. A hood obscured his face in the dim light.

"Zyed?" Haddad squinted, noticing the bruised and swollen mass of flesh that enveloped his left eye. The boys hadn't visited his flat in the week since Fabrice and his thugs thrashed Zyed against the pavement. Haddad was worried that he'd gone too far, exposed his hand in firing at the bastards. He'd surely saved Zyed's life that night, but had he also scared the boys away? Now, looking at that defeated, mangled wretch on his doorstep, Haddad had his answer. And he knew at once what the boy had come back to learn.

"I wasn't sure if I'd ever see you again."

"No," Zyed dipped his head. "It's okay. I can go if—"

"Never," Haddad lifted the boy's chin. "You are *always* welcome here." He brought Zyed inside and bolted the door behind them. "Show me what they did to you." Haddad tugged the hood from Zyed's hair and ducked down to meet the boy's sad green eyes. Rusty brown scabs marred his brow and the bridge of his nose. A black and blue splotch ran along the side of his face. "Does it hurt?"

Zyed offered no reply; a tear streaked toward his jaw.

"Come sit." Haddad sat the boy next to him on his tattered sofa. "Where's your brother? Where is Sajid?"

"I sent him to school," Zyed sniffed.

"How is he?"

Zyed shrugged.

"Has anyone bothered you?"

Zyed shook his head.

"Good," Haddad said. "What did you tell your grandmother?"

"I told her the truth"

Haddad was alarmed for a moment. "You told her about the gun?"

"No," the boy shook his head again. "We haven't said anything about you. I just told her some men tried to rob us and I protected Sajid. She wasn't happy that I got into a fight."

"You were right to defend yourself," Haddad frowned.

Zyed looked at the floor. "I didn't defend anybody. If you hadn't come, I don't know what would've happened. Thank you, Badi, for saving me. You were right—we are brothers."

"It was only by the will of Allah," Haddad dismissed with a grin. "He has great plans for you."

The two were silent for a minute before Haddad asked, "Would you like to smoke with me? Or have a drink?"

"No," Zyed answered firmly. "I don't want to do any of that anymore. Since that night, I've been reading from the Quran. And I have questions."

"*Alhamdulillah,*" Haddad happily patted the boy's shoulders.

"You told us before about someone you knew who gave himself to a martyrdom operation. Ali Saffedine?"

Haddad nodded. "That was his name in life. Now, my brothers know him as '*al-Shahid al-Ammar,*' and he smiles upon us from Paradise, alongside all *shaheed,* and the prophets, and even Allah."

"Did you know others like him?"

"Many."

"Why did they do that? Why did they give their lives?"

"Oh, but they did not give their lives," Haddad inched toward him. "They gave their bodies, a temporary vessel that God gives us in order to walk upon this earth for but a short while. When He commands, the Quran says that we are called back to our true home, to live for eternity in Paradise. My brothers merely answered His call."

Zyed held for a moment, feeling the pain, the quiet agony he fought to subdue that ran throughout his own body—a weary and broken vessel that the boy was all too eager to shed. "Did it hurt?" he asked.

"Never." Haddad shook his head. "It's as simple as falling asleep."

"Something took their pain away?"

"God did, my brother."

Zyed's eyes ran over the flat. "You said you fought for Hezbollah. These *shaheed* did too?"

"They certainly did. And plenty more still fight."

"Why?"

"This was in my youth," Haddad hoisted his legs beneath him, "about the same age as you and Sajid. My village was tucked in this little valley in southern Lebanon. I wasn't as fortunate as you to have a brother from birth, but Allah was good to grant me two in life. One was Ali Saffedine, as we then knew him, and the other was Omar Othman. We were inseparable, the greatest of friends. But as you know, our village and the whole country was under occupation."

"By the Zionists?"

Haddad nodded. "They came with tanks and mines and artillery. They bulldozed homes, murdered women and children. We vowed not to be powerless. We rose up in jihad against the Zionists and formed our own army to fight them, an army under the banners of Almighty God."

"Hezbollah?"

"That's right," said Haddad. "We were foot soldiers in the service of an unwavering commander, and in time—with the martyrdom of many *sha-heed*—the Islamic Resistance spilled the Zionists' blood and ran most from our lands, but more brothers are still fighting today. And it was all due to our commander, the greatest man I have ever known."

"What was his name?"

"Ibrahim al-Din."

Zyed's eyes widened. "You fought for Abu Dokhan?"

"Yes," Haddad admitted with a humble laugh, "and I still do."

"I never knew that."

"But, Zyed, you cannot tell a soul," Haddad urged, "not even Sajid."

"Brother Badi, I would swear before God never to break your trust."

"Good," Haddad pressed his hands to his knees.

"I want to be a martyr, a *shahid* like your brothers."

"Wouldn't we all?"

But the boy was serious, much more so than Haddad realized. "I mean it," Zyed's gaze narrowed, "I want to join a martyrdom operation."

"Zyed," Haddad scoffed, "it isn't that simple. There must be orders."

"Why?" he raced. "Why not here, in France? In Clichy-sous-Bois? In La Forestière? There are *kuffar* everywhere. Why can't we kill them as Allah says?"

Haddad struggled to contain him. "Martyrdom is a gift that must be given."

"And what if life is a gift I did not want?" Zyed cried and doubled over.

Haddad rubbed his hand along the boy's heaving back. "Zyed? Please, Zyed. Look at me."

But the boy's trembling hands masked his scarred face. "Every day since we came here, I told myself it was not true. I said I was taught to put my faith in God, and that it couldn't be true. It was evil," he croaked. "And then I fell in that street. And they beat me. I knew I was going to die. But then I saw him." Zyed sat upright and wiped his nose with his sleeve. "I saw *him.*"

Haddad looked on.

Zyed shuddered, staring away into the void. "And he was exactly what that lunatic told us. He touched me as they kicked and punched, and he felt more real than you do now. He was blacker than anything I'd ever seen. He didn't have eyes. But he looked at me. He looked inside of me. And, for a second, he took my pain away. Not just the pain I felt then in that street, but all of it—all the pain I'd ever known. It was gone. He knew my name. And he called to me. I knew if I went with him, I'd never feel pain again. All I had to do was say yes, and I could go with him. Forever. I wanted to. But then I heard those shots, the bullets hit the street, and I saw you come and pull Fabrice off me."

Zyed took a deep breath, collecting himself.

"And then he was gone," the boy struggled to explain. "All the pain was there. I knew I was alive…but I didn't want to be. Now, every night when I close my eyes, I call for him. *Come back.* But then I open them. And he's gone."

Haddad pulled away and came to his feet. "Wait here, Zyed." He went to his galley kitchen and filled a glass under the faucet. The boy genuinely frightened him, but Zyed's commitment to martyrdom also excited Haddad. He and his brother were the first promising recruitment target Haddad was given in the years since al-Din's group sent him to the miserable slums outside Paris. Much had changed since then. Hezbollah did not easily strike abroad anymore; politics in Lebanon overcame the will to fight. Haddad resented that the Islamic Resistance had stuck him here, but the boys presented an opportunity that he couldn't overlook. An eager *shahid* in Europe, a walking clothes hanger for a suicide vest, might prove useful, especially if the rumors he'd heard were true: that Hezbollah's ranks roiled with disgust at the clerics in the Security Quarter, itching for the next war—the last war.

Before Haddad could report back to his controller in Beirut, he needed answers to the questions that were left burrowed under the boy's skin. He needed Zyed to bear what scraps of his soul remained.

Haddad sat beside the boy again and wedged the glass in his trembling hands. "Drink this," he said, "and breathe."

Zyed gulped the water down, wiping the remains from his lips.

Haddad imposed himself next to the boy, leaving scarcely an inch between them. "Zyed, if not I'll understand, but can you share with me what happened to you and your brother in Syria? You've never told me how you came here."

"No, it's okay," he cleared the snot from his nose. "I should've told you before. I can't be like this with Sajid. I have to be strong for him."

"You don't have to be strong here," Haddad smiled. "You're always safe with me, my friend."

Zyed panted for a moment, letting the familiar demons come for him, and then he began. "We're from Nubl, on the road between Aleppo and Turkey."

"I know where that is," Haddad said.

"The war left us alone for almost four years. The army protected us. We're all Shias, like you, so there were always bandits that tried to come and raid the town, but the soldiers were good to us. Whatever they were doing in the rest of Syria, we didn't know, we didn't care. We heard some stories, but mostly we were told that the rebels were terrorists, sent by America and the Zionists. And as for Daesh," Zyed used the Arabic term for ISIS, "they were so far away. For years, the war was only something we saw on TV. But that changed."

Haddad tried to look him in the eyes, but the boy's focus was elsewhere.

"The rebels came at sunrise. Sajid and I were sleeping, and we heard the blast. It woke us. The house shook, and I thought it was an earthquake, but I knew we never had one of those before. Down the street I heard men shouting, and I heard their rifles. I remember Sajid was screaming, but over him I heard a moan. It was weak, but for some reason it stood out to me over the noise. Our parents slept in the next room and I just went there without thinking. I opened the door, and all I could see was gray dust, over everything. I heard that same moan, but louder this time. As I turned my head, I saw that where there should've been a wall, there was the sun, and smoke. I looked down, and in the dust I saw bones, and blood, and what looked like meat we got from the butcher. That's what it smelled like, too. I saw a face staring back at me from the dust. It looked like my father's, but it wasn't his anymore."

It struck Haddad how calmly Zyed spoke, like it was a sequence of events he'd trained himself to regurgitate without any recognition of the weight of the words that fell from his tongue. The details, to him, were coldly familiar.

"Across the room was my parents' bed, where the moans were loudest. I moved through the gray dust and it covered me. The bed was red, and squirming, but I knew that was wrong—their sheets were white. Sajid was still screaming in the next room. But the moans... When I was little I saw a cow get split open by a bus, and those sounds it made, that's exactly what this was. I looked at the bed, and it was my mother. She looked back at me, and she was still there, she still knew me. There was a piece of metal that tore through her waist; her legs were on one side, the rest of her on the other. I touched it for some reason and it burned my fingers. Half of her moved like tentacles, like squid you see getting chopped up in a market; and as she moved, the bed turned redder, and her face and her eyes, that still clung to me, turned the same shade of gray as the dust around us. I watched her sink into that gray dust for I don't know how long. I only looked away when Sajid came in, and when I looked back, her eyes were closed, and there was nothing left to see."

The boy smirked. "Sajid shit himself."

"But we couldn't stay there," Zyed continued. "Worse noises were coming up the street. We had to run. I took Sajid's hand and we went, where the wall should've been, into that sun. And we ran, and ran, and ran across the field. I turned back once. There was smoke rising over the town, flashes and flames. We kept running. Sajid fell. I pulled him up and I slapped him. We kept running. If I cried, I don't remember. I couldn't. I had to be strong for the both us. Somehow I knew that if I cried, we would die. But we shouldn't have made it that far."

"You escaped the rebels?"

The boy nodded.

"I wanted to live," Zyed shook his head, as if it were a foolish notion to which he'd long ago grown wise. "We must have run twenty kilometers. It was dark by the time we collapsed. We came to a riverbank and hid in the reeds. It was winter and the water had frozen over. I took a stick and poked holes in the ice so we could drink, and I dug as much as I could into the dirt and pulled out bugs to eat. I didn't sleep that night, or any others. We spent four days in those reeds until I convinced Sajid that we had to keep moving. I don't know where we were supposed to go—any place that wasn't where we were then. Not an hour after we started walking, the rebels captured us. It was a different group, not the ones that hit Nubl. They were kind to us. For some reason I told them we were from Aleppo and ran away from home. I think they wanted to ransom us to the government, so they tied us up in one of their trucks, and took us to the city. But they didn't last very long."

Haddad touched the boy's arm. "You don't need to tell me everything. If it's too hard, then—"

"But I want to," said Zyed. "It reminds me why this world has to end."

Haddad eased off.

"When we came to Aleppo, the army attacked the rebels who took us. I pulled Sajid under the seats. Bullets shattered the windows. Both of us were soaked in blood. Somehow we crawled from the truck and into the rubble. It took us a few days to get away from the fighting. We kept moving back, as far from the gunfire as we could get. When we heard shooting in front of us, we found a different way. That kept us alive, for a while, until we found what was left of that church—the Cathedral of the Forty Martyrs."

Haddad's saw the boy's larynx quiver in his throat. Zyed paused, panting again, fighting for composure, and he pressed on—not away from the darkness, but straight toward it, and gaining.

"Sajid didn't want to set foot in that cathedral, but I made him. He said it was an evil place. But we had to, night was coming and I thought we wouldn't survive another in the open. I'd been in churches before, smaller ones, and they're always full of gold and cloth and paintings. This one had none of those things. It was darker inside than out. Most of the ceiling had caved in, soot covered what was left, and I remember looking up at these huge stone arches that had been ripped apart to almost nothing. But we could hide, which I guess is what mattered. We found stairs in the rubble, going down, and we followed them under the cathedral. We felt safe down there, and we slept, both of us."

Zyed waited to find the words. "That morning Sajid woke up screaming. A man stood over us, but it's not right to call him that. He, um, didn't look like a person. His hair, and beard, and nails, and the smell—he wasn't like anyone I'd seen, or hoped to see. And his eyes… He could see us, somehow, and when he opened them all the way, they were like sour milk. And there were thin scars, raised scars—two over each socket—that cut into the lids and the skin around his brow. But he could still see, just not well. We panicked, we both did, but something told me he wouldn't hurt us. He said he'd been a priest, Armenian, and those ruins above used to be his. His name was Father Avraam."

The boy purged his lungs and struggled. "The first two weeks with Father Avraam weren't bad, compared to what we had before. He shared his food and water with us, but he kept to himself. Sajid never wanted to look at him. I got the feeling the priest had been down there since the war started, or at least until the fighting came to the old part of Aleppo. When everyone ran, he stayed. He didn't seem to know much about what was happening outside, and he didn't seem to care. He said we were always free to go whenever we wanted, but he begged us only to leave at night."

"Why?" Haddad asked.

The boy's jaw tightened. "Because ghosts walk the streets at night. Aleppo, he said, belonged to the dead, and only the dead know mercy. That should've been enough for me. I should've taken Sajid and left, but I didn't. I was so tired of running. In a way I knew the priest, and while I dreaded him, I still dreaded him less than what I didn't know outside. But it only got worse. Every night was worse. Eventually I got the courage to ask him about his eyes. I expected him to tell me that he was tortured, or that an animal had done it. But nothing I could have imagined came close."

Zyed shivered. "Father Avraam said he took a razor and did it to himself. He tried to scratch out his own eyes, because—as he told us—this was no longer a world he wanted to see. And then the priest told us everything. He told us that God was dead, that there was no heaven, no Paradise, only an eternal hell right here on Earth that we're doomed to suffer again and again. He told us that 'life is an infinite festival of massacres.' I'll never forget that. Somewhere in those tunnels, the priest said, a shadow had come to him, and that shadow was the only truth he still believed in. How'd he put it?" Zyed struggled. "He told us that it was 'the raw singularity' that forces all mankind to stand naked before the silent, unblinking void.' It offers us a gift—an escape from the massacre, from the conscious life none of us have ever asked to know—and all we need to do to have peace is to let it take us into that void. Just say yes and it all ends."

"No," Haddad implored, "that priest was evil, delusional, full of lies."

"Either way," Zyed said, "it went on like that. For weeks, months—I really don't know how long we were down there. Sajid wouldn't go near him, and whenever I mentioned him, Sajid cried. Each time Father Avraam spoke about the shadow, he became a bit more commanding, like he expected something from me. I don't think he liked Sajid; the priest thought he was weak."

"How did you ever get out?"

"One week it sounded like those tunnels would fall on us—explosions outside, every few minutes. Gunfire, too. It never stopped. Of course, I learned that Daesh pushed into the city and that Turkey invaded the country to end the war. But down there, we had no idea. As the fighting got worse, so did Father Avraam. A few days passed and we didn't see him, which was strange. One night he showed up again, out of the blue. He came to where we were sleeping and starting shouting at Sajid. It horrified us; whatever he said, it wasn't in Arabic. I settled the priest down, and he disappeared back into the tunnels, but I knew after that we had to leave. I couldn't keep Sajid down there. Even if it meant going up into the fighting, I had to get him out. Still, it got worse."

Zyed hunched over. "The next day, I tried to plan how we would escape. I spent hours listening to the bombs and the shooting outside, and I noticed that at dawn it was almost silent. The fighting must have stopped for prayers. So I told Sajid that we'd leave the next morning, find a break in the lines and hopefully the army would save us. I hoped. But first we had to get as much rest as we could. That same night I woke up, again, to Sajid screaming. I saw Father Avraam there in the darkness, pouring something over him. It smelled like petrol. I shoved the priest to the floor, took Sajid and ran. Even with his eyes the way they were, he still managed to chase us. We shot up to the surface and into the light as a Daesh patrol moved past the ruins. I never expect to see them so far into the city, but I recognized their black flags, and I'd heard the stories. Before they spotted us, I dragged Sajid into what I guess was once a chapel and waited for them to pass. Then Father Avraam came up the stairs. He saw them too. But he didn't run. He charged right at them, dropped on his knees, and cried out for death. I almost smothered Sajid to keep him quiet. I tried to look away, but I couldn't. I wanted to see what they would do to him.

"One of the terrorists," Zyed continued, "I remember, with a red beard, looked in charge. He stopped the patrol and they surrounded the priest. Father Avraam was still on knees. He spat at them, chanting, *'Death! Death! Death!'* They laughed at him, and I saw one kick him in the head. He fell over, and even on his back, he kept shrieking, *'Death! Death! Death!'* They brought him back to his knees and the one with the red beard pulled a knife from his belt, stood over the priest and gripped his hair. And then started sawing. I saw his blood spill over the ruins. He didn't scream, and I only heard his last cry once that blade was buried in his throat. After they left, we snuck through the fighting and found the Turkish Army maybe a mile outside the city," Zyed said. "They drove us to a United Nations camp and we told them our grandmother lived in France."

Haddad was still. He couldn't pinpoint a single word that might begin to shape an adequate response. Luckily he wouldn't have to.

Zyed shifted at the end of the sofa, still glaring into the void, and ran his palm through the beaded sweat on his forehead. "Could I have another?" Zyed lifted the glass.

Haddad carried the glass back to the kitchen while the boy kept speaking.

"After I left Sajid at school this morning, I took a bus to the RER station in Gagny. I bought a ticket, but I didn't want to go anywhere. I sat near the end of the platform, watching all of these blank faces come and go. None of them saw me. For a minute, less than that, I was happy. I told myself I must be invisible, unreachable to everyone and everything in this world. And I realized: this is how the dead must feel; this is how Father Avraam must feel right now. And I asked myself, why would anyone not want this? Forever. Just…to be left alone. To let it all end. I saw the trains rushing in. But I couldn't do it. That shadow was right there in front of me, its black hand ready to lead me onto the tracks…"

Haddad returned and handed him the glass. "This is evil," he said. "Zyed, that priest lost his mind in those tunnels and he filled yours with lies."

"Was it a lie when your friend became a martyr?"

Haddad hesitated. "No. He gave himself to a purpose."

"Then give me a purpose!" Zyed cried. The glass slipped from his hands and shattered. His voice gave and loosed an appalling wail.

Haddad swallowed the boy in his arms and pressed Zyed's head against his chest. "I'm sorry this happened to you."

At first Zyed's sobs were stifled as the last dignified shred of him struggled to hide his grief. And then the gates fell. His legs melted onto the floorboards, the rest of him held only by Haddad's strength. The boy's eyes bled pain and his voice cracked, the cries yielding to silence. Zyed gasped into Haddad's chest, "I miss my mother!"

"I'm sorry," Haddad muttered in his ear.

"I want to go home and I can't," he cried. "I want this nightmare to end, and for as much as I scream, *'Wake up! Zyed, wake up!'* I'm still here."

"I'm sorry."

"And that shadow!" Zyed wailed. "That shadow's all I see. I want him to take me. I want to go. I want to just let go. But I can't!"

"Zyed, you are my brother now and always…"

"I can't do it alone. I tried. I won't go with him alone!"

"You won't," Haddad vowed with a whisper. "You won't die alone."

CHAPTER 34

FREEMAN'S HAND HOVERED over the end table, ready to swat the source of the monotone chirps that coaxed him awake. He grasped his BlackBerry and tilted it up to view the harshly radiant screen. The phone pulsed in his fingers, it was only two in the morning and the caller ID merely proffered: "Unknown."

He knew nothing good would come of this.

Mary was turned away from him, still fast asleep. Freeman picked the phone off the table, cupping his palm over the speaker. He swung his legs out from the bedspread and started quietly into the hallway. Midway down the stairs, he pressed the BlackBerry to his ear. "Hello?"

"Director Freeman?" asked a female voice in a tone more alert than anyone should be at that hour.

"Yes?"

"Please hold for the president."

Those five words struck Freeman like lightning. His spine straightened and his eyes fluttered back to life. He cleared his throat. Maybe something good would come from this—and maybe not. Freeman left the White House mostly empty-handed. Operation PACER hadn't been aborted in an avalanche of ridicule and condemnation, but its birth was hardly assured. But the president didn't give bad news; his minions were perfectly capable of that. Perhaps Freeman was about to get the answer he wanted, or perhaps he would have to mount a last-ditch defense. Why else would the leader of the free world call him at home in the middle of the night?

Freeman made for the sitting room, his path marked by dim LED lights dotting the house. The line clicked twice and the president's voice rose on the other end.

"Ryan? You there?"

"I'm here, Mr. President."

"Ryan, this is Andrew Paulson," he stated the obvious.

Freeman's head spun back toward the kitchen. His security detail's shift commander peered out from the basement stairwell.

"Everything okay, sir?" the officer asked.

"It's fine, thanks."

"Sorry?" said Paulson.

"Oh no, sir," Freeman stuttered. "I was just talking to one of the guys on my detail here."

"Right," the president paused. "How are you? Were you sleeping?"

"I was, but that's no problem..."

"Of course. It's late." Paulson stood in the Treaty Room, his personal study on the second floor of the family quarters, watching the traffic floating along Constitution Avenue as sparse red and white orbs beyond the South Lawn. "Listen, I won't take much of your time."

Freeman came to the picture window where Isaac's flowers once sat.

"I've put some thought into this Iran business," the president continued, "and I'm green-lighting your op."

"Okay," Freeman accepted. "We won't fail you, sir."

"This is only authorization to bring in JSOC's operators, contact Gorani and prepare the details—cross the T's and dot the I's. We're not launching just yet. State has priority to see if they can't work something out with Khansari. I'm cautiously optimistic that they can, but one way or another, what the IRGC is doing can't stand."

"I totally agree."

"You know, Ryan," Paulson glanced over to Larry Dawson, waiting in a nearby chair, "Angela speaks highly of you."

"That means a lot coming from her."

"Right," the president's voice wavered. "We haven't exactly had a moment to sit down man-to-man. I'm sorry about that. But I wanted to make sure you're aware that I'm grateful for the hard work that you and everyone at Langley does for this country. It's an honor to have you in my administration, and please know that the American people are safer because of your service."

"Thank you very much, Mr. President."

"Okay, well I don't want to take more of your time. We'll talk soon."

"Goodnight, sir."

The line went dead and Freeman was left holding his phone, staring into the serene gloom lingering above Highland Drive.

• • •

Atop a snow-capped spur of Mount Hermon called "Mitzpe Slagim," on the northern shoulder of the Golan Heights, three geodesic radomes sprouted from the barren ground. Each golf ball-shaped fiberglass enclosure housed a range of electronic monitoring and communications intercept antennas. The ground station's location, seventy-three hundred feet over the Upper Jordan Valley, allowed the sensitive equipment to wring the whole gamut of electromagnetic signals from the atmosphere like a sponge. The surrounding air hid its share of secrets, too. At the intersection of Israel, Lebanon and Syria, Mount Hermon was the highest summit in the region and straddled a tangled knot of demilitarized zones and contested international borders. On a clear day, it was even possible to glimpse Damascus with the naked eye.

This position made the installation atop Mount Hermon Israel's first warning against a surprise attack from it's enemies to the north. A cordon of elite reservists from the IDF's Alpinist Unit patrolled the slopes with customized skis and armor-plated Snowcats and guarded several thin tunnel portals blasted into the mountainside. Inside those tunnels, teams of soldiers worked in continuous shifts to record, interpret and analyze the haul. Dressed in loose-fitting olive fatigues, most were practically still children between eighteen and twenty-two, conscripts in mandatory service to the IDF, but all were fluent in Arabic and English. They clutched headphones to their skulls and read computer screens with attentive eyes. In a shift, the soldiers would eavesdrop on the radio chatter of the UN peacekeeping forces watching the Golan and the Lebanese border, intercept diplomatic communications from Damascus, and even sometimes monitor the encrypted conversations between Hezbollah units dug into their bunker complexes around the Litani River. However, those soldiers manning an outpost of Unit 8200, the IDF's signals intelligence agency, did not just collect the scraps of information that happened to float their way, they also had a mission to target certain individuals moving on the ground who'd piqued Israel's attention.

Working with its counterparts in Mossad, Unit 8200 had clandestinely installed taps on the key network switches of Lebanon's Internet service providers and mobile phone operators, giving Israeli intelligence the capability to monitor each shred of unencrypted data originating within or passing through the country. Virtually every cell, landline or satellite telephone and web-connected computer inside Lebanon was within reach, and the soldiers on Mount Hermon could cast their nets as broadly or as tightly as necessary with just a few taps of their keyboards. One soldier, an analyst for Unit 8200, sat at her terminal with a tasking order forwarded from the headquarters of the IDF's Military Intelligence Directorate—known as Aman—at Camp Herzog in Herzliya. The order listed phone numbers and email addresses that would be used to support an operation down the slopes in Lebanon. The analyst utilized a software program based on the National Security Agency's XKeyscore, which established parameters for the network taps to siphon any data connected to those numbers and addresses. She typed each one into the proper fields on her screen, setting "selectors" for the taps to monitor, and let the program run.

Now any time a message was sent or delivered to those phone numbers and email addresses, any time a call was placed, any time an online chat was initiated or a website was visited, the taps would record it in real-time and save it to the massive servers at Camp Herzog. While she wasn't cleared to know, all that data was attached to a single man.

At midday, Turkish Airlines Flight 1865 landed at Rome's Fiumicino Airport from Istanbul. Still fresh from the two-hour hop over the Aegean and Adriatic seas, passengers swept up the jetway and into Terminal 3, joining the other dregs arriving from around the globe. Most were Asian or American tourists coming to swarm Italy's ancient sights in the off-season, and more still were business travelers or Europeans rushing to connecting flights home. Most were harmless, but one did not share their benign intentions.

Dressed casually in jeans and towing an aluminum suitcase, Ruslan Baranov moved like a wolf camouflaged in the flock. He knew that this was one of the riskiest moments of the mission, both for him and the fourteen other members of his team arriving throughout the day from Tunis, Algiers, Cairo, Rabat and Amman. Crossing into Europe, while easier than in decades past, was still a serious undertaking. The EU's Schengen Agreement removed the internal border controls of its twenty-six signatories, allowing unrestricted movement of goods and people between them, but it had also strengthened their external borders with standardized procedures and technologies. If Baranov and his men could get through, which he was confident they would, the team would have full, anonymous reign over the continent.

The herd bottlenecked at passport control, diverting into two lanes: one for EU and Schengen passport holders, and a second for all other nationalities. Baranov held a Latvian passport, expertly forged by the GRU with a carefully curated legend of visas meant to deter interest in its holder. As Latvia was an EU member state, he moved into the former lane, bypassing immigration and customs. But there were other obstacles: a pair of Carabinieri military police officers stood with navy blue berets, body armor and Beretta AR90 assault rifles, scanning the crowd; surveillance cameras panned overhead, watching for the physiological signs of nervousness. But Baranov and his team were trained to shrug those tells aside, to look thoroughly mundane and forgettable. It worked flawlessly. Coming into the terminal without an ounce of scrutiny, he boarded a Leonardo Express train to Termini Station, buying his ticket with cash.

From the station, in the *rione* of Esquilino, Baranov walked a few kilometers to an address on Via Mario dè Fiori, a narrow cobblestone street near the Spanish Steps. On the top floor of a three-centuries-old building that leaned over the cobbles, was a flat kept by the GRU's residency in Rome for transient officers. It was spacious, although a bit worn and furnished with plastic tables and chairs. Yellowed newspaper covered the windows. Baranov was first to arrive.

The remainder of Baranov's team trickled in over the next four hours. They entered Italy undetected using Danish, German, Polish, and Lithuanian passports. Kazanoff had deployed nearly half of his contingent to Europe. Among them were some of the GRU's most vicious and capable killers. All had seen years of combat in Russia's most recent and officially disavowed entanglements. Some were pulled from the ranks of the *"Umarovtsky"*—the private army of Chechen president, Ramzan Umarov—a militia whose unorthodox methods were equally feared and renowned. Others had served in the 10th and 22nd Spetsnaz Brigades, the masked "little green men" who ran the Georgians out of South Ossetia, seized the Crimean peninsula from Ukraine and worked incessantly to foment an armed insurgency in the Donbass. None had families to their names and few would admit to caring if they lived or died; they were tools, instruments of death whose work could be as precise or blunt as their commander wished. And their current commander had dispatched them with one very blunt objective: ignite war in the Middle East.

Once they all arrived—fifteen dour men packed into the flat's front room—Baranov began the briefing. Kazanoff gave precise instructions for their mission, and they knew he wasn't a man to fail. When contacting local GRU residencies for support on the ground, the men were to explain that they were part of a classified operation directed personally by General Trubnikov in Moscow. If the matter were pressed further, anyone questioning was to be swiftly reminded of his place. Baranov's team would be divided into four sections: The first, consisting of two men—Glazkov and Bezhaev—would stay in Rome to operate the communications net. A secure, burst transmission radio in the flat would link the team back to the farmhouse in Zarayeb. At a set time, a Spetsnaz operator from each section would use a different prepaid SIM card, one for each day of the mission, and place a call to either Glazkov or Bezhaev, who would select a random location in Rome and wait for their calls. Each section would give a report, which would in turn be transmitted back to the Beqaa Valley via encrypted radio. A list of code words was made for operational security. The second section—Zaytsev, Ratskov and Lazarev—would catch a flight to Athens the next day with two million euros in traveler's cheques. Their objective would be to purchase a yacht for sale by a bankrupt media mogul and standby in Greece for additional orders. The third and fourth sections, the bulk of the team, would prepare their equipment and depart together for Paris. Once the targets Kazanoff had given were identified, the third section—Vlasiyev, Ibragimov, Pokhrovskii, Isayev and Dratchev—would remain in France for execution. Meanwhile, the fourth—Akhmadov, Kakiyev, Ignatev, Kotov and Baranov, himself—would move on to Germany and liaise with their local contact in Germany. Their objective, by far the most important to Kazanoff, would be to retrieve what they only called "the *ranet*" and ready it for extraction back to Lebanon.

The Volvo's headlights raked the alleyway and illuminated the service exit. In a few moments, Nina could toss him back in the pond, free to undulate through the muck and snatch another unsuspecting minnow in his jaws.

She'd driven a countersurveillance route through the hills of eastern Beirut, bringing Colonel Samir Basri—TOPSAIL—up to speed on the mounting operation to force a defection of Walid Rada. To keep the colonel from a full-on revolt, Mossad and Nathan Cohen's involvement in the operation wasn't mentioned. For all he knew, this was strictly a CIA endeavor. Basri, to Nina's minor astonishment, didn't much mind. As chief of the Internal Security Forces' *Bureau d'information,* the colonel had a wealth of assets at his fingertips, and for the right price he was more than willing to sit on his hands while the storm passed. But for Nina, Basri had only one request: no one dies in Lebanon.

It was a promise she did not intend to break.

Nina pulled into the alley behind Basri's flat on Rue Gouraud and threw the Volvo in park. "Thanks for your help," she stared at the golden haze ahead.

"It'd be a shame to waste Uncle Sam's money." He plucked a fat envelope from her hand.

"Just keep your people out of Machgara, don't provoke Hezbollah, and when it all goes down, play dumb. Play dumb, Samir," she reiterated.

"I should manage that just fine," Basri smiled.

"This'll all be over soon."

"Will it?"

Nina cast a look off the rear-view mirror.

"Will it be over soon?"

She rolled her eyes. "What the fuck are you talking about?"

"Have you ever asked yourself how this ends?"

Nina paused. She hadn't. Not even once—from the moment she'd waded into the mosquito-infested swamps along the York River at the Farm, to when she'd first watched a JSOC team kick in a door at the time and place of her choosing, to just then when, she'd bribed a treasonous child molest-er—did Nina ever think to ask herself how this all ends. Perhaps, some-where in her mind, she couldn't bear to. Maybe that thought was just too terrifying. After all, if it did end—like a dog chasing its tail—what the hell would she do?

Better to not be so pensive. "What kind of bullshit question is that?"

Basri sat upright. "Let's say, just because, that you do get Rada to defect and Hezbollah doesn't shoot you all to bits, you fly him back to Washing-ton and all's well… What happens then?"

Nina shrugged. "We drill him until there's nothing left."

"And you just walk away?"

"No," she grew annoyed.

"Then what?"

She looked back to the haze. "I don't know."

Basri touched her shoulder. "Remember what I said about stabbing flags in the ground. The storm tends to blow them loose."

"Never took you for a poet," Nina spat sarcastically.

"No, me neither," he said. "But a bird sung me a song that the caul-dron's brewing in the *dahieh*. That's all."

"And you're just telling me this now?"

"I know you don't like rumors."

She bit her lip. "What happened?"

"Marwan Kadi was summoned to the Security Quarter. You know, he's—"

"Commander of the Fajr Unit. Thanks, I'm aware."

"Right, well, Wissam Hamawi and all the show-offs on the Shura Coun-cil were there," said Basri. "They wanted him to present a plan on how his cadres intend to disarm with the Islamic Resistance come summer. Gaza was raised. Kadi wants Hezbollah to open a northern front. It didn't go well. He stormed out and Hamawi's tried to reach him for days."

"Cool story," she said.

"Kadi makes a dangerous enemy for the clerics. He commands three thousand men at arms spread around Beirut; they could seize the city before anyone could mobilize to stop it. With the right friends—"

"I know," Nina cut him off.

Basri opened the car door an inch and stopped. "Ask yourself again, Ni-na—how does this end?"

It surprised Harris at how quickly Maggie had availed herself of Z's condo. The living room furniture was completely rearranged since his last visit, and much of it looked brand new. When Harris blindly reached into a cabinet, expecting to find the chipped whiskey glasses that had rightfully sat there for years, he found plates, and not made of paper, but pristine, polished porcelain. Confused, Harris froze until Maggie floated over and happily pointed out where the new glasses were stashed, as if—silly him—he didn't know. And Harris wouldn't dare think what travesty Z's bedroom must have become. From what Harris understood, Maggie didn't even live there—yet. It frightened him to think about that eventuality, although he felt selfish to admit it. A woman like Maggie, or at least one like she seemed, was an overdue addition into the life of Harris' skirt chasing, gun-toting best friend. They both seemed to genuinely care for each other, which was more than Harris could say for some of Z's other "hit and split" exes. Better still: Z was happy around her. Some industrious soul needed to grab the reins and steer Wilmer Zapata into adulthood, and if Maggie was up for that challenge, Harris could only wish her well. But he swore there was absolutely nothing wrong with those old glasses.

Z was in his element that night. It was an old habit to use his boisterous personality to take disconnected groups of friends and mold them into one over charred meat and copious amounts of alcohol.

Luckily for Harris, his designated driver didn't have a choice.

Creedence Clearwater Revival's cover of "Susie Q" came over the Blue-tooth speakers. Harris plopped an ice cube in his glass and spun around from the countertop. "Sandy, what guitar did John Fogerty use in this song?"

"Rickenbacker," she answered from the living room.

"Did Fogerty write it?"

"No." Sandra beat this interrogation before.

"Who," he refilled the glass with Jameson, "did?"

It took her a moment. "Dale Hawkins?"

"Fuck, leave her alone," Z wrapped his arm around her shoulder, "she's sober!" and laughed.

"I knew I married you for a reason." Harris moved back to join them and leaned over the sofa to kiss her before taking a seat on the carpet.

"Wait, wait," Sandra said as his legs bent, "grab me that."

Harris picked up a throw pillow—which was certainly new—and passed it to her. She wedged it under her lower back for support.

"Alright, guys," Z looked to Whitford and Farah, "so about that badass shot Bryce took..."

"Go ahead, you tell it better," Farah deferred.

Whitford wiped the beer from his mustache. "Right, this was 2010, Ja-mie?"

"August 2010."

"Shit, that long ago already?"

"Yup," Farah nodded.

"We got sent out from J-bad to Gardez," Whitford said. "Admiral Wade and the ambassador were coming in from Kabul for a sit-down with the governor and the PRT commander. The embassy wanted to make a big thing with the press, so we got fucked right there on OPSEC. Anyway, they marked us for security. So we set up in the battlements of that gnarly old fortress right in the middle of town. I got my MacMillan Tac-50, but the humidity was so bad we couldn't see shit. Down the street in front of me, I had overwatch on the governate building and the ANP headquarters. To my left, I could see down the Khost Road maybe eight hundred yards toward Camp Lightning, and after that it was just a blur. The plan was for Wade and them to come in on a helo to the camp and then take a convoy up to Gardez. Eventually, we get the radio call that they'd touched down. We're listening in on the net, and I know they're coming up the road, but I still can't see a damn thing past eight hundred yards. Then I notice a dust cloud at the bottom of my scope. It's this shit, Russian Izmash sedan; ugly-ass green color. I notice the car's back axel is sagging almost to the ground. It's driving south down the Khost Road, right to where the Humvees are heading. So I'm like, 'Fuck, do I try and disable this thing?' The ROE cleared us, but I didn't know if I had the shot, and the farther it went down the road the more it got swept up in that haze. Once the car got to eight hundred yards, all I could see was dust and I fired a round. Thought I'd missed."

"Bryce hit the dude from the back window," Farah explained. "The round went through the seat, struck him center-chest, into the steering column and pierced the engine block. At eight hundred yards."

"Shit," said Harris

"Yeah," Whitford shrugged. "Turns out the driver was hardcore Taliban; intel was hunting him for weeks. They found the trunk packed with shells."

"And then catch what Wade did," Farah added.

"Oh, right," Whitford smiled. "That night, we're back at J-bad around the fire pit and Wade storms up, drops a thirty of Corona in the dirt and says: 'Next time, you pop that motherfucker at two hundred yards!'"

Z burst into laughter and slapped his knees. "Yo, that dude's a legend." He lurched up from the sofa. "Robby, help me with the grill."

Harris came to his feet again and followed Z outside. The patio was small and fenced-in on three sides from the adjacent condo units. Z placed a tray by the grill and lifted the lid, loosing tongues of flame and a whiff of sizzling meat. "Hey, these fumes aren't gonna put you on the deck are they?" he jabbed, giving the burgers one final flip before sliding them on the tray.

"Might," Harris hiccuped.

"What do you think of Maggie?"

Harris tightened his arms against his torso, fortifying himself from the cold. "She's great, dude."

"You think?" Z looked pleasantly surprised.

"Absolutely," Harris forced back another hiccup.

"Seriously, I can't remember the last time I felt this way about a girl."

"I'm happy for you."

"Her and Sandy seem to get along." Z switched off the gas and scraped away the gristle. "They've been talking a lot."

Harris didn't entirely endorse that theory: that Sandra and Maggie would somehow become inseparable and get their nails done together and they could all go out on double dates and laugh for hours and forget that the restaurant was shutting down around them. It wouldn't happen, no matter how much Z pressed his love-struck delusions. Harris knew his wife better than Z knew his girlfriend, and Sandra was simply being nice. "Yeah, that's cool," he lied.

"Man, this'll sound weird, but I've had a few, so fuck it," Z said, closing the lid. "I've always been jealous of you and Sandy."

"Really?"

"It's just like—I dunno—like you guys walked out of a fucking Viagra ad. You're like that old couple they show walking through a field, or some shit."

"Okay," Harris chuckled.

"Not that I need Viagra, or anything, I'm just saying," Z assured. "But it's always weighed on me. You guys are perfect; you have each other's back."

"We're far from perfect," Harris shook his head.

"No, but everyone thinks that. So you are. And I want that."

Harris watched him struggle.

"What you two share is rare, for anybody, but in this line of work, it's damn-near fucking impossible. Somehow, you two have done it."

"It's not easy."

"That doesn't matter," Z insisted. "I want that, for me. If I'm ever downrange again, and I fall, I want to know that someone cares. Sure, I got my teammates and more family than I can count. But once that casket goes in the ground, what's left of me?"

Harris leaned against the clapboard siding. "Z, we all care."

"That's why I left the squadron for Green Team; I couldn't do it," Z admitted. "And that's why I want you to come with me. Because, to tell you the truth: I'm scared."

After dinner, they sat around Z's coffee table. Sandra looked down to her husband on the carpet. "Should we tell them?"

Harris thought for a second and clenched his teeth. "Eh, I dunno."

"Maybe not," she grinned.

"Tell us what?" Z barked.

"I mean, if they want to hear," said Harris.

"No, you can't leave it now," Farah added.

"Alright, I guess we'll tell them."

"I guess," Harris shrugged. "You do it."

"Okay," Sandra took a breath. "We're having a girl."

"What!" Z leapt from the sofa and swallowed her in a bear hug while the others cheered. "That's so great!"

"But we've only told our parents," she laughed.

"I love you guys, you know that, right?" Z kissed her forehead.

Whitford leaned over and slapped Harris' back. "Nice, man."

"Hold on," Z bounded up the stairs, returning in a moment with a box of Padrón cigars from Nicaragua. "I've been saving these for a reason. Everybody outside, we're hitting the beach."

"But it's cold out there," Maggie claimed.

Z was already moving for the door. "So put a coat on."

He led them to the back of his development where cement steps mounted the seawall and descended to the beach. Nine hundred feet down the shoreline, the Lynnhaven Fishing Pier reached into the inky mouth of the Chesapeake. Clouds masked the stars and the winter wind buffeted the sand. As they strolled toward the pier, Harris saw the sodium lamps atop the trestlework causeway of the Bay Bridge-Tunnel glowing three miles in the distance. In the opposite direction, several freighters were moored off Cape Henry, waiting for clearance to sail into the port of Norfolk; their running lights shining like a spectral fleet.

"Sandy, I know you got a pre-existing condition," Z called through the wind, "but, Mag, you want a stogie?"

"I'm alright, babe," she yelled at Sandra's side, watching Z respond with a shrug and vanish with the pack into the darkness under the pier.

The wind was gentler beneath the planks. Z took the Padróns from his coat and passed them around, each singeing the tips with a torch lighter. Harris drew the blue flame from his cigar and puffed into the air, listening to the surf wash through the pylons.

"Alright, Robby, this one's for you," Z purged the smoke from his lungs, looking to Farah and Whitford. "Gents, nobody knows what we do, nobody understands our fight, our drive. Nobody but us," he said, drawing on the cigar. "That's our brother right there—always, until the end. Damn few."

"Damn few," they echoed.

"Z can't say enough about your husband," said Maggie, as she stood with Sandra at the water's edge.

"They really do love each other. Z's a good guy," she nodded, "the best."

"He said they met at BUD/S?"

"And they've been attached ever since," said Sandra.

"I don't think I've heard anyone call Z by his first name," Maggie smiled.

"No," Sandra snickered, "me neither. I remember once we were at a dinner, I'd known him a while, and some two-star at our table mentioned a 'Wilmer,' and I said, 'who?'"

"I really like him."

"That's great," she welcomed, "he's earned it." There was a short silence, and she said, "Where do you work?"

"I'm a manager at the Victoria's Secret in the Lynnhaven Mall."

"Oh, right," Sandra nodded.

"It's a job," Maggie said humbly. "You?"

"Secretary, at the veterinary hospital in Bayside."

"That's awesome."

"Yeah, it's a job."

"You must really have your hands full," Maggie added. "Z told me about your son."

"Yup," Sandra sighed. "Ben's a piece of work."

"I'm sorry," she dismissed, "I shouldn't pry like that."

"No, it's fine. I'm—it's normal for me." Sandra dug her hands in her pockets and fixed her eyes on the black waves. "These first few years are torture. It's all about milestones: 'Mine's walking. Mine's talking. Mine said the funniest joke the other day.' For each of those missed milestones, it's hard not to grieve for the child you never had. And the guilt can just paralyze you. But I don't let it. I don't have time to grieve. I know that God is letting us borrow Ben for only a while, and when He decides to take him home, I don't want one second wasted. The same goes for Robert. I can't say how much longer we have together, so we focus on enjoying the time we've been given."

"Wow," Maggie breathed.

Sandra only watched the waves.

"I probably sound dumb saying this," Maggie continued, "but it's so intimidating, not to mention a little scary, you know, dating a guy like Z—all the guns, and secrets, and war stories. You're never really allowed in—"

Sandra cut her off. "That's just their job, it's not who they are."

"Isn't it hard though, having a relationship with a man like that?"

"I wouldn't recommend it, if you just want a merit badge."

"I've been reading a lot online—"

"Don't do that," Sandra turned to her, slightly frustrated. "If you stay with Z, you'll see. There're cliques, the wives and girlfriends clubs. Stay away. They only sit around, feeling sorry for themselves and acting like their lives are one big soap opera, but they wouldn't know what to do if it wasn't. They *choose* to let their husbands' or their boyfriends' professions define them. Don't."

Maggie scrunched her face. "Guess I never thought of it that way. And it just awes me how they can get up and face that danger."

"It's a brotherhood. That's cliché, but it's true," Sandra answered. "I still remember when that Chinook went down in Afghanistan a few years back. Fifteen men died that day, and Robert knew all of them. He got a text message and was just in shock. He stayed in our room all day. Sobbing. It was horrible. I've only seen him like that twice: after Ben was born, and the day his brother drowned. And then there were the funerals…"

"I don't ever want to be there."

"Stick it out and you will," she said soberly. "I was raised pretty religious, so however Robert processes it through that locked box of his, I still can't understand, but I respect him for it. I've been there too."

Sandra shivered and buttoned her lapels over the bare dip in her jugular. "Robert and I are both from San Mateo, the Bay Area; we met in middle school," she continued. "When I was fifteen, I got involved with a guy from our neighborhood. It started out great, as they all do, and then after a few months, he showed me what he really was. I still remember the first time he kicked me, and how I convinced myself that it was my fault. He was smart about it, too; where he put his hands on me. I wore long sleeves and heavy makeup, stopped in gas station bathrooms to wash the blood off my thighs, and I must've 'tripped' down the stairs more times than I can count. But his words were always worse. And I believed him. Staying was a conscious decision I made, because anything, in my mind, was better than being alone. I was in disbelief. I kept telling myself it was just temporary, that it was okay to wait it out because that wasn't really him, or that we were too young. I brainwashed myself. And it never got better."

"I'm so sorry," Maggie muttered.

"Robert was there the whole time, but I just looked him over. He was that nice kid I talked to between classes. He denies it, but I think he always knew. He was there for me in that subtle way of his, never acting like I was some shrinking violet that needed saving. He was just…my friend." Sandra looked back to the waves. "It got worse. I can't tell you the awful things he said to me, how much I cried, how much I dreamed that this existence couldn't be mine, how much I pleaded that there must be more to love. On my eighteenth birthday, after he held me down again, I snuck away once he'd passed out. And I drove straight to Robert's."

Sandra heard Z's unmistakable booming laugh and saw them emerge from under the pier. "So," she said to Maggie, "comfort him, love him, and try your best to understand the unexplainable—but never forget that he is not the definition of you."

• • •

Andrei Minin was ready to watch them stack like kindling.

A goose-stepping honor guard from the Kremlin Regiment paraded down the center aisle, bearing over their epaulets the white, blue and red tricolor of the Russian Federation and the red and yellow field of the People's Republic of China. The flags were installed on stage, and as their titles were heralded to the hall, Dmitri Lavrov and his Chinese counterpart, Han Jing, entered from the side to an eruption of camera flashes. The regiment's band dutifully performed the national anthems of each country to the risen crowd. Both presidents then took their time at the rostrum—approximately an hour by the hands of Minin's watch—spouting flowering words on the "renewed commitment" to deepening Sino-Russian economic ties. From his chair in the front row, Minin silently mouthed Lavrov's best lines as they were spoken. He'd written them himself.

To pass the time as they droned on, Minin admired his surroundings. Vladimirsky Hall in the Grand Kremlin Palace was one of the old red fortress's gems and typically reserved for treaty signings such as this. It was a triumphant, octagonal room fit for the tsars. The walls and pilasters, clad in rose-colored marble, stretched to a gigantic bronze chandelier and a vaulted ceiling in the shape of a cupola, decorated with gilt ornaments and symbols of the Order of Saint Vladimir, a red-enameled gold cross and a star. Karetnikov scarcely used it, preferring the more expansive Georgievsky Hall for those moments when he needed to elevate himself on an equal pedestal with God. Minin plainly remembered one such day, a transparently masterminded piece of propaganda akin in the Russian consciousness to when Napoleon barged into Notre-Dame and crowned himself emperor. The self-proclaimed Crimean People's Republic, liberated from Ukraine's vice by Vyasheslav Trubnikov's little green men, had just voted for independence in an election that was undoubtedly organic, as all state-owned media declared. Karetnikov, quick to generously rescue Crimea's Russian-speaking brethren, welcomed their leaders into the Kremlin and hastily signed a treaty cementing their ascension into the Russian Federation in total defiance of Europe and NATO's impotence. Minin knew that act, more than any other in Karetnikov's tenure, was his proudest—the moment he usurped the norms of modern statecraft and revealed how truly hollow the West's guarantee of security was. In a way, Minin also knew they were here today because of that achievement, and without Karetnikov because of Minin's actions. It was Karetnikov's hubris and arrogance that charted the course, but it would be Minin's own determination and charm that paved the road ahead. And that road would be sprinkled with the crushed skulls of those sitting amongst him.

Minin craned his neck to see down the row. It was the familiar faces of the cabinet, many of whom he recalled sitting dumbfounded around that conference table across Ivanovskaya Square on the night Karetnikov's plane slammed into the ground. Minin knew most of them were not long for their posts, and some still were not long for their lives. Foremost in his eyes was Uri Popoff, Karetnikov's faithful foreign minister who, if the rumors fluttering around Moscow were true, intended to resign and challenge Lavrov for the presidency. An ill advised decision if ever Minin heard one. There was also the Chinese delegation, Gazprom's management committee, and senior members of the Federal Assembly, who were assured to unanimously confirm the agreement the very next day.

Now that sufficient time was given to mourn Karetnikov, and his visage was relegated to the pantheon of tsars where it belonged, the state could return to the normal order of business. After a delay, the memorandum of understanding both countries agreed to nearly three weeks earlier would finally be signed. Its passage would secure a thirty-year deal, worth four hundred billion dollars, that would ship thirty-eight billion cubic meters of Russian natural gas to China annually. Using a network of pipelines dubbed the "East-Route," Gazprom would pump gas from its massive Kovyktin and Chayandin fields locked in the recesses of eastern Siberia to the metropolitan sprawl surrounding Beijing and the Yangtze River delta, reaching the doorsteps of 250 million people. Once the pipelines were constructed and reached full operational capacity, the deal would satisfy one-fifth of China's yearly consumption of natural gas. It was a revelation, lauded in both countries' press as an answer to China's reliance on coal and Russia's disposition to over-regulated European energy markets. But in that grand hall, as they congratulated themselves, only Minin knew the truth. That agreement was not a final outcome, but an impetus, an opening for the Kremlin to maneuver closer to Beijing, and an excuse to hand Russia the keys to China's front door so that Minin could fill the void once the Persian Gulf was consumed.

As their speeches concluded, and the chief executives of Gazprom and the China National Petroleum Corporation (CNPC) were brought onstage to ink the memorandum in the presence of their heads of state, Minin considered how they managed to reach this far.

In the final week of negotiations between Gazprom and the CNPC at the Mandarin Oriental in Shanghai, the Chinese declared that in any arrangement, they would only agree to pay half of the going European market rate for Russia's gas. To buttress their argument, they claimed that a consortium of Central Asian energy monopolies, led by Turkmenistan, had offered the same rate. The Chinese demanded that Gazprom match the price or the deal would collapse. In Moscow, Karetnikov was furious, but Minin thought to call Roman Ivanov, whose Vidar Group in Geneva held exclusive tender contracts to sell Russian seaborne crude. Ivanov immediately flew from London to Ashgabat and made Turkmenistan's notoriously corrupt president, Dhzuma Ovezov, a proposal: the Vidar Group would purchase the lot of Central Asia's natural gas exports at the standing market rate for the next fifty years and secure a grant from his friends at the Asian Development Bank to modernize Turkmenistan's lagging infrastructure. To sweeten the deal, Ivanov brought twenty suitcases of freshly printed British pounds sterling for whatever use Ovezov saw fit. With the added promise of a trip to Ivanov's hunting lodge in Scotland, Ovezov was hooked and quickly forgot about the Chinese. But there was another obstacle. Arseni Sokoloff, the Vidar Group's co-owner who held an equal stake to Ivanov, was vehemently opposed to chaining his firm to Ovezov's incompetence. Sokoloff had to go. Minin turned to General Trubnikov at the GRU and asked him to handle the situation. And handled it was. "The American," as Trubnikov called him, doused Sokoloff in kerosene and torched him alive in his own bed. China lost its alternative, and several days later, an agreement with Gazprom was reached.

Now the deal was done—with Karetnikov himself tossed upon the lapping pyre. Signatures were scrawled, hands were shaken; they rose with thunderous applause. But Minin sat, stone-faced.

He still recalled the nausea that overcame him when he learned of Sokoloff. Since then, murder had become par for the course. Trubnikov confessed he hadn't heard from the American in at least a week and they'd no idea what he was planning down in Lebanon. And from what Minin saw, he had no illusions of the deathly masterpiece to come.

Zyed felt the Makarov's weight. His finger ran along the trigger guard; the grip filled his palm. The boy tucked the pistol in his jacket pocket. Haddad showed him how to use it: release the safety, pull the slide and let it spring back into place. The magazine afforded eight nine-millimeter rounds. Enough to put any man down, Haddad said. But Zyed didn't intend to use a gun.

Fabrice stood only a few hundred feet away across the parking lot, ringed by the other fawning grunts who had punched and kicked and taunted Zyed. They followed Fabrice's every step, but Zyed wanted him alone—to take his time. The boy crouched back behind the bushes. Not tonight.

CHAPTER 35

THE BAY WAS cloaked that morning in a curious stench of salt, boat exhaust and festering garbage—an unpleasant reminder of the dragging sanitation workers' strike. Seven miles south of Athens, the port of Zea cut an oval-shaped notch into the rocky coast of the Piraeus peninsula, forming a sheltered harbor that lead into a narrow inlet before the Saronic Gulf. Cafés and tourist shops ringed the quay and a network of floating docks prodded into the cloudy water. A few dozen sailing skiffs and motor yachts were moored to the docks. In recent years, the boats rarely, if ever, slipped their lines for the open channel. Flagrant displays of wealth in Greece only invited the ire of the penniless public, not to mention the scrutiny of government tax assessors. As their hulls collected rust and algae, many of the boats' owners sought to sell them out of personal or financial necessity, and sometimes both. One such vessel sitting in the marina was the *Calliope*, a ninety-eight-foot flybridge yacht manufactured by Princess International in Plymouth, England.

The owner was an ostentatious Greek media mogul whose portfolio once included two tabloid newspapers and a television station. However, Greece's economic collapse and a sharp drop in advertising revenue, coupled with a rather bitter divorce, decimated his net worth. The mogul's attorney fees were hemorrhaging his accounts and he scrambled for cash. Ditching his yacht was a logical place to begin. An ad was placed online and, to the astonishment of the mogul's broker, was answered almost immediately by a terse individual claiming to represent a Ukrainian oligarch. The man wanted to view the yacht as soon as possible and emphasized utmost discretion. Several days later three broad chested men, with accents to match, promptly met the broker on the quay and identified themselves as members of the oligarch's security team. The broker took pains to inflate *Calliope*'s luxurious fittings and amenities, but the men had other concerns.

They asked for demonstrations of the hydraulic aft bathing platform and the transom garage underneath and took interest in the size of the storage compartments on the lower deck. The men were also clearly well versed in the mechanics of the yacht, appearing to be familiar with the engine room and the eleven-thousand-liter capacity of her fuel tanks. Not once, the broker noticed, did they ask about price. It would have all seemed exceptionally strange, but the broker was desperate for a sale.

The broker climbed up the ladder to the main deck, having just highlighted the master stateroom—with Ratskov, Zaytsev and Lazarev in tow. "As you can see, this is just a brilliantly sociable saloon. It's right in the heart of the boat, with these lovely views to starboard *and* port," the broker gestured to the oversized windows on either side. "Fantastic if you're in the Med."

The three Spetsnaz operators barely squeezed the tops of their heads beneath the ceiling. They tried their best to feign interest.

"You've got your TV right here, recessed behind the sofa, but that pops up at the touch of a button. The boat is just roomy and it flows beautifully."

Lazarev nodded.

"Calliope has been a delight for the owner, and I'm sure your client would be lucky to have her," the broker concluded.

"The asking price is one-point-five?" Zaytsev asked.

"One-and-a-half million euro, correct," the broker humbly confirmed. "But we're open to offers, of course. The owner is eager to sell."

Zaytsev turned to the others and they spoke for a moment in some Slavic language the broker didn't understand. Ukrainian—or Russian.

Ratskov's mouth twisted, speaking in English, "We'll offer two million to take possession of the vessel today. Is this acceptable?"

The broker's face went flush. "I'm sure it would be *quite* acceptable to the owner. If you have a letter of credit from your client's bank, we can arrange a wire transfer at my—"

"Our client is wary of the banking system in this country," said Zaytsev. "Would traveler's cheques be an acceptable form of payment? Unsigned."

The broker smiled. "It so happens that I have the deed in my car."

Ruslan Baranov pinned a map to the dashboard. It outlined Paris' 1st arrondissement in particular detail. The Seine ran as a slender blue strip down the bottom. Bordered by the river's right bank were the Tuileries Garden in green and Place de la Concorde in beige. Baranov traced his fingertip along Rue de Rivoli, dragging westward from the Louvre to the intersection of Rue de Castiglione. He tapped on the flimsy paper; the Hôtel Meurice sat at the meeting.

Baranov drew his eyes back to the windshield. The E25 highway stretched out before him atop a concrete viaduct fording a glacial fissure of Italy's Aosta Valley and the river Dora Baltea. Fir trees canvassed the layered alpine crags ahead, building to a colossal massif of drifting snow shrouding the naked peaks of Mont-Blanc, the mightiest spine of the Alps. Behind the range was France.

At the wheel of the Citroën C3 was Magomed Akhmadov and sitting behind Baranov was Kakiyev. The remainder of his section, Ignatev and Kotov, followed three miles back, judging by their last radio call. They had left Rome at dawn and took a direct, thirteen-hour route to Paris. The other section bound for France—Vlasiyev, Ibragimov, Pokhrovskii, Isayev and Dratchev—boarded a Thello sleeper train from Milan and should have already been in the city, activating a pair of safe houses and a storage unit with the assistance of the local GRU *rezidentura*. Baranov was confident that he and his men managed to infiltrate Europe without attracting attention from the security services; he'd run countersurveillance from the minute he'd landed in Rome and was sure if his men were being followed, they would know. He planned to report as much to Kazanoff.

"We're coming up on the border," Akhmadov uttered.

A series of winding approach roads with various gates and inspection stations preceded the Mont Blanc Tunnel. Police and customs officials closely monitored the tunnel on both ends, but Baranov knew their focus was on inspecting the giant lorries passing through the artery, not an unassuming Citroën.

"This car's registered in Brittany," he said. "How's your accent?"

"It'll pass."

Akhmadov slowed at the tollbooth, mouthing *"bonjour"* and *"merci"* to the collector, before pressing the gas and accelerating into the tunnel's shade.

An Airbus 321 landing at Beirut airport from Frankfurt screamed over the cinder block, plaster and frayed wire hive of Ouzai. As the hollow whine relented, Anwar Sabbah alighted from the Isuzu Trooper and let his sunglasses rest on his shirt's top button. The armed guards in the alleyway knew their commander's aide-de-camp by sight and escorted Sabbah into the house. Up the creaking stairs and around a corner, he found Ibrahim al-Din right where he left him the previous day: a gray waste pooled over the cushions, gazing tediously at the television screen.

"What is it?" al-Din hummed, not bothering to look away.

"Yesterday a message was saved in an email drop-box we've occasionally used for European operations…"

"So?"

Sabbah cleared his throat. "Well, it was from Badi Haddad."

Al-Din gave an indignant huff.

"He had some interesting news," Sabbah said. "Two Syrian boys of fourteen and nineteen—Shias, orphaned in the war—have taken a liking to him. The oldest knows of Haddad's role with us. He says the boy's expressed interest in a martyrdom operation."

Al-Din scratched at the scruff edging the corners of his mouth. "Boy would be better served putting a bullet in his brain."

"Haddad writes that the boy's quite sincere. He asked if there are opportunities here, or perhaps back in Syria." Sabbah knew it was an absurd notion.

"Don't they have news in France?" spat al-Din. "Doesn't he know we're afraid of our own shadows?"

Sabbah dipped his head toward the floor. "But the Russians are in Paris. It occurred to me that Haddad might help—should they need a patsy."

Al-Din drew his attention from the screen. "Check first."

"Um," Sabbah's voice shivered, "must *I* go to him?"

"No," al-Din answered. "Use his courier. Gelayev."

Sabbah nodded. "Thank you."

Al-Din pulled himself off the cushions, sweeping the wrinkles from his tunic, and smoothly stepped to an open window. "But you'll go to Paris."

"Of course."

"Reaffirm our commitment to Haddad; promise grace despite his misgivings; assure him it's in the past. And then do as the Russians say."

"May I speak freely?" asked Sabbah.

"Always." Al-Din shone in the afternoon light.

"It worries me…what he'll do to you." Sabbah had no need to elaborate on whom, exactly, he meant. That much was clear to both men.

A cloud passed before the sun and the radiance cloaking al-Din faded to something pallid, and bare. "I've been a witness for too long," he said. "For twenty-three years, my friend, I've watched the world change. Usually right here, from this window. I've watched entire wars be won and lost. I've witnessed whole countries fall. I've seen great men stripped of glory. The whole time, only a witness, forced to watch."

Al-Din turned his head to Sabbah, his eyes tinged with sadness. And then his tone dropped, scorched with equally turbulent undertows of rage and hope. "I'm tired of watching."

With nightfall, a gale swooped down from the mountains to the east, pelting the camp with dense, watery snow. The weather soured by the minute, although such erratic and violent shifts weren't uncommon in that part of Kurdistan. But the camp's *khajakji*—the local word for smuggler—had been jumping around nature's hurdles for generations, and would sometimes even use it to their advantage. Their efforts continued unabated through the storm as it had every night with an almost ritualistic intensity. Lorries idled in lacerated tracks of mud, their diesel engines grumbling with loose serpentine belts, as workers scurried around in the glow of headlights to unload contraband hauled up from rented warehouses in nearby Choman. Inside the tents, withering men wrangled over dates and prices around oil lamps, etching their agreements onto scraps of paper with dull pencils. Horses stirred in the snowy muck and fussed with bulging canvass sacks draped from their backs. Around crackling fires, the khajakji chugged cans of Turkish beer and warmed their limbs by the heat, girding themselves for the uncertain hours of cold and darkness ahead. Although hardly an ideal way to make a living, for many, it was a fundamental way of life in the villages dotting the Iraq-Iran border, and often the only option to provide for their families. The border, as they saw, was merely a geopolitical construct drawn by nations in the dirt, just another step in thousands taken on their journey. And as far as they were concerned, it was all only a single country: Kurdistan—two halves of one *Rojhelat*. It had been this way to enterprising Kurdish families for generations, and while the mechanics were largely unchanged, the contraband was decidedly modern.

Beneath the moldering tents were cases of alcohol brought from Europe and meant for deprived consumers with remarkably refined tastes: Absolut vodka and various blends of Irish whiskey, Johnnie Walker Red Label and French cognac, Pinot noir champagnes and Fratelli Bellini chianti from Tuscany. The destinations for most of it were the underground drinking clubs of Tehran, where young, elite Iranians gathered to embrace a "hedonistic" lifestyle outlawed by the Islamic Revolution—although the mullahs were rumored to partake, themselves. Iran's ban on alcohol created a maddeningly lucrative environment for the smuggling ring's organizers. From the camp near Choman, alone, two-and-a-half million dollars of booze was transported over the border every day. In Iraq, a bottle of Absolut from Sweden was worth only eight dollars, but a few short miles over the border in Iran could fetch as much as twenty. While the profit margin for those running the camp was gigantic, the payoff for the khajakji was far more meager, and the risk was saddled entirely on their shoulders.

Considering that, one young khajakji stood at the fire, harboring a secret.

Swara was in his mid-twenties and had been hauling illicit goods into Iran since he was old enough to carry the load, as his father and grandfather had done before him. For a hundred thousand Iranian rials, or roughly three US dollars, Swara could make as many as three trips over the border in a day. What he carried on his back did not concern him, so long as there was a healthy market for it in the towns over the mountains. Swara had smuggled anything from tea, tires, fuel, clothing, makeup, computer parts and even satellite dishes, which were especially popular in Iran. The thaw in relations between the mullahs and the West over the past months put a dent in his business. As waning sanctions brought a flood of trade into Iranian ports, it was cheaper, and safer, for merchants to stock their shelves legitimately. But the smugglers knew that the ban on alcohol, and the demand for it, would not change any time soon. Swara also knew the lengths taken by the Border Guards to stem the flow.

Most of the older and more established khajakji crossed the border with small packs of horses wending along hidden trails through the mountains. The Iranians knew those trails, too, and while some guards could be bribed to look the other way, a few took their jobs quite seriously. Swara was told around the fire that snipers picked off sixteen horses on the previous night. If the snipers were kind, they would drop the horses into the mud with a single shot to the head; if not, the khajakji would have to put the animals out of their misery, often with any blunt objects they could find. Swara was too poor to afford his own, and honestly thought the beasts were more trouble than they were worth. The horses were cumbersome, easily frightened, and gaping targets for the guards and their thermal riflescopes. Once he'd even seen a horse step on a landmine and instantly shred five of the animals, their owners with them. Swara preferred to make himself a nimble target, easily eluding the snipers in the barren hills. As they prepared to embark, Swara knew he'd need every trick at his disposal.

To make ends meet for his family, Swara occasionally ran errands for some friendly Americans at their compound in Erbil. Months would pass without word from them, and then unexpectedly a car would appear and an American would ask him for a favor, often running a message to a PJAK commander or an Iranian dissident over the border. He always obliged, both out of America's support for the Kurdish people and the hefty price they paid. In one trip, he could match half-a-year's salary smuggling alcohol, but it also came with difficulties. Under no circumstances, the Americans urged, could any of his fellow khajakji ever know about his errands. The Iranian Border Guards were another matter: Swara's stomach turned at the thought of what they'd do if he were caught. Yet he did it anyway, and on that night he would once again deliver a message from the Americans, this time in the form of a peculiar device.

Swara was given a phone that could bounce its calls off satellites and instructed to hand it to a particular person the Americans suspected was in a village locked deep in the Ushnu-Sulduz Valley. He kept the phone buried in his rucksack and didn't dare show it to the other khajakji loitering around the camp. Swara suspected it was worth thousands of dollars, although to look at it, it appeared to be dead. Still, the Americans said that with the phone they could track his every move through the mountains. After ditching his tins of whiskey in Piranshahr, Swara was given money to take a bus north to Oshnavieh, and from there could make his way into the valley, and to Palanjar. The Americans showed him a picture of the person he was meant to find: a hulking man with a billowing black beard tied into three prongs. In Palanjar, a dwindling village of meek shepherds and their even meeker wives, a figure like that would stand out. But Swara recognized the man as soon as the picture was placed before him; anyone in that part of the world would. It was Major General Jamil Gorani, the Dark Lion of Kurdistan, and the Americans desperately wanted to speak to him.

As his friends tracked Swara through the mountains, they assured him that a signal would remotely activate the phone once he reached Palanjar, and with it, General Gorani could securely communicate with the Americans. Swara took them at their word, and waited for his half of the bargain.

The coals at the fire's base hissed in the driving snow. With conditions on the mountain deteriorating, the khajakji trusted that the Iranian guards would hole up in their barracks for the night. If they moved quickly, all of their loot could cross the border. They abandoned the fire to die and readied their horses.

But Swara would walk alone. He tied a checkered *keffiyeh* scarf over his face, leaving only his eyes exposed to the cold, hoisted the canvas pack over his shoulders, and set off into the hills in search of the Dark Lion.

After clearing the North River Tunnels, Morteza Ghanbari stood patiently in the enclosed vestibule while the floor plates and rubber diaphragm swayed between cars on approach to track seven at New York's Penn Station. Once the train stopped and the side doors opened, he stepped onto the subterranean platform, past the panting New Jersey Transit locomotive and took an escalator up to the main concourse. At five in the afternoon, the tide was surging into the station, not out. Ghanbari jockeyed against the throng through the low-ceilinged catacomb, past a Hudson News and a Dunkin' Donuts, and amid indecipherable scratches over the PA system. Emerging into the light at the taxi stand on Eighth Avenue, he hailed a yellow cab from the stream and directed the driver uptown, to the home of his old friend, Harold Lansing.

An Iranian expatriate—liberal by the mullahs' standards—Dr. Ghanbari was a frequent sounding board for American policies in the Persian Gulf and a respected alternative voice in the vacuous echo chamber between New York and Washington. His specialty lie in taking the contemporary difficulties of the region and framing them in the shared history of Islam and the Middle East in a way that was digestible to a layman, explaining how these crises often metastasized over millennia, and showing how they might be resolved with a greater understanding of that history. While the conversation on Iran was maddeningly dominated by hollow talking heads, their claims usually rooted in xenophobia and gut-mined "truthiness,"

Ghanbari actually held the expertise to support his claims. Once a member of the Iranian parliament, he resigned his seat in the *Majlis* after receiving death threats in the wake of the 1999 student protests and fled to Europe. After a brief tenure at the London School of Economics, Ghanbari came to Princeton University and was eventually named the Dayton-Stockton Professor of History. At Princeton, he joined the American Iranian Council and led the charge after September 11th to foster dialogue and understanding with Tehran, which often meant fighting to hold his countries of birth and adoption back from the brink of war. It was an arduous, ceaseless battle. Ghanbari's greatest desire was to simply enlighten policymakers in the belief that Iranians were not the sniveling bearded boogeymen of 1980s action movies; to convince them that scores more Iranians sought iPhones than nuclear weapons. But like the Midtown Manhattan traffic that afternoon, the tide was frustratingly against him. While a number of think tanks or lobbying groups could pack a room in the Rayburn House Office Building with promises of stale danishes and supermarket coffee, filling Congressional staffers' minds with the gospel of impending doom, Ghanbari struggled to get a fraction of attentive ears. His first true victory came with passage of the JCPOA and the possibility of that nuclear agreement paving the way for rapprochement between the United States and Iran. During the months of negotiations in Switzerland and Vienna, Ghanbari practically kept a cot at CNN's studios in the Time Warner Center, consistently reminding the other panelists on the realities, and limitations, of Iranian politics. The country was not an absolute dictatorship—like Saudi Arabia, or even Russia—where Ayatollah Khansari could simply do as he pleased, regardless of how the law was written. Iranian politics, like in any state, was fraught with a myriad of factions, some of which were quite formidable. He always argued that those who most wanted a nuclear weapon and confrontation with the United States, such as Qasem Shateri and his Quds Force, were also the voices in Tehran most vehemently opposed to negotiations. Once a deal was reached and sent to Congress for approval, Ghanbari took his message to the Capitol, enduring hours of questioning before the Senate and House foreign relations committees. His pleas remained unchanged. In Washington, he was aghast at the degree to which those policymakers touted the talking points and generalizations spun by a legion of lobbyists committed to destroying the agreement. All of it, he knew, was done at the behest of a foreign power; orchestrated in Jerusalem by Dennis Roth, Prime Minister Arad's spin doctor. Ghanbari suspected that, like the Saudis, Arad knew the cold fact that Israel reached the pinnacle of its strategic footing in the Middle East, and the only way to maintain it was to likewise preserve the status quo. A rapprochement between the United States and Iran did not fit that bill. Yet despite all the shady ad dollars and frightening rhetoric, Dennis Roth and his master failed: the JCPOA ultimately became the law of both countries. For it, the Iranian people were feeling a well-deserved reprieve. As President Behrouz Rostani promised in his election campaign, fifty billion dollars in unfrozen oil revenues were pumped into Iran's crippled economy. Buying bread, rice and soap might no longer cost a week's salary. Dangerous shortages in pharmaceuticals might be filled. A chance to eat at McDonald's was the least of Iranians' concerns. It worked, or at least Ghanbari's contacts told him as much. Rostani kept his word: That fresh cash did not flow into the coffers of Shateri and his minions, and Iran wasn't pursuing a nuclear bomb. But, if Harold Lansing summoned Ghanbari to a secret chat, he knew all was not well in paradise.

The cab rounded Columbus Circle and inched up Central Park West. Ghanbari and Lansing first met nearly twenty years ago, back when he was in the Majlis and Lansing was working on the Dayton Accords. When Ghanbari left Iran, Lansing was one of the first Westerners to reach out and encourage him to come to the United States. While the following decade saw Lansing shuttled between postings in Seoul, Warsaw, Washington and Kabul, the two reconnected after Lansing retired from the State Department in 2006, taking a job as managing director at Kissinger Associates, where Ghanbari already advised part-time. His prevailing judgment was that Lansing was a walking cliché, a noble statesman and an optimist who still clung to the rare belief that dialogue could bridge the gap between civilizations. During the darkest days of the Syrian civil war, Ghanbari was present when Lansing resigned from Kissinger Associates and returned to Washington as Secretary Weisel's personal envoy to bring some resolution to the catastrophe. Although that war's climax was far bloodier than anyone would have wished, its outcome was, at the very least, amicable for the West: ISIS was chased underground, Syria's borders remained largely intact, and Iran's hardliners would not reap the spoils. That last fact frightened Ghanbari; he knew Qasem Shateri was not a man to accept defeat. As the cab crawled along the 65th Street Traverse, he pondered why his friend sought his help. Ghanbari's current focus was in monitoring the implementation of the JCPOA and its economic effects on Iran. Lansing's brief was making peace between the Syrians and the Israelis. The only adequate explanation, Ghanbari thought, was that the administration had finally realized that, in the Middle East, every piece on the board was interconnected.

His cab pulled to the curb at 834 Fifth Avenue, an art deco co-op dating to the 1930s opposite the Central Park Zoo. Ghanbari paid the driver and walked past the doorman into the lobby, where an attendant was expecting him. The attendant called upstairs and escorted Ghanbari to an elevator, keying it for a unit on the eleventh floor. When the doors slid open, Lansing waited in the foyer.

"*Salam,* Morteza!" Lansing happily spread his arms.

"*Salam,* Harold," Ghanbari smiled. "How are you? It's been too long."

"Well," Lansing huffed, hanging Ghanbari's coat in a closet, "I've been busy."

"You've been lucky," Ghanbari quipped.

"I get that a lot these days." Lansing showed his friend into his home. The apartment, in combination with his wife's money, was the fruit of his payday upon leaving the State Department—serving on the boards of the Carlyle Group and the Council on Foreign Relations, and advising Fortune 500 companies through Kissinger Associates. The apartment boasted six thousand square-feet on the building's west façade, overlooking the park, with eleven-foot ceilings and meticulously preserved pre-war details. Ghanbari couldn't help but note that Lansing had done quite well for himself.

He greeted the ambassador's wife, Patricia—they'd met on numerous occasions—while she put the finishing touches on dinner, and followed Lansing into the living room.

"Can I get you a drink?" he asked.

Admittedly a bad Muslim, Ghanbari replied, "Anything red that's open."

The chimneypiece was decked with pictures: Lansing with the president of Afghanistan, standing under the wing of Air Force One on the flight line of some desert airfield, and strolling with Avi Arad beside the Western Wall of the Temple Mount in Jerusalem.

"Pay no attention to that 'mantle of ego,'" Lansing returned with two glasses of Château Lascombes, handing one to Ghanbari.

"Oh, I've seen worse."

They sank into two leather armchairs in the dying light from the park.

"How's the semester going?"

Ghanbari sipped his wine and set the glass on an end table. "My grad students have a fifty-page midterm due tomorrow, so their night's probably not as good as mine," he snickered, adding, "I've only got three courses for the spring: Islamic World, Imperialism and Reform in the Middle East, and Themes in Islamic Cultures. Faculty issues and those Congressional testimonies wore me out in the fall. My undergrads and I talked about your deal getting Hezbollah to disarm last week."

Lansing was intrigued. "Really? How'd they take it?"

Ghanbari shook his head. "Educated youths are pessimists."

"Sounds like a lot of uneducated adults."

"You should come down one night and speak."

"Sure," he said. "That'd be fun."

Business had to be brushed aside for the moment. Patricia made lasagna, which Ghanbari welcomed on a bitterly cold February night. They each shared the latest anecdotes with Ghanbari on their grandchildren—ages seven and twelve—who recently visited from Palo Alto over Christmas. After clearing their plates, and with a fresh glass of wine, he and Lansing went to the sunroom that opened onto a balustraded terrace. With the sun now firmly cowled by the buildings of the Upper West Side across Central Park, both men could only see each other against faint shadows and through the flicker of candlelight.

Lansing sipped from his glass and crossed his legs in the wicker chair. "How's life inside right now?"

Ghanbari knew exactly what the ambassador meant. "It's a mixed bag, Harold," he said with some sadness. "The nuclear agreement's begun to change many lives; normal people's lives. Rostani has a lot of capital in the streets for it. He'll likely stick around through the next elections, provided the Guardian Council doesn't give him the boot and his allies hold their seats in the Majlis." Ghanbari referred to a twelve-member group that wielded a number of powers in Iran, most notably the responsibility to ensure the compatibility of legislation with Islamic law, and the capability to vet and approve candidates for public office. Without their consent, one could not run for president, the Majlis, or the Assembly of Experts; and as the Guardian Council consisted of conservative clerics, one could not gain their consent without holding similar views. It was part of the vicious cycle in Iranian politics that maintained the regime's control.

"Would they?" Lansing asked.

"Give Rostani the boot? Probably not," he pondered, "but more than one of the ayatollahs on the council are close to the military, so we'll see if they have a grudge for pushing those negotiations."

"The Revolutionary Guards, you mean?"

"That's right," Ghanbari nodded. "Why? Has the JCPOA failed already?"

Lansing's lips contorted in an uncomfortable smile. "Hardly."

"Honestly, I only hear good things. People are committed."

"So where does this 'mixed bag' come in?"

Ghanbari cocked his head. "The Green Movement is dead, Harold."

Lansing gave a few sympathetic nods.

"The whole opposition is either in Evin or under house arrest," he continued. "I'm told the Pasdaran saw the writing on the wall with the negotiations and made sure that those who'd surely demand further reform didn't have a platform to demand it. If they find so much as an active VPN client on your hard drive, they'll toss you in a cell. It's a scary time. Syria's spooked the Pasdaran; they won't let their control slip like that again. And then there's the whole matter with Mehdi Vaziri. You heard about it, I trust?"

Lansing allowed another curt nod.

"Just like that," Ghanbari snapped his fingers. "Gone."

"Well where'd he go? People don't just vanish," Lansing observed.

"No, they don't," he said. "Certainly not people like him. Not without help. It's a state secret; you won't find it in the news over there. Someone tunneled into Vaziri's house in Tehran two weeks ago, right under the Pasdaran. There's a rumor that the *Etelaat-e-Sepah,* the IRGC's intelligence arm, discovered that a fishing dhow took him and his wife across the gulf to the Emirates. From there, who knows?"

"Someone does."

"Exactly."

"So what happens now?" Lansing asked. "They can't just let him go."

"I'm told," Ghanbari uttered his usual refrain, "that the Pasdaran are searching through Europe for him: Vienna, Holland, Denmark, Paris. They think that Mossad took him with the cooperation of a European intelligence service."

Lansing crossed his arms and pressed back in the chair. "Well, it would make a good spy novel."

"Wouldn't it?" Ghanbari set his wine down. "So is this when you reveal why you asked me to visit? You're not so spontaneous."

Lansing also set his wine down and bent in closer. "This Gaza mess..."

Ghanbari shook his head. "Disgusting. All of it."

"It's my fault."

Ghanbari shot him a look of incredulity.

"Ahead of the Annapolis conference, I wanted to make some precedent by which Arad had the political will to negotiate with the Palestinians. I met with Hanna Sayigh and asked him to use what influence he had with Hamas to leverage Islamic Jihad into freeing Moshe Alder."

"Goodness, Harold."

"It didn't work," Lansing admitted.

"No, it didn't."

"And you know why."

Ghanbari certainly did. "It was Shateri, and his man in Khartoum. I forget his name now."

"Rasoul Gharib Abadi," Lansing said. "You heard about that firefight the Royal Marines found themselves in on that ship off Somalia? That was bait."

"I'd believe it," Ghanbari sighed. "This is blowback, Harold—for the nuclear program, for Syria, for Hezbollah, all of it. If I asked for an example on a test, this is basically what I'd look for."

"The White House wants to try a new approach, something that can isolate the hardliners while empowering Rostani and his allies."

"Good luck with that," said Ghanbari. "To use one of your expressions: Tehran's already sold the farm. Don't expect them to keep giving."

"Oh, no," Lansing shook his head, "we're planning to give, too."

Ghanbari blinked. "So where do I come in?"

"Okay." Lansing sat back. "The president and Secretary Weisel have asked me to restart negotiations with Tehran right where we left off when

Damascus fell. We want to keep pursuing that agenda, but we're prepared to make some serious concessions, only if the Iranians are ready to match them. Where do you come in? I need an intermediary, a trusted go-between who can bring a message to the supreme leader and bypass the IRGC."

"But, Harold," he said, "Khansari hasn't been seen in public in almost six months. I'm told he's ill."

"So whose word is strongest in the supreme leader's absence?"

He thought for a moment. "Saeed Mofidi. You know of him?"

Lansing couldn't say for sure if he did.

"I didn't think so," Ghanbari said. "Few in the West do."

"Who is he?"

"Saeed Mofidi is essentially Khansari's advisor on foreign affairs and security. His office sits outside the Pasdaran apparatus, although he's a retired general. Mofidi speaks for the ayatollah on a range of issues, and rumor has it that he holds 'pro-Western' views. For a worker so close to the queen, I get the feeling that he resents the hive."

"He's honest?" Lansing fished for the right answer.

"Absolutely."

"Good," Lansing nodded. "So I need an intermediary who can bring a letter to Saeed Mofidi on behalf of the president of the United States. I told Weisel that you could recommend someone. Say, in Europe, I figured."

Ghanbari shrugged. "I could do it myself."

Lansing's eyebrows arced. "You?"

"Why not? Who could you trust more than me?"

Lansing had to admit that Ghanbari was right. "You can get to Tehran?"

"I've dual citizenship," he reasoned. "And my mother lives in Tehran. She's ninety-three years old; I don't need an excuse."

"How would you contact Saeed Mofidi?"

"Ayatollah Abdolhossein Moezi," Ghanbari finished his wine. "He's imam of the Islamic Centre of England and Khansari's representative in London. I'd ask him to make the introduction."

"Use encryption."

"Of course."

"Good, good," Lansing breathed.

"What am I supposed to sell?"

"You're not going to sell anything," said Lansing. "That's my job. Simply state our terms to Mofidi, tell him that the United States would like to discuss it further, and ask him to bring it to Khansari."

"But what are the terms?"

Lansing offered his hand. "Only if you'll agree to do it."

Ghanbari accepted.

"A draft of the letter's in my safe." Lansing rose and left the room.

Ghanbari stood too, moving to the thin panes of glass barring the cold.

By now, the prevailing force in the sky over the city was darkness. Looking south over Central Park, from the classical gabled roofline of the Plaza Hotel, to the sheening glass monoliths racing into the air along 57th Street, the Midtown skyline twinkled with thousands of multi-colored incandescent embers, and Ghanbari felt the overwhelming premonition that Manhattan burned before his very eyes.

Lansing returned after a moment, holding an open envelope, and noticed him taking in the view. "Beautiful, isn't it?"

From his office in Beit Rahbari that morning, Mofidi watched the world slowly unravel on live television. During the previous night, an Al Jazeera producer and his cameraman were perched on a rooftop in Rafah, filming what they believed was an engagement between Sayeret Matkal, an Israeli special forces unit, and fighters of Islamic Jihad. The target, the producer claimed to the studio anchor in Doha, was a clandestine Qassam rocket launcher buried under a farmer's field. In the middle of the broadcast, the roar of a jet engine pierced over the producer's microphone, and after a moment, their feed went black. An F-15I dropped a five-hundred-pound bomb on the roof. As dawn broke, every major news network around the globe picked up that thirty-second clip preceding the crew's death, playing it on a loop for the gawking masses to parse over their breakfasts. At a press conference in Tel Aviv, the IDF's spokesperson claimed it was an accident, offering his condolences to Al Jazeera and the victims' families, while cautioning other journalists not to encroach on an active military operation. Few bought the IDF's account. Qatar's ambassador at the UN pressed for a full and transparent investigation, while the correspondents on Fars—Iran's semi-official press agency—as Mofidi watched, denounced the strike as but another example of Zionist crimes against humanity in "occupied Palestine." There was no discernible end to the carnage in Gaza. While the IDF whittled away at Islamic Jihad's stockpiled arms and infrastructure, Hamas leadership both in Gaza and Doha refused to arrest Azzam al-Nakhalah. Although with collateral damage like the dead Al Jazeera crew, beginning to stack, it was becoming politically impossible for Hamas to abet the Israelis, even if they wanted to. Despite the unprovoked murder of Moshe Adler, popular opinion in the Middle East was now firmly on the side of Islamic Jihad. It astonished Mofidi at how easily Avi Arad took the bait. He also knew that the longer Hamas defied Israel's demands, the more they risked IDF tanks and ground troops plowing over the armistice line. Mofidi suspected that Qasem Shateri bargained on it.

It was the sprawl of Shateri's ambitions that filled Mofidi with dread. Gaza was but a gory sliver of it. In Iraq, Hashid Shaabi's militias cemented their gains, exerting control over the countryside seized from ISIS, expelling anyone who presented a military, political or ethnic challenge; Unit 400, *al-Quds'* hit squad, stalked the cities of Europe, monitoring dissidents whom Mehdi Vaziri might make the dire mistake of contacting; and in Tehran, Shateri tasked Hossein Taeb and the Etelaat-e-Sepah with torturing Vaziri's family in case a useful confession bled from their wounds. Amongst it, Mofidi felt powerless.

As he thought more, he came to see that notion wasn't quite true. On matters of Iran's armed forces and foreign policy, Mofidi spoke for a man whose words were second only to God, and as none could sanely claim to have heard from Him in eons, Ayatollah Khansari's would have to suffice. However, the supreme leader was a shell, although few knew it. Secluded behind the walls of his estate in Mashad, Khansari spent his waking moments in a haze, attended to by a trusted regiment of doctors who fought to allay his worsening dementia.

But, as Mofidi realized, Khansari could still wield a pen. While whatever words that pen produced could be credited to the supreme leader, they could just as easily be Mofidi's own. And with that signature, Mofidi would have the heavenly endorsement he needed to end Shateri's rampage.

It *was* a pleasant thing to behold the light—but only briefly—until the occluding umbra shone its flares and scorched his retinas. Mehdi Vaziri understood that now, and while a part of him was still thankful to be recalled to life, a waxing element wished they kept him sedated in that trunk.

His French bodyguards, from the National Police's *Service de la protection* (SDLP), mostly let him sleep and kept to their command post in the spare bedroom down the hall. The Israelis were not so kind, although when they came, they also brought his medicine. In a sense, he appreciated that; it was the only way to rouse his wife, Fatemeh, from bed. At nine in the morning, a Mossad doctor came to suite 102/103 of the Hôtel Meurice and gave them each a fifty-milligram ephedrine tablet. That greased the wheels. After a light breakfast, the doctor gave them each a dosage of clonazepam to aid with any anxieties that came throughout the day. Often, despite the medication, Fatemeh would fall into hysterics and the doctor would hook her to an intravenous drip of propofol, relegating her nearly comatose. A few times, he prayed that she wouldn't wake.

Vaziri didn't exclude himself from those evil thoughts, in the quiet moments when the shadow came. It was never supposed to be like this. A few years ago, he helmed the most powerful political opposition movement in Iran since the overthrow of the shah in 1979. In hindsight, Vaziri felt naïve to even attempt to oppose the mullahs, and he knew that he and his companions had only gotten so far because the system allowed it. Like throwing a switch, the regime's enforcers crushed any dreams of a democratic process in Iran. Yet Vaziri also knew, strangely, that he was lucky. The others, the brave men and women who'd marched with him and rallied the people to be heard for want of their basic rights, were all gone: dead, nearly dead, or in a prison cell and wishing for death. When the Israelis contacted him through a sympathetic Pasdaran soldier guarding his house and began plotting to secure his freedom, Vaziri thought that, away from Iran, he could galvanize what opposition remained. Now he saw what a pathetic undertaking that was. Instead, he was an indentured servant to an intelligence agency of a country he loathed, his mind a natural resource to be stripped of worth; and the Hôtel Meurice, a place where he and his wife were supposed to rediscover life, felt like their tomb.

Once the drugs settled, more Israelis came from their embassy. It was clear that the Mossad *katsas'* interest in him was fading. During Vaziri's first days in Paris, their barrage of questions persisted for hours, and their faces were warped with interest. They hung on his tales of the Green Movement's intricacies and his dealings with the regime. The Israelis seemed most fascinated by details on personalities, those slight ticks of human depth that illustrated Iran's leaders, making them all the more vulnerable to Mossad's deception. Although they never revealed their hand to Vaziri, he could sense that for some questions, the Israelis already knew the answers and they merely tested his knowledge and honesty. Despite his disdain, he never lied to them. He hadn't a choice. What little remained of his life rested in their hands. After two weeks, their questioning now lasted only minutes, and their curiosity to his answers was insipid. Perhaps, Vaziri reasoned in his more lucid moments, his answers didn't shed light in the right corners of the Iranian regime. The *katsas* always pressed him on the Quds Force, the Intelligence Ministry, the orders of battle of the police forces in Tehran—but how was he to know? Over time, his hosts turned their attention to the future: specifically, what was to be done with the Vaziris now that Mossad made the regretful decision to extract them from Iran. The French grew tired of providing security in a major five-star hotel in the middle of their capital, and the Israelis just wanted to put the whole matter behind them. But he and his wife spending out their days in Israel was an altogether repulsive prospect for Vaziri. Israel orchestrated the wholesale murder of Palestinians. On that belief, he and the Iranian regime did not differ. The thought of accepting an Israeli passport and living falsely as one of them disgusted him. But what else, his hosts argued, was he to do? Where was he to go? Iran? Surely the regime's enforcers would take him back; the *katsas* already told him that Iranian intelligence officers were scouring Europe. Vaziri knew that they would never stop hunting, that he and Fatemeh would never be safe from their death squads. In Israel they would have a fighting chance, but he was not prepared to yield.

Vaziri's head throbbed—a side effect, the doctor explained, of the drug cocktail necessary to ease his mental wanderings. He felt dirty, not just on that morning, but on all of them, persistently itching at some imaginary grime. It felt like an army of invisible bugs encamped on his skin, and their ghostly feet refused retreat, no matter how often he scratched or showered. Despite this, his mind fought for its grip on sanity and tried to make sense of their latest round of questioning.

He sat opposite a *katsa* named Ezra in the sitting room of suite 102/103 on an antique Louis XVI chair. Looking out from the row of French windows, rain clouds formed over the Tuileries Garden across Rue de Rivoli. Ezra placed a digital voice recorder on the coffee table and flipped to a clean page in his notepad. An SDLP officer went to pull the drapes as Vaziri's eyes trailed him.

"No. Why must you close them?" Vaziri asked with an agitated whine. "I can't. There's no light, no air. I can't breathe."

The officer paused, holding the fabric midway along the rod.

Vaziri placed his head in his hand. "I'm sorry."

"It's fine," Ezra dismissed the Frenchman with a wave. He crossed his legs and held a pen between his fingers. "Today, I'd like to go back over the initial protests on June 13th, 2009. That afternoon, you and Mousavi spoke. Can you elaborate on your conversation?"

Vaziri didn't remember any conversation that day. He massaged his forehead and squinted from the pain. "No. I want to call Nima and Roya. Yesterday you promised. You promised I could call someone."

Nima and Roya Banisadr were Iranian documentary filmmakers who had produced several features on the regime's human rights abuses and persecution of religious minorities. Their films had premiered in festivals at Cannes, Venice and Sundance, garnering considerable media attention and even an Academy Award nomination. The husband and wife lived in the affluent suburb of Wassenaar in the Netherlands. Before his house arrest, Vaziri made a point to keep in touch with the couple and closely followed their work. Now being free, in a sense, he could not wait to hear their voices after years of silence.

"Please let me call them," Vaziri implored. "Let me have a conversation with anyone that isn't you."

Ezra weighed the risk. "I found their number."

"Wait," Doku Vlasiyev gripped the headphones, "they're making a call."

Merely twenty meters over Rue de Castiglione from Le Meurice was the Westin-Vendôme hotel, which also fronted the Tuileries Garden at the intersection with Rue de Rivoli. From a deluxe room on the hotel's first floor, the Spetsnaz operators had a clear view of their target's suite in the adjacent building. The Russians had shooed away room service and repositioned the furniture to fit their needs. Peering through a hole in the curtains on a tripod was a Spectra M laser microphone provided by the GRU residency in Paris. The microphone bounced an invisible infrared beam off a window of suite 102/103 across the street, reading the minute vibrations made by human voices against the glass. Converting those slight variations back into an audio signal, the Spetsnaz operators could hear every word spoken by Mehdi Vaziri and his hosts.

"You mean his security?" Baranov sat on the bedspread behind Vlasiyev.

"Nyet," the Chechen pecked at a laptop keyboard, manipulating the interface of a multi-band equalizer software program. "It's for him."

"For Vaziri?" Baranov's spine straightened.

"Yes." Vlasiyev lifted another pair of headphones off the desk. "Listen."

Next to Vlasiyev was Pokhrovskii, who was fluent in Persian, and sat ready with a legal pad to make a rough translation while the audio was recorded to an external hard drive. Baranov pulled the headphones over his ears. The windows of the Hôtel Meurice were dual-paned, which was beneficial for heating costs, but did not aid their purposes. Through Baranov's headphones, the return audio was wracked by static, like a muffled humming noise, which Vlasiyev explained earlier was the resonate frequency in the cavity between the glass. In a moment, however, he recognized a man's voice.

"Nima... Can you hear me?"

Vaziri struggled to contain himself.

"Who is this?" Nima Banisadr demanded. An unknown number rang his phone at breakfast. He answered, against his better judgment, and discovered a Persian-speaking man on the other end, asking for him by name. Roya loomed in the doorway, a concerned glare on her face.

"It's Mehdi. How—how are you? *Halet chetore?*"

"Mehdi?" Banisdar's voice cracked in disbelief. "Oh my god!"

Vaziri laughed. "I've missed you, my friend."

Roya's look of concern turned to shock. "Mehdi *jon,* where are you?"

Banisadr fumbled. "I heard terrible, awful lies."

"I'm well, Nima. I can't say, but I'm alive. I'm free."

"What the hell is he saying?" Baranov stood at the desk.

Pokhrovskii scribbled over the pad. "Pleasantries: 'I'm alive. I'm free.'"

"Who did he call?"

Vlasiyev shook his head. "Can't confirm. 'Nima'-somebody."

Baranov ripped off the headphones. "Find out."

CHAPTER 36

IN THE FINE, frigid rain that mantled the night sky, it looked as if the grim, brownish façades of the towers were weeping. The twin high-rises of La Forestière loomed over him from both sides. As his eyes climbed ten stories to their rooftops, rain dripping through his lashes, he saw roughly a dozen lights of varying colors: greens, blues and yellows; more windows were darkened, the glass mended with tape and rags or long-ago shattered, left to fall and scatter on the fractured pavement. The cold, February downpour chased the rabble inside, leaving the parking lots and walkways eerily quiet.

Over that void, Zyed Bata reigned.

The boy had studied his target. For the past two nights, after Sajid was asleep, he stalked Fabrice. Using the surrounding estates' warren of overgrown vacant lots, the shade of faulty lampposts, and his target's own inebriation for cover, Zyed learned that Fabrice was a creature of habit. Around eleven, Fabrice came down from the flat he shared with a few other African boys on one of the tower's upper floors, some of whom Zyed remembered from his beating. They hung in the parking lot between buildings, laughing and bumping rap music from a Renault. Girls came and went. Tendrils of hash smoke rose from the crowd. Bottles of cheap booze were passed around. One night, Zyed watched a BMW pull into the lot—rare in Clichy-sous-Bois. Fabrice reached inside the open window, exchanged words with the driver, and pulled away with a lump of tinfoil in his hand. By one in the morning, most of the boys trickled back into the towers, but some wandered with Fabrice amid the empty streets. Zyed prowled after them through tangled weeds sprouting alongside the roads, darting from one shadow to the next. He kept his distance, holding off as far as he could without losing sight, but Fabrice's sheer size made him nearly impossible to miss. The group ran a circuit through the *banlieue's* blight, haunting the neighboring estates of Cité des Bosquets and Le Chêne Pointu. As they entered the flats, Zyed would dip behind a car and wait, glaring at the vestibule for their return. After a while, he would again see Fabrice's bald scalp jutting up from the others. Each time they left an estate and made off down the street, he noticed their stagger worsen. Their speech was loud and slurred, and Zyed could creep within thirty meters of them, in the full glow of a lamppost, without being spotted. Gradually, as he watched Fabrice feebly stumble down the pavement, he shed his fear.

Now Zyed thought he finally had a chance. That night, when Fabrice came down from Le Chêne Pointu with his posse, he had a girl in tow. Zyed figured that she must have also been in her late-teens and from one of the estate's West African immigrant families. Overhearing their chatter, he learned that the girl's name was Tippi, and Fabrice could not keep his hands off her. After a drunken stroll back to La Forestière, they crowded around the Renault. Fabrice unfolded the lump of tinfoil on the hood and placed a slim glass pipe between his lips. He drew the flattened foil to the stem and ran it over a lighter. Zyed heard a sizzle and saw Fabrice's face illuminated by the flame; he thought it was heroin, but he wasn't certain. Tippi took the next drag, followed by the three other boys with him. After their first hit, Fabrice took Tippi to the vestibule steps and made out, digging his hand down her jeans. The others lingered in the parking lot for nearly an hour, smoking hash and swigging vodka. Fabrice and his woman returned to the Renault after a while and took another hit from the glass pipe. Slurred mumbles fell from their mouths and they ambled like clumsy, wooden puppets attached to uneven strings.

Zyed crouched behind a nearby row of cars and peered with hateful eyes. The Makarov sagged in his jacket's front pocket. It was Haddad's idea to wait. He explained that attempting to confront Fabrice sober, for a man of his strength, was suicide—and although that was exactly what Zyed wanted, he had to finish the job. Better to wait, Haddad explained, and let them lose their senses. With the pistol Haddad gave, he could rush out and execute all of them on the spot, but Zyed didn't intend to make it that easy.

Fabrice did not deserve mercy, and a bullet to the temple was just that. To make him pay, to make him suffer, Zyed needed to get Fabrice alone, but he didn't know how.

And then came the rain.

The first drop from the black abyss overhead landed on Zyed's neck. Echoing on the roofs and streets, it rolled in from the west. One drop turned to two and within seconds multiplied by a thousand. In the downpour, Zyed reached for the ski mask folded in a cap over his hair and pulled down, aligning his eyes and mouth with the holes cut into the ribbed fabric. Poised on the balls of his feet, Zyed edged up to the front bumper for a better view. As the rain drummed on cars and shattered against the pavement, the pack ahead stumbled for the entrance to the nearest tower block, where Haddad lived.

In the light shining out from the vestibule, he watched them take cover under the narrow canopy. The three boys who were with Fabrice all night slapped their hands together, turned into the vestibule and made a right, stepping out of view. Zyed knew that corridor opened onto the spiraling stairwell that led to the upper floors. Now in his sights, there was only Fabrice and Tippi, alone. Frozen under the canopy, they held each other close.

Zyed was restless as the rain soaked his clothes. He'd never get a more perfect moment to strike. Le Chêne Pointu was nearly a kilometer down the street, a fifteen-minute walk at best. If Fabrice took Tippi home, through the rain, Zyed could catch him oblivious and exposed; leave him gutted in a drain until dawn. Zyed drew the Makarov from his jacket, chambered a hollow-point round and released the safety. The boy felt his heart rage inside his chest.

Fabrice locked his lips with Tippi's and filled his hands with her rear end. They turned their backs to Zyed and started for the vestibule. Zyed sprung out from his cover. He panicked. If they went upstairs, he would never find them in the tower. He wanted it over, wanted Fabrice dead—so that he, too, could die. Zyed leveled the Makarov at Fabrice's back; the iron sights tracked his lumbering frame. Zyed slid his index finger against the wet trigger.

But inside the vestibule, they turned left.

Zyed lowered the gun at his side. Rain seeped through the ski mask, drenching his cheeks like tears. Left, he knew, led to another stairwell that descended to the basement. It struck Zyed in an instant, as he heaved and gasped: this was fate, a sign from that black shadow.

His eyes ran up the tower's weeping façade, over the doused windows. An icy gust shrouded Zyed, and with it, a ghostly hand pressed into his back. That familiar touch had only ever drug him along, but now it urged him ahead.

Zyed marched into the vestibule. Graffiti tags and mold painted the walls and bare wires dangled from the ceiling tiles. A solid steel fire door stood to the left. He forced down the handle and slowly drew it open. The stairwell was lit by a single, flickering bulb and plunged into the ground for nearly fifty feet. He let the door ease shut, careful not to make a sound, and listened for a moment. A slopping noise with an occasional pant and a moan resonated off the damp concrete. Zyed crept down the stairs. He paused on the first landing and gripped the Makarov firmly in his hands. The noises from below grew more distinct. He heard Fabrice's accent. Easing down the final steps to the floor, he flattened his spine against the wall and tip-toed to the frame of an open doorway. Looking in from the side, Zyed saw a portion of the room ahead—a murky cavern of pipes, manifolds and machinery. The noises came from the other side of the wall.

Zyed wrapped his finger around the trigger and swung through the doorway.

Fabrice stood with his pants undone and Tippi's face in his crotch. He noticed the ski mask in his periphery and jerked his head to the right. A rush of terror smacked him, but there was only enough time to loose a deep cry before Tippi flinched and the muzzle flash burst in their eyes.

Zyed fired once. The bullet caught the left hinge of Tippi's jaw. It expanded with the pressure, shattering bone and ripping off the lower half of her face. She fell on her side, twitching, as Zyed stepped forward.

Badi Haddad parked his Skoda Octavia along Boulevard Beaumarchais, a bustling thoroughfare of bars and cafés, which at that late hour saw enough foot traffic that any surveillance unit would be pained to tamper with it. He filled an hour roaming the incoherent streets west of Place de la Bastille, through the city's 2nd and 3rd arrondissements. Using the healthy sense of paranoia instilled in him in the training camps of southern Lebanon, he interrogated the passing Parisians: looking for familiar faces, too much eye contact or too little, and watching for responses to his sudden changes in direction. Haddad had never detected either passive or hostile surveillance on him; he'd been in Europe for too long, and if the French meant to give him trouble, or even knew of his existence, they would've already gotten around to it. With both hands dug into the pockets of his topcoat and his shoulders arched against the cold, Haddad strolled anonymously up Rue Saint-Denis.

Charted by the Romans in the first century, it was one of the oldest streets in Paris and a center of the June Rebellion of 1832, as depicted in *Les Misérables*. But now there were no barricades, only vice. Less renowned than the tourist traps and scam artists of Pigalle, Rue Saint-Denis was a seedy red-light district. Prostitutes openly mingled on the sidewalk, dressed in over-the-knee boots, fur-collared coats and mini skirts, smoking cigarettes and chatting during lulls in traffic; neon signs hung over the cobbles, peddling sex shops and peep shows; pitch men trawled the glow, luring passersby. But Haddad was wholly indifferent to their wares. He had been communicating over the past few days with an old controller in Beirut, a fellow *mujahid* whom he'd fought under during the insurgencies of the nineties. After Zyed's visit, Haddad saved a draft message in an encrypted email account he was instructed to use only in case of utmost emergencies. At the time, he wasn't sure if he would receive a reply.

Haddad was part of a network of sleeper agents embedded in Europe by Hezbollah. Alongside others in Greece, Spain and Italy, Haddad's mission was to prepare caches of weapons and explosives and burrow into society until orders came from the commander of foreign operations, Ibrahim al-Din, that an attack was underway on the continent. At that point, Haddad would be charged with logistics in support of the team sent from Lebanon that would physically execute the operation. But no orders were ever given. The Quds Force and Hezbollah's leading clerics neutered al-Din's Special Research Apparatus and forced him into retirement. The tentacles they stretched out from Beirut were left to whither and die, and Badi Haddad was roundly forgotten, until now.

The draft he saved to the account detailed Zyed's willingness for a martyrdom operation and asked if any opportunities were available somewhere in the Middle East. Haddad expected his query to be in vain, and made it largely out of sympathy for Zyed—and also for him to see if anyone was still listening. To his shock, they were. A response came within hours. It denied that any operations were underway, but it asked for more. Haddad gave a full account of his time in Europe to that date: his assessment of any scrutiny paid to him by French security services—there was none—and the state of the caches he maintained in the country—Haddad kept six rented storage sheds outside Paris under various identities. Once the volley of questions were satisfied, another reply came, instructing him to communicate with a different, more secure platform. Haddad bought an air-gaped laptop, one that was never connected to the Internet, and booted it with a USB thumb drive using Tails OS. Tails was a Linux-based operating system that functioned like a computer-in-a-box, which ran entirely off the thumb drive and didn't save any data locally on the laptop's hard drive. By forcing all of its outgoing connections through Tor, a web browser that encrypted Internet traffic through a global network of volunteer servers, Tails allowed Haddad to talk with his controller in total anonymity. Switching their communications to Pidgin, a secure instant messaging service, Haddad was finally told the truth: No chances for martyrdom were available in Lebanon or Syria, but there was another opportunity. On the final exchange with his controller, Haddad learned that this whole time he was speaking to "Dhu al-Faqr," the *nom de guerre* of Ibrahim al-Din's most trusted lieutenant, Anwar Sabbah. And he intended to pay Haddad a visit.

As instructed, Haddad turned down Passage de la Trinité, a crooked alleyway sliced discreetly amid the parade of capitalized sex. Stepping down the alley a few dozen feet, Haddad heard a faint, rumbling bass and spotted a massive fleshy cube of a man swaddled in a velvet blazer, sentineled beneath a lit sign that summarily proffered: *"Les Dames."* After surrendering the compulsory thirty euros for admittance, the bouncer opened the door and pointed Haddad down a narrow flight of steps toward a glaring cauldron of neon lights and electric noise.

A manic staccato of synthesized rage boomed off speakers. Haddad maneuvered along a low-ceilinged corridor into a windowless room ringed with semicircle booths teeming with unseemly men who were either enthralled or detached at their entertainment. Topless women danced on raised platforms and swayed around poles. Green lasers oscillated with the heavy bass. Strobes glinted in the darkness. Multi-colored spotlights painted the musty haze. Haddad's eyes narrowed in the onslaught. Beyond the bar, he noticed, there was another room. Dhu al-Faqr would be inside, the final message read, wearing a dark suit. Alone.

Haddad waded between the undulating strippers and their perspiring fans. Sitting at a booth near the emergency exit was a man dressed in a tailored blazer and trousers with the top two buttons of his shirt undone—all in black. His face was turned from the crowd, but as Haddad came beside him, he recognized it as the malleable mask of Anwar Sabbah.

"Brother Badi," Sabbah smiled and inched down the booth, motioning to a patch of worn, artificial leather. *"Fadlak."*

Haddad eased himself behind the table, sitting close enough that they could hear each other through the clamoring music.

"Aucun français," Sabbah declared; *"al-'arabiyyah."*

Two girls wandered up to their table, as if someone whistled them over, and squeezed into either end of the booth. Wearing only a G-string and stilettos, their skin appeared oddly synthetic in the haze and their breasts were masterfully sculpted to hide the implant scars.

One ran her manicured fingernails through Sabbah's hair and crooned, "Buy us drinks, honey?"

Sabbah's eyes rolled. He took a five-hundred-euro note from his pocket and held it over the table with a thud of his elbow. "Get your own damn drink," he said. "And leave us. Tell your friends."

She snatched the bill from his hand and the pair sauntered away.

"Loathsome cunt," Sabbah huffed into a glass of San Pellegrino and gin.

Haddad noticed that he looked genuinely offended, his eyes trailing the girls with disgust as they melted into the crowd.

Sabbah slid an ashtray in front of him and lit a cigarette. "Abu Dokhan sends his regards," he said in Arabic, snapping the lighter shut.

Haddad's jaw hung slack for a moment. *"Shukran,* brother. I pray that Abu Dokhan and all the *mujahedeen* are well."

"I will be truthful, as I believe you deserve it," Sabbah said, "but the Islamic Resistance has never been so close to defeat."

"Syria?"

Sabbah nodded, tapping away the ashes. "Two thousand *mujahedeen* were martyred before Damascus fell... For nothing. You know what happened: Daesh went mad, and the Turks were forced to intervene. Then the Americans came. Before we could dig defensive lines around the city, those terrorist battalions were all around. The brothers who weren't cut-off fell back to Lebanon. The Pasdaran wanted to send reinforcements through Iraq, but they were overruled. In our defeat, Wissam Hamawi is content to humiliate us even more."

"You're really disarming?"

"No," Sabbah ruled with a puff, "that will never happen. There are greater tides about to wash ashore."

Haddad gauged what he meant, but Sabbah was in no mood to be coy.

"We are planning a coup," he said; "Abu Dokhan and others. We mean to rid the party of Wissam Hamawi and the clerics, set the resistance back upon the straight path, and declare war on the Zionists. I'd like you to play a role."

"Uh, yes, I'd be honored," Haddad stammered. *"Alhamdulillah."*

"Good." Smoke purged from Sabbah's lungs, and he spun an artful lie. *"Hajj* Qasem is directing this operation from Tehran; Ibrahim—Abu Dokhan—is merely an executor of *al-Quds* will. Like old times, brother."

"Like old times," Haddad grinned.

"First we must eliminate a traitor, a friend of the Zionists, and an enemy of the Islamic Revolution." Sabbah's finger jabbed the table. "In Paris."

"Who?"

"Mehdi Vaziri."

Haddad shot a look of surprise.

"Oh yes, brother." Sabbah pulled a smartphone from his pocket. "The Zionists arranged his defection from house arrest in Tehran. Mossad's debriefing him in the city with the cooperation of the DGSE." He passed Haddad the phone.

Sliding his finger over the screen, Haddad scrolled through a collection of photos. He knew they were taken only a few blocks away. Haddad saw the arcaded sidewalk along Rue de Rivoli opposite the Tuileries Garden, commissioned by Napoleon. Flicking to another photo, Haddad noticed uniformed porters, flags dangling over awnings, and a string of gold leaf letters that read, "Le Meurice." Lastly, he saw a corner of the same building, standing above a Chopard boutique at the intersection with Rue de Castiglione."

"Vaziri is a guest of the Hôtel Meurice," Sabbah said, sliding the phone back into his pocket, "in suite 102/103, posing as a Brazilian sugar baron. The suite hasn't been serviced in two weeks, the hotel's security manager barked at housekeeping for asking questions, and at least five plainclothes *Police nationale* officers are in the lobby at any given time of day."

"You want me to kill him?" Haddad dropped his voice despite the noise.

"I want your boy to kill him. I want you to assist."

Haddad folded his hands on the table. "Zyed's in a dark place. He confuses the idea of martyrdom with death. He's a disturbed boy."

Sabbah rolled his eyes with a detached shrug. "Makes no difference to me. It is an act of mercy, then."

"How?" he stuttered. "How should we do it?"

"Your caches; what's their state?"

"I keep sheds around Ile-de-France; six in all," said Haddad. "I've spread forty fifty-pound bags of ammonium nitrate between them. That's... Twenty-three hundred kilos? But they've sat for years. I can't say they're any good."

"No," Sabbah shook his head, "fertilizer is quite stable at room temperature; there shouldn't be any decomposition. What else?"

Haddad thought. "Five hundred kilos of acetylene and liquid nitromethane I stole from a racetrack, seven crates of Tovex sausages, eighty spools of shock tube, a few hundred blasting caps."

"Good, that's fine," Sabbah took a pen from his jacket and opened a napkin. "You're going to get a box lorry—rent it, steal it; I don't care. Mix the ammonium nitrate and nitromethane in barrels, add the acetylene for brisance." He drew a crude outline of the truck's bed, making the barrels in the shape of a letter T. "Tamp the explosives along the front side of the lorry, like this; like a shaped charge. You understand? It explodes up into the hotel."

Haddad nodded.

"But you must distribute the weight evenly, or else it'll list, or an axel will crack. Okay? Build it like that," Sabbah gave over the napkin. "Zyed drives the lorry, of course. Have him come down Rue de Rivoli, gaining speed, and ram through the arcades and into Chopard. Vaziri's suite is above."

"I can do this," Haddad studied the design.

"Good. You remember your training?"

"Näam," said Haddad. "Quite well."

"Your boy will be with God," said Sabbah, "whether he wants or not."

Haddad waited as Chehab took a drag on his cigarette.

"Now we must talk about you," he said, tapping off the ash. Chehab reached inside his jacket and removed a creased envelope, passing it to Haddad under the table. "Inside are two passports: a French and an Iranian. We've taken an old photo of you and doctored it to account for age. Both have visa histories and will pass biometrics. You'll also find three cash cards with a total balance of twenty thousand euro. Draw in small bills on separate cashpoints. On the day of, drive to Séte and book round-trip passage on the ferry to Tangier, using the French passport to bypass the visa requirement. In good weather, it's a forty-five-hour crossing—toss your identification cards overboard. Once in Morocco, you can take a train or bus to Casablanca and then purchase a one-way ticket on a flight to Beirut with the Iranian passport."

Haddad stuffed the envelope in his coat pocket. "When?"

"Don't know." Chehab crushed the cigarette in the tray. "But it could be any day, so start preparing. I'll message you forty-eight hours in advance.

One more thing… That day, in the public car park on Rue de Berri, off Champs-Élysées, there will be a dark blue Fiat Linea with the plate number '524 BXL 75.' A key will be taped in the rear driver's side wheel well. If we attack in the morning, you should have time to reach Séte before the seven-thirty ferry departs; if not, get as far from Paris as possible and wait. There's a Carrefour near the quay where you can abandon the Fiat. Understood?"

"Understood," Haddad breathed.

"Excellent," Sabbah took his hand and slapped it against Haddad's, giving a firm shake. "You will be a fugitive in the West for the rest of your life, but we will protect you. Abu Dokhan will reward you properly."

"Then I will see you again in Beirut," said Haddad, realizing with joy that he was finally coming home.

"In Beirut, brother," Sabbah nodded. "Either you return as a martyr, or carrying the banner of victory."

"Inshallah," he smiled.

"Now off with you," Sabbah waved. "We can't leave together."

As Haddad left, Sabbah waited fifteen minutes and finished his drink before wadding through the writhing mass of flesh.

Blood gushed from Fabrice's crotch. He wailed a hideous, angry cry, building to a guttural shriek as he realized what was happening. Fabrice's fingers tensed like claws and his hands rose to his face. His pants fell on his ankles as he tilted forward in shock—his eyes not on Zyed, but on Tippi. Her jaw was in pieces and her cheeks dangled in shreds. Flopped on her side, she gently twitched in the growing pool around her. Her eyes rolled back into their sockets.

Before Fabrice could utter a coherent word, Zyed fired again.

The bullet struck his right kneecap, tearing apart bones, cartilage, muscle fibers and nerves. He dropped like a stone, gripped his lower thigh and flailed on the ground in searing agony.

Zyed came closer.

Fabrice rolled on his stomach and tried to crawl toward the far wall on his forearms—struggling with every inch to get away, to buy more time.

Zyed snatched his ankles and drug him back with a smear of blood. He ripped the ski mask from his face and roared, "Look at me!"

Fabrice cried, grasping for each centimeter of concrete. *"Non! Non!"*

"Look!" Zyed hunched over him, pressed the Makarov into the pit of Fabrice's left knee and squeezed the trigger.

Fabrice almost snapped his spine recoiling from the blast. His vocal cords were hoarse. *"S'il vous plaît!"* he yelped. *"S'il vous plaît!"*

He was ready. Zyed tossed the gun to the opposite end of the room and fought to steady his hands. His stomach was bound in knots. His face was flush and his skin tingled. His heart pounded. This was it.

Zyed crouched over Fabrice's naked pelvis and drove his right knee into Fabrice's lower back. Gasping, he took a spring-loaded knife from his jacket, pressed the switch and released a six-inch, serrated blade from the handle. He smiled. Zyed fantasized about this moment. There was no turning back.

Fabrice squirmed, shrieking, and Zyed forced down more of his weight.

Zyed brought his left hand over Fabrice's scalp and jammed his index and middle fingers up Fabrice's nostrils as far as they would fit. Fabrice moaned as Zyed pealed his head off the floor, exposing his throat, and slashed with his right hand.

The blade's serrated edge dug into the skin, and Fabrice made a gargled cry. Blood spilled from his jugular as his feet drummed on the floor.

Zyed grit his teeth. He sawed vigorously, severing the carotid arteries and tendons attached to the clavicle and pulling open the widening gash in Fabrice's neck.

Fabrice screamed savagely and Zyed spotted tears dripping into the blood. After maybe seven seconds, the alarm and distress in Fabrice's eyes began to fade, the screams subsided, and his head drooped forward in Zyed's hand.

Zyed kept cutting into the cartilage around Fabrice's trachea and esophagus, but when he reached the muscles near Fabrice's spine, the knife's edge got caught in the sinew.

Zyed gave up. He wrenched the blade loose and rose to his quavering feet. His face was drenched with sweat, and his legs and hands were soaked in blood. A thin pool settled over the floor, running into the stairwell. Zyed saw the extent of what he had done. Tippi's skull was unrecognizable. The bits of flesh pinning Fabrice's head to his shoulders were twisted and mangled.

Standing over them, his chest heaved for air. It was nothing like he expected. Zyed sensed none of the rage or sorrow that consumed him over the past weeks. In a way, he felt cheated, denied of the catharsis that was owed him. He thought of his parents, and the fate dealt to them. It was almost identical. He felt nothing—not pleasure, not anger, not guilt, not sorrow. His station in the universe was unchanged; he was still Zyed Bata, a boy adrift and helpless in a vast sea with no one coming to his rescue; a spectator to the endless festival of massacres.

Only now, he counted one to his name.

South down Rue Saint-Denis, toward the Seine, a blustery wind rattled Sabbah's bones. A huddle of prostitutes across the street clutched their fur collars. It sounded from the west, echoing on the porcelain chimneys and mansard roofs. A single drop broke on the cobblestone at Sabbah's feet, and then thousands. Unmoved, Sabbah lifted his umbrella as the prostitutes dashed for cover, opening the canopy into the downpour. He kept on through gathering streams and shallow lakes of light, with only the sound of dripping from the eaves for company. Sabbah strolled through the rain, crossing over to Boulevard de Sébastopol and finally to Rue Pernelle. Tour Saint-Jacques loomed above. The Gothic sixteenth-century belfry sat isolated in a square of barren, white mulberry trees; its pale gargoyles snarled and sobbed in the amber cascade. His eyes fell back to the street, where parked cars flanked either side of Rue Pernelle. He stood on the cobbles, scanning the rows of drenched metal, when two headlights flashed once in the darkness. Sabbah stepped around the rippling puddles toward the Citroën C3, collapsed his umbrella, and slid through the open passenger door.

Ruslan Baranov sat behind the wheel.

"How'd he take it?" the Russian asked.

"Like we thought," answered Sabbah as the engine turned over.

"He has the passport?"

Sabbah nodded.

Baranov switched on the headlights and eased off the curb. "An asset of ours with Europol flagged the biometrics and listed features for facial recognition. He'll get held for secondary screening if he tries to leave the continent. You told him about the Iranians?"

"Yes," Sabbah muttered. "Let's hope we don't need it."

"Leave that bit to me."

The Citroën slipped into early morning traffic. Baranov followed a circuitous route toward Paris's northwestern suburbs, crossing Boulevard Périphérique into Levallois-Perret and spanning the Seine at Pont de Courbevoie. Passing a cemetery in Nanterre, the landscape became oddly postapocalyptic. In the glossy shadow of the glass and steel high-rises of La Défense, Sabbah saw a drifting warren of rusting, corrugated tin shacks; ramshackle garages covered in faded, peeling paint; and dour, empty warehouses. Barriers of ivy and razor wire fences carved the terrain. Shipping containers were stacked and butted together at strange angles, marking seemingly endless fields of salvage—mangled heaps of tailpipes, racks of doors and mountains of chassis. Yet hardly a kilometer away, in full view of the detritus, Sabbah eyed the vast Carrara marble frame of the Grande Arche de la Défense, reflecting the towers' glimmering light. But as they drove, to his suspicion, not a living soul could be seen.

Baranov picked a prepaid cell phone from the cup holder and dialed a number, placing it to his ear. He mumbled after a few rings, *"Ya odnu minutu iz…da,"* and hung up.

Turning into a scrap yard, Baranov eased on the brakes.

Sabbah saw a large Quonset hut ahead. Its metal door rolled open and a silhouette stepped outside. Closing a few feet, Sabbah recognized the silhouette as Ignatev, one of the Chechens he'd spotted swirling around the farmhouse in Zarayeb on the night he accompanied al-Din. Ignatev wore a load-bearing vest over a black sweatshirt and wielded an AK-103—an upgraded derivative of the *Avtomat Kalashnikova*—equipped with an American-made Magpul stock, a shortened, dimpled barrel, an accessory rail and a forward grip. It wasn't, Sabbah knew, a weapon commonly brandished on the streets of Paris. But again, he'd long ago been shown that these men weren't common foot soldiers.

Baranov pulled the Citroën into the hut while Ignatev heaved the door shut behind them, masking any trace of their presence. As they rose from the car, Sabbah saw a half-dozen other Spetsnaz operators dressed in plain-clothes, and none armed like Ignatev. They kept at their work, ignoring his arrival. A black Land Rover Freelander SUV sat near the hut's far wall. Its hatch was lifted and in the trunk was an industrial-grade concrete saw and sledgehammers. On a nearby table, a pair stood over several more rifles and sidearms, snapping ammunition cartridges into magazines. Lastly, occupying the most space in the hut, was a dark blue Fiat Linea with the plate number 524 BXL 75. Its hood was raised and the dashboard was disassembled in sections on the floor. A few operators tinkered with the engine and the exposed wires in the steering column.

Sabbah pointed to the guns. "What are those for?"

"Some of us are headed to Germany in the morning."

"To—"

"Yes," Baranov grinned, "but first we must make a detour."

Zyed made no attempt to hide Fabrice and Tippi's bodies and left them where they lay. What would come next, or how he'd move forward, was an alien concept. It never occurred to him, nor did he care. He wanted Fabrice dead, and now he was. Zyed climbed the stairs and left through the vestibule. As he reeled through the empty parking lot to the adjacent tower, the rain fell with fury. He stopped midway and opened his palms, letting the cold drops wash away the blood. It hardly made a difference.

Coming up to his grandmother's flat on the adjacent tower's sixth floor, he took off his shoes and quietly stepped into the small room he shared with Sajid, sitting at the edge of his brother's bed. Zyed gave him a gentle pat on the leg.

Sajid awoke with a startled jerk.

"It's me."

Sajid squinted and recognized the outline of his older brother. As his eyes adjusted to the pale light, he noticed Zyed's hands and pant legs. He shot up in bed and pointed, "What is that?"

"Shhh," Zyed held a finger to his lips. "She'll hear you."

"What is that?" Sajid whispered.

"Blood."

Sajid's glared at his brother's hands, certain he was dreaming. "You—"

"I killed Fabrice."

"Oh!" Before Sajid could voice another syllable, Zyed dove over the bed and slapped a bloodied hand over his mouth.

"Shut up," Zyed spat as Sajid gave a muffled whimper. "You have to shut up. If I take my hand away, promise you'll be quiet?"

The boy nodded and his brother pulled back.

"How?" Sajid whined, wiping his mouth with his T-shirt.

Zyed replied nonchalantly, "I cut off his head."

Sajid's shoulders dropped. "You're not lying." He scanned the room, looking like he was about to be sick. "Why? How could you?"

"I had to."

"How—"

Zyed placed another finger on his brother's lips. "I had to, Sajid," he said. "For us."

"Think of *Jaddah,*" Sajid invoked their grandmother. "You'll kill her."

"I don't care," Zyed coldly shook his head. "I don't care if she dies."

Sajid's eyes welled. "What happened to you?"

Zyed folded his hands and looked down at his lap. "This world is cruel. What mother and father told us, what the imams told us—it's all lies. God is a coward. He's stranded us in this eternal hell and promised rescue. But God is dead, and no one is coming to save us. It goes on like this, eon after eon; all of us characters, condemned to suffer in a story we did not ask to play. There's no happy ending waiting for us, just agony. We, alone, can choose to end it. We, alone, can choose to finally wake up, Sajid; to go home."

"You sound like him," Sajid muttered.

"And he was right," Zyed admitted with a calm nod. "You know that."

Sajid was frozen.

"I hate it here," Zyed casually declared. "I can't stay. I won't. It's not just this estate, or this town, or this country; it's all of it, this whole world. It's us. It has to end. We're piles of rotting meat that think we're special. And I won't be a witness anymore."

"What are you saying?" Sajid's lips cracked, and his voice teemed with pain—with resigned disappointment that twilight was upon them.

Zyed's head rose as he caressed his brother's leg through the sheet. "I'm saying that I want you to die with me.

CHAPTER 37

"THAT'S HIM? THAT'S our guy?"

The back of Nathan Cohen's head bobbed from the driver's seat. "That's our guy."

Nina leaned forward and studied the modest house sitting fifty meters beyond the windshield. A short, portly man with thinning black hair and a full mustache fastened the latch of the front gate and strolled along the deserted side street—wholly oblivious to the unflinching apparatus that stalked his every move. She thought Walid Rada was physically underwhelming, but after weeks, Nina could finally put a face to the name.

Rada followed the street's slope downhill, gradually sinking into the pink horizon above Machgara's concrete and terracotta skyline. The *muezzin's* call to prayer from the loudspeakers of the nearest mosque ended only a few minutes earlier, and with the coming surge into the streets, Cohen knew it was safe to bring his operators out from cover.

He lifted the radio off the center console. "All stations, all stations, this is control. Beta One is out, out, out from the trap; approaching blue one. Who has eyeball?" Cohen's team peppered Machgara with a series of spot codes, or waypoints, which they used to track Rada around town. "Blue one" was the first spot code between his home and his office at the Jihad al-Binna Foundation.

The radio crackled in response, "All stations, this is Sierra One. I have eyeball toward blue one. Who's backing?"

"Sierra Three—backing."

"Sierra Two—roger that."

"Sierra One—Beta One still straight toward blue one."

"Sierra Two—roger that."

"Sierra Three—roger that."

"Control—copy all. Foot traffic is sparse. Keep your distance," Cohen said and set the radio down, looking to the rugged laptop on the passenger seat. The screen displayed a map of Machgara overlaid with each spot code and three gradually shifting markers, identifying the real-time locations of his operators.

The Israelis used floating-box surveillance to not just follow Rada, but to physically surround him, blending seamlessly into the environment. The "box" of Mossad *katsas* floated with Rada, moving as he did. It was a tactic that made it exceedingly difficult for the target to escape, if he even knew he was being watched. As a bureaucrat whose only real purpose was to shift funds between accounts and see that Hezbollah's construction projects remained on track and within budget, Rada made himself a soft target. He was nothing like the shrewd chameleons of the Islamic Resistance who, if lost even once, could stay underground for decades. For Mossad, Walid Rada was easy prey.

Cohen pointed up an adjacent street to a parked utility van marked with the logo of Électricité du Liban, the Lebanese national power company. "If we're lucky, we'll get inside today."

"These collects are interesting," said Nina, leafing through a folder.

"Yeah, homeboy's got some weird tastes."

Using their taps on Lebanon's Internet service providers, Unit 8200 monitored Rada's web traffic. For roughly two hours late each night, he visited a slew of hardcore pornographic sites. Rada tried to use a virtual private network to cover his tracks, but he used his VPN to connect through the browser and not the other way around. It was a sloppy mistake that Unit 8200 exploited all too often. Nina ran her finger down the log, reading the URLs with an adolescent grin.

"I got a friend coming up from Tel Aviv; she specializes in that sort of thing," Cohen said. "I'll use her for the approach. At the very least, we'll get his attention."

Unit 8200 also syphoned off his text messages, emails and phone conversations. That same night, before getting online, Rada spoke for nearly twenty minutes to the director of al-Ajarha Association, a veterans' benefits charity for Hezbollah fighters. It was the first time, since Unit 8200 started listening, that he called someone inside the party from his cell phone. Nina could discern from the transcripts that al-Ajarha's director clearly wanted to keep the conversation as brief as possible, but Rada kept him on the line. He knew that the director recently met with Secretary-General Hamawi in Beirut and wanted any scrap of information on the investigation that might have been revealed on the embezzlement from Rada's office. But if the director had any insight, he wasn't about to share. Rada saw the director as one of his only friends, he made that much clear, but at this late stage any association to Rada was toxic. He was desperate.

"Can I bring these to the embassy?" Nina asked.

"Yeah, those are yours."

In a moment, Cohen's radio scratched to life.

"All stations, Sierra One. Left, left, left toward blue three. Sierra Two, can you?" In parlance, Rada turned left on his walk to the office. Sierra One was asking if Sierra Two could take up the eyeball position behind their target.

"That's a roger," came the reply from Sierra Two.

"Sierra Three—backing."

Cohen clicked at his screen, following their maneuvers.

Neither said a word of what happened between them the other night. Nina woke the next morning in her room at the Tango Inn with a simmering headache and a stomach toiling with regret. It was difficult to face Cohen, to consider how he might have interpreted her advance. But Cohen was a professional, they both had a job to do, and whatever he thought remained locked inside his head.

They sat in the car for nearly twenty minutes, listening to the radio transmissions. Rada took the same route to work that he used the past several mornings that Cohen's team tracked him. The *katsas* positioned a fresh plot-up around Jihad al-Binna's office and waited to do it all over again come the afternoon. After a few days, Cohen thought he had a firm grasp of Rada's habits and daily life. It was rather predictable and mundane—a monotonous routine pursued by most bureaucrats around the world—but that just made Rada easier to snare. Yet there was one blind spot in their understanding of Rada's life. Cohen still hadn't a clue what happened when he went inside his home and shut the door, away from technology. He needed to know how Hezbollah's scrutiny affected Rada's relationship with his wife, Yusra. Did she stand beside him? Did she loathe him? The answer would be critical when the time came for Cohen to pitch his defection. To find out, he needed to drill eyes and ears inside their walls.

Cohen checked the time.

Like clockwork, a plump, homely woman wrapped in a purple headscarf emerged from the house, towing a beaming little girl with burgundy locks. It was Rada's wife, Yusra, and their four-year-old daughter, Eshe. Yusra fastened the gate and headed toward town, Eshe skipping beside her. Also prone to habit, Yusra left twenty minutes after her husband to bring Eshe to school and then always took her time perusing the market.

"Here we go," Cohen breathed, lifting the radio. "All stations, all stations, this is control. Beta Two and Beta Three are out, out, out from the trap. Sierra Four, you are clear for approximately thirty mikes. Execute."

"Sierra Four—roger," the radio crackled.

As Yusra and Eshe sank into the horizon, five men appeared from within the Électricité du Liban utility van, dressed in matching coveralls and hauling Pelican cases. Each was from Mossad's Neviot unit, specializing in technical surveillance and covert entry. They stormed toward the house.

Cohen smiled as they disappeared from view and craned his head around to see Nina. "I'll highlight the juicy bits."

Her eyes met his. "Thanks, killer."

Lansing was exhausted. He cut down the narrow corridor on the first floor of the West Wing and turned into the crammed anteroom adjoining the Cabinet Room and the Oval Office. The president's personal secretary sat behind a large mahogany desk, tapping away at her keyboard. Lansing wiped the bead of sweat slipping along his brow. "Hi, Carol," he breathed.

She looked up from her computer. "Good morning, Ambassador."

"I'm so late," he checked his watch. "Have they started?"

"Not yet, but they're all in there—"

A booming voice rumbled from the Oval. "Harold?"

Carol smiled at him.

Paulson appeared in the curved doorway. "Harold, come on in."

Lansing adjusted his grip on his briefcase and offered out his free hand. "Mr. President, my apologies…"

"Not necessary," Paulson touched Lansing's arm and swept him inside, "Angela showed me your emails." The Oval Office was drenched in sunlight from the South Lawn, washing over the *Resolute* desk. Sitting in one of two caramel-colored leather high-back chairs was Weisel, and on the end of the beige sofa next to her were Freeman and Larry Dawson. Across a coffee table between them, on the end of an identical beige sofa, was Tanner, his yellow notepad ready on his lap. The vice president, thankfully, was away at a campaign rally in Greenville, South Carolina. "Help yourself," Paulson motioned to a porcelain carafe on the table.

"You made it," Freeman exclaimed.

Lansing shook his head. "My Acela must've sat on the tracks for forty minutes—some signal problem in Philly. Next time, I'm driving."

"That's what happens when you criminally underfund Amtrak," said Paulson, dropping into the chair next to Weisel. "Well, let's get started."

Tanner spoke up. "Sir, I thought we'd begin with CIA's preparations for Operation PACER."

"Ryan?" asked Paulson.

Freeman shifted on the sofa. "Our focus for the moment is establishing contact with General Gorani. About two days ago, our asset left a smuggling camp near the border in Iraqi Kurdistan. We gave this asset a secure sat phone and instructed him to deliver it to Gorani in Palanjar—then we'd wait for a call. Using the phone, we were able to track our asset along the way. I can tell you he reached Palanjar late last night. Our GPS fix on the phone has been stationary since then, but no call as of yet… But we're waiting, sir."

"Ryan, how confident are you that Gorani will want to talk?" Paulson said.

"Persia House seems to believe that the hard part is simply getting Gorani on the phone; at least that's what I'm told by our officers who've worked with him in the past. Once that's accomplished, we can sustain a dialogue and ease Gorani into the operation. If he's determined to take a pound of flesh from the Iranians—and from what we've seen, he is—then working with us would have clear benefits." Freeman glanced at his notes. "I also spoke with Admiral Wade earlier. He's settled on an NCO from DEVGRU to command our liaison element, if we're able to get a hold of Gorani. Wade's headed to Virginia Beach in the next few days to make the offer in person. And, of course, we're waiting on word from Mossad that they've gotten Alireza Fakhrizadeh's autopsy report. That's about it on our end, sir."

Paulson nodded. "Okay thanks. You'll let us know if Gorani calls?"

"That minute."

"Harold, you were able to meet with Dr. Ghanbari?" Tanner asked.

Lansing nodded. "That's right, Morteza came up for dinner. It was interesting, to say the least. We talked about politics in Tehran after the JCPOA, and it's essentially as we've imagined: Rostani's been given a lot of capital in the streets, but naturally the IRGC is feeling backed into a corner. The Green Movement's in tatters, which we knew. Khansari's involvement in the day-to-day operations of government is ceremonial, which we knew. There's a question if the Guardian Council will block Rostani's reelection, but given that the public credits him for sanctions relief, it seems unlikely. I brought up our proposal to restart negotiations and asked who he thought might be an acceptable intermediary. He volunteered himself."

Tanner set his pen down. "Sorry, Ghanbari's offering to go to Tehran and give Khansari our invitation?"

"Well, not exactly," Lansing said. "I asked who is best suited to speak for Khansari, given his condition—someone whose authority could bypass the Revolutionary Guards. He suggested the supreme leader's security advisor, a retired general named Saeed Mofidi."

Freeman felt like molten lead seeped into the pit of his stomach. His eyes darted over to Weisel, whose own were ready to meet him. They held each other's gaze with an unspoken look of dread, cursing fate.

"Apparently, Saeed Mofidi holds pro-Western views," Lansing explained. "He was a crucial voice in convincing Khansari to keep negotiations moving forward. Chances are, he'd be happy to see them start up again. Dr. Ghanbari would arrange a meeting with Mofidi in Tehran, explain our position, and ask that he present it to the supreme leader. From there, CIA's asset could ensure that Khansari sees it through."

"Ryan, Angela—do you know anything about this Mofidi fellow?" Paulson asked.

Weisel nodded, slack-jawed and numb, scribbling something at the bottom of her notepad. She tore off the bottom quarter of the page, folded it, and handed it to the president.

"Y—yes," Freeman stammered and cleared his throat, "Saeed Mofidi is one of the more liberal, reformist minds near the supreme leader. That's right."

Paulson took the page and read it in a single glance.

Mofidi is CIA.

"Okay, thank you, Harold," Paulson swallowed and passed the note over the sofa's arm to Tanner. "So what's the plan going forward?"

Weisel swore in her mind as the scrap drifted farther away.

Tanner took the scrap from between the president's fingers and opened it in his lap. Weisel saw his eyes widen for less than a second and drift over the coffee table toward Freeman, who looked down at his lap. Tanner folded the paper again and slipped it in with his notes, out of sight. Weisel bit her lip—but it was too late. Freeman missed the entire exchange. By the time he looked up again, it was all over.

"What's the plan going forward?" Lansing echoed. "Morteza has dual citizenship, so when he flies to Tehran, he doesn't need to worry about a visa. His mother is in her nineties and lives in the city, so he has a reason for travelling."

"How's this all happening?" Weisel interrupted. "I mean, how is Ghanbari getting in touch with Mofidi? What's the plan there?"

"Ghanbari's friendly with the imam of the Islamic Centre of England, Ayatollah Abdolhossein Moezi," said Lansing, "Khansari's representative in London. The request to meet with Mofidi went through him."

Freeman shook his head. "Then the Rev Guards almost certainly know Ghanbari's coming. The only question to them is why."

"Would they interfere?" Dawson asked.

The D/CIA shrugged. "Hard to say. Not overtly; not unless they knew."

"Okay, so let's assume Ghanbari meets with Mofidi and agrees to pass our offer to the supreme leader," Paulson said. "Then what?"

"May I?" Weisel raised her hand.

Lansing yielded. "Go ahead, Angela."

"Harold and I have already worked on this," she said. "Before Ghanbari reaches Tehran, CIA would get word to its asset that Khansari must agree to resume talks. Correct, Ryan?"

Freeman nodded. "We're working on that now."

"Okay," she continued, "so we can predict that there would be some discussions between Saeed Mofidi, President Rostani and Javad Zanjani. As this is strictly a backchannel negotiation, for now, Harold would represent us at an initial meeting to discuss an agenda for follow-on talks. Providing that goes well, we would announce renewed negotiations, likely after Annapolis, and I would take point. As for that initial meeting, our proposal to Saeed Mofidi would suggest Villa Tatiana, our ambassador's residence in Geneva—it's quiet, away from the press."

Paulson rubbed his chin. "Eli and Larry, how's our legal coverage?"

"Well, as Angela said, it's a backchannel," Dawson explained. "And we're clearly empowered to conduct this nation's foreign policy. We're not discussing a treaty or any radical shifts to our alliances—this is merely a formality on an agenda for future dialogue. I don't foresee a problem."

"Congress doesn't need to know, if that's what you're asking, sir," Tanner said. "If Harold's meeting in Geneva goes well, and Weisel takes point on future dialogue, we'll go from there. They won't be pleased, but when are they ever?"

Paulson smirked. "Good point."

"Andrew, I think we're fine," Weisel added.

"Okay," the president nodded, "okay, very good. Well done, everyone."

Nina sat with her legs crossed before Tom Stessel's desk. She listened to the progressive ticking of a clock on the wall and twiddled her thumbs. On each page turn, the Beirut Station chief passively signaled his contempt with a bowing frown. Stessel parsed Mossad's plunder through every scrap of Walid Rada's life and exhaled through his nose.

"What's this? This bank account?"

"We think that's where he stashed it," Nina said.

Stessel's eyes rose from the page. "The Iranian aid funds?"

"Yep."

When Unit 8200 compromised Rada's VPN, they discovered that, between the pornography, he occasionally visited the website of the Lebanese Swiss Bank. Intrigued by his behaviour, Unit 8200 breached the bank's servers and found that Walid Rada held an account there, albeit under a different name. The account was opened three years prior and was immediately hit with varying cash deposits over a nine-month period. The highest recorded balance, after the rash of deposits, was two million dollars—the same amount stolen from Hezbollah. Since then, the account collected interest and saw only sporadic activity. But there was one exception. Every few weeks, the account logged direct withdrawals of three thousand dollars to a nightclub called *"Le Piége"* up the coast from Beirut in the resort town of Jounieh, which was commonly known as a front for prostitution. And then three months ago—as Hezbollah took stock of its losses in Syria and realized its war chest was short two million and change—the withdrawals ceased.

Mossad had Rada cornered. He was guilty, that much was certain, but the Israelis now also knew that so long as Rada remained in Lebanon, he couldn't risk retrieving the money he stole. Likewise, so long as Rada hid behind his VPN, Hezbollah hadn't the technical capability to prove his guilt. Mossad could secure Rada's cash for him and see that he and his family lived comfortably in Israel, or they could leak evidence of his betrayal to Hezbollah. The choice would be his.

Stessel still wasn't impressed. He closed the report and after a pregnant pause said, "Just for the record, I think this is utter bullshit."

Nina bobbed her head and pretended to jot a few words in her lap with her pen. "Mmhm, m'kay, yup…noted." She didn't care anymore—there wasn't a damn thing Stessel could do to stop her, and he knew it.

His frown turned to a pursed look of scorn.

"Any questions, Tom?" she gaily asked.

Stessel leaned back in his chair and scratched his temple. "Yeah, when's this motherfucker gonna be out of my country?"

"They're planning to approach him tomorrow afternoon on his walk home. As you saw, if he rejects the recognition code, the op will be aborted. If not, he'll be instructed on how to contact us. Nathan wants to get him to a hotel here in the city to pitch him as soon as possible. From there, it's up to him. All the details are in there; Mossad's put all the assets in play. My guess? Hopefully—Rada will be sitting in a safe house in Istanbul this time next week."

"You with him?"

Nina smiled. "You're cute."

"All right, whatever. Just get it done." He leaned forward. "One condition: Do not leave this post again without a GRS detail. Understood?"

"Done."

The choked streets of north Tehran descended from below the mountain's brow like a tangled web of raw nerves, pulsing and firing with vivid electrical currents: neon signs and traffic signals, headlights and lampposts; all burning like a lit fuse under unfurling, incendiary smog clouds ignited by the dying sun; sounding above the dirt beneath with a low and distant moan gradually swelling and increasing to rage; shifting and wavering like the brittle spinal cord of a nation laid upon a fraying fabric of lies that was about to snap.

Jack averted his eyes from the listing light. He jogged down the sloping switchbacks toward the base of Jamshidieh Park, scanning the branches in his periphery—wary of what might lurk within. His dead-drop, the peculiar rock beside a trail in the park's summit, was just refilled. The one-time pad stashed inside would allow CITADEL to decode a new message scheduled to broadcast from Camp Arifjan the following night. It would warn him that Morteza Ghanbari was bound for Tehran with an offer the ayatollah ought not refuse.

The back of Roya Banisdar's neck prickled with dread. Her gut sank. The blood boiled in her face. She listened again—and knew fear.

Someone was in the house.

She sat up in bed, pulling the sheets taut against her chest. The room was dark, plunged into a vivid, thick blackness that seemed alive. Her eyes scanned the pall. Nima, her husband, was asleep beside her, yet she could scarcely see him lying only inches away. The room was darker than usual; the soft sheen of the streetlamps that normally painted the window curtains was gone.

She looked at the door. It was shut. She held still, training her ears. And there, again, she heard it—a low creak sounding on the wooden stairs.

Her mouth felt like a desert. Her heart was pounding. "N—Nima... Nima," Roya stammered, wrapping her trembling fingers around her husband's shoulders, "wake up."

He rolled onto his side and groaned.

She shook him. "Nima, get up now."

Nima eased open two weary slits.

Roya leaned in and dropped her voice to a panicked whisper. "I think someone's inside the house."

"What?" Nima threw his eyes open and sat up next to her.

"Listen," she pleaded.

Both held still, together, in the darkness.

Another creak on the stairs—this time closer.

Roya could tell he heard it too. Nima became as pale as a ghost and shot his hand out to the lamp on the nightstand. He turned the knob beneath the bulb—nothing, only a dead click. He turned it again—nothing. Nima sat up against the headboard, his breaths growing labored.

"Call the police," she gasped.

Nima took his cell phone off the nightstand and held it in his hands. The top left corner of the screen read, "No Service."

There was a muffled thud in the hallway outside their door—a footstep. It sounded almost deliberate, taunting.

He froze for a moment, shaking. "Get under the bed."

"What?"

He placed both hands on Roya's shoulders and looked her in the eyes. "Get under the bed—right now, and stay there."

Roya began to cry. "But what about you?"

"Just do it. Please. Get under the bed and don't make a sound."

Tears ran down her cheeks. "Okay. Okay."

"Go."

As quietly as she could manage, Roya went prone and squeezed herself into the tight gap between the box-spring and the dusty planks. She inched ahead on her forearms, struggling to glimpse the small, dark patch of her bedroom visible from the floor. The springs above her whined as she saw Nima's bare feet touch the ground, slinking cautiously, fearfully to the door.

And then, without any attempt to conceal the noise—boastfully—came the gentle rhythm of boot heels, echoing slow and steady with every step.

Roya smacked her hands against her mouth, fighting to control her breath: quick, labored shivers that wet her palms. She felt her heart in her chest; veins throbbed in her temples.

With a final thud, the footsteps stopped, just beyond the door.

Roya had never been so frightened. It warmed and chilled her all at once; paralyzed her in its smothering embrace. She kept her hands to her mouth, trying not to scream. She held for a second that seemed like an hour, waiting for the door to open. Nima stood still, his feet planted to the floor.

But there was nothing. Silence.

Nima's voice trembled, speaking Dutch. *"Ik heb de politie gebeld."* I've called the police, he lied. "They're coming."

There was no reply.

He whispered into the darkness. *"Hallo?"*

Silence.

He paused, and asked again, in Persian, *"Dorood?"*

Before the final syllable left his mouth, the door burst back violently on its hinges and smashed into the wall with a loud crash. Roya saw the lower half of a man stepping through the doorway. Nima yelped with a thud and dropped, his forehead striking hard against the floor. Roya could see him only inches in front of her. Blood poured from a gash in his skull and his eyelids flickered wildly. He let loose a pained moan as the man reached down, grabbed his ankles, and dragged him over the threshold.

Roya screamed.

The man stomped back into the room, his boots thundering on the boards. Dropping down on one knee, he calmly tilted his head under the bed. He wore gloves and a jumpsuit; a black balaclava masked his face. The man gazed directly at her with two metal tubes lit with the pale green glow of night vision goggles. His powerful arms sprung out and snatched her.

Roya wailed and squirmed as the man's fingers dug at her armpits. She tried to force her legs around and kick at him, but he was too strong. His hands latched around her and pulled her out from under the bed with ease. On her back and flailing her legs, smacking against the bed-frame, she was helpless as the man wrapped his arms around her waist and hoisted her to her feet.

As she struggled, Roya heard the man call to someone.

He spoke Russian.

Baranov shouted to Akhmadov and Kakiyev as they trudged up the hallway. "Grab him," he ordered. "Take him downstairs."

Both lifted Nima, stunned from the blow, and carried him off.

"Please, God!" Roya pleaded. "Please, God, no!"

Baranov threw her over his shoulder—her hair dangling over his back, her legs thrashing in the air and her nails clawing at his neck. She cried out for her husband, sobbing. "Nima! Nima!"

The Russians planned to leave a spectacle. It was meant to be gruesome, to maximize impact and presumptions of guilt, and each second was timed. Ignatev and Kotov held overwatch in the driveway, training their suppressed AK-103 rifles at the desolate street. They had six minutes to finish the job.

Baranov hauled Roya down the stairs to the living room. Ignatev and Kotov had Nima pinned to the floor. Dark red blood was smeared over his face. He saw his wife struggle. *"Roya…run"*

"Nima, please!" she screamed.

"Run. Run."

But she couldn't. Baranov held her like a vise. "Outside," he barked.

They dragged Nima down the driveway and into the middle of the pitch-black street. Power was cut to the entire block and cellular signals were jammed. If the neighbors were drawn to their darkened windows by the commotion—as the Russians intended—there was nothing they could do but watch.

"Help us!" she bawled as Baranov wrestled her outside. "Please, God! Someone help! Help!"

"Put him on his knees, facing her," Baranov commanded, now in English.

Kotov shoved Nima on the ground as Ignatev gripped the back of his shirt and hoisted him upright. And then the Chechen pulled a knife from his belt.

Baranov heaved Roya back over his shoulder and forced her to her feet. "Stand up," he hissed in her ear. He then locked his left arm around her neck, squeezing her chin in the pit of his elbow.

"Please, you don't have to do this. You can walk away. God will forgive you. Please, sir, you don't—" Tears streaked down Roya's face as she felt a knife caress her hip. She found Nima a few feet ahead in the darkness, weeping as she muttered, "I love you."

"I love you, too."

The blade pierced Roya's gut. Her eyes darted down to her stomach. Blood seeped through her shirt as the serrated metal shard emerged from inside her, hovered in the air for an instant, and dove back through her skin. She felt a dull throbbing with the first stab, building with each thrust to a writhing pain that overwhelmed her senses. Roya gasped in shock as Baranov plunged the knife into her again, and again, and again, severing arteries and puncturing organs.

She heard Nima's helpless wails.

Baranov pulled out the knife one final time and released his hold around Roya's neck, letting gravity lure her to the ground. "Do it," he said with a detached certainty.

Ignatev took his knife and slashed across Nima's throat. Blood sprayed from the wound, and in a moment, he fell forward. Lifeless.

Baranov took a few steps toward Nima and heard a whimper at his back. He turned around. Roya was face down in a crimson pool, her fingers grasping at the pavement. The Russians stood around her, some laughing.

Kakiyev sauntered over. "Quick, fuck her, while she's warm."

Baranov watched her with an ounce of pity. He leveled the muzzle of his pistol over the back of her head and fired, lighting the street with a white flash. The shot rang in the night, and she was still.

CHAPTER 38

FREEMAN FOUND THAT foul news often came with the rain. Watching from his windows on the southeast corner of Langley's Old Headquarters Building, the sky was somber and bloated. An angry wind caught the branches shrouding the George Washington Parkway. The storm came in during the night, anchored itself above Washington, and refused to relent without exacting its due.

"Here's what we know, Ryan," Grace Shaw spoke from the sofa at his back. "At two-eleven a.m., the Dutch national grid operator, TenneT, registered a power failure over a square-mile residential section of Wassenaar. Around that same time, KPN, Vodafone and Deutsche Telekom noticed that their cell towers covering the same area abruptly dropped all active connections and didn't log any others for approximately fifteen minutes. GSM, LTE, CDMA: all bands went down at once. Landlines, too. Internet service providers also observed their bandwidth tank in that same square mile."

"A little chunk of the Netherlands got sent back to the Stone Age," added Pete Stavros from the opposite couch.

"Fifteen minutes later, all of these systems came back online," she said. "Within seconds, the regional constabulary got maybe a dozen calls from a street right in the center of that outage. Local cops in Wassenaar reported sporadic radio interference as they responded. They found both lying in the road in front of their house—Nima and Roya Banisadr."

CIA's station in The Hague was given crime scene photos by a liaison at AIVD, the Dutch intelligence service. The glossy pictures were arranged on the coffee table and showed the couple face down in merging pools of blood. Freeman really had no desire to study them, but Shaw waded into her own account.

She took a breath. "Preliminary from the coroner says Roya was stabbed

433

in the abdomen seventeen times. COD was a single gunshot wound to the back of the head. No casing was found, but bullet fragments were pulled from the pavement. Ballistics will take time, but it's not promising. Nima's throat was cut from left to right. He also had a head wound that police believe he suffered in the bedroom; there's a blood trail to support that. The lack of defensive wounds would suggest that they were held from behind. Police don't think they tried to run, but were forced into the street and murdered there—almost staged. The coroner also found that Roya was six weeks pregnant."

"Witnesses?" asked the D/CIA.

"We're still getting those reports. The few I've read paint the same picture: neighbors woke up, heard screaming; their house had no power, and they couldn't get cell service. One guy looked out his window and saw five masked men—all in black, with long guns and NVGs—dragging the Banisadrs down their driveway. He described their murder pretty well. Another witness up the street saw a dark SUV speeding away. For what it's worth, a gray Opel Antara was found torched near a wind farm in Zeewolde about three hours ago; the interior was incinerated, so it's another dead end. National Police have taken over the investigation, and AIVD's looking into the blackout. Hague COS says the Dutch are pretty spooked by it." Shaw shook her head. "I just can't wrap my head around why they paid so much attention to Roya."

"Because they could," Freeman came back from the windows and sat around the coffee table with Shaw, Stavros and the surly chief of the Counterterrorism Center, Roger Mathis, "...whoever did this, I mean."

Mathis glanced over to Stavros. "Care to guess?"

Freeman gave the C/CTC a grim look, although he plainly saw the writing on the wall. CIA knew that Shateri's hit men, Unit 400, were dispatched to the Iranian embassy in Vienna to wait for a lead on Mehdi Vaziri. By now they should have expected *Hajj* Qasem to be a man of his word.

"We knew this was possible," Mathis persisted.

"Not like this," Stavros chewed at his thumbnail. "This is different, it's not like them. It's too... You know what I mean."

Freeman crossed his legs. "Do we know how long Vaziri was on the phone with the Banisadrs?"

Stavros shrugged. "Inside a minute."

"The Mossad officer with Vaziri at the Meurice made the call with a secure line that routed back through Israel," Shaw noted. "Was it encrypted on the Banisadrs' end? Sadly, no, but the Iranians couldn't have traced it back to Paris. We know from CITADEL's reports that the Etelaat-e-Sepah is watching dissidents Vaziri might contact. So there you have it."

"And that was the first time Vaziri's reached out to anyone?"

Shaw nodded.

"That was stupid," Freeman scoffed.

"Tell the Dutch to start ripping out the Banisadrs' light fixtures; they might be surprised what they find," Mathis observed.

"Either way, Vaziri can't stay in Europe," said Stavros.

"No," Freeman agreed, "and the French will be itching to get rid of him. He'll have to swallow his pride and take an Israeli passport."

"Ryan, don't you think the Dutch should be read-in on this?" Shaw asked. "Without knowing about Vaziri, they're playing with an arm tied behind their backs. The Europeans should be aware of what they're up against. Chances are, we haven't seen the last of this."

Freeman's lips tensed. "That's Isaac's court, but I'll call him and touch base." He looked away. "Benny told me he might go to Paris and force Vaziri to come back with him. I'd bet it's a priority after last night."

"It's the violence that gets to me," breathed Stavros. "The Iranians have strangled, shot and poisoned their share, but…"

Shaw finished his thought. "Even the Russians don't butcher pregnant women in the street."

"Okay," Freeman loosened his tie. "Pete, how are we handling Gorani?"

It was a busy night at Langley. At four in the morning, Eastern Time, a call was placed from the satellite phone that CIA smuggled over the border to Palanjar. The sole duty officer at Persia House off Corridor C nearly considered it a prank, but before he hung up, the young, well-spoken voice on the other end claimed to be Niyaz Gorani, the eighteen-year-old son— by birth—of Major General Jamil Gorani. Niyaz correctly answered the recognition code given to Langley's courier, and declared that he would be negotiating on behalf of his father. The duty officer arranged a time for the chief of the Iran Operations Division to call back and negotiate on behalf of the United States government. Niyaz happily stated that he looked forward to it, and the line went dead.

Now it fell on Stavros to reel in the Dark Lion of Kurdistan: one of the biggest fish in the region, and the only man they could rely on to thwart Shateri's nuclear ambitions. After the slaughter in Wassenaar that same morning, the task held a foreboding importance.

"It's interesting," Stavros' shoulders tightened. "My analysts can't stop talking about it. Niyaz is the last person we suspected Gorani would trust to speak to us. All through the Nineveh offensive, Niyaz held no leadership role. He was just a foot soldier like the others. A kid with a Kalashnikov."

"Maybe his old man doesn't see talking to us as a priority?" Mathis said.

"Or maybe Niyaz stepped up after his big brother, Arjen, was killed?"

"Also by *Hajj* Qasem's hit men," Shaw added.

"The kid's still just a mouthpiece for his dad," Freeman shot. "What's our play, here?"

"We have the duty officer's recording. My analysts are combing through it. I brought in a voice specialist from S&T to look at his emotions—they were all genuine. Niyaz seemed skeptical of our motivations. He said America's been quick to offer support to his people, only to let them get slaughtered once it comes to building a sovereign Kurdish state. And he was upset that Weisel condemned his father's treatment of ISIS prisoners in Mosul. We need to convince him that this time's different, that we're not operating under media scrutiny like in Iraq, and that we're not using them as human shields for the Rev Guards."

"His dad was literally cutting people's hearts out, and half of them weren't even ISIS. What did he expect from us?" Freeman said with a hint of astonishment. "Tell him, working with the bad to kill or capture the worse is a time-honored tradition of US foreign policy. Tell him that."

Shaw beamed.

Freeman rubbed the bridge of his nose. "So you're ready for this?"

"Absolutely, boss," Stavros nodded. "We're calling him back at six, I'll have a copy of the notes I'm using on your desk at five."

"Thanks, Pete," said the D/CIA. "Have we heard from the courier?"

"Courier's still dark," added Stavros. "Once he comes back across the border, we'll debrief him in Choman and makes sure he gets paid. We're hoping he'll have some valuable nuggets on the state of Gorani's men."

"How's planning with the JSOC brass?"

"Seamless," he nodded. "Our people work well together. We've charted Iranian Border Guard patrols around Palanjar and shortlisted a few drop sites. Flight plan's been mapped. And the good news is that the mountains scatter radar coverage, so the team will be clear below thirty thousand feet. The 427th at Pope's earmarked a C-41 for the drop, and that'll be on standby at Incirlik when we're ready to launch."

"I told the president that Wade's decided on an NCO from DEVGRU."

"Yeah, he's a chief petty officer from Red Squadron," Stavros continued. "I don't have his name with me, but he filled in for Delta on the raid in Tartus that netted Ali Mamlouk. Wade hasn't offered him the job yet, but he wants to do it himself, so he's waiting for a spot in his schedule to head out there. If he accepts, he'll come up here for a briefing and then it'll be on him to pick the three other operators in the element."

"What do you think, Grace?" Freeman looked to Shaw. "We should recall Jack for that, right?"

"For the briefing?" She thought for a moment. "Yeah, they should meet in person beforehand. But that's if IOD think CITADEL would be fine on his own for a couple days."

Freeman shot another grim look across the coffee table. He'd address that other glaring problem in a minute.

Stavros nodded. "We're broadcasting to CITADEL tonight about Morteza Ghanbari flying in to visit him. He's been advised that Khansari needs to at least consent to an initial meeting. Depending on how that goes, I don't expect CITADEL would need to contact us for another few weeks. We can recall Jack."

"Good," said Freeman as he scratched his scalp. "Since we're on that, how do you guys feel about Ghanbari?"

Upon Freeman's return from the White House yesterday, the news that Ghanbari had selected Saeed Mofidi as a trustworthy partner in Tehran was met with a small uproar by the D/CIA's brain trust. Both Shaw and Stavros were bewildered that, all of the people in Ayatollah Khansari's inner circle, the Princeton academic picked the one in Langley's pocket. No doubt, Ghanbari chose well. There was no Iranian more loyal to American interests than Saeed Mofidi, but Langley's interest was in diverting attention far away from their most valuable asset. However, Freeman couldn't go back to the White House and reveal that Mofidi and CITADEL were one in the same. It was a conundrum. Yet all they could do was pray for the best, and prepare for the worst.

"I'm still confused how this happened," Shaw shook her head.

"Harold Lansing was tasked by Angela with finding an intermediary who could deliver our terms to restart negotiations directly to the supreme leader, bypassing Shateri and the Rev Guards, who would scuttle it at the first opportunity," Freeman explained, again. "To find this mythical unicorn, Harold consulted Dr. Ghanbari, who volunteered to go to Tehran and personally deliver our terms. Given that Khansari's off in Mashad, recovering from his last stroke, Ghanbari recommended that he should speak to—who else?" He shot out his arms. "You guessed it."

"Well, Ghanbari's a smart guy, I'll give him that," said Mathis.

"Too smart," Stavros countered. "Do we know when this is happening?"

"Tomorrow morning," Freeman said flatly. "Ayatollah Moezi in London arranged the meeting. Ghanbari's arriving on a flight from Dubai and going straight to Beit Rahbari to see our man. He'll be in Tehran for about three weeks to visit his mother and cover his tracks."

"He'll be dripping in surveillance from the minute his plane hits the runway," Shaw added.

"Exactly, which is why it's good he's seeing Mofidi."

"You think so?"

Freeman shrugged. "He's got pull with the president, the foreign minister and the Assembly of Experts. The mullahs in Qom respect him. He can get Khansari alone in a room whenever he wants. And he's one of the few people that Shateri can't make disappear. It guarantees our terms are accepted."

"So what happens after he gets the ayatollah's consent?" asked Stavros.

"He'll have to consult with Rostani and Zanjani; that's a given," Freeman answered. "And he may have to meet with Harold Lansing in Geneva. Look, guys, all that matters is that this ends without anyone beyond this room knowing what Saeed Mofidi truly is."

They sat in silence for a moment, and Freeman could sense that his optimism wasn't unanimous. "Roger?" he asked to the C/CTC.

"Yes, sir?"

"Lebanon."

Mathis nodded. "I had a nice powwow with Nina Davenport earlier. She walked me through the situation on the ground, and I think Mossad has a solid grasp on things. Beirut COS has been looped in, so hopefully Near East won't be too pissed. I'll let Grace handle that." He pushed a thin, bound report over the table. "That's the ops plan for you. Extract's been considered."

Freeman crossed his arms. "Enlighten me."

"If," Mathis tilted his head, "if, Rada agrees to defect and can bring his wife onboard, Mossad will get them Turkish passports and seats on the next MEA flight from Beirut to Istanbul. Debriefing will occur at a local safe house *with* Nina in the room, so nothing's secondhand."

"And you think they can dodge Hezbollah's CI?"

"Mossad's run this show before," Mathis dismissed. "They know the Beqaa Valley, they know Lebanon, and they know their enemy's capabilities better than anyone. Plus, Nina tells me they've roped in the IAF for support."

"Guess they're not screwing around," Freeman smirked.

"No they are not. Mossad wants this dude."

"Okay," Freeman checked his watch and calculated the time difference with Tel Aviv, "let me ring Isaac before it get's too late over there. Thanks, guys."

Once they filtered from his office, Freeman placed a call through his secretary to Mossad's campus in Herzliya. As he waited for Isaac's voice to break through the electric chirps in his ear, Freeman thought of Jack.

He hadn't been home in over a year. In the spare moments they shared, Freeman watched Jack grow from a timid and lost little boy into a young man who was—what else could Freeman say?—distant, and still lost. In clouded glimpses through chinks in his armor, Freeman saw something missing; and while each reminded the other of what was stolen from them, both understood that void could never be filled. He cherished what time they had together, although each moment now, bitterly, felt like the last.

It was his duty to protect Jack, to honor a promise made long ago.

And it haunted him that one day he might fail.

• • •

Walid Rada felt the noose tighten.

It began with the best intentions—or at least that's how the justification spun in his mind. Three years ago, their refrigerator unexpectedly died. Rada and his wife, Yusra, inherited it as a wedding gift from her parents. The damned thing was nearly half their age, had broken numerous times over the years, and did not owe them a cent. It was time to push the capricious hunk of metal to the curb. Ever demanding, Yusra insisted that Rada have it replaced as quickly as possible. But how was that to happen? Their budget could scarcely handle the basic expenses to sustain life, much less absorb the shock of shelling out thousands on a new refrigerator. Yusra pecked and badgered for days until the thought hit him—mountains of cash passed through Rada's hands every week.

Back then Hezbollah was embroiled in Syria's raging civil war. Wissam Hamawi and his Shura Council trucked the Islamic Resistance's legions over the border to fight and die in a vain attempt to prop up President Hafez Jadid's regime. To support the war effort, Qasem Shateri cut the party a blank check. Chartered Iranian cargo planes landed nightly at Beirut Airport, bursting with arms and cash. Millions were dispersed to the party's middle management: to the unit commanders fighting on the ground, and to the numerous aid organizations that kept Lebanese Shia faithful to Hezbollah's cause. A chunk of those funds were given to the Jihad al-Binna Foundation and the al-Ajarha Association, which both tended to the families of the party's dead; all of it entrusted to Walid Rada's care.

Awash in Iranian cash, what was a few thousand skimmed off the top? Hezbollah would never miss it. And so, he drew just enough from a Jihad al-Binna account to cover the cost of a new refrigerator. Not a cent more. His stomach churned for weeks after the decision, expecting the party's enforcers to swoop down and whisk him away. But they never came. Rada was relieved, elated, emboldened. Yet Yusra, who knew nothing of his crime, never once bothered to thank him. She kept on with her shallow little life, offering affection only when it benefited her, and assuming that even the stars were an entitlement.

Over the following nine months, Rada returned for more. He took another hundred dollars, then two hundred, a thousand, five thousand, and so on until the exact amount he'd stolen was irrelevant. Like an unhinged junkie, fistfuls of cash were stuffed into his pockets and briefcase as he left his office each day, wrapped in cellophane and crammed into a dusty crawlspace above his daughter's bedroom ceiling. The ease with which he could steal from the venerable Hezbollah and their Iranian masters stunned him. There were no curious calls or visitors from Beirut, no audits or asset freezes; the party's eye was fixed solely on the catastrophe unfolding in Syria and left blind to the deception under their very noses. Walid Rada, who never reckoned himself a particularly devious character, escaped scot-free.

After several weeks of unabatedly looting Jihad al-Binna's accounts, he ran out of hiding places. Wary of a house fire, an inquisitive wife, or worse, a raid by Qasem Shateri's gunmen, Rada was forced to turn to that inexorable bane of all men accursed with ill-gotten capital—a bank.

However, Rada could not simply waltz down to Machgara's branch of Crédit Libanais and deposit a fortune vastly greater than his meager salary allowed. He'd be arrested within the hour. Undeterred and bolstered with an air of confidence by his stroke of luck, he hatched a plan.

Yusra's older brother was severely mentally disabled—a crippled, drooling creature as Rada saw on scattered occasions, and an embarrassment that his in-laws paid an order of Maronite nuns at the *Hôpital psychiatrique de la Croix* in Jall al-Dieb to powder over the blemish on their otherwise flawless family. With a signed letter of attorney Yusra previously had drafted, Rada visited the Lebanese Swiss Bank in Hamra and opened a high-yield account in his brother-in-law's name. Discreetly transferring his loot to the account over several weeks, Rada choked to discover with the final deposit that he had stolen just over two million dollars from his employer. He nearly panicked at the extent, the severity of his crime. If Hezbollah ever caught him, Rada knew, it would mean death for him and a life of misery for his wife and child. For the first time, Rada regretted what he'd done. He wished that goddamned refrigerator was never theirs; he wished that he could return every cent and pretend that none of it happened.

For a while, he did just that. Rada abandoned his account at the Lebanese Swiss Bank and let it collect a few incremental ones and zeros behind the decimal. By day, he kept to his role as a dutiful Hezbollah *apparatchik,* managing the construction crews and social outreach teams with which the party honeycombed the Beqaa Valley's desolate villages. By night, he begrudgingly dragged his weary, fat-laden bones up the sloping side streets on the western edge of Machgara, and was forced to tolerate Yusra's painfully familiar indignant whinging and the incoherent, mind-numbing babble oozing from Eshe's lips. Each day, Rada bit his tongue to the point of blood to distract from the monotony until the hour came that he could acceptably slip from consciousness, only to rise again with the sun's mocking rays and inch life's boulder up time's hill.

Rada's one ounce of pleasure came from sex—and more the idea of it than the physical act. The notion that it would come from Yusra was laughable, and was frankly agreeable to him, given the sights her veiny thighs and gravity-stricken breasts offered. Rather, he did the job himself.

Once they'd gone to bed for the night, Rada would lay on his side, facing away from Yusra and wait, wide-eyed in the darkness, until he heard her snores. Then he would ease off the mattress and creep downstairs, take his laptop from a table, and lock himself in the bathroom. Sitting on the lowered toilet seat, with headphones tucked into his ears, he would surf to those murky corners of the Internet and watch, for a few hours, a parade of young girls from Europe and America. The next morning, those fantasies would remain a vague sketch in his daydreams—an airbrushed and silicon-padded mirage in the desert of his life that gradually wore thin against the grains of reality. The luster of those unreachable girls beyond his computer screen faded, but his urges did not. Rada wanted more; he wanted the real thing.

Then one day as he sat at his desk in a haze, another idea struck him; possibly leaping from the same sharp nerve ending that told him he could plunder the Party of God's war chest without consequence.

Rada would hire a prostitute. Their numbers swelled with the influx of refugees escaping Syria. Over a million settled in Lebanon, and among them were scores of young women widowed, orphaned, separated, abandoned; perhaps all four, it didn't matter. Desperate and alone, they turned to the source of income their bodies could provide. Prostitution in Lebanon was officially illegal but was widely tolerated so long as it was done quietly and with the necessary bribes. Catering mostly to Gulf Arabs, garish nightspots dotted the liberal neighborhoods of East Beirut and ran up the coast to Jounieh and Byblos. Their websites and flyers promoted fresh dancers with exotic, Western-sounding names and dressed merely up to the limit of what was socially permissible in Lebanon. Patrons to the clubs would come for private dances with the women, and after a few exorbitantly expensive drinks could even arrange a "date" at a nearby hotel. What happened during that date, as the club owners made clear, was between two consenting adults—one of which only had to look the part. And Rada, as his newfound shrewdness reminded him, sat on a mountain of offshore cash.

He found a website for a club just off the coastal highway in Jounieh. It's lit marquee read *"Le Piége"* beside the silhouette of a busty, long-legged woman in twisting neon bulbs. Rada drove out sixty miles the next after-noon, stopping in Hamra along the way to withdraw three thousand of Hezbollah's Iranian blood money, and within hours had a date in the adja-cent hotel. For once, the sketches that drifted through his mind were more than a mirage.

Rada returned every few weeks when he could spin an artful excuse to Yusra. He sampled the menu like a wine connoisseur, dropping an addi-tional three grand with each date. Infinitely more vivid than thrusting pixels on a screen, the girls at *Le Piége* did not bicker or complain, truthfully would not utter a word if he asked, and on command, rode him damn near into the floorboards.

But then that war across the border in Syria came blazing to an abrupt and blood-soaked end. Hezbollah limped away in defeat, and soon cleaved from Iran by Lebanese popular opinion and the rebels in Damascus, was forced to take stock of its losses, finally looking inward to the deception under its nose.

The call came from Rada's friend, the director of al-Ajarha Association. A sheikh who oversaw Hezbollah's Executive Council, himself third-in-command to Secretary-General Wissam Hamawi and responsible for the party's social affairs, arrived at al-Ajarha's office in the Security Quarter with members of Unit 910—Hezbollah's counterintelligence arm once overseen by Ibrahim al-Din—and launched a barrage of pointed questions. An audit was made of party finances, tracing every available penny at its disposal after the war. Of the Iranian aid funds given to party charities, X amount was recorded as expended, and so simple arithmetic would affirm that the remaining balance should be Y. But within that balance there was a discrepancy, a chasm two-million-dollars wide. Where, the sheikh demanded, did all that money go?

Without a ready answer, the director of al-Ajarha posed the same question down the line: Where did it go?

Rada staged a masterful performance that day, pledging ignorance as perhaps only the most revered actors or pathological liars could. Despite the convincing show, Rada's friend implored him with an ominous chill: Find it.

Naturally, Rada never could locate the missing cash no matter how vigorously his office searched. For three months and up to the current day, he kept spinning the wheels, redirecting and misdirecting; glimpsing "Zionist" plots and accusing fraud at every strand of Hezbollah's spidering web but his own; berating his staff for their incompetence, knowing full well that each assigned lead was a dead end; proclaiming his outrage and deep sense of betrayal at the sheer, unmitigated gall taken by any *mujahid* who would rob the Islamic Resistance like some skulking Jew in the night; hearing his every word land more hollow than the last; witnessing lifelong friends and colleagues distance themselves as if he were a parasitic dog; panicking; dreading; playing the game all the while until the inevitable hit.

And hit it did.

Just over two weeks ago, a convoy of Isuzu and Nissan SUVs converged on Jihad al-Binna's Western Beqaa Branch. Unit 910 officers, backed by two-dozen Islamic Resistance fighters, swarmed the center of Machgara. Equipped with body armor and Kalashnikovs, they cordoned off the surrounding streets, turned away traffic and pedestrians, and corralled Rada and his staff into a room at gunpoint while others tore through the building. The *mujahedeen* seized everything but desks, chairs and cleaning supplies. Filing cabinets were emptied into boxes; hard drives were ripped from their housings. As the men kept on their rampage, Unit 910 pulled Rada's staff one-by-one into a separate room, questioned each person, and then sternly ordered them to head straight home. Rada was humiliated. His office was rendered a barren shell. He tried to reach his superiors in the Security Quarter to consult them on what had just transpired, but none would take his call. That night, Yusra wouldn't let him hear the end of it. She pleaded, demanded, screamed at him to tell her what he'd done, but he kept to the familiar, failing story and feigned total ignorance.

The following morning a fraction of Rada's staff trickled back into work. To do what? He couldn't begin to tell them. There was nothing left. But he mustered a smile for the lingering few who would still listen and assured them it was all a mistake, a misunderstanding that the sheikhs in Beirut would sort out in time. After a few days, he said, Hamawi himself will come to apologize. Rada lied, as he now only knew how.

Within, Rada toiled not with guilt, but with fear that he was nearly caught. The swaggering, shrewd, deceitful corner of his mind dropped its rifle, shed its uniform and fled post. The self-preservationist camp charged ahead. His life, a surging faction of his mental civil war argued, was over. Yet he still clung to hope. They never bothered to question him during the raid. One could assume that was because Rada was their key suspect and Unit 910 intended to collect evidence before his own, grueling interrogation, but Rada—self-preserving even on the threshold of hell—reasoned that it was because Hezbollah now only doubted his competence as a manager. He swore his tracks were covered. The account with Lebanese Swiss was off-limits. Whenever he referenced the bank's website to transfer another payment to *Le Piége,* he encrypted the connection through a VPN in Norway. Only he, Yusra, and her parents knew that his brother-in-law existed, and Hezbollah was not about to interrogate nuns running an asylum. Both, he assured himself, were safe from the party's reach. At worst, he would be dismissed in disgrace; and it might even be the final tug that spurned Yusra to divorce him. Rada could live with that. Better yet, as he analyzed the trees despite the forest, they neglected to search his house. If he were truly under investigation for embezzlement, surely the *mujahedeen* would ransack his home.

So Rada kept on for the past two weeks, in a self-induced fog of ignorance. There was a cruel irony, he thought, that to try and retrieve the money he stockpiled and flee the country might very well be the only thing that could get him caught. Hezbollah couldn't prove his guilt otherwise. It was a foul stasis of his own doing, and almost comically apt. Nevertheless, he woke each day since, buttoned a suit over his gut as he always had, and wandered down Machgara's hills to sit, for exactly eight hours, in an empty office, awaiting that exonerating phone call he knew would never come. No one throughout the party, or frankly the world, as he could see, wanted anything to do with him.

But Walid Rada was so wrong.

At dusk, he followed the sloping street uphill with Machgara's terracotta skyline at his back. Rada's legs were bowed, his head tilted down in contemplation of another night with Yusra. In his office, it was a day nearly identical to all the recent others. He sat at his desk, no computers, no papers, and only a single working phone, with plenty of time to think on his sins. Gently swinging his briefcase and with slow, meager steps, he arched the rise of the hill on the town's western end. Home was a few meters ahead.

Rada hardly noticed the woman waiting along the curb in front of him. She wore a black, Persian-style *chador* of the sort that was popular in Tehran. In that conservative, Shiite enclave of Lebanon, it wasn't uncommon to see women dress modestly in public and cover themselves from view lest they invite a scolding from their jealous husband or a local Hezbollah official. Her whole body was swallowed in the loose cut of dark fabric with only the woman's face exposed in the folds. She stood alone, which was odd at that hour, but nothing too alarming. As Rada inched closer on his stroll, he saw her hands moving under the fabric. Her face gave the unmistakable impression that she was lost, almost as if it were rehearsed. He gave her another glance and then quickly shifted his eyes back to the road. Coming nearer as he made for home, Rada saw her passing in his periphery, and then, just as the two were perpendicular, he noticed the woman take a single step forward.

It slightly startled Rada, and he eased back on his heals.

"*Law samaht,*" the woman muttered in Arabic. Excuse me.

Rada stopped in his tracks, scanning her. The woman came right toward him now, her *chador* disturbed by the movement of her hands beneath. Fingers slid through the folds, and then her whole right hand was exposed, holding a thin, glossy and black half-sheet of paper. The text was turned away from him, against the fluttering cloth.

"What?" Rada warily asked.

The woman smiled. He could see her face fully in the twilight. Her teeth were white as chalk and straighter than any woman's he'd seen in the Beqaa Valley. Her skin glowed with life and her cheekbones gently sloped to a fine point at her chin. Her turquoise eyes stared him down with knowing confidence. Rada struggled to decide whether to fear her or adore her.

"Excuse me," she said again, now within reach of him, "*Monsieur* Rada?"

Rada froze as a calm tremor drummed in his legs. She knew his name. The woman eased herself against Rada's side, letting her *chador* block any view of her hands from the east, down the slope and back toward town. Huddled together, the woman flipped the paper over to show him.

"Monsieur Rada, where might I find this?"

Rada blinked in disbelief, and after a second, when his brain processed that it was indeed real, that he did read what he suspected, his eyes bulged.

The woman held a flyer for Le Piége in Jounieh. A photo of a topless girl pressed against a metal pole was emblazoned on the front. Overhead was that familiar logo and the silhouette in neon light.

"Where might I find this?" she repeated, her voice unwavering.

His mind raced. It wasn't possible. He told no one. Jounieh was sixty miles from Machgara and the possibility that a random, shrouded woman standing on his street at dusk would have such a flyer, much less approach a stranger for directions was absurd. Rada hadn't a clue who this woman was, but he wanted to be rid of her.

The woman's left hand now emerged from the *chador*. In a fluid movement, she brushed it against his suit and slipped a card into the open seam of his jacket pocket.

His eyes rose to her with shock and fear. He pressed his own hand against the pocket she touched. In a way, he understood, and his desperate, survivalist instinct urged him to trust her. "Get away from me," Rada stepped back on the pavement. "I—I—I don't know anything about that," he stammered. "Get away from me."

Rada stormed off at a hurried pace just shy of a run. He looked back only once and saw that the woman was already gone. He reached home a minute later and bolted the door behind him.

Rada's hands trembled in the frigid water. His fingers twitched, tingled with shock as he ran them under the faucet. He wanted to furiously scrub his joints, to cleanse the filth settled beneath his skin, but he couldn't.

Eshe scratched on the bathroom door and jiggled the locked handle. "Papa, you okay?"

"Fine, *habibti*," Rada called. He wet a towel and laid it on the back of his neck, controlling his breath with short sips of air. Someone found him; someone knew what he'd done. Someone—*they*—knew where he lived, knew his family, knew his vices, his weaknesses.

They could destroy him. They could save him.

Rada's suit jacket hung from a hook on the door, and the card the woman slipped inside now sat against the vanity mirror. Its finely written text gazed at him. He read it maybe a dozen times in the five minutes since he'd barricaded himself in the bathroom. Its words cut to his core, offering an escape...or a trap.

Walid, it began, we know what you have done. We can help you. Go to the cemetery in Haret et-Tahta tonight. Walk east, past seventeen headstones on your right. You will find the eighteenth marked with orange chalk. Beneath it will be a unique rock. Open it. Press # to reach us. We are waiting. Think of Yusra. Think of Eshe.

Who were they? Rada had his suspicions. Western spies, perhaps? Certainly not the ISF's Intelligence Bureau, he knew. They would have simply passed evidence of his crimes to Wissam Hamawi, lest they offend Hezbollah. Or maybe it was the party, itself? Rada couldn't shake that thought. Maybe it was a trap, a dangle by Unit 910's inquisitors to lure Rada in and seal his own indictment.

"Walid, supper!" Yusra beckoned from outside.

Either way, the instructions were clear. They wanted to hear from him tonight. Something sat in that cemetery below town, waiting for him: an open hand of mercy, or a clenched fist of vengeance.

"Walid!"

"I'm coming!" he snapped.

Rada had to know. He memorized the card's instructions—*pass seventeen headstones on the right; orange chalk on the eighteenth*—and tore it to shreds, flushing the evidence down the toilet.

At dinner it was a struggle to maintain idle conversation. He picked at his food, only able to eat a few bites and offered curt, distant replies to Yusra's questions. Rada plotted how he could get away that night without drawing her suspicion, how he might move through Machgara undetected, how he might explain himself if questioned, and how he might die if caught. Midway through the meal, Rada dropped his fork on the plate as if he had a striking realization.

"I forgot my wallet," he declared, cursing his clumsiness with a bite to his lip. "I left it on my desk."

Yusra finished chewing. "Get it tomorrow."

"No, I can't," Rada shook his head as he tossed a napkin off of his lap. "I'll be up all night worrying."

Yusra sat back in the chair as her husband rose from the table. "Do you really have to go right now? We're eating, Walid."

"Yes," he insisted, feigning annoyance as he typically would.

Eshe watched the exchange with a puzzled look while Yusra swore under her breath. Rada fetched his jacket from the bathroom and threw open the front door, pausing before he left.

"Be back soon."

Pale moonlight lit the crests of Mount Lebanon's engulfing massif. Stepping down the slope, Machgara was laid out before him, soaked in shades of shadow. Rada kept descending the hill, passing homes and shuttered shops until he came into Haret et-Tahta, the "lower town" set in the valley near the banks of the Litani River. He chose not to eye his surroundings for surveillance. If it were a lure by Hezbollah, the trap was already sprung, and Rada was good as dead. There was no use in fighting anymore.

Machgara's cemetery sat almost on the eastern fringe of town. Rada entered through a gap in the waist-high stone wall that guarded the perimeter. Letting his eyes adjust, he stood for a moment on the gravel path that meandered through a field of withering stones. The graves faced due south, toward the *qiblah* in Mecca. *Walk east, past seventeen headstones on your right.* Rada turned his head. The markings were simple, per Islamic custom, and many bore the names of Machgara's old families: Ghazal, Mehsen, Baroud—Rada. He began counting, putting a headstone behind him with each wide step. His shoes pressed against the gravel; branches rustled above. *Five stones,* he counted—and in a few paces—*nine, thirteen*—closer now—*fifteen, seventeen.* And then there he was: the eighteenth headstone. He crouched low, setting his nose nearly against the grave.

A slash of coarse orange dust marred the stone. Rada felt lightheaded. Now he had to find the rock—*unique*—whatever that meant. Still crouched, Rada ran his hand over the wet grass, struggling to discern any form in the darkness. After a moment, his fingers brushed an object that felt not like any rock, but rugged plastic. *Unique,* he thought. Rada picked the rock from the ground and stood, scanning the cemetery, but he was still alone. He inspected the rock, turning it over in his hands. It appeared more like a thick, jagged bit of concrete than any rock. Its exterior was undeniably plastic, but painted to match the same tone of gray as the headstones. To any layman, casually wandering along the path, it would have looked like a chunk fallen from the decrepit graves. Rada squeezed its center, looking for a seam, and with a tug, it popped in half. Hidden inside was a small black device that looked like mobile phone. It featured holes for a microphone and an earpiece, like any normal phone, but lacked a screen and had only a single button on its surface: a hash key.

Rada wondered where he should make the call. Home was out of the question, and he could always be overheard from the street. Standing in the cemetery, in the company of the uninterested dead, was the safest option—his only option.

He steadied his hand, pressed the hash key, and touched it to his ear.

Under the moonlight the Mediterranean angrily charged ashore, crashing against the sea wall in Batroun with glowing silver spray.

Nathan Cohen answered on the first ring. "Monsieur Rada," he smiled, "listen very carefully…"

It took almost a day for their bodies to be found. The rusty stench of congealed blood lured an eight-year-old girl into the basement. Fabrice and Tippi's remains were in an early stage of rigor mortis: their limbs stiffened like a board; Fabrice's partially-severed heard turned a deep shade of purple. The girl ran like hell to her parents and for five hours La Forestière's residents gawked around the stairwell, debating what to do. A typical response anywhere else would have been to phone the police within seconds, but not in Paris's *banlieue*. *"Les archers,"* as the police were known in the suburbs, were universally despised, and more than a few in Clichy-sous-Bois would rather quietly bury the bodies in a field and be done with it than bring in the state. Finally, an elderly Algerian woman who'd lived in La Forestière longer than any could remember put an end to the discussion. She would make the call.

The *Préfecture de police* came in force that night. Clichy-sous-Bois was infamous for spates of unrest, and the police never set foot within its boundaries without backup. Pulsing lights and sirens swarmed the estate. Armed officers stood guard in the parking lot. Two riot control companies and the *départemental* gendarmerie group were placed on alert with water cannons and tear gas. Judicial Police inspectors combed the towers, knocking on each door, most of which went unanswered. Fabrice was not widely admired—a crude and obnoxious grunt who haunted the estate—and the few boys who did flock to his side all held warrants, and Tippi's family were more concerned with avoiding deportation than catching their daughter's butcher. Repulsive as their deaths were, it wasn't gruesome enough to overcome La Forestière's repulsion toward the government. Nobody talked. The local tabloids caught wind of the murders and used the grisly details to sell papers, but the story would never gain traction. Despite Fabrice's beheading, there was no credible link to terrorism: the teenager was hardly a target for ISIS and there was not a single boastful word of credit for the act. It was as if they died in a vacuum. The lives of two poor African immigrants in a community many French deemed savages were not worthy of justice. In time, without any leads, the inspectors would banish the case into their archives to collect dust. And by then, Zyed Bata would be long gone.

Sajid couldn't look at his brother the same way. He was timid around Zyed and cautiously chose his words, speaking only when necessary. While he wouldn't admit it, in his heart, the boy was terrified. Sajid's closest friend, his own flesh and blood, had become something altogether alien, and monstrous.

Zyed spoke constantly of death and made it abundantly clear that he wanted his brother to join him. He had a calm, blithe air about him; lacking fear and remorse, Zyed looked to his own blank future with a sense of quiet, idle peace. And he took his brother's hand, shoulder-to-shoulder, drawing him nearer to the abyss with every word—certain that there was no other way.

"Imagine you have cancer," Zyed recently told him.

Sajid wasn't ready to go into that cold blackness. But he felt like a helpless passenger, strapped into a roller coaster as it climbed the tracks, waiting for the slow crest and the swift, imminent fall.

If Sajid had a shell, he'd crawl into it. From the back seat of Badi Haddad's Skoda Octavia, the passing amber streetlamps seemed to illuminate a distant world—one safe and familiar, full of life; and one he would never know.

Haddad led the boys far from Clichy-sous-Bois, driving aimlessly for over an hour through the empty streets south of Paris, avoiding highways and glancing in his mirrors. They'd crossed the Seine a few kilometers back and Sajid now spotted signs for Orly Airport. He only wanted to be left alone, not to think about dying, but Zyed wouldn't have it.

"I love you, Sajid; to the moon and back, deeper than the sea and higher than the sky," his brother said from the passenger seat. "It's totally painless for *shaheed*. God tells us. You just have to do it. The more you put it off, the more you worry, the worse it becomes."

Zyed waited for a reply, but heard only silence. "Carried by angels to Paradise," he smiled. "How could that be bad?"

"Please," Sajid muttered. "Just...please."

"It's *Jaddah*," Zyed nodded. "You're worried about *Jaddah*. You're afraid that she'll be sad." He smirked, confidently. "She knows we're in a bad place. Trust me. I'm not saying she wants us to do it, but how could she not accept it? She knows there's nothing she can do for us. *Jaddah's* tried helping, but there's a point when there isn't anything that anyone can do to save us. We have to save ourselves." Zyed was sure of it. "This is it, Sajid. This is the only way."

For a moment, only the humming engine broke the air.

"I love you," Zyed repeated.

Sajid forced back tears. Desperate to change the subject, he turned to the only brighter topic at hand. "How will the police not catch you?"

Zyed scoffed.

Haddad adjusted his grip on the wheel. "You heard the rumor that Fabrice shorted the Albanians a few thousand? The PJs will sniff down that road for two months, at least."

"By then it'll all be over," Zyed grinned.

Sajid wiped the corner of his eye.

Haddad checked his mirrors again.

"Enough with this spooky shit, Badi," said Zyed. "Where are we going?"

"I want to show you boys something."

Haddad drove along Avenue du Maréchal-Leclerc, past squat warehouses beneath Orly's flight path at the very edge of the Parisian metropolitan sprawl. Turning down a narrow access road, a lit sign marking a Shurgard self-storage center came into view. He stopped at the gate and tapped a keycard against the console. As the gate wheeled itself open, Haddad pulled into the facility. Two-dozen red rolling shutter doors lined the warehouse, each an individual storage unit. Haddad squinted in the light of the sodium lamps, reading the numbers beside the doors. After a minute, he pressed the brake and forced the car to a gradual halt. He turned to the boys. "This is it."

"It's what?" Zyed replied, a tad impatient.

"You want martyrdom, right?" Haddad popped open his door and rose into the night.

With that, he had Zyed's attention. Zyed got out of the car and motioned for his brother to follow. It wasn't an invitation.

Haddad turned a tumbler lock and hoisted open the metal door about five feet, holding it in place on his shoulder. "In, quick," he beckoned. Once the boys ducked inside, Haddad pulled the door closed behind them, plunging the space into darkness.

The boys recoiled, shielding their noses.

"I have five more lockers like this around Île-de-France," said Haddad.

"What the fuck is that smell," Zyed yelped.

Sajid gagged. It was a pungent, acrid odor like burning plastic.

Haddad threw a light switch, and answered, "Ammonium nitrate."

Fifteen bags were stacked neatly against the left wall, and to the right sat seven cardboard boxes, each reading in block letters: *"Danger Explosif."*

"About two-hundred-kilos worth," Haddad explained. "And over there, those are Tovex sausages; very stable explosives. There's more of it—lots more."

Zyed looked on, emotionless. Sajid, too, was fully resigned.

"You want martyrdom?" Haddad smiled. "This is how."

CHAPTER 39

By October of 1989, Europe sat on a precipice. Throughout the Eastern Bloc—in Poland, Hungary, Bulgaria, Czechoslovakia, Romania and East Germany—the oppressive threads that stitched together four decades of communist reign were unraveling.

It began in Poland the previous summer. Following a series of general strikes at coal mines and shipyards, the pro-Western trade union, Solidarity, was legalized and permitted to stand in general elections. On the fourth of June, the popular earthquake long feared by Moscow hit. In the *Sejm*, the lower house of the Polish parliament, Solidarity won each seat up for contest; in the senate, all but one fell to the trade union; and with bitter humiliation, prominent communists failed to attain even the minimum amount of votes required to secure their reserved seats. That August, two coalition partners of the ruling United Worker's Party defected to Solidarity, forming a government and bringing democracy to Poland for the first time since World War II.

Cracks were always wont to spider along the Iron Curtain. In 1953, striking construction workers in East Berlin swelled into an uprising across the German Democratic Republic. Soviet tanks and the *Volkspolizei* quelled the revolt, killing five hundred in a single day. Over several weeks in 1956, militias battled the Hungarian regime in the streets of Budapest, but again the Soviets intervened and thousands died. Once more, in August 1968, the Kremlin's domination of Eastern Europe was challenged with the liberalizations of the Prague Spring. Moscow responded in kind. Twenty-seven divisions of the Warsaw Pact—half-a-million troops, six thousand tanks and eight hundred planes—stormed into Czechoslovakia and viciously overthrew the reformist government. However, the willful capitulation of the Polish People's Republic to Solidarity was the greatest blow to the Soviets yet: a fissure in the façade of eternal control, a sudden and irreparable halt of the spinning wheel. But there were no blazing divisions, no Russian tanks and soldiers patrolling the streets; the leaders of Poland's new democracy weren't rounded up, flown back to Lubyanka Prison and tortured. Caught in the ceaseless current of change, Moscow was silent.

Elsewhere in the Warsaw Pact, high inflation, surging poverty and inequality spurred the proletariat in Bulgaria, Romania and Czechoslovakia to voice their discontent in ways that were unthinkable only a few months prior. But it was Hungary that would prove to be a linchpin.

Met with the same economic slide as its neighbors, the Hungarian Politburo voted in May 1989 to dismantle large sections of its 240-kilometer border fence with Austria, allowing scores of East Germans vacationing in Hungary to escape into Europe and rejoin their splintered families in West Germany. The political and social cracks in the Iron Curtain were now a physical reality that any eye could see. That summer thousands more fled over the border, destabilizing Czechoslovakia and the GDR. Through August and September, simmering discontent in the Eastern Bloc rose to a rolling boil. Come October, demonstrations against communism were endemic. In Prague, Budapest and Sofia, the old regimes would not survive a month. In Bucharest, Romania's hardline dictator pleaded for Soviet troops to intervene and rescue the dream of World Socialism, but his cries were ignored, and on Christmas Day he was put before a firing squad.

In the German Democratic Republic, *Die Wende* or "The Turn" was fully underway. By September, thirty thousand East Germans managed to flee into the West before the GDR banned travel to Hungary, and thousands more camped on the grounds of the West German embassy in Prague. On October 3rd, the GDR shut its border with Czechoslovakia, sealing the country off from its neighbors and severing any remaining avenue of escape. In response, East Germans took to the streets. After five successive weeks of demonstrations in Leipzig, the GDR's general-secretary issued "shoot and kill" orders to irregular militias, the *Stasi,* and the National People's Army. Despite rumors of an impending massacre, on October 9th, seventy thousand protested for reforms. Officers on the ground defied direct instructions to fire at the crowds. On October 16th, more than a hundred thousand marched through Leipzig as the military stood idly by. Within forty-eight hours, the general secretary was dismissed in a palace coup, and in a week three hundred thousand demonstrated in Leipzig. By the first of November, the Czech border was reopened and East Germans were allowed to travel directly to West Germany. But those concessions were not enough. The demonstrations grew and on November 4th, half-a-million demanded their freedoms in East Berlin's Alexanderplatz. Unable to stem the flood into the west and unwilling to soak the streets with blood, the GDR allowed citizens to enter West Germany through existing checkpoints. Finally on November 9th, the Berlin Wall was swarmed by jubilant crowds and broken apart in great chunks.

The Soviet empire in Europe was roundly toppled.

Late that October, while the world crumbled, a foreign solicitor appeared in the Austrian town of Wildalpen. Home to roughly six hundred, the quaint village was isolated on a hairpin bend of the Salza River and flanked on all sides by the steep granite faces of the central Alps. Sited away from popular ski resorts, major highways and rail lines, Wildalpen was unaccustomed to outsiders and the solicitor made no attempt to blend in among the locals. The *Bundespolizei* recorded his entrance a day earlier off a flight from London with an Argentinian passport, although his name given at customs was as disposable as cheap socks. The solicitor registered at the Imperial in Vienna and drove to Wildalpen the following morning in a chauffeured Mercedes S-Class from the hotel's motor pool. Dressed smartly in a dark three-piece suit and polished loafers, he went directly to the village's *Rathaus* and warmly greeted the clerk—the two had spoken on several occasions by phone—before presenting a briefcase with his clients' immigration papers. Four thousand schillings greased the Austrian bureaucracy to approve what applications couldn't be forged. After several minutes of polite conversation and a few purposefully illegible signatures, the solicitor returned to his Mercedes and vanished into the mountains, never to be seen or heard from again. The seat booked on his return flight to London was empty.

The next week, a newly married Argentinian couple landed from Buenos Aires with fresh Austrian passports that labeled them Ernst and Carla Kubin. Ernst's birth certificate, as provided by his solicitor, showed that he was born in Argentina in 1962 to Austrian parents who were Nazi Party members given asylum after the war, both of which were also conveniently deceased. Ernst and his new Argentinian wife, his solicitor declared to immigration officials, only wanted to finally return home and atone for his parents' sins. Granted citizenship, the couple purchased a house in Wildalpen with Ernst's inheritance and eagerly awaited their new life together. Yet not all was as it seemed.

From his office in the sprawling Soviet embassy in East Berlin, as Russian diplomats and military attachés wrung their hands with trepidation and quietly raged at the Kremlin's inaction, a young Russian officer watched the same slow crumble that autumn and saw, not catastrophe, but opportunity.

Colonel Vyasheslav Trubnikov commanded the GRU's Second Direction, responsible for agent intelligence in Berlin. After several years of leading Spetsnaz efforts to assassinate *mujahedeen* figures in Afghanistan, he was given a hefty promotion despite his age and ordered to Germany, where it was hoped that his tight military discipline and operational mind would serve the GRU well in its bitter turf wars with the KGB. He did not disappoint. Answering only to the director at the Aquarium in Moscow, Trubnikov saw the divided German capital as an eager child might see a heap of tinker toys on the floor—assembling form from the chaos just as easily as he could create it. Less than a year after arriving, Trubnikov kept representatives in each of the GRU's covers in the city: the Soviet ministries of Foreign Affairs and External Trade, Aeroflot and TASS, the Merchant Navy and the Academy of Sciences. He held a direct line to the commanding-general of the GSVG—the Group of Soviet Forces in Germany—in Wünsdorf, and was friendly with his opposite number at the East German Main Directorate for Reconnaissance, or the HVA. From the embassy, Trubnikov placed agents at every hotel and diplomatic facility in the city, and reigned over a network of listening posts monitoring allied communications opposite the wall. And with Moscow's blessing, he didn't let that barrier of concrete and razor wire slow him down. In a direct affront to the KGB's traditional jurisdiction, Trubnikov sent his officers into West Berlin.

For two years before the popular revolts washed the Soviets away, Trubnikov built his outpost of the GRU into it's own fully-fledged, and largely autonomous, intelligence agency. As his spies trawled West Germany's political, economic and security circles, Trubnikov set his eyes on Brussels and recruited assets within NATO and the European Union. While his rivals screamed of unwarranted overreach, the heavyweights in Moscow hadn't seen such rich and timely intelligence from the West in decades, and after each Politburo meeting the KGB's fearsome chairman left humiliated.

By September 1989, as mass demonstrations and feckless leadership eroded Soviet control of its satellite states, Colonel Trubnikov was at the peak of his influence. A faction of generals and party hardliners, outraged at the Kremlin's refusal to militarily intervene, quietly recalled Trubnikov to Moscow. They met in secret at a dacha in the birch forests west of the city. Into the early morning the cabal hatched a plot, an insurance policy of sorts to soften the blow once the inevitable came. In order for their plan to succeed, they needed a distraction. Trubnikov recently penetrated a deep-cover intelligence ring in East Germany run jointly by the Americans and the British, turning one of its own as a double. He was confident that he could use his mole—this American—to stoke the flames, to make enough noise in Berlin that CIA and MI6 would be drawn to the false light and left blind to the GRU's efforts behind their backs. Trubnikov would use, as he explained to the dour old men of that dying world order, the black art of sabotage and deception that served them so well in the past...

Trubnikov would use active measures.

And so it was done. While butchered and burnt bodies appeared in the back alleyways of East Berlin, drawing out Langley and London's best to make sense of the carnage, the true operation got underway.

Ernst and Carla Kubin were hardly settled in Wildalpen when it became time to move. After only two months, they sold their house in December 1989 and left town before the snows made it difficult to travel. With Austrian passports, they freely crossed the border into West Germany without much scrutiny and arrived in Heidelberg. Situated in Baden-Württemberg, the town was at the southern end of the Rhine Valley, the densely populated engine of the German economy, and host to a number of American military facilities. The couple quickly rented a flat and before New Year's Ernst took a job at an automotive parts company a hundred miles south in Freiburg, as were their instructions. Now embedded into the fabric of West Germany, Carla safely contacted their handlers at the Soviet embassy in East Berlin.

Legally married for their operational cover, Evgeny and Olga Mirov—which were their true names—prepared the way for Trubnikov's follow-on force. They kept to themselves, not shunning their neighbors, but avoiding interest. For those first few weeks, Olga outwardly played the part of a bored housewife becoming acclimated to a new home, purchasing furniture and exploring Heidelberg. Behind closed doors, Olga maintained radio contact with Berlin, updating the GRU and Trubnikov of the reality on the ground while establishing a support network entirely separate from any the Soviets currently maintained. For Evgeny, taking a job two hours away in Freiburg allowed his "wife" to explain his prolonged absences and give himself an excuse to drive aimlessly through the wooded ranges of the Black Forest between, searching.

Bordered by the Rhine Valley to the west and south, the forest spread over two thousand square miles in Germany's southwestern corner. With vast expanses of heavy fir trees over broad hills and mountains, dotted with countless lakes and streams and ignored by man unlike anywhere in the country, the forest was the perfect place to become forgotten. Evgeny spent weeks systematically patrolling the wilderness, marking his tracks on a map and snapping pictures of potential hide-sites for Trubnikov's analysts to examine. Then one frigid morning in late January 1990, Evgeny found it. Near the base of the Belchen, the fourth highest peak in the forest, he discovered an old cottage down an unpaved road.

It must have sat abandoned for decades, Evgeny thought, cupping his hand to peer through the dusty windows—at least since the fifties. From the outside, it appeared like a kind of cuckoo clock brought back from a nightmare. Its steep, pitched roof sagged over rotted timbers, and its Tudor beams and stucco walls were weathered against the elements. Evgeny checked his map and saw that the closest structure was five miles away. It would be perfect. He heaved his weight against the front door, breaking it open with his shoulder. Inside, the cottage had only three rooms, mired with dust and cobwebs. He searched with his flashlight, finding a set of stairs that led into the ground. Evgeny followed it down into the basement. With only the dull beam of light in his hand, he saw a bare dirt floor and ceiling of exposed beams. Four walls marked the cottage's foundation, Evgeny discovered: red bricks packed neatly into the earth.

Olga radioed the news. Trubnikov dispatched a Spetsnaz unit, which inserted into Western Europe through the port of Rotterdam in late February, moving into Germany and up the Rhine on a barge for cover. On the twenty-fifth, Evgeny led the unit into the forest. A storm battered them with wind and snow, and as they went higher into the hills, Evgeny fought to keep warm. But the Spetsnaz operators did not flinch. Heavily armed and dressed for battle, they brought with them what they only called the *"ranet"*—the satchel. It took two men to carry and was roughly the size of a trunk, sealed with an air- and watertight gasket. Evgeny was never told what sat inside the locked, stainless steel case, but the operators guarded it around the clock. At the cottage, they held a perimeter and nailed boards over the windows. In the basement, the Spetsnaz operators took industrial-grade concrete saws and cut away a section of the brick wall. Evgeny saw them dig into the foundation, making a cavity large enough for the trunk to fit. The *ranet* was then placed inside and the wall rebuilt over it with fresh bricks and plaster, masking any trace of their passing.

For almost twenty-six years, the trunk—the *ranet*—never left that cottage. Evgeny saw to it. As Germany reunited, as the Soviet Union and the KGB splintered, the Mirovs stayed put in Heidelberg. The GRU survived the Cold War and was never broken apart, but given the task of executing President Mikhail Karetnikov's dirty wars in the Russian Federation's near abroad—a task for which its current director, Colonel-General Vyasheslav Trubnikov was well suited. Evgeny and Olga Mirov, still wed by law, still "Ernst and Carla Kubin" to their neighbors, were part of the GRU's European network of "illegals," Russian non-official cover intelligence officers buried deep within their target country. Middle age and familiarity to those around them—a general sense of amnesia as to how the couple ever came to Heidelberg—enhanced their covers. While counterintelligence officers focused their hunt for Russian spies on German politics and industry, the Mirovs kept their heads low. Olga contacted their handlers only when necessary and traveled to Moscow once in the last five years to be trained on how to operate their new radio. Evgeny was now a manager at the same automotive parts company, commuting to Freiburg twice a week, and passing through the Black Forest along the way.

As he spied the wooded depths and misty crowns beside the road, Evgeny kept wary of the secret he held, and was perpetually troubled by the thought that one day it would inevitably rise to the surface.

And so it would.

Almost to the anniversary of that operation, Evgeny Mirov was summoned with a radio call on a shortwave frequency occasionally used by Moscow. The encoded message directed him to a certain location at a certain time for a meeting with "representatives."

Evgeny waded through the same, biting February chill. Heiligenberg—or, "the Mountain of Saints"—rose just to the northeast of Heidelberg, over a steep valley bearing the river Neckar. At nearly three in the morning, he climbed the trails on the mountain's deserted southern slopes. Sparse gaps in the tree line revealed the town below and across the river to the ruined ramparts and curtain walls of Heidelberg Castle. Evgeny left behind his flashlight, using the clear night sky to find his way, but even in that dim glow, he knew he wasn't alone.

Along his periphery, almost from the minute he left his car, the faint sound of branches snapping in the distance met his ears, and his eyes caught brief glimpses of shadows prowling amid the trees. Deceitful figments of his imagination as they might have been, Evgeny knew that this time they were distinctly real, and stalking him as he climbed. The dark sounds and sights were with him the whole way, breaking off at Heiligenberg's summit. Then Evgeny heard not a single noise, although a part of him wished he did.

Coming upon the trail's end, the bare trees opened on to the *Thingstätte,* a sprawling amphitheater on the mountain's brow. Designed by the Nazis in the 1930s for grand propaganda presentations, the amphitheater was built to hold twenty thousand, with fifty-six stone tiers of seating rising a full twenty-five meters in a wide semicircle over a stepped platform. But there remained nothing grand about the place.

Evgeny stopped, looking down the length of the center aisle through his frosted breath. Knee-high weeds sprouted from cracks in the slabs and moss covered the seats. He scanned the murky glow, vaguely recognizing the outline of the platform below. He struggled to catch sight of the shadows that stalked him, to hear a sign of their presence, but he failed. The green hands of his watch struck three, the time Evgeny was told to arrive.

Midway down the aisle, Evgeny sat on a cold, damp slab and waited. A minute or two passed before a stirring atop the platform ahead, an inky break in the darkness, drew his attention.

Green eyes peered out from the night.

That was Evgeny's initial, fearful reaction. The outline of an automatic rifle followed, then arms and shoulders, legs and a torso: a man all in black; armed, with a balaclava masking his face. Those two green eyes, watching him with spectral glints, Evgeny now knew, were night vision goggles. The blackened man stood silent and motionless on the platform, the rifle resting in his arms. And then far to the left, in the corner of Evgeny's eye, emerged another, virtually identical, and watching.

Footsteps sounded at Evgeny's back, advancing down the aisle. Instinctively, Evgeny turned. Two more green-eyed figures loomed at the top of the stairs. But another man—different from the others—wearing a gray scarf, a waxed cotton field coat and jeans, his eyes and face bare to the wind, calmly approached, unarmed as could be seen.

Evgeny rose to greet the man as he came nearer.

"Sidyet," the man commanded in Russian. Sit.

Evgeny did as told, and in a moment the man sat on the slab next to him. But Evgeny looked forward, only stealing a slight glance at the man's face. Finally, he drummed up the courage to speak. "I don't know you."

The man looked forward as well, surveying the watchful green dots that surrounded them. "I serve an old friend of General Trubnikov," he said softly. "That makes us friends." A moment passed in silence, before the man added, "My name is Ruslan Baranov."

"You're with the directorate?" Evgeny said into the wind.

"I was." Baranov nodded toward the dots. "Them, too."

"Why are you here?" Evgeny shivered.

Baranov kept his gaze forward. "Where is it?"

Evgeny trembled in the cld. "In the forest, near the Belchen."

"You'll take us there."

"Tonight?"

"Tomorrow."

"There's a storm coming," Evgeny warned.

"I know."

"Some of those roads will be impassable."

"Which is why we need to go tomorrow."

"Okay," Evgeny rubbed his arms and dipped his head. "Okay, I will bring you tomorrow. When and where?"

"Your flat in Freiburg. Dusk is at six. We'll come to you."

"Why?" Evgeny heard himself ask. "Why do you need it?"

Baranov turned to him for the first time, looking Evgeny dead in the eyes. "We are returning it home for decommissioning. It is not safe."

"What do I tell my wife?"

Baranov gave a passive shrug. "You've already told her about this meeting. Why not tell her the truth? It won't matter in the end. After tomorrow, you will both be recalled to Moscow and allowed to retire with full pensions," Baranov continued. "Perhaps you can marry for love?"

Evgeny nodded.

"I see your watch works," he stood. "Wait five minutes and leave."

CHAPTER 40

JACK WAITED BY the broad, glass façade of the terminal at Imam Khomeini International Airport, staring out over the tarmac and into the arid, semi-desert plains south of Tehran. Glittering in the morning sun, an extended jetway interrupted the brushed gold livery of the Boeing 777 that would ferry him to a bitterly short repose from Iran's harsh glare. Emirates Flight 972 to Dubai had just begun boarding, with precedence given to first class. Hovering by the maze of stanchions at the gate for thirty minutes, Jack surveyed a ménage of Arab hustlers in pressed suits and Persian dilettantes toting Chanel and Hermès scarves that scarcely passed for *hijab*. The mullahs were glad to be rid of them, Jack mused with a silent huff, although the sentiment was surely mutual.

The lie he told people at the moment was that he—not Jack Galloway, but Simon Marleau, a Swiss national contracted to the Arab Banking Corporation's office in Tehran—was taking some time to visit family back home. Simon had gone on short-notice holiday before, whenever Jack was summoned to Langley.

With takeoff scheduled for eleven that morning, he'd arrive in Dubai just past one. After a two-hour layover to relax in the lounge, he'd board another flight to Switzerland, arriving in Zurich by eight. There, Simon would stay behind, letting Jack move unseen to Washington.

It was a sound plan—allowing him to shed his false skin and stand bare in the reality he no longer knew.

But Jack still hadn't escaped Iran. The Islamic Republic's main portal to the outside world, he knew, was a valuable chokepoint for the regime. All of it—from the flight controllers to the janitors—was ultimately governed by the Revolutionary Guards' watchful eye. Imam Khomeini Airport was a point of pride for the Pasdaran, not to say a lucrative cash spigot. Hours after its inauguration in 2004, IRGC troops simply stormed the terminal and seized it, drove trucks onto the runway and scattered incoming flights. They never left.

Cameras overhead and teams of spotters sifted the crowd. Everyone entering or leaving Iranian airspace was checked against two watchlists: one issued by the Ministry of Intelligence and Security (MOIS), and another curated by IRGC Intelligence, the *Etelaat-e-Sepah*. Protocol dictated that most on the list were granted entry into the country, only to be trailed during their stay and arrested at the airport before departure. Still others had their passports confiscated at immigration and were forced to attend questioning at MOIS offices. But the Iranians were deeply petrified of their watchlists being compromised on the Internet, so much so that they resorted to recording the details of everyone entering and leaving the country by hand, and driving the records into Tehran to be transcribed onto the internal networks of MOIS and the Foreign Ministry. Their paranoia cost them a twelve-hour delay. Even so, Jack dreaded each footstep from check-in to the gate. If they came for him, he wouldn't try to run; there was nowhere to go. If it ever got that far, Jack could only hope for a swift drop through the gallows.

So as the gate agent's voice tannoyed that business class boarding was underway, Jack breathed an invisible sigh of relief. Yet only when he crossed into the 777's fuselage and found seat 9A, watching the flight attendant seal the cabin door a few minutes later, did Jack crack a smile—brief, but undeniably real.

After pushback from the jetway, Emirates Flight 972 slowly rolled toward the hazy black tape laid over the sand. It held on the taxiway for a moment, and Jack watched from his portside window as an identical Boeing 777 swooped down upon the runway.

Beyond the starboard wingtip, wrapped in ozone and refracted ultraviolet light on the northerly horizon, the Alborz mountain range sat as a distant, immediate black mass. Morteza Ghanbari felt a sense of déjà vu at the sight—comforting just as it was troubling, like witnessing a once murky dreamscape rendered in reality's honest stare—and he knew that he might never wake.

Outbound from Dubai, the Boeing 777's undercarriage skidded along the tarmac, thrusting him forward in his chair. Emirates Flight 971 was over an hour behind schedule, for which the purser was convincingly apologetic as she welcomed the flight's three hundred passengers to the Islamic Republic of Iran. Ghanbari had been in transit for nearly twenty-seven hours. He wanted to arrive in Tehran early in the morning, allowing time to freshen and mentally prepare for his meeting at Beit Rahbari in the afternoon. To manage that tight schedule, he'd been forced to catch a much earlier flight from New York, arriving in Dubai the previous evening and spending the night at the Sheraton along the creek. The plan worked to some extent; his body had at least a vague idea of time and he didn't feel like a gaseous lump of sweat and stale clothes, but the delay in spanning the Persian Gulf took those strategic preparations and shredded them. It was nearly noon, and Ghanbari still had to wait through customs and immigration, brave Imam Khomeini Airport's infamous taxi rank, check-in to his hotel, and yet somehow wage diplomacy between his spiteful countries of birth and adoption. As his plane was towed to the gate and its passengers freed to disembark, Ghanbari fought the urge to charge right down the aisle.

But Ghanbari anxiously waited his turn, clutching his suitcase. Locked inside, within the pages of a Quran he carried when travelling, was a sealed envelope containing two letters printed on White House stationery. One was written in English and the other was translated into Persian, but both carried identical sentiments and bore the signature of the president of the United States. The message's words, carefully selected and addressed to the supreme leader of Iran, Ayatollah Ali Mostafa Khansari, might finally shatter the long impasse between both nations—but if first intercepted by the wrong hands, might spell death for the messenger.

And so Ghanbari tightened his grip. Coming off the jetway, he was immediately struck by stern signs and high walls corralling him deeper into the terminal. Arriving passengers were split into separate lanes for men and women and he sorted himself into the appropriate queue. Hundreds from the morning's influx of flights waited at passport control. Behind a rampart of bullet-resistant glass, ten women drenched in black *chadors* sat in individual glass booths, each calling forth a single passenger, soberly stamping their passports and buzzing a door that led to immigration and customs. Surveillance cameras loomed over the crowd and police with clubs stood sentry in their bottle-green uniforms. Ghanbari knew well that the Pasdaran permeated every square inch of the airport, casting inquisition on all who came and went, but he wasn't nervous. As he reminded himself countless times: this was home. For a respected Iranian academic and former member of the *Majlis,* Tehran was no more dangerous than walking Princeton's campus after dark. He took his passport in his hand, inching forward in the queue.

Ghanbari had not lived in Iran for sixteen years, nor had he set foot in the country for three, but he still held an Iranian passport kept current through their interests section at the Pakistani embassy in Washington. Although he also carried a US passport, Ghanbari opted to use the former when entering Tehran, bypassing the cumbersome visa ordeal. It was safer, he reasoned, and less liable to suspicion. Likewise, Iranian law did not recognize duel citizenship, and so long as Ghanbari stood on Iranian soil, all the lofty rights and privileges afforded to him as an American were useless.

Still, he felt secure.

After twenty minutes he was hardly any closer to the veiled women behind the glass. Ghanbari started to become agitated, nervous even, as his regimented schedule trickled through his fingers. He did the math, calculating in his mind how he could still make his meeting that afternoon, when he felt a slight tug on the back of his left sleeve. Ghanbari turned and saw a man beside him, looking him straight in the eyes. The man wasn't a police officer, but in a plain suit with the top button of his shirt collar undone, he wore a uniform all the same. Close-cropped salt-and-pepper hairs clung to the man's jawbones, and stark lines marked the shaven skin of his lower cheeks and upper neck. In Iran, a beard signified two things: government affiliation, or piety. For this man, it signaled both, and told Ghanbari that he stood before an officer of the Revolutionary Guards.

"*Doktor* Ghanbari?" the man asked with an affable crack of his pale lips.

"Yes, that's me," Ghanbari hurriedly replied.

His lips widened to a full smile. "*Doktor* Ghanbari, I am with the Etelaat-e-Sepah. Would you please come with me?"

Ghanbari felt his stomach drop. A few paces behind the bearded man, two more men materialized in the crowd, staring him down. "Is there a problem?"

"No, no problem, just a peculiarity with your return flight that we wish to clarify," the man gestured to the stagnant horde, "and this queue…"

Ghanbari froze for a moment. The only way IRGC Intelligence could spot a "peculiarity" with his return flight, if indeed there was, was if they combed the Emirates passenger manifests three weeks in advance. That only meant the Pasdaran were expecting him, and asking why he returned to Iran.

"Please, *doktor*," the man held his smile with an outstretched, welcoming arm into some invisible path through the crowd that only he could see, "right this way."

The bearded men escorted Ghanbari to the front of the queue, through a door in the glass barricade at passport control, and down an anonymous hallway into the terminal's bowels. After walking for a minute or so, he was shown into a spartan room furnished with a wooden table and two chairs. Ghanbari felt the handle of his suitcase dig into his palms and beads of sweat stick to his brow.

"I'll need your papers, *doktor*," said the smiling man.

"Of course." Ghanbari's customs form and the boarding pass for his flight from Dubai were tucked in the spine of his Iranian passport. He offered it over.

But the man hesitated, purring through his yellowed teeth, "Both, *doktor*."

Ghanbari struggled to affect an easy grin. He unzipped the front pocket of his suitcase and removed his American passport, surrendering both.

"*Merci, doktor,*" the man said. "Please make yourself comfortable. This should only take a moment. With another smile, the man turned, and left.

As the door shut, Ghanbari heard a lock click into place. He was alone, bounded by four bare wells, until his eyes rose to the camera lens peering down from a corner of the ceiling. Ghanbari cursed himself. He had barely set foot on Iranian soil and already failed. For a moment, he thought of diving into his suitcase, tearing the letters to bits and swallowing them whole. But then sanity quickly returned. There was no turning back now, he knew. Ghanbari had to stay the course, even if it cost him his freedom.

He sat in silence, knowing his every flinch and utterance was monitored. Instead, Ghanbari did all that an animal caught in a trap could—wait for fate to run its course. Minutes slipped by, then an hour, and another, when finally Ghanbari heard the lock tumble. The door opened and the man appeared behind it, but he was no longer smiling. He churned with embarrassment, fumbling his words.

"*Doktor* Ghanbari," the man stammered, "please accept my deepest apologizes. I was unaware that you had official business at the Leader's Household."

Ghanbari stood from the table. "Uh—yes—thank you." He wasn't sure what more to say, or what they wanted him to say.

"It was just a misunderstanding with the airline, and it's all been resolved. It won't happen again, *doktor,*" the man declared. "Here are you papers."

Ghanbari took back his passports.

"I've taken the liberty of arranging a car that will bring you to your hotel, compliments of the state."

"Thank you," Ghanbari said again, lifting his suitcase's handle.

"Enjoy your stay in the Islamic Republic of Iran, *Doktor* Ghanbari," the man gave a short nod in his direction. "And welcome home."

Ghanbari was escorted out to the main arrivals halls with no less than a dozen apologizes along the way. The *agence,* a black Peugeot—as hired cars were known in Persian—waited along the curb outside the terminal a few meters behind the chaotic swarm of the taxi rank. The driver greeted Ghanbari by name and already knew his destination: the Espinas Hotel.

As the Peugeot zipped north along Freeway 7 toward Tehran, Ghanbari thought he knew the guardian angel watching over his shoulder. It had to be Saeed Mofidi. Only the ayatollah's extended arm could clear away the Pasdaran like that, and none represented that arm more so than him. Mofidi had to be serious, he thought, and just maybe he wouldn't leave Tehran empty-handed.

• • •

A light snow blew from the dour clouds over North Tehran late in the afternoon, coating the stone pathways throughout Beit Rahbari in a thin white blanket; dewing Mofidi's shoulders. Fat, hooded crows massed in the tall pines—hundreds of them, bowing the branches and scarring the bark with their claws—jeering and cackling at the old man below.

But Mofidi ignored his loathsome audience. He was incensed.

A meeting of Iran's Supreme National Security Council (SNSC) just adjourned after running at least an hour over schedule. As usual, the familiar faces were in attendance—all of them even more loathsome in Mofidi's eyes just then than the feathered shit factories squawking overhead. President Behrouz Rostani presided; the speaker of the *Majlis* and the chief justice were in attendance, as was Foreign Minister Javad Zanjani with his colleagues, the ministers of the Interior and Intelligence; and of course, the chief of staff of the Armed Forces sat at the table alongside the commanders of the Artesh (Iran's regular army) and the Revolutionary Guards. But absent from that gathering of bearded mandarins was the most zealous one of them all, the one whose name they invoked almost as often as God's, and whose actions nearly drove Mofidi's heart to seizure: Major General— or simply *"Hajj"* to his subjects—Qasem Shateri.

Hajj had little time or patience for formal meetings, the mandarins extolled in a distant, reverend, almost mythical tone. Best to let him sow the seeds of revolution in the field, the mandarins acquiesced, while they huddled in Tehran to meditate on grander designs and guidance that would surely please Ayatollah Khansari once he returned from Mashad, with prayers for his health.

It was all a farce, Mofidi wanted to scream through the aches in his chest. The scrawls of a toddler were "grander" than anything that huddle could devise, and while the mandarins meditated, Shateri daubed a masterpiece of blood across the Middle East—blood that soon might be the mandarins' own.

Mofidi saw the gathering storm on the horizon. Eight days ago, a string of photographs and video clips surfaced on websites and social media accounts run by Hashid Shaabi, the umbrella organization for Shiite militias in Iraq. A particular video featured dozens of soldiers, dancing and cheering before jeeps and armored personnel carriers, crying *"Allahu Akbar!"* against volleys of gunfire into the sky. One photo displayed a few dozen stern-looking men gathered around on cushions, some dressed in camouflage fatigues with others wearing black and white turbans. And another depicted at least a hundred fighters arrayed on the carpeted floor of a mosque, all recumbent in prayer. Highlighted at the foreground of each posting was Qasem Shateri: the valiant commander making a glorious return to the battlefield where nine months earlier thousands of Shia liberated Iraq from ISIS's brigands and their treacherous collaborators. Or so the story went,

Mofidi thought, never mind the loss of Syria and Hezbollah or the disastrous consequences for Iran's strategic footing.

His triumphant appearance at Camp Ashraf, a sprawling Hashid Shaabi stronghold in Iraq's eastern Diyala Province, was a staged homecoming of sorts for Shateri, a propaganda dog-whistle for any who could hear the faint patter of war drums building again to a steady rumble.

But Mofidi heard it well.

Behind the walls of Camp Ashraf, after being received like a savior, *Hajj* Qasem held an audience with the generals of Hashid Shaabi's principal militias and the political and religious chiefs of Iraq's largest Shiite tribes. Mofidi identified their faces in the photographs. By Shateri's right hand was his personal envoy to Baghdad and commander of the Quds Force's Ramazan Corps, Brigadier General Jamal Jafaar Taghavi, but who was better known by his *nom de guerre,* "Abu Mahdi al-Mohandis." At *Hajj's* left was the man rumored to be his closest friend, a powerful Iraqi politician and commander of Hashid Shaabi's largest militia, the Badr Organization, Haider Mohammed Hatem. Seated beside them were various *seyyids* and *hojjatoleslams* from Iraq's Shiite heartland, and officers proudly bearing the patches of the militias Asa'ib Ahl al-Haq, Saraya al-Khorasani and Kata'ib Hezbollah. Their discussions were unknown to anyone not in attendance, but given what Mofidi just learned, he had his suspicions, and he hoped they were wrong.

The SNSC session, from which Mofidi stormed away, was called over two crises currently confronting Iran. Israeli airstrikes in Gaza was the first, but the second were the lingering protests in West Azerbaijan and Kurdistan provinces and the spate of assassinations that followed. The regime's press outlets tried to suppress the story, but word still got through. People took to the streets, outraged by Farinaz Katani's suicide in Mahabad. Local police and Basij units kept a lid on the demonstrations, but amid the simmering unrest, five Pasdaran officers were murdered over the past six weeks. With the first, a Badr Organization lieutenant was found shot along the shore of Lake Zarivar; next, two captains of the IRGC's provincial Saberin Unit were targeted by a sniper outside a restaurant in Piranshahr; and then a car carrying the assistant defence attaché of the Iranian consulate in Erbil was overtaken on the highway and raked with bullets; finally, Brigadier General Taghavi's aide-de-camp was blown apart in broad daylight.

Someone combed the borderlands between Iran and Iraq, picking off the most senior Revolutionary Guards that could be found. The brass was suitably spooked, the Pasdaran's commander reported to the council, and while steps were taken to increase security in those provinces, it was only a matter of time until five murders became six or more.

Who could be responsible? The Etelaat-e-Sepah looked over the border into northern Iraq and pressed their spies within the Kurdish intelligence services, the peshmerga forces of the KDP and PUK, and inside the PKK and PJAK camps on Mount Qandil. The resounding answer was unanimous: Jamil Gorani—the Dark Lion himself—and his band of "sons."

Mofidi subdued a satisfied smirk during the meeting. For him, it was a particularly ironic, if not the least bit karmic, display of cosmic justice. Gorani's revolt against the Kurdistan Democratic Party and Ezzedine Barzani after the deaths of his wife and eldest son was well known to Mofidi. After all, it was Shateri who personally ordered a hit squad from the Badr Organization with Barzani's tacit approval not to intervene. They failed to put the lion down, and now Gorani sought revenge. *How fitting,* Mofidi thought.

Yet now *Hajj* Qasem, speaking through the mandarins on the SNSC, seized on Gorani's rampage as a pretext for a long-overdue offensive into Kurdistan's *Rojhelat,* wiping clean another slate of opposition. Maybe Shateri even planned it that way, Mofidi wondered, deliberately goading an angry lion. The IRGC's commander presented a detailed plan for the council's recommendation and Ayatollah Khansari's ultimate approval. Spring's coming thaw would create the perfect conditions for a push through the border's valleys and mountain passes. In roughly four weeks, by the end of March, five Pasdaran provincial corps from West and East Azerbaijan, Kurdistan, Kermanshah, and even as far south as Ilam, would mobilize with Artesh artillery units, fighter aircraft and attack helicopters. The operation called for twenty thousand to surge into the border region. As PJAK rebels fled into the hills, IRGC Saberin commandos would pursue them back into Iraq, while their safe havens on Mount Qandil were pounded from the air. Estimates were three weeks with minimal casualties, and when the smoke cleared, any Kurdish resistance in Iran would be decimated.

The operation was acceptable enough to Mofidi, the Pasdaran were routinely deployed to burn away the overgrowth along the border, and he told the council he would present it to Khansari when he next visited the supreme leader in Mashad. His suspicions would have stopped there, but looking in tandem with the chaos in Gaza, Shateri's unexpected return to Iraq uncloaked the truth to Mofidi—a truth that would have also revealed itself to the mandarins on the council, if only they had eyes to see.

In Gaza, the carnage only worsened. Airstrikes were due to reach into the twelfth night without either side showing any willingness to relent. IDF fighters, helicopters and artillery bombarded the strip, whittling away Hamas and Palestinian Islamic Jihad's munitions stores and launching positions. However, once that Al Jazeera crew was killed on live television, the modicum of Arab sympathy Israel enjoyed for Moshe Adler's execution evaporated. Emboldened by a private message of support from Qatar's emir, Hamas' prime minister in Gaza, Fawzi Abu Musameh, and the chief of the al-Qassam Brigades, Khader Issa, outright refused any demands to surrender Islamic Jihad's Azzam al-Nakhalah before a complete halt to Israeli strikes. But from his war room beneath Tel Aviv, Avi Arad was targeting the wrong people.

As the Iranian intelligence minister once more revealed to Mofidi in his assessment of the situation in Gaza, al-Nakhalah continued to take orders—like the one to execute Adler—from Colonel Rasoul Gharib Abadi in Khartoum, Shateri's lieutenant for North Africa. Hamas had zero say in the matter, and with their leadership pushed into hiding by the airstrikes, al-Nakhalah held *carte blanche* over the strip's jihadists like never before. Scores of Hamas foot soldiers, the intelligence minister eagerly reported, were disgusted by their leaders' cowardice and reluctance to fight back against the Zionists. One senior al-Qassam officer, Bassam Sinwar, commander of their Northern Gaza Division, openly defected with his men and arms to Islamic Jihad, firing rockets at Ashkelon earlier last week in a show of allegiance. Time was on their side, the minister declared. Popular support in the Middle East would prevent Hamas from yielding to the Israelis, and while Avi Arad desperately needed to exact justice for his soldier's execution, he would inevitably order IDF tanks and ground troops over the armistice line into Gaza. *Inshallah*—God willing—as Shateri and his allies prayed.

Bodies of women and children would pile up. Homes, schools and hospitals would crumble and burn. Cameras would capture every tragedy. Outrage would swell, and the Israelis would be unmasked to all as the bloodthirsty monsters that Iranians always knew they were. No Arab head of state would dare sit across from Avi Arad at the negotiating table.

It was now so obvious to Mofidi. *Leave an opportunist with no opportunities,* Mofidi cursed as he marched through the flurries, *and he just might create his own.* Shateri played the only cards he had left. The plot unraveled in Mofidi's mind. In Iraq, Shateri returned to muster his troops and set them loose under the cover of a counterterrorism sweep. It would begin when Hashid Shaabi advanced north in a pincer striker against Mount Qandil. As fighting continued, Shiite militias would capture the Kurdish oil fields at Baiji and Kirkuk, severing the highways and blocking peshmerga in Erbil and Sulemaniyah from responding if—when—Hashid Shaabi mounted an assault on Baghdad. In Gaza, Shateri brilliantly manipulated the Israeli psyche. Mofidi still couldn't decide if the *Catarina A* and her cargo was a lure, but it didn't matter. The gambit worked. Its seizure gave Islamic Jihad an excuse to execute Adler and invite Avi Arad's predictable wrath. Hamas' reputation would be tarnished, the Israelis would go too far—they always did—and the bloodshed would make it impossible for Syria's delicate new government to forge peace with Jerusalem. And there it would be. *Hajj* Qasem would single-handedly restore Iran's strategic primacy in the Middle East.

What could make Shateri so confident that he would attempt to manage two simultaneous wars at opposite ends of the Arab world? What made him so bold, so brazen to do it before everyone's eyes? What secret did he hold?

Mofidi stopped in his tracks, exhaling an icy cloud. He already knew.

The Quds Force was about to be a nuclear power. That was Shateri's secret, the fountain of his gall. It struck Mofidi, as he held in the drifting flakes. All around him inside that compound's beige stone façades—in the Leader's Household, in the Presidency, in the Assembly of Experts, in the Guardian Council, in the ruling organs of the Islamic Republic of Iran—men went about their work thinking that they were in control, assuming that they mattered, all the while ignorant that they were not worth but a single atom. Another had come along years ago—quietly, without uttering a sound—and stole their country, their revolution away. But they never noticed, they couldn't see, and so they just kept working, unassuming, while they controlled nothing at all.

Mofidi kept walking toward his office. There were still good men in Tehran, reasoned and patriotic men who loved their country, who knew its proud history, who weren't content to allow the fevered fantasies of a zealot sweep it off a cliff and fall to ruin. Mofidi had to reach them, convince them to stand together against "Hajj Qasem" and his delusions that would destroy them all. But before Mofidi could confront Shateri, he had to silence the voices in Tehran that perpetually cried for war, and he had to end Shateri's quest to build a nuclear bomb. And he thought he knew how.

Last week, Mofidi received a fax from Ayatollah Abdolhossein Moezi, imam of the Islamic Centre of England and the supreme leader's representative in London. The fax's cover page was handwritten in Persian and forwarded a letter from Professor Morteza Ghanbari of the American Iranian Council at Princeton. Ayatollah Moezi explained on the cover page that the professor was an honest man and a good Muslim and vouched for him. Reading the professor's letter, Mofidi learned that Ghanbari was traveling to Tehran for three weeks to visit his ailing mother, and while in town, he humbly requested a few minutes of Mofidi's time. Mofidi knew the professor's reputation. He knew that as a moderate member of the Majlis, Ghanbari fled Iran in the turmoil following the student protests of 1999—the same protests that took Mofidi's son, Omid. Now comfortably relocated in the United States, Mofidi appreciated the work Ghanbari did to bridge the gap between Washington and Tehran. The American Iranian Council attempted to broker countless deals over the past decade, but only with the JCPOA to stringently limit Iran's nuclear program, did they finally make some progress—at least until Damascus fell. Ghanbari wrote in his letter that he wanted to speak to Mofidi about the economic benefits of the JCPOA and the deluge of foreign corporations seeking to tap Iranian markets. Mofidi found room in his schedule and set a date, thinking little more of it, until a much different message reached his ears.

Only last night, with the latest broadcast from Kuwait, Mofidi was told by his friends at CIA that Morteza Ghanbari was sent by the White House with a secret proposal to restart negotiations between the two nations. Through the grid of encoded numbers, Mofidi was instructed to ensure that this proposal made it into Ayatollah Khansari's hands. He could guarantee that much, but whether it went any further, Mofidi could only promise that he would try.

He crossed the compound and breezed past the checkpoints, shaking away the snow from his jacket. As Mofidi bowled into the anteroom outside his office, his secretary introduced him to Dr. Ghanbari, who by that time had been perched on the sofa for nearly an hour. He took the professor's hand, greeted him in an almost awkwardly soft voice, and ushered Ghanbari into his office. Shutting the door behind them, Mofidi removed his loafers and set them on a mat before slipping on a pair of plastic sandals. He could sense his guest stir; the sandals were ubiquitous beside the doorways of most Iranian homes, but weren't typically found in offices, and certainly weren't expected for Beit Rahbari.

Ghanbari took a seat on another imitation leather couch like the one outside. He eyed Mofidi, and realized that he was nothing like he expected. His voice was quiet and he carried a gentle demeanor. As he observed Mofidi closer, he noticed that his gray suit jacket didn't quite match the shade of gray on his trousers, his white shirt was slightly browned, and the loafers he'd removed were scuffed and battered. Mofidi seemed to him more like a quirky member of the Princeton faculty than the security and foreign policy advisor to a reclusive ruler who was often compared to Hitler.

"*Salam,*" Mofidi said with a quick nod, taking an opposite seat.

"*Salam,*" Ghanbari echoed. "Again, it is a privilege to meet with you."

"How was your flight?"

"Long," smiled Ghanbari. In his lap was a folio containing the sealed envelope with President Paulson's letters. "But it was okay."

"You came from New York?"

"Yes."

Mofidi leaned into the armrest. "Very crowded, I'd imagine."

"No," said Ghanbari with a slight turn of his head, "no more than Tehran."

"I always wanted to go there," added Mofidi, "to New York—to see the Statue of Liberty, Times Square."

"Maybe you will one day."

It went on like that for some time. Iranians called it *"ta'arouf,"* a kind of polite, back-and-forth small talk that went in circles. Often frustrating and incomprehensible to both sides, the niceties were a long-winded overture to any conversation, even serious negotiations. The point was usually lost on Westerners.

The office tea man arrived during the exchange with a tray balanced on his palm. He arranged the silver pot and cups with a bowl of sugar cubes and departed as quietly as he appeared. Mofidi was bent over the tray, pouring a cup for his guest, when Ghanbari mouthed the first consequential sentence.

"A peculiar thing happened at the airport. I ought to thank you."

"What's that?" Mofidi's eyebrows tightened and he leaned back, offering over the teacup.

"I was detained at immigration," Ghanbari revealed, "by the Etelaat. They held me for maybe two hours, said something was wrong with my flight home. When the guardsman returned with my passports, he was all upset and apologetic, said he didn't know I had business at the Leader's Household. I figured word got to you and you chased them away—so thank you for that."

Mofidi was frozen. He stared at Ghanbari with a bewildered look in his eyes, finally declaring, "I did nothing of the sort."

Ghanbari's head dipped. "You didn't?"

"No," Mofidi denied, "I've been in meetings since seven this morning. Nobody's told me a word about you."

Ghanbari's back straightened. "I—I don't know then."

Mofidi rose from his chair. "Would you like to hear some music?"

"What?"

"I think I'll put some on." Mofidi crossed his office to a credenza that was placed directly beneath a smoke detector on the ceiling. Sitting amid dust and some family photos was a small Japanese stereo and a stack of CDs. "Do you like Tchaikovsky?"

Ghanbari was puzzled. "I don't mind."

Mofidi placed a disk in the tray, crossing his office again as the horns, woodwinds and trumpets of the composer's Symphony No. 4 filled the room. He sat on the sofa, directly next to Ghanbari. "Morteza, it isn't safe. Why are you really here?" Mofidi asked as his voice became lost in the noise.

Ghanbari understood what was happening, and while he was slightly amused by the scene, he couldn't help but feel frightened. "I was asked to deliver a letter to Ayatollah Khansari from President Paulson," he muttered.

Mofidi hovered half a foot from Ghanbari's face. "Where is it?"

The professor pointed to the folio.

"Let me see."

Ghanbari handed over the envelope. Mofidi quickly ripped open the seal with his thumb, removing four canary-colored linen pages folded in thirds.

"One's in English, the other's in Persian," Ghanbari added.

Mofidi took the letter written in his language and unfolded it.

Ghanbari watched Mofidi's eyes as they began to slowly trail down the page. After a few seconds, he saw Mofidi's hand tremble.

"What—" Mofidi stammered. "What is this?"

"It's exactly what it says…"

"This is real?" Mofidi breathed. "They're serious?"

"Very much so."

Mofidi read the letter a third time, and only then did he believe. President Paulson began by addressing Ayatollah Khansari, thanking the supreme leader for Iran's faithful efforts to implement the JCPOA. But then the president's attention shifted to more pressing matters. He lamented how the last rounds of negotiations between their two nations so hastily collapsed in Vienna as news reached either side that Damascus was overrun. Paulson assured Khansari that he wished the Syrian civil war could have reached a more orderly end and gave his hopes that one day soon Tehran and Damascus could rekindle diplomatic relations for the betterment of the Middle East. The president stated his desire before leaving office to resolve America's great impasse with Iran once and for all, settling their disputes, allowing no wound to fester. To demonstrate his sincerity, Paulson outlined three points that the United States was prepared to discuss—a diplomatic quid pro quo that might set the stage for normalization. First, the US would recognize Iran's right to intimate but stabilizing involvement in Iraqi politics and in the Persian Gulf; in exchange, Iran would pledge support for Iraq's unity government and help disband the Hashid Shaabi militias. Second, Iran would impose a moratorium on supplying matériel to groups that call for Israel's annihilation, commit to supporting a two-state solution with Palestine, and back Hezbollah's transition to a peaceful political party in Lebanon; in exchange, the US would call upon Israel to abolish its nuclear weapons and work to establish a WMD-free zone in the Middle East. Third, the US would lift its remaining unilateral sanctions ahead of JCPOA provisions if Iran disbands the Revolutionary Guard Corps and dissolves its overseas activities. If this track was followed, Paulson assured, the United States could normalize relations with Iran. The letter closed with an offer to privately discuss these terms in Geneva as soon as possible, and with Paulson's deepest wishes for peace to come, he signed his name.

Mofidi dropped the letter in his lap and eased into the sofa as Tchaikovsky's trumpets blared through his office. He was just handed a blueprint to obliterate Shateri and every single one of his plots—to make *Hajj* Qasem irrelevant.

"Is this acceptable?" Ghanbari asked after a moment.

Mofidi snapped out of his daze and reminded himself that he still had a role to play. "I don't know," he stated. "What happened in Damascus was unacceptable. His Excellency is in no mood to hear the president's pleas."

Ghanbari blinked. "Is it possible to at least discuss this with him?"

"I suppose," Mofidi shrugged. "His Excellency is at his home in Mashad for the time. I'm due to visit him in a few days. I will show him this letter—what he'll say, I can't promise—but I will show him. I'll send a car to your hotel when I have an answer."

Ghanbari reached out for Mofidi's hand. "Thank you, sir."

Mofidi clutched the professor's hand and pulled him in, masking his voice in the melody. "How long are you staying in Tehran?"

"Three weeks," he replied with some nervousness.

"That's too long," Mofidi shook his head. "Do be careful."

"I'll try."

Dusk settled. A fiery palette split the westward horizon, sinking peacefully at the Mediterranean's angry swells; headlights and streetlamps silently broke the waxing darkness far beneath her feet; traffic hummed and voices echoed all around; and as the last sliver of sun fell beneath the waves, unwaveringly prompt, the *adhan* rose in layered cries from loudspeakers of the surrounding mosques, summoning Beirut to prayer.

Nina disregarded the call. She held a commanding view on the flat's balcony, stretching from the American University's limestone façades, palms and cypress trees to the shimmering glass high-rises lining the Marina District. While the *muezzin* wailed, she watched the neighboring buildings, scanning dozens of rooftops and hundreds of windows. Behind each, Nina knew, there might have been eyes, watching in return.

A deceptively warm breeze for late February swirled around her. It caught her hair. A nearby police siren broke the cries, seizing Nina's attention.

Her eyes darted right, toward the source, but then they froze.

A white light flashed.

Nina spotted an adjacent apartment building across the street. Most of its windows were darkened, but she swore the light came from within, somewhere on the middle floors. She held her gaze and waited. Then, just long enough, as if she were meant to see, the light flashed again. Twice.

"I wouldn't hang out there too long."

Nina's head spun as a door slid open at her back. It was Nathan Cohen, filling a narrow gap in the curtains. She stared at him.

"Are you coming in?"

Nina thought to tell him, but what could she say? A light merely flickered across the street—it could've been anything. "Yeah," she nodded.

Cohen pulled the door shut behind her and made sure the curtains covered the glass. The flat was one of a handful periodically used by Mossad officers passing through Beirut and, like the safe house in Batroun, was austere with shabby, mismatched furniture. As Nina entered, she saw Lotz—a technician from the Neviot unit and part of Cohen's "film crew"—

mounting a clock to a wall facing the sofa. Ortega, the head of her GRS detail, stood silently by the dining table; Tom Stessel had given him a direct order to keep Nina in his sights.

She tucked her hands into her pockets. "Is he close?"

The radio clipped to Cohen's belt crackled. "All stations, Sierra Two. Beta One is right, right, right toward red five. Closing—two hundred meters."

Cohen pulled the radio to his mouth, "Control, copy that," and looked to Nina. "He's right down the block."

"You ready for this?"

"He wouldn't have come this far if he hadn't already made up his mind," Cohen answered. "He just doesn't know it yet."

Cohen paused for a moment, knowing she wouldn't appreciate what he had to say. "Listen, Nina—I need you to keep out of sight."

She glared at him.

"I don't want him to see you. Just stay in the back with Lotz and Ortega. You can watch everything on the monitor."

Her lips tightened.

"Please..."

"Fine."

"Thank you," his shoulders dropped.

Nina sighed. "Is the audio running?"

"Tape starts rolling the minute he comes through the door," said Lotz. "I put one mic in the clock with the camera and another in that smoke detector, just to be safe. It's all wired to hard drives in the bedroom."

She dug her hands deeper into her pockets. "Well, big boy," Nina said to Cohen, "looks like you got this thing. Don't fuck it up."

Ortega trailed her down the short hallway to the bedroom. Lotz was only a few steps behind. Pelican cases were laid on the bare mattress. Several laptops and a monitor sat on a folding table in the corner with a jumble of wires, and, as in the living room, the curtains were drawn. Nina took a chair at the table and pulled a set of headphones over her ears, watching the monitor intently. She eyed the sofa in the living room through the high vantage afforded by the pinhole camera disguised inside the clock. Cohen stood within view, and then crisply in her headphones, Nina heard a knock at the door. Cohen glanced up at her through the camera lens and stepped from the frame.

Walid Rada stood in the open threshold.

"As-salamu alaykum, Monsieur Rada."

Rada looked around Cohen, peering into the flat. *"Wa 'alaykum."*

"Hal tatakallamu alloghah al-enjleziah?" Cohen asked. Do you speak English?

"Enough."

Cohen cast out his arm. "Please, come in."

Rada entered with tight, rigid steps. His head moved from left to right, inspecting every visible inch of the flat.

"I'm Nathan," said Cohen, bolting the door. "We spoke on the phone."

Rada stood in the middle of the living room with his back turned to Cohen. "You are Mossad?"

"I work for the Israeli government, yes." He came up past Rada and sat in a chair beneath the clock, gesturing to the sofa with an open hand. "Please."

"A Zionist spy," Rada mused as he sat.

"I guess it's a matter of perspective."

"No," Rada crossed his legs, "...it's not."

Cohen brushed the barb aside. "Mr. Rada, it's good to finally meet. I—"

"Why are you people following me?" Rada interrupted. "Whatever you're after, I want nothing to do with it."

That, Cohen knew, was utter nonsense. If Walid Rada truly had no interest in the cadre of "Zionist" spies tracking his every move, he would not have come fifty miles to Beirut—into the heart of Hezbollah's counterintelligence web—only to say, "Thanks, but no thanks." Rada was in total denial. It was Cohen's job to turn Rada's eyes toward the grave situation confronting him and his family while something could still be done to save them.

"If our ways upset you then I apologize, Mr. Rada, but it's come to our attention that you're in a bit of trouble. And that's putting it mildly. In fact, we think that your family's lives are at stake."

Rada gave a restrained smile. "Trouble? Our lives at stake? Really?" He breathed dismissively. "But I've done nothing wrong."

Cohen already caught his hook into Rada's mouth. Now he only had to reel him in, and there was no time to be gentle. He leaned over the coffee table between the two and opened a manila folder, removing the first page. "Mr. Rada, you can look at these if you want—they're pretty interesting— but let me just read the first few bits, if you don't mind."

"What is that?"

"This is a statement from the Lebanese Swiss Bank in Hamra. It appears that in 2013, your brother-in-law opened an account there. That's really interesting because I've heard he eats through a tube and shits in a bag. Is that true?"

Rada's face went flush.

"It also appears your brother-in-law is quite wealthy," Cohen observed. "In fact, he's so wealthy that only a few months after opening his account, it recorded a balance of—let me get this right—two million, one hundred thirty-one thousand dollars and change."

"Stop."

"Wait, there's more," Cohen held up a finger. "The only withdrawals noted on this statement are for a club just up the beach. *Le Piège.*' Have you heard of it? Rumor is, for the right price, their girls do more than just dance. Now, I wonder if the nuns were wheeling him over from the psych ward for a visit?"

"Stop!" Rada insisted.

"Would you like to see for yourself?" he offered the page, but Rada wouldn't take it. "No? That's fine." Cohen set it back in the folder and was silent for a moment. He stared at Rada, who looked down at the carpet, his breaths growing more labored by the second. That mask of denial had shattered.

"Mr. Rada. No, I'll call you Walid," Cohen said. "I mean you no harm. I know everything about you—about Yusra and Eshe, too. I could read out transcripts of every word uttered in your home for the last two days. I know about each website you've visited, every phone call, email or text you've sent—especially your porn fixation. I know how miserable and ungrateful your wife is, and how you've tried to please her for years. I know you despise the skin you live in. I know how flawed you are, Walid…and I know all about your sins."

Rada's head was still down, but Cohen heard him sniffle.

"Even still, Walid," he dropped his voice, "I want to help you. But please, do not mistake me for a fool."

Rada eased upright. His eyes were red and sunken and his hands trembled. He reached into his jacket. "May I smoke?"

"Go ahead, light up." Cohen knew of Rada's habit and came prepared. He pulled a lighter from his pocket. "Here, use mine."

Rada placed a cigarette between his lips and leaned toward the flame. He took a long drag and then finally asked the question Cohen was waiting to hear. "What do you want from me?"

Cohen pointed to Rada's forehead. "Everything in there that I don't already know."

Rada pushed the smoke from his lungs. "Like what?"

"You were involved in the construction of nearly every bunker in the Beqaa Valley. There's a start."

"Why should I betray my brothers to a Zionist spy?"

"Because your 'brothers' will kill you," Cohen shrugged, "and this Zionist spy won't."

Rada took another drag. "You can protect me?"

"Yeah, I can protect me. And Eshe. Even Yusra, if you want."

"In Lebanon?" Rada was skeptical.

"No," Cohen admitted. "First in Istanbul. And then, eventually, in Israel."

"Piss off," Rada spat. "No—no, I will not go to Israel. Never."

"Okay, fine," Cohen sat back in his chair. "You can walk out that door whenever you like. Go back to Machgara; I won't stop you. But I can't promise that folder won't get dropped off at Al-Manar." Cohen spoke of Hezbollah's in-house television network. "That might speed things up."

Rada's eyes burned like embers.

"Or, you can stay," offered Cohen, "and we can talk about how you and your family could be granted Israeli citizenship, be given a house that's much nicer than the one you have now, and have all of your crimes forgiven. We can even talk about securing the money you've stolen—which is, after all, how you've gotten into this mess. So, it's your choice: You can live in our world or you can die in yours."

Rada turned his eyes toward the curtains.

"Walid, we can give you a life worth living." Cohen paused and leaned in again. "I want to tell you something about myself."

Nina was riveted. She gripped the headphones tighter and stared into the monitor. Over the scratchy audio, she heard Cohen press his case.

"My wife had a baby girl last month," he confided. "And I learned that when you become a father, as you are, something becomes vividly clear. You realize—it just pops into your head one day—that you would do anything, *anything*, to keep your child safe. Every decision, every mistake you've made that's sculpted your life up to that very second, it all goes out the window. The only thing that should matter anymore is her—her future. Walid, you've already set yourself down a path and there isn't much else you can do to change it now, but at least give her a fighting chance. Don't let your decisions, your mistakes, define her future; let her have a chance to make her own life free of your sins."

Nina heard Rada begin to weep.

"Give Eshe a fighting chance, Walid. Let her try. There's nothing here for her, or you, or Yusra—only pain. You know that. Come with us and let some good stem from your mistakes. Let Eshe live without your shadow, without any of this politics, without any fear. It's time, Walid—to finally admit what you've known for a long time..."

Nina watched Cohen come over the table, place a hand on Rada's back, and whisper coldly into his ear. *"You're fucked."*

Two hours in Dubai quickly became five. Jack spent most of that purgatory monitoring weather reports from the plush comfort of the Emirates business class lounge. Frigid temperatures and high winds had wracked central Europe for the better part of the week, but in the last twenty-four hours a blustery squall named Cyclone Petra roared down from the Alps, blanketing tracts of France, Germany, Switzerland, Lichtenstein and Austria in nearly a hundred centimeters of snow and ice. Airspace over the continent rapidly shut down throughout the day and Jack was convinced he would spend the night in the terminal, but by nine that evening the blizzard had dissipated enough that some airports could clear their runways.

Emirates Flight 85 finally landed in Zurich at midnight. Jack swept through the largely vacant arrivals hall and presented himself to the Swiss Border Guards as Simon Marleau, and with a Swiss passport to match his legend. His passport was duly stamped without fuss—a crucial part of the scheme to re-enter Iran without suspicion—and he hailed one of the few lingering taxis outside. During the twenty-minute drive along the A1 motorway into town, Jack saw just how much havoc Petra had wreaked. Cars were spun around and left abandoned along the highway's shoulder; over-burdened tree branches as thick as a man's thigh were snapped like twigs; power lines dangled and transformers sparked on their poles; city plow crews and *polizei* worked through it all, determined to make the mess a distant memory by morning.

His taxi cut down Bahnhofstrasse to one of Zurich's *"grande dames,"* the one-hundred-seventy-year-old Hotel Baur au Lac. The maintenance staff was still busy shoveling out the driveway and sidewalks as Jack paid his driver and went through the revolving door into the ornate, marble-floored lobby. Posing as Simon Marleau—a yuppie, expatriate account manager for the Arab Banking Corporation returned home on holiday—Jack was forced to suffer the harsh indignity of booking a junior suite for the duration of his cover's stay in Switzerland. A bellhop escorted Jack to his room on the second floor, overlooking the Schanzengraben canal. The Bangladeshi porter offered to unpack his bags, but Jack wouldn't have it, so he tipped the boy well and sent him on his way. And then, alone in the suite, Jack stood idle for a moment—happily realizing that he had absolutely no idea what a human being in that situation should do next.

He browsed the room service menu, but at that late hour the offerings were slim and he wasn't too hungry either, having eaten in the Emirates lounge and again on the flight. Coming from the Islamic Republic of Iran, the only option, as Jack saw, was to get piss-drunk. Luckily, near the bottom of the menu was a Glenlivet 18 single malt Scotch. He lifted the phone off the nightstand and ordered a whole bottle. Rubbing his palms together like a giddy kid on Christmas morning, Jack found a white terry cloth bathrobe in the closet, tied it tight around his waist, and flopped onto the bed, as he understood idiots often do. After a few minutes, a waistcoated attendant appeared with a polite knock on the door and delivered the whiskey on a silver tray.

Jack dropped a couple ice cubes into a glass, cracked open the bottle, and got straight to work. Old re-runs of *The Big Bang Theory* dubbed in German kept him company for the next several hours, and when he finally slipped away into a drunken stupor, something altogether unthinkable happened: Jack Galloway slept through the entire night, spinning deceitfully peaceful dreams.

CHAPTER 41

ALL EVGENY MIROV could do now was pray.

Baranov rose from beside him and climbed the amphitheater's center aisle as calmly as he arrived, his footsteps growing softer by the second. As commanded, Mirov sat on the damp, moss-smothered slab in the company of the black wraiths that infected the silver pall upon the mountain's brow. They held their perch, cradling their rifles and watching him from all sides. It was unlike anything he had ever seen. Over twenty-six years of a secret life, Mirov counted his share of meetings with handlers, but none compared to this. Never had they come in such force or presented such a sheer rampart of menace. There would be no boasts, no threats, no parlays, no reprieves, only deeds; those Russians, whoever they were, were inhuman, wholly indifferent to the terrestrial planes over which they traipsed like wildfire: irrepressible and silent. They sapped Mirov's heart and wordlessly begged him to question all he knew. And then, once Baranov had gone—synchronized to the second—the wraiths turned their green eyes and dissolved into the inky void. Mirov knew it then. Lurking behind those spectral glints were the unblinking eyes of Death itself.

After another five minutes, Mirov mustered the courage to stand. When he did, knees trembling like gelatin, he raced down the mountain and soon came to the foot of the Alte Brücke, a stone arch bridge leading over the river Neckar into Heidelberg. It was almost five in the morning, but the sun was absent on the horizon. Clouds gathered in its place, tethered low in the sky by burgeoning payloads of snow and ice, casting a gray, predawn half-life over the town. Mirov crossed the river and wandered aimlessly through long, narrow streets. He didn't want to go home just yet. He wished that he could simply walk away from all he'd done, to start over. But he knew he couldn't; from that moment to his last, Mirov would shoulder his regret like a contagious disease. At five-thirty, shopkeepers and deliverymen made brief appearances on the cobbles to accomplish any small task that might be squeezed in before the storm. By six, Mirov came to rest on a bench in the Marktplatz and forced himself to admit that he couldn't sit there forever. He took the tram home and found that Olga had just woken. She had a rash of questions: What was so urgent that Moscow required an in-person meeting? Why weren't they contacted on a routine frequency? Who was the handler? Were they in danger? What would happen now?

As Baranov allowed, Mirov was truthful and answered what he could. Moscow was launching an operation to recover the *ranet*, that trunk they'd hidden away in the Black Forest all those years ago, Mirov explained, and he was to guide the team up the mountain and to the cottage. Afterward, they'd be recalled home and granted retirement with full rank and pension. "Ernst and Carla Kubin," a lie perpetrated for twenty-six years, would finally end.

What did it mean for them?

He hadn't a clue.

Mirov needed to leave before Cyclone Petra made that impossible. Heidelberg expected twenty centimeters of snow and it would only get worse farther south. In the Black Forest, toward Switzerland and the Alps, wind speeds were predicted at forty knots with gusts reaching seventy, and up to a hundred centimeters—over three feet—were due to fall throughout the day and well into the night. After the operation, Mirov told her, he would likely have to stay in Freiburg for a day or two until the roads were cleared. Then, suspiciously, he switched on the TV in their living room, turned the volume as high as it would reach, and sat Olga down beside him on the sofa. Dropping his voice nearly to a whisper, Mirov first made her promise that she would do exactly as he was about to say, without deviation, no matter the consequences. Reluctantly, she agreed.

By noon on the third day, if he hadn't returned home or contacted her, Mirov instructed Olga to gather the artifacts of their false life. He told her to take their forged Argentinian birth certificates that labeled them Ernst and Carla Kubin, their German identity cards, their Latvian passports used to travel back to Russia, even their encrypted satellite radio and codebook, and go immediately to the Baden-Württemberg LfV—the State Office for the Protection of the Constitution, the local counterintelligence agency, in Stuttgart—and reveal all. Mirov wanted her to detail every minute of their service to the GRU in Germany. Tell them where he went and why. Leave no rock unturned, no secret unspoken. She was to bear the whole truth, beg for clemency, strike a deal if possible, and accept any punishment they gave her. If Mirov vanished in the storm, Olga would bring their house of lies crashing down.

If she followed her training and trusted her instincts, Mirov was certain that she had a long, happy life before her. But, if he did not return in three days, she had to assume he was dead. Mirov made her promise again.

That premonition shook her to the bone. Olga was frightened, for him more than herself. She truly cared for Evgeny Mirov, even loved him, although she cursed that she hadn't the nerve to tell him. After a quarter-century of callous deception and deceit, Olga still could not lie to her heart.

They said their goodbyes. At two in the afternoon, the clouds let loose and thick snowflakes began drifting with the wind. Mirov eased his Volkswagen Sharan up the on-ramp onto Autobahn 5 as a dark gray and white curtain straddled the highway. There were hardly any other cars on the road beside the occasional *Landespolizei* cruiser with slow convoys of plows and salt trucks. He reached Karlsruhe, the next city south of Heidelberg, in under an hour. By four in the afternoon—just as the round peaks and fir trees were building on the horizon—the gray curtain dropped. Visibility fell by the minute and dense snow eddied around the Volkswagen, charging at the windshield before rising effortlessly back into the air. Mirov held the steering wheel with both hands, sensing the tires fight desperately to grip the pavement. He reached Offenburg ninety minutes later as darkness crept over the hills and valleys, and two pale orbs appeared at his back.

Mirov looked in the rear-view mirror. Headlights pierced the snowfall. They hovered ten meters behind him in the same lane, silent and unblinking. Mirov squinted in the mirror for a better view. It was a black Land Rover.

He knew it was them—the wraiths.

They stayed with him all the way, holding that same distance. There was no longer any need for subtlety or subterfuge: Mirov saw them and they saw him. The world seemed barren and deserted, abandoned in the storm, and theirs to shape.

It was after six o'clock when they finally arrived in Freiburg. Night fell and Petra was furious. Mirov led them over snow-laden roads to his flat on the outskirts of town. The Land Rover rolled alongside his Volkswagen and Mirov pulled the key from the ignition, telling himself that it would all be okay.

Baranov rapped on the driver side window and barked, "Inside."

There were five Spetsnaz operators with Baranov: Akhmadov, Ignatev, Kotov and Kakiyev. All came into Mirov's flat without speaking, dressed in UF PRO tactical clothing, camouflaged and waterproof for the worst that winter might conjure. Each laid a canvas rucksack on the living room floor and got to work preparing their gear while Baranov brought Mirov into the dining room.

"How are you, my friend?" Baranov asked with an attractive grin.

"W—well," Mirov stammered, "thanks."

"I need you to look at something for me." Baranov placed a tablet on the table. A topographic map covered the screen, showing the rugged wilderness south of Freiburg that splayed out undisturbed all the way to the Swiss border. Various waypoints were overlaid on the map, each another coordinate monitored by GLONASS, Russia's satellite navigation system. "Where is this cottage, Evgeny?"

Mirov interrogated the map for a moment and pressed a finger to the hamlet of Münstertal. "It's just there, by that village," he said. "The cottage is on the northern front of the Belchen, about a third of the way to the summit. There's a paved road, Schauinslandstrasse, which follows a pretty direct route through the Oberried-Hofsgrund pass. Münstertal's only thirty kilometers from here if we take the pass—a two-hour drive with the weather. From there, we have to follow a dirt track up the mountain, and I can't guarantee that it will even be passable."

"I'll make it passable," Baranov vowed.

"The longer we stay here, the more difficult that becomes."

"No," Baranov took a glance at this watch, "it's too early. We'll wait two more hours and then make our move."

It was eerily similar to what Mirov remembered of that night—February 25th, 1990. Like the Spetsnaz operators that came before, these men were also dressed for battle. They wore steel-toed boots and pulled load-bearing vests with ammo pouches over their insulated jackets. Their AK-103s were fitted with red dot sights, sound suppressors and coated in white paint.

Mirov was given an identical set of camouflage clothing and told to put it on. It all fit him perfectly. When it came time to move, Baranov's men pulled white balaclavas over their faces, hoisted their rucksacks back on their shoulders, and went outside to warm the Land Rover, leaving Mirov and Baranov alone in the flat.

"You and I are taking your car, Evgeny," Baranov said flatly.

"Mine?"

"You lead the way and my men will follow." Baranov placed his hand on Mirov's shoulder. He flinched, and Baranov pulled away, eyeing him with a cross between amusement and concern. "Oh you're afraid. Aren't you, Evgeny?"

"No," Mirov muttered.

"Yes, you are." He shook his head, "But you shouldn't be." Baranov touched Mirov again and this time he held steady. "See?"

Mirov gently nodded.

"You and I are casualties of the same hypocrisy. Tonight, it ends."

Harris knew that noise. It was unmistakable, a tone that pierced through the air sharper than a bullet shattering the sound barrier, and each time he heard it, without fail, Harris felt a small tingle of relief.

After all—the dead have nothing to cry about.

Harris forced himself awake with a few weary blinks and stared at the blackened ceiling. He took his arms out from under the comforter and sat up against the headboard. As his eyes adjusted, he saw an unruly brown clump of Sandra's hair beside him. Harris kept absolutely still, training his ears down the hallway, and waited for a moment. Then, it pierced the air again: Ben's cries.

"I got it," Harris said to no one, and rose from his bed.

Snow blew horizontally in the pass so thick that Mirov could hardly see ten feet beyond the windshield. The blizzard conjured a universal diffusion infinitely more disorienting than the gusts and eddies of the day; it was a thickening blackness, night itself descending layer by frigid layer.

"I can't see the damn road!" Mirov complained.

"Keep going, we're five kilometers from Münstertal," Baranov called from the back seat. He held the tablet in his lap, watching them inch along Schauinslandstrasse on the map. On the seat next to him was an FN Herstal Five-seven pistol with a round loaded in the chamber.

"We should not be here, it's too dangerous."

"Shut up and drive!" Baranov spat.

Mirov felt the winds batter the Volkswagen. The Land Rover followed at a good distance and only its headlights were visible. Chains wrapped around the tires of both SUVs kept them from careening into the guardrail. Their route through the pass took thirty minutes longer than expected and they reached Münstertal by eleven. Power lines leading into the valley were down, washing the village in darkness. The Volkswagen's wiper blades snapped rapidly back and forth, scarcely clearing the windshield before heavy flakes covered it over again. Mirov leaned forward with his chin just over the steering wheel, peering through the blitz.

"You need to tell me when to turn."

Baranov set his eyes on the tablet's glare. "A hundred meters ahead on the left. Before the monastery."

"How am I supposed to see that?"

"Turn now, damnit!"

Mirov cut the wheel, fishtailing the back tires and sending the Volkswagen into a spin. He released the brakes and recovered, barely making the trail.

Baranov quickly radioed Akhmadov in the Land Rover and in a few seconds he saw their headlights slow and turn into position behind them. They drove across an open field for another kilometer until the trail sank into a towering stockade of fir trees burdened with fresh snow. Mirov eased the Volkswagen to a crawl as the hood gradually inclined on the Belchen's northern slopes.

"How close are we?" asked Mirov.

"Close."

The tires groaned up the hillside between broad timbers coated with hoarfrost. A short distance up the mountain, Mirov pressed the brakes to a halt. Mangled tree limbs as large the Volkswagen had fallen, blocking the trail.

Baranov reached for his pistol and leaned into the door. "Don't move."

Harris stepped over Boomer and crossed the hall into his son's room. The sobs grew louder and more painful as he nudged open the door. In the dark, Ben laid in the folds of his Batman-themed bedspread with his little hands pressed tightly to his eyes.

"Buddy, what's up?" Harris asked and scooped his son into his arms.

Of course, the boy couldn't answer. Ben's lungs heaved and his skin glistened with a cold sweat.

Harris held Ben against his chest and gently rocked him back and forth. "It's okay," he whispered. "It's okay, Daddy's here."

The boy's cries fell to a dull whimper.

"Daddy's here, pal."

Harris brushed Ben's shaggy blond bangs away and kissed his forehead. "Did a monster scare you?"

It only stalled them. Before Mirov had even a second to contemplate an escape, the Land Rover crawled up from behind and Baranov coolly explained their obstacle. In minutes, Akhmadov and Kakiyev revved chainsaws and dug the whirling metal teeth into the branches with a guttural groan. They cut the limbs into manageable chunks, dragged them from the trail and tossed them into the woods. Baranov came back to the Volkswagen once it was done, shook the snow off his shoulders, and ordered Mirov to drive.

The trail curved ahead and after another kilometer Baranov pointed through the gusting white barrage to some indiscernible edifice out in the dark. "There," he said, his breath frosting the window, "I see it."

Mirov pressed the brakes again and the Volkswagen lurched still.

"We're here," Baranov keyed his radio, and then turned to Mirov. "Out."

The air stung Mirov's throat and snowflakes piled on his lashes. He watched them sail like gray shadows into the blizzard, rifles trained against the night, and fan out around the cottage. Like the day Mirov found it, the house's pitched roof sagged under the weight of the snow; the stucco walls were pockmarked and sheathed in ice; and after twenty-six years, Mirov was surprised— if not even disappointed—that it still stood.

"It's in the cellar?" asked Baranov, his voice muffled by the cold.

"On the eastern side," Mirov answered. "Behind the wall."

The Spetsnaz operators finished the sweep around the perimeter and stacked at the door. Akhmadov thrust out his foot, splintering the wood and launching it back on the hinges. One after the other, the four dipped their barrels into the darkness and stormed through the doorway.

"Let's go," Baranov grabbed Mirov's arm and pushed him forward.

Osvobozhdat! he heard them bark as they cleared each room. Mirov entered with Baranov inches at his back. Chemlights were cracked and dropped on the timber floors, bathing the cottage—and the wraiths—in a neon green shade.

"Down," Baranov commanded them.

Ignatev lit the cellar with another chemlight. Mirov went toward the eastern foundation and searched the bricks. After a few moments, he found a section near the center of the wall—approximately four feet on each side—where the bricks appeared newer, and not nearly as cracked and discolored as the rest. Mirov stepped back and pointed. "It's there."

Akhmadov barged forward and marked the section with chalk while the others went back outside to fetch the concrete saw and sledgehammers.

"There aren't any monsters in here. Want me to show you?"

Ben anxiously clung to Harris' sleeve.

"Come on, dude, let's check it out. Mommy's sleeping, so we gotta be quiet." Harris held Ben with his right arm and tiptoed to the closet, tapping his knuckle on the particleboard. "Hey, monsters, you in there?" He carefully slid the door aside and tilted his shoulder just enough so Ben could look through the clothes hangers and storage bins. "Nope, don't see any."

Ben tried to form a word and pointed into the hallway.

"Oh, out there?" Harris wondered. "I hope not."

Harris carried his son down the hall and cracked open the door to the spare bedroom. It was empty. "Still no monsters."

Ben cooed and clicked his tongue.

"What about the living room? Think we should check?" Harris pressed his nose to Ben's. The boy bounced in his father's arms. "Yeah, you want to?" Harris laughed. "All right, here we go."

They crept down the stairs and searched the living room, the dining room, and even the kitchen. Finally, with a cautious squint into the laundry room and out onto the patio, Harris looked at his son and could positively declare, "Well, looks like we're safe."

Ben's tears had dried and his breathing steadied.

Harris climbed the stairs again. "See, I told you there weren't any monsters in here," he boasted. "Not while Daddy's home." He carried Ben back to his room and sat on the bed, still holding his son close.

He couldn't let go just yet.

"Are there monsters out there somewhere?" Harris asked. "Sure there are. But real monsters don't have scales, or wings, or ten eyes; they look just like the good guys. That's how they hide. When the monsters hurt people, your dad and his friends go out in the world and find them. They're scared of us, and when the monsters see us coming, they turn and run real fast. But we catch them, and we make sure they never hurt anyone again."

Ben rested his head on his dad's chest.

Harris threaded their fingers together and sighed, "But you don't ever have to worry about those monsters, buddy. I'll never let them get you."

Beyond the boy's bedroom window, a streetlamp rose like an island of light adrift in an endless black sea. "Can you see that?" Harris lifted Ben's arm and pointed out to it. "That's how I know us good guys are winning."

Smoke and dust flooded the cellar. Orange sparks spilled over the floor.

Mirov watched through a respirator mask as Kotov wielded an industrial-grade Stihl concrete saw in his hands and laid its sixteen-inch, diamond-tipped circular blade into the wall. It loosed a deafening, metallic scream. Kotov sliced along the chalk lines, leaving a square of chewed and shredded mortar in the foundation. It took fifteen minutes to complete all four cuts. The sparks cooled and died and the blade's scream reverberated through the cellar as Kotov finally backed away. Akhmadov and Ignatev then approached with sledgehammers and heaved the twenty-pound iron heads at the wall. After several blows, the mortar binding the bricks together began to fracture. The wall wavered and then crumbled in jagged chunks on the dirt floor. Baranov cracked a chemlight and stepped forward as the dust settled, revealing a cavity in the foundation. He dipped his head, searched amid the dull neon glow, and smiled.

"When your uncle and I were little, your granddad used to drive us to the ocean at night," Harris explained to Ben. "We'd sit on the beach, dig our toes in the sand, and watch the stars floating in this blackness that went on forever. They looked so tiny against it all. One night, your uncle asked why the universe was made with so much more dark than light. So your granddad told us that once, a long time ago, there was only dark, until *poof*—out of nothing—one lonely little star appeared in the sky, floating all by himself. But from that star—*poof*—there came another, and another, until a whole bunch of stars floated in the sky. Your granddad said that even though there was still so much dark, now that first star wasn't as lonely, because he knew he didn't have to face it by himself anymore. As long as the stars floated together, the dark wasn't so scary."

Harris kept his eyes on the streetlamp.

"Then your granddad told us to look out into the ocean. It was all black, just like the sky, but he said that if you tried really hard, we could spot one little light on the water. I found it before your uncle. It was a buoy, shining in the night. He said that if we were ever afraid, no matter what, wherever we looked—either in the sky or out to sea—we could always find at least one tiny light, and we would know that we didn't have to face the dark alone."

Harris kissed the back of his son's head.

"You're my light, Ben."

"Get the battery."

Kakiyev opened his rucksack and handed Baranov a four-volt battery attached to two electrodes. He set the chemlight on a shattered brick. Inside the cavity, within arm's reach, was one end of a stainless steel trunk. Baranov knew this next step was critical. At the trunk's opposite end was an old booby-trap designated by the GRU as *molniya,* or "lightning" in Russian. The device consisted of an extremely sensitive pressure trigger wired to a small explosive charge. If the trunk was moved or touched in any way, the trigger would sense even the minutest shift in pressure and detonate the explosive, destroying the trunk and showering the unlucky soul attempting to retrieve it with molten shrapnel.

So Baranov held his breath and inched his hands into the cavity.

He took the electrodes attached to each of the battery's contacts and gingerly placed them against the steel, allowing an electrical current to flow through the case. Mirov and the others were gripped in a tense silence. Baranov held the electrodes still, and listened. After a minute that passed like an hour, he heard five audible clicks sound in quick succession from within the trunk. He breathed again with relief. The charge was disarmed.

"Help me bring it out," Baranov stood. Ignatev came forward and they both grabbed the handle and pulled with all their strength. It gradually slid out from the cavity. "Okay, now let's set it down." Kotov took the bottom and the three carefully eased it onto the dirt floor.

The trunk, the *ranet,* weighed approximately ninety kilograms with its lead-lined exterior shell and sat sixty by twenty centimeters. It was made of stainless steel and devoid of any markings. After a quarter-century of hibernation, Mirov thought, it looked totally unscathed.

"I need a reading," said Baranov.

With that, Baranov undid the trunk's two heavy latches and raised the lid. Any view Mirov had inside was blocked, although he recognized the

Geiger counter that Akhmadov hastily removed from his pack. The plastic device fit in Baranov's hand and he methodically waved it over the trunk's interior. As he did, Mirov heard the counter burst alive with a rapid ticking noise that filled the cellar. Mirov's stomach dropped; suddenly he understood what they had been hiding all these years—and he knew the wraiths weren't bringing it home.

"It's good," Baranov casually announced. "Let's move before the storm gets any worse." He shut the lid and secured the latches while Ignatev and Kotov bounded back outside to guard the cottage's perimeter. Akhmadov and Kakiyev lifted the trunk and lugged it upstairs.

"Are we done now?" Mirov asked. "Am I out?"

Baranov patted his back and led him to the door. "Soon, my friend."

Mirov could scarcely see the night through the snowfall. It blanketed everything now: the trees, the cottage, the SUVs. He walked ahead and made out the Land Rover's frame. Its rear hatch was raised, the trunk was placed inside, and the four Spetsnaz operators stood around it with their rifles aimed at the ground. He stumbled with his next step. Mirov's eyes fell to his boots. A black bag rested in the snow. It was nearly six feet long and a zipper ran down the middle.

"Thank you, Evgeny," Baranov's voice echoed from behind.

His legs were frozen.

"This is our gift to you."

He couldn't take his eyes off the bag.

"Open it."

Mirov's lips quivered. He knelt down in the snow. He felt sick. His head spun with fear. Mirov swallowed and unzipped the bag. He first saw what looked like clear plastic, but as Mirov pulled down another few inches, his heart skipped a beat.

It was Olga, gazing up at him with lifeless eyes.

"You show me that I don't have to be afraid," Harris muttered. He knew Ben could only comprehend a sliver of what he said, but Harris kept on; he needed to at least try. He ran his fingers through the boy's hair. "I hope you understand how much we love you, Ben."

The streetlamp shone through the window.

"The night you were born, you were so small that you could've laid right in my palm," Harris continued. "The doctors took you away before we could even get a glimpse of you. I stayed up in the hospital that whole night. Outside the waiting room there was a streetlamp in the parking lot just like that one. I sat by the window and watched it for hours. I cried and cried. As I looked at the light, I remembered what your granddad told me, and I called out to your Uncle Ben for the first time in years. I said, 'Ben, wherever you are, if you can hear me, I could really use your help.' I told him my son was sick, that we named you after him, that I didn't know what would happen, but I asked him—please, please, please—if you slipped away that night...please, help you find your light."

He exhaled and wiped a tear away. "I'm not sure what I did to deserve it, but you soldiered through, buddy. And you know what? For those next one hundred and thirty-six days before we could bring you home, all the nurses in the NICU wanted to take care of you. They told your mom and I that whenever they came to your incubator, you were staring up at the ceiling lights. When we finally did bring you home, you would wake up screaming in the night for months. Then, just as we opened your door, you stopped. We'd come to your crib, and you'd be smiling on your back, looking out the window there—right at that streetlamp."

"I miss your uncle more than words can say," Harris confessed, "but whenever I see you, I also see him." He looked down and noticed that Ben had fallen asleep in his arms. He placed one last kiss on his son's forehead and tucked him in bed. "And I know that he saved you...just like you saved me."

A plastic bag was tied over Olga's head. Her skin was marred with cherry-red welts and a horrific expression was frozen on her face.

Mirov staggered away and cried an anguished shriek.

Baranov lurched forward and seized him. Mirov felt the bag slip over his head and pull taut around his neck. He gasped, sucking the plastic into his mouth and nose. It covered his eyes as he struggled. His lungs burned and with every panicked breath there was no air, only heat, and pain. Spots danced in his vision like fiery imps. His head throbbed.

All the while, the wraiths stood before him, watching motionless, indifferent, and unblinking—melting back into wispy black shadows.

He didn't want to fight anymore. Soon his mind was peaceful. His eyelids grew heavy. With the next, ultimate, gasp, his legs gave; and Evgeny Mirov fell down, and down, and down, nearer to the cold.

CHAPTER 42

MOVSAR GELAYEV SPED through acres of arid farmland to that barren hilltop outside Zarayeb with a fresh trove of secrets transmitted from Moscow. He let his motorcycle rest on its kickstand. The Beqaa Valley sat a thousand meters below, and in the morning sun he could clearly see the crooked fingers of snow capping the Anti-Lebanon Mountains and the Syrian border. Gelayev removed his helmet and walked toward the cinder block house, carefully watching his step—the slopes were mined. Past a few trucks and SUVs parked under camouflage nets, he spotted the barn, which was sealed and under guard until Ruslan Baranov returned from Europe. A Spetsnaz operator standing sentry by the door let Gelayev in the house and he quickly found Kazanoff at work in a back room.

Maps and photographs were tacked to the walls and splayed across a large table. Kazanoff heard Gelayev's footsteps, and as the Russian entered, his spindly arm was outstretched. Gelayev handed Kazanoff a USB drive, who then took it and plugged it into a laptop on the table. Gelayev turned and went to leave.

"Stay."

Gelayev's boots stuck to the floorboards. He slowly turned back around.

Kazanoff pecked at the laptop's keyboard and, without uttering another word, drifted into the hall.

Gelayev heard a printer rustling. His eyes drifted up to the walls; maps of Lebanon plastered an entire side of the room. One depicted downtown Beirut. Gelayev looked closer. He noticed the Grand Serail, where the prime minister lived and worked; the Parliament Building on Nejmeh Square; Baabda Palace, the president's official residence; numerous key government ministries and military barracks spread throughout the city; all outlined with red pencil. On another map, he recognized Beirut's southern suburbs. The *dahieh,* where Hezbollah's ruling clerics kept their offices in the Security Quarter, was clearly marked. Gelayev looked to the opposite wall and saw maps of Riyadh and Saudi Arabia's Eastern Province, equally latticed over in red.

He moved toward the table. Three photographs were arranged by the laptop. They showed an apartment building, which Gelayev thought might have been located in the neighborhood near the American University of Beirut. Captured at the center of each—standing on a balcony and looking toward the camera lens—was a woman with long auburn hair.

Kazanoff floated back into the room with a thin stack of papers. He set them on the table, picked one from the top of the pile, and silently passed it to Gelayev. It was another photograph, snapped hastily in poor lighting, and showed the bottom quarter of a page ripped from a yellow notepad. A crease ran through the middle, and as Gelayev squinted, he read Secretary of State Angela Weisel's scrawled handwriting. Her note was candid, and to the point:

Mofidi is CIA.

At sunrise, a Dassault Falcon 50 operated by Meraj Airlines—which provided executive transport services for the Leader's Household—lifted off the runway at Tehran's Mehrabad Airport and set a course into the distant fringes of Iran. It flew east over the peaks of the Alborz Mountains that girded the Caspian Sea toward the blunt, dusty slopes of the Kopet Dag at the southernmost advance of Central Asia. The jet's sole passenger sat along the starboard fuselage, sipping tea and idly watching the terrain below. About an hour into the flight, Saeed Mofidi put his cup down and looked out, far beyond the wingtip, and saw a beige smear appear on the horizon. It was the blazing Haj Ali Gholi salt flats, and Mofidi knew that within that pale waste, shrouded somewhere in the haze and burrowed deep beneath the earth, sat Qasem Shateri's deadliest secret—the spring watering his dreams of empire—itching to see the light.

Before it could, Mofidi intended to choke that fountain dry.

After ninety minutes, the Falcon touched down on schedule at Mashad International Airport and taxied to the military apron. Mofidi took his briefcase and descended the airstairs to the tarmac. It was a few degrees warmer than in Tehran and the air was noticeably clearer without the capital's noxious blanket of smog. Situated three kilometers from the civilian terminal building, the northwest corner of the aerodrome was home to the IRI Air Force's 141st Tactical Fighter Squadron, which was responsible for defending the airspace over Iran's desolate frontiers with Afghanistan and Turkmenistan. As Mofidi's eyes adjusted to the sun's glare, he spotted two hardened aircraft shelters made of reinforced concrete. An F-5E fighter was parked in a fast launch position beneath each shelter with cockpit canopies raised and Russian A-11 Archer air-to-air missiles mounted to hardpoints on the wings. At the opposite side of the apron, behind a watchful perimeter of Pasdaran soldiers, Mofidi saw the customized Airbus A330 of the supreme leader. He thanked his pilots and the veiled stewardess and walked to a waiting Peugeot 508 that whisked him to the Ghadir Expressway.

Like Shiraz and Esfahan to the west, Mashad was an incubator for renowned figures of Persian art and literature, such as the poet, Fernandowsi, whose *Shahnameh* is considered the national epic of Iran. Once a small outpost of the Abbasid caliphate along the Silk Road, Mashad's population exploded during the 1980s with refugees fleeing the Iran-Iraq war. The tide never receded. For Mofidi and countless other faithful Muslims, Mashad was a holy place akin to Mecca or Jerusalem. Roughly twenty million pilgrims converged on the city each year to pay their respects at the Shrine of Imam Reza, the eighth imam of Twelver Shias whose martyrdom in the ninth century is still grieved over a millennium later. Everything in the city, from the entrenched ring roads to the subway lines and the markets, orbited that colossal shrine. With its thriving population and local economy, Mashad sprouted from the eastern desert like a modern, chaotic oasis. Yet rivaling in importance for the Islamic Republic's zealots, Mashad was also the birthplace of Supreme Leader Ali Mostafa Khansari, and was still a retreat when political intrigue or the ayatollah's poor health—and often both—made Tehran too harsh for the old man to endure.

The Peugeot took an interchange to the Kalantari Expressway and drove north along the city's abrupt western limit. Mofidi sent Khansari to Mashad two weeks earlier at the consensus of the ayatollah's eldest son and medical team that the dry air might help staunch the recent slide in his mental awareness. With Khansari away from the capital, Mofidi schemed that he could speak in the supreme leader's absence and work with greater latitude. He had been proven wrong. The Quds Force's adventures in Gaza, Sudan, Iraq and Europe had spun out of control. To end the madness, to prevent a wider conflict, Mofidi needed the ayatollah more than ever.

Khansari's residence in Mashad was a sprawling three-hundred-thousand-square-meter estate called Malek Abad. Its high walls disguised lush gardens and guesthouses, a racetrack and a horse stable, an indoor swimming pool and a gymnasium, a mosque and outbuildings for staff, and even its own hospital. Soldiers of the IRGC's Ansar-ol-Mahdi Force—the unit that also protected Beit Rahbari in Tehran—stopped the Peugeot at the first gate. After a routine inspection, the car was waved through and rolled along a winding, tree-lined driveway to another checkpoint. Mofidi noticed that there seemed to be armed guards standing everywhere he looked—two hundred in all. He felt a sense of relief for Khansari's safety, but soon realized that those guns could be ordered to turn inward just as easily as they faced out.

Once clear of the second checkpoint, the Peugeot stopped by the palatial main house. As the driver came around to open his door, Mofidi spotted a familiar face waiting for him. It was Dr. Marandi, the ayatollah's personal physician. Mofidi stepped out of the car and immediately offered his hand.

"*Salam, doktor!*" Mofidi smiled.

"*Salam, Baradar* Saeed," Marandi welcomed. "How are you?"

They embraced and pecked each other's cheeks like old friends.

"Fine. Stressed, but fine," answered Mofidi. "And you?"

"There are good days and bad," the doctor admitted.

Mofidi's smile melted away. He eased closer to Marandi and nearly whispered, "How is he?"

Marandi grimly shook his head.

"Tell me."

The doctor also lowered his voice. "It's worse than when he left Tehran. His Excellency—" Marandi stopped and glanced at the nearest guards, "he no longer recognizes me, his nurses, his maids, the butler. We're strangers now."

Mofidi's eyes also shot to the guards. "Where is he?"

"The stables."

"Show me. I need to see him."

The pair strolled along a pathway between the trees. After several wide paces, Mofidi noticed that the guards followed at a distance. His jacket sleeve brushed Marandi's and he asked, "Has Mojtaba visited?"

Hojjatoleslam Mojtaba Khansari was the ayatollah's eldest child and only son. While his daughters had been married off as trophies to loyal businessmen and politicians, Mojtaba shouldered the responsibility of continuing the family legacy. As a respected scholar and a rising seminarian at the prestigious Qom *Hawza,* Mojtaba could one day be a formidable player in Iranian politics with a seat on the Assembly of Experts or the Guardian Council all but guaranteed. However, while his father still lived, Mojtaba elected to work firmly in the supreme leader's shadow as a valuable confidant with no hidden agendas or baggage to speak of; for the time, Mojtaba existed solely to serve his father. Mofidi admired him for just that reason and saw Mojtaba as one of the precious few he could trust to place loyalty to the country over personal ambition or religious zeal.

"He came last Thursday," said Marandi. "When Mojtaba first saw him, well…the past few weeks haven't been kind. He spent the night in his father's room, and when he left for Qom in the morning, I'm afraid he had tears in his eyes."

"He didn't know his own son?"

Marandi's head shook.

"What of his wife?"

"Khojasteh's taken residence in the guesthouse since they arrived. She walks in the garden in the afternoons, but otherwise I haven't seen her."

Mofidi swore.

Two years ago, Khansari suffered a series of small strokes in his sleep. None was particularly debilitating in isolation, but repeatedly and in quick succession, they exacted an irreversible toll. The frequent interruption of the blood supply to the temporal lobe of his brain starved his nerve cells of oxygen and induced the onset of dementia, of which his family already had a history. The initial symptoms were so mild that he wasn't diagnosed until six months later. Mofidi would never forget that moment. After a marathon briefing on the most recent nuclear negotiations with the United States, the supreme leader was asked for guidance. His response typically would have been sharp and resolute, but instead, Khansari mumbled several unintelligible words that lethargically trailed off into nonsense. Mofidi and others around the table quickly moved the conversation along as not to draw attention, but the deed was done. The ayatollah was no longer himself, and his aides could do little but watch him shrivel and die.

For the next several months, Khansari's day-to-day memory was not affected. He could function normally and manage the country with his advisers' assistance as he always did. Yet during policy briefings, or in meetings with foreign heads of state and diplomats—any time that complex issues were discussed—Khansari seemed totally lost. After a few minutes of discussion, one could see his eyes fog over, and he would sit there, politely nodding whenever he assumed it was appropriate. In particular, Mofidi recalled one meeting with Mikhail Karetnikov, when afterward Khansari pulled Mofidi aside and asked who it was that he'd been talking to for an hour. That was when Mofidi first felt afraid for his boss, when the Russian president's face was erased from Khansari's memory, and when Mofidi realized what dark, uncharted territory they were about to enter. That night, Mofidi broke the news in a letter to Langley.

In time, the supreme leader gradually lost his grip on reality. The names and faces of important clerics and ministers, military officers and faithful devotees, and how they were all connected to him began to fade. Khansari's speeches and sermons became tightly scripted and choreographed, lest he stand idle at the podium and forget where he was or why. Negotiations on Iran's nuclear program continued in Geneva and Vienna while his closest aides conjured the illusion that the ayatollah was firmly in control of Tehran's position. The Syrian civil war raged toward its bloody conclusion, hundreds of Iranians died fighting and thousands more looked to the *vali-e faghih* for validation that theirs' was a just martyrdom, but none came. Cracks appeared in the charade, and through them slipped Qasem Shateri and his allies in the Revolutionary Guards. Now those cracks were torn to gaping fissures that threatened to rip the country apart from the inside.

Iran was about to burn and no one held a water hose.

"His Excellency is up all through the night," Marandi informed. "He usually falls asleep in his wheelchair at about eleven in the morning, and then we'll put him in bed where he'll lay until maybe eight in the evening, if we're lucky. I'd give him a sedative for the insomnia, but I'm concerned he wouldn't wake."

"Don't do that," Mofidi shot. "If he won't sleep, then so be it."

Mofidi spotted the stable just ahead. He could see through the open timber doors and straight down the row of stalls. More soldiers stood by the stable, two of whom Mofidi recognized as Cheyzari and Nejat. Both were decorated IRGC officers and had protected Khansari for thirty years; Mofidi knew them to be as loyal as men come. They saluted as he approached.

"*Salam,* brothers," he answered their salutes. "I've come from Tehran to consult His Excellency on a matter of national security. The sensitive nature of this matter did not allow me to utilize telephones or couriers. I need only ten minutes of His Excellency's time—alone."

Cheyzari and Nejat never left Khansari with anyone but immediate family members. They weighed Mofidi's request with suspicion for a moment, and then Cheyzari asked, "Is this approved?"

That struck him as an asinine question. Above Mofidi, who else could approve such a thing? "Of course," he gave an exacerbated look. "Ten minutes."

"Ten minutes," Nejat echoed and let Mofidi by with a slant of his head.

Mofidi inched through the door. Dry hay crushed beneath his soles. The stables stretched on for a hundred meters and housed seventy horses, with thirty-five stalls on either side. As he stepped deeper along the row, he saw some horses lying in the stalls while others stood with their broad necks jutting over the tops of the metal doors.

A withered man sat in an electric wheelchair before a stall about midway through the stable. His ashen skin hung slack from his bones and a wiry gray beard dangled from his chin. A black turban was tightly wrapped atop his head and gold-embroidered clerical robes flowed down his wheelchair and fell into the dusty hay. It was Ali Mostafa Khansari. The ayatollah's left arm was outstretched as high as it could reach and his hand was placed on the muzzle of a gorgeous white Arabian stallion called Zuljanah. Named after the steed of Hussein ibn Ali, the third imam of Twelver Shiism who was slain at the Battle of Karbala in 680 AD, the horse was Khansari's prized possession.

Mofidi stopped to collect himself. *"Agha?"* he called.

Khansari slurred something indistinctly. He kept caressing Zuljanah's coat and beheld the horse through his round spectacles as if Mofidi wasn't there.

"Agha?" Mofidi called again, this time a bit louder.

Khansari stirred in the chair and briefly took his hand from the horse. He mumbled under his breath, and then returned to petting Zuljanah.

Mofidi was frustrated, even in shock. He cautiously approached and dipped his head so that he might catch the ayatollah's gaze. Khansari was mumbling again, and Mofidi strained his ears.

"Beautiful creature."

"Agha, it's me. It's Saeed," said Mofidi in a clear voice. "I've come from Tehran to speak with you. Would you like that?"

Khansari's eyes never left the horse. Zuljanah affectionately nuzzled down at him with each gentle stroke. "Beautiful creature."

"How are you feeling?" Mofidi asked. "Are you enjoying Mashad? I heard your son, Mojtaba, visited last weekend."

"Beautiful creature."

Mofidi's stomach sank. He'd known that Khansari's condition worsened by the day, that it was just a matter of time now, but to actually witness it in person was devastating. He wasn't prepared for it. He could no longer pretend it wasn't true. It broke Mofidi's heart to see a man he served—and betrayed—for years so shattered and helpless; to see a man who was so reviled and compared to the worst despots of history reduced to a shell; to see that it was all true while millions remained oblivious.

If only they knew that this is what they feared, Mofidi thought.

Mofidi reached into his briefcase and removed a pen and two single-page memos. Khansari's name and title—second only to God—were typed at the bottom of each page. The few inches above were left blank for his signature.

He loomed over the ayatollah's wheelchair while Khansari remained enraptured in Zuljanah's presence. "I have something for you to review," he proposed. "Since you've been away, *Agha,* there has been renewed conflict in Occupied Palestine. The Zionists have assaulted Gaza with planes and artillery. They mean to destroy our brothers in Hamas and Islamic Jihad. Nearly a hundred have died and I'm afraid scores more could follow if we do nothing—"

Khansari groaned. "Have pity on my people."

Mofidi held the memo before Khansari's spectacles. "This first statement would demand that Prime Minister Arad order an immediate cessation of hostilities against Occupied Palestine so that humanitarian aid may reach civilians. It also bars Major General Qasem Shateri and the Quds Force from furnishing any matériel support to resistance groups in Gaza for the next six months. The second statement would give your blessing for renewed negotiations with the Americans and would recommend that I represent Your Excellency at an initial meeting in Geneva."

He knew that Khansari hardly understood a word he said, but it assuaged his conscience that he at least tried to explain the terms.

Khansari huffed and stroked Zuljanah's coat. "Beautiful creature."

"If I could see your hand, *Agha.*" Mofidi took Khansari's other arm and placed the pen in his palm. Molding his skeletal fingers around it like a corpse, Mofidi held his swollen knuckles and quickly formed the ayatollah's wavy signature across the bottom of each page. *"Merci,"* Mofidi said gratefully and returned the memos to his briefcase.

Khansari's attention was drawn to that last word. *"Merci,"* he muttered, and eased his head up to the man standing above him, as if he only just noticed, and locked his eyes on Mofidi's. They held there, at once heralding an encroaching doom and a melancholy recollection of a life once lived. To Mofidi, those eyes almost begged for help, for a merciful end. And then, effortlessly, something shifted. Those eyes knew fear, confusion, and beheld only a stranger.

The ayatollah's mouth cracked open. "Who are you?"

The buzzer blew off the loudspeaker atop range control.

Harris dragged his muzzle up from the low ready position and squeezed the trigger twice. A pair of 5.56 rounds burst from the Heckler & Koch 416's barrel and pinged against the steel plate. Within a millisecond, his red dot sight swung an inch right and painted the two adjacent targets. He fired again, hurling a double tap twenty yards over the grass into each silhouette at center mass.

Then, instinctively—as the rifles' reports screamed in his head—Harris dropped his left arm through the sling, wrapped his right hand around the barrel's forward vertical grip, tucked the 416's buttstock against his left shoulder, and fired, striking the three targets again.

An acrid, sour whiff of burnt gunpowder met his nose. Harris safed the rifle, dipped its muzzle to forty-five degrees, and sprinted downrange. He spotted Z running in his periphery.

Both stopped at the fifteen-yard line and leveled their guns at the targets. Flames leapt from the barrels in rapid succession, six times on their left shoulders and six times on their right, sounding with a metallic clap as the bullets hit.

They lowered their rifles again and dashed ahead.

At the ten-yard line, after sending another double tap into each target, their thirty-round magazines ran dry. They let their rifles drop on the sling and immediately reached to their right thighs. Harris drew his SIG Sauer P226 service pistol from its holster and bounced three nine-millimeter rounds off the targets at close range—two in the chest for safety, one in the head for certainty.

The buzzer blew again. "Cease fire, cease fire!" the loudspeaker boomed.

Harris flicked the safety switch and returned his SIG to its holster. He felt the 416's barrel simmer through his vest. Gunpowder was caked on the muzzle and the rifles' waning roar still echoed off the dunes. An icy wind from the Atlantic swept the smoke inland to the marshes around Lake Redwing.

"Time is twenty-five-point-six," Z read from his wrist.

"Not bad," Harris hung his earmuffs around his neck and strolled into Z's lane, "but I need to see if this new girl of yours and all these throw pillows and shit that came with her made you soft."

Z already stood before his targets. "Fuck, sometimes I surprise myself," he turned to Harris and beamed behind his Ray-Bans.

Harris counted twelve dents punched into the sternum of each steel silhouette with a single security round placed between the eyes. He nodded, accepting that his wallet would take a beating on their next trip to the Lynnhaven Pub. "Looking pretty tight, buddy."

Z shook his head and lamented, "Man, I just wanna go outside the wire and do infidel shit with my friends."

The range safety officer's voice broke through the loudspeaker. "Chief Harris, can I see you a sec?"

Harris turned around and faced the control pavilion.

"Have a date?" Z wondered.

"Wasn't planning on it."

They walked back up a dirt path to the pavilion and found the RSO at his booth. "What's up?" asked Harris.

"Got a call from your squadron commander," the RSO informed. "He asked for you to meet him in the team room."

Harris gave a mystified, slightly annoyed look to Z. "Right now?"

"Sounded like it."

"He say why?"

The RSO shrugged. "Just the messenger, Chief."

"Fuck," Harris tightened his jaw.

"It's no problem, Robby," Z offered. "Leave your shit with me."

"You'll square it away?"

"Just go, dude. I got it."

Harris unclipped the 416's sling from his load-bearing vest. He left the gun with Z and made the short jog down Regulus Avenue to the fenced compound that housed DEVGRU's head shed. Harris found that Red Squadron's team room on the second deck was empty, which was unusual for a weekday when no major trainings were underway. The door to his squadron commander's office was shut. He knocked, preparing himself for some administrative ambush, and immediately received a reply.

"Come on in."

As Harris turned the knob and eased the door open, his eye first caught three stars stitched into the lapel of a woodland-camouflage Navy working uniform. With another inch he saw the name patch over the uniform's breast pocket.

Startled, he snapped to attention and saluted. "Good morning, sir."

Vice Admiral Eric Wade, commander of the Joint Special Operations Command, calmly returned the gesture. "At ease, Chief. Relax."

Harris widened his stance. His entire chain of command sat before him: the squadron commander and master chief, even DEVGRU's CO. A folder was opened on the desk and it seemed like they had been speaking for some time—about him, Harris quickly understood.

"Gentlemen, I thank you for your time," said Wade. "If you could give the chief and me the room, I'd appreciate it."

As they filed through the doorway, the two senior officers shook Harris' hand and his master chief gave him a stiff slap on the back. None offered a word of clarification, but their eyes hinted to Harris that today would be radically different than the last.

"Have a seat, Robert. I want you to be comfortable," Wade said casually.

"Thank you, Admiral." Harris took a chair before the squadron commander's desk. Looking down, he remembered the vest wrapped around his torso, the dirty boots on his feet and the loaded sidearm strapped to his leg. It wasn't the manner in which he wanted a private sit-down with the legendary commander of JSOC, but the admiral hardly seemed to mind.

Wade cracked his knuckles and began. "You know that feeling when you think you know someone without actually meeting them?"

Harris realized that Wade wanted a response. "Yes, sir."

"That's how I feel about you." Wade sat back and crossed his legs under the desk. "I've heard a lot about you recently."

"All good things, I hope," Harris tried to smile.

"Well," Wade thought, "the CO here told me all about your son and that your wife is expecting. Is that right?"

"Yes, sir. A girl this time around."

Wade smacked the desk. "Outstanding. Congratulations, Robert."

"Thank you, Admiral," Harris nodded, trying to figure out why the hell he was sitting there.

"Let's see… What else do I know about you?" Wade picked the folder off the desk, placed it in his lap, and leafed through the pages. "I've read your personnel file," he said. "I know you enlisted fresh out of high school. BUD/S, Class 235 soon after that. You've served fourteen years in Naval Special Warfare, eight of those in SEAL Team 3, and six here at DEVGRU. I see deployments to J-bad, Kandahar, Baghdad, Anbar, J-bad again, Djibouti, Jordan—Abbottabad; looks like we've chewed you up and spit you out."

"It's felt like that sometimes," Harris grinned, "but it's been an honor, sir."

"What's next?"

Harris cleared his throat. "Um—I'm sorry, sir?"

Wade deliberately pronounced each syllable. "What...is...next?"

"For me?" he stammered. "For my career?"

"Correct."

Harris caught himself in the middle of a shrug. "Well, I just came off deployment about two weeks ago—"

"I know."

"So I'm getting acclimated to the squadron and our workup schedule. Beyond that," he shook his head, "I'm really not sure, sir. My wife and I have talked about it since I've been home, but our concern right now is this baby on the way."

Wade cocked his head inquisitively. "What do *you* want?"

Harris thought for a moment. "May I speak freely, Admiral?"

"I'd expect as much."

He breathed and shook his head. "To be honest, sir, everyone has an answer to that question but me."

"Okay," Wade smirked and straightened his back. "Answer this for me: Do you see yourself in this line of work for much longer?"

"If I'm being honest, sir—no. I don't," he admitted.

"I understand," Wade nodded. "Completely. You're only thirty-three and sitting at E-7. You've been around the world a few times and have probably seen your life flash before your eyes once or twice. You've got a disabled child who needs his dad, another on the way, and a wife whose patience with all this bullshit is running thin. You wake up every morning and ask when this lucky streak is gonna run out. So before you're just another VA statistic, you'd rather cash out while you still can. The only problem is, you've been at this game so long, the thought of doing anything else scares the piss out of you. Is that right?"

Harris blinked. "Yes, sir."

Wade leaned over the desk. "I'm asking you to hang on a little bit longer."

"Why?"

Wade eased back. "Like I said, I've taken the liberty of getting to know you from afar. I heard how you rogered up when Delta was short a few operators in Syria, and I know what happened on that op in Tartus. I respect that. The TF commander in Hama speaks highly of you, Bragg speaks highly of you, and naturally everyone here speaks highly of you. So I figure they can't all be wrong."

"Thank you, sir."

"What I'm about to share with you has to stay pretty vague—I need you to understand that."

"Of course," said Harris.

Wade held for a moment. "CIA is planning an operation that requires a four-man element drawn from our Special Mission Units and placed under their Title 50 authority. Director Freeman has asked that I recommend an individual to lead this element in concert with his officer already in-country. After lengthy due diligence, it is my intention to recommend you."

The blood in Harris' face ran hot and cold at once. The hair stood on his arms and neck. The admiral's words ricocheted through his mind and rang in his ears. Although he couldn't show it, he felt dread. He knew the consequences.

"This is voluntary," Wade explained. "I'm not ordering you."

It briefly occurred to Harris that he could simply decline, but the question fell from his tongue, "What's the op?"

"It's a long-term surveillance operation with the possibility of a targeted killing inside a hostile foreign country at which the United States Government is not officially at war," said Wade.

"That narrows it down a bit," he smirked.

"Beyond that, I can't say more unless you accept."

Harris looked away. "How long would I be gone?"

"Two weeks? Three months? However long it takes."

Harris' eyes fell to his lap. "If I have a choice, Admiral—"

"Here's what I'm prepared to offer," Wade asserted. "First, the three additional operators in the element will be yours to pick. You name them and I'll clear it with my J1; it doesn't matter if they're on deployment, we'll get it done. Second, when you get home, there'll be a promotion to master chief waiting for you. Now you can stay in the squadrons on that rate, transfer to Green Team or staff duty, or you could even retire. Whatever it is you decide you want to do, go with God. You've served your country well and you don't owe her a dime."

Harris weighed his options. Leaving on Sandy again, voluntarily, before their daughter was born would crush her. He didn't want that. Yet again, retiring from the Navy at the rank of master chief, with its pension and benefits, was an offer he couldn't ignore. It seemed right to Harris, to try his luck one last time.

But then Harris remembered that night in Tartus—how one, simple mistake had saved his life—and he thought of Ben. Both were dumb luck.

"When do you need an answer, sir?" he asked.

"By the end of the day," Wade replied. "You'd have to drive up to Langley later this week and get briefed by their people. My J2 has been involved in the planning, but there're details with comms and insertion they need to settle. Just tell your skipper what you decide and he'll contact me."

"I appreciate this, Admiral. I really do," Harris shook his head, "but I'm not sure. I have to think about my kids."

Wade was gathering himself to leave, but as Harris uttered that last sentence, he froze. The admiral's posture relaxed and his eyes narrowed. "Whenever I went out to BUD/S, I would always give the trainees the same speech. You know what I would tell them?"

"No," Harris warily breathed.

"I said that most men go through their whole lives as spectators," Wade explained. "Spectators to the world and its indiscriminate nature, to its chaos, to its evil. I told those trainees that while their friends and neighbors, their parents and siblings, their wives or girlfriends, while the overwhelming majority of the human race—even you up to that moment—are forced to live as spectators, and even casualties, to the world and its turns, men like us choose to make a change. Men like us choose not to watch, but to act. We are privileged to go out into the world and change it, to shape it, to fight so that even one day is a bit less cruel. I told them that while we've had it drilled into our heads that we fight for God and country, for the Constitution and our freedoms, one day you're going to find yourself out there, and you won't fight for any of that bullshit—you're going to fight for the few people you love most in this chaotic world, and on that day, you're going to win."

Wade paused and stared Harris down. "You're worried about your children, Chief? That's fine. Get out there, and help us shape the world you want them to inherit."

Haddad placed his forearm on the steering wheel and turned to face the boys. "Remember what I told you," he said. "Just do as I say and it'll be over in five minutes. Understood?"

"You can count on us, Badi." Zyed was eager to prove himself.

"Sajid?"

Sajid passively nodded. He would dissolve into his seat if he could.

"You need to say the words," his brother demanded.

"Fine," Sajid conceded. "Sure. I'm ready."

"Okay," said Haddad. "Sajid, you'll come and watch my back. Zyed, stay with the car and keep your eyes on the road. If you spot anyone coming, just flash the headlights. If all goes to plan, we'll be home for prayers."

"We got it," Zyed assured.

Haddad looked to Sajid. "Let's go."

Their objective, a twenty-four-foot Mitsubishi Fuso box truck, sat a hundred meters ahead in the dim moonlight. Haddad had spent several days canvassing the cities within two hours of Paris—Compiègne, Beauvais, Évreux, Orléans—until finally, just that morning, he discovered a charming little bakery set along Rue de Magneux, a quiet residential street on the outskirts of Reims, only a ninety-minute drive east of Clichy-sous-Bois. The bakery's delivery truck was parked on the curb outside the shop without a single surveillance camera in sight. A quick Internet search confirmed that the truck's axles could support the three-ton payload he'd discussed with Anwar Sabbah. Haddad was sold; he returned to La Forestière to gather the boys and seize the truck that very night.

Reims was desolate at that late hour.

Haddad tucked a thin metal slim jim inside his jacket, rose from the Skoda Octavia, and strode confidently down the street with Sajid on his heels. At the Fuso, he hoisted himself up on the cab's entry step and peered through the driver side window. "Go and keep lookout," he whispered to Sajid.

Sajid crept around to the rear bumper and hid in the shadows. As told, he watched back up Rue du Magneux with his gaze fixed on the Octavia while Haddad wrestled the lock. Sweat beaded over his brow despite the wintry breeze and he felt his heart thumping inside his chest. He stood there for what seemed like ages, until Zyed signaled.

The Octavia's headlights flashed.

Haddad plunged the slim jim between the window and the weather stripping and carefully slid the tool back and forth inside the door panel. After searching a few moments, he felt the notch catch hold on the locking rod. With another slight tug, the lock pin popped up.

"*Badi,*" he heard Sajid gasp.

"What?"

"Someone's coming."

Another car had turned the corner and now rolled down Rue de Magneux.

"Get behind the wheel," Haddad ordered.

The boy dove to the sidewalk and ducked behind the truck's wheel well. Haddad opened the cabin door and went prone on the floor, slamming it shut behind him. Sajid was curled in a ball and listened while the car rumbled past. He then peeked around the wheel and saw two red taillights sinking in the dark. Sajid came out from hiding and knocked on the cabin door, telling Haddad that they were clear.

Inside the cabin, Haddad took a deep breath and turned his attention to the Fuso's steering column. It was an older model truck—1998 by his search on the VIN—and wasn't fitted with the anti-theft devices that Mitsubishi now placed on its vehicles. Hot-wiring the truck would be child's play. He pulled a flathead screwdriver from his jacket and removed the bottom panel of the steering column. With the ignition cylinder exposed, Haddad found a pair of red wires leading to the battery and a pair of brown wires leading to the starter. First, he stripped the red wires with the tip of his screwdriver and twisted them together. The truck's interior lights fluttered to life. Next, he stripped the brown wires and gently touched the exposed ends. The engine turned over and rumbled beneath him. Haddad smiled.

He reached over and unlocked the passenger door. Sajid climbed inside. With Zyed trailing in the Octavia, they drove west alongside the early morning traffic on the A4 Autoroute, toward Paris, and Haddad's storage units peppering Île-de-France.

The operation launched at midnight.

In the rusty mélange of the Negev desert, an airman waving lighted wands lured a heavily modified Gulfstream G550 business jet from its hangar at Nevatim Air Force Base. It received immediate clearance for takeoff and climbed rapidly to forty-one thousand feet—well above the cruising altitude of commercial airliners. As the Gulfstream banked to starboard and sped north over the Mediterranean, six mission specialists of the Israeli Air Force's 122 "Nahshon" Squadron were busy in the aft section of the cabin. From their workstations, the specialists activated the EL/W-2085 multi-band airborne early-warning radar housed in a bulbous dome on the belly of the fuselage. After twenty minutes, the Gulfstream loitered a few miles off the Lebanese coast and flew in a narrow loop with its unwavering eyes trained to the night.

An hour earlier, at Tel Nof Air Force Base on Israel's southern coastal plain, an Eitan UAV glided off the runway and followed a pre-programmed flight path over the West Bank, the Sea of Galilee and the Golan Heights, and crossed into Lebanese airspace by Mount Hermon. From their virtual cockpit at Tel Nof, the drone's pilots took control of the forward-looking infrared (FLIR) camera mounted between the undercarriage and peered into the pale blue hills.

Pulling the strings, deep beneath downtown Tel Aviv in a bunker called "the Pit," was Benny Isaac. Packed inside a control room before him were analysts, intercept operators and imagery experts from the General Staff Intelligence Directorate; operational planners from Mossad; a liaison element from the IDF Northern Command; and even the commander of the Israeli Air Force, who'd momentarily stepped away from orchestrating the ongoing bombardment of Gaza. The view from the Eitan's camera was projected on a large screen at the front of the room. A dozen more screens eavesdropped on Hezbollah radio chatter or monitored Lebanese army and police frequencies from remote SIGINT sensors hidden throughout southern Lebanon. Another screen mirrored the detailed radar image transmitted from the Gulfstream orbiting above the Mediterranean and displayed the precise, real-time geolocation of any vehicle moving within a search grid on the ground.

Isaac watched it unfold live through the glare on his wire-rimmed eyeglasses, stoic and unmoved. On the main screen ahead, the hills yielded and the picture of a flat, chalky expanse materialized. Someone in the room announced that the Eitan passed over the Beqaa Valley. In another few moments, a car heading along a dirt road came into view, lit only by the heat of its engine and the three warm-blooded bodies inside. The Eitan banked around to pursue and its camera swiveled, reacquiring the target. All that military machinery and technological wizardry, Isaac knew, could only achieve so much. Success or failure—life or death—in the coming hours, now rested solely on the team below.

CHAPTER 43

HE HAD COME so far. He surveilled the target; he burrowed inside the target's mind, heard his most private thoughts, uncovered his darkest secrets and witnessed the world through his eyes; he approached the target and demonstrated power, then comforted the target as an old friend and revealed the better life that they could build together; he earned the target's trust and convinced him to reject all he knew for an as of yet intangible future, and did so with such skill that the target brought his family along for the ride; he had manipulated the target to betray his own country and religion and live the remainder of his days with an eye turned over his shoulder. He had come so far, and now the fate of three people—Eshe, Yusra, and Walid Rada—was set precariously in his hands.

Only now Nathan Cohen had to exfiltrate them from Lebanon.

Cohen pressed the night vision binoculars to his eyes again and watched the southern horizon. A gentle breeze blew. There was no moon that night and high clouds thick enough to block most of the light that bled from the stars. *Good weather to run,* he thought—*or hunt.* It was so dark that his binoculars displayed more receiver noise than an actual image; the mountains appeared like a green heap in the distance with bits of white static flitting across his eyes. He frowned and let the binoculars dangle from his neck.

After Cohen prevailed upon Rada to defect, he returned home with the unenviable task of convincing his wife to do the same. Cohen gave him a prepaid cell phone and instructed Rada that if Yusra refused to join he must call as soon as possible. If he wanted to stay with her, Rada would let the phone ring once and the operation would be aborted; if he wanted to continue without her, let the phone ring twice. If he succeeded in the impossible, Rada was to pack a suitcase for each of them—the only keepsake from their past lives—and meet at one o'clock in the morning in a vineyard ten miles north of Machgara on the opposite end of Lake Qaraoun. From there, they'd be given Turkish passports and tickets for the next Middle East Airlines flight from Beirut to Istanbul. No call was ever made, and so the exfiltration proceeded as planned.

Looking south, Machgara's lights reflected off the clouds. He heard a car door close and footsteps crunch in the soil.

"It's almost zero-one-hundred," said Nina.

"I know that."

"So where is he?"

Cohen held his tongue. "He isn't traveling alone," he reminded her. "Give him some time. He'll make it."

Nina dug her hands in her pockets. "Can I hang out here with you?"

"Yeah."

There were two cars backed down a row in the vineyard—one for Cohen to drive the Radas to Beirut and the other for Nina's GRS detail, which Stessel demanded stay at her side. Bird nets covering the vines masked their position from the surrounding hills, and Cohen knew an IAF drone circled overhead. With the added benefit of a few armed CIA heavies on the ground, he felt fairly secure. Even still, staring down a dirt road that led toward Machgara, Cohen wanted to get out of there as soon as possible.

Almost as that thought left his mind, Nina pointed into the darkness and asked, "Do you see that?"

Cohen squinted. "No."

"*That,* right there."

He brought the binoculars to his eyes. Emerging from the murky green mass ahead was a car with its headlights doused. "I think we got 'em." Cohen lowered the binoculars and cracked a chemlight at his feet.

The engine's moan grew faintly louder against the breeze as the car rolled up the rutted trail toward them. It came to a stop in another minute, but Nina saw only black through the windshield.

"*Salam,*" Cohen called.

Just then, Nina remembered standing out on the balcony of Mossad's safe house in Beirut—and the three white flashes.

Cohen stepped to the driver's side window with a wide smile.

Nina held her breath.

"Piss off!" The front passenger door swung open. A plump woman in a purple *hijab* stormed out of the car. "No!" she spat inside. "Do not touch me. Do not speak to me. Do not even look at me." The woman cursed in Arabic and went around to the back seat. She leaned into the car and rose a moment later with a little girl asleep in her arms.

Nina's shoulders dropped. It was Yusra and Eshe.

Rada got out of the car next and wrapped his arms around Cohen. Nina noticed that his eyes were damp and glossed over. For a man only a few hours from freedom, he appeared exhausted and utterly defeated. Rada turned from Cohen and glanced at Nina standing idly in the road. For a fleeting second, he wondered about that fair-skinned, auburn-haired woman and why he had never set eyes on her before. She etched an indelible impression on his mind, like those flawless and unreachable girls beyond his laptop screen.

It was done in less than ten minutes. Cohen unscrewed the license plates off Rada's car and stripped the interior of any personal markings. When dawn came to Lebanon it would be as if Walid Rada and his family simply vanished in their beds. Days would pass before Hezbollah's agents, or anyone, would notice. Cohen drove them back to Beirut to rest for a few hours before their final escape. The GRS detail took a different route through the hills, and as they raced back to the embassy, all Nina could remember were those three white flashes.

That morning the clouds gave way to blue skies and a radiant sun. Nina met with Tom Stessel first thing and went over her plan to spend the week in Istanbul for Rada's debriefing. Stessel was content to see her leave, if only for a few days, and was happier still to finally get the Counterterrorism Center's hands off his turf. If it weren't considered bad form that early in the day, Nina would've also reminded Stessel that he could go fuck himself.

She hid her eyes behind aviator sunglasses, tied her hair in a ponytail, and tucked what remained under a baseball cap. Ortega took one of the more nondescript SUVs from the embassy motor pool and dropped her a few blocks from the Charles Helou Bus Station in Gemmayze. Nina walked the rest of the way and hailed a taxi to the airport, bartering a price with the driver in hurried Arabic. It was six in the morning.

As the taxi sped down the Airport Road, Nina saw the cinder block jungle she'd watched for so long grow at either side, mere feet from the highway. She saw the banners immortalizing martyrs slain in Syria and in the south; extolling the airbrushed likenesses of Ayatollah Khansari and Secretary-General Hamawi; and heralding that great foretold war when Hezbollah will eradicate Israel from the earth, shatter America's military might and punish all who oppose them. To the grizzled old clerics who still held Hezbollah's reins, those banners were red meat tossed to the bloodthirsty, humiliated ranks—hollow echoes and broken promises of conquests that would never come.

At least not while those clerics ruled.

Nina looked to her right. A lush golf course ran from the highway's edge nearly to the Mediterranean. Yet something blocked it from reaching the waves. There was another jungle out there, as she noticed: grayer than the others and ensnared in its own hive of wires and dust, stretched like canvas over a rocky promontory beside the sea. It was a jungle called Ouzai, and

Nina swore that if Ibrahim al-Din—her white whale—ever staggered out of the depths and returned to the light, he would surface from within.

The taxi driver navigated around a cloverleaf interchange and followed the departure signs up to the concrete and glass terminal at Beirut airport. Nina tipped the driver just enough to dissuade scorn and avoid praise. The curb was jammed with other taxis and hotel shuttles. Baggage trolleys and valets littered the sidewalk. She took her suitcase in tow and followed the awning. In a few paces, she read a sign for Middle East Airlines and found Cohen waiting under it, just like he told her. About thirty feet away, beneath the same awning, Nina spotted the portly, balding figure of Walid Rada. Yusra stood beside him, swaddled from head to toe in a gray *abaya* so that only her face was visible. Eshe was held in her mother's arms.

Nina and Cohen turned their backs to the family; they'd link up again on the ground in Istanbul. "How were they last night?"

He shook his head. "Rough You ready for this?"

Nina looked at him from the corner of her eye. "Are they?"

They walked through the automatic doors and into the terminal. A departure board suspended from the ceiling displayed the outgoing flights for that day, listing destinations to Frankfurt, Cairo, Athens, London, Dubai, and so on. Midway down the board, Nina found Middle East Airlines 265 to Istanbul, scheduled for takeoff without any delays at 8:35 A.M.

It was six-thirty in the morning.

Anwar Sabbah heard a commotion outside. Car doors sounded, opening and closing. He went to the window and looked down. A Nissan Patrol was parked in the alleyway. Two brawny Russians stood by the SUV—Knight's Armament PDWs hung on slings at their sides—and a third was moving to the rear passenger door. Sabbah's own guards stirred, agitated by their unexpected guests. The Patrol's door eased open and a pale figure rose into the sun with a stooped gait and shuffled steps.

He strode into the next room and roused al-Din from his sleep.

"It's him," Sabbah sputtered. "He's here."

Al-Din sat up in bed. Boots echoed on the floor below. The guards protested but were roundly ignored. Soon, the boots climbed up the stairs, and just down the hall. Then that same pale figure appeared in the doorway.

"My friend," Kazanoff's voice soughed like the wind, "I've something to share…"

To minimize chances for a mistake, Cohen printed Rada's boarding passes and gave them to him at the safe house. All Rada needed to do at security was present their Turkish passports and seem thoroughly dull. Yusra's *abaya* was part of that plan. Besides, the ISF company that patrolled the terminal had much bigger fish to fry. In Cohen's mind, the greater threat would come once they landed in Istanbul. The border police at Atatürk Airport were on high alert for foreign fighters attempting to return from Syria. Cohen rehearsed a cover story with Rada and had faith in his ability to perform, but in the unlikely event that they were held for secondary screening, Cohen made Rada swear that he would keep his mouth shut while Cohen leaned on his contacts at Turkish National Intelligence to get them released. They were almost free, Cohen promised earlier that morning, and the next step was to board that plane. But first they had to clear security in Beirut.

Nina and Cohen stood together before the checkpoint, which was more like a horde than an orderly procession. For some unexplained reason, two of the three checkpoints servicing the terminal were closed, forcing every passenger attempting to leave Beirut that morning to squeeze through one. Nina scanned the crowd and estimated at least three hundred people: Arabs and Westerners, old men and women, small children—all crammed together like cattle, snaking around the stanchions and spilling into the check-in hall. The police and customs agents did their utmost to manage the crush, but they were overwhelmed. All they could do was stand and wait while each person trickled through one at a time. Nina lifted her chin and scoured the herd. She and Cohen were nearly halfway to the rampart of magnetometers and X-ray machines. The Radas were somewhere in the ranks of flesh at their backs. She'd lost sight of them, and in that dizzying cross-section of mankind, everyone looked the same.

"Don't do that," Cohen nudged her elbow. "Look forward."

"I can't see them."

"They're back there," he reassured. "We'll check on them at the gate."

She dipped her head.

"Don't worry, they'll be okay."

Nina checked her watch. It was nearly seven o'clock when the lights above flickered and died.

Lebanon's Coastal Road briefly passed through a tunnel beneath runway 16/34 at Beirut airport, which was partially built on landfill protruding into the Mediterranean. However, before the road reached the tunnel, it first bisected Ouzai, which ran right to the airport's perimeter.

A convoy raced across that jungle—a Toyota Hilux and a Land Cruiser pickup truck, an Isuzu D-Max and two Ford Rangers. All had heavy machine guns bolted to makeshift mounts in the beds and were manned by fifteen of al-Din's most seasoned fighters. The convoy stormed down Ouzai's narrow streets and skidded into a rubbish-strewn vacant lot bordering the perimeter fence, standing ten feet high and topped with razor wire.

Haze danced over the airfield all the way to the terminal building nearly a mile in the distance. Business jets sat on the general aviation apron, hangars rose from the mirage and hulking airliners crawled along the flight line.

Sabbah's voice sizzled in their radios. "Unit 2, sweep around the terminal and disable as many planes as you can. Engage anything standing in your way. Today, we give glory to God!"

Two fighters took a pair of five-foot steel pipes loaded with PETN plastic explosive from the Hilux's bed and dashed to the chain-link fence. They slid the pipes through the bottom of the mesh and unspooled detonator wire across the lot. The pipes burst in an orange flash, shaking Ouzai with a violent thud. When the smoke cleared, a five-meter section of the fence laid in mangled scraps.

Al-Din's militiamen mounted their guns. The trucks revved through the smoldering gap and made straight for runway 17/35 just as an EgyptAir Boeing 737 swooped in on final approach.

The control tower howled at the pilots to pull up. Shedding altitude by the second, the 737 glided to Earth at one hundred and forty knots. From the cockpit, the pilots spotted the five trucks charging down the runway. Without a moment to spare—as the landing gear hovered just yards above the trucks' guns—the pilots shoved the throttle to full power, retracted the flaps, and sent the plane soaring skyward.

As jet engines screamed overhead, four blacked-out Dodge Chargers with the Internal Security Forces' insignia emblazoned on the doors and wailing sirens tried to outflank the trucks. Speeding alongside the lead Hilux, a police officer waved out his window and demanded they stop at once.

A militiaman in the bed of the Ford Ranger directly behind the Hilux cocked his DShK and swung the weapon around, placed the police cruiser in his sights, and pressed the trigger. The muzzle nearly exploded. 12.7-millimeter rounds ripped across the Charger, punctured the engine block, shredded the tires and shattered the lightbar on the roof. It spun out of control, sparks flying from the stripped rims, and careened off the runway and into the grass. "*Allahu Akbar!*" the militiamen shouted and pivoted the DShK ninety degrees, firing a second burst and disabling another cruiser. The remaining pair quickly broke their pursuit and turned back toward the hangars. Only six hundred meters of open tarmac sat between al-Din's men and the terminal.

The control tower closed the runways to incoming flights and ordered a full ground stop on the airfield. Beyond that, there was little they could do. A Lufthansa Airbus A321 was frozen on the taxiway. The ZPU-2 anti-aircraft gun on the Hilux took aim with its dual barrels and opened up, tearing the stabilizers on the aft end of the aircraft to bits.

"*Allahu Akbar!*" the militiaman screamed.

Crossing onto the apron at full speed, the trucks split off and fanned out around the two piers that jutted from the terminal building. There were a dozen planes parked beside the gates—all entirely exposed. The fighters in the Toyota Land Cruiser and the Isuzu D-Max took the east pier while the others in the Hilux and the two Ford Rangers took the west. Pivoting around on their gun mounts, the militiamen held on the trigger and fired swaths of ammunition, unleashing deep, bellowing cracks. Airliners marked in the liveries of Etihad and Emirates, Qatar Airways and Air France, Turkish Airlines and Royal Jordanian—every one that sat by a gate was struck. High-caliber rounds chewed apart tailfins and ripped through engines. One volley at an A320 owned by Middle East Airlines punctured the starboard wing, spilling jet fuel on the concrete. It caught a spark. Flames lapped at the fuselage and smoke billowed over the piers.

Fire engines raced from the far side of the airfield and police sirens cried in the distance. They had done their job. Not a single airliner could make it off the ground—that much was certain. The trucks turned around and sprinted back to Ouzai at ten past seven, totally unscathed.

Sabbah pulled a black balaclava over his face and chambered a round in the Kalashnikov that stood between his legs.

"Electricity is down in the terminal," Unit 3 reported over his radio, "but backup generators are unaffected."

"Position your men on the interchange," Sabbah replied. "Response time is fifteen minutes. Hold them off if need be."

"Inshallah, I will kill whomever interferes."

The seven men with him wore woodland camouflage Lebanese army uniforms, Kevlar vests and balaclavas, and were armed to the teeth with AKM and Chinese Type 56 assault rifles, flashbang grenades and enough ammunition between them to repel a battalion. Three rode in his Isuzu Trooper and the other four followed immediately behind in another SUV. Each had memorized a grainy surveillance photo of a portly, balding man. It would be a difficult task to pluck one individual out of hundreds, but Sabbah assured his men that with the proper entrance, they could flush out their target.

The SUVs tore up the approach road and screeched to an abrupt halt outside the terminal. The drivers stayed and kept the engines running. As Sabbah jumped down from the Isuzu and advanced under the awning with his men, he heard sirens and the opening, thunderous reports of anti-aircraft guns sowing havoc on the tarmac.

He breezed through the automatic doors and into the check-in hall. Power was cut not three minutes earlier and the emergency lamps had only begun to switch on, casting an eerie scarlet half-light over the terminal. They discreetly lowered their rifles and moved like a fog to the security checkpoint. There were hundreds, just as he expected, all massed together and nervously gawking at the ceiling, wondering where the light had gone.

But Sabbah knew how to get their attention.

He took a flashbang from a pouch on his vest, pulled the pin from the fuse, and gently rolled it toward the crowd.

A searing flare burst over Nina's eyes, overwhelming the photoreceptor cells in her retinas. Her ears burned right through to her brain as if they were being skewered with a thousand molten daggers. She would have fallen if Cohen hadn't first yanked her to the floor.

Nina felt his arm reach across her back and pull her tight against his body. "Fuck!" she cried, and reeled at the concussive force rumbling through her head like colossal shockwaves, each more powerful than the last. Her eyelids blinked and fluttered wildly, but she saw only a dazzling white light scorched into her vision. Her ears rang like hellish church bells, but through them—and over mounting screams—Nina heard a muffled, yet altogether unmistakable sound: the sharp, immediate pop of Kalashnikovs.

"Down! Down! Down!"

Sabbah held the Kalashnikov next to his head and fired up at the ceiling, raking the rifle back and forth. The hardy few who didn't drop instantly at the flashbang fell to the floor.

His men sprayed the X-ray machines and magnetometers ahead, sending the customs agents diving for cover.

More shots rang out from the check-in hall. A bullet whizzed inches past Sabbah and lodged in a cement column. Two police officers rushed at them with pistols drawn.

"Right!" Sabbah barked.

Their AK barrels swung around.

"Legs!"

They fired below the officers' waists, shredding their kneecaps and causing both to tumble forward and hit the ground face-first.

"Stay down!" one of Sabbah's men roared as the officers rolled in agony.

Cohen pressed all his weight into Nina's back. His training took over and he ran through a mental checklist of everything—anything—he could do to fight back. But what was there? He was unarmed and disoriented, surrounded by scores of civilians. It was a tactical nightmare. Fighting wasn't an option. All he could do was ride out the storm and pray that he and Nina survived. In the next instant he tried to understand what went wrong, who betrayed them and why. But he suppressed the urge. That day would come soon enough.

Five seconds after the blast he regained some semblance of sight. Cohen glimpsed up over the shrieking bodies. He looked back to Nina. Blood trickled from her ear canal.

"Six," he told her. "Long guns and body armor. Masks."

They had been inside the terminal for less than four minutes, Sabbah estimated; still plenty of time, but not enough to play games with these people. As the gunfire ceased, so did their screams, which subsided to dull moans or even bated silence. It was enough for his demands to be heard.

"We are here for Walid Rada," he shouted, "branch chief of the Jihad al-Binna Foundation." Sabbah and his men prowled between arms and legs, waving their muzzles over the fallen crowd.

He lowered his voice. "If you are not *Monsieur* Rada, we have no interest in you whatsoever so long as you do not interfere. If your travel plans have been inconvenienced this morning, know that we offer our sincerest apologizes and wish you a safe journey whenever that may come."

He paused, searching for any telling sign. "If you are Monsieur Rada, I promise that no harm will come to you or your family…" He looked down, reached to the floor, and grabbed a handful of cotton fabric. "But I cannot say the same for him."

Sabbah took a handsome Arab man in his thirties and dressed in a tailored suit and pulled him to his feet. "Here, stand there," he pointed to a spot on the floor, then shouldered his Kalashnikov and aimed it directly between the man's terrified eyes. "If you're unable to see, I am holding a rifle to this man's head."

Whimpers rippled over the crowd.

"I will count to five, and if before that time you do not reveal yourself to me, Monsieur Rada, I will lay a bullet through his brain."

"Please," the man choked.

"And then another—and another," he vowed, "until you choose to face your destiny." Sabbah cracked his neck and placed an eye behind the iron sights. "One."

Faint cries radiated up from the floor.

The man lifted his hands. "You don't have to do this."

"Two."

"Whoever you're looking for, I'll help you find him."

"Three."

"Please," he bawled to the crowd, "for the love of God, just stand up."

"Four."

He panted and muttered the first syllable of the *shahada* under his breath.

The round sheared off the top of the man's skull, throwing him dead on the tiles in a cloud of red mist. A clap echoed, and they screamed.

Nina saw the man drop.

"Monsieur Rada, you disappoint me!" Sabbah hollered over their screams.

She clenched her eyes shut, hoping it was all a nightmare, but it wasn't. Nina gazed at Cohen and listened on, horrified, enraged, and utterly helpless.

"That man died for your avarice and your cowardice," Sabbah boomed, "so that you may lie and cheat your way through life even one more—"

"No! Stop!"

Nina looked up. A woman in a gray *abaya* shot from the crowd. Sabbah's men trained their rifles at her. "Oh my god," Nina gasped. It was Yusra.

"That's him!" Yusra croaked, leveling her finger down at a shivering lump. "That's my husband! Take him! Take him!"

Nina felt numb.

They swarmed in and peeled Rada off the floor, bound his wrists with zip ties, and threw a black hood over his head. The same was done to Yusra, and even Eshe, who cried out in anguish for her mother. Nina and Cohen both watched on, paralyzed, as they were swept out the doors, tossed into the SUVs, and whisked away.

CHAPTER 44

UNEXPECTED AS CYCLONE Petra was when he'd been called home, Jack instead used it to his tactical advantage. During the previous day—the first of "Simon Marleau's" holiday in Switzerland—while sub-zero winds battered the city, Jack steeled himself against the blizzard and stalked Zurich's snow-choked, deserted streets and hoped to unmask any minders who might've trailed him from Tehran. He was relieved, although maybe a tad disappointed, to spot none. Back at the Baur au Lac, the hotel staff took the storm as a pretense to become better acquainted with their few lingering, stranded guests. Jack made a point to avoid the unnecessary attention and spent the remainder of the afternoon under self-imposed exile in his suite, ordering room service and downing another bottle of Glenlivet 18: slipping into unconsciousness, for he knew all too well what the next day would bring.

That following morning, just as he feared, the alarm clock on his bedside table cruelly reminded him that it was the twenty-fifth of February.

He nursed his hangover with a few Advil and a liter of mineral water and ventured from the hotel in search of breakfast. Snow and ice were still sheathed around church steeples, rooftops and tree branches, but life in Zurich was beginning to show signs of normalcy. Jack walked the promenade that ran along the frozen Schanzengraben canal to a coffee shop called La Stanza. It was full of bankers and insurers rushing to their offices. He ordered a cappuccino and a croissant and waded to a table at the rear of the café. The day's issue of the *Tages-Anzeiger* sat on an adjacent chair and he opened the paper, pretending to read, although his eyes peered over the pages to the transient crowd. Above the noise and the clattering cups and plates and spoons, a television played on the wall. It was tuned to N24, a German news channel, and displayed a bright red Chyron that read: *"Flughafen Beirut Angegriffen."* As the anchorwoman and her guest tried to com-

516

prehend the developing situation, the screen cycled through footage of a charred airliner doused in fire-retardant foam, a pulsing sea of emergency lights, and soldiers deployed around the terminal. Jack took stock of the news from the corner of his eye, but his attention was fixed on each new face that came through the doorway.

Satisfied that he hadn't detected an Iranian surveillance team, Jack finished his breakfast and went to the main branch of Rahn & Bodmer, a private banking firm that dated back to 1750. He introduced himself to the receptionist in French as Simon Marleau and was shown to a comfortable sitting room. In a few moments, an attendant delivered a safety deposit box and left him in privacy. Inside the box, among other things, were a US diplomatic passport and a wallet containing a District of Columbia driver's license and various credit cards—all under the name of Jack Galloway. He took the contents and replaced it with anything that branded him as Simon Marleau. After the box was returned to the vault, Jack hastily returned to his hotel, grabbed a bag he'd packed the night before, and hung a "do not disturb" placard from his suite's door. While Simon Marleau would ostensibly remain in Switzerland for the next few days, Jack Galloway took a train to the airport and boarded a flight to Heathrow before flying on to Washington, and a bittersweet homecoming.

Minutes upon returning to Beit Rahbari after his pilgrimage to Ayatollah Khansari—or what was left of him—Mofidi sent word to the Quds Force's headquarters on the grounds of the old American embassy. His message was clear: Qasem Shateri and his devoted minion, Colonel Rasoul Gharib Abadi, were summoned to Tehran at once.

In less than twenty-fours hours, they arrived in Mofidi's office. Shateri had begrudgingly slithered away from the mounting plots at his forward command post in Iraq, and Colonel Abadi—chief of the Quds Forces' operations in North Africa—had flown in from Khartoum, where he was posted under diplomatic cover as the Iranian ambassador to Sudan. Mofidi's justification for convening them on such short notice was that the supreme leader had asked for an urgent report on Islamic Jihad's performance on the battlefield in Gaza and *al-Quds'* efforts to support their fight. His true intent, however, was to neuter them both with a stroke of Khansari's pen; Mofidi had been up through the night, imagining the look on Shateri's face. But thus far Shateri said little during the discussion, instead deferring to his lieutenant as Abadi gave an exhaustive account of PIJ's resistance to Israeli air strikes and special forces raids. The colonel recounted the events as a proud father might boast of his successful children. It made Mofidi sick to an extent, knowing that Abadi's unsanctioned retaliation resulted in the execution of that Israeli soldier, Corporal Moshe Adler, and thrust them all into a war that neither side was fit to fight.

"The brothers of Islamic Jihad are steadfast in their commitment to repulse the Zionists from Gaza," Colonel Abadi gladly explained. "No doubt His Excellency would be overcome with joy at the news; the *mujahedeen* have fought bravely, with conviction, and by the grace of God some have even been blessed with the sweet gift of martyrdom."

Mofidi leaned his head against his fist. "But not too many?"

Abadi cleared his throat. "No, *baradar.*"

"Tell me about Hamas' role," said Mofidi. "We were briefed in the last Security Council meeting that some brothers from al-Qassam Brigades rebelled against Khader Issa's direct orders not to intervene."

"Yes," Abadi replied with a confident nod, "an entire unit of al-Qassam—the Northern Gaza Division—defected with their commander, Bassam Sinwar. Issa and Fawzi Abu Musameh's refusal to lend their arms to the fight against the Zionists disgusted Brother Bassam. After discussions with Brother Azzam," the colonel referred to Azzam al-Nakhalah, chief of PIJ's military wing and Moshe Adler's executioner, "Brother Bassam pledged allegiance to Islamic Jihad and fired rockets at Ashkelon."

"And what happens when the dust settles and Hamas gathers its forces that haven't switched sides?" Mofidi asked. "Are Brother Azzam and Islamic Jihad prepared for a civil war inside Gaza?"

The colonel's nose tilted up. "Should such a war come, Hamas will find itself severely outgunned and swiftly crushed."

"What makes you so certain?"

"Our unwavering support."

"Like our cruise missiles seized in the Gulf of Aden?" Mofidi's eyebrows arched. "That kind of support?"

Shateri leaned over the table and lent his voice for the first time. "Yes."

They locked eyes in mutual contempt. Mofidi felt his heart beating. He knew it was time to strike. "His Excellency sees it differently."

"Does he?" Shateri smirked.

"He does."

"That His Excellency sees anything at all is incredibly amusing."

Mofidi ignored the insult. He opened a folder on the table and slid on his glasses to read the memos he'd forced Khansari to sign in Mashad. "This afternoon, the supreme leader will issue a statement demanding that the Zionist armed forces bring about an immediate cessation of hostilities against Occupied Palestine so that humanitarian aid may reach civilians." Mofidi brandished the page so they could see the signature. "I've already discussed it with President Rostani, Foreign Minister Zanjani, and will shortly bring it to the attention of the Supreme National Security Council."

Shateri's blood simmered.

"Regardless of whether or not this demand is met, His Excellency has determined to bar the Quds Force and the Intelligence Ministry from providing matériel support to resistance groups in Gaza for the next six months."

"Let me see that." Shateri's arm shot over the table.

"Of course, *baradar,*" Mofidi obliged.

While Shateri's eyes ran down the page, Mofidi went for the second forged memo, the one that would sting the most. "Now, I wanted to share this with you before anyone else, *Baradar* Qasem," he smiled. "A letter was recently delivered to me from Washington by a representative of President Paulson. This letter detailed the president's frustrations at the manner in which our negotiations collapsed after Damascus fell to the rebels. I promptly delivered it to His Excellency, who has likewise used his repose in Mashad to reflect on this country's impasse with the United States. After consulting with myself, His Excellency has elected to accept the president's offer to send an envoy to Geneva for talks on the possibility of restarting our dialogue. His Excellency has also decided that I would be best suited to represent our interests at this meeting. Like I said, I haven't yet informed the council, but before I did, *baradar,* I thought I would at least give you the courtesy of hearing the news first." Mofidi could hardly contain himself.

Shateri gently set the memo on the table. "Oh, you thought you'd give me the 'courtesy' did you?"

"I did."

Shateri's eyes rolled to Abadi at his side. "Leave us."

The colonel rose off the sofa and saw himself out.

Mofidi curled his quivering fingers into a fist. He steadied his breath and felt his scalp tingle with fear. Shateri's stare pierced his skull, and as he heard the door latch click shut, Mofidi summoned the nerve to confront him.

"Everyone is so frightened of you," Mofidi slowly shook his head, "but not me. You don't scare me. There's nothing you can take from me that hasn't already been stolen."

Shateri crossed his legs and held his gaze.

"I know what you've done. I know—"

"You know nothing," Shateri calmly breathed.

"I do," Mofidi declared. "That ship in the Gulf of Aden, the *Catarina A?* I know you planted it as bait. You wanted it found, just like you wanted an excuse to execute that soldier so Avi Arad would overreact and you'd have a new battle to fight with the Israelis. The Banisadrs murdered in Europe— I know that was your men searching for Mehdi Vaziri, wasn't it?"

Shateri cracked an amused smile.

"What happened in Beirut this morning?"

"That's absurd," he dismissed.

"I know what you're planning in Iraq, too. With the militias?" Mofidi was taken aback at his composure, at his ability to look the man dead on and hold his ground. "And I will stop you."

"No," Shateri nearly sung and swung his head in disappointment.

"I will." Mofidi felt his veins flood with rage. "I will!" he swore. "I won't let you drag us into a war we aren't prepared to win. I won't stand by and watch you tear this country apart. I won't allow it."

"And how exactly will do you that?" Shateri picked the memos off the table and held them up in the air. "With these?" He drew a lighter from his jacket pocket, threw his thumb down the wheel, and set a fluttering orange flame to the corner of the pages. "You think these will save you?" he curiously asked. "A piece of paper?"

Mofidi's recoiled in his chair. The flame consumed the memos, rendering Khansari's scrawled signature to blackened curls of ash.

Shateri left the smoldering remains on a metal tray. "I heard a story recently," he added, "about your son, Omid."

All the strength Mofidi gathered shattered in an instant.

"The jailers at Evin Prison told me all about him; how he'd been arrested working with the *monafiqeen* groups, and all. They also told me something I thought you'd like to hear," Shateri grinned. "The night they brought your son out in front of the firing squad, one of the executioners must've had jittery hands. The first round—this is funny—it missed by an inch or so. It struck your son right here," he pointed, "on the side of his eye socket, blew out the cartilage and a chunk of his skull, but the eye itself hung down your son's face. The shot didn't kill him right away, of course, so when the executioner went to fire again…his rifle jammed. Would you believe that luck? They said it took maybe ten minutes to get the damn thing cleared. And your son laid there the whole time." Shateri shrugged his shoulders. "Awful way to die, I'd imagine, wouldn't you?"

Mofidi couldn't move. His eyes welled.

Shateri stood and went to leave. "Either way, he surely deserved it. All traitors do. Did you know that they also say it's an inherited trait? Treason, I mean. It runs in the blood." Shateri held by the door and looked suspiciously upon Mofidi. "I wonder where he got it?"

Mofidi trembled. A tear ran down his cheek. "God damn you."

Shateri smiled. "Have fun in Geneva."

Nine police officers were wounded, four critically. In the terminal and on the tarmac, nearly twenty passengers and groundcrew were struck by shrapnel or treated for smoke inhalation. One person, a thirty-four-year-old real estate developer from Dubai, was killed: executed with a single shot to the head. Thirteen aircraft were disabled, with one destroyed by fire that spread to a large section on the east pier before it was doused. It was hailed as a miracle that more didn't lose their lives, but Nina knew better. The gunmen used incredible restraint in their assault, and it was no accident that so few were harmed. They stormed the airport with one specific target in mind, seized him and his family, and withdrew as swiftly as they appeared. The only reason that Nina, Cohen or any of the hundreds in that terminal survived was because someone allowed it. She was convinced who that someone was—that she had witnessed the dramatic return of Ibrahim al-Din to center stage. Only none could see the writing on the wall, and over the ensuing hours, Lebanon rapidly devolved to its old habits.

The prime minister convened his cabinet in an emergency session that ran throughout the day. After news broke that the attackers had emerged from and retreated to Ouzai, Hezbollah immediately mobilized in Beirut's southern suburbs and broadcast over its television station, Al-Manar, that any attempt by government forces to enter Shia neighborhoods in pursuit of the suspects would be "tantamount to an act of war." Checkpoints in Haret Hreik and Bourj el-Barajneh were reinforced with extra men wielding AK-47s and RPGs. In parliament, members of the pro-government March 14 Alliance openly accused Hezbollah of orchestrating the attack, railing that it had drastically crossed a line and should immediately expedite its planned disarmament. Hezbollah and its affiliates across the aisle were infuriated and some in the party even called for mass demonstrations until the prime minister issued a formal apology. The White House, the UN, the EU and the Arab League all pleaded for calm, but as nightfall approached, many feared the worst was still to come. Shops and restaurants in downtown Beirut closed early, streets were deserted, and troops formed a cordon around the government buildings on Serail Hill. The Lebanese Armed Forces were deployed to maintain order, but their commander had no intention to pick a fight with Hezbollah and assured that his units would only respond if directly attacked. Yet one crucial voice remained silent: Sheikh Wissam Hamawi. Hezbollah's secretary-general hadn't issued a statement during the standoff, not a single word either claiming or denying responsibility for the airport assault.

After giving a full account of what she'd witnessed that morning to both Stessel and Roger Mathis back at Langley, Nina rushed up the coast to Mossad's safe house in Batroun where Cohen had taken refuge. She arrived just before sunset as waves gnawed on the old Phoenician seawall. He answered the door holding a loaded sidearm.

"Has Hamawi talked yet?"

"No."

Nina looked over his shoulder and saw empty beer bottles dotting the coffee table. "I'm assuming you got enough of those to share?"

Cohen gestured toward the kitchen with his gun. "Get me one."

She went to the refrigerator and pulled out two bottles. Ortega followed her inside and posted by the doorway. "It was him," Nina announced. "Those were al-Din's people at the airport. He took Rada."

Cohen groaned. "You don't know that."

"Then who else did?" She sat next to him on the sofa, popped the caps off both bottles and passed one to him.

"Any *hadji* with a gun?" he swallowed. "Unit 910? The Fajr Unit? Take your pick; Hezbollah's been watching Rada for weeks."

"No, they came from Ouzai," Nina insisted. "Marwan Kadi's outfit won't go there."

She had told Cohen about the three flashes she'd seen from the balcony on the night Rada was pitched. He wasn't angry; if she told him earlier he would've written her off as overly paranoid. Nina didn't dare tell anyone at Langley or the embassy that she'd been spotted. It didn't matter much. To last six months in Lebanon, Cohen said, without being identified by Hezbollah was an exceptional feat. Besides, he reasoned, they only had a picture of her—no name, no affiliation—and likely tagged her as an Israeli. In his initial postmortem, Cohen surmised that Hezbollah's counterintelligence apparatus identified one of his surveillance operators as they entered the country, tracked him to the safe house in Beirut, and thus made Rada as he arrived at the flat. It was a start, a way to ascertain how so much had gone so wrong—but it got them no closer to learning what fate befell Walid Rada and his family.

They expected to hear an answer any minute. Al-Manar announced earlier that Wissam Hamawi would hold a press conference that afternoon, his first public comments since the airport was stormed. What the secretary-general would say was anyone's guess, but his silence thus far only stoked the flames. Nina and Cohen stared at the TV in anticipation. To fill airtime until Hamawi's appearance, an Al Jazeera reporter broadcasting from Martyr's Square in downtown Beirut attempted to moderate two opposing members of Parliament as they lobbed accusations at one another.

"How'd your COS take it?"

"Stessel?" Nina huffed. "He was just happy to say 'I told you so.' CTC's having a collective stroke; I swore Mathis would puke. What about your people."

Cohen shrugged. "Isaac was pretty indifferent to be honest."

"Really?"

"Yeah, it takes a lot to faze the old man. He's always seen worse."

"Wait…" Nina pointed to the TV.

The reporter took the cue from the producer in her ear and interrupted the sparring politicians, announcing that Hamawi was about to speak. The shot broke away and turned to a podium set before a sky-blue backdrop with the Lebanese and Hezbollah flags. Secretary-General Wissam Hamawi then walked into the frame—a stocky, middle-aged man in a black turban and silk clerical robes—straightened his glasses, and looked into the camera.

"Bismillah hir-Rahman nir-Rahmin," he began, and paused, presuming that all those watching would recite the same. In a moment, his eyes rose back to the camera, and his pale lips cracked; there was no need for preamble. "At approximately half-past-six this morning I was notified that Walid Rada, a party member who was under investigation for embezzling a large sum of money set aside for humanitarian aid and construction projects, was attempting to flee the country with his family. Our investigators informed me that *Monsieur* Rada was presently sighted at Beirut airport and intended to board an unknown flight abroad."

"No..." Nina muttered and felt Cohen's hand touch her back.

"Given time constraints and a lack of actionable information," Hamawi continued, "it was clear that cooperation with government security services was not possible; if we were to retrieve Monsieur Rada before he fled the country, extreme measures had to be taken. At that point, I instructed the Islamic Resistance to use any method at their disposal to place Monsieur Rada in custody."

"He's lying," Nina blurted.

"An operation was launched to prevent any aircraft from departing and to search for Monsieur Rada in the terminal. With some regrettable property damage and a most unfortunate loss of life, I am happy to report that Walid Rada has been apprehended and will face the full weight of God's justice for crimes against the faithful and the oppressed of Lebanon."

"Turn it off."

"In the coming days, it is my intention to make full amends—"

"Enough, Nathan!"

Cohen clicked the remote and the TV fell silent. "Nina, please..."

"He's lying," she stood and brushed her hair back. "That motherfucker's lying, I know he is!"

"Why would Hamawi do that?" Cohen gestured to the hissing screen. "Why would he just take responsibility and put Hezbollah in a such a shitty position when it's been battered enough?"

"I don't know," Nina turned around, her cheeks red and her hair frizzled. "He—he's covering, he's saving his ass. How shitty would it look to come out there and admit he doesn't control his own troops? Huh? What about that?"

Cohen scoffed.

She doubled over and gripped her head. "Jesus Christ."

"You should sit down."

"I don't want to," Nina snapped. "Don't tell me to fucking sit down!"

"Okay fine, I'm sorry," Cohen shot off the sofa. "I'll pound around too," he stamped his feet on the floor. "How's that, huh? We both will."

"Don't even!" she roared.

"This is crazy," he nearly laughed. "Why, because of al-Din, because of some relic from twenty years ago? Nobody wants to hear about that."

"Yes," Nina regained her composure, "that's exactly why."

Cohen's shoulders dropped. "Al-Din is gone. Okay? He's long gone, either dead or wasting away in some cinder block shack somewhere. And I can promise you...he is not a threat to anyone. He's not your problem."

"He is my problem," her eyes widened. "And he's your problem too."

"See, this is what you do," Cohen shook his head. "You pick one of these guys out of a lineup, out of some creepy rogues' gallery, and you obsess over them to the point of delusion. You've done it in AfPak, in Yemen and Somalia—you do it better than anyone—and now you're doing it here. Why? I don't know, I guess it must occupy some void you have deep down." As soon as Cohen heard those last words fall from his mouth, he regretted them.

Nina looked him dead in the eyes—for the first time, defeated.

"Don't you see?" Cohen offered. "Don't you see what you're doing to yourself, Nina? Don't you see what you've missed? What you've lost? This is all you have in the world...and it breaks my heart."

"You're so wrong," she forced back tears. "This is on you and me. You and I have to go find him—for us."

"Nina, there is no us."

For a time only the waves could be heard crashing against the seawall.

She turned back to Ortega. "Can you give us a minute?"

"Sure, Nina," Ortega nodded. "I'll be outside.

"What do you want from me?" Cohen asked once the door closed.

She trembled and sat back on the sofa. "I don't know."

"Nina, I have a family of my own."

"It's not that, Nathan," she sniffed. "It's not that."

"Then what?"

"I don't know," her voice cracked.

Cohen sat a few inches beside her. He said nothing, just listened.

"You told me that you and I are always meant to say goodbye," Nina murmured. "I believe that. I didn't accept it until you said it, but I think I've always believed it. I believe it anytime I see two people together, and happy, like we were. Like I'm not. Somewhere I think I've hated myself all these years for what I did to you. Seeing you again just forced me to admit it."

She looked up at him. "I'm not here to try and take you away or ruin what you've found with someone else; I'd only hate myself even more. For twelve years, Nathan, I've thought about you every single day. I think about what would've happened if I'd stayed, if I even had the decency to call you. I think about what we'd have, what I'd have, and I wonder if I'd be happy. I wish I could change the past, but I can't, and I hate myself for it." Nina wiped her eyes. "So there it is. That's the truth."

Cohen put his hand on her shoulder. "For the record, I think you're last the person alive who should hate herself. You've given me more than I could ask for in a lifetime, Nina. But I have to go home now. I can't do this for you. Whatever battle this is, you have to fight it yourself. You have to let go of these ghosts you carry. We need to say goodbye—and you need to accept...we've failed."

Jack's connecting flight from Heathrow touched down at Dulles at four-thirty in the afternoon. Once clear of customs and immigration, he caught a shuttle near baggage claim that delivered him to Enterprise Rent-A-Car. He booked a Toyota Camry for the next five days, although he didn't anticipate needing it that long, and drove east along the Toll Road and Interstate 66 toward Washington, enduring an immense sense of déjà vu. Crossing the Potomac on the Roosevelt Bridge, he saw the city's monolithic white shrines beyond his windshield: the Lincoln Memorial and the Washington Monument, the Kennedy Center and the Watergate Building, all laid before the dying winter sun. He followed Rock Creek Parkway into Northwest DC and Adams Morgan, a cosmopolitan neighborhood renowned for its night-life. After parking the Camry on a quiet side street lined with nineteenth and early-twentieth century row houses, Jack towed his suitcase to the front stoop of The Beacon, a condominium at 1801 Calvert Street. He entered discreetly and climbed two flights of stairs to Apartment 204—and home, although he dared not call it that.

It was a one-bedroom apartment with a galley kitchen and a tiny living room overlooking Adams Mill Road before it turned toward the gauntlet of bars and clubs on 18th Street. An accountant at Langley promptly paid his rent and utilities each month. There were no personal items, no photographs or memories on display, and a millimeter of dust coated the furniture. It wasn't home by any stretch of the imagination. As Jack saw it, the apartment was merely a hotel room without whiskey on call. As Jack saw it, he had no home.

Worst of all, it was utterly silent.

Jack dropped his suitcase by the door and spotted a note placed on the kitchen countertop. He stepped into the kitchen, picked the note off the granite, and read, carving a smile on his face.

Put some stuff in the fridge this morning. Not sure what you wanted.
Dinner's at eight tonight.
Maybe we'll see you?
—Ryan

• • •

It was a promise she made before the whole ordeal began...

"No one dies."

She distinctly remembered saying those words; uttered right alongside all the lies she told to keep the truth from her asset, whose trust she worked painstakingly to earn, whose cooperation was pivotal to her mission in the country. She believed those words when she said them. They weren't lies like the others. But now people *had* died in Lebanon, and she felt it in the pit of her soul that scores more would follow before the end. With grim portent, that thought brought her to a confounding question her asset had asked.

"How does this end?"

She masked with derision the cold realization than an answer had never occurred to her, that even the very question had never occurred to her. Only now, with the dead beginning to mount and her lies unraveling, Nina Davenport was forced to confront that question—"How does this end?"—and admit to herself that now, more than ever, she hadn't the faintest idea.

Earlier in the day, Nina signaled to her asset that she needed to have an emergency in-person meeting later that night. The protocols ran as rehearsed. After returning from Cohen's safe house in Batroun, Nina chose an embassy vehicle and ran a countersurveillance route from the compound in Awkar through the hilly streets of East Beirut, discreetly escorted by Ortega and the GRS detail in a trailing Mitsubishi Pajero. Once certain that neither the *Sûreté,* Hezbollah, nor any of the myriad militias that flew a flag in Lebanon were following her, Nina drove on to the neighborhood of Gemmayze and the elegant colonial edifice off Rue Gouraud that housed the top-floor flat where Colonel Samir Basri—commander of the ISF's *Bureau d'information*—entertained his distasteful sexual fixations—which, Nina often reminded her asset, the US federal government had funded for the past six months.

Fifteen minutes after the time when protocol dictated that Basri would come down for their meeting, TOPSAIL still had not shown. Idling in the darkened alleyway behind the building, Nina digested each passing second with growing dread. She turned the ignition key and grabbed her radio. "Just give him a bit," she said as the Volvo's engine rumbled quiet.

"Roger that," Ortega replied from the Pajero. "Still clear in the street."

"Copy." Nina dropped the handset on the center console and leaned her head against the window.

Her eyes crawled up the stone façade. The lights in Basri's flat were out. She ran through every possible excuse, bargaining with her own mind: Maybe Basri was still at his office in the Khoury Barracks, inundated with ISF's response to the airport attack? Maybe he was home with his family and unable to sneak away? Maybe Basri was kidnapped by Hezbollah and laid dead in a ditch somewhere in the Beqaa Valley? Even that notion was more palatable than the truth she tried to subdue. However, as several more minutes dragged, she realized the absurdity of her silent pleas.

When she recruited Basri—her first major victory since arriving in Beirut—he made it clear that he did not view his new relationship with the Americans as an act of treason, and nothing would convince him otherwise. As Basri saw it, he was merely assisting CIA in its desire to bring lasting stability to Lebanon, to calm the tempestuous waters of his country by undermining the foreign winds and radical currents that conjured storms for generations. He made his private disdain for Iran known and pledged to Nina that he would do anything to disarm its proxies and purge Lebanon of Ayatollah Khansari's influence. The only thing that trumped that sense of scorn in Basri's mind was his hatred for Israel: "an illegal, murderous, genocidal regime that laid waste to Lebanon whenever it was most politically and militarily expedient." Nevertheless, promoting the respect Basri enjoyed from Lebanon's political and religious factions and the access it afforded him, Nina persuaded the lily-white consciences of CIA's lawyers and operational managers to open their bottomless wallet and turn a blind eye to the dapper colonel's tastes for the finer things in life and his penchant for the taut pelvic muscles of underage girls. Spying, she argued, was no enterprise for saints. For six months, her gamble paid off: Langley was no longer blind to the hidden intrigues of Lebanon's security services; Station Beirut was back in business; and in time, Colonel Basri gave CIA a preciously rare opportunity to recruit a source within Hezbollah. In her cynical pursuit of that opportunity, as she was trained to do, Nina mouthed countless lies to mine Basri's brain—until an unforeseeable squall blew in from the horizon and stripped those lies bare.

Nina assured Basri that the operation to coax Rada's defection was strictly a CIA endeavor. Because of her lies, he agreed to look the other way with the guarantee that no Lebanese lives would be lost. She made him a promise, and for once she truly meant every word of it.

Only then that squall blew.

With Rada's capture it could only be assumed that Mossad's hand would be discovered, and Basri would learn of his complicity in a Zionist plot.

When Basri came to her with news of his passing glance outside Hamawi's office in the Security Quarter, swearing that he set eyes on Ibrahim al-Din after lying dormant in the shadows for twenty-three years, as certain of what he spotted as if he looked in a mirror, she believed him. Yet their cries fell on deaf ears.

That morning—as she saw columns of black smoke rise once more over Beirut, as she heard bullets zip inches over her head, as she felt a sensation of pure helplessness and defeat while masked men dragged Rada and his family away—Nina understood that she and Basri were right all along: Ibrahim al-Din was alive and well in Lebanon, prowling just beneath the surface.

She looked up at the windows.

The one soul who would believe her, who might stand beside her toward whatever unknown, horrific end awaited them, was gone.

Nina was paying the price for her lies.

With equally-grim portent, in that dark alley, Nina came to accept the harsh truth that Cohen tried to place before her as delicately as he could…

She had failed.

The Volvo's engine turned over. Nina slipped the brakes and reached for her radio. "Let's go," she sighed, "he's not coming."

Yet one question hung in her mind like a gull-pecked corpse in a roiling sea of detritus, adrift in the passing storm's wake, but floating only a short distance from shore, while even blacker clouds loomed on the horizon…

What became of Walid Rada?

Ryan Freeman yanked the cork from a bottle of Napa Valley Cabernet Sauvignon when the doorbell rang. He set the bottle on the countertop and started through the living room. For an instant, as he pulled the door open, Freeman asked himself if what he saw was real, and as his senses confirmed it, he beamed a loving smile.

"Those guys told me I was in the right place." It was Jack, pointing over his shoulders with his thumb to the two armored Chevy Tahoes parked outside Freeman's home on Highland Drive in Silver Spring, Maryland.

"You made it," Freeman gushed, throwing out his arms. "Come here, kid!" He swallowed Jack in a warm hug and then pulled away a few inches, admiring that face he hadn't seen in over a year.

"I picked these up," Jack held out a bouquet of blue pansies. "Wasn't sure what else to bring, really."

"They're great," Freeman shook his head at the flowers, elated and still in a slight sense of disbelief. He gave a quick wave to his bodyguards standing in the driveway and ushered Jack inside, shutting the door behind him. "Honey, look who showed up," he called.

Freeman's wife, Mary, emerged from the kitchen. "Jack!" she cried and hugged him, planting a kiss on his cheek. "We're so happy you came."

"I got you these," Jack handed her the bouquet. "Wasn't sure…"

"Thank you, they're beautiful," Mary smiled and went to fetch a vase.

Standing in the foyer, Freeman let it wash over him, eyeing Jack from head to toe. "I just can't believe you're actually here," he shook his head and laughed.

"Here I am," said Jack with an awkward chuckle.

"Well, come in and have a seat." Freeman took Jack's coat and showed him into the living room.

Freeman's home was a picturesque brick colonial constructed in the 1930s and set back from a tree-lined, residential road. Each room was meticulously and tastefully decorated, and as Jack looked around from the sofa beside a crackling fireplace, he thought that the house seemed to have sprung from a magazine.

"Can I get you a drink?" Freeman asked.

"Sure, whatever you got."

"I literally just opened this bottle of red that Mary picked up," Freeman said as he went to the kitchen. "It's some organic, biodynamic, whatever."

"Sounds great."

Freeman returned a moment later with two wine glasses, placed one in front of Jack on the coffee table, and sat in a high-back chair.

"Um... Thank you, for the invitation," Jack said before he sipped.

"What else were you gonna do?"

Jack smiled although the well-meaning comment struck a tad too close for comfort. He shook his head, "Probably not much," and took a large gulp.

"How was the trip?"

"Long," he answered. "I came through Zurich, like usual."

"Ah, you got stuck in that blizzard?"

"Yup," Jack nodded. "Although it worked out for CI."

Freeman glanced over to Mary moving in the kitchen. "We'll talk about all that stuff later," he drank. "I swung by your place this morning."

"Yeah, thanks. I really appreciate it."

"Was it all okay?"

"It was more than okay. Thank you." There was a short pause while Jack wondered what else to say, and then it came to him. "*Director* Freeman!" he exclaimed. "I haven't seen you since the big promotion."

Freeman scoffed. "That's for the best."

"How's it been?"

"This past month," the D/CIA shook his head. "Well, you already know."

"Yup," Jack took another gulp.

Mary came into the living room and joined them in another chair by the fire. "The steak's just resting, so we can eat whenever."

"Yeah," Freeman's eyes widened, "Mary cooked up—" He looked to his wife. "What exactly is it called?"

"*Côte de bœf.*"

"That's it..."

"With Brussels sprouts," she added. "And a surprise for dessert."

"You guys didn't have to do all this," Jack offered.

"It's nothing," Freeman replied.

Jack wanted to change the subject. "How's Valerie?"

"She's doing great," smiled Freeman.

"Val started her last semester at Juilliard," said Mary. "She'll get her BFA in May, and then right after that she got a role as an understudy for a big production of *Othello* they're doing at the Lincoln Center. So it's pretty exciting."

"That's great."

Mary neglected to mention that Valerie graduated high school at sixteen to join Juilliard and was the youngest person to ever be accepted by the famous conservatory. It wasn't an exaggeration to call their daughter a prodigy. From the few times they met, Jack had memories of Valerie has a gleeful little girl, and as he was nearly twelve years older than her, it was always an open secret that she had a bit of a crush on him.

"And you're still at Georgetown, Mary?"

"That's right," she grinned.

"Actually," Freeman interrupted, "you're looking at the new Villani Chair in Economics at Georgetown College. She runs the whole damned department."

"Wow."

"Thank you," Mary modestly dipped her head.

The small talk went on for some time. As Jack thought to pull them, Ryan and Mary offered more interesting tidbits about their lives and all the relatively fortunate things that happened to them since he was last in the country. Jack enjoyed listening to them—he truly did, and he was genuinely happy to hear that this family he loved was faring so well. But there was nothing of the sort to be said of Jack. He offered nothing and nothing was asked. Freeman knew enough—where Jack was and what he did on a daily basis—but none of it could be shared with Mary, and so there was simply nothing to say.

After a while, Mary beckoned them to the dining room. They ate steak and Brussels sprouts and carried on their conversation. Jack drank more than his share of wine—nearly two bottles—and was silently plotting his options for later that night. Once they finished dinner, Ryan and Mary assured him that he should absolutely stay put while they cleared the dishes. Jack sat alone at the table for a few moments while they disappeared into the kitchen. He finished another glass and felt sufficiently buzzed when the couple reappeared, holding a cake, and singing.

"Happy birthday to you. Happy birthday to you," they sang in unison. *"Happy birthday, dear Jaa-aack. Happy birthday to you!"*

Freeman placed the cake in front of Jack. Two lit candles molded into a three and a one protruded up from the icing. It was an ambush—that was the first thought that popped into his drunken mind. Jack was at a loss for words.

"Holy shit, you guys."

"Happy birthday, Jack," Mary hugged him.

He shook his head. "You really didn't have to do this."

"We wanted to," Freeman said. "You shouldn't be alone tonight."

With that, Jack was forced to reconsider his plans.

He downed another glass of wine with his slice of cake, and as Mary took the dessert plates away, he turned to Freeman. "Where's your bathroom?"

"Oh, use the one in our bedroom," Freeman pointed toward the stairs. "The plumbing's been funky in the other two. Down the hall, first door on the right."

"Thanks." Jack eased from his chair and climbed to the second floor. He found the bathroom just like Freeman said. As Jack flicked the light switch, he caught a glimpse of himself in the mirror. His face was flush, weary bags hung beneath his eyes, and a glaze of sweat covered his forehead. Standing there, Jack thought of his plans again. Then, without much hesitation, he reached for the mirror and popped it open. On the medicine cabinet's shelves, he saw a tube of toothpaste, cotton swabs, various skincare products—and an orange prescription bottle. Jack picked the bottle off the shelf and read the label: Percocet. He unscrewed the cap, tapped out three white tablets into his palm, and then set the bottle precisely where he had found it. He stuffed the painkillers in his pocket.

As the toilet refilled and Jack trudged downstairs, gripping the railing, Freeman met him in the foyer and placed a hand on his back. "Hey, let's talk."

Freeman showed him into the library where they sat in two leather chairs beneath the ticking hands of a grandfather clock. "Are you going up to visit your mom?"

Jack quietly shook his head.

"Okay. You're going in tomorrow morning?" the D/CIA asked.

"Yeah," Jack raked his hair aside.

"Pete and Grace will brief you. Unfortunately, I have to catch a six-A.M. flight out of Andrews."

"Where you headed?"

"Tel Aviv," said Freeman.

"Beirut?"

"Yup."

"That's a clusterfuck," Jack shook his head.

"You don't know the half of it. Between you and me, that was our recruit Hezbollah seized. So I'm going over to have a chat with Benny Isaac and see what we can salvage. My hopes aren't too high."

Jack forced down a hiccup. "What's going on, Ryan?"

Freeman glanced back to the living room before leaning in and lowering his voice. "You're leading an op to sabotage Haj Ali Gholi."

"By assassinating Alireza Fakhrizadeh?"

"That's right. Paulson will sign the order."

"Shit," Jack turned his eyes to the bookcases, "I knew you were up to something."

"Pete and Grace will bring you up to speed," Freeman reiterated. "All I can say here is that the Quds Force is on a war footing, Jack. What our man in Tehran is telling us is true: Gaza, Sudan, that freighter off Somalia, Iraq, dissidents murdered in Holland—it's all connected. Shateri needs to be stopped before we're facing some serious casualties."

"How?"

Freeman dropped his voice nearly to a whisper. "We've made contact with a force in-country that might help get the job done. JSOC is loaning us a four-man element to run liaison; they've been planning it with us for a few weeks. The guy Wade picked to command the element is coming up tomorrow as well. You'll meet him at the briefing, work out the kinks, and wait for the NSC."

"How's it been received at the White House?"

"They're onboard—for the most part. Secretary Weisel's run interference since the beginning. And State has another play in the works designed to isolate Shateri and the IRGC."

"Paulson's letter to Khansari?"

"Yup," Freeman nodded. "Our man's going to Geneva."

"He'll be fine," Jack assured.

"Let's hope," the D/CIA pressed back in his chair. The grandfather clock tolled the hour, and once the chimes subsided, he asked Jack, "How are you? I know tonight can be pretty hard."

"I'm okay," Jack looked down at his feet.

But Freeman didn't believe him.

Jack held his gaze at the floor. After a pregnant pause he muttered, "Do you ever think about him?"

Freeman leaned closer. "Jack, I think about your dad every day. He's always with me."

With his eyes still dropped, he gently shook his head. "That's not who I meant."

Freeman's spine straightened and his lips pursed. The hair on the back of his neck stood on end. "No—I never think about him," he said. "And neither should you... Jack, he is gone, and he is *never* coming back."

There was no reply.

"Jack, how'd you get over here?" he asked above the clock's quiet ticks. "I hope you didn't drive."

"Metro."

"Alright, wait there, okay?" Freeman rose from his chair and walked into the foyer.

From the library, Jack heard the front door open and felt a chill draft touch his skin. After a minute, the door shut and he overheard Freeman and another man whose voice he didn't recognize speaking in the foyer.

"Listen, do me a favor," said Freeman. "I need you to drive Jack home."

"Of course, sir," the other voice replied.

"Don't leave him until he's inside his apartment. Alright?"

"Understood."

He heard footsteps coming toward the library.

"Jack, this is Doc," Freeman told him as they entered, "He's the head of my detail. Doc is going to take you back to your place."

"Sounds good," Jack slapped his knees and stood.

Freeman held Jack's arms. "Happy birthday, Jack," he said. "I'm glad that you spent it with us." He looked Jack in the eyes and saw tears building on his lashes.

Without a hint of warning, Jack wrapped his arms around Freeman and pulled him in tight. "Thank you," he said. "Thank you. Thank you. Thank you."

"I love you, kiddo," Freeman choked and kissed the side of his head.

"Goodbye," Jack let go and passed through the doorway.

It always felt the same. Whenever Jack left a room, Freeman was afraid that he had seen him for the last time. Jack was burning himself out before the world's eyes, and in rare bursts of startling intimacy he desperately needed someone to notice.

GRAVITY

DOC DROVE THE Chevy Tahoe along Colesville Road through the corridor of low-rise office blocks and chain restaurants in downtown Silver Spring. Traffic was scant and every few moments he glanced in his rear-view mirror, watching his passenger and remembering Freeman's very specific instructions.

"Just drop me up here, chief."

Doc could smell the wine on Jack's breath. He pressed the brakes at a red light. "The director told me to bring you home."

Jack's face tensed and he turned his eyes toward the window. "Drop me at the Metro and circle the block for ten minutes."

There was no reply. The light turned green and the Tahoe eased ahead.

Jack leaned forward in his seat. "Dude, you're doing what, fifteen, at best? I could just jump. Don't make it hard."

Doc squeezed his thick fingers around the steering wheel, and after a labored silence, he begrudgingly allowed, "Fine."

"Thank you," Jack eased back with an indignant sigh.

Through the intersection, Doc slid the Tahoe along the curb and unlocked the SUV with a resounding *click* through the cabin.

"Take it easy," said Jack as he leaned in against the armored door.

"Yep."

Stepping onto the sidewalk, Jack heaved the door shut and watched the Tahoe pull away with the next gap in traffic, fading into the red wash of taillights. A hundred yards ahead, the Silver Spring Metro station sat on a platform spanning the road. Jack stuffed his hands in his pockets and crossed the street, just then beginning to feel the alcohol latch his feet to the pavement like magnets. The station's mezzanine was surprisingly empty for a Friday night. Typically, yowling cliques of teenagers from suburban Maryland flocked into the city, swarming Gallery Place and Chinatown until

534

early in the morning. But Jack saw no trace of them. The cold drove them away. He tapped his card against the faregate and rode an escalator up to the platform. A CSX freight train lumbered past on the adjacent track, a mile-long parade of creaking rust; the lights of Silver Spring glowed below; the station's brutalist concrete canopy stretched overhead like a gull's wings, masking the stars; and Jack shivered, feeling a haze settle behind his eyes.

The display board suspended from the canopy read that the next southbound Red Line train toward Shady Grove was due in eight minutes. Jack didn't mind the wait. He thought he was alone, but looking over the terracotta floor tiles, Jack soon saw otherwise. Far at the station's northern end, a young couple was pressed against a concrete pylon beneath a broken light fixture, their lips locked together.

A dark wind blew. Jack felt the Percocets in his pocket, and then, he decided that he didn't want to do it anymore.

Once the CSX train cleared the station and continued its slow march toward Anacostia, it became mercilessly still. Jack loathed the silence. For him, the dull tones of life—any life that wasn't his own—gave an escape, a point of focus, a way to drown out his own hateful thoughts. But in those quiet moments, with only a void between his ears, Jack heard the gentle drum of his monster prowling near, and then he knew: there was nowhere to hide.

And Jack wished that he didn't have to face it alone. Not tonight.

It felt like lead weights were tied to his feet. Jack knew he was drunk. His knees were weak, a daze bubbled behind his forehead, and his skin became comfortably numb to the cold. He turned, and the world turned with him. He strolled to the edge of the platform, his legs rumbling with every step, and stopped only when he felt the rubber bumps of the tiles under his soles.

To Jack's right, headlights broke the darkness, charging toward the station. He heard the third rail sizzle alive as a rush of frigid air swelled over the platform, the headlights still gaining.

A six-car train came to a halt on the platform. Jack stepped into the second car as the doors slid open on a chime and chose a seat along the starboard bulkhead, resting his head against the window. After another chime and the pre-recorded announcement of, "Step back, doors closing," the train accelerated with an electric moan, heading south into the District of Columbia.

The Washington Metro's Red Line charted a course that resembled a long and narrow hairpin, bending beneath the city with caps in the northern exurbs of Montgomery County. Speeding away from Silver Spring, Jack could only see faint hints of light in the darkness: glowing homes through bare trees and traffic drifting like timbers in a river. After three minutes, the train stopped at Takoma—no one got on—and again at Fort Totten, where a few transferred from the Green and Yellow lines. It took off again, whining over the rails for several moments, until a massive Byzantine dome and Venetian bell tower lit by floodlights briefly emerged in the distance beyond his window. The train slowed, and Jack looked up and read "Brookland" proudly painted in white lettering over the façade of a brick building. The doors slid apart with the usual refrain and a tide surged in.

Jack's head spun to the left at the sound of their voices. There must've been two dozen by his count, all in their late teens and early twenties. They packed his car, taking the remaining empty seats or gripping the poles along the center aisle, chattering and gleefully carrying on—drunk, like him, although in a much brighter state of mind. And they all vaguely looked the same, as Jack noticed: the boys all wore button-up shirts and reeked of cheap cologne; and the girls mostly wore variations of a loose, sequined top with tight jeans. The cold hardly seemed to bother them. One redhead on stilettos plodded into the car like part of a chain gang and took the seat beside Jack. Her back pressed against his arm, flooding his nose with a fruity aroma. She unzipped the clutch purse bound to her wrist and brandished a driver's license to her friend behind them.

"So—like—what do you think?" she asked.

Her friend pinched the card between her polished fingernails and passingly declared, "I mean, you're probably fine. The bouncers don't even care as long it's not expired and the picture isn't, like, a black girl, or something. Is that your cousin?"

"Yeah, she gave it to me over Christmas. But she's twenty-six, do you think that's too old?"

"Nah, you're fine," her friend assured.

Jack listened to them and kept his head against the window, letting the soft vibrations rattle his skull. His eyelids slowly grew heavy and the whole car seemed to totter in his mind. Normally, he would have desperately wanted them to shut up, even gotten off that train and waited for the next, but their blather was the only thing keeping Jack from weighing his options.

The redhead glanced to her friend between pecks at their phones. "Should I get with Connor tonight?"

Her friend gave a detached shrug and kept typing. "Why not? I'm staying at Tyler's, so go for it."

The redhead reached back without looking and dug her bony elbow into Jack's side. She turned, barely noticing him, and affected, "Oh, sorry."

On the viaduct just past Rhode Island Avenue station, a large portion of downtown Washington came into view and he saw the Capitol dome over the rooftops, gleaming white through swathes of scaffolding. At Union Station, the train went underground and the herd disembarked in unison, surely moving on to greener pastures at the bars on H Street.

The train was now, again, largely empty—and silent. As it slid through the blackened tunnel between Metro Center, Farragut North and Dupont Circle, Jack made a decision. He knew how, and he knew when.

It was just after eleven-thirty when the train arrived at Woodley Park. Jack got off, tapped his card again on the faregate, and came to the escalators, rising two hundred feet to the surface. It was easily ten degrees cooler than in Silver Spring, but Jack didn't feel the chill. He walked down Connecticut Avenue from the station's exit and turned left on Calvert Street, toward the bridge over Rock Creek Park.

The bridge was shrouded in fog so dense that the streetlamps seemed to levitate like orange orbs above the sidewalk. As Jack went to cross, wisps of clouds dissipated before him with still infinitely more hovering at all sides. A few cars drove by with only their lights visible. He heard voices passing somewhere on the opposite side of the bridge, happy and jubilant voices disembodied in the haze and muffled by the cold air.

Jack was alone—surrounded, but utterly alone.

He stopped at a small alcove two-thirds over the span and, without much thought, stepped up onto the ledge. An iron fence rose to the top of his chest. He wrapped his fingers around the bars and looked down. There was nothing, only weary stone arches wading in a gloomy sea. Yet somewhere down below—forty meters, Jack guessed—was a shallow creek bed.

I should jump, Jack heard himself think. It startled him at how casually the idea popped into his mind, but with another second he began to rationalize it. *Forty meters. I'd probably be dead on impact.* That much was good. The fence didn't go above his chest. *I could climb over this. And if I jumped from here, I'd hit the creek.* He scanned the fog at his back. *No one would know.*

Jack gasped. His eyes welled. He thought it again.

No one would know.

He could throw himself from that bridge right then and there and no one would know. No one would know for hours, maybe days. No one would stop him. Jack was surrounded—but no one knew him, and no one would save him.

He came down from the ledge and sat in that alcove, pulling his legs beneath him. His heart pounded. It was the only sensation reminding him that he still clung to life. The rest—his thoughts, his memories, his emotions—only made him numb.

And he sat there in a ball on the cold pavement, gasping, with tears running down his cheeks. Laughter sounded somewhere in the haze. He didn't want to live this way, and for years Jack screamed at himself that it wouldn't always be, that it couldn't, that one day it would get better. But it never did, and the more he screamed otherwise, the more he began to truly believe that it was all a lie. And when that shadow came for him—promising an eternity of rest, offering to let it all end—each time it became harder to resist.

Jack stood up and nearly vomited. He froze for a moment, forcing the nausea away, and kept walking. Crossing into Adams Morgan, it took only a short stumble along Calvert Street until he was "home," if he could call it that, at The Beacon. Jack buzzed himself through the front door and trudged up two flights of stairs to his apartment. That daze behind his forehead began to build into a splitting headache, and he knew that the only solution was to keep drinking.

And so he did. Jack dropped his keys by the door and kept the lights off, feeling around in the darkness until he reached the kitchen and plucked the unopened bottle of Jameson that he bought before heading to Freeman's off the counter. He didn't bother with a glass. Jack unscrewed the cap and took a long swig, wincing as he swallowed. He stumbled toward the bathroom and began filling the tub. He kept drinking. Light from the street bled in through the windows with the low roar of the bars and clubs on 18th Street. But Jack hardly noticed. He took the Percocets from his pocket, placed them on a shelf over the tub, and stripped down to nothing. After the tub was full, he shut off the spout and eased into the water with the Jameson bottle in his hand. He didn't cry anymore, but as he took one swig after another, he did once stop to ask why he kept doing this to himself.

He couldn't find an answer, the room spun, and he drank again.

He heard the monster's gentle drum, and he wished, just this one night, that he didn't have to face it alone. He wished that someone would call, that someone would knock on his door, that someone would barge in and save him from himself. Who? He didn't care. Someone.

More than anything—Jack wanted his father.

He drank. But did he? Was it actually his father that Jack wanted or some other "idea" of his father that his mind created to fill in the gaps? He couldn't find an answer; he didn't know anymore. It shamed him to think of it, to know a person's absence better than their presence. What little he knew, what little scraps he remembered were quickly fading. Jack no longer remembered the sound of his father's voice. He had never told anyone that. When he went to summon those memories, nothing came, and it terrified him. When all was said and done, when his father was nothing but a shade, what would Jack have left?

He didn't want to face it alone.

But that's how it always was. Jack imagined his future and saw absolutely nothing; his entire life, he thought, was already behind him. It was his share of the quiet agony we all suffer, a false twilight brought on by the fact that we crave what we've lost and we covet what we've never known.

Jack reached up to the shelf and downed the three Percocet tablets in a single gulp. He didn't want to die, but he didn't want to live either. He wanted to hover on the threshold between and wait for one side to reach out and grab him, praying that the right side chose first.

He set the bottle down and rose from the bathwater. His head felt lighter than air and the walls whirled around him. He couldn't see. Jack picked up his right foot and went to step forward, but his toe caught the tub's edge. He stumbled. His hand grasped at the shower curtain, ripped it from the hooks, and he collapsed, slamming his head against the tiles. Splayed facedown on the floor, he felt a searing hot pain rip through his skull. Jack groaned, he couldn't move, and then all went quiet—but only for a moment.

Looking through the bathroom doorway ahead, Jack could see his whole apartment washed in a morose pall. The familiar chill came. It was bitterly cold, like slabs of ice pierced his veins. His grip on consciousness began to blur. Jack tried to fight, but he knew it was pointless. There was nowhere to hide. He felt a force pull him into the floor, hugging him like a straightjacket. His mouth was sealed shut, and if he tried to scream no one would hear. The hair on his arms and legs, soaked as they were, bristled. A vibration swelled from some dark, unfathomably low place in his mind. A quake shook his apartment, and although nothing moved, he heard the floorboards and furniture, the pots and pans in the cabinets, rattling all around.

The vibration rose in his ears, and then fell to screams.

It blazed like a furnace, buildings crumbled to rubble, and through their thousand wails—writhing in the red waves of hell—no help would come. And then it stopped, a cold wind reaching down to snatch them away.

White noise replaced the screams. In the darkness through the open doorway, before Jack's very eyes, a shadow materialized in his living room. From a flat singularity on the wall, it grew into the three-dimensional silhouette of a man. Gaunt and lanky and blacker than the darkest night, its feet touched the floorboards. It curiously stepped toward the bathroom with its disjointed gait; its left hand convulsed in violent spasms. Jack was paralyzed, lying naked on the tiles as it crept closer: forced to gaze into the silent, unblinking void.

The Black Emperor—his monster—had come to claim him.

It called to him, it's hand outstretched in an offering of eternal peace.

As it came closer, Jack saw its placid, emotionless face, and it revealed all its horror in a glimpse. It was like a mirror. Within that shadow Jack saw his own skull inside his skin. Behind the skull—only blackness, nothing; someone was there, and yet no one was there. It sliced the spoiling flesh and peeled back. Underneath was the doleful apotheosis of the universe, a raw singularity of chaos that bubbles at the center of all infinity with creaking desolation—an endless festival of massacres, a carnival where all the rides are moving, yet not a redeemable soul occupies the seats.

And then Jack knew, its slow thighs slouching nearer, there was no escape.

It lurked at the dark heart of creation, an unseen force that drags all things kicking and screaming to their fitful ends, toward a deathly torrent washing over the falls. Jack swam ceaselessly against that current all his life, more desperate with each stroke, but now the lure was insurmountable: lapping at the bare soles of his feet, hawking a merciful end.

Jack didn't want to face it alone. But he knew no help would come.

Blood ran from his head and charted a delta between the tiles. Jack had never felt so cold. His eyes dimmed. His monster loomed over him, reaching to the floor with its convulsing hand. All he had to do was let go, to gently slip away, and it would carry him over the falls and across the horizon to a shoreless plain free of pain, free of fear, free to dream better dreams.

Somewhere within that abyss, the shadow promised Jack in an unspoken whisper, was his father—made whole again and ready to welcome his son. Just let go, it beckoned as Jack's eyelids closed, and let it end.

Walid Rada was thrust into a maelstrom.

The harsh odor of ammonium met his nostrils and roused his mind. A fiery glare whirled in his vision, and suddenly, it all began to reel. Up was down, forward was backward, and left was right. He thought that he was falling, stripped of any sense of three dimensions. He tried to move, but his muscles were like cement. It felt as if his every molecule was being squeezed through a grater and stretched apart into infinitely smaller strands.

Rada swore that he was in hell. He clenched his eyes shut and prayed for it all to stop, but the more he struggled, the worse it became. His legs flailed and he heard dirt skidding beneath his feet. His hands tensed into claws and he felt his fingernails scratching at metal. His shuddering vocal cords loosed an impulsive scream. Cool air filled his lungs. Clinging to sanity, he gasped, and he forced his eyes open.

The night sky hung miles overhead—a thousand bleeding stars arcing from one edge of the horizon to the next like a dark, glittering tapestry. In that instant, he realized that he couldn't be in hell, that he was still alive. Yet he was wrong, and the truth of his fate was far worse than he could imagine.

Walid Rada, or what remained, haunted a purgatory between.

His last memory was of lying in the back of a speeding car with that hood pulled over his head. He remembered men shouting at him before feeling a few drops of liquid land on the fabric covering his mouth. His mind was blank after that moment. Rada regained his balance, although he was still lightheaded and felt his stomach roiling just beneath his throat. He went to lift his arms, but they wouldn't budge. He realized that he was sitting and lurched forward to pull himself up, but his legs were frozen. He thought of Yusra and Eshe, recalling their looks of sheer anguish while they were dragged away. His eyes fell to Earth, and in that moment, the reality of his situation flooded back all at once.

Rada was bound by zip-ties to a metal chair locked into a slab of concrete on the dirt floor. Weathered limestone walls open to the stars above flanked him at all sides. It was unnaturally quiet and not even a breeze blew. Rada knew he wasn't alone. The hair on his neck stood like spines. He felt something, a presence holding passively in the darkness at his back, invisible and smothering.

He heard a stifled crack. There was a brief flash behind him, followed by a hollow hiss near the ground and a brilliant, blazing red light that washed over the crumbling limestone. Breaking that light, to Rada's dread, was a shadow projected on the wall before him. It was the black, featureless silhouette of a man, standing silent and unblinking. Its arms and fingers were held along its narrow torso, and its left hand faintly twitched. White smoke unfurled toward the sky and a persistent sizzle echoed between the walls. Rada tried to speak, but each attempt fell from his tongue as an unintelligible murmur.

It gazed without eyes. The shadow slightly cocked its head to the side and looked upon Rada like some frail curiosity. "I've been watching you," it said with a monotone sigh.

Rada shivered. "I—I—I—I did it," he confessed, "I stole it. I took the money and hid it in an account I opened in my brother-in-law's name. It's still there, all of it. I—I'll give you the number. Anything you want, it's yours," he panted as the words stumbled over one another in a mad rush to the exit. "It was all me. My family had nothing to do with it. My wife never knew until the end."

But the shadow was unmoved.

"The Jews! You want to hear about the Jews!" Rada blurted. "There was a team of them—Mossad, I think. They approached me and threatened my family if I didn't do what they wanted."

The shadow turned and contorted on the wall, then Rada heard something scraping in the dirt.

"I met them at a flat in Beirut, near the American University. I can take you there. One was in charge. Cohen. That was his name. Nathan Cohen."

The shadow melted away. A man appeared at Rada's side, placed a chair in the dirt and sat in front of him. The burning flare cast back on the man's face, illuminating the pale, gaunt regions of waste and fatigue in a rippling red glow.

Rada paused at the sight of the man's shallow, indifferent eyes. "There was a woman, too," Rada said. "She was a redhead. I don't know her name."

"I do."

Rada's lips quivered. "Who are you?"

David Kazanoff crossed his legs and set his spindly hands in his lap, and answered, "Your monster."

"Do you have my family?"

"No."

Rada felt sick to his stomach. "Where are they?"

"At home and at peace," Kazanoff dismissed. "As you will be in time."

Rada took a deep breath. He was possessed with a strange sensation that he had seen Kazanoff before, as if the man's face and mannerisms were a vague amalgamation of each living person he had ever laid eyes upon, stitched together somewhere deep in his subconscious. He found the man's unwavering voice oddly soothing. When Kazanoff spoke, Rada felt that he had chosen those words himself in the millisecond before Kazanoff said them. With every utterance, Rada trusted him more. "You work for Hezbollah?"

Kazanoff calmly shook his head.

"Why are you holding me?"

"I'm not. You were gifted into my care so that I may save you."

"Save me?"

"From yourself."

"No," Rada spat. "No, I want to go home."

"So go," Kazanoff shrugged. "Stand up."

"You tied me to a chair," Rada croaked.

"No, I didn't."

"Then who did?"

"You did," said Kazanoff. "I'll show you." He took a knife from his jacket pocket, flicked the serrated blade open and cut the zip-ties around Rada's wrists and ankles. "Stand up."

Rada leaned his torso forward, but nothing followed. He pressed his feet against the concrete slab, expecting his legs to lift him upright, but nothing happened. Rada grimaced. He wrapped his hands around the chair's armrests, shifted his weight into his forearms and pushed with all his strength—three times—but nothing came. "Help me," Rada grasped out.

"I can't," Kazanoff replied as he sat again.

"How—" Before Rada could finish the syllable, he winced and doubled over, gripping his head as a searing pain shot through his skull.

"Be still and it'll pass."

Rada groaned and caught his breath.

"Stand up, and you can go home," Kazanoff promised. "Wake up, and you can go home."

"Wake up?"

"Yes," Kazanoff nodded. "Think—how did you come to me, Walid?"

Rada swore he knew, but as soon as Kazanoff spoke, his mind was filled with doubt. He trembled. "You're not?"

"No," Kazanoff knowingly shook his head. "All that exists is empty space...and you."

Just then, he sensed an icy wave of peace fall over him like a smallpox blanket. Rada felt drawn to Kazanoff; whoever or whatever the man was, he knew he could not harm him. Rada wouldn't resist. Bathed in the red glow, he watched the spasms mount in Kazanoff's hand.

"When I was a boy," Kazanoff started placidly, "I had certain curiosities that didn't come naturally to others my age. Relationships were difficult for me. I was terribly lonely—until I found Alex. We made quick friends, and in time I thought we were inseparable. I fell for the fatal music of his voice. We spent an entire summer together, passing our days on the beach or in the woods. He made me drunk with the simple joy of lingering at his side, of gazing into the paradise of his eyes, of feeling the ecstasy that coursed through my veins with his touch. I had never known happiness like that. But to my dismay, it became clear to me that Alex did not feel the same way. As that summer fell to autumn, he spoke to me less and less, and with curt and sterile words that stung me in ways I never knew possible. Although I tried to forget, I still thought of Alex all the time, despite my fears that he thought of me not at all. Until one day..."

Kazanoff steadied his twitching hand, and then continued. "One day, before the cold settled in, I persuaded Alex to walk with me on the beach as we once did. Although the sun shined and the waves were deceptively tame that day, I knew a storm churned far out to sea. We sat at the foot of a cliff for at least an hour, not saying much of anything, until I pointed at the waves—and as I did—we heard a hideous wail. A young woman thrashed about in the surf, struggling to reach her little dog that bobbed and yelped just above the surface barely a few feet away. They fought hopelessly with each labored stroke as the current lured them deeper into the great blue abyss. Alex wanted to help, but I compelled him not to. So he sat there, frozen in my rapture, while the last trace of them sank beneath the swells. He sobbed when they vanished. It seemed so pure to me: in their place was vacancy. Once his tears dried, I told Alex the truth. Would you like to hear it, too?"

Rada swallowed. "What?"

"God is dead," he revealed, "and His death was the life of this world."

"I don't understand," Rada's head shook.

"Alex was never the same once he heard the news, and neither will you," said Kazanoff. "But that one truth binds the brotherhood of suffering between everything alive. God is dead; He killed himself, and the turbulent wake of His suicide echoes through eternity and tugs at our strings like an undead, imbecilic puppeteer that sustains the fitful ruckus of the universe. And a puppet is but a child's toy, a thing of parts pieced together into hunks of spoiling flesh on disintegrating bones. God is a black emperor unjustly lording over all our fates. God is a more absurd character than I could ever be."

Kazanoff shifted in his chair. "Watching that woman and her dog drown was as bland to me as if they were so many rats in a storm drain. Alex was quite taken aback when I told him. But there was no need to grieve. They were merely unwitting marionettes forced to play their roles in a cast of billions that is so dull and ignorant and trivial and conceited, so diseased and rickety, so worthless all around. They had no value. That knowledge alone, I told Alex, is the blossom of all human wisdom. When we left that beach, he could no longer turn away from me. He came to me day after day, night after night, now conscious of the lies that had been eating away at his soul like a pestilent marrow. The life Alex once knew and cherished now seemed false and scripted; the body he inhabited smelt rotten and crumbled at the touch. We made a pact that we would end it together. We had to escape, I told him, for to be alive is to inhabit a nightmare without hope of salvation. We had to wake up, and the only way was to further God's blueprint for bringing about an end to His creation. We had to die, by our own hand, like God did."

"How?"

Kazanoff fixed his gaze on the mist in Rada's eyes. "With fire."

Rada choked.

"We emptied a can of kerosene over our heads. There was no need to say goodbye; we were going home. We each took a book of matches. I stepped several paces from him. Alex lit his, and with that first spark, he was swallowed whole. I watched the flames consume him...and I vowed to love him always.

Kazanoff stretched out his arms. "Now you sit before me."

"I have to die?"

"No, Walid. You have to wake up."

"And go home?" he muttered.

"Of course," answered Kazanoff. "The life you know is an endless festival of massacres. The world you inhabit is an utterly horrifying place, and yet you've convinced yourself that the lines you drew in the sand and called 'home' were somehow different. What have you done, that you are punished so? Nothing at all, except being born into a foolish, loathsome story. Were it up to me, Walid, the pages of that story would still be blank. Think about it: your self-murdered God could have done this literally to anyone, but He chose you. And why?" he shrugged. "Because God is an entertainer who needs His audience to know terror. Don't you see now?"

Rada gave no reply.

"It goes on like this," he said. "None of God's characters have even a modicum of control over what they are, and yet He curses them to believe they do. You are all ignorant that God is the cause of your suffering, but that makes it nonetheless true. It's a game: God stands a row of bricks on end a few inches apart; God pushes a brick, it knocks its neighbor over, the neighbor knocks over the next brick, and so on until all the row is felled. This is human life. Under this tyrant, only the dead know mercy. Scores are doomed to live and suffer between the spine of their creator's scrawls, but you have been placed into my care and gifted the right to free will. Just let go, Walid, and it all ends."

Rada's head was spinning. He wanted to believe him, if only to make it stop. "This is a dream?"

"A nightmare," Kazanoff replied, "and when you wake, Yusra and Eshe will be standing there to welcome you."

"I'm ready," Rada nodded, "I want to go home."

"I knew you would be," Kazanoff grinned. He rose from his chair and returned a moment later with a jerry can. Kazanoff unscrewed the cap, held it above Rada's head, and dipped it forward.

"Wait," Rada panted.

Kazanoff stopped.

"Thank you."

Kerosene poured out over Rada's scalp, dripped through his lashes and soaked his clothes. Kazanoff set the empty can in the dirt and handed Rada a matchbook. Rada's fingers trembled as he tried to tear one loose.

"Will it hurt?" he asked.

Kazanoff smiled. "It's as painless as gravity."

Rada struck the match and was instantly engulfed. Flames sucked the oxygen from his lungs and scorched his throat; his hair curled and smoked. He felt his flesh blister and melt on his bones. Rada screamed in unfathomable agony, but it was far too late. Before his bubbling eyes, he saw Kazanoff leaning against the wall—tranquil and indifferent—as life evaporated from his body. Once the fire consumed him, all that remained in Walid Rada's place was vacancy.

CHAPTER 45

HARRIS HEARD THE mattress creak. Fingernails tickled his scalp.

"Hey…" Sandy's breath warmed his ear.

Harris groaned, holding his eyelids closed.

She kissed his cheek, "Time to get up," and pecked at his neck.

"Little lower," he grinned.

Sandy slapped his shoulder. "Come on, lazybones." She got up on her knees and snatched a pillow out from under his head. "Last shot."

"You're so mean!" Harris squealed and moved to shield himself.

"Get. Up." She walloped him with the pillow. "Right. Now."

Harris turned over as Sandy giggled with each blow, grabbed her arm, and yanked her down next to him. "That wasn't nice," he pressed his lips to hers.

"Oh, really?"

"Nope," Harris kissed her chin. "I'm telling your mom."

"Go ahead, I'll dial," Sandy laughed.

Harris worked down her neck. "On second thought…"

She twirled his hair. "Don't you have top secret macho stuff to do?"

"Damnit." He stopped at her chest. "What time is it?"

"Six."

Harris crawled up and kissed her again. "Oh well," he sighed. "You got lucky this time."

"I bet." Sandy rose off the bed. "Where you going?"

"Just a training thing down the coast," he lied. "Z's coming, too."

She opened the drapes. "Guys want dinner later?"

"Nah, don't worry about us. I'm not sure when we'll be back." Harris swung his legs off the bed. "Go shower first. I'll get the munchkin."

• • •

Yellow bile erupted from his throat. Jack clung to the toilet bowl—legs splayed across the bathroom floor—as his stomach contracted in violent waves. He heaved a half-dozen times until only air retched free of his seething gut. His eyes watered and his nose ran; a sharp pain rang inside his forehead like cymbals. Once he caught his breath, Jack flushed the toilet and slowly came to his feet. It would be wrong to say that he was particularly relieved: another morning came and Jack was still there; like most, he heedlessly accepted the gift. He remembered almost nothing of the night before, and while the damage hinted enough to fill in the blanks, the pain told Jack that he was still alive. The bathtub was full but the Jameson bottle sitting on the ledge beside it was not. His knees were bruised and a section of the tiles where he had lain all night were crusted over in dried blood. His head throbbed. Jack hobbled to the sink and looked in the mirror. Rusty stains marred the right side of his face, streaking from his brow to his neck. He carefully touched his fingers to his scalp, parted his hair, and discovered a two-inch gash.

"You're getting heavy, dude," Harris said as he carried Ben downstairs.

They came into the living room. A rose-colored sky shone over Minneapolis Drive. He let Boomer into the backyard before placing Ben on the sofa. Harris turned on the TV and played a *Looney Tunes* Blu-ray. Ben never tired of the old cartoons; no matter how many dozens of times he had watched them before, he could still sit for hours, sending fits of laughter through the house.

While Ben sat enthralled at the epic clash between Wile E. Coyote and The Road Runner, flapping his hands and clicking his tongue, Harris made a pot of coffee and reflected on the lie he told Sandy. There was no training mission down the coast, and Harris made Z swear that he would play along if Sandy somehow brought it up. When Z demanded to know why Harris asked him to lie to his wife, he promised to tell him as soon as he could. Until then, only a handful knew that Harris was summoned up to Langley, much less why—although, to be honest, neither did he. Boomer barked at the patio door.

After thirty minutes he had breakfast ready, and when Sandy met them at the kitchen table, Harris did his best to feign a smile.

Blood circled the drain. Jack turned off the shower faucet and wrapped a towel around his waist. He swallowed a few Ibuprofens with a swig of Jameson and steeled himself for the impending, unpleasant task.

Jack dipped his head and looked in the mirror. He had a much better view of the gash with the blood washed away. The wound was already clotted over and it wasn't nearly as deep as he originally feared. Jack could handle it himself and none would be the wiser. He squirted a bit of hydrogen peroxide into a gauze pad and—taking short, steady breaths—dabbed it on his scalp. It stung like hell. Jack grunted and his face tensed, wincing to suppress the pain. After removing the gauze, he gingerly pinched the gash together with his fingers and sealed it shut with a thin strip of super glue.

Harris kissed his family goodbye and backed out of the driveway by seven-thirty. He intended to make it home before dark and told Sandy that his cell phone might be switched off for most of the day, but promised to text her before he and Z started back—another lie to shield the others.

Instead of driving to Dam Neck as usual, Harris took Interstate 64 northbound toward Newport News and Richmond. He crossed the Hampton Roads Bridge-Tunnel just as the morning rush began. On the causeway approaching the southern tunnel portal, looming beyond his windshield, Harris spotted the USS *Bataan* amphibious assault ship as it inched along the main channel. He had forgotten that Z's old ship was ordered by the Pentagon to end its pre-deployment workup a few weeks early and head to the Persian Gulf. Navy harbor tugs pressed against her towering, steel-gray hull. An MH-60 Seahawk hovered overhead, and sailors in their dress blues manned the rails around her flight deck, undoubtedly frozen stiff in the driving winds. The additional escort ships of the *Bataan* Amphibious Ready Group (ARG) were also putting to sea. Back at Naval Station Norfolk, the USS *Mesa Verde,* a *San Antonio*-class transport dock, eased from her berth and would follow down the channel at a ten-minute interval. Several miles east at Joint Expeditionary Base Little Creek, the *Whidbey Island*-class dock landing ship, USS *Gunston Hall,* was getting underway. In two hours, the ARG would rendezvous off the Virginia capes and make for Morehead City, North Carolina to embark the twenty-two hundred men and women, aircraft and equipment of the 24th Marine Expeditionary Unit before sailing across the Atlantic.

He was three hours from Langley. Sinking into the orange glow of the tunnel, Harris sipped his coffee and readied a Fleetwood Mac playlist for the miles of highway ahead—speeding toward a mission of his own that was still all too uncertain.

The main lobby of the Old Headquarters Building at Langley was swathed in shades of gray and white Georgia marble; a large granite agency seal— which measured sixteen feet in diameter and featured an eagle, a shield, and a sixteen-point star—was inlaid on the floor. Along the right wall of the lobby was a field of 115 chiseled stars flanked by an American flag on the left and a flag with the agency's seal on the right. An inscription above the field read: "In honor of those members of the Central Intelligence Agency who gave their lives in the service of their country." To Jack, one of those stars might have been his entire universe.

He would never forget that day—once the funeral and the memorials and the ceremonies ended, once the sympathy cards and the phone calls and well-wishers disappeared, once the mountains of food and flowers spoiled and wilted, once all went quiet—when Freeman brought Jack to see it for himself.

It was Christmastime, he remembered. Jack and his mother recently moved to live near her family in New Jersey and so they drove down to Washington to visit Freeman before the holidays. Nearly a year had passed, Jack almost seven, and he had just begun to truly understand who his father was and what he did—and why he was never coming home. It was late at night, snow flurries fell outside, and the lobby was empty except for the two of them. Freeman took Jack's hand, led him up to the Memorial Wall, and placed his finger on the star—a freshly carved chink in the marble—that symbolized his father. Below the field was a black Moroccan goatskin book enclosed in a steel and glass frame. It listed each star, ordered by year of death, and when possible displayed an officer's name. Freeman pointed to the year—1990—and a gold star, beside which read: "Michael Patrick Galloway." It was for his dad, Freeman told Jack, so that no one who entered the building would ever forget his name.

But Jack noticed something peculiar. Another star sat directly beneath his father's in the book, only there was no name written. He asked why and Freeman explained that several of the fallen officers were operating undercover and so their names must remain secret, even in death. However, what Freeman didn't explain was that some names were best left unwritten, unspoken, and forgotten.

After twenty-six years, Jack stood before the Memorial Wall in service to the same agency for which his father sacrificed his life. Michael Galloway had no headstone—his ashes were scattered in the sea—and so, to Jack, it was his father's grave: a gray star etched into a cold slab of marble. As a man, Jack now understood what his father died for.

Without fail, the wall was his first stop on each visit to Langley. Yet it always unsettled him. When Jack looked at his father's star, he felt another gazing back at him. When he read his father's name in the book, it was impossible not to notice the blank space beneath it: an unwritten name, best left forgotten.

• • •

Near the high-rise offices, luxury hotels and sprawling shopping malls of Tysons Corner, Harris took Exit 46B off Interstate 495 to Dolley Madison Boulevard in McLean, Virginia. He drove past residential subdivisions and fast food chains for nearly five miles until a sign planted beside the road announced: "George Bush Center for Intelligence, Next Left." He turned at a traffic light and found several more signs brandishing the usual warnings: "Restricted US Government Installation; Photography Strictly Prohibited;" and, one that Harris heeded, "All non-badged visitors must keep right." With the concrete and glass gatehouse clearly ahead, Harris pulled off the entrance road into a separate lane and stopped at a metal box equipped with an intercom and a pinhole-size camera. Harris rolled down the window when a disembodied voice crackled, "How can I help you this morning?"

"Yeah, hi," he leaned toward the box. "I'm Chief Petty Officer Robert Harris from JSOC. I have an appointment at eleven."

"Can I get your social security number, please?"

After reciting the nine digits, the voice replied, "Pull up to the barrier, sir."

Harris eased off the brakes and drove twenty-five feet to the gatehouse, stopping at an erect steel barricade. A uniformed guard in a broad-brimmed hat with an M4 across his chest stood nearby while two more led a German Shepherd around Harris' Jeep and inspected the undercarriage with a mirror. Another appeared by the window with a clipboard.

"Photo ID please?" the guard asked.

He offered over his DOD Common Access Card. The guard made a few glances and matched the picture with his face. "If you could just sign this form," the guard handed the ID back and reeled off regulations as if from a recording. "It gives consent to search your person or belongings while on the premises. You'll also need to surrender your cell phone and any other cameras or electronic devices you may have in your possession; you can pick those up here when you leave. Do you have any questions?"

"Nope," said Harris as he jotted his signature on the clipboard and picked his phone out of the cup holder. It was a familiar routine.

The guard then passed him a bright orange card printed with a large V. "Okay, this is your visitor's badge, please keep it visible at all times; your parking permit, that can go on your dash; and a map of the parking facilities. You're cleared for the VIP lot, so just stay to the right and you'll see the signs. Enjoy the rest of your day, Chief."

"You too." Harris rolled up his window. Once the barrier retracted into the ground, he pressed the gas and continued along the entrance road past bare oak trees as the Old Headquarters Building gradually appeared through the branches. The VIP lot sat just left of the main entrance to OHB. Harris parked his Jeep in an empty space, took a breath, and followed the sidewalk up to the lobby.

He stepped over the granite seal on the floor, passed the Memorial Wall, and presented himself at the security desk at the far end of the lobby. A receptionist checked his name on the appointment roster and placed a phone call. After a minute, beyond the row of turnstiles, a professorial-looking man rounded the corner and came down a short flight of steps toward the lobby.

"Chief Harris?" the man asked.

"Good morning."

"I'm Peter Stavros, head of the Iran Operations Division. It's nice to finally meet you." They shook hands over the turnstiles.

"Pleasure."

"Let's get you to the office, the whole crew's ready for you."

Harris felt slightly intimidated. He remembered that this was all for him—out of JSOC's entire range of tier-one operators, Admiral Wade chose him.

Stavros entered his ID card into the turnstile and punched in a code. Then Harris inserted his visitor's badge into the same turnstile and two metal bars slid aside. They made small talk as Stavros escorted him through the building and eventually arrived at a cypher-locked door in Corridor C. Stavros tapped his ID against the reader and led Harris past a life-size poster of Imam Hossein and through a bustling warren of cubicles to another locked door.

Inside, Harris counted a dozen people packed inside a conference room. A large LCD screen and a whiteboard were mounted to the far wall, and a topographic map laid flat on the table at the center of the room. He instantly recognized the mountainous terrain of the Iran-Iraq border. As he entered with Stavros, everyone looked up from their tasks and fixed their eyes on him. It briefly occurred to Harris that he should turn on his heels and run, but he already knew that it was much too late for that.

Stavros made the necessary introductions: first up was the vaunted Grace Shaw, deputy director for operations; next came Stavros' own deputy at Persia House, Marcia Lath, and the handful of CIA analysts, operational planners, and JSOC Intelligence Brigade personnel attached to the task force; finally, Stavros brought Harris around to the back corner of the table, and said, "And this fellow here is Jack Galloway. He runs our HUMINT asset in-country."

Harris leaned forward and offered his hand. "Nice to meet you."

"Same," Jack accepted.

He took a chair next to Jack. The lights dimmed and Lath stepped up to the screen. She clicked a remote and a PowerPoint slide appeared, showing a desert valley with two tunnel portals punched into the mountainside. "Late in January," she began, "overhead reconnaissance detected this previously unknown facility bordering the Haj Ali Gholi dry lakebed in Semnan

Province, which lies approximately two hundred miles east of Tehran…"

Lath brought them up to speed on that dusty patch of the Dasht-e Kavir desert that haunted the US Intelligence community's best minds for weeks. Aided by the PowerPoint presentation, she detailed it all: the two tunnel portals labeled Monet and Picasso, the rotating IRGC security force and the ongoing excavation work under the cover of darkness, the mysterious flights from Tehran that landed in the valley, the surrounding geography and how it all seemed tailor-made to foil detection. She then revealed how CITADEL—the agency's primary HUMINT asset in the country—had baited Major General Qasem Shateri and inadvertently shredded the veil of secrecy around the site with a few choice words: "I would be honored to inform His Excellency that Doctor Fakhrizadeh has extracted fifty kilograms of plutonium-239 and the appropriate amount of tritium. God willing, he intends to assemble and test a device in the summer." With that, Lath explained, the pieces all fell into place. It was CIA's current judgment that the Monet portal housed a twenty-megawatt reactor to reprocess plutonium from spent uranium fuel rods and a fabrication workshop; Picasso, meanwhile, was an incomplete test site designed to mask the signatures of an underground nuclear explosion. Another slide offered a quick background on Dr. Alireza Fakhrizadeh—namely his education by the Soviets at Chelyabinsk-70 and renown as Iran's own Robert Oppenheimer, his expertise in constructing an atomic bomb small enough to fit inside the trunk of a car, and the convenient timing of his demise before Mossad could assassinate him. If Fakhrizadeh indeed faked his death before an Israeli hit squad could do the job, as CIA believed, then the truth of Haj Ali Gholi was unassailable. Beneath that mountain, with the blessing and protection of the Quds Force, Dr. Fakhrizadeh had nearly finished his life's work and was only months away from completing a personal batch of nuclear weapons for Qasem Shateri—and all without Ayatollah Khansari's knowledge or authority.

The Western world's worst fear had finally come true.

Any doubts Harris had of his role in the mission to come evaporated. He thought of Ben, Sandy and their daughter. If CIA and JSOC were headed into Iran to sabotage that place, he wanted to be a part of it.

With the next several slides, Lath outlined the tangled strategic realities on the ground in Iraq with the Hashid Shaabi militias, the Kurdish peshmerga forces, and the rebel groups encamped on Mount Qandil. She narrated Jamil Gorani's role in the offensive to retake Nineveh Province and Mosul from ISIS, how those efforts led to the murder of his wife and eldest son, his renouncing of the Kurdistan Democratic Party, and the rash of assassinations targeting IRGC officers across the border. Lastly, she revealed how Persia House established contact with Gorani through the help of a local smuggler, before handing the remote over to Stavros.

A reconnaissance image covered the screen, detailing a stepped village of mud houses climbing up opposite ends of a narrow, rocky gorge. "Jamil Gorani and his group are operating out of Palanjar in the Ushnu-Sulduz Valley, which lies roughly five kilometers east of the Iraqi border and seventy kilometers north of Mahabad," Stavros said. "As you can see, it straddles the Gadar River and sits near the tri-border of Iran, Iraq and Turkey, solidly within the Kurdish tribal areas of those three countries. Census data indicates that most young people have left the village in recent years. The few old shepherding families that remain take guest right quite seriously and are sympathetic to the idea of a Kurdish state. They have little contact with outsiders, and as our communications with Gorani indicate, they're entirely loyal to his cause—if you wish to call it that."

Stavros cleared his throat and went to the next slide. "IOD has been in contact with Gorani via a secure sat line for several days. After some tense negotiations we were able to break down the barriers a bit and get him to open up. Gorani claims that he has fourteen men with him in Palanjar. Most hail from his tribe in Bardarash, but there are apparently a few Sinjari fighters in there as well. A real hodgepodge, it seems. Gorani says his men are determined to make the Iranians bleed, but the isolation in Palanjar is taking its toll—their weapons and equipment are failing, ammunition is dwindling. That, of course, is where we come in."

He clicked the remote. "We've labeled it Operation PACER. This mission has three primary objectives. First, a four-man team led by Chief Harris here from DEVGRU will insert into the valley and rendezvous with Gorani. Once in Palanjar, the chief's team will gauge their morale, readiness and operational security. If everything checks out, IOD's forward cell in Erbil will work with JSOC to ferry the necessary arms and supplies over the border. That includes three million dollars paid to Gorani for his services. Second—while the team in Palanjar trains Gorani's men on tradecraft and surveillance—Jack will return to Tehran, make contact with his asset, and task CITADEL to use his leverage within the regime to gain access to the Haj Ali Gholi facility under the guise of an inspection tour for Ayatollah Khansari. It's our hope that while at the facility, CITADEL will come into contact with Alireza Fakhrizadeh, if he is in fact still alive. Getting CITADEL inside is critical to closing our intelligence gaps. For instance, we still don't entirely understand how the facility was built, how it's funded, how many individuals work there, how the Quds Force obtained the spent uranium fuel rods and the material to operate the reactor, or who else in the regime knows that this place exists. There are still plenty of unknowns to settle before we can make a sound determination of just what exactly we're facing and how to counter it. Jack, does this all seem feasible to you?"

"Pretty much," Jack thought aloud.

"Good," Stavros nodded. "Chief Harris, here's where your paths collide."

"Hit me."

"Once you've determined that Gorani's men are ready, and once Jack's placed CITADEL inside Haj Ali Gholi, the third objective calls for us to use Gorani's men to surveil and eliminate Fakhrizadeh. Now, the president is willing to authorize you to do that, but we're also prepared to deal with any eventuality that confronts us. Basically, we'll cross that bridge when we get there."

"This is a top priority for the director," Shaw added, "and anything you boys need, you will get it."

The necessary arrangements were made. Harris' four-man team was officially code-named "VALENCIA." Luckily, given IOD's continuous dialogue with Gorani, the team's housing situation in Palanjar was squared away. However, the weather wasn't so predictable. Spring rapidly approached, which in that part of the world meant torrential downpours and melting snowcaps that would engorge the streams and rivers in the valley and create more than enough mud for any man to see in one lifetime. Harris was already consigned to the fact that they would be dirty for weeks on end. IOD would handle their communications link back to Langley and the Joint Operations Center in Erbil. All of the remaining equipment needed for the mission—weapons and ammunition, clothing and gear—was available back at Dam Neck. They put the final touches on the team's insertion plan, made a list of any further requirements that needed to be addressed, and adjourned at one o'clock with their marching orders. Jack would fly back to Tehran via Switzerland in the morning and arrange an in-person meeting with CITADEL. Harris, meanwhile, would return to Virginia Beach, recruit the three remaining members of his team—he knew exactly who he would pick—and then somehow break the news to Sandy.

Jack took off at the first opportunity. Harris trailed him through the cubicles and caught up to him near the Imam Hossein poster.

"Hey man, wait a sec," Harris called.

Jack stopped in his tracks and turned around. "What's up?"

"Wanna get lunch?"

Jack stared Harris down for a moment.

"Is the cafeteria here any good?"

"Not really."

Harris shrugged. He could take a hint.

"But I know a better spot in town," Jack gestured to the door. "How about I meet you at the gatehouse in ten?"

Harris smiled. "Sounds like a plan."

• • •

Miraculously for midday, they found two parking spaces opposite Holy Trinity Church on 36th Street in Georgetown. Jack slid his rented Camry along the curb and Harris squeezed his Jeep in behind.

"I've never been to this part of DC before," Harris mentioned as he rose from the driver's seat and met Jack on the sidewalk.

"Yeah. Virginia's a shithole."

Harris wasn't sure what to make of Jack. On the way over, down the GW Parkway and across the Potomac, a part of Harris began to regret asking Jack to lunch. It seemed like the polite thing to do at the time—they were headed downrange together—but the more he thought about it, the less he wanted to try and put a dent in Jack's armor. Comments like that one told Harris all he needed to know: Some people just didn't want friends.

As they crossed N Street, Jack pointed toward the gothic spires of Healy Hall a few blocks away. "I went to school there."

"Wow. Georgetown?" Harris fished for a conversation starter. "Lots of memories, I bet."

Jack turned with a slight twinkle behind his sunglasses. "They're more like lessons."

Harris wished he had just gotten back on I-95 and went home. "Where you taking me?"

"It's just up here. A cozy little spot called The Tombs."

Jack showed Harris down a short flight of steps into the cellar of a Federal-style townhouse beneath the 1789 Restaurant. Coming through the door, The Tombs reminded Harris of a bunker. It was warm and dimly lit and full of muddied voices. A fire roared inside a brick hearth. Memorabilia from Georgetown's storied history covered the walls.

"You can sit anywhere you like," a bow-tie-clad waiter called.

"I gotta show you something." Jack took Harris over to a dark corner and bent toward a picture on the wall that showed roughly two-dozen men in tank tops and shorts huddled together along the Potomac's edge. A sign at their feet read: "Hoyas Crew, Class of 2007." He pointed to a beaming, boyish face jutting up from the middle row. "See that strapping young lad there?"

"For real? You rowed?"

"Yeah."

"Me too."

"No shit! Where at?"

"San Mateo High," Harris admitted. "But still."

"That's cool, man."

Harris watched Jack smile for the first time.

They eased into a booth just as a waiter swung by and asked, "What can I get you to drink?"

"Jameson," said Jack. "On the rocks."

Harris did a double-take. "Make that two."

The waiter took their order and went back to the bar.

Harris saw Jack take stock of everyone sitting near them, scanning their eyes and scouring their intent, not unlike a machine. He still hadn't a clue of what to make of Jack. "Did you serve at all?"

"In a uniform?" Jack made a final glance at the crowd. "No. No, I've been with the company since right out of college. I did an internship in Ryan's office and then went to the Farm."

"Ryan?"

"Sorry," Jack paused. "Director Freeman. He was good friends with my dad near the end. Looked after my mom and me for a while."

Harris tightened his lips. "I take it he passed?"

"Yeah."

Their waiter returned and set two glasses on the table. "Are you guys ready to order?"

"Um," Jack peeked at the menu. "Hanger steak. Medium rare."

"Just a Caesar salad for me. No chicken. Thanks."

"So, yeah," Jack added with a sigh as the waiter stepped out of earshot, "my dad was with the company, too. He died when I was five—it's been twenty-six years yesterday, actually. Ryan put down the guy who did it."

Harris looked to his lap. "I'm sorry."

"Eh," Jack shrugged, "it was a long time ago. So what's up with you? Tell me your story."

"Me? Shit…" Harris' eyes widened and he thought for a moment. "Well, I'm from the Bay Area—San Mateo. I enlisted fresh out of high school; started at Team 3 in Coronado and been with the command for about six years. I've flown around the world a couple times. I'm sure you can guess where." He sipped his whiskey. "My son, Ben's, in kindergarten. He's autistic, so—um—he can't really speak and he gets pretty fixated on stuff. But I swear he's the most beautiful thing I've ever seen. My wife is expecting a girl around the end of May, so we're excited about that." Harris thought again. "I dunno, what else is there?"

"Siblings?"

"I have a little sister back in California, although we don't talk too much," said Harris. "And my brother, he died when we were teenagers."

Jack ran his finger along the rim of his glass. "I never knew my brother."

Harris pressed into the leather padding on the bench and crossed his arms. "You ready for this, man?"

"Are you?"

Harris affected an uneasy grin. "Isn't it your turf?"

"Oh, it's nobody's turf," Jack drank. "I'll tell you a secret, Robert. There's something brewing. I don't know what yet, but it's coming like a freight train. And once it hits," he shook his head, "you and me will be right on the tracks."

Harris arched his eyebrows. "Hey, I say bring it."

"Okay," Jack nodded.

Harris dropped his elbow on the table and raised his glass. "But you know what? At least we'll have each other."

Jack clinked his glass against Harris'. "Until then, I guess we're just two guys drinking in a fucking basement."

CHAPTER 46

THE C-37A'S ENGINES gave a high-pitched whine as it taxied to the military apron at Ben Gurion International Airport. Freeman unbuckled his seatbelt and leaned forward to see out the cabin window. It was well after dark and the runway lights twinkled in the distance. After eleven hours in flight, Freeman was ready to claw through the fuselage.

Freeman had worried about Jack all morning, and it wasn't until Grace Shaw called during a refueling stop in Germany to update him on the PAC-ER briefing at Langley that he put his mind at ease, assured that Jack at least survived the night. Now his thoughts agonized over a greater problem. His scheme to enlist Isaac's help in obtaining Alireza Fakhrizadeh's autopsy report rested on a deal which had—quite literally—evaporated into a cloud of smoke over Beirut. Walid Rada was gone, and with him, went any incentive for Isaac to cooperate. Touching down in Tel Aviv for the second time in as many weeks, Freeman was left to do little but pray that his gamble would hold against the wave of chaos erupting from Lebanon.

A handful of Suburbans unceremoniously met the D/CIA and his security detail on the apron. Shrugging off the jet lag, he descended the airstairs to the tarmac and climbed into the second SUV.

After thirty minutes, Freeman arrived at a fortified campus of spare concrete buildings a few miles north of Tel Aviv that hid discreetly between the Glilot Interchange and a Cineplex. While the existence of the complex was technically a state secret in Israel, it was commonly known to any of the motorists who whisked by on the highway as the headquarters of Mossad. Clearing the checkpoints, the Suburbans crawled up to the front entrance. Waiting on the steps—a graying frame buttressed by a hooked cane in the blunted glow of floodlights—was Binyamin Isaac.

Freeman stepped out of the SUV and shook Isaac's bony, knotted hand. "Good to see you again so soon, Benny," he said.

Isaac's beady blue eyes narrowed behind his spectacles. "Really?"

The old man's embrace was surprisingly firm, verging on painful. "Sure," Freeman smiled, hiding his discomfort.

Isaac released his hold. "Come, Ryan," he turned, "let's get this over with." He keyed an elevator off the lobby that climbed to the top floor. It was nearly eight o'clock and the bulk of Mossad's headquarters staff had already gone for the night, leaving the featureless corridors eerily vacant. Isaac led Freeman down the corridor and through the secretary's anteroom to his spartan office overlooking Israel's coastal plain.

Once the door shut behind them, Freeman made his move. "Benny, I can't apologize enough for what happened in Beirut."

Isaac set his cane against an armchair and eased himself down. "Why?"

"What?" His demeanor caught Freeman off guard again.

"Why would you apologize?"

"We fucked up," Freeman admitted as if it was brutally obvious.

"Hardly," he dismissed. "These things happen."

Freeman sat on the adjacent sofa. "It doesn't concern you that Hezbollah captured Rada after he's been exposed to your officers?"

"It might if Hezbollah actually took him."

"What makes you think that?" Freeman grinned to hide his frustration.

"Well, what makes you think Hezbollah's telling the truth?"

"You're getting at something here, so just—"

"When Hamawi came out on television and took responsibility for storming the airport," Isaac interrupted, "did he produce any evidence that Hezbollah well and truly took Rada? Did he say anything about ever prosecuting him?"

Freeman thought for an answer.

"Why not just put Rada in front of a bloody camera? It's not hard," he continued. "But no. It's been almost forty-eight hours and not one of our sources in Lebanon can confirm that, yes, Hezbollah has the man in a cell. It's as if he simply vanished—*poof*, gone, into the ether. Hamawi has no better idea of what happened to Walid Rada than we do, and it terrifies him that we may all become wise to the fact that he does not control his own party."

"Who does?" Freeman warily asked.

Isaac shrugged. "No one at the moment."

"So you're not upset?" Freeman looked down at his hands.

"Quite the opposite. This merely gives us an opportunity to pour salt in Hezbollah's wounds," Isaac ruled. "Rada is already dead."

Freeman wiped his face. "Did your people find it, Benny?

"Yes," he pressed into the chair. "A *sayan* in the Tehran police got hold of it from the city mortuary. We have a copy. It's in Persian, and a few of the photographs are—well, I think we did our job—but it's yours. A deal is a deal."

"Can I see it?"

"Before you leave," Isaac glanced at the credenza behind his desk. "I'm told you're not staying long."

"No," Freeman shook his head, "once we're done here, I'm heading back to the airport."

Isaac seemed disappointed. "You must be exhausted. Would you like a coffee?" he offered.

"Sure, thanks."

Isaac reached for a phone on the end table at his side and dialed the canteen downstairs, placing the order in Hebrew. "It'll be a minute." Isaac set the phone back on the cradle, scratched at his leg braces, and asked, "Could I get your opinion on something?"

"Yeah, absolutely," Freeman leaned in.

"It's troubled me."

"Go ahead."

"Ali Mamlouk…" Isaac began and took a sudden glance at his watch.

Freeman wondered if he was walking into a trap, although for the life of him he couldn't figure out what it might be. Something about Isaac disturbed him. He was nothing like the playful menace who cooked Freeman breakfast on his last trip to Tel Aviv. The old man who received him that night was a shell: cold, aloof, and peculiarly unnerved.

"My people had a chat with him in Hama," Isaac said of the former head of the Syrian National Security Bureau and close confidant of President Hafez Jadid. Driven underground after the civil war's barbarous conclusion, Major General Mamlouk was captured in Tartus earlier that month by JSOC's Task Force OLYMPIA and held prisoner at Hama Air Base. To sweeten their deal to get a hold of Alireza Fakhrizadeh's autopsy report, Freeman arranged for Mossad to have access to Mamlouk before he was shipped off to face trial at The Hague. Unknown to Freeman or anyone in CIA at the time, Mamlouk was an Israeli asset during the civil war, reporting back to Mossad from within the regime's inner circle—until Qasem Shateri unearthed his plans for a palace coup in Damascus and placed Mamlouk under house arrest.

"Wade told me," Freeman nodded.

"Did he tell you what we learned?"

Freeman shook his head.

"No, of course he didn't," Isaac affected his familiar grin. "Anyway, Mamlouk opened up to us, and I'm told he was quite surprised to see us after all this time. We asked about the sarin precursors—"

"Benny," Freeman rolled his eyes. He knew where Isaac was going, and as far as he was concerned it was a crackpot theory without basis in reality, debunked by every Western intelligence agency. But Isaac wouldn't drop it.

"Hear me out, Ryan," he insisted. "When we pressed him, Mamlouk swore that the regime possessed 581 tons of precursor agents—DF and isopropyl alcohol. Match that against the 580 tons the OPCW accounted for and destroyed in the Med..."

"Just like I told you," said Freeman. "So is it done now?"

"Not at all," Isaac countered. "That's one ton still missing."

Freeman bit his lip.

"Mamlouk was already under house arrest when Jadid was torn apart. We have to take him at his word. Of course, he's on his way to The Hague now and has lawyers out the ass, so he's as good as gone. I'll admit we've hit something of a dead end, and my *katsas* in Damascus haven't done much better."

"Benny," Freeman blinked, "why is this bothering you?"

Isaac was still for a moment. "I'll tell you the truth, Ryan..."

Freeman braced himself.

"Those cruise missiles seized on the Gulf of Aden, the ones your man in Tehran got wind of, the ones *Hajj* Qasem tried to base in Sudan—we've seen them before."

"In Syria?" Freeman nearly whispered.

Isaac nodded. "Late last June, a freighter linked to the Quds Force docked at Latakia. A *katsa* observed ten, forty-foot shipping containers being offloaded and placed on trucks. Our overhead reconnaissance followed the trucks back to the Syrian 155th Brigade's garrison on Mount Abu al-Ata in Qutayfa. At the time, we judged that the containers were likely each retrofitted to store and launch Soumar cruise missiles based on a reverse-engineered Russian design—just like the containers aboard the *Catarina A.*"

Freeman's eyes were fixed on the old man. "You're sure, Benny?"

"Positive," he said. "Now, a few weeks later, on the night of the uprising in Damascus, we intercepted a call from the Iranian embassy to the commander of the 155th Brigade. Our analysts identified the voice in Damascus as Qasem Shateri. In that call, we recorded Shateri authorizing the use of chemical weapons against IDF units in the Golan Heights."

Freeman was stunned. "Why have I never heard this before?"

Isaac continued. "It's like a page out of Saddam's playbook in the Gulf War: drag Israel into the conflict and it becomes politically impossible for Turkey, or Jordan, or the Saudis to fight beside us; shatter the alliance."

"Those warheads were armed with sarin?"

"At least five by our count," he said. "We met in the Kirya with the PM. Avi wanted Sayeret Matkal to raid the base and seize the containers, capture the evidence intact, but there wasn't nearly enough time to plan the operation. So the IAF scrambled F-15s and targeted the bunkers where we thought the containers were being stored. You remember that strike?"

"Yeah."

"Good man," Isaac grinned. "BDA could only verify that three of the ten containers were destroyed—the other seven, we don't know. I tried to get men on the ground to confirm, but the situation was just too fluid. For what it's worth, the Syrian personnel who survived the attack all fled their posts. The next morning, a local rebel commander in Qutayfa radioed a *katsa* that armed, Lebanese-accented men were spotted on the base. We had another source reporting that seven trucks were later seen driving toward the Lebanese border. Officially, we—the Israeli intelligence community—believe that the missiles were taken back to Iran on a Mahan Air charter out of Beirut. But personally, I don't buy it for second."

Freeman nervously shook his head. "You don't think…"

"I do, Ryan," Isaac said. "I think those missiles are still in the Beqaa Valley, in storage for a rainy day. There are caves in the valley large enough to hide them, far off the grid, in places where the Lebanese army won't dare go. And I'll tell you something else: I think Ibrahim al-Din is still very much alive, and I think he took them, on Qasem Shateri's orders. I think they're working together—I think they have for a long time—and I think they're behind the airport attack. I can't prove it… Yet. But I think al-Din took Walid Rada, one of the few men who could help us locate those missiles. And I think you do as well, Ryan."

Freeman felt his stomach turn.

"Do you know now why I accepted your offer?"

Freeman's face went flush. "Benny, I'm sorry."

"Like I said," Isaac tightened his lips, "it isn't your fault. It's Shateri's."

There was a knock at the door.

"Yes?"

A steward entered with a tray.

"Just there, on the table," Isaac smiled. "Thank you."

The steward placed the tray down and quietly let herself out.

Freeman leaned in from the sofa and grabbed the carafe.

"No, no," Isaac swat his hand away with a huff. "You're a guest."

"You're too much," Freeman backed off.

Isaac poured two cups, set one on a saucer and passed it to Freeman.

"So this report—" Freeman added as he steadied the cup in his hands.

Isaac sipped his coffee. "We may have located Azzam al-Nakhalah. Have I told you that?"

Freeman knew Isaac was deflecting, but he also knew it was often best to humor the old man and let him come around in time. "How?"

But Isaac only grinned, unwilling to give away his secrets. "Send out all your dogs and one may return with prey."

Freeman arched his eyebrows and placed his coffee on the table.

"A source who works one of the smuggling rings through the Sinai helped us identify a young woman in Deir al-Balah. Apparently Brother al-

Nakhalah enjoys this woman's bed on occasion—when he's not murdering our soldiers. Shin Bet placed the girl's house under surveillance. We'll pay him a visit next time he stops by."

"And will that put a stop to this mess in Gaza?" asked Freeman.

"That's up to them," Isaac said after another sip, "to Hamas, to Islamic Jihad, to all of those bearded jackals. Once I leave Azzam al-Nakhalah to rot, I'll come for Colonel Abadi, and then one day I'll come for *Hajj* Qasem himself. So that's up to them, Ryan. How soon do they want to die?"

Freeman crossed his hands in his lap. "The White House is concerned."

"About a ground invasion?"

"Yes."

"They shouldn't be," Isaac assured. "That won't be necessary."

"And we can count on seeing Avi in Annapolis?"

"With bells on," the old man smiled.

Freeman nodded. "Is Mehdi Vaziri coming around?"

"Another dead end, I'm afraid," Isaac grimly shook his head. "The whole thing was a mistake. He has next to zero current intelligence value; anything he can tell us, we've already known for years. And the French are getting tired of it. What happened to the Banisadrs spooked them."

"I've never seen the Iranians do anything like that."

"No, neither have I," Isaac agreed. "Shateri orchestrated that scene, too. Out of their embassy in Vienna. His orcs are stalking Europe—searching. They'll never stop. We can't keep hiding Vaziri and his wife in the middle of Paris. The risk is too great and I don't expect the French to shoulder it. So, it's fallen in my lap to convince them to come to Israel. I'm going to Paris to do it person. If I can't persuade them, we'll just have to drug them and bring them back anyway," he shrugged. "But I won't waste any more time on these people."

"So this report?" Freeman tried his luck again. It was getting late.

"Yes, of course," Isaac pressed on his cane and came to his feet with a grunt. "Just a moment." He hobbled to the credenza behind his desk and opened a cabinet, revealing a small safe. He crouched down and spun in the combination. "It wasn't too hard to find, actually."

"I'm glad to hear that," Freeman said from the couch.

Isaac shut the safe and stood upright with a sealed manila envelope in his left hand. Making his way back to the chair, he eased himself down again and offered it to Freeman. "It's yours, Ryan."

Freeman reached out to take it, but Isaac's grip wouldn't budge.

"When you find Doctor Fakhrizadeh," the old man's eyes simmered, "make sure he stays dead."

Freeman froze.

"And do not ever mistake me for a fool again." Isaac released his hold.

"I won't," Freeman muttered.

"Good." Just as Isaac eased back in his chair, the phone on the end table at his side chirped. He answered on the second ring.

Freeman's hands trembled. His palms were glazed over in a cold sweat.

Isaac held the phone to his mouth and mumbled a few terse words in Hebrew. Freeman watched and squirmed slightly in his chair. Once something was supposedly agreed upon, Isaac placed the phone back on the cradle and smiled at Freeman across the coffee table, massaging the serial number tattooed on the inside of his left forearm that had stretched and faded with age—grayed, like him.

"Can I show you something?"

Freeman hesitated at first, still shaking. "All right."

"Walk with me."

They left the office and went slowly, Isaac balanced by his cane, down the desolate corridor flanked by doors marked with vague acronyms. "Do you recall what I told you last we met, about those unpleasant decisions we make?"

"I do."

Isaac stopped at a door and punched in a code on a keypad above the lock. "Here's what comes of those decisions."

The door opened upon a buzzing operations center. Freeman saw it through the electric glow of computer monitors. A pitched floor held five tiers of workstations split by a center aisle. Support personnel moved about the room, hurried in their manner but hushed in their words, speaking only in purposeful whispers. Still, Freeman found the tempo stifling. At the base of the room was an imposing screen covered with flight data, mechanical readouts and a soaring, monochromatic vantage over the dusty streets of Khartoum from the FLIR camera of an Eitan reconnaissance drone.

A Mercedes SUV sat in the crosshairs, its headlights sweeping ahead.

Isaac kept his eyes on the screen. "Men like you and I, Ryan, are sculptors. We're given these rambling blocks of stone, quarried from the most uncivilized places on Earth, and then directed by our betters to mold it into something much more...agreeable. So we dutifully take our chisels and we chip away until out of this incoherent, ghastly mess emerges 'truth'—like a rotting corpse revealed in the thaw."

The Mercedes moved easily through the maze of rooftops. Khartoum's evening rush had already subsided and the stream of motorbikes and taxis flowed with little resistance. A Toyota pickup crawled a dozen meters behind the SUV, driven by operatives of Kidon, Mossad's infamous hit squad. It had trailed the Mercedes from the airport.

"Who's in the car, Benny?"

"Our mutual friend, Colonel Abadi," Isaac casually replied. "He's just returned from Tehran—had a meeting on Islamic Jihad with Shateri and Saeed Mofidi, I believe."

A lump formed in Freeman's throat.

The Mercedes slipped into the diplomatic quarter in the well-heeled streets around the International Stadium.

"One might say the sculptor's most important tool is the chisel. It cuts away at the excess, measured and controlled," the old man continued. "But they're wrong. It's the hammer." Isaac pointed at the screen. "Do you see that sedan parked just ahead?"

"Yes," Freeman's voice trembled.

"And do you see that walled villa right across the street?"

"Yes."

"That's the Iranian embassy. Keep watching the sedan." Isaac turned to Freeman. "It's the hammer that knows when—and how—to apply force."

The Mercedes was three blocks from the embassy gates.

"When Abadi had our boy executed," Isaac said, "he did it with a simple phone call. With one call, Abadi was his judge, his jury, and his executioner. Now, with a phone call."

Two blocks.

"I am his judge."

One block.

"I am his jury."

The Mercedes pulled to the gates and the sedan across the street burst with a brilliant white light that consumed the screen, temporarily blinding the Eitan's camera. There was no sound to match the carnage. The light quickly retreated, revealing two twisted, smoking, burning wrecks of metal. A flaming silhouette lurched free from the Mercedes' rear passenger seat, staggered, and fell limp at the gates.

"And now I am his executioner."

Baranov was camouflaged in the low brush. Aided by a slim sliver of moonlight, he looked down from the dunes and scanned eighty meters of open beach. The Ionian Sea gently washed over the shoreline ahead, although farther out on the inky swells, Baranov saw only darkness. He laid an arm over the *ranet* resting on the ground at his side, and waited.

Kotov was crouched a few feet behind him and kept the suppressed barrel of his AK-103 trained toward the guardrail of the E90 motorway. The Spetsnaz operators had been on the move for four days, carefully and methodically covering eighteen hundred kilometers from the Black Forest, through the Austrian and Italian Alps, past Rome and Naples, before finally reaching their extraction point along the eastern coast of Calabria. Only the two of them would escort their precious cargo off the continent; Ignatev, Akhmadov and Kakiyev were busy hiding any trace of their operation. As he and Kotov separated from the others, Baranov made it clear: they all had to leave Europe as soon as possible.

With forewarning of that encroaching chaos in mind, Baranov checked his watch again. The glowing green hands were joined together. It was midnight. He took a small Maglite from his coat pocket, leveled it toward the sea, and clicked it on in two short bursts. Just then—a short distance down the beach—three quick flashes replied in the night.

"It's time."

Kotov dropped his rifle on its sling and came to Baranov. They grabbed the handles on either end of the *ranet,* lifted all ninety kilograms of the trunk's stainless steel shell, and made their way over the dunes. They crossed the beach as the moonlight gradually illuminated a Zodiac rigid-inflatable boat sitting in the breaking surf. Another Spetsnaz operator dressed in a full wetsuit and wielding a Knight's Armament PDW stood beside the tender. As Baranov and Kotov approached, they recognized that it was Zaytsev and set the *ranet* on the compacted sand.

"Privyet, moy droog," Baranov greeted him with a firm handshake.

"Where are the others?" asked Zaytsev.

"Covering our tracks," Baranov answered. "Vlasiyev and the rest are still in Paris. They'll fly out separately."

Zaytsev nodded. "Let's move."

Baranov and Kotov placed the *ranet* in the Zodiac and then all three men eased it into the surf, hopping in one at a time once the waves caught its keel. Zaytsev ripped the outboard motor's starter cord, steered the boat over the swells, and sped from the Italian coast.

A kilometer offshore, Baranov spotted the swaying hull of a ninety-eight-foot flybridge yacht—the *Calliope*—sitting low on the waterline. Her hydraulic swim platform was raised, revealing a transom garage at the yacht's stern just wide enough to stow the Zodiac. As Zaytsev skillfully maneuvered the tender alongside, two more Spetsnaz operators—Ratskov and Lazarev—tossed a line and helped secure the Zodiac in the garage. With Kotov's help, Baranov pulled the *ranet* aboard and stowed the trunk in a compartment below deck that wasn't already crammed with extra fuel and provisions for the cruise ahead.

Calliope's engines rumbled to life and within minutes she sailed into the open sea. It would take another three days to cross the eastern Mediterranean, toward Lebanon—and Kazanoff.

"Gotta give the old man credit, he kept his end of the bargain." Freeman held the secure telephone's handset to his ear as he passively gazed at the stars beyond the cabin window. After refueling at Shannon Airport in Ireland, the C-37A continued on over the North Atlantic. Approaching the coast of Newfoundland at thirty thousand feet, the Gulfstream hit a patch of rough air, jolting the fuselage every few moments. It was the only thing keeping Freeman awake.

Weisel remained in her small cherry-paneled inner office on the seventh floor of the Truman Building, watching distant shadows dance through the floodlights cast on the Lincoln and Jefferson memorials. "You had no control over what happened in Beirut, Ryan."

"Yeah, and I'm beginning to worry that neither did Hezbollah."

"How so?"

A water glass trembled at his fingertips. "Isaac made a good point. When Hamawi took credit for the airport attack, notice that he never gave any proof that he actually had Walid Rada in custody; he never said anything about prosecuting him, or parading him in front of the cameras."

"So who the hell does have Rada?"

"That's what worries me, Angela."

Weisel crossed her legs. "Either way, you guys got what you needed."

"Yep," Freeman looked to the satchel at his feet that held the envelope containing Fakhrizadeh's autopsy report.

"Just so you heard me say it: Iran's gonna make a lot of noise about losing their ambassador, and Paulson wasn't happy."

Freeman shook his head. "Isaac totally ambushed me with that. He wanted me to watch. If we stick to the car bomb angle, we have plausible deniability."

"At least that's one more off his list," she sighed.

"Yeah, but Shateri won't take this lightly. We'll see blowback somewhere down the line—and sooner rather than later."

"I don't know what to expect anymore."

"How's everything on your end?"

Weisel swiveled her chair away from the windows. "Harold's heading out to Geneva tomorrow afternoon. He's meeting with Mofidi at Villa Tatiana the next morning. Listen, I'm sorry how this went down."

She could sense Freeman's unease through the phone.

"We'll do all we can to keep it quiet," Weisel assured.

"I appreciate it, Ange."

"Did you hear about the storm coming?"

"Which one," Freeman scoffed.

"No, I mean a real one," she said. "We're supposed to get a nor'easter next week—a foot of snow between here and New York. It'll be bad."

Freeman shook his head. "Figures."

"What time do you get in?"

"Wheels down at Andrews around three."

"God bless," she checked her watch. "Well anyway, take care, Ryan."

"See you soon, Angela." The line went dead, and the cabin rattled.

• • •

In the Cola neighborhood of Beirut, dawn was reluctant to break. Lost in the city's urban sprawl, the neighborhood's main intersection was divided in two by the heavy and bleak concrete pillars of an elevated highway running between downtown and the airport. At five-thirty that morning, buses, taxis and minivans were parked beneath the overpass, ready to depart for Baalbek, Tyre, or even Damascus. In the weary half-light of buzzing sodium lamps, none saw what hung just above their heads.

As rush hour gradually spun to life, Cola became more hectic and disorganized. Cars, delivery trucks and pedestrians mobbed the intersection; the first busses and taxis rolled away; and the hollow whine of engines and tires echoed between the pillars. At sunrise, as the *muezzin* of the nearby Hamra Mosque evoked the call to prayer, an elderly woman pointed up at the overpass and shrieked in horror. In minutes the highway above was closed to traffic in either direction and the intersection was choked with flashing lights and ISF police cruisers.

Walid Rada's charred corpse dangled from the guardrail.

Suspended only by ropes tied around his shoulder joints, he appeared like a shadow, a marionette without its puppeteer. The flames ate away his features, leaving a skeletal form of carbonized muscles clinging to bits of blackened bone, dusty ash and clenched teeth, frozen in an eternal, agonized rictus.

He stared without eyes.

Carved unevenly across his chest, like undercooked meat, was a message conveyed in English with one, simple word—an admonition for all to come...

Peace.

Those last days were indistinguishable. The sun was either up or down; it rained or it didn't. None of it had even the slightest bearing on him. As far as he was concerned, the universe was merely a passing tragedy staged beyond the windows of his gilded cage, and he was but a reluctant spectator eager to break for the exit. To Mehdi Vaziri, life slipped like ash through his fingers.

In those last days he became convinced—this was how it felt to be a ghost.

Vaziri was no longer that defiant figure in a green silk scarf who marched through Tehran with thousands in opposition to Ayatollah Khansari's regime. In a matter of weeks he had aged beyond his years. His bones were bowed in despair, and a haunted look settled behind his eyes. He became suspicious and resentful of the French National Police officers guarding his suite and of the doctors who came with their pills and syringes. They watched him constantly—through cameras embedded in the walls, through microphones hidden in the light fixtures. They watched him when he slept and when he ate; when he sat for hours on end, leering out at the Seine and the Tuileries Garden; when he went to relieve himself, he could count the seconds until one of his bodyguards gently tapped on the bathroom door, just to check if he was all right. Yet Vaziri reserved the brunt of his scorn for the Israelis. Like a child that tired of its new plaything and left it to collect dust in a corner, Mossad now rarely sent its people from the embassy. When the *katsas* did come to speak with Vaziri, they no longer had any interest in his accounts of the Green Movement, nor did they seek his input on the mindset of Iran's leaders. For both, there was a palpable sense of regret that their relationship ever began. Some days, Vaziri even wished that he was still under house arrest. At least then, if he were to die a prisoner, it might be in his own bed.

When Ezra came one morning and coldly broke the news that Nima and Roya Banisadr had been murdered, Vaziri almost shattered the bathroom mirror and slit his wrists. He held himself responsible. Vaziri knew that the ayatollah's spies scoured the continent for him, and with one, well-intentioned phone call—a kiss of death—he enveloped them in his own cursed fate. The future, it seemed, had passed him by, and Vaziri resigned that he would never be free. The only question, then, was what to do with the time he had left.

But he still clung to some shred of dignity, to the notion that he could choose. Fatemeh, for her part, was already gone: slipped fully beneath a tide of depression, self-loathing and barbiturates. She didn't care what happened next. After the Banisadrs were murdered, Vaziri's *Police nationale* detail doubled the number of plainclothes officers standing watch in the lobby, any vehicles that loitered along the curb outside Le Meurice were promptly shooed away by hotel security, and Ezra aggressively insisted that he and Fatemeh come to Israel. He admitted that they would be safe there, far beyond the reach of Qasem Shateri's hitmen. They would have a semblance of freedom in Israel, but it would be bitter at best, and whatever remained of their lives would be tainted with the sting of treason. To him, that fate was worse than death.

A cloud hung over Mehdi Vaziri that morning. The bread and cottage cheese on the table before him went stale; his tea ran cold. His only appetite was for a swift end. In those last days he felt the executioner's blade at his neck—and he almost welcomed it.

"You should eat," Ezra urged from the high-back chair across from him.

"I'm not hungry."

Ezra clicked his pen and set his notepad on the table. "Mehdi, I wanted to ease into this, but I'm not sure how, so I'll just say it," he began with some hesitancy. "The French are revoking your visas. They want you and Fatemeh out of the country by the end of next week."

Vaziri dipped his head.

"We've tried to stall them, to convince them to wait," Ezra attempted to reassure, "but they're set. It's too dangerous to keep you in Paris."

"We aren't contagious. You brought us here."

"No, of course not," said Ezra. "But you're guests in this country—we are, too—and Mossad can't take the risk of something happening to you here. You *must* come to Israel."

Vaziri didn't reply.

"Your safety is important to us, Mehdi. We value the sacrifices that you and Fatemeh have made to join us," Ezra continued. "To make the case, to clear any doubts that may remain, our director-general—Binyamin Isaac—is coming here, to the hotel, at noon tomorrow. He wants to speak with you in person, and it's his wish that you and Fatemeh will return with him."

Vaziri turned his eyes to the windows.

"I'm sorry that it's come to this…but there's no other way."

The curtains rustled in a room on the first floor of the Westin-Vendôme hotel. Behind them, a Spectra M laser microphone was aimed over Rue de Castiglione to the windows of suite 102/103 at Le Meurice, reading the vibrations on the glass. Doku Vlasiyev sat on the bedspread while Pokhrovskii monitored the audio signal and rapidly translated the conversation by hand.

"Shit," Pokhrovskii muttered as he scribbled across a page.

"What is it?"

"Binyamin Isaac. He's coming tomorrow. Noon."

Vlasiyev's spine straightened. "I'll make the call."

"Hold up," Harris panted as the frigid air singed his throat.

Z jogged in place on the wet sand. "I know you're not quitting, *ese.*"

"Fuck no." Harris pressed his hands to his hips and caught his breath, admiring the fearsome beauty of the sea. The Atlantic was swollen and gray, rising and falling on turbulent swells that crashed ashore with a biting wind. Despite the sour weather, they had run alongside the dunes for a mile and a half from the ranges by the command's head shed to the northern perimeter fence of Dam Neck Annex that crossed the beach and gradually sank beneath the roiling surf.

Harris bent over and massaged his calves. He had been wide-awake all night. While Sandra slept soundly next to him, Harris stared up at the ceiling and asked himself how he could possibly summon the strength to tell her that he was leaving again. He also questioned—more than once that night—his own sanity. But it was done. The pieces were set on the board and the players awaited their order to move. Harris was headed to Iran and his focus now was on recruiting the remaining three operators in the team. He planned to break the news out there on that beach, just the two of them, but Z spoke first.

"So have you thought about coming over to the cadre?"

"Huh?" The question caught Harris off guard.

"Green Team," Z called over the wind. "The guys are stoked about it."

"Well…" he turned to waves.

Z planted his feet in the sand. "Come on, dude."

"Just listen for a minute."

"What are you waiting for?"

"Hear me out," Harris insisted. "Please just listen." A gust sheared the crests off the dunes. Grains of sand stung their faces and a light snow began falling from the clouds above. "Last week we were on the range and I got paged. Do you remember that?"

"Yeah," Z replied with an irritated nod.

"Wade was in the team room when I got there—"

"For fuck's sake, you gotta be kidding me, Robby."

"Please, Z," Harris held out his hand. "He said CIA is planning an op and needs a JSOC element to go downrange for a few months and get it done. Wade asked me to lead it."

"Is that why you wanted me to lie to your wife?"

"I drove up to DC yesterday and sat in on a briefing at Langley," Harris continued. "It's for real, man. And I have to do it."

Z crossed his arms. "Where?"

"I can't."

"Where?"

"Iran," Harris revealed with a slip of his tongue.

"Jesus-fucking-Christ," Z's head shook.

"I'm commanding a four-man team. The other three are mine to pick. Z, I'm asking you, Farah and Whitford to come with me."

"Why are you doing this?"

"What?"

Z dropped his arms. "Robby, if I had what you've got, I'd walk away from this bullshit and never look back. You've got the perfect girl who's head-over-heals for you. You've made the sweetest kid I've ever seen. Why are you doing this, Robby? Just tell me why."

Harris' eyes welled. He knew how foolish he was. He couldn't answer.

"Why, Robby?"

"I don't know," he said. "Okay? I don't know."

"Talk to me, buddy," Z lowered his voice. "Tell me what's going on."

Harris took a deep breath. "A few weeks ago, in Syria, we raided a safe house in Tartus. I was part of the roof team, led the stack up to the door.

We breached it, but the helo pilots put us on the wrong house. We went around the alley and gave overwatch to the other Delta guys inside. After the firefight, once the smoke cleared, I went inside; saw what we'd done," he paused. "Upstairs, there was a PKM aimed at the door. I would've come right through there if the pilots hadn't screwed up. It would've sawed me in half. I haven't been able to get that out of my mind. And I've asked why countless times. Why'd they make that mistake? Why'd I survive? Why am I still here?"

"Robby—"

"And I can't find an answer," Harris choked back tears. "It was dumb luck. I can't explain it…just like I can't explain this. But I have to go. I have to do this—and I know I can't do it without you."

"Does Sandy know?"

"Not yet," Harris shook his head. "She'll probably divorce me."

Z relaxed his shoulders and gave a smirk. "Well, maybe," he said. "But I'm sure as shit not letting your stupid ass go this one alone." He swallowed Harris in his arms and pulled him in tight. "I just hope you realize that you are, by far, the dumbest motherfucker alive."

"Yep," Harris nodded as Z pulled away, "I have you to remind me."

Just then Harris caught something in the distance. Far up the shoreline, beyond the perimeter fence, an old woman stood on the beach tossing bread to the swarming gulls. Her back was turned to him and the icy wind played with her hair. Harris understood then, in that moment, the gift that Sandra had given him. It was an appreciation for ordinary life; for the faith in our quiet, shared humanity when all around seemed gray and foul; for the strength to stand defiant against the storm and keep to something as simple and trivial as ripping up a bit of bread and throwing it to the gulls; for the belief that any of it mattered. Harris understood then what he fought for. It wasn't for God or country, but for the dumb luck that allowed a woman like Sandra to love him with all her heart—and he promised that if that same dumb luck carried him home just once more, he would hold on and never let go again.

Nina burst through the door with rage in her eyes.

The station's meager staff instantly went silent and warily looked up from their desks. Al-Jazeera echoed from a television mounted to the wall; a grainy cell phone video of a body dangling from a highway overpass played on the screen with a breaking news Chyron. She clutched a manila folder and scanned over the tops of the cubicles for her prey.

Tom Stessel stepped from his office to see what was wrong.

"You!" she barked.

"I have nothing to say to you," he huffed disdainfully.

"Give me what I need to find al-Din," Nina came toward him and jabbed her finger at his chest, "or get the *fuck* out of my way!"

Stessel was shocked. "Have you lost your goddamn mind?"

"Oh," she shook her head, "a long time ago, motherfucker."

"You're finished," he hissed.

"Fuck you!"

The whole station gawked at them. "Get out," Stessel went flush. "I'm calling the ambassador. *And* Langley."

"You're such a prick," she sneered.

"If you're not out of Beirut by tomorrow night—"

"Look at this!" Nina ripped a photograph from the folder and flung it in Stessel's face.

He picked it up. "How did—"

"It's Rada!" she spat before he could utter another syllable.

Stessel was disgusted at the sight. The photo was taken in the back of an ambulance and showed Rada's charred corpse staring out from the open seam of a body bag. "What is that?"

"That says 'Peace,'" Nina turned to her audience, "carved into his fucking chest." She lowered her voice. "And it's not in Arabic, it's not in Hebrew. It's in English. It's a message. To you, to me— to all of us." Nina's words hung over the room. She glared at Stessel. "This is the work of a psychopath, and I promise you, we have not seen the end of it."

The clouds broke, and in the waxing moonlight, Anwar Sabah first spotted the Nissan Patrol, its headlights doused, emerging from fields below. It drove slowly—its engine a dull rumble lost in the night air—and crept up the hillside toward them.

Al-Din stood a few paces ahead of Sabbah; a guard hovered at his back. Five more were fanned out in a protective cordon around the SUVs and the bunker entrance, cradling their Kalashnikovs.

In another moment, the Patrol came over the rise and stopped. Sabbah felt a lump in his throat. A breeze swallowed him; the hair on his neck stood on end. Three Spetsnaz operators dismounted—all in black with rifles slung from their chests—and silently scanned the area. One went to the rear passenger window and knocked. The door opened, and Kazanoff stepped out.

Al-Din flung his cigarette to the dirt and took Kazanoff's hand. "All of this belongs to Abu Ali," he said, pointing to the swath of cannabis and poppy fields that ran clear on to the outskirts of Baalbek, sixteen kilometers east. That rugged stretch of Lebanon sat inside the realm of Hassan "Abu Ali" Meqdad, leader of a powerful Shiite clan that held strongholds in South Beirut and the Beqaa Valley. The clan was entrenched in the Lebanese drug trade and enforced its stake over the country's underground with a militia that boasted two thousand armed men in their ranks. Coincidently, al-Din's third wife was a daughter of Hassan Meqdad, securing a quiet alliance between the two.

He turned Kazanoff's attention to a cinder block structure jutting out from the hillside. "Jihad al-Binna dug dozens of these bunkers all along this edge of the valley. The Islamic Resistance used them to stockpile arms and matériel," al-Din explained. "After the July War, Hezbollah ordered them evacuated for more secure shelters farther north, around Hermel. Abu Ali seized this territory shortly after. Now he looks after it for us."

"What do you have for me?"

Al-Din cocked his head to the side. "A gift."

The cinder block structure disguised the bunker entrance to look like any of the mundane outbuildings dotting the farms across the valley. Its rusted door was tall and wide enough to fit a truck. Al-Din's men heaved the door aside and switched on an electric lantern. Sabbah followed them in.

Past the bunker entrance, carved into the hillside like a yawning mouth, sat seven forty-foot shipping containers lined up in a neat row. The lantern's glare played in the darkness. Kazanoff stepped toward a container and laid his hand on the cold corrugated steel wall.

"There are four missiles to a container," al-Din breathed. "Twenty of the warheads carry four hundred kilos of high explosive; the remaining eight are loaded with sarin, one of which can create a cloud three kilometers long and five hundred meters wide—killing everything below. Enough to consume a city."

Kazanoff looked back to al-Din. "Or an army."

He was supposed to have forty-eight hours. Instead, Haddad had less than a day. Around noon, he received an encrypted instant message on his Pidgin account. It was from Anwar Sabbah, and coldly revealed that the director-general of Mossad was due in Paris to meet with Mehdi Vaziri at noon the very next morning. Eliminating both Binyamin Isaac and his turncloak defector in one strike was not, the message explained, an opportunity that they could let slip away. Haddad was instructed to assemble the bomb as quickly as possible and prepare the brothers for martyrdom.

Giving an alibi to their grandmother, the boys joined him and retrieved the box truck they had stolen from the bakery in Reims and emptied Haddad's storage units. They then drove two hours and forty minutes east of Clichy-sous-Bois to an abandoned open-pit slate quarry near the commune of Rimogne in the Ardennes forest along the Belgian border. It was dusk when they arrived.

At three in the morning—after hours of arduous, dangerous work—the bomb had finally taken shape. Haddad clicked on a flashlight and shined it over the cargo bay. Held in place with wooden boards nailed to the floor were sixteen fifty-five-gallon plastic drums arranged in the shape of a letter T with the top flush against the front of the cargo bay, closest to the truck's cab. Each drum weighed roughly five hundred pounds and was filled with a mixture of ammonium nitrate fertilizer, acetylene and liquid nitromethane. An intricate web of blasting caps, shock tubes and wires connected the drums to a single electric fuse that ran through a fish-tank conduit between two holes drilled into the cargo box and the cab. That, in turn, was soldered to a set of batteries in the rear of the cab and finally to a switch taped under the dashboard. Haddad was proud of his creation; once the bomb detonated, he assured the boys, it would incinerate an entire block.

Zyed gushed that evening. He promised Haddad every few moments that he would not fail, that he would see the mission to the end. Sajid, however, was another issue.

Since Fabrice's murder, the boys spent practically all of their time in Haddad's flat. They pored over the Quran, studied the words of the Prophet Mohammed, and listened intently to Haddad's stories of the martyrs he fought alongside in Lebanon. The praise and adoration they received in death was far sweeter than any earthly pleasure they knew in life. The Islamic Resistance would exalt the boys' names for all time, Haddad foretold. Zyed and Sajid Bata: the heroic *mujahedeen* who slew the Zionist spymaster. Millions of Muslims across the world would rise up and cheer at their success. That promise seemed to persuade Sajid, but he was not eager to die. Then again, Haddad thought, what fourteen-year-old was? In the end, it mattered little to him. As long as Sajid got in that truck with his brother, what went on inside the boy's head was meaningless.

And if not—Haddad would kill him anyway.

After a final inspection of the bomb, Haddad shut the truck's rear roller door and snapped a heavy padlock over the latch. Zyed and his brother followed in the Skoda Octavia. Reaching Clichy-sous-Bois, Haddad pulled the truck into a far corner of the parking lot at the E Leclerc shopping center off Boulevard Gagarine and left a note covering the VIN plate: *"Not abandoned. Please do not tow. Needs battery and cable."* At La Forestière, they rehearsed their plan one final time before going their separate ways.

The faint glimmer of light was mounting in the sky. Neither of the boys slept. Zyed stood before the window for hours, smiling at the sight of his final sunrise. Sajid hid beneath his bed covers, wide awake, and praying that dawn might never come—his eyes wet with wasted tears.

CHAPTER 47

BUT DAWN CAME.

"It's time, Sajid."

Imagine you have cancer. That was how his brother once described it, how he justified it, how he coped, how he held his tenuous grasp.

Death is guaranteed. It works patiently, unprejudiced, at its own pace. Sajid witnessed it more intimately than most his age, and he understood that, overwhelmingly, it calls before its victims have agreed to let go. It selfishly, rudely drags us over the threshold without empathy, for better or worse. One by one, as it exacts its toll, every living thing is destined to die alone. We accept this, aware from our initial conscious thought that our communal, private fate will not come at a time of our choosing. If we are lucky, we blind ourselves with a blissful parade of artificial, chemically induced emotions to subdue any tickle of the inevitable, all the while stealing anxious glances at a clock without hands.

We unconditionally surrender to the whims of an indifferent universe.

Zyed preached that they were offered a gift. They had an opportunity to thwart that cruel nature, a chance to subvert the guarded plots of their author and opt for their tale to end before it was fully told. Unlike billions before and countless scores to follow, they had a precious chance to die together.

"Wake up." Zyed Bata loomed over his brother's bedside.

Sajid hadn't slept in the few hours since they returned. His covers enveloped him like a coffin and he dug his head between his pillows, tasting the salt of his tears. He wished it would all go away. If he just laid there a while longer, clenched his eyelids a bit tighter, Sajid thought, perhaps he would wake up, the sun warming his face, and realize that it had all been a nightmare. Perhaps his brother, his closest friend, his partner in their shared life, would be sitting across the room, spinning a soccer ball and ready to greet him with a smile. But Sajid heard raindrops pelting the window. He sensed Zyed towering above him like a shadow. He felt his gut bubbling with dread. It told Sajid that he had already awoken into something far more terrible than any nightmare.

His blissful parade had come to an end. It was time to decide.

He wasn't ready to die, but he couldn't bear the thought of enduring life alone in a world scarred by his brother's madness. With that, Sajid understood what Zyed meant. He imagined that he had cancer. His fate was outside his control, but looking forward beyond that morning, Sajid's path in life was littered with such horrors that whatever faceless unknown waited behind death's door could not possibly be worse.

It was time for Sajid to choose. He felt Zyed's weight at the foot of the bed. He shuddered, seeing only infinite blackness between the folds of his pillows. A steady hand massaged his legs through the covers, and he heard the familiar, fatal music of his brother's voice.

"Don't let me die alone."

Mofidi eased his arms into the sleeves of his suit jacket. From the fifth floor of the Hotel President Wilson, he could see straight to the snow stirring on the crests of Mont-Blanc and the Chablais Alps. On the lake, whitecaps charged at the shore and shattered all through the night, leaving the naked branches of the plane trees dotting the quayside entombed in a fresh coat of ice. Looking south toward the entrance of the river Rhône, the Jet d'Eau protruded out into the harbor and shot a column of water over a hundred meters in the air where it fell into a cloud of spray. He pulled the lapels taught against his collar and admired the view, trying to suppress a troublesome thought that echoed between his ears. It was only a few words, spoken by Qasem Shateri. Mofidi paid it little attention at the time, but it clung to him, and the more he replayed it in his mind, the more it rang like a threat.

Have fun in Geneva.

He picked his tea off the coffee table and settled on the sofa. Al-Jazeera English's *Newshour* played on the television. It lightened his mood. A panel discussed the results of Iran's parliamentary elections that had trickled in piecemeal over the past several days. The returns in Tehran alone suggested a stunning upset. Reformists and moderate conservatives captured an early lead and barred several prominent hardliners from returning to the *Majlis*. In the Assembly of Experts, the body charged with supervising Ayatollah Khansari's activities, all but one of the sixteen seats allotted for Tehran went to allies of President Rostani. For Mofidi it was a godsend, yielded by a tremendous sense of goodwill the people felt for Rostani and his moderate allies who championed negotiating the JCPOA with the United States.

To aid his reelection hopes next year, Rostani would depend on a supportive parliament to help enact his lofty campaign promises. Also, as Mofidi clearly saw, the elections sent a message to zealots like Shateri that the people still had a voice and were not so easily deceived.

The news from Tehran bolstered Mofidi's faith in his mission that morning. He knew he was a marked man. Ayatollah Khansari's signature scrawled across a piece of paper was supposed to protect him, but Mofidi was not keen to test his luck. There was a resourceful faction, unmoved by elections back home, determined to see that his trip ended in disaster. Mofidi came quietly to Switzerland on a commercial flight, giving last-minute notice to Iran's diplomatic mission in Geneva, and was accompanied only by his regular driver, Babak. Nevertheless, it was impossible not to notice that a silver Volkswagen had trailed them from the minute he touched the ground. Inside his hotel room, Mofidi said next to nothing, kept off the phone, and assumed that anything he had not personally packed in his suitcase was bugged. He took no chances against *Hajj* Qasem's reach, and he counted the seconds until it was all over.

Mofidi saw the time at the bottom right corner of the television screen. He was scheduled to meet Harold Lansing in less than an hour. If anything sinister lurked behind Shateri's threat, it was long overdue to reveal itself.

There was a knock at the door. He set his tea down and crossed the room, pressing his eye to the peephole. Babak stood in the hall, alone.

As Mofidi unlocked and opened the door, Babak greeted him with a nod.

"We should go, *baradar.*"

A late winter squall raged over the North Sea and blanketed a swathe of northwestern Europe stretching from Denmark and the Low Countries down to the Pyrenees mountains in the south. That morning the fiercest bands of wind and rain fell over Île-de-France, sowing logistical havoc in the crowded skies above Paris. Dozens of flights were arriving from Asia and across the Atlantic or from elsewhere in Europe, and each waited for clearance to descend upon the runways at Charles de Gaulle, Orly and Le Bourget. At a nondescript office park in Athis-Mons, in the city's southern suburbs, air traffic controllers attempting to choreograph this spiral kept peeled to the radar, watching for breaks in the storm when it was safe for the flights to land. However, one curious blip flitted over their screens. Its transponder identified the aircraft as a Bombardier Global 6000, and its tail number was registered to a South African shell corporation. The business jet neglected to file a flight plan with Eurocontrol that morning and had soared over the Mediterranean at forty thousand feet, well above the operating altitude of commercial airliners. The controllers at Athis-Mons watched it circle Paris for the better part of an hour, waiting for the weather to subside, and overheard its pilots speaking to the tower at Villacoublay Air Base with abrupt, coded radio transmissions. And then, at precisely ten o'clock, the controllers noticed the jet's altitude on their screens begin to gradually drop.

Benny Isaac watched as thick gray clouds dimmed the cabin and raindrops streaked past the windows. The Bombardier's fuselage rattled and heaved in the crosswinds. He looked out and saw the starboard wing trembling. After a few tense moments, the jet pierced through the canopy and glided over saturated fields and villages. The airfield appeared next. Isaac heard the landing gear and flaps extend. It hit the runway, and the breaks screamed. Isaac was jolted forward in his seat while the engines groaned and the wing swung toward the taxiway. He unbuckled his seatbelt and checked the time. Isaac would be late to his meeting at the Hôtel Meurice, but the delay was only a minor annoyance; he knew Mehdi Vaziri hadn't anywhere else to go.

Three black, armored Peugeot 508s and a security detail from the French National Police's *Service de la protection,* or SDLP, met the Bombardier on the apron at Villacoublay Air Base, seventeen kilometers south of Paris. Isaac descended the airstairs with the help of his cane and a bodyguard, wearing a tweed flat cap and Mackintosh trench coat to shield him from the rain. He ducked inside the middle Peugeot and was off, out the gates, bound for Le Meurice.

The boys got dressed without speaking a word. When they came into the living room, *Jaddah,* their grandmother, hovered before a portable electric stove on the countertop and seared lamb kebabs in a pan. The smell almost brought tears back to Sajid's eyes. He wanted to savor it, to remember, in what spare moments remained.

"Are you hungry?" she asked.

"Not now,*"* Zyed answered for them. "We're going to mosque."

Jaddah turned the skewers. "You should eat first."

"There's no time."

She shrugged and looked up from the stove, studying Sajid with a disapproving frown. He wore only a light windbreaker zipped to his chest, jeans and tattered tennis shoes. "Is that any way to speak to God?"

If only she knew, he thought. *If only God gave a damn.*

"You'll catch a cold," *Jaddah* persisted.

"It's okay," Sajid answered meekly.

She shrugged again. Zyed came over, tightly wrapped his arms around her and pressed his cheek to hers.

"Zyed," she said with a hint of alarm, "what's wrong?"

"Nothing," he whispered. "Everything is right."

Sajid stood by the door, diverting his eyes. He knew that if he looked, he would give it all away. "Zyed—"

"See you soon," he let go. "I love you, *Jaddah.*"

They descended six flights of stairs to the vestibule. There was a brief lull in the rain and the bloated, gray clouds above hung precariously low in the sky, nearly shrouding the tower. The boys crossed the parking lot and found Haddad emerging from the driver's side of his Skoda Octavia. He came around and embraced Sajid, who awkwardly kept his arms stiff at his side. "Today is going to be a beautiful day," Haddad promised.

"Did you do it?" Zyed demanded to know.

Haddad scanned the adjacent tower where his flat was and answered with a wry grin, "Oh yes."

"Good."

"Come," Haddad moved to his car, "and let's give glory to God."

Sajid squeezed in the back as the Octavia pulled out of La Forestière and made for the roundabout at Boulevard Gagarine. There was an overnight bag on the seat next to him, stuffed so full that the zippers barely clung together. He wanted to feel angry and betrayed. While he and Zyed were meant to die today, Haddad fully intended to eat a meal that night and slither off to whatever future he designed for himself. Haddad had plans beyond that fateful morning, and they were built on the presumption that his naïve marionettes would dutifully dance beneath their strings. Sajid shot a scornful glare through the headrests. They were talking about God again—a metaphysical inkblot hijacked to prescribe and remedy mankind's invented ills: spiritual, personal, political, maniacal. Sajid never fawned over football stars or pop singers; his brother was always his hero. He respected Zyed, envied him, trusted him, worshipped him. But that babbling fanatic in the passenger seat was not worthy of anyone's admiration, and while Sajid so desperately wanted to hate him, he was not deserving of that either. Rather, Sajid could not help but feel something different. For the first time, he pitied the hollow, ravenous monster his brother had allowed himself to become. For the first time, Sajid felt sorry for him.

It wasn't going to end this way, he swore. He wouldn't let it. For all the wicked spells Haddad had cast, Sajid still loved his brother. He still believed that while Zyed's mind was spoiled, there must be some good left inside of him, some shred he could hold on to—anything to guide Zyed from darkness, back to light.

At E-Leclerc, the old white Mitsubishi Fuso sat just as they had left it earlier that morning. Haddad walked around the box truck a few times, inspected the tires and the chassis, checked beneath the hood and jiggled the padlock on the roller door. Sajid almost darted across the parking lot and screamed to the passing shoppers for help, but couldn't bring himself to abandon his brother. If he was going to save Zyed, he needed to do it alone.

"Get in," Haddad called once he finished his search.

Zyed nearly sprung from the Octavia and climbed inside the cab, taking the steering wheel in his hands. Sajid trailed with a few slow, deliberate paces. Any minute now, he half expected to hear a swarm of incoming police sirens and see men with assault rifles leap through the bushes. But Sajid only heard the rain.

"Oh wait, my bag," Haddad said as Sajid came around to the passenger door. "Grab it for me, will you?"

Sajid went back to the Octavia and lifted the bag off the backseat. It was heavy, and sagged at the end of his arm. He saw the Makarov bulging through the black canvas fabric and then noticed an open pocket on the side. He stole a glance and spotted a small booklet bound in burgundy leather. It was a passport. Sajid looked closer. On the cover, embossed in gold, he saw something written in English—which he didn't understand—and in another language he knew as the swirling Persian script, but which he oddly couldn't read. It stumped him for a moment until he then noticed, also on the cover, a distinctive coat of arms: four sharp crescents and a sword joined at the base. Sajid recognized it immediately. It was the emblem of the Islamic Republic of Iran.

He felt enraged. He felt abused. He felt determined.

It was eleven o'clock and they had exactly an hour to reach their target. Sajid clambered inside and sat on the edge of the passenger seat between Haddad and his brother. He held the bag on his lap and skimmed his finger over the Makarov's frame. Once they were all in, Zyed dipped his head under the steering column and rubbed a few exposed wires together, bringing the engine to life.

While Sajid watched his brother, he noticed the detonator switch taped beside the ignition. A single red wire ran from the switch, along the steering column to the floor and then disappeared beneath Zyed's seat. Sajid traced the path. To his left, he looked down into a narrow gap splitting the driver's and passenger seats. In the gap, nearly invisible amid clumps of sand and dust, the wire reappeared and led to a strip of clear plastic fish tank tubing, which in turn fed through a tiny hole no wider than a dime that Haddad had drilled into the rear wall of the cab. The previous night, as Haddad and Zyed built the bomb, Sajid was lost in a daze, but he recalled crucial bits of the blueprint they followed. He remembered that Haddad had drilled another hole directly opposite the cab into the front wall of the cargo box where it connected to the maze of blasting caps and shock tubes, and finally to the sixteen fifty-five-gallon drums of ammonium nitrate. The plastic tubing was meant to protect the wire as it hung over the open chassis—a sole electric fuse linking nearly four thousand kilograms of explosives to the detonator. Without that fuse, the bomb was merely a science experiment. He kept an eye on the wire. He could reach it. One firm tug would rip it in half.

Zyed slipped the breaks, and Sajid made his decision.

There it was again—the silver Volkswagen. It was the same car Mofidi noticed once he arrived in Switzerland last night, and it had intermittently trailed them since they left the hotel. It was no coincidence. Shateri's orcs had caught his scent. They were watching, and they wanted him to know.

Mofidi turned back around; there was nothing he could do. Babak drove up Route de Suisse, which followed the shoreline of Lake Geneva, into the Canton of Vaud. His mind ran through the Americans' proposal that he would discuss with Harold Lansing: First, if Ayatollah Khansari expressed support for Iraq's unity government and vowed to dissolve the Hashid Shaabi militias, the United States would recognize Iran's right to have a stabilizing influence in regional politics. Second, if Iran imposed a moratorium on sending arms to Palestinian terrorist groups like Hamas and Islamic Jihad, the United States would call on Israel to abolish its nuclear arsenal. Lastly, if Iran disbanded the Revolutionary Guard Corps and its overseas activities, the United States would lift all of its remaining unilateral sanctions and begin the process of normalizing relations with Tehran. All that Mofidi and Harold Lansing had to accomplish that morning was to agree on a framework for future dialogue—to set the stage for the real negotiations yet to come. But others, like *Hajj* Qasem, did not see it that way. This proposal, if followed through, would sound a death knell for their pursuits of empire.

And the Volkswagen stalking Mofidi only proved their fear.

In the village of Crans-près-Céligny, about twenty minutes north of Geneva, Babak made a sudden turn down a driveway leading into the tree line. After announcing themselves to an intercom, an iron gate wheeled aside, and Mofidi spotted an American flag whipping in the wind. Villa Tatiana was the residence of the US ambassador to the United Nations in Geneva and sat on eighteen acres of tended woodland. Babak drove past grand sequoia trees dotting the grounds to a late neoclassical residence that fronted a private cove along the lake. Two Chevy Suburbans were parked in the driveway, and as they pulled up, Mofidi saw Harold Lansing waiting on the front steps.

"Mr. Mofidi…" Lansing came down the steps as he emerged into the cold.

"Ambassador." Mofidi took his hand.

"Or should I address you as, 'General?'"

Mofidi gave a sheepish grin. "I haven't been one of those for a long time."

"Well, on behalf of President Paulson and the American people," he nodded, "it is my distinct honor to meet you at last."

"Likewise," Mofidi said. "And on behalf of His Excellency Ali Mostafa Khansari and the people of Iran, it is my hope that this is the beginning of a prosperous relationship."

Lansing extended his arm toward the steps. "Let's get started then."

On Voie Georges-Pompidou—a two-lane highway hugging an embankment along the Seine in Paris' 16th arrondissement—traffic seemed to crawl forward a few inches at a time. Isaac's motorcade had just passed beneath the steel trestlework of Pont de Bir-Hakeim when the Peugeots were stymied by another clot of exhaust and brake lights. The storm picked up again, churning the river into a seething, muddied artery of undulating swells and whirlpools the color of rotting flesh. In the backseat of the middle 508, Isaac put his elbow on the center console and tinkered with the air vents while sheets of rain drummed on the roof. He still hoped to stay on schedule and reach Le Meurice by noon, but with each bottleneck they encountered, that became increasingly unlikely. Flipping on the emergency lights and slicing right through was out of the question if they intended to keep a low profile, and the embankment was the most direct route to the city center. There was little Isaac or his French hosts could do but be patient.

"How much longer do you think?" Isaac asked his driver, an SDLP officer.

"Hard to say, *monsieur,*" he glanced in the rear-view mirror. "The on-ramp ahead has everything jammed, but once we merge…twenty minutes, maybe."

Isaac exhaled.

"Apologies, *monsieur.*"

"Not your fault." He stared out at the raindrops trickling down his window. Over the Seine, barges clung to their moorings along the quay and the Eiffel Tower stood frozen in a gust that battered the treetops.

Wiper blades smacked across the windshield.

"Eight rounds in here," Haddad slid the magazine back inside the Makarov's grip, "and one in the chamber," he pointed at the ejection port. "That makes nine. Remember that. Nine is the magic number."

"Okay," Sajid nodded.

He moved his finger along the slide to the safety catch. "If it's up like this, the safety's engaged. Push it down," Haddad did, "and you'll see this red dot. Bring the hammer back until you hear it click." Then he pointed to the front and rear sights. "Line these up, and pull the trigger. Think you got it?"

Sajid opened his hand for the gun. "What's not to get?"

"You're a natural," Haddad slapped the boy's shoulder, "like him."

Zyed's eyes were peeled on the drenched blacktop ahead and fought to maneuver the lumbering old truck through the veering traffic exiting Boulevard Périphérique, a busy ring road marking the border between central Paris and the inner suburb of Hauts-de-Seine. The junction emptied onto Place de la Porte Maillot, and coming around that, to Avenue de la Grande Armée, a broad thoroughfare leading straight to the Arc de Triomphe.

"Hold that just in case," Haddad told him.

Sajid felt the pistol's weight: a tool of steel and polycarbonate, rubber and grease, pieced together in a way that hoisted his brother up from his lowly station in life, set him on a pedestal, and emboldened him to murder. Now Sajid held that same tool, and he knew that time to use it was running out.

Zyed barely moved. His knuckles were white around the wheel.

Yet Haddad was serene. "Let's run through it again—"

"I know how it goes, Badi," Zyed interrupted. "Gain speed, ram into the arcades, the switch is right there."

"But you must hit the corner."

"I know!" he snapped.

Sajid sensed that his annoyance came, not from being questioned, but because Haddad thought he showed any sign of hesitation. Zyed had that much respect for Haddad. He wanted to prove himself, to earn the praise of the *mujahedeen* in Lebanon.

Haddad tapped on the door panel. "You're stressed."

"I'm not."

"You must have no uncertainty."

"I don't!"

There was tense silence as the truck reached Place Charles de Gaulle, where twelve straight avenues fanned out from the Arc de Triomphe like points of a star. Their heads all turned as they circled the monument, and while no one spoke, something changed inside the cab. Their mood became eerily somber. There was none of the confident pretension, the air of assurance that littered Zyed and Haddad's boasts of martyrdom over the past weeks. They radiated the exact opposite: doubt, sorrow, and fear. Despite all their faith and zeal, neither of them had any idea what would happen next. All they could truly know was that the end drew near.

Haddad pointed forward. "It's not far."

"Where?" Zyed asked.

"Rue de Berri."

They drove east down Champs-Élysées—named after the paradise for dead heroes in Greek mythology—past banks and glittering boutiques set inside some of Haussmann's most renowned façades. After a few blocks, Haddad announced without preamble, "Pull over when you can."

Zyed eased the truck along the curb. The intersection with Rue de Berri sat just ahead. Sajid kept some frail hope that Haddad might still put a stop to it, that he might see them as anything more than a tool like the gun in his hands. But Sajid only prepared himself for disappointment.

"I guess this is goodbye," Haddad said as he picked his bag off the floor.

"Not goodbye," Zyed resolved.

Haddad must have felt something then. His face tensed, almost shedding tears, whether by pride or guilt—or both—he didn't reveal it. He swallowed Sajid in his arms first and then reached past the boy, tightly taking Zyed's hand. "You are better men than I."

Zyed held his embrace. "Thank you for all that you've taught me."

Haddad's eyes welled. *"Allah yusallmak."* May God protect you. With that, Haddad dipped his head, leaned into the door, and climbed to the street.

Sajid watched his brother give a labored sigh and turn back into traffic. He had never felt so afraid, even as he ran through the fields while his home went up in flames. And he knew, even then, sitting in that cab, he still wasn't alone. He tried to speak, but nothing came—only hot, trembling breath. His gut rolled in knots. His blood sizzled up in red splotches on his cheeks. He felt the gun. He saw the wire down at his side. He had to say something, and in that moment, Sajid Bata found his courage, he found his voice.

"Zyed…"

Mehdi Vaziri retched the remains of his breakfast into the toilet. He steadied his knees and straightened his spine, gripping the edge of the marble vanity, and flushed. A member of his detail cautiously scratched at the door.

"Mehdi?"

"Fine, Pascal."

"Should I get Ezra?"

"Non!"

"I'll be in the corridor."

"Merci."

His elbows trembled. His skull felt like it was packed with shards of glass. Bent over the sink, he turned on the faucet and wet two fingers, trying to scrub the bitter taste from his mouth. It hardly made a difference. After splashing a few handfuls of cold water on his face, he caught his breath and warily looked in the mirror. Wispy tendrils of blood unfurled through the white of his left eye like an oily slick, slowly encircling the soft amber of his iris. It almost seemed as if his body was giving up, privy to a secret his mind was not.

Vaziri dried his moldering mask with a washcloth and stepped back into the bedroom. He saw rain falling steadily beyond the windows into the manicured white mulberries hedging the Tuileries Garden. He heard the groveling engines sitting at the traffic light on Rue de Castiglione below. On the bed, Fatemeh remained in her sarcophagus of cotton linens, rendered comatose by a forest of prescription bottles on the end table. A thin film of drool glistened in the corner of her lips and puddled out onto the duvet. She had shit herself one night last week. Vaziri only discovered it once he eased in beside her, and when he tried to wake her to get her clean, she hysterically fought him off. Compared to the life she had spun for herself behind those spackled eyelids, the one waiting when she opened them was far more terrifying. There was nothing in the life she was given that still held any value; all she needed, she could dream all her own.

Fatemeh was lucky, he thought. Soon she might not have to choose.

The eastern terminus of Champs-Élysées opened onto Place de la Concorde, a sweeping public square of over twenty acres that symbolized the beating heart of Napoleon's imperial capital. A seventy-five-foot yellow granite obelisk wrapped in Egyptian hieroglyphics and crowned by a gold-plated apex sat at the center of the soaked cobbles, in the spot where numerous aristocratic heads were liberated from their necks. Twin monumental fountains made of cast iron and gold leaf marked the northern and southern ends of the square, the rain spilling over their vasques. The Tuileries Garden extended east of the square, bordered by the Seine, the baroque pavilions of the Louvre, and the bowed roofline of the Hôtel Meurice peering over the naked treetops.

Just before reaching the square the Mitsubishi drifted right, onto an off-ramp that sloped into a brief tunnel where it merged with traffic on Voie Georges-Pompidou and continued inching along the embankment between the Seine and the Tuileries' balustraded perimeter wall.

Sajid placed his finger on the Makarov's trigger guard. The hammer was pulled back and the safety was disengaged. *Nine,* he remembered, and knew that there was not a moment to spare.

"Zyed…" he muttered.

"What?"

"Why are you doing this?"

Zyed looked up from the windshield and shot him a dagger. "What?"

"This," he reiterated. "Why?"

His brother glanced at the gun in his hands. "Give it."

"No," Sajid said calmly without a second of hesitation.

Zyed punched the steering wheel. "Give me that fucking gun, Sajid!"

"No."

Zyed's nostrils flared. His eyes rapidly switched between the traffic and his brother, back and forth, at a loss. "Badi wanted to kill you, you know?" he cruelly pointed out. "Because he knew you would try some shit like this. He wanted to do it last night. At the quarry. He wanted to cut your throat and toss you in the back. But I stopped him!"

"So?" Sajid said with an impassive shrug. "Would it have made a difference?"

It took Zyed a moment to respond. "You wouldn't become a *shahid.*"

"But you don't want to become one either…"

"I want martyrdom!" he spat.

Sajid tightened his hold on the gun. "You keep saying that, but you don't."

"I do!"

Sajid turned and opened his chest to his brother. "I know you," he declared, sensing tears build under his eyes. "It's only me here, Zyed. Whatever it is you think you have to prove, whatever it is you think you have to become, I want you to know that you don't. You don't have to—because it's just you and me right now. You don't have to be afraid."

"I'm not afraid!"

"Yes you are," he said softly. "You've always been afraid. You're afraid right now. I am, too. And I want to tell you that it's okay. It's okay, Zyed." The first tear fell. "It always has."

Taillights flashed on ahead of them. Zyed pressed the brake. "You don't know a fucking thing about it," he hissed.

Sajid shook his head. "I don't. But I wish I did," he wiped his face. "I wish I knew what happened to you. Because the Zyed I know, my best friend, my hero, my big brother—you're not him…" his voice cracked, "and I want him back."

Zyed sniffed and painted his glare on the road. "Any world that would do what this one's done to us is not worth saving. Worse than that—it's not worth seeing, it's not worth hearing, it's not worth knowing. It's not worth opening our eyes when the end's already been written and we just sit here waiting." He punched the steering wheel again and bit his lip, fighting to keep control.

"That's not true."

"It is!" Zyed howled and looked to his brother. "But we get to choose. We get to escape—you and me, together. And this is how."

"By murdering all these people?"

"They chose too."

"I don't believe that," Sajid looked to the cars stopped around them.

Zyed's eyes burned; his voice smoldered. "Then you haven't seen what I've seen."

Traffic started moving again. The truck rounded the corner onto Avenue du Général-Lemonnier at the foot of the Louvre's Pavillon de Flore. Scarcely seventy meters ahead, the avenue descended into a tunnel beneath the Tuileries and Place du Carrousel. The intersection with Rue de Rivoli sat on the opposite side.

"The shadow?" Sajid asked flatly.

Zyed tensed at the word. He wouldn't dare speak of it.

"You think a shadow on the wall spoke to you?" Sajid pressed. "You think it actually put those horrible things in your head? You think it wants you to do this right now?"

"It told me the truth."

"Then here," Sajid offered out the Makarov. "Blow your brains out."

The shade of the tunnel fell over the truck. It stopped roughly midway through. A logjam of red brake lights three lanes across stretched up to the portal of gray daylight ahead.

Zyed's attention was locked on the gun.

"You're afraid." Sajid brought the gun back to his lap. "All those things Badi told you, about Islam—about martyrdom and the *mujahedeen*—you don't really believe any of it, do you?" he coldly realized. "It's all just bullshit you've swallowed to convince yourself—"

"Shut up!"

"—that you're not staggering alone into nothing. You're too afraid to do it yourself. You need a reason," Sajid grit his teeth. "You need someone to promise that *anyone* will care about you once you're gone."

"Enough!"

"Badi doesn't care about you, Zyed. The *mujahedeen* don't care about you, Zyed. But I do. I care about you—I love you, Zyed. *Jaddah* loves you. And one day when you get married and have little kids of your own, they'll love you too. Badi thinks you're just a tool. And if you do this for him, the only way you'll be remembered is as a murderer and a coward."

Zyed seethed. Traffic was still frozen.

"A shadow on the wall isn't real. What you think it tells you to do isn't real," he insisted. "You! You're real, Zyed. I'm real. *Jaddah* is real. What you're doing right now and all these people you plan to kill are real!" Sajid looked at the wire on the floor. He made his peace. "But I'm sorry, I won't die for you."

Isaac's motorcade stumbled upon another clot of exhaust and brake lights.

"We'll be at the hotel in five minutes, *monsieur*," his driver said. "It's only a couple blocks once we get through the light."

"Thank you." Isaac kept staring out the window. He looked up and admired a pale stone edifice as it crawled by, weeping in the rain.

"This is all the Louvre, *monsieur*," his driver pointed to their right. "And that part next to us is the 'Pavillon de Flore.' That's why this tunnel ahead is always backed up. The entrance to the parking garage under the museum is through here, so it's always a mess," he said. "Always."

The motorcade inched inside the tunnel, breaking Isaac's view of the park. It was jammed, just like his driver said—all three lanes blocked. He glanced behind him. Their chase car stopped a few inches off the rear bumper, and in front of his Peugeot, the lead car was just as close. Further up in the tunnel, Isaac counted no less than six tourist coaches, two-dozen more compact cars, and—sitting maybe four rows ahead—an old white box truck.

Sajid dove for the wire beside him. But he missed. He hovered less than an inch from the floor when he felt Zyed's open palm land against his chest. It shoved him back across the seat. He clung to the Makarov, tensing his fingers. Within a second, Zyed had yanked up the emergency brake and dove on top of him. The back of his head hit the door panel. His teeth crunched together with a sharp *click*. Zyed's fist flew toward him like a meteor and struck his left eye socket. His vision blurred for a moment, pain rippled through his skull, and in that haze another blow followed. Searing, throbbing—one after another. He felt his cheekbone crack. Zyed was screaming.

He had to get him off. *The Makarov!* Sajid noticed it in the corner of his eye, clenched in his right hand. He had to hold on. Whatever happened, he couldn't let go. Sajid took his left hand and swung at his brother. He hit Zyed dead on the side of his face. But he hardly budged. The blows were relentless. His eyes dimmed. Zyed's screams blunted. With his last ounce of strength, Sajid turned the gun against his brother.

Zyed saw the Makarov moving. He lashed out, smacked the barrel toward the windshield and wrapped both hands around Sajid's arm. "Let go!" he barked, pounding his brother's hand against the dashboard.

"No!"

Sajid's fingers were glued to the pistol grip.

"Let go! Let go!" Zyed howled. "You won't take this from me!"

Straddling Sajid's waist, Zyed latched his hands around the Makarov's slide and wrestled for control. He pried Sajid's arm back, slowly leveraging the muzzle toward his brother.

Sajid struggled. "Wait. Wait, Zyed. Wait. Stop." He saw the gun turning, inch by inch. Zyed growled and hissed inhuman sounds. Spit foamed over his gritted teeth and dripped off his bottom lip. His eyes and nostrils flared.

Red veins bulged on his temples. Sajid no longer recognized him. In that moment—through pain and rage, through agony, sorrow and regret—Sajid felt clarity.

Maybe it was best.

He relaxed his grip. Sajid stared down the unblinking void of the barrel.

The next thing he remembered was his brother's voice…

The sound was unmistakable to Isaac.

Pop!

Barely had it registered in his ears when, looking between the front seats and through the windshield, Isaac caught a brief halo of white light reflect off the dark concrete tiles. He froze—it couldn't be. But as the sound echoed through the tunnel, Isaac realized that it absolutely was. He heard gunfire.

His detail sprung into action. *"Des coups de feu! Le camion jusqu'à trois rangées!"* the radio squawked. The driver's head jerked around, searching the road behind them for an escape. An officer in the passenger seat pulled a SIG Sauer 2022 from his jacket and vaulted into the back. "Sir, you need to get down!" The officer grabbed Isaac by the collar, forced him against the seat and laid his weight on top of him. As he went down, he caught a glimpse of the lead Peugeot in front of them. Four men were crouched on the pavement and took cover behind the open doors. Their sidearms were drawn and trained on the truck ahead.

"This is the price you pay." Zyed calmly eased off his brother. The Makarov was in his hand. Smoke hung in the cab.

Sajid was slumped against the door. Blood spurted from his jugular and powder burns marred the left side of his neck. He clutched the wound, but it would make no difference. The round tore clean through, severed the artery, and exited out the window behind him. He sleepily eyed his brother—his murderer—on the driver's seat, and said nothing, only faintly gurgled as his airways flooded. He felt numb.

"Montrer vos mains!"

Zyed looked in the side-view mirror. "Fuck!" he punched the wheel.

"Sortez du camion avec vos mains!"

"No," he whispered and began rolling down his window. "No, no, no."

"Maintenant!"

With a deep breath, he steadied the Makarov and leaned out the window.

It was mostly quiet, but through the dissonant buzz in his ears, Sajid heard a flutter of muffled pops, the crash of copper and lead ricocheting against aluminum, concrete and steel. Men were shouting. After a few seconds, Zyed yelped and quickly pulled back inside the cab. He tossed the Makarov on the dashboard and pressed a hand to his ribcage. He gave heaving, labored breaths. Blood wept through his jacket.

Men kept shouting behind them.

The tunnel ahead was clear, emptied by the shots. Zyed groaned with the gears. The truck slipped its emergency brake and crawled forward. In seconds, rain pelted the windshield. Zyed forced the truck into a wide, skidding left turn onto Rue de Rivoli and plunged his foot on the accelerator. The engine revved, and with it, the truck careened down the street, veering through traffic. Zyed scoured the arcaded façades, searching for his target. It was all a wash of stone until he spotted the gold leaf letters that read, "Le Meurice." He looked over one last time. Sajid's eyes were closed.

The truck was at full speed now. Zyed saw the corner of the hotel at the intersection with Rue de Castiglione. He took the wheel and cut it hard to the right. The tires screeched, hardly gripping the pavement. The front of the truck was just feet from the arches. Bodies scattered in every direction.

Zyed felt the impact next. It launched him over the wheel. Stone cracked and glass shattered and steel twisted. At first he saw only blackness, and then a narrow shaft of light pierced the rubble. He blindly reached along the steering column until he felt the detonator switch at his fingertips. Then he said a prayer. To whom or what, it didn't matter. Nothing could hear him.

A horn sounded in that hollow deep.

The parquet floor shuddered beneath Vaziri. Dust plumed past the trembling windowpanes. Alarmed, he stepped to the windows fronting Rue de Rivoli. Cars were stopped all along the street. People ran toward the hotel; others were frozen on the sidewalk, their mouths gaped in shock. A horn blared below.

"Get back!"

Vaziri turned. It was Ezra, charging down the hall.

"Get back!"

A wave of molten glass washed over his face. A brilliant white light engulfed him. Vaziri looked down. The floor didn't shudder anymore. It was gone.

Isaac's motorcade had backed out of the tunnel, whipped around in a synchronized three-point turn, and raced along the shoulder of Voie Georges-Pompidou toward the Israeli embassy on Rue Rabelais. Darting around opposing traffic, the Peugeots sped up an on-ramp to Place de la Concorde and swerved onto the cobbles. Isaac was pinned facedown on the backseat.

He heard the sirens wailing and his detail shouting over the radio. He tried to make sense of what was happening. His mind began searching for answers.

But then all of it became unnecessary.

Isaac heard the roar.

And then he felt it.

It was a deafening sound. The concussion buffeted his bones and rattled his eardrums. Isaac pushed the bodyguard off of him and climbed up to see out the window. He looked east, over the Tuileries. A blazing fireball climbed above the naked treetops. Lateral sheets of stone and metal and blacktop launched into the air, mangled and flaming. The buildings on Rue de Rivoli—stretching from Place de la Concorde to the Louvre—wobbled from side to side. Their façades crumbled at the pressure and toppled over into the street. Lost in the dark heart of it all, shrouded in a surging mountain of fire and smoke and ash that reached higher into the sky, was the Hôtel Meurice.

It was meant for him, Isaac knew; another piece felled on the chessboard. Yet this time it was different. This was no longer a hushed bout played in the shadows. This time dozens, maybe hundreds, with no discernible role to play—unwitting, innocent pawns—were tossed to the pyre. The game was now indelibly changed, and the cost of failure burned before his eyes.

Someone had made their move. The next would be Isaac's.

Waiting a mile away, Haddad never saw the blast. He heard its low rumble and felt the ground quake under his feet. Before the mushroom cloud had risen, he crossed Champs-Élysées and walked, eyes straight ahead, along Rue de Berri. He refused to look back, never stopped to gaze at his work. It happened, the boys were gone. That was all he needed to know.

He was focused on a more immediate concern. In a few hours, Badi Haddad would be the most wanted man in Europe, and each passing minute increased the likelihood of his capture. But Haddad had no intention of letting that happen. He looked to the future with much greater plans. In Beirut, Anwar Sabbah promised him, he would either return as a martyr, or carrying the banner of victory. After years of toiling in obscurity—dead or alive—Haddad was finally coming home.

Yet despite all his boasts of martyrdom and praise for the glory of *shaheed*, Haddad was not without his personal preference. He enjoyed this world too much to abandon it in a suicidal blaze. It was best to help others down that path. Like the boys, he paused to consider, as sirens cried in the distance.

After a short stroll along Rue de Berri, Haddad spotted a lit sign hanging over the sidewalk that marked the entrance to a public parking garage in the basement of the Hôtel Warwick. He turned past the hotel and walked down the garage's ramp. Sabbah had explained that a car would be left in the garage on the morning of the attack. He described it as a dark blue Fiat Linea with the plate number, 524 BXL 75. A key would be taped in the rear driver's side wheel well. Haddad would use it to make his escape.

The garage was quiet, and at that time in the morning the spaces were mostly filled with cars of hotel guests or commuters working in nearby offices. Haddad searched around in the dim glow of sodium lamps. The Fiat Linea was a compact sedan, a ubiquitous design in Europe. He checked the colors and the grille emblems, weeding out the imposters as he walked by, until finally he spotted a suitable candidate. He read the license plate: 524 BXL 75.

It was parked on its own in a far corner of the garage. A wide column shielded it from the passing gaze of a surveillance camera. Haddad eyed the Fiat. He slid along the wall and stuck his hand inside the wheel well. There it was, just as Sabbah promised. He tore the key loose and unlocked the car, placed his bag on the backseat, and smiled as the engine effortlessly turned over.

"On dvizhetsya." He's moving.

In a Citroën across the garage, Pokhrovskii lowered a pair of binoculars.

"Khorosho," Doku Vlasiyev mumbled, watching the Fiat pull away. He glanced at his watch. "Five minutes…"

"Da."

Haddad paid with cash at the automated ticket machine and tried not to look directly at the pinhole camera above the credit card slot. Once the arm barrier rose, he drove up the ramp and turned left down Rue de Berri. It took a moment to master the headlights and windshield wipers, but once he did, the Fiat sailed confidently along. It was ten past noon.

The math was simple. If he drove straight on, with a full petrol tank, Haddad could reach Sète on the Mediterranean coast in seven hours, which would give him just enough time to abandon the Fiat and catch a ferry to Tangier before it left that night. He would use the counterfeit French passport Sabbah had given him to purchase the ticket. That was only the first leg of his escape plan.

Still on Rue de Berri, he approached Rue d'Artois and crossed over without having to stop. After several more meters, Haddad spotted a traffic light that turned yellow just as he came to it. He pressed the brakes and waited at the intersection with Rue du Faubourg Saint-Honoré. He heard more sirens cry. Within moments, a convoy of fire engines, ambulances and police cruisers zipped through the intersection like a blaring haze, racing in the direction of the Hôtel Meurice. He struggled to give it a second thought.

Once clear of Europe, he could blend in among the other passengers for the two-day crossing to Morocco, and if he made it that far, Haddad was essentially free. After taking a train to Casablanca, he would use the Iranian passport and board a direct flight to Beirut.

The light changed to green. It tickled him to think about it. In three days, he would be home. He took his foot off the brake and pressed the accelerator. As the Fiat inched forward, the engine's temperature warning light flashed red, but Haddad never saw it.

It startled him. The dashboard gauges exploded. Bits of shattered glass and boiling plastic showered him, lacerated his face and scorched his eyes. The side windows burst into the street. Flames leapt from the air vents. It felt like a furnace. He kicked his feet and flapped his arms, but everywhere he was burning, melting. The Fiat rolled idly through the intersection— smoke billowing from within—mounted a curb, and crawled still in the rain.

CHAPTER 48

"SO THAT'S IT? You're just not gonna talk to me?" Harris chased after her.

"I don't know, Robert. What is there to say?" Sandra swung her purse over her shoulder and marched downstairs. Harris had just told her that he planned to leave again. She knew better than to ask where or for how long—those answers were classified. It didn't matter; she was furious all the same. She went into the kitchen, storming straight past Ben who munched on a bowl of Cheerios at the dining room table.

"Please just sit for a minute." He was on her heels.

A squirrel on the patio had teased Boomer into a frenzy. The dog jumped up on his hind legs against the sliding glass door and barked.

"It's a squirrel, Boomer," Harris tried to calm him.

"I have to go." Sandra was due in early at the veterinary hospital. She snatched her lunch bag off the countertop and dismissively glanced at Ben's half-made sandwich. "You can figure this out."

The dog kept barking.

"Boomer, it's a goddamn squirrel!" Harris yelled and saw that Sandra had started down the hall. He went after her. "Wait!"

"I have to go."

Harris caught up to her and slammed his hand against the door just as she reached for the knob. "Please wait," he exhaled.

Sandra stared him down.

"Please."

An all too familiar whimper rose from the dining room.

"Ben's crying."

Harris dropped his arm. Sandra opened the door and left.

He nudged the door closed behind her and then ambled, defeated, back down the hall. WVEC, the local ABC affiliate in Hampton Roads, hummed on the television in the living room, and just as Harris entered, a breaking news graphic flashed over the screen.

At the Olive Tree restaurant in the Tango Inn, a small collection of American embassy staffers ignored their lunches. The television on the far wall broadcast CNN International while a banner across the bottom of the screen announced: "Massive Explosion Rocks Central Paris." The anchors struggled to make sense of it all, parroting whatever vague update a producer fed into their earpieces while endlessly replaying a shaky, twenty-second video clip that had been posted to Twitter in the last few minutes. Narrated by the broken ramblings of a French woman, it showed dozens of bloodied and soot-covered Parisians—some wearing shredded clothes—all hysterically running or staggering in disbelief from a smoking inferno at the far end of a city street. The anchors and a correspondent who joined in over the phone already began speculating about a plane crash or even a ruptured gas line.

"ISIS," one brave Foreign Service officer dared venture.

But Nina Davenport knew better—not that anyone cared.

Standing at the back of the crowd, watching as Paris burned, Nina crossed her arms and breathed, "This is how it starts."

"What the hell happened?" Freeman burst through the cypher-locked door guarding the entrance to room 7-F-27, CIA's Operations Center on the seventh floor of the Old Headquarters Building. The digital wall clocks displayed the time for Damascus, Moscow, Islamabad, Beijing, Singapore and Greenwich Mean. It was 6:27 A.M. in Washington. Meanwhile, a bank of televisions tuned to the three major American news channels, including the BBC, Al Jazeera and France 24, had all begun to reach a grim consensus.

"There's been a major explosion in Paris, sir," the senior duty officer pointed to the screens with his chin. "It already broke across the networks."

Freeman stuffed his hands in his coat pockets. "What do we know?"

"NORAD reported it first; two DSP satellites copied the flash at just past 0600 here—noon over there. Must've been pretty big," said the SDO. "Not fifteen minutes after that, NSA generated a CRITIC reporting SCE Paris had intercepted local police and EMS responding to calls that an explosive device detonated at a hotel in the 1st arrondissement—"

"The Hôtel Meurice," Freeman shook his head. "Motherfucker."

"Sir?"

He felt his stomach turn. "Anything else?"

"Not much. We haven't been up that long. FBI and NCTC are on-line. DIA and Homeland Security touched base and NSA activated DECKPIN. I'm told NRO has an ONYX bird passing over Paris in about thirty minutes.

Weather's been bad all morning, but we'll see what they get."

Four of the screens above simultaneously rolled the same snippet of carnage. "Listen, I want you to get ahold of Mossad's liaison in town and don't hang up until he confirms that Benny Isaac is alive. Understand?"

"Yes, sir."

"Good." Freeman nodded. "Alright, I want Shaw and Mathis up here the minute they get in the building. Once you're done with Mossad, I want the COS in Paris on the phone. Alert all stations. Put the word out that if they've got it, I want it. Okay, I'm taking over the conference room," he started walking. "And if Sheridan or Tanner calls, you patch 'em through!"

"Got it!"

Freeman tossed his coat over a chair and opened the blinds in the conference room, looking down at the snow flurries falling in the courtyard. On the table, the secure telephone's faceplate had several buttons each corresponding to one of the various operations centers throughout the Beltway: the Pentagon, Fort Meade, the White House, etcetera. He lifted the handset, thought for a moment, and then punched the only one that made sense.

"State Ops."

"This is Director Freeman at Langley. I need to speak with the secretary."

"Just a moment, sir," a disembodied female voice replied from a gray cubicle in Foggy Bottom. The line chirped.

"Ryan?"

"Ange."

"What the hell?" Weisel sighed as her motorcade rushed down Rock Creek Parkway.

"That's what I said."

"Terrorism?"

"It's looking like it."

"What've you got?"

A watch officer handed him a cup of coffee. "Eh, not a lot," he confessed. "We're kinda in a holding pattern here. You guys?"

"Same. I ordered DS to activate our crisis management cell, and the embassy is running a headcount. Paulson's been briefed. The RSO in Paris fired off a cable; my chief of staff just forwarded it to me. It's bad, Ryan," she said. "Real bad."

"Dozens?"

"Hundreds." Weisel practically felt his spine shiver through the phone. "Jesus."

"Are you thinking ISIS?"

Freeman brushed his hair back. "No, but we're about to wish it was."

"How so?"

He glanced out over the operations center and nervously began, "Angela, they hit the hotel where Mossad was debriefing Mehdi Vaziri. Isaac is supposed to be there right now."

"You don't think—"

"I do," Freeman nodded.

"Oh my god."

"And who is Lansing meeting as we speak?"

Weisel paused. "Ryan, I can't contain this."

"No one can," he admitted. "Not anymore. That's the point."

"What should we do?"

The words made Freeman sick to utter. "End it."

Mofidi and his new American counterpart got on swimmingly. They had been talking for over an hour in the drawing room at Villa Tatiana, sipping tea and establishing a feel for one another's personality before carefully wading into negotiations. Both were enthusiastic and believed that, just maybe, if they kept talking, the world might become a better place that day.

Lansing was about to offer that they have lunch brought in when a young State Department staffer uneasily crossed the drawing room and passed the ambassador a note. "I have a phone call," he read with a tinge of annoyance. "Would you excuse me a moment, Saeed?"

"Absolutely, take your time."

"Thank you." Lansing rose from his chair and stepped into the hall.

Mofidi was thoroughly impressed with the ambassador. Lansing was of the rare breed of Western diplomat who made a point of listening twice as much as he spoke, and when he did there was not a hint of backhanded flattery or an iota of condescension. He took pains to grasp the Iranian psyche, the breadth of Persian history and the richness of its culture. He saw Iran for what it was: a maddeningly vivid and complex tapestry of religions and ethnicities fueled by predictably self-defeating human bias and passion; and he admitted that in one lifetime a man could only hope to comprehend scarcely half of it. He attempted to negotiate, not from a position of moral superiority or imperial hubris, but as a citizen of another country that was regrettably marred by the same afflictions. Lansing freely confessed that the United States of America was just as imperfect as the Islamic Republic of Iran. And his strategy worked.

For his part, Mofidi wanted to validate the ambassador's noble impression of his countrymen. He wanted to do right by Lansing. There was a personal connection now, and Mofidi intended to make a dent before the fanatics who happened to share his nationality proved Lansing wrong.

A whistling gust rattled the windowpanes fronting Lake Geneva. The weather had steadily soured since Mofidi arrived, stirring the lake into a turbulent boil and shrouding his view of Mont-Blanc behind a pale gray wash. Lansing then reappeared in the drawing room, seizing his attention.

Lansing didn't sit. "That was Secretary Weisel," he said rigidly.

"Oh?"

"She had terrible news. There's been a terrorist attack in Paris."

"That's awful."

Lansing nodded, searching for the words. "I'm afraid—"

"No, you can't…"

"It appears that elements of your government may be involved," Lansing struggled to say. "Until we have all the details and have determined who is responsible, I must put our discussion on hold." A Diplomatic Security Service agent entered the room. "This gentlemen will escort you to your car."

Mofidi gripped the armrests. "Please!" he shot up from his chair.

"I'm sorry." There was genuine regret in Lansing's eyes. "Goodbye."

Lansing slowly turned and disappeared into the hall again, leaving Mofidi frozen on the carpet. It felt as if a bomb exploded right where he stood. His jaw hung open; his neck was bowed in defeat. The room seemed to blur in a dull haze. It was useless to argue, to lob retaliatory accusations, to try and explain. Mofidi would only confirm what Lansing and the Americans suspected. It struck him then—a shockwave blowing in the windows and collapsing the ceiling on top of him. Like the wind against the glass, Shateri's threat rang in his ears.

Have fun in Geneva.

It was the *Catarina A* and her cargo, baiting the trap. It was the execution of Moshe Adler, luring Israel back into a strategic and political quagmire in Gaza. It was the militias roving the countryside in Iraq. It was the suspicious glare of Khansari's guards in Mashad. It was the legion of spies and hitmen trawling Europe for any trace of Mehdi Vaziri. It was the Banisadrs, dragged from their bed and gutted like cattle. It had unfolded before Mofidi all along, and now—with the pieces set on the board—he saw Shateri's intentions clear as day.

Mofidi numbly moved with the DSS agent into the foyer.

How plausible was it that Vaziri broke free of his house arrest? How impossible a feat was it for Mossad—despite its legendary talents—to tunnel three hundred meters under Tehran, through rock and dirt and sewer lines and power cables, without a soul noticing? How likely was it that the company of armed Pasdaran soldiers enforcing Vaziri's sentence, who surrounded his home with high walls and steel gates, who watched him with cameras and patrols, were all desperately inept as he vanished into the night? How fortunate was it that Vaziri and his rescuers were given a head start until dawn when the regime finally cast its dragnet? How miraculously and breathtakingly absurd was the entire ordeal?

Unless someone stood by and let it happen.

Mofidi choked back his grief. "Where is the restroom?"

The agent pointed to an alcove by the entrance.

"I'll just be a minute," he said, and crossed the foyer.

Mofidi didn't bother to turn on a light. He flattened his spine on the bathroom door. It was all Shateri. Mofidi was convinced.

Shateri planned for Vaziri to escape, to watch where he ran and hid, to hold up the last glimmer of hope for millions of Iranians and slaughter him. He wanted to stoke their outrage. He wanted them to protest while the regime's enforcers mowed them down in the streets. He wanted international condemnation, sanctions and embargoes. He wanted to set Iran on a collision course with the West, to cement the United States as their eternal enemy and cast any moderate Iranian as a traitor. He wanted war, and that morning—as a nuclear weapon sat within his grasp—Shateri lit the fuse.

Mofidi's eyes welled; his knees quivered, and gave.

He collapsed against the door, pressed his trembling fingers to his eyelids, and sobbed. Cowled by that vast darkness, he realized the cost of his blindness. Mofidi saw what loomed on the horizon, and he felt like a butterfly beating its wings upon the wall of a hurricane.

Minin launched up from behind his desk. "You did this!" he snapped.

Snowflakes dewed the epaulets of Colonel-General Vyasheslav Trubnikov's wool greatcoat. He disregarded the indictment and set his peaked cap on a side table, then calmly removed his gloves.

Minin crossed his office. His shoulders dropped. "What have you done?"

"*Andruishka,*" Trubnikov breathed and touched his cold hands to Minin's arms, "what have *we* done?"

There was no reply. Minin couldn't hide his guilt.

"What did you expect?" The general's brow tightened.

"Not this."

Trubnikov shot him a look of disgust. He raked an eye an over Minin's ornate office. "How did you get here?"

Minin recalled the scene where Mikhail Karetnikov met his end: a field of scorched earth and toppled fir trees lacerating the snow; mounds of twisted aluminum and steel; blazing pools of jet fuel; and a Russian tricolor streaked with soot and dried blood. They had done that, too.

Trubnikov strolled past the windows overlooking Senate Square in the Kremlin and pointed to Nikolai Ge's painting, *Quod Est Veritas?*, hanging above the fireplace. "That's new," he blithely observed.

"It was a gift from Roman Leonidovich."

"Sit down," he added as he sank into a leather armchair. "We need to talk."

Minin padded over and joined him.

Trubnikov took a folded piece of paper from his coat pocket. "Read."

It was an article printed off the website of the *Badische Zeitung,* a regional newspaper in Freiburg. Minin glanced at the headline: *"Heidelberger Paar sterben an Kohlenmonoxidvergiftung im eingeschneiten Auto."* He was fluent in German, but didn't see how it was of any concern to him. "What is this?"

Trubnikov looked at the fire. "Keep going."

Minin shook his head. He read the headline, "Heidelberg couple die of carbon monoxide poisoning in snowbound car..." and then went silent.

The article revealed how three days earlier—in the aftermath of Cyclone Petra, which had dropped a hundred centimeters of snow on southern Germany—the Baden-Württemberg *Landespolizei* discovered two bodies inside a Volkswagen Sharan that was buried in a six-foot snowdrift along a back road near the town of Münstertal. Investigators identified the remains as Ernst and Carla Kubin—ages fifty-three and fifty-one—of Heidelberg, and blamed acute carbon monoxide poisoning when their car's tailpipe became blocked with snow as the likely cause of their deaths. Neighbors in Heidelberg remembered them as quiet and unassuming, the article said, and seemed genuinely disturbed at the couple's tragic and surprising fate. The Kubins settled in Germany twenty-six years ago from Austria and Argentina and had no known next of kin. A spokesman confirmed that police in Baden-Württemberg were still investigating their deaths, but suspected no foul play.

"What the hell does this have to do with anything?"

Trubnikov's eyes were fixed on the embers feeding the flames. "Ernst and Carla Kubin, were actually Evgeny and Olga Mirov," he said. "Both were original officers in my European illegals network. I sent them to Germany."

"For what?" Minin asked.

Trubnikov took a deep exhale. "To hide a nuclear weapon."

Minin crumpled the paper and tossed it in the fire.

"It was 1989. I commanded the Second Direction, responsible for agent intelligence in Berlin," Trubnikov explained. "Everything had gone to hell that summer, and in September I was quietly recalled home for a meeting. It was the old guard, the true believers. They knew the end was near, that Gorbachev was feckless and refused to stop the bleeding, and they asked that I help. Remember, these men were convinced that the West conspired to destroy us; that once Germany reunified, NATO would push east and finish us off. In many ways they were right," he justified. "So I suggested an insurance policy. Our Special Purpose units had access to certain devices designed to operate outside the safeguards of the KGB and the General Staff. It could disappear and hardly a soul would notice."

"So you gave them a bomb?"

"An RA-115 Atomic Demolition Munition with a one-kiloton yield," he said flatly. "Very durable; built to last years without maintenance. A single man can arm the weapon and detonate it. It was perfect. We quietly removed one from a depot and smuggled it into Europe through Rotterdam. Only the Rhine Valley made sense: there were the NATO bases around Stuttgart, their headquarters in Belgium, French tank divisions across the river—all within a day's drive. Evgeny Mirov was tasked to select a hide site. By February he found an abandoned cottage in the Black Forrest. To keep the CIA off our scent, I asked the American to create a diversion in Berlin. That was how he came to work for me."

Minin froze.

Trubnikov crossed his legs. "We hid the bomb in the foundation, and that was the end of it. The Mirovs stayed in place, collected what information they could from the community, and kept an eye on the cottage. Until now."

"Who knows about this?"

"With Evgeny and Olga dead, the only two people left alive who know that bomb exists are me," Trubnikov hesitated, "...and him."

"Oh my god." Minin raked his hair back.

"When we saw that article, I sent a team to the cottage. It's gone."

Minin looked like he was about to be sick.

"I haven't heard from Lebanon in almost three weeks."

"We are not prepared for this." Minin stared at the floor.

"We are."

"What do we do?"

"We stay the course. We control what we can," he said. "In Paris, the American delivered precisely what he promised. Once they stitch together the clues, the backlash against the Iranians will be overwhelming. After the OPEC conference, you get Lavrov to withdraw our ambassador, and no one will bat an eye. Then we pivot to the Saudis. Have you spoken to Roman Leonidovich?"

"He's sending a plane in the morning," Minin chewed his thumbnail. "I have to tell him—about the bomb."

"Fine," Trubnikov shrugged. "He'll tell you exactly what I have."

"I can't just watch."

"Then shut your eyes." Trubnikov stood and started for the door.

"What about the cabinet? I can't keep them from Lavrov forever."

"Leave that to me. I'll deal with it."

"How?"

Trubnikov turned and grinned. "Umarov."

• • •

ONYX-5 sailed through the abyss of space in geosynchronous orbit four hundred miles over the Earth's surface. As its flight track crossed the nimbostratus clouds blanketing Western Europe, microwave pulses emitted by the synthetic aperture radar antenna on the underside of the satellite's bus pierced the storm and illuminated a target grid below. Echoing back to the bird at the speed of light, the results were measured and processed, and then downlinked to the NRO's Aerospace Data Facility-Southwest at White Sands Missile Range in New Mexico. The composite image produced by the satellite depicted a scene not witnessed in Europe since the darkest days of World War II.

Snowflakes eddied through the courtyard of the Old Headquarters Building with an opening band of the nor'easter churning its way up the coast. Freeman, Shaw, Roger Mathis and Pete Stavros were packed in the conference room as an analyst from the Counterterrorism Center soberly doled out the details.

"Just here, on the southwest corner of the hotel, we can observe a crater approximately twenty-eight feet in diameter and seven feet deep," the analyst circled a spot on the monochromatic image generated from the ONYX satellite's radar waves. "The energy required to form a crater of this size is roughly equivalent to three tons of TNT. A detonation of this magnitude produces a radially propagating air-blast wave, which is clearly indicated *here* and *here*. This would produce a maximum pressure of ten thousand psi at the area closest to the detonation and a minimum of nine psi at the northeast corner of the hotel."

"Emanating out from the epicenter, there's been a full structural failure of the Hôtel Meurice: all six floors and the ceiling has collapsed into the street, exposing this inner courtyard. Moving farther east along Rue de Rivoli, we can observe major damage to the façade stretching for approximately seventy meters; and moving west, we see a similar radius across Rue de Castiglione, with severe effects on the adjacent Westin hotel."

"Does this confirm that the bomb was delivered in a truck?" asked Mathis.

"I'm confident," the analyst agreed. "There's a uniform arc of shrapnel in the Tuileries Garden, which would suggest a detonation seated alongside the hotel rather than from within."

Apart from the smoldering remains of the Meurice, the image revealed the outline of police cruisers, ambulances and fire engines choking the streets. Burnt out cars and chunks of debris ringed the hotel, and an inky haze of smoke and dust clouded the air.

Freeman popped an Advil and massaged the bridge of his nose. "This backs up what Isaac told me. The truck was stopped in front of his motorcade. He heard a weapon discharge and when his security detail went to respond, the driver leaned out and opened fire. The truck sped off, and a few minutes later, Isaac saw the hotel go up."

"If they were going after Isaac, like he thinks, why not just set it off in the tunnel?" asked Shaw.

"Maybe they didn't know he was back there?" Freeman shook his head.

"They were targeting the meeting," Mathis added. "Isaac *and* Vaziri."

"Well, they got one," said Freeman. "They're gonna wish they got both."

Stavros crossed his arms. "The second bomb doesn't make sense."

"What do we know about that?" Freeman asked down the table.

"Station chief hasn't heard much," answered Shaw; "DGSE's being pretty quiet about it. Last we heard, witnesses said it rolled through the intersection and went up in flames. Bomb squad found five jerry cans of ANFO in the trunk, so it looks like a dud—triggering charge failed to detonate the rest."

"Police recovered a body, but no word on the identity," Mathis noted.

Freeman tossed his pen on the table and leaned back in his chair. "So when the president asks me who did it, what do I tell him?"

The room was silent. No one wanted to say it out loud.

"Don't all speak at once."

Mathis stared down at the table. "I wish we could pin it on ISIS…"

"No," Shaw cut in. "If it were anywhere else in Paris on any other day, I'd say the same thing. But—with the Banisadrs, with everything we've heard from Tehran about Vaziri, with Isaac just smoking their ambassador in Sudan—we knew this was coming."

"Not this bad," Stavros said.

"Once we get names of the bombers, it'll all fall in place. Until then we're just treading water," she exhaled. "We'll find out a lot more real soon."

It was dusk in Paris; the rain subsided, a lifeless fog settled in its place, and through it, *les archers* came charging. Dozens of pulsing lights and sirens swarmed Clichy-sous-Bois. The National Police's Republican Security Company No. 4 from Pomponne arrived in riot gear and cordoned off a five-hundred-meter radius around La Forestière. Officers from the local commissariat swiftly evacuated the towers and canvassed the neighboring estates, ordering residents to stay indoors. Snipers dotted rooftops and the steady, rhythmic beat of rotor blades sang in the twilight. A pair of SA 330 Pumas attached to the Special Operations Command's Joint Helicopter Group set down in a field beside Le Chêne Pointu, the cabin doors on either side of the olive drab fuselages slid open, and out poured thirty masked commandos, all clad in black. Deployed from their barracks at Château de Bel-Air in Bièvres, the team from RAID—France's domestic counterterrorism unit, known as *"Recherche, Assistance, Intervention, Dissuasion"*—was driven in a convoy of PVP armored trucks to a command post established at Gymnase Henri Barbusse, directly across the soccer pitch from La Forestière. The team studied schematics of the northern tower, marking points of access and egress, noting the diameter of the stairwell and counting the number of steps between each landing, until a call came from the Interior Ministry, and the operation launched.

The commandos rolled in the PVPs along Boulevard Emile Zola into La Forestière's parking lot and stopped at the vestibule steps. They swept inside and climbed to the ninth floor, then methodically started down the hall, filed behind a ballistic shield as their flashlights played in the darkness, right to the doorway of the flat. A commando brought up a fiber optic camera attached to a telescopic pole and fed it along the threshold. The FLIR image displayed on a tablet confirmed their intelligence that the flat's sole occupant was gone—his charred corpse laid under a tarp on Rue de Berri. As the camera retracted, the team leader radioed that they were ready to breach. A commando trudged up the hall with a steel battering ram and set it above the deadbolt.

The team leader lifted his gloved fist and whispered, *"Trois."*

Muscles tensed all along the hall.

"Deux."

Rifles steadied.

"Brèche."

The ram swung out like a pendulum and struck the door with a metallic thud. As the door hurled back on its hinges, the team leader barked, *"Allez!"* and turned his body toward the frame. In that pitch-blackness, the flashlight mounted on his rifle illuminated jagged wooden shards flying in the air. A warm breeze rushed in at his back, and suddenly it wasn't dark anymore. He felt his jumpsuit ignite, and through his iron sights, saw a surging tide of flames.

"Of course, René." Paulson sat hunched over the *Resolute* desk in the Oval Office, enduring a tirade from his French counterpart. "Absolutely... mhmm," he nodded, and gave a few mystified blinks. "Well just—okay, I see—well just let me assure you that whomever is responsible will be brought to justice." Paulson scratched his chin. "I know. I've already ordered the FBI to assist in any way we can... Oh, you have to go now?" His eyes widened. "Alright that's fine. Our offices will stay in touch... Right. Please don't hesitate to call. Okay—we'll talk soon. Take care." Paulson slammed the phone down. "Laniel wants to invoke Article 5."

"Against Iran?" Tanner nearly gasped.

"Yeah."

Article 5 was the *casus foederis* clause of the North Atlantic Treaty, NATO's founding document, and declared that an armed attack against one alliance member would be considered an attack against all.

"Laniel's angry and he's getting ahead of himself," Weisel judged from her perch on the sofa. "We should meet for consultations before that. In Paris."

"That's good," Dawson agreed.

Tanner looked up from his notepad. "First we need all the facts."

As they streamed in throughout the day, those facts consistently suggested the worst. A state of emergency was declared and, as night set in, thousands of troops were on the move across France. In Paris, the 1st arrondissement was sealed off and much of the city was a ghost town. Police searched passengers boarding flights and randomly stopped cars at the border. Mobile phone service had crashed and electronic gantries along surrounding highways urged motorists to keep clear of the city. It took nearly six hours for the fire brigade to douse the inferno raging around the Hôtel Meurice, and now rescue crews turned their efforts to combing the remains. 167 people were confirmed dead on Rue de Rivoli, although that number kept climbing each time a body was pulled from the rubble or another slipped away in a hospital bed. During a news conference, the mayor breathlessly warned that casualties could reach as high as four hundred. With each passing hour, it became bitterly evident that Europe had not faced a deadlier day since World War II.

Yet while Parisians picked up the pieces and the world mourned, an investigation got underway. There were now three crime scenes spread around the city and its suburbs. At the intersection of Rue de Berri and Rue du Faubourg Saint-Honoré in the 8th arrondissement, a forensic team probed a dark blue Fiat Linea. The front half of the sedan—the engine block and the dashboard—was burned down to a skeleton of scorched steel and melted plastic, but the rear half was relatively intact. To the investigator's surprise, twenty-five gallons of ammonium nitrate were hidden in the trunk and somehow failed to detonate. The body of the would-be bomber was found slumped behind the steering wheel, charred from the waist up. Once an EOD squad made the Fiat safe, they carefully placed the corpse on the street and did what any curious person would: they checked the man's pockets.

In his wallet was a driver's license belonging to "Nazih Taha" with an address in a notorious housing estate. An overnight bag sat on the backseat, also unscathed by the fire. Inside, beside a change of clothes and an envelope stuffed with cash, they found two passports: one French and one Iranian. Police descended on Clichy-sous-Bois and, with seventeen dead RAID officers to show for it, the carnage of the day now had a face and a name.

"What do we know about these guys?" asked Paulson.

Freeman cleared his throat from the sofa opposite Weisel. "Nazi Taha is—or was—a Lebanese national. We can confirm that now. His residence permit was issued in October of 2000, and he occupied that apartment shortly thereafter. It's not clear if he had a job, there's no indication of him filing taxes, but he managed to eat and pay his rent. There's a bit more on the brothers: Zyed Bata, age nineteen, and Sajid Bata, age fourteen."

He shuffled his papers.

"The UN recorded them arriving at a refugee camp in Turkey last June. Their asylum application listed their place of birth as Nubl, a Shiite village near Aleppo," Freeman continued. "The brothers claimed they were or-phaned in the civil war and wanted to live with their grandmother in Clichy-sous-Bois. The Interior Ministry approved their request and they arrived at Charles de Gaulle soon after. Now the grandmother, Rima Bata, has lived in France for at least twenty years. The Judicial Police have her in for ques-tioning, and she confirmed that the boys knew Taha. They're interviewing everyone they can at their housing project. I should add that last week a man and a woman were found murdered in the basement of the tower where Taha's flat was. There aren't many details, but the man was behead-ed."

Freeman noticed Weisel shaking her head.

"It does look like Taha radicalized the boys and planned this thing, but the French are looking for outside connections. We've been told that the second bomb—in the Fiat—detonated prematurely and failed to trigger the more powerful explosives. As for the passports in the car, the French one was labeled a forgery with Europol; can't be certain about the Iranian one, but it's concerning."

"So we should make the obvious conclusion," said Tanner.

Geoffrey Sheridan, the director of national intelligence, sat on the cush-ion beside Freeman. "I'm not comfortable putting it on Hezbollah—this type of attack, killing civilians on such a scale, it goes against their tactics."

"Ryan, was this a targeted assassination against Mehdi Vaziri and Benny Isaac?" Weisel asked bluntly.

"I would think so. At least that's how Isaac sees it—"

There was a knock on the curved door leading to the anteroom.

"Yes?" Paulson called.

The president's secretary nudged the door open. "Sir, I have Ambassa-dor Lansing on the line. You wanted to speak to him?"

Weisel straightened her back.

"Put him through." The phone chirped after a moment and Paulson placed the call on speaker. "Harold?"

Lansing's voice rose through the room. "Mr. President?"

"Harold, you're on with Larry, Eli, Angela, Director Freeman, Dr. Sher-idan and myself," he almost shouted. "What happened in that meeting?"

"I—I don't know, sir," Lansing stuttered. "Mofidi and I spoke for about an hour. Everything was going well and then Secretary Weisel called and told me."

Freeman stared at his lap.

"Nothing seemed strange at all?" Paulson hovered over the phone.

"Nothing," Lansing swore.

The president shot a glance at his staff. "Okay, Harold, you get back here right away before this blizzard hits."

"Heading to the airport now, sir." The line clicked off.

"That probably has a lot to do with it," Freeman looked up.

"Why?" Paulson asked, lingering by the windows.

"Mehdi Vaziri defected early this month as part of a joint operation by Mossad and the DGSE. He refused to go to Israel, so they were debriefing him at the Hôtel Meurice."

"That was stupid."

"Maybe, sir," Freeman consented. "The Iranians, specifically the Quds Force, were aware of this and we have reason to believe that they've been searching for Vaziri since his escape. One report from Tehran claimed that IRGC Intelligence put several European dissidents under surveillance in the hope that Vaziri might try to contact them. He did. Vaziri placed a call from his hotel to the documentary filmmakers, Nima and Roya Banisadr. A few days later, they were dragged from their home in the Netherlands and stabbed to death. Almost zero evidence was left behind. Because of the threat, Benny Isaac went to Paris this morning to convince Vaziri to come back to Israel. Hardly a day earlier, Mossad eliminated Iran's ambassador in Khartoum, a known Quds Force officer. At the same time Isaac was in Paris, Lansing had this meeting with Saeed Mofidi in Geneva," he gestured to Weisel. "I don't think it's all a coincidence."

"He's right, Andrew," she agreed.

"Mr. President, I think this is the next evolution in an escalating pattern of aggressive behavior by Qasem Shateri and the Quds Force. They've lost Hezbollah and Syria and now they're lashing out. We've seen them attempt to transfer cruise missiles disguised in a shipping container to Sudan. We've seen them execute Moshe Adler and provoke a conflict in Gaza. We've seen them murder their own citizens in Europe. Trying to assassinate two men by wiping out a city block is only the next step. Why is Shateri acting so bold?" Freeman leaned in. "Because he's about to have a nuclear weapon."

Dawson crossed his arms. "Sir, I think our backs are against the wall."

An encouraging nod from Weisel told Freeman he should keep going. "If we green-light PACER, it gives us an operational capability in-country. It allows us to sabotage this program before it advances any further, while Angela works to target Quds Force assets abroad and isolate their political supporters in Tehran. Right now, Shateri's running the table—we can change that."

It was silent in the Oval; no one spoke against him.

Paulson stood before the windows as snowflakes dusted the crabapple trees in the Rose Garden and breathed with resignation, "Do it, Ryan."

Harris never expected the call to come so soon.

He sat on the living room floor, watching the same reports that had echoed across every news network since morning. It was now four A.M. in Paris and the anchor manning CNN's helm stood before a nearly deserted Place de la Concorde. Most of the talking heads on his television screen had pinned the bombing on remnants of ISIS that survived the bloodbath in Syria and regrouped in Europe. This was the Caliphate's grand return to the stage, they warned, although a sense of suspicion was mounting that after seventeen hours no group had claimed responsibly.

But Harris knew better.

This was a grim ritual for him. He indulged his obsessive-compulsive tendencies on the night before deployments, repacking his personal gear again and again, compressing the bulk and weeding out unnecessary items. After fourteen years he had it down to a science, although this time was a bit more complicated. VALENCIA would operate in Palanjar for several weeks until JSOC could safely drop the remainder of their equipment along with the arms and cash promised to Gorani over the Iranian border. Until then, anything the team needed to survive would be strapped to their backs as they jumped from a C-41A at twenty thousand feet. Each time he emptied his rucksack and started fresh, Harris grappled with the pesky reality of physics, factoring in his own body weight and the weight of his weapons, clothing, parachute and oxygen tanks that would all conspire to send him plummeting to Earth. Sandra always kept him company through the ordeal, but on that night, Harris sat alone.

Once his rucksack was squared away, Harris placed it by the front door and turned to the next step of his ritual. He switched off the television and sat at the dining room table, opened his laptop, and began typing.

Harris usually wrote three letters: one addressed to his parents and his sister, one to Sandra, and one to Ben. But now he wrote a fourth—to his daughter. He printed the letters when he finished, signed and dated them, sealed each in a separate enveloped, and wrote, "To be opened only in the event of my death," across the front.

His phone vibrated in his pocket. It was a text message from Z, and told that he was on his way. Harris held the envelopes in his hands and nervously eyed the blackness at the top of the stairs, steeling himself to say goodbye.

Harris climbed the stairs. Light bled through the frame of his bedroom door. He nudged it open without glancing over at the bed and quietly placed the envelopes in the top dresser drawer, where they always went. He stood there for a moment, bowed his head, and muttered, "Please speak to me."

"It's fine, Robert." Sandra sat up against the headboard, reading a paperback.

"It's not." Harris came toward the bed. "Z's coming. We're gonna drive in together so we don't leave two cars on base. This is it, Sandy."

"Okay," she said stoically and turned a page.

Harris eased in beside her. "I can't leave like this." He ran his hand along her thigh. "I have to fix it."

She didn't pull away.

"Tell me what to do."

Sandra snapped the book shut and pinched the bridge of her nose. "Please don't, Robert."

Harris shook his head. "Sandy—"

"Every time it's the same," she hesitated and then began with a shudder in her breath. "I listen for that doorbell to ring. I ask myself if I'm strong enough."

"You are."

"I ask myself if I can do it alone. But I don't believe it anymore."

"That's not true."

Her face tensed. "No matter how much I pray for you, I have no guarantee that God will save you. I think these terrible thoughts. If death were inevitable, what way would be the least worst for you? What way would be the least worst for me? Could I bear a day without you? And I know I can't."

Harris wrapped his arm around her and pulled her against his chest.

"Please don't go," she cried.

He rubbed her heaving back. "We've done this before. I'll come home and we'll survive like we always have."

"Not this time," she wailed. "Not this time!"

Harris felt her tears bleed through his shirt. "Sandy, what's going on?"

Sandra wiped her eyes and sat up. "I have this dream," her voice trembled. "It's you, and Z, and Jamie, and Bryce. You're running through the trees. They're burning. Everything's burning. Men are chasing you—like shadows. And the last thing I see... They kill you... All of you. You die, Robert."

Harris grabbed her by the shoulders. "Listen," he looked her in the eyes, "that's not going to happen. That's not me. I'm coming back. Understand?" He kissed her. "And I need you to remember, Sandy—if you forget everything else. I love you forever... Okay? I'm coming back."

"Okay," she sighed.

He brushed her hair aside. "After this, I'm done. I'm out."

Sandra took a tissue from the nightstand.

"That's a promise. After this, it's just you, and me, and Ben—and our girl."

"Ava," she smiled.

"What?"

"We're calling her Ava."

"Okay, you got a deal," he laughed. "I can't wait to meet her."

They held each other for what seemed like a lifetime. Harris stepped into Ben's room and hovered there for a while, watching his son's chest gently rise and fall in the warm glow of the streetlamp. Z arrived by eleven. Harris squeezed his rucksack in the Mustang and kissed Sandra goodbye. As they pulled away into the darkness, Harris looked back and saw her standing in the driveway, one last time.

From Dam Neck Annex, a van shuttled them through the back gate of Naval Air Station Oceana to an apron on the far side of the airfield. A hulking C-17 Globemaster sat idling in the drifting sleet while the Air Force crew ran their pre-flight checks. The nor'easter steadily intensified up the coast, and just a hundred miles south, parts of the Outer Banks were being pummeled with gale-force winds and storm surge.

Harris jumped out of the van with his rucksack. He looked up into the open cargo bay where the rest of their gear was strapped to the deck and spotted Peter Stavros plodding down the ramp.

"Chief Harris…" he called through the rain.

"Good to see you again, Pete."

They shook hands. "Is this the team?"

"Yeah," Harris turned. "Petty Officers Bryce Whitford and Jamie Farah, and Chief Wilmer Zapata, but you can call him Z. Guys, this is Peter Stavros; he runs Iran Ops at Langley. His people put this whole thing together."

"Nice to meet you boys," Stavros nodded.

"Likewise."

"Pleasure."

Stavros looked out into the night and pointed. "That would be the admiral."

A staff car drove along the taxiway and stopped by the aircraft. "Evening, gentlemen," said Wade as he emerged from the backseat.

The SEALs saluted.

"Okay, couple things before you get airborne," Wade approached. "You've got this bird to yourselves all the way to Turkey. Once you touch down at Incirlik, the 427th will pick you up for the hop into Erbil. We'll VTC there and handle the last mission briefing. Weather should be great for the drop. Understood?"

"Check, sir," the SEALs echoed.

"Excellent." He went around the group and gave each of them a firm handshake. "Godspeed, gentlemen."

Wade's car pulled away and they climbed inside the cavernous belly of the C-17. Harris dropped his rucksack on the deck and took a bench seat along the fuselage. Farah and Whitford fished out their sleeping bags and searched for a quiet corner of the cargo bay to pass the eleven hours to Turkey. Stavros slipped in his headphones. The ramp retracted with a hydraulic groan and the cabin lights dimmed, washing the bay in a cool blue glow. Harris felt the aircraft moving beneath his feet. Z came over and buckled himself into the adjacent seat.

The engines powered up.

"You clear shit up with Sandy?" Z looked straight ahead.

"Pretty much."

"What about the baby?"

"Her mom's staying with her."

"Sounds like it all worked out, Robby," Z patted him on the back as the C-17 turned onto the runway. "Just imagine how she'll look once she pops it out."

"You're an asshole."

The engines screamed and thrust them forward.

"Well…you got me there."

The C-17 lifted off the ground and soared skyward, rattling the fuselage.

"How'd Maggie take it?"

Z hesitated for a moment. "She broke up with me."

Harris put his hand to his mouth and shook with laughter.

"Really?"

"I'm sorry."

"Eh," he shrugged. "Fuck her."

CHAPTER 49

MININ WADED THROUGH the downwash. A pearl white Airbus H175 helicopter sat a few meters ahead on the tarmac, its rotor blades stirring the
morning's frigid air against his face. Three hours earlier, a Dassault Falcon
7X business jet in Roman Ivanov's fleet took off from Vnukovo Airport in
Moscow and quietly spirited him to Lugano, a city in southern Switzerland
near the Italian border. Hastily closing the gap to the helicopter, he climbed
inside the H175's cabin and sank into a hand-stitched leather seat along the
starboard side of the fuselage. The helicopter soon lifted off the ground,
dipped its nose and flew southwest at 285 kilometers per hour, passing the
glacial cut of Lago Maggiore and skirting Milan's western suburbs. The hills
then melted away and Minin stared out at seemingly endless swathes of
green meadows and rice paddies. Forty minutes into the flight the terrain
rose again at the base of the Maritime Alps, marking the French border.
Minin saw the snowy crests and forested slopes of the Mercantour massif
below, and then, far out on the horizon, he saw the Mediterranean. After
another twenty minutes, the helicopter crossed the Paillon Valley and soon
began bleeding altitude over the final mountainous rampart that plunged
into the sea. The pilots hooked around the medieval village of Èze and
banked to port. The Mediterranean splayed out before him with distant
swells glinting in the sun. Now heading east, the pilots continued their descent. Then Minin caught sight of it. Perched like an eagle's nest atop a
promontory smothered by olive, almond and cypress trees and Aleppo
pines eleven hundred feet over the sea, the ochre façade and terracotta roof
of Villa Lou Sueil gleamed.

The helicopter's landing gear deployed and gently set down on an asphalt pad next to a tennis court. As the rotor blades whined still, the copilot
slid open the cabin door. It was unseasonably warm that morning, even for
the South of France. The humidity weighed on Minin as he stepped out and

spotted Ivanov's private secretary, a thin man in a tailored waistcoat, approaching him.

"Premier Minin," the secretary offered his hand, "welcome to Lou Sueil."

"Thank you," he said, smoothing the wrinkles from his suit."

"Just this way please. His Lordship is eager to see you."

Minin followed him along a path of finely crushed gravel that snaked between swaying palm fronds, flowering hedges and sprays of white, cream, blue and purple irises to the back terrace where a teenage boy trawled the pool for debris. He knew Lou Sueil's reputation; there were whispers over the years of lurid parties in the eighties that roared on until dawn, featuring brigades of scantily clad men and mounds of cocaine. But old age had tamed Roman Ivanov, and now, unlike Cliveden House, hardly anyone saw beyond the villa's high walls. Lou Sueil was his sanctuary, where the Oracle of St James's lounged in the Riviera sun, and plotted against the world.

The secretary led Minin under a long ivy-strangled arbor and down a flight of stairs carved into the cliffside to a belvedere terrace overlooking the sea. Ivanov sat at a wrought iron table in the shade of a lemon tree, reading a newspaper behind a pair of horn-rimmed Prada sunglasses. The breeze played with his feathery white hair. "Good morning, my dear," he acknowledged them as they came down the steps.

"Lord Ivanov, may I present Premier Minin," his secretary announced.

"Yes, I see," Ivanov folded the paper. "Would young *Andruishka* fancy a coffee, or perhaps a scone?"

"I'm fine, thank you."

"That'll be all, Sebastian," he said with a smile.

His secretary gave a slight bow and floated up the stairs.

Minin was stunned by the view. His eyes followed the shoreline from the rocky breakwaters around Cap Ferrat in the west to the urban sprawl of Monaco clinging to the hills in the east. Yachts were moored along the coast and a flock of gray herons soared through the azure sky. Perched atop the balustrade rimming the terrace were marble busts of the goddesses Aphrodite, Rhea and Hebe, gazing silent and timeless over the Mediterranean.

"I trust you had no trouble in Lugano," Ivanov said once his secretary was out of earshot. So there would be no evidence of Minin's trip to Europe, Ivanov had called an old friend on the Swiss Federal Council and arranged for immigration officials to ignore his plane upon arrival that morning.

"Not a soul," Minin replied. "Walked right off."

"Splendid," Ivanov removed his glasses. "Join me."

There was an empty coffee cup and saucer on the table beside a small leather-bound book bearing the title, *Michael Robartes and the Dancer* by the poet William Butler Yeats. Minin took the seat across from him.

Ivanov picked up the salmon pink front page of that day's *Financial Times* and proclaimed, "'Hundreds killed in Paris carnage.'" He flopped the paper on the table, lifted *Le Figaro* and melodramatically gasped, *"L'Horreur."'*

Minin tightened his lips. "I wasn't expecting this."

"Come now."

"When Mikhail Borisovich..." He shook his head. "But now—all those faces, all those names I don't know."

"Light a bloody candle."

Minin looked away.

"We point," Ivanov spread his arms, "and the American abides."

Minin shivered at that.

"When will they link it to the Iranians?"

"They may have already."

"How has Lavrov taken it?"

"He phoned Laniel yesterday," Minin breathed. "The Foreign Ministry released a statement condemning the attack, but we haven't placed blame. People are beginning to ask questions."

"So long as they get their answers before OPEC sits down," Ivanov nodded. "You're leading the delegation to Vienna? Prince Farid is keen."

"Yes," replied Minin. "We'll recall our ambassador from Tehran the minute I return. The next day, Lavrov will announce that we've cut ties."

"How will you deal with Uri Popoff and the others?"

Minin rubbed his arm. "Trubnikov is enlisting the Chechens."

"Good," huffed Ivanov. "Let them do their worst."

Minin felt his stomach turn. "Vyasheslav told me something yesterday," he muttered. "Something disturbing."

Ivanov held for a moment. "And?"

"I don't know how to say it."

"Speak, boy."

Minin's eyes were glazed over. "The American has a nuclear bomb, small enough to fit in the boot of a car. The GRU had one buried in Germany—and he took it. We don't know where it is. We don't know the target. We don't know when. He won't answer our messages. Vyasheslav said it's been weeks since he's gotten a reply. I can't sleep. I watched a video of that explosion in Paris yesterday, again and again. I was at a restaurant last night. All those people around me. It made me sick."

Ivanov showed no emotion.

Minin stared at the horizon. "They have no idea what's about to happen."

Ivanov reached for the book on the table and flipped to a yellowed, dog-eared page. He sighed, and then read aloud:

Turning and turning in the widening gyre
The falcon cannot hear the falconer;
Things fall apart; the centre cannot hold;
Mere anarchy is loosed upon the world,
The blood-dimmed tide is loosed, and everywhere
The ceremony of innocence is drowned;
The best lack all conviction, while the worst
Are full of passionate intensity.

Surely some revelation is at hand;
Surely the Second Coming is at hand.
The Second Coming! Hardly are those words out
When a vast image out of Spiritus Mundi
Troubles my sight: somewhere in sands of the desert
A shape with lion body and the head of a man,
A gaze blank and pitiless as the sun,
Is moving its slow thighs, while all about it
Reel shadows of the indignant desert birds.
The darkness drops again; but now I know
That twenty centuries of stony sleep
Were vexed to nightmare by a rocking cradle,
And what rough beast, its hour come round at last,
Slouches towards Bethlehem to be born?

Minin heard those verses before; it was Yates' "The Second Coming." Ivanov had read it to him weeks earlier, when he first proposed murdering Karetnikov. Even now, his cold indifference was unshakeable.

"*Andruishka,* it's time you appreciate the strange predicament of our enemy," Ivanov closed the book and drifted to the balustrade. "It's one thing to wage war against poppy farmers and suicidal teenagers, but quite another to accept the challenge of a nuclear power with the world's largest territory and richest deposits of natural resources. Europe and the United States, in their decadence, have reached the final stage of their degradation where only material comforts matter, who have been rendered breathtakingly impotent by decades of inert existence. They will lose their heads in this inferno—all of them. But one by one, as the fires die, you and I will have forged the next era of Western civilization."

"It's interesting," Freeman said as he opened his binder. He would've smiled if their moods weren't so grim. "The Israelis have only been on the ground a couple hours and they've already blown this thing open." He looked up the conference table; most of the National Security Council's eyes were locked on him. The vice president was busy campaigning through the Deep South ahead of the next day's Super Tuesday primaries and the secretary of defense was in Japan, but the rest of them were there. Paulson, Weisel, Tanner, Dawson, Sheridan, Admiral Benson from the Joint Chiefs, and even Harold Lansing, who had just returned from Geneva—they all hung breathlessly on his words. Freeman swallowed, and continued. "Isaac informed me that Mossad's team are working closely with the DGSE and French law enforcement. Concerning 'Nazih Taha'—the third bomber who expired on Rue de Berri—it seems that the Lebanese birth certificate he used to receive a French residency visa was forged. I'm told it compares to other birth certificates produced by a Sicilian counterfeiting ring that was broken up in 2011. Now here's the interesting part: Tissue samples taken from the body were run against Israeli databases and returned a conclusive match with a known Hezbollah officer named 'Badi Haddad.'"

That vaulted enclave of the White House Situation Room was silent for a dragging second; only the air vents droned overhead. Then Weisel gave a heavy sigh, and Paulson cleared his throat. "So you're telling me Hezbollah is responsible? Is this what CIA is reporting, Director Freeman?"

He chose his next words carefully. "Mr. President, this is the information that Binyamin Isaac has shared with us."

"And he was nearly killed in this attack?" Tanner tried to insinuate.

Freeman nodded. "He was, Eli."

"Well don't stop now," Paulson folded his arms. "What do we know about this Haddad fellow?"

"There isn't much," Freeman flipped to the next page. "IDF Intelligence has records showing that Haddad was imprisoned at the Khiam Detention Center by the Israeli-backed South Lebanon Army in 1998 during the occupation. It's thought he was held at Khiam until Hezbollah overran it in May of 2000. Mossad lost track of him, but we know 'Nazih Taha' entered France that October. Like I said, details are sparse, but it was noted during his interrogations that Haddad was, at the time, a member of the Special Research Apparatus, a foreign operations and intelligence unit commanded by Ibrahim al-Din."

"Ibrahim al-Din?" Tanner echoed down the table.

"You'll know his work..." Freeman breathed soberly. "He blew up our embassy in Beirut twice—in '83 and '84—*and* attacked the Marine barracks that same year, hijacked TWA 847, bombed the Israeli embassy in Buenos Aires in '92 and brought down the Khobar Towers in '96; not to mention masterminded hundreds of other kidnappings, hijackings and ambushes over the last thirty years. Before bin Laden, no other terrorist had murdered more Americans. Interpol issued a red notice in '97 and," he gestured to Weisel, "State has an outstanding five-million-dollar bounty on his head."

"If you had to guess, Director Freeman," Dawson tapped his pen, "would you say he orchestrated this attack in Paris?"

Freeman shrugged. "It's complicated. Al-Din was always an Iranian operative; Hezbollah was a flag of convenience. After September 11th, Qasem Shateri ordered the Quds Force to scale back their 'terrorist' activities in favor of more conventional military operations abroad. It's been thought that al-Din was essentially forced into retirement around that time. There hasn't been a confirmed sighting of him in twenty years. That may have changed this month."

"Beg your pardon?" the president shook his head.

"One of our agents in Beirut claimed to have seen him. We can't verify it."

"Well, Director Freeman, I think that just became a priority."

"There's more," Freeman looked back to his binder. "The Iranian passport that was in Badi Haddad's possession: Another passport with the same number was used by a suspected Quds Force officer entering Thailand two years ago."

Dawson turned to his boss. "Andrew, it's time we consider—"

"I already have, Larry," Paulson cut him off.

"Ryan, if I may," Weisel shifted in her chair. "If CIA can conclude that the bombing yesterday was a targeted assassination against Mehdi Vaziri and Benny Isaac, can it also conclude that it was executed by Ibrahim al-Din on Qasem Shateri's orders?"

Freeman hesitated at first. "Probably."

A shockwave rippled over the table.

"We need more evidence," he continued, "but in context of Shateri's behavior since Damascus fell, it's impossible to dismiss it."

"Thank you, Director Freeman," Paulson muttered. "So what now?"

"It's only a matter of days, maybe hours, until the French publically accuse the Iranians. They'll bring it up at the UN and push a resolution through the Security Council. We'll go from there," Weisel thought aloud. "Assuming Laniel wants to invoke Article 5—and I don't see why he wouldn't—NATO will have to meet for consultations beforehand. The logistics need to be hammered out, but I'd bet the meeting will be in Paris. It makes a clear statement."

"How will this affect Annapolis?" asked Tanner.

"Hard to say. That's up to Avi and the Syrians."

"We need to smooth that over, Angela," Paulson stressed.

"I'll reach out." Weisel looked down the table. "Harold, what about Ghanbari?"

"Yeah, I called him on the plane," said Lansing. "Tehran's had protests since the news broke that Vaziri was killed. Morteza's flying out tonight."

"Good," Paulson nodded.

"FEST team should've taken off from Andrews by now. RSO and the legal attaché at the embassy are handling liaison in the meantime." Weisel referred to the Foreign Emergency Support Team, an interagency crisis group drawn from the State Department, the Pentagon, the FBI and the Intelligence community, which was deployed in response to terrorist attacks against American interests or allies overseas.

"What about your people, Director Freeman?" asked the president.

"They're en route to Erbil and will insert tonight if the weather holds."

Paulson cracked his knuckles. "Angela, how rough will this get?"

Weisel pursed her lips. "A lot can happen in Paris. There're too many moving parts. How will the Iranians react? What other evidence comes forward? How far does Laniel want to prosecute it? I mean, Andrew—we're talking about a clear act of war. What about the Chinese and—"

"The Russians." Freeman snatched it off her tongue.

"Kremlin's been quiet…just like after Gaza."

"Why?" Dawson wondered.

"Well, we know Lavrov was planning to dump Tehran even before all this happened," she pointed out. "Can't imagine he'll back out now."

"Vienna's gonna be a bloodbath," Freeman added.

"Andrew, think about it," Weisel turned to him. "If the Russians join OPEC, and then cut ties with Iran because of this attack, what's stopping Rostani and all the moderates in Tehran from taking Shateri to the woodshed?" With that, a duty officer entered and quietly handed Weisel a note. She read it in a glance, and her face went pale. "Jesus Christ."

"What?"

She drew her eyes up to Paulson. "It's Lavrov's chief of staff."

Weisel stepped into the Watch Center. The call was transferred to the Situation Room director's office. She shut the door and steadied her trembling hand around the phone. It chirped once, and she answered. "This is Angela Weisel."

"Madam Secretary, this is Andrei Minin. I hope I'm not disturbing you. It's early in Washington, is it not?"

She recognized the eloquent, flawless English. "Not at all, Premier Minin."

"Please. To you, I am only Andrei."

Weisel couldn't help but smile. "What can I do for you, Andrei?"

Minin sat in the humming cabin of Roman Ivanov's Dassault Falcon, admiring the snowy peaks of the Alps below. "I must convey a message on behalf of the Russian Federation," he said. "In light of recent events, please do not mistake our silence for apathy. President Lavrov has every intention of honoring our arrangement. In due time, we will make our intentions known. And—Angela?"

"Andrei?"

"I would very much like to see you again."

• • •

The bells of Notre-Dame tolled at noon, marking twenty-four hours since the bombings. For sixty seconds across France—in schools and businesses, in parliament and atop the rubble of the Hôtel Meurice—life fell to a stand-still.

A script detailing how mankind displays its collective grief was dusted off. The death count hovered at 248, mostly guests or employees of Le Meurice, and spanned more than fifty nationalities. From a beachhead staked on Place de la Concorde, the international media narrated the trage-dy across a breadth of languages like the strings of some macabre orchestra. Their cameras panned over the same backdrop. A makeshift memorial around the obelisk and the fountains had steadily grown since yesterday afternoon. There were heaps of lilies and carnations, roses, daffodils and tulips; gulfs of handwritten posters and cards with messages of sympathy, solidarity and perseverance; stuffed teddy bears, candles and French tricol-ors; all of it drenched and wilting. That morning an anonymous Parisian was filmed floating around the obelisk as she attempted to relight the can-dles that had been extinguished in the rain. A CNN crew jumped at the opportunity and swept into the crowd to interview her, but the woman spoke little English and shied away from the anchor's advances. Yet be-tween those manufactured, heartwarming glimmers of humanity, the full scope and gravity of the attack was just being felt.

The prevailing wisdom on television screens across the globe shifted with the hour. Every moment in the short lives of Zyed and Sajid Bata was stripped down by a bevy of talking heads and rebuilt in the mold of two young Arab men who had slipped between the cracks of European society and were drawn to a radical interpretation of Islam. Sajid was an early fan favorite: a naïve and impressionable fourteen-year-old boy led to jihad by his older a brother, a character with whom viewers could empathize. Zyed was framed as the villain, the more religious and ideological of the duo. Last night, after the botched raid in Clichy-sous-Bois, the police report detailing the murder of Fabrice and Tippi was leaked to the press just in time for the primetime broadcasts and was met with outrage. It should have been a clear "red flag" for French law enforcement, a failure by security services to "connect the dots," as the talking heads proclaimed. After the explosion at La Forestière, the talking heads could hardly contain their excitement. Agence France-Presse first broke the news that the flat targeted in the op-eration was rented by the man killed on Rue de Berri. Within minutes, all the talking heads concluded that this Lebanese immigrant, Nazi Taha, fit the role of the would-be "third bomber." Whether his device failed to det-onate properly or if he got cold feet was still up for debate. Since then, the Interior Ministry and the Paris prosecutor's office released few details that could confirm those assumptions either way, but for the talking heads, si-lence in lieu of speculation was unacceptable. However, hours after arriving in Paris on a chartered El Al flight, Nathan Cohen already understood, within that silence rang whispers of war.

He cleared a checkpoint manned by a platoon of the 3rd Marine Infantry Parachute Regiment and continued along Rue du Faubourg Saint-Honoré. Police cruisers and all-terrain army trucks lined the street. Two hundred meters ahead, at the intersection with Rue de Berri, sat the burned-out husk of a Fiat Linea. Forensic investigators of the National Gendarmerie's Criminal Research Institute milled about the car, dressed from head to toe in Tyvek coveralls. He walked right up to the barricade tape and watched them work. Badi Haddad's corpse had already been removed from the scene and was taken to the laboratory at Quartier Lange in Pontoise. Photographs of the body showed that flames ate away most of Haddad's features, revealing a skeletal visage of charred bone and muscles; it gazed without eyes. But Cohen noticed something familiar. In that gruesome rictus he saw the same expression of hopeless agony etched upon the face of Walid Rada, and Cohen feared it was the same artist at work.

It was a calm afternoon on the northern shoulder of the Golan Heights, but inside the guarded tunnels beneath the summit of Mount Hermon, a young IDF intelligence analyst watched his computer screen come alive.

A tap covertly installed on a telecommunications switch in the basement of the Lebanese Parliament Building on Nejmeh Square in Beirut activated with a preset selector and called back to the fiberglass radomes sprouting over Unit 8200's ground station. The raw SIGINT data crawled across the analyst's screen and identified the subjects: Subject One, whose phone number was the targeted selector, was Nawar al-Sahili, leader of Hezbollah's Loyalty to the Resistance Bloc in parliament; and Subject Two was none other than the party's secretary-general, Sheikh Wissam Hamawi. The analyst trained his eyes to the glow and eavesdropped on a conversation unfolding forty miles north.

"Was this us?" al-Sahili croaked. "Stop these fucking games and tell me."

The sheikh's voice trembled. "I'm not sure."

"How? Do you know what they are saying—about us, Wissam? The *mujahedeen* want us dragged through the streets."

"I've heard the rumors," Hamawi muttered with resignation.

"They're not rumors, damnit!"

The sheikh was silent.

"The airport was ours, our citizens, our land. But this is different. So I'll ask one more time." The analyst heard al-Sahili exhale. "Was it us?"

"…It was Abu Dokhan."

• • •

Morteza Ghanbari awoke shortly after dawn and sensed that he overstayed his welcome. There was a thunderous roar outside his hotel room: Engines revved and backfired; men chanted about the revolution and Islam, about Shiite saints and ayatollahs. He rushed to the window and looked five stories down. It was the Basij, the regime's fanatical paramilitary enforcers. At least fifty of them rumbled along Keshavaraz Boulevard in a wide phalanx of motorcycles, cloaked in riot gear and brandishing batons, howling in the early-morning light. Their show of force continued throughout the day. The Basij fanned out across Tehran, prowling the city's restive neighborhoods. The battle lines were drawn. In Laleh Park and Haft-e-Tir Square, groups of young people unfurled green banners, waved flags and wept around photographs of Mehdi Vaziri. The crowds spread like wildfire and within minutes the Basij descended upon them, swinging their batons and scattering them back into the streets. Internet chat rooms and social media applications lionized Vaziri and his cause and buzzed with cries for a "day of rage."

Ghanbari knew what would come. Every action would necessitate an even fiercer reaction. One ripple in Tehran would build into a tidal wave and wash over the country, drowning hundreds in its wake. Harold Lansing called en route from Geneva, and both agreed: It was time for him to leave.

He rang his ninety-three-year-old mother across town and apologized for cutting his visit short, but promised to call again once he was home. To his relief, there was still space aboard an Emirates flight leaving for Dubai at eight that evening. Ghanbari booked a seat, emailed the details to his assistant at Princeton, and then arranged for a car with the concierge desk. He spent the rest of the day locked in his room, glued to the television. A yellow Samand taxi arrived later that afternoon, and as he ducked inside, motorcycles echoed all around.

His driver rushed down Freeway 7 through the arid fields surrounding Imam Khomeini International Airport south of Tehran. The blazing sunset offered a modest distraction. Lansing had explained what happened in Geneva, that Saeed Mofidi was emphatic about Iran's innocence. Right or wrong, it wouldn't matter. Ghanbari knew they failed. All that concerned him now was ensuring his country didn't come apart at the seams. He gazed off at the sun.

But to make a difference, he first had to make it home.

Ghanbari was jolted forward in his seat. A muffled crunch tore through the taxi. He spun around and saw a tan Toyota Land Cruiser hovering off the rear bumper. The SUV's windows were tinted, even the windshield.

"Madar kharbeh!" the driver swore. He pressed the brakes, ranting into the rear-view mirror, and drifted to the shoulder.

Ghanbari felt his gut plummet. "Don't stop!" he pleaded.

But it was too late. The Land Cruiser kept on their tail. Another SUV overtook them on the left and crept into their lane, both gradually forcing the Samand off the highway.

The taxi crawled still, boxed in on either side. Men in balaclavas poured from the SUVs—six of them, all with Kalashnikovs trained at Ghanbari's head. And they called for him.

"*Doktor* Ghanbari…"

One moved toward his door.

"…please step outside."

It was dark when they arrived in Erbil. After a brief stopover at Incirlik Air Base in Turkey, Harris and his teammates rendezvoused with an aircrew of the 427th Special Operations Squadron and transferred their gear to a waiting C-41A transport for the short flight to northern Iraq. Landing in a C-41 was sobering. The twin-engine aircraft's undercarriage hung mere inches below the fuselage, and when it touched down the whole cabin shuddered with a jarring scream as if the belly was scraping against the runway. Harris suppressed the pain darting up his spine and tried to shrug off his jet lag, but after nearly thirteen hours in the air, the damage was done. The crew chief lowered the ramp on an isolated apron, and Harris felt a cold draft sweep through his hair.

Parked by the hangar ahead were a collection of helicopters and fixed-wing aircraft: a UH-1N Huey and a Sikorsky S-61, three decommissioned Marine Corps CH-46s and two Cessna 208 Caravans, all painted in a blue and white color scheme. The small fleet was the forward deployed detachment of Embassy Air Iraq, operated by DynCorp on a State Department contract, and just one cog in the stealthy American machinery at work in Erbil.

Stavros was first on the tarmac and checked the reception on his encrypted Iridium satellite phone. Farah and Z hauled the team's gear off the plane while Harris, Whitford and the C-41's crew chief handled the rest of the equipment strapped to a pallet on the deck. Stored in wooden crates on the pallet were fifteen AKM rifles with folding stocks and fifteen Browning nine-millimeter Hi-Power pistols. Other crates held thousands of rounds of ammunition, magazines and sound suppressors for each weapon, along with holsters and pouches, cleaning kits and webbing. Another three crates contained hundred-dollar bills, all used and non-sequential. The money was packaged into bundles of ten thousand, wrapped in cellophane into bricks of a hundred thousand, and packed ten bricks to each crate, totaling three million US. Months of hit-and-run attacks and isolation in Palanjar took a toll on Jamil Gorani's militia, and the Central Intelligence Agency hoped that their tribute might earn the favor of the Dark Lion of Kurdistan in their mutual crusade against the Revolutionary Guards.

After breaking down the pallet, Harris trudged off the ramp with the last crate and set it on the tarmac. The others stood under the C-41's tail.

"Okay, thanks, Marcia," Stavros said into the sat phone. "We'll VTC in a minute." He ended the call and lowered the handset. "That was my deputy."

A pair of armored Suburbans and a Toyota Hilux turned onto the apron. "That for us?" Whitford pointed with his chin.

Stavros squinted as the headlights gained. "Yup."

The convoy drove over and stopped. The drivers—three contractors with CIA's Global Response Staff detail in Erbil, and retired special operators themselves—hopped out and helped load everything in the Hilux. After several minutes they took off again along a dusty road toward a fortified compound just beyond the airport's northern perimeter fence. Anti-vehicle berms, coiled concertina wire and watchtowers sprouted from the surrounding field. Several miles west there were still hand-dug trenches where the Kurdish peshmerga had repelled ISIS, beat their hordes back across the Nineveh plain to Mosul and eventually purged them from Iraqi soil. Discreetly advising the Kurds at every step, summoning laser-guided bombs onto the terrorists' tanks and artillery pieces, strangling their finances and systematically assassinating their leaders, was a JSOC Expeditionary Targeting Force, or ETF, which operated from the compound. At its height early last year, the ETF was a two-hundred-man element, comprised of a full Delta squadron and a host of intelligence and support assets. Since ISIS lost its base in Syria and was driven underground, JSOC's contingent in Erbil gradually dwindled to a rotating force of fifty tier-one operators and support staff. Their standing mission in northern Iraq was to work with the various Kurdish security services to finish off what remnants of ISIS still lingered and mop up the mess they left behind. Yet since Damascus and Raqqa fell, another threat was mounting in the north. Without a common enemy in ISIS, Iraq's fractious politics was reverting to its self-destructive nature. The Hashid Shaabi militias dominated the territory north and east of Baghdad. The Quds Force riddled the Kurdish government with spies at every level. Iraq was slowly unraveling again, and Qasem Shateri meant to glue the pieces back together to his liking.

In the floodlights, Harris saw the Iraqi and Kurdish flags flapping against a jet-black, starless sky. The lead Suburban doused its headlights and weaved with the convoy through a series of concrete chicanes. In a sandbag bunker overlooking the checkpoint, he noticed a peshmerga in an olive drab uniform—no older than twenty, and surely a seasoned fighter—resting her toned arms on the top of a fifty-caliber belt-fed machine gun. A barrier was raised for the convoy as it sped by. The compound was a rambling hodgepodge of prefabricated offices, warehouses and repurposed shipping containers that had been hastily expanded with each surrounding town that ISIS conquered. Much of it was built around three conjoined modular trailers in an eastern alcove of the perimeter fence that housed the Joint Operations Center, or JOC. On the northern side was a grouping of "B-Huts," simple plywood structures used as barracks for the American operators and staff assigned to the ETF, and on the southern side was a helicopter landing pad and a firing range. It didn't make for a pretty postcard, but the compound was meant to be functional, and secure, and after withstanding countless mortar barrages and more than one truck bomb charging at the gates, it was certainly tested.

As his Suburban pulled up to a trailer across a clearing from the JOC, Harris spotted a short, hard man in his late-thirties, with a thinning pate of red hair and a flat nose, and wearing a T-shirt and jeans, standing to meet them.

"The fuck is that?" Z mumbled beside Harris' shoulder.

"He's mine," Stavros answered from the passenger seat.

Stavros was the first one out again; by the time the SEALs climbed out, he and his man were already talking. "Gentlemen, this is Elliot Flanagan. He watches our friends over the border when they rear their ugly faces around town," Stavros said, and made the introductions down the line.

Flanagan, a veteran operations officer from Gloucester, Massachusetts, ran Persia House's station in Erbil. He and his small staff managed one of several listening posts that the agency established around Iran's periphery, attempting to peer through fractures in the blank façade, and sometimes creating them. Beyond his charge to monitor Iranian activities in northern Iraq, he was tasked with balancing a precarious relationship with the much larger CIA station in Baghdad, JSOC and the State Department, not to mention the locals. "Welcome to Kurdistan, boys."

"Shame we're not sticking around," said Farah.

"No, we gotta get you airborne again," Flanagan agreed.

"Still got four hours," added Harris.

"Lath is on-line with everybody back home," Flanagan looked to Stavros. "We could run through the briefing now and then give you guys a bit to get yourselves together. GRS will bring your stuff to a B-Hut. We'll secure the weapons and the cash, and I've locked down a cage so you guys can store anything you can't carry on the jump."

Stavros deferred to Harris.

"Let's do it," he nodded.

"We lucked out with OPSEC," Flanagan said as he led them into the trailer where his station worked. "Asayish was all over here earlier today, and Delta's on a rotation, so the whole place is pretty quiet. Nobody will ask about the new faces." Asayish was the fledgling Kurdish intelligence agency. It was a running assumption with Western officers that any information given to them might as well be forwarded to Tehran.

They began a final video teleconference with Operation PACER's planning staff at Langley and Admiral Wade's headquarters at Fort Bragg. Director Freeman was busy at the White House. For the next few hours they ran through the mission and every possible contingency. At 0100 that morning, Harris and his team would return to the airport and depart on the C-41; the aircrew was well briefed. They would climb to twenty-four thousand feet and head for the designated drop zone (DZ), approximately fifty-three miles northeast of Erbil, near the town of Soran, and still well inside Iraqi airspace. At 0200, VALENCIA would execute a High Altitude, High Opening (HAHO) jump and deploy their parachutes five seconds after exiting the aircraft. This was designated Waypoint 1 and given the code name "Anaheim." While the C-41 returned to Erbil, the team would drift under canopy for twenty-five miles to a landing zone (LZ) on a ridge overlooking the Gadar River positioned three miles behind the Iranian border. This was designated Waypoint 2, and upon reaching it, Harris would pass "Burbank" over the radio. VALENCIA would then maintain radio silence and follow a route along the Gadar River for approximately five miles until they reached a rendezvous point (RV), which was designated Waypoint 3, and would signal their arrival with "Compton." Sunrise in the Ushnu-Sulduz Valley was set for 0655, and the team should make the RV by 0620 at the latest. At 0630, the team would link-up at the RV with Niyaz Gorani, Jamil Gorani's son, and be transported the rest of the way to Palanjar. A recognition code was established, and with positive identification of Niyaz, Harris would pass "Wildfire."

The window of opportunity to launch was narrow. The lunar phase stood at third-quarter, which wasn't optimal, but the night's thick cloud cover over the region compensated. Once the SEALs dropped through, the clouds would shield their silhouette all the way to the ground. Conditions would only worsen for the next two weeks, and with the stormy mood gripping the White House, waiting any longer wasn't an option. It had to be tonight.

Other assets were in play. Wade borrowed an RQ-4 Global Hawk reconnaissance drone that was currently en route to the skies over northern Iraq from Al Dhafra Air Base in the UAE. The drone would shadow the C-41, providing a live video feed of the jump, and then loiter along the border, monitoring the radio frequencies of the Iranian Border Guard Command. The route along the Gadar River to the RV outside Palanjar was plotted to avoid their patrols, but if those patterns unforeseeably changed, the drone's SIGINT sensors would give Harris forewarning. Radar coverage was sparse in far western Iran—the most advanced systems blanketed Tehran—but the Khatam al-Anbia Air Defense Base operated an old, Soviet P-80 BLACK NET installation near Tabriz. Four men floating over the border under parachutes would appear like birds on their scopes, but NSA's Office of Tailored Access Operations would clear the skies nonetheless.

The only unknown in the equation was Jack. He arranged an extremely rare face-to-face meeting with CITADEL to plant the seed in his agent's mind about personally penetrating Haj Ali Gholi. Their talk was set to happen sometime that same night, in Tehran, but none at Langley would know the outcome for at least two more days. Until then, Jack was dark.

The VTC concluded at ten o'clock. Stavros stayed in the trailer while Harris and his men followed Flanagan to a B-Hut that was used as a kitchen and a makeshift mess hall. The offerings were slim with JSOC between rotations. There was an unopened case of Almaza beer from Lebanon in the refrigerator, and oddly enough several bottles of Israeli Goldstar, yet downing one—or twelve—was out of the question for them. Harris found a tin of strawberry jam tucked behind the bottles and reached for his Gerber multi-tool. Whitford dug through the pantry and pulled out a jar of peanut butter and then a plastic bag of pita bread. He gave it a glance for mold, but it turned up clean. Harris carved open the tin. Whitford shrugged at them.

Z had his feet up on a flimsy plastic table and huffed, *"Fuuuuck you."*

"Gimme," Farah said with a confident smirk. He drew a custom-made Daniel Winkler knife from a sheath on his hip and cut open the hollow pocket in each loaf of bread, then spread in a heaping portion of peanut butter and jam.

They sat around the table together—no plates—and ate.

It helped that their mouths were full. It gave them an excuse. There was no talk of home, no talk of the mission, no talk of what they were about to do or of the men they were about to confront.

There was nothing more to say. Except for Z.

His eyes crept up from the table. "Pretty shitty last supper, huh?"

They all chuckled.

At eleven, Harris grabbed his toothbrush from his rucksack and a bottle of water and went around to the back of the plywood hut where the GRS stowed their gear. It struck him that this was the end. This was the last time Harris would run that ritual. Since BUD/S all those years ago, a belief was drilled into his head that he was simply doing his job, that this was just the next mission. But tonight was more than that. Harris would make it home again, or he would die.

Either way, it was over.

He spat into the gravel and stepped back inside the hut. His teammates were spread out, readying their gear with obsessive detail. It all had to be perfect; even the slightest malfunction could cripple the mission. Harris laced up his boots, tied them in a double knot and tucked the loops against his ankles. He slid a gray flight suit over a black turtleneck sweater and digital camouflage pants. The rigging for his RA-1 parachute and oxygen tanks went overtop of that. Z came over to check his work. Harris stood with his hands on the back of his head while Z methodically inspected and tightened each fastening. After finishing the primary chute, Z moved to his chest and yanked at the reserve chute to see that it was fixed to his torso harness, cinching his crotch straps with a hefty tug.

Harris winced. "Warming me up for an Iranian prison, bud?"

Z cracked a slight grin. "Chief, I'm just looking out for kid number three."

By midnight, everything they could've prepared before boarding the plane was finished. Encryption codes were entered into their radios. Their long guns and sidearms were secured against their ribcages, and their drop bags were packed and zipped shut. All they could do now was wait.

Stavros rapped on the door at quarter-to-one and let himself in. The satellite phone was in his hand. "It's a go."

The Suburbans whisked them back to the airport. The C-41A sat on the apron. Its ramp was extended, and the props were turning.

"...It was Abu Dokhan."

The subject hesitated. "Then maybe it's time he went away."

Cohen paused the recording and tried to gauge her reaction.

In Beirut, in her room at the Tango Inn, Nina's hand was pressed to her mouth. She gently shook her head, turned her eyes from the screen and muttered, "I knew it."

At the Israeli embassy in Paris, Cohen eased back in his chair. "So have you heard of this guy before? Badi Haddad?"

"No," Nina looked at her laptop, "but I bet I've heard of his friends."

Cohen nodded. "It's bad here."

"It's all anybody here's talking about."

"Hezbollah?"

Her lips pursed with disappointment. "Nobody wants to say it."

"Anyway, word is that the French are going public tomorrow. They're accusing the Quds Force of sponsoring al-Din," he said. "You're gonna have some awkward stare-downs in the hallway."

"I just can't believe it's real," she breathed.

"Nina, I owe you an apology. We all do," said Cohen. "You were right all along—and I never should've doubted you." He looked into the camera, and for a moment their eyes met. "I think your white whale is back."

"Harold, this is going to move faster than any of us can imagine," Weisel said from her office in the Truman Building. "I need you in New York."

Lansing listened through the Bluetooth connection in his rental car. "Absolutely, Madam Secretary." He struggled to see out the windshield. The nor'easter intensified since noon. Amtrak's Northeast Corridor was closed and every flight from Richmond to Boston was cancelled. Lansing inched along the eastern spur of the New Jersey Turnpike over the Meadowlands and the Hackensack River. The sun had just set and the Manhattan skyline shone as a discordant glow on the horizon, lost in a dizzying wash of snow. He was maybe twenty minutes from the Lincoln Tunnel, and he counted each passing mile marker.

"I want you to dig in with Lisa's staff and help her run interference in the Security Council," she continued, referring to Ambassador Lisa Tully, the US representative at the UN. "The Russians may play ball, but the Chinese won't."

"I can do that," he answered over the rhythmic thwack of wiper blades.

"President Laniel is expelling the Iranian ambassador and pulling his own from Tehran in the morning," said Weisel. "Afterward, he's addressing a joint session of parliament at Versailles and will present their evidence connecting the bombers to the Revolutionary Guards. I'm told his first act will be to convene NATO and invoke Article 5. We'll go from there, but we're working with the Treasury to draw up some options; I want Shateri to suffer. In the meantime, our priority is keeping Annapolis on track. Avi needs to leave happy," she sighed.

Lansing frowned. "I'd like to sit that one out if you don't—"

Headlights burst through the snow. It was a Greyhound bus, sliding out of control in the southbound lanes. Before Lansing could react, the bus vaulted over the concrete median and careened toward him.

All Weisel heard was a scream.

CHAPTER 50

THERE WAS GREAT power in letting go.

Something had shown him that—a visitor in the night, a voice inside his mind that left a chill on his neck and made his hair stand on end; something faceless that ambled on the cold void he knew, and beckoned.

Jack Galloway weighed his surroundings with a wary intent: a few muted women, their bodies engulfed in the deep, black obscuring fabric of a *chador;* the cliques of men, young, old and plenty indescribably lost somewhere in the gap between; and their voices—the usual voices, the normative patterns—at times bated in stoic resignation toward the news coverage on the television screen suspended from the far wall, at times silenced by an assuaging drag on a water pipe, at times hushed in acquiescence of the CCTV camera suspended to the other; at no time content.

The café was the only business still open on Tajrish Square. The other storefronts were shuttered and dark; their owners left hours ago, dreading what dawn might reveal. Jack checked the time and discreetly wiped his DNA from a coffee cup with his shirt cuff. He dug his hands inside his coat, gripping a knife in his pocket, and stood, catching whispers of riots and martyrdom as he weaved a path through the tables. Outside, raindrops flittered like sparks through the harsh, crimson burn of a neon sign.

He trawled the glow, looking right, and then left.

Tajrish Square was desolate. The usual sulfurous noise was gone; there were no hawking vendors, no mingling packs of indulgent young men and women braving the suspicions of the morality police. All around the city, streets were drenched in shadow.

Tehranis kept behind closed doors that night. Most hunkered down in their flats and waited for the tide to pass; some hoped for a swift and merciless response by the regime to the disorder and anarchy of the day; still more bided their time until morning, emboldened to set out again and make their voices heard; while others intended to avenge Mehdi Vaziri with violence.

For Jack, it simply offered a decent cover. He strolled toward the street corner, cowled by the darkness, as a metro bus rumbled up behind him.

It was being called the storm of the century. Earlier in the afternoon, a blocking ridge of high-pressure in Newfoundland stalled the nor'easter off the Outer Banks, where it exploded and intensified far beyond predictions. Sustained hurricane-force winds battered Hampton Roads and pushed a wall of seawater up the Chesapeake Bay. Power grids were falling like dominos. Thousands were stranded in airports. That evening, forecasters called for four feet of snow between Washington and New York. Blizzard warnings and flood watches were issued as far north as Maine. Governors from Virginia to New Hampshire declared states of emergency and mobilized the National Guard. FEMA was put on standby. All along the eastern seaboard, over fifty million people sat in the storm's path.

Freeman witnessed its fury up close. He rushed home after finishing at the White House to change into a fresh suit and have dinner with Mary. Shaw called shortly after he arrived with an update. JSOC reported that VALENCIA was deploying at seven, their time. He kissed his wife goodbye, and by five o'clock was headed back to Langley. His motorcade rolled warily down Interstate 495 near Bethesda. The two Chevy Tahoes hadn't passed another vehicle for miles, not even a plow truck. In the lead SUV, Doc's knuckles were white around the steering wheel. The agent beside him monitored the radio and their GPS position on the dashboard screen. Freeman turned and peered out the rear window. Snowflakes swirled in the headlights of the Tahoe behind them.

"There's another bend ahead," said the agent in the passenger seat.

"How far?" Doc asked.

"Maybe a thousand yards? It's just through this overpass."

"Got it."

The agent relayed it to the chase car, and the radio replied, "Hey, be advised—we're seeing emergency lights running up our six."

"Okay, copy that."

Freeman turned back around. Pulsing red and blue shades flickered off the noise barrier bordering the highway. Another pair of headlights appeared behind the chase car. The red and blue shades radiated just overtop of them, illuminating the blowing snow.

"Troopers," the radio crackled.

Kicking up snow with the chains wrapped around its tires, a Maryland State Police cruiser quickly overtook the Tahoes and beat them to the overpass. As the lights spiraled beyond the windshield, Doc leaned over the wheel and pointed. "You see that, sir?"

Freeman pressed against the door. "See what?"

"Hold on."

Once through the overpass, he saw it for himself.

The sky was painted orange.

Freeman looked out his window as the Tahoes cleared the bend. A semi truck was overturned diagonally across the opposite side of the highway. Fire engulfed the trailer and danced on the wind, igniting the surrounding trees. Glowing embers drifted with the snow.

Doc steered toward the right shoulder, away from the blaze, and slowed.

The state police trooper was the first to respond. He stood just outside his cruiser, stopped along the median, and shouted into his radio.

The Tahoes crawled past. Freeman's eyes were peeled to the flames as they climbed skyward. An ember landed on his window, and he felt the heat.

The C-41A bucked and swayed in a patch of rough air over Mount Safeen. Harris sat on a red nylon bench that lined the fuselage, shackled by the pull of his parachute, oxygen tanks, rifle and drop bag strapped between his legs. Ordered by weight, Farah was squeezed to his right, with Z and then Whitford sitting farther aft. None had said much of anything since takeoff and passed the time idly listening to sporadic radio traffic. Their headsets used bone conduction technology to channel transmissions into their inner ear canal, filtering out the roaring propellers. In his right ear, Harris heard the troop net, which handled communication with his teammates and the aircrew. In his left ear, Harris monitored the command net and the chatter between Langley, Fort Bragg and the compound in Erbil.

Fifteen minutes into the flight, Harris read the altimeter on his wrist. He watched the needle creep above twenty thousand feet, and then a message from the copilot broke in his right ear.

"Thirty minutes."

Down the bench, the SEALs pulled on Gentex helmets and fastened the attached oxygen masks. Harris felt the rubber flange tighten around his airways. He reached for a valve and turned, hearing a burst of pure oxygen sweep up the delivery tube and fill his lungs.

Brakes hissed at Jack's feet. He climbed the front stepwell and walked down the aisle, taking a seat by the metal bar that divided the men's and women's sections. There were only two other passengers on board: a man in a yellowed shirt near the driver and a veiled woman, who Jack assumed was the man's wife, seated a few rows behind the bar. Neither gave him a second glance. Its engine groaned and the bus continued east, stopping once more along Niavaran Street, where no one boarded.

As the brakes hissed again at the following stop, the man in the yellowed shirt turned around and stared right through him. Jack tensed his fingers around the knife in his pocket. The woman floated up the aisle, fanning Jack with her veil, and accompanied her husband down the steps.

Jack's shoulders dropped.

Jack got off at the next stop and walked one block to Ammar Street, opposite Mehr Park. He took his time now, reading the trees and the shadows. Jack had run his gauntlet through the city, luring his phantoms into carefully selected chokepoints, patiently driving them into the open, but none revealed themselves. He was free of surveillance; his phantoms were either figments of his imagination, or they plied the darkness better than he.

Jack came to a handsome villa surrounded by a white limestone wall. The lights inside were doused—save for one. Suspended in a window on the upper floor was the soft orange flicker of a candle. He ducked alongside the villa, out of view from the street, and hoisted himself over the wall.

"He has company."

Movsar Gelayev switched off the television and padded across the darkened flat to a window. Peering through the curtains on a tripod was a Zeiss spotting scope and a Nikon DSLR camera. He pushed the curtain aside and looked out over North Tehran, then drew his eyes six stories down through the bare branches of Mehr Park to a handsome villa on Ammar Street. The villa's gate was shut and the garden lights went dark at their scheduled time an hour earlier. "His driver never comes this late," the Spetsnaz operator noted skeptically.

"It's not that," Israilov blinked in the electronic glow of a laptop screen. "Someone just went over the wall."

Gelayev stepped toward the dining table and sat beside the other Chechen. The screen displayed the vantage caught by the spotting scope's lens, showing the villa in varied shades of green.

"Where?"

"There," Israilov tapped the screen with his fingernail.

"Someone *climbed* over the wall?"

"*Da,*" he said. "A man. Average height. Slim build."

"Did you get a photo?"

"*Nyet,* it happened too quickly."

Gelayev stood. "Keep looking."

• • •

There was fear in Ibrahim al-Din's eyes.

Sabbah never noticed that before. Al-Din sat like a corpse in the front passenger seat since they hastily left Beirut, rendered paralyzed and speechless by the thoughts boiling over in his mind. He clutched his left hand in his lap, fighting to hold it still as his bones gently twitched.

On that barren hilltop outside Zarayeb, Sabbah parked the Isuzu Trooper near a small collection of off-road trucks and SUVs hidden under camouflage nets. A dozen Spetsnaz operators were fanned out in defensive positions, establishing clear fields of fire down the mined slopes to the gray-blue valley floor below. The Russians were protecting something, and as he saw them, Sabbah grimly accepted the truth.

It was real.

And they meant to use it.

Al-Din shook his daze and stepped out of the Isuzu. Sabbah went around the hood and followed him. Three men with rifles slung across their chests blithely advanced on them from the barn, silhouetted against the pale moonlight.

Sabah eyed the wraiths, and the wraiths gazed back.

He knew the trio from Paris: Kotov, Ignatev, and Ruslan Baranov.

A fourth man walked between them, his spindly arm outstretched.

"I have a gift for you…"

His voice scarcely broke the wind, and Sabbah knew him, too.

Kazanoff took al-Din by the hand and turned back up the hill.

"Come and see."

Freeman gleaned each passing update through a subdued symphony of clacking keyboards, hushed whispers and terse radio traffic. The air inside the Operations Center at Langley hung at an almost stifling degree. He stood with his sleeves rolled up and his arms crossed, sweat gluing his shirt to the small of his back, and waited.

A buzzing matrix of screens canvassed the wall ahead. One showed a map of the Iran-Iraq border and marked the waypoints between the DZ and Palanjar. Another monitored current radar and weather data. The largest displayed a live video feed of the C-41A at twenty-four thousand feet through the unblinking gaze of a Global Hawk that had arrived on station several minutes earlier. Piloted from its ground station in Nevada, the hulking drone trailed the C-41 to the drop zone north of Soran. It's onboard FLIR camera painted the heat of the aircraft's twin engines in white and its fuselage in gray; the frigid mountains in the background were swathed in black.

Shaw, Roger Mathis and Marcia Lath hovered a few paces away, listening to the incoming chatter from Erbil and Fort Bragg. Lingering at Freeman's side was Eli Tanner, who soldiered the blizzard and crossed the Potomac just so he might personally inform the president if, as he put it, anything went wrong.

"How much longer?" Tanner quietly asked

Freeman nodded to a digital clock that was counting down on the wall. A display beneath it read, "Time on Target."

Just then, the copilot's disembodied voice sounded over the speakers.

"Ten minutes."

Harris wiggled the circulation back into his toes. He drew on his oxygen supply in quick, successive breaths through his mask, gradually purging the nitrogen from his bloodstream. The temperature plummeted near their jump altitude, and Harris felt goose bumps prickle the hair on his forearms.

"I say again: We are ten minutes from the DZ," the copilot echoed in his right ear. "Course is zero-four-seven. Winds at altitude are one-two-five knots at zero-niner-four. LZ coordinates are three-seven degrees, four-one point eight-niner minutes longitude, four-four degrees, five-one three-five point four-niner minutes latitude. Elevation is seven-zero eight-three feet. Set that in your jump boards. All checked?"

"Check," was the reply four times.

Harris looked aft and gave a thumbs-up sign to the jumpmaster.

Jack moved low through the gardens to the patio door. He crouched down, cupped his hands around his eyes and peered through a window into the villa's sitting room. He gently knocked on the glass, and in a moment, saw a figure emerge from the blackness.

Saeed Mofidi cracked the door open. "Come in, my friend," he whispered, warily scanning the gardens.

"Thank you," Jack said as Mofidi locked the door behind them, "for all you've done for us. Please know we appreciate it."

"I don't need to be thanked." Mofidi eased onto a cushioned chair bathed in the orange glow of the city lights outside.

Jack helped himself to a corner of the opposite sofa. He pensively rubbed his hands together, hesitating to speak. Finally, he summoned the nerve. "I need to know what happened in Geneva."

Mofidi made a heavy sigh.

"Saeed, did you know? Did you know about Vaziri?"

"If I knew, you would have known," he replied. "And if you knew, I'm assuming that none of it would have happened."

"Did Khansari?"

Mofidi shook his head. "The supreme leader knows nothing and no one but the ghosts in his head."

Jack looked at the floor. "I was afraid of that."

"I've been warning you for months."

"I know…" Jack drew his eyes up. "This will unravel everything we've worked toward. No more talks, no more backchannels. It's all gone, Saeed. Do you understand that?"

Mofidi nodded. "And do you understand who that empowers?"

"That's why I'm here." Jack leaned in and lowered his voice. "Men are entering Iran tonight—and I'm asking you to help them."

The barn's corrugated metal door was rolled open.

Sabbah watched Kazanoff lure al-Din inside. He followed them, with the wraiths on his heels, and heard the door groan shut.

Halogen lamps were placed against the cinder block walls. A diesel generator droned in the corner and fans in the ceiling pulled air through aluminum ventilation hoses in the roof. Four iron posts were stabbed into the ground and connected by welded trusses, forming a large box that nearly swallowed the interior. Weather-sealed plastic sheeting hung from the trusses and a concrete floor was spread between the posts.

Placed on the floor behind the sheets—lit by the harsh glare of the lamps—was a stainless steel trunk.

"Two minutes."

The jumpmaster balanced against the shuddering fuselage.

The SEALs lurched off the bench and came to their feet. Harris reached for the goggles on his helmet and pulled them over his eyes. He planted his boots to the deck and braced himself.

"One minute to drop."

The ramp yawned open, and the winds howled.

"I need you to go to Haj Ali Gholi," Jack explained. "I need your eyes."

"How could I possibly—"

"Have Khansari sign an order," he said. "Just like with Geneva."

Mofidi stared uneasily.

"Go under the pretense that you're performing an inspection of Project 260 on the supreme leader's behalf. We need you on the inside to see what our satellites can't. If Alireza Fakhrizadeh is alive and working there, we need you to confirm it. Use your position to ask questions. Take note of the facility's layout, the number of employees, the posture of the security force, the operation of the reactor and the fabrication workshop. Memorize everything you can."

"And then what?"

"We'll figure out how to destroy it. And if Fakhrizadeh is running the program, we'll destroy him too," Jack said flatly. "For good this time."

"Is that where your men come in?"

"Exactly."

Mofidi nodded. "Okay, I will help you."

Jack took his hand. "We owe you a debt, Saeed."

"Consider it paid."

"I'll be in touch. Take care of yourself."

"And you, my friend."

Mofidi unlocked the patio door. He held by the windows for a moment after Jack left and watched the American disappear back into the garden.

"That's him," Israilov hurriedly pointed at the laptop screen. "He just went over the wall again. He's heading north. I got a photograph."

Gelayev's frame parted the curtains. "Go down and follow him."

"My gift to you…" Kazanoff swept his hand over the trunk.

Baranov unlatched it and began to raise the lid.

Al-Din trembled.

"…and with it we will drag them all to hell—kicking and screaming."

A small red light blinked on next to the ramp. The wind swirled around Harris' legs. He heard the flaps extend, violently rocking the fuselage as the aircraft slowed to one hundred fifty knots.

"Thirty seconds."

Harris flexed his fingers inside his gloves.

"Ten seconds to drop."

The red light switched to green. The jumpmaster held up his thumb.

The SEALs waddled down the deck under the weight of their gear. Harris kept his eyes over their shoulders as they inched aft. He saw Whitford drop into the night, followed by Z, and Farah, until Harris was alone on the ramp. The wind tore at his flight suit, tempting him to the edge.

A pale moon rose in the sky, bleeding out over a sea of silver clouds.

Three parachutes blossomed below.

Harris toed the precipice, yielded, and plunged into the abyss.

•   •   •

Freeman watched four warm specks cross the screen.

"Load clear, four jumpers," the copilot called over the speakers.

"Copy that," another voice replied in the ether. "Anaheim. I say again: Anaheim. VALENCIA is en route to LZ."

Tanner went to gather his coat. "There. It's over."

"No…" Freeman said with sadness in his voice. "This was only the beginning."